"I would like to dedicate this novel to my husband, Ken, the love of my life, and to my loving family"

❖

Thanks also to my editor, Roy Robins, without whom I would not have been able to complete my novels.

A resounding Thank You to Toby Meyer for providing such stunning artwork for the covers of both of my books, and for being the first friend to read my novels and love them!

Sincere thanks to Nigel Dickson, who assisted me in uploading my novels to Amazon and with the design of the books. His computer-savvy, knowledge, and patience were invaluable.

And finally, a heartfelt Thank You to my readers, each and every one of you. If one of the places or spaces described in my novel feels very different, or even at odds with, your personal experience of it, feel free to preserve your own experience of that place or space.

This novel is just that, a novel. Names, characters, business, events, and incidents are the products of my imagination.
Any resemblance to actual persons, living or dead, or actual events, is purely coincidenial.

Copyright © 2023 Yvonne Spektor
Cover designs © 2023 Toby Meyer
Picture credits; Dreamstime, Shutterstock, Images by StockSnap from Pixabay, T.Schmidt and Toby Mayer
All rights reserved. Used with permission.

No part of this book may be reproduced or used in any manner without the prior written permission of the copyright owner, except for the use of brief quotations in a book review.

ISBN 978-1-7392966-1-2

Safi's Journey So Far

Safi's loving family had warned her that life outside of Brighton could be dangerous. And now she was discovering for herself how dangerous things could be …

Until the night she met Sasha Rubicov, the handsome, enigmatic son of one of Russia's most infamous oligarchs, the most reckless and exciting thing 18-year-old Saffron Asher-James had accomplished was the journey from her Brighton birthplace to the energy and allure of New York City.

Talented, Manhattan-based architect Daniel Asher is Safi's first cousin, and (along with his life partner, Dax) he welcomes the dark-haired, bright-eyed ingénue into a world of high society and exquisite good taste.

Of course, Daniel has an ulterior motive: he is hoping that Safi (as everyone knows her) will be able to facilitate a reunion between himself and his father, Rupert, who long ago spurned his son on account of his homosexuality.

It is at the launch of Manhattan's Rubicov restaurant (designed by Dan) that Safi is introduced to Sasha, who is 10 years her senior and by far the most attractive man she has ever met. Sasha oversees his family's American concerns; he is at once powerful and vulnerable to outside pressures, pressures Safi cannot (and, from Sasha's perspective, *must not*) understand. Sasha's world is one of polish and privilege – and unimaginable peril.

A passionate love affair soon consumes them both. When Sasha is called back to Russia to manage his family's major holdings, Safi decides she cannot live without him.

Sasha proposes marriage, a proposal frowned upon by Yvetta Rubicov, Sasha's emotionally troubled, self-destructive older sister, who manages art galleries in Russia's major cities.

Yvetta becomes pathologically envious of Safi, who she is convinced has taken her place in the Rubicov family's affections and intends to wrest control of her galleries. Along with her lover, the East German temptress Fritzi, Yvetta schemes to sabotage Safi.

Moving to Moscow, a stranger in a chilled and chilling landscape, not understanding the language and so much else, Safi feels truly alone for the first time in her life. The country is inscrutable – but then so is the Rubicov family. Why, for example, is Safi accompanied everywhere she goes by a bodyguard? And how did the family really make its money?

Becoming increasingly emboldened and out for blood, Fritzi and Yvetta organise for their criminal accomplice to ransack the Rubicov family's Moscow estate, tying up and traumatising Sasha's mother and stealing priceless antiques. Later the two women attempt acts of extortion and intimidation on the family's flagship restaurant, and attack and drug Sasha's stepmother in London.

But it is Safi they truly want to target.

The stress takes its toll on Sasha, who becomes increasingly absent and aggressive towards Safi, who herself begins to reconsider their relationship.

After an investigation, Fritzi and Yvetta are brought to book: Fritzi is threatened with arrest and warned off having any further communication with Yvetta, who is committed to a high-security psychiatric facility in Colorado.

But Fritzi and Yvetta's devotion for one another is not to be underestimated. Fritzi manages to escape Yvetta from the facility – and the two are on the loose again.

The Rubicov family discover that Fritzi, who is wanted by Interpol, has been illegally dealing in stolen antiques. Meanwhile, Sasha, who has been quietly moving the family's assets offshore, is arrested by the Russian government.

Safi now finds herself utterly alone, out of her depths, and in grave danger. In *Safi: Book Two*, the adventure continues …

Part 1
Chapter 1

Everything – Russian politics, the economy, the way business was done – was changing and, in order to survive, the Rubicov family had to change, too. Stay on top of things and somehow come out on top. But it was difficult to have the upper hand when your legs were cut out from under you. The present government was as unpredictable as the last, with spies almost everywhere: not only inside of the country, but also out in the wider world.

Politics was a dirty game; those involved played for high stakes. No one felt safe from Putin and his network of cronies. An outspoken critic of Putin had recently been murdered; everyone was nervous during elections. No one wanted to rattle the bears cage or get caught up in a political purge. As for Mika Rubicov, his top priority was to keep his younger, recently imprisoned brother Sasha's profile low while working tirelessly for his release. Mika would do this with whatever ammunition the Rubicov family had in their arsenal – an arsenal which, it seemed to Mika, was quickly being depleted.

Mika hoped that Fritzi – his sister Yvetta's lover, who the family had discovered was a criminal wanted by Interpol – might present them with a bargaining chip, making her years of irritation work in their favour. Some priceless items had gone missing from a very valuable collection owned by the Rubicov family, and others had been stolen from exhibitions and replaced with fakes: Fabergé eggs and jewel-encrusted clocks, snuff boxes and other jewelled objects from the reign of Czar Nicolas II, that, if found and returned, would go a long way to put them back in favour.

Mika's father, Alexi, was uncharacteristically nervous. DuPont's plan to capture the smugglers working with Fritzi was far more important than Fritzi herself; it would give the Russian authorities a long-awaited break in apprehending a successful smuggling ring from siphoning literally billions of dollars out of their country's coffers, through their trade in precious metals, stones, and artefacts.

Knowing how insecure the family were in the new Russia, the Rubicovs had invested abroad for many years. The most traditionally Russian of the three Rubicov children, Mika had never wanted to leave the country, but if it became impossible to run their Russian enterprises or remain safe, they would have no choice but to leave. The way Mika perceived it, the family would be uprooted like an ancient tree that's soil no longer sustains it.

And the Rubicovs would not be alone. Many Russian oligarchs had relocated and rebuilt their lives in London, New York, and elsewhere in Europe. This would be far from ideal, but the family was nothing if not pragmatic and forward-thinking. In order to survive, financially and otherwise, you had to stay on your feet and adapt at every opportunity. They had long planned for this possibility, even eventuality. Mika was safe in Florida at the moment, his other home, far from Moscow.

He had an apartment in St Petersburg and limited funds in the bank; when the time came to move more permanently, he would not be encumbered by what was left behind. The family had tried to diversify as much as possible, but this had come at a high price for Sasha. Through his underground network, Mika learnt that a sting was possible on his family. Alerting Sasha, Anna, and the rest of his family to imminent danger and long-term risk had been his job, but somewhere something had gone very badly wrong.

Sasha had been in the midst of negotiations with a Russian conglomerate, selling off shares in their natural gas and oil companies. The media company had slowly been scaled down, selling off contracts to the Russian media, but the last of the programs had been confiscated and banned by the authorities, making no profit for the Rubicov holdings. Sasha was finishing off a sale of their gas, oil, and metal industries to a Russian concern; money had left the country and the lawyers were finishing up. Sasha had been on his way to the airport to fly out of the country to meet Safi a new life was waiting in New York. Safi had no idea and it was a smart move to send her out of the country before the hammer and sickle came down on their heads. Leaving Russia for good had happened, and they were now forced to close down all their business dealings that could hurt their standing with the Russian government. Selling their mining concerns to a Russian company was much less profitable than continuing to operate in the country, but it was a loss they were prepared to take. Apart from the restaurants, Yvetta's galleries in Moscow and St Petersburg was all the family had left. Most of their homes and properties had been put on the market. All the groundwork had been done for the family to make their move abroad.

Alexi had worked tirelessly behind the scenes for years to extract their holdings from any Russian control; it had been an enormous undertaking that he and the family lawyers had only just completed with relative success and very few penalties. All of this was up in the air now that Sasha had been apprehended before his flight could leave the tarmac.

When Valentina and the restaurant in London had been targeted, Mika had immediately wondered whether it has been a warning from the Russian authorities. Once Fritzi's trademark fingerprints had been found to be the cause, his concerns had dwindled. Unfortunately, it had taken his mind from the danger that still obviously lay in their path, closer to home. Selling off or pulling out of the country most of their major assets and making way for the family to relocate abroad was seen by the government as a slap in the face. They did not approve of major players moving off their radar, where they could not be watched or called upon to contribute to various coffers. Certain politicians liked nothing more than milking big concerns to keep their own coffers full.

Oligarchs were often made scapegoats and made to pay for the wealth they had accumulated after the end of communism. It was considered a tax and a small penance to pay to the police and a fledgling Russian democracy. Some disgruntled authorities had got wind of the Rubicovs' financial dealings. Mika believed that the authorities, deciding they had not been notified or paid favourable recompense, were taking their vengeance out on Sasha, who would pay the price for Mika's oversight.

Driving down his palm-lined Florida driveway, watching the pink sky rising over the ocean and leaving his magnificent waterfront mansion behind for New York, Mika had doubts about his brother's safety: he had to secure his release at any cost.

Mika and Kolya, who flew in from London, arrived at DuPont's New York apartment to be met by a hoard of undercover art insurance officers and a number of other unidentified people discussing the sting that they hoped would crack open the smuggling ring no one had been able to infiltrate.

Mika and Kolya took a back-seat to the discussions. They learnt that some agents were to go undercover for a period to help infiltrate the illegal art market. The plan was that the agents would release small artefacts into an unsuspecting art market. DuPont's call to Alexi about the operation had afforded the Rubicovs an opportunity to get back in Russia's good graces. The Russians dispatched their own people to join the Americans in apprehending Fritzi and her gang of smugglers; the art market managed to work across international borders.

Watching from a corner of the room, Mika and Kolya quietly discussed the new order of authority they found in working together. It was an excellent opportunity for Mika to make valuable headway with the Russians present, to negotiate for Sasha's release with the authorities holding him in Moscow. But Kolya was of the opinion that they should sit back and watch the race to apprehend Fritzi unfold. If the Russians were able to get ahead of their American counterparts, they would then have greater leverage when asking for favours in return. No one had quite as much information on Fritzi as the Rubicovs had; giving the Russians the upper hand could only be beneficial.

The buyers arrived at DuPont's offices to purchase the fake artefact. Once the bogus papers for the sale had been signed and handed over, the authorities were ready to wire the money into the account they had been provided. The buyers were told to resell immediately after the sale was made. It all depended on the news reaching the right ears before the price was set for the resale. The sting unit would release word into the market about the resale of the artefact. The smugglers would hope to siphon off a large percentage for imparting the highly confidential information about the artefact being back on the market. The insurance officer would offer twice the original price, which meant it was highly sought after.

The authorities had to wait for the sting to take hold; it would be the moment that would bring major movers out of the woodwork. The authorities would set those movers against each other by confusing the players into play for ever-higher stakes.

Chapter 2

Safi woke from a fitful sleep and made her way down to breakfast. Over coffee she encountered Valentina: beautifully turned out and ready for a normal day at the ballet, or wherever it was she went to help the Russian contingent settle into their newfound lifestyle in London. Safi stared at Valentina in bewilderment. How on earth does she manage to look so calm when my life is falling apart? Safi thought. Surely, she must feel her husband's pain about his son being incarcerated in a Russian Gulag? Okay, so Sasha was not technically her son, but still … there was now worry enough to go around.

Valentina stretched across the table, taking Safi's hand. She held it until she forced Safi to look her in the eye. Not blinking, Safi watched her mouth move.

'Sasha be free soon, you see,' Valentina began haltingly. 'Alexi and Mika will not rest until then. You must be strong. Continue work, be strong for Sasha. Work is only medicine now.'

Dazed, Safi stared at Valentina with her calm exterior. Safi's own mind was in complete upheaval, more lost than ever, her world turned upside-down.

She felt like an automaton going through the motions. Brushing her teeth in the shower, her mind flew from one scenario to the other, settling on none. She felt stateless. Voiceless. Joyless. Worthless. Unmoored. Absolutely empty; and then full of unspeakable, confusion, self-doubt.

Without Sasha she did not belong anywhere. Her head ached, felt as though it had been bled dry. There was no one she could speak with. Sasha was locked up somewhere in Moscow, her parents were in Australia, and the two D's were in a baby-centred world all of their own.

Pete had listened patiently, but this was beyond even his comprehension. She had lost everything. In a split second her life had changed. One moment it was moving along perfectly, and the next the bottom seemed to have dropped out of her world.

DuPont and Alexi understood in some way, though how could they actually empathise with what she was experiencing emotionally? They were both frantically busy trying to save Sasha and keep the family together. Besides, no one would understand her complete loss of confidence, lack of belonging, constant sense of alienation. Going back to Moscow was off the cards; remaining in London seemed superfluous since she had no friends to speak of, and the international art world was not exactly waiting for her with open arms. New York was an option, but did she really want to continue without Sasha? The very idea tore her apart. She would rather think of just about anything else. What was the point of life without Sasha? Never had her thoughts been so dark, even during the darkest months of her first Russian winter.

She needed space, she needed to discuss her needs with someone objective, someone who she could trust with her doubts and fears about almost everything she had valued beforehand. She wanted what no one could give her: wisdom and the guidance to do the right thing. She needed this for her own peace of mind, yet she felt useless and weak, a dull, throbbing, trembling nothingness at the core of her, unable to garner even the smallest spark of anger or fight to understand her own selfish needs.

She had no energy anymore, no optimism, no zest for life. It was as if all her most authentic and well-endowed characteristics – her inner life, her utmost Safiness – had been sucked right out of her. And replaced with – what? Nothing, that was what. Suddenly everything went dark. Sasha had been her life up to now, and now she had no life, no energy or interest in anything. And yet her mind still raced.

Should I cut and run? But what about Sasha? Don't I love him enough to sit this out? Who do my loyalties belong to, the Rubicov family or me? What does it mean to be loyal, or to love someone, truly? What do I stand for? How can I figure any of this out when I don't even know what I want?

That was the worst, turning all of that anger and fear inward, towards herself. She needed to know what she wanted before she could plan her next steps.

She looked up at Valentina as the thoughts raced through her mind. She shot up from her chair. 'I must speak to Anna,' Safi said.

'I think you tell Alexi,' Valentina replied. 'Anna has gone to a villa in the South of France with family.'

Safi wondered why she felt the need to speak with Anna. After all, Anna must also be devastated over Sasha's predicament. Safi had to remember that she did not have exclusive rights on her grief over Sasha. She could not be selfish. This was a family affair and everyone was hurting, even if in very different ways. Still, under the circumstances, it was difficult not to be selfish. If anyone knew what the family was dealing with, Anna did.

Alexi had been on the phone making deals with government agencies, but he had to wait until noon before he could liaise with Mika or DuPont in New York: the time difference was an irritation he could do without. He walked to the kitchen and sank down heavily in his chair. Safi noticed how haggard and exhausted he appeared. She felt guilty for her own self-pity, but could not shake the sadness she felt at the situation she found herself in.

Suddenly these people felt like strangers to her. She needed to be with her own family, yet she felt beholden to Sasha to remain put. She could feel their need for her presence, even if it were just to remind them that they still had a part of Sasha with them. Sasha had always been buoyed by her sunniness, but there was nothing sunny about her now; not anymore.

'You slept well,' Alexi said. 'Hope not so tired, yes? We must accomplish more today. I need you to be in the office today, Safi. We need to move your art operation to New York City. That is where you want to be, right?'

Safi's mouth opened; she knew she was speaking but had little control over what she was saying.

'I don't know what I want.' The tears started to flow down her cheeks. 'I feel completely lost without Sasha, I seem not to belong anywhere now.'

'I know this a shock,' Alexi said slowly, his gaze even with hers and his sensitive eyes exhausted-looking, red-rimmed and puffy but nonetheless alive with feeling, 'but Safi, he is alive, yes, and you are not alone. You part of our family. We see this through together, fight together for Sasha.'

She shook her head as if she understood what he was saying, though her heart and her mind could comprehend nothing. She was still in a haze, and perhaps he was too, for he glanced away from her for the first time, as though his attention had moved on from her. She did not want to lose Alexi's goodwill and his trust, but she also did not want to make hasty promises she could not fulfil, and right now she felt incapable of everything, even the simplest things like talking and moving felt heavy and confusing.

She felt as if her world had collapsed. Before moving to Moscow, she had been warned that Russia was very different from the life she was used to back home in Britain, but she had not realised the degree to which this was true. Everything about Russia was different, from how people addressed one another to the inscrutable inner workings of the government. In Britain, you could see Parliament operating out in the open on television. In Russia, it seemed, everything that happened, happened in the darkness.

She did not understand their world, where everything could turn upside-down at the whim of the powerful. No law broken, no crime committed, but to broker nonetheless for someone's life. Everyone making deals, no one – not even the very rich, it appeared – entitled to basic rights. It was an alien world to Safi. It made no sense to her because she was a foreigner, but those who had lived here all of their life could not explain it to her, either. She felt more scared and helpless than she ever imagined possible, not only for herself but for Sasha as well. For months now, Sasha and her had felt like one person, and with half of her gone she too felt imprisoned and at sea. His pain was her pain, and her pain was too great, right now, to bear.

'It seems so hopeless,' Safi said, and he made eye contact with her again. 'They have all these grudges against you and the family. Why would they free Sasha? I can't understand your country or it's political system, where no law seems to matter. They do what they want when they want. They give and take away anyone's livelihood and freedoms on a whim. Everyone seems to be in the State's pocket. No one is safe inside or outside the country. How will we fight this, Alexi?'

Alexi could not argue with her synopsis of the present government, but to him the workings of the State were, if not altogether explicable or predictable, at least a lot more familiar. To get by, everyone played the same games and lined the same pockets and repeated the same lies. You became dulled to the dirty dealings of the State after a while – that is, until the State came for your family. He knew that, with enough influence and bargaining power with the contacts they had in their inner circles, he would be able to make a deal to suit them all.

What he did not know was how to explain this to a young, foreign girl who felt she had lost the person she loved. To try to explain Russia to a non-Russian was perhaps like explaining the concept of colour to someone born blind. But Safi had value to the family; they needed her not only for Sasha, but to keep the gallery going outside of Russia.

Valentina asked to speak with Alexi in private. Safi remained in the kitchen, picking joylessly at the scrambled eggs and bacon the cook had just put down in front of her. She did not have the heart to say she had no appetite. She felt she had disappointed everyone enough by her lack of resolve and her downcast demeanour. Her stomach felt as if it was knotted into a tight ball.

Alexi returned to the kitchen and, over a second cup of coffee, tried to give Safi's mood a lift by regaling her with anecdotes of past skirmishes he had had with the Russian authorities, skirmishes that, in the end, had been resolved for both parties. But this only increased Safi's anxiety. She thought about how irretrievably corrupt the country was, about how everyone went around in circles – and to what end?

Alexi added that, with Safi's help, he was sure they could manage to do the same for Sasha. She knew he was trying to involve her, trying once more to make her feel a vital part of the family and a part of this infernal system that was currently trying to tear them apart.

She followed Alexi to his office. It was close enough to noon to call Mika. Alexi felt Safi's interest would spike if she became involved with the authorities and the sting to catch Fritzi and her gang of thieves. It would bring Safi into direct contact with dealers and the world she loved and had spent three almost four years much of her young working life building the gallery into a viable concern.

Alexi was in frequent touch with the doctors at the Swiss clinic, and Yvetta's progress reports all seemed encouraging. The last thing he wanted to happen was for Fritzi to worm her way back into Yvetta's life. He had the sense that Fritzi was an addiction Yvetta had not fully kicked; it was imperative that the two women never be in contact again. He did not put it past Fritzi to find a way into the clinic.

The success of the sting was important to Alexi for more than one reason. It would bring an end to his fears for his daughter's wellbeing where Fritzi was concerned. And it should enable him to cut a deal with the authorities in Russia. It all depended on the success of the sting. Alexi felt sure that a successful sting would reach the ears of the people who mattered, standing the family in good stead when they reached out to make a deal.

Mika was the first to speak on the open line, bringing them up to date on his progress. He spoke in English for Safi's benefit. Alexi noticed that she was now sitting on the edge of her seat following the proceedings. She asked to speak with DuPont, wanting to clarify whether the authorities agreed to allow the artefact to be put on the market again even though it had been established as a fake. The expert in the field had alerted one or two other buyers who had interest in the figurine to put in a high bid for the artefact when it returned to the market. When the bid was accepted, they would then follow the sale, waiting for Fritzi and her gang to make contact with DuPont.

They would introduce another stolen fake and insist DuPont find a buyer for it. Releasing it back onto the market and hoodwinking the dealers into believing that it had been put up for resale by the owner – this way they would double their investment on the fake.

The whole scenario was becoming hugely complicated, though everyone felt confident the money could not be moved without the authorities being able to follow where or to whom it went The buyers and the dealers had been briefed and knew the role they were expected to play.

The catch was luring them out of hiding to drop off the artefact before the money was deposited into their bank account. The whole deal was to take place in a couple of hours. They were all playing for high stakes. The dealers in the know would double the price for resale, but the artefact would have to be physically in their hands before resale, making the criminal syndicate a tidy extra million dollars.

Alexi and Safi were now completely immersed in the sting, and they were both nervous wrecks. If they missed the pickup or the drop-off, the whole scenario would collapse, alerting the network. The smugglers would go underground once more; it would take years before they were presented – if ever – with an opportunity to crack the network wide open again.

The phone on Alexi's desk sprang into life, the red light flashing. He pressed the conference call button, and they were on speaker with Kolya. This time they were speaking in Russian. Alexi listened for a few moments, then asked if Kolya could try to speak in English so Safi could understand.

Reluctantly, hesitating often, Kolya related in broken English what was happening.

'Woman contact owner and offer $50,000 more for artefact.'

'That's good,' Safi said, 'did they accept?'

'Owner ask why sell for only $50,000 more? Market price fetch double.'

Staring at Safi, neither sure whether this was going to work, Alexi asked, 'What happened?'

'Woman threaten spread rumour artefact fake if not sell. Owner meet woman Waldorf Hotel, 1pm.'

'That's in five hours,' Safi said.

'Da, undercover policeman many at hotel, wait. Owner ask meet in suite at hotel, make exchange.'

'Okay,' Alexi said, 'we wait for your next call.'

Excited but cautious, they both took a break for lunch. Alexi had calls to make. Safi returned to the kitchen for company. She did not want to be alone. All she could think of was calling Sasha to fill him in – an impossibility, of course. Not being able to speak with him was becoming more painful and frustrating than she imagined.

Valentina was out for the day but the staff were in the kitchen and Safi felt at home in their company. They did not mention Sasha. Safi knew that the staff kept their ears close to the ground when things were happening in the household, and somehow pulled together in a comforting, conspiratorial way to make everyone feel cared for. This time felt no different.

Still an emotional wreck, she was in no state to make calls, but she felt that she needed to keep in touch with the two D's, and her folks would wonder why she had not mailed recently. Safi sat at her laptop, nibbling at the salad, when she noticed three emails she had not opened since her arrival back in London.

One of them had an address she did not recognise – she wondered why it had not gone into spam. Taking a chance, she opened the email. Wide-eyed with shock, she realised the message was from Sasha. It consisted of only a few lines, but she knew immediately it was from him.

NYC 2D's 791 SR. Not so much words, but code. She sat staring at the screen. It did not take long for her to work out what he wanted her to do.

Go to NY, be with the two D's, and stay in his apartment, number 791. 'SR' stood for Sasha Rubicov. She ran back to the office. Alexi was on a call but she did not care. She barged in and pushed the iPad across the desk to him.

'*Look*,' she said, 'it's from Sasha.'

Alexi hung up and pulled the iPad closer. 'Clever boy,' he said, smiling. It was a long time since she had seen him smile like that. 'He has managed to get someone to send you this message. This is wonderful. It means there is someone on his side helping. We have a contact.'

Safi felt elated. She wanted to tell Sasha she loved him and missed him – but dare she? She hesitated suddenly and said, 'What if it's not Sasha? How should we answer? Can we trust this person?'

He had written in a code that only they could understand. Maybe she had to do the same.

'Well, this person has written Sasha's message. We must work out carefully the information you send.' So much was happening in such a short space of time, Safi found her head reeling, not sure she was able to cope with all of the information crashing down on her from all sides of the world, New York and Moscow, with little or no control of the outcome. All of these disparate threads somehow tied together to reveal a larger pattern – but what?

It was 6pm but only one o'clock in New York, and they had not heard anything from Kolya or Mika. The sting would be happening soon. They would soon know if it had been a success. Safi typed quickly and then handed the iPhone over for Alexi to read. *Chelsea spring, NY Summer Fall 4U X.*

'It's good,' he said. 'Does not tell the reader anything, but gives him an idea where you are and will be and what you are hoping for. Send it and we will see if Sasha is able to reply.'

Safi pressed 'SEND'. She had barely had time to breathe when Alexi's phone buzzed. They both stared at it for a few moments before Alexi pressed the conference button. A strangled voice came on the line.

'Schweinhund, you will not get away with this.'

Then an American voice said, 'I think you should rephrase that, don't you?'

It was Mika who came on next.

'We have Fritzi, as you can hear. We think she is working alone in New York; once she has been interrogated, we will know more.'

Alexi banged his hand down on his desk in delight.

'Keep us informed and keep her in chains. She is like Houdini so watch her.'

They could hear Fritzi cursing in German. '*Shize.*'

Even though Safi had only met her once, there was no mistaking Fritzi's larger-than-life personality. Safi knew it had to be her, arrogant in attitude to the end. 'You will regret this, Rubicov bastard. I learnt plenty about your so-called empire from Yvetta. I will find her, you will all pay.'

Alexi did not bother to reply. He was relieved to find that Fritzi obviously had no idea where Yvetta was, hoping that it would remain that way forever. He was happy for Fritzi to believe his daughter had let her down. It was now up to the FBI to hand her over to Interpol and the Russian authorities. Perhaps the FBI would keep her for transgressions perpetrated on US soil. Alexi did not care where she landed up, as long as they threw away the key. She could rot in hell as far as he was concerned.

'Do you think Fritzi's capture will lead them to her underground contacts in the art world?' Safi asked. 'If they do not manage to get what they want from her, will it be enough of a bargaining chip for them to release Sasha?'

Alexi did not know the answers to Safi's questions, but he hoped that having Mika part of the negotiations would enable Mika to put the word out amongst the contacts he still had left inside the police and the Kremlin. Words in the right ear could do for Sasha what it had done in other, similar situations in the past. The Russians were undergoing strenuous times, and any additional bad press abroad would surely be something they would prefer to avoid. It was a waiting game: the family would have to have patience and wait for the machinery to move, hopefully in the right direction, before any of their recent efforts could pay off.

'Safi, all we can do is be patient,' Alexi explained, 'and when I say 'patient', you have to realise these things can take a long time.'

Safi stared at Alexi. She had been stupid enough to think that, after Fritzi was caught, Sasha would be released within a week, would be back beside Safi and in her arms again. Realising her naïveté, she looked up to see the pain in Alexi's face. His eyes were dull, his complexion grey, he showed his stress in a different way; the cracks were showing.

Well, Sasha made it clear he wanted me to go back to NYC,' Safi said, trying to put a brave face on it, 'and I think that's what I ought to do. If you do not mind, I really have no one here now that my folks are spending six months of the year in Australia. I do not want to upset them, or have them come back because of me, so I am not going to tell them about this, until we know more.'

'Yes, agree,' Alexi said, sounding eager to tie the conversation up and return to the business of the family's Russia crisis, 'you will have much to do in NYC. I will try to have Mika and Kolya help you purchase a new gallery once we have found the right property. I am sure DuPont and Zack will lend a helping hand.'

Suddenly she felt exhausted. Valentina knocked on Alexi's office door. Safi made her excuses and went to her room to arrange her flight back to New York.

On her own once more in New York, the city seemed alien without Sasha. Neighbourhoods and restaurants they had visited together, bright shiny places, now looked worn-out and lifeless – or was that just her? DuPont was being an absolute gentleman, helping her choose suitable premises in Chelsea. The premises were small but a good start to build up her new collection, and the perfect area to become accustomed to the high-energy art market. With Zack's guidance, she could offer a different kind of gallery space, and her New York artists would be happy to provide her with work to open her doors to the public once she managed to get sorted.

Planning for the opening of the new gallery took up all of her time. At first she resisted staying without Sasha at the apartment in the Rubicov building, but she did not have the time to search for her own place. Alexi had given her the option with the purchase of the gallery the Rubicov company would be happy to purchase an, apartment of her choice, if she did not want to remain in Sasha's apartment, for now. She worked all hours of the day and night – and that was a good thing, distracting her from depressing thoughts and feelings. The gallery – the idea of the gallery, *her* gallery – became a kind of friend to her. Something hopeful and positive to fill up a future with and give her something to live for and look forward to.

Her body felt as heavy as a sack of bricks when she sank down on their bed at night. She had moved Sasha's pillow lengthwise, waking at dawn with her arms and her legs entwined around it. Somehow it made being without him less lonely. Since the coded text she had sent they hadn't heard a word.

Kolya had returned to London where he now worked for Alexi once again. No one had a timeframe for Sasha's release, but all, including Anna and the rest of his family, encouraged her to keep busy. To open the gallery would be what Sasha would want.

Her own family were more sceptical. Once Safi broke the news to them about Sasha's arrest, they were initially too shocked to have any opinion. But the more Leonard and Fiona spoke with their daughter, and to Dan and Dax, they began to doubt whether Sasha would ever be released. Fearing for their daughter's future, they tried to encourage her to socialise and not to isolate herself, or to make the gallery her whole existence. She deserved to have a life while she waited for his release.

The two D's were devastated, too. They took charge of Safi's wellbeing, never leaving her alone on weekends. She became part of their family once more, entwined in their everyday lives, immersed in their excitement as the surrogate became closer to having their baby. Neither Dax nor Dan wanted to know the sex of the baby. The nursery took on a magical yellow hue with rainbows, rabbits, and other small animals adorning the walls and the bassinette bought from Giggles, the must-go-to baby store which became their weekend haunt.

The shelves filled with every baby book they could find; toys were stacked up waiting to be opened, including every baby practicality one could possibly need, all bought at giggles. Safi wondered what was left for anyone to buy for the baby shower, which Dax was organising with more joy than any mom-to-be could have managed. The surrogate was to have an elective caesarean, something her gynaecologist had recommended was the best option for everyone.

Safi still managed to spend time with Pete, who kept her sane with his endless patience, listening to her mindless chatter and offering her his dusting cloth to dry her occasional tears.

Weeks, then months, went by without a word about Sasha's situation. Anna, Alexi, and even Mika kept in touch, always encouraging her to be hopeful. Then, one night just as she was drifting off to sleep, her cell phone rang. Safi picked it up but all she heard was breathing. She kept saying hello but heard nothing in response, just breathing.

She cut off the call, staring at the cell, expecting it to ring again. But nothing happened. Safi convinced herself that it was a wrong number, or someone who had not realised their cell was on. The next night, at the exact same time, as she drifted off to sleep, the same thing happened. Breathing. Nothing. And again, the night after. Shaking with fear, she called Mika in Florida. He had given her his direct line on the private cell he only used for family. Mika picked up immediately. Through her distress he managed to patch together what had happened for the last three nights. There was a long pause before he responded.

'I will be there tonight when it happens again. Have you mentioned this to anyone else?'

'No, but I am now petrified.' Indeed, her hand – and along with it her cell phone – was still shaking. 'I have no idea what's going on. Is someone watching me? Maybe someone is following me. Isn't that what they do in Russia if they suspect you? Next thing I will disappear and no one will know where I am.'

'This not case,' Mika said, somewhat awkwardly, truly a man of few words, 'but we need to find who and why you get calls.'

'When you home I will be there. Now you sleep. I see you tomorrow.'

The line went dead and Safi made a stiff brandy from the drink cabinet. Her senses spinning, she fell into a deep sleep.

Mika was waiting in the Rubicov club when she arrived home from work. He insisted on taking her to the Rubicov restaurant for dinner.

'You need fattening up,' he said. He had never seen her so thin, she needed to eat, not fade away, before Sasha was free. 'You get ill, then what?'

Safi found his concern for her wellbeing amusing and decided to humour him by trying to eat a hearty minestrone soup with crusty homemade bread. At Mika's insistence, they shared a fettuccini with truffles. It was more than she had eaten in weeks. Her stomach felt as if it would burst. They discussed the gallery, how the location suited her, whether the new artist they had opening it would pull in as many clients as Safi successfully managed in Moscow. They spoke about their favourite restaurants in Manhattan. They spoke about some of the many ways that Moscow and Manhattan were worlds apart. They discussed everything, as it happened, but Sasha and the call that she both hoped and feared would come later that night. He plied her with wine throughout the meal. He probably wanted her to be relaxed while they waited until midnight for the call to come again. Safi doubted she would be restrained enough not to fall apart when the silent caller rang again. She found it nerve-wracking not knowing whether it was Sasha trying to call, or someone on his behalf, or just a wacko trying to frighten her. And what if – a new thought – the caller was somehow one step ahead of her and did not call tonight while Mika was there?

They returned to Sasha's apartment just before 11.30. Only a half hour to wait for the call. She still felt shivery with tension. Once in the apartment, Mika asked for Safi's cell, tested the ring, and plugged it in to make sure the battery was charged. They put the cell on the table between them, where Sasha and Safi first sat staring at the lights snaking far below, on her first real date, when Sasha so elegantly seduced her, or did she seduce him?. From his jacket pocket Mika removed a pad of paper and a ballpoint, both of which bore the Rubicov logo, and set them down on the table near the phone. They sat on the swing chairs facing the New York skyline, where down below the yellow cabs snaked along the streets and the neon signs glowed brightly on storefronts. Leaning into the chair, she felt her eyes growing heavy.

She woke with a start. At first, she had no idea where she was; seeing Mika in the swing chair alongside hers soon brought her back to reality. It should have been his younger brother, Sasha, who she opened her eyes to. Safi felt darkness pressing down on her, her heart lifting and falling with increasing speed. She felt, too, the pulse of the night, the strangely quiet room. The moment stretched and flexed, endless and impossible. Everything was pulled taut: their faces, their eyes, their breathing – everything. Distended and deformed. Even their movements exaggerated in their clumsy attempts at restraint. She closed her eyes again reflexively, then opened them sharply. She felt dizzy.

Mika attempted a smile, but again his nervousness revealed itself. Nothing had changed. He tapped his fingers on the table three times. Then three times more. A rhythm was established. Tap-tap-tap. Tap-tap-tap. She told herself to breathe. Eleven fifty-nine. She looked at her phone. She tried not to look at her phone. *Breathe*. Tap-tap-tap. Tap-tap– His fingers hovered. She waited for it but it did not come. The seconds suspended, time agonising her situation anew, and felt hopeless all over again. The more she tried to rationalise her predicament, the less confident she became about ever seeing Sasha again. She had asked people to stop regaling her with horror stories, they were too much to bear.

She looked at her watch. Eleven fifty-five. Five minutes to go. She needed to be alert, collect her emotions, to be ready – but for what? More dead-ends, more disappointment, more desolation and loneliness. Taking a deep breath, banishing negative thoughts from her mind, she made her way to the kitchen and poured two cups of espresso from the coffee machine. She could tell that Mika, who was used to dealing with all kinds of intrigue, was showing signs of nerves, as he kept pulling his fingers through his thick greying hair. After all, it was his brother and her fiancé who was locked up in a Russian prison, while the rest of his family were safely out of the country. She tried to steady herself, but felt she would come undone entirely. Eleven fifty-eight. They looked at each other; neither spoke. She could in its sudden slowness. Then dropped down like a guillotine. Tap. Thank God. Some sort of closure, at least, but then it all began again. *Breathe*. Tap-tap-tap. Twelve o'clock. Mika was no longer smiling. Everything had changed. A sound that wasn't tapping or breathing and then her head began to spin.

Her cell vibrated on the table, its shrill ring pierced their dulled senses into sharp focus. *Breathe*. But it was too late to breathe now – everything had come too far. Safi waited for Mika's sign before she lifted the cell to her ear, saying a tentative hello. Both watched each other closely to read any sign that may give the caller an identity. 'Hello,' she said again. 'Hello?'

Mika took the cell, plugged some device he had into the charging slot at the bottom, and gave the cell back to Safi. He mouthed, 'Speak, say anything.'

'I do not know who you are,' she said slowly, finding the words, 'but why are you calling every night at this hour? Surely it would be better to tell me what you want than to say nothing?'

The cell was on speaker. They waited. Again, the seconds seemed to bleed away, but at least the call had not yet been aborted.

'Starbucks, 80 Delancey Street,' a flat, disembodied electronic voice said, 'the Lower East Side, six p.m. tomorrow.'

Mika's eyes locked with Safi's. He grabbed the pen and paper and wrote the address down. Safi sat with the cell in her hand for what seemed like ages after the automated voice had rung off.

'But that sounded just like a recording.'

'It is recorded message held near cell. I check now if cell belongs to anyone, but probably pay-as-you-go cell. I will send someone to Starbucks to watch over you. I will not go, maybe they recognise and run. Someone not Russian, maybe lady. I will make arrangements. Not worry, she will know who you are.'

'But what do you think this is about, Mika? Is it about Sasha? Or something unrelated?' He sat in silence for a moment, then he shrugged his shoulders, non-committal.

'I have Yvetta's apartment. Goodnight, Safi, I will call you later today.'

He was gone, leaving Safi in a state of panic. She was fired up, excited, but not sure why. She was sure at last she would have some word of Sasha.

Once in bed she tossed and turned, endless scenarios playing through her mind and sleep for ever at bay. As she finally dozed off she was aware of dawn breaking through the shutters.

The day at the gallery passed by in a distracted haze. The only thing on her mind was the meeting that evening. Mika had called to tell her to sit by a window if she could; he would have security both inside and outside the coffee shop.

She tried to walk into Starbucks with a relaxed confidence, ten minutes early ordering a latte and finding a seat by the window. She set up her laptop like so many others around her, hoping to attract little if no attention from others in the coffee shop. There were no more than a dozen people spread around. Not wanting to make any obvious observations of the clientele, she sipped her coffee as she scanned the room, seemingly with disinterest, relieved that she could not pick out the security people Mika had placed around.

A smartly dressed woman in a red coat entered, stopping at the door to look about. She moved smoothly to the counter, made eye contact with the barista before ordering. No, Safi thought, not her. Safi returned to her coffee and computer screen, looking up intermittently to see whether this woman may be her contact – she seemed not to be. The coffee shop was filling up with people picking up take-outs on their way home and Safi found she was not able to distinguish anyone in particular. The chairs around her had mostly been taken up when a man, wearing a NY baseball cap brushed past, almost knocking a chair over at her table. Apologising as he straightened the chair, he moved on to a table at the back of the room. That was when Safi noticed a folded white paper lying under the chair he had knocked over. She bent down to retrieve the note and return it to the man who had dropped it on his way to what she thought was another table. But when she looked for him she realised that he was no longer in the coffee shop.

She placed the note on the table and continued to sip her coffee, trying to act unflustered and at ease. With an easy, fluid, unobtrusive moment she picked up the note and opened it. It was from Sasha. Shocked, she dropped the note and took a sharp intake of breath. She needed to calm down and not draw attention to either herself or the note. She nonchalantly dropped the note into her briefcase, folded the laptop away into her bag, lifted her long camel coat from behind the chair, and left Starbucks, hoping to find Mika close by. As her bag brushed against her on the busy street, the letter became the only object that mattered. She felt prickly hot sweat break on her forehead.

With every step the bag became heavier; she felt the full weight of her fatigue, or her anxiety, her feet shaking, too, now. The street was a blur of activity now – cold sweat prickled in her brows, and her mouth felt dry. She tried to walk faster but instead stumbled, almost fell. From somewhere, a car horn sounded. There were voices – many voices – speaking in languages she could not understand. All of a sudden, she realised she did not know anything, but that the message in her bag was of crucial importance. This moment felt as loaded as her laptop bag. She hurried on. At the corner of Allen Street, she was about to hail a cab when she spotted Mika.

He had a limo and was waving to Safi to join him. But she kept on walking. She was sweating heavily now. Her plan was to ignore Mika and hail a cab, where she would be able to read the letter in private. But she thought better of the wild plan and joined Mika in the back of the limo. As it sped off Mika lent over to tell her not to take the note out until they reached the safety of her apartment. There they could go over it with a fine-tooth comb for any hidden code or agenda. She felt her stomach turn. Dizzy and drenched in sweat, she leaned over to touch the window, desperate to hold on to something.

The glass felt warm, surprising her. She thought of sliding down the window and sticking her head out, like a dog, revived by the fresh air. But the windows appeared to be locked. The windows were tinted but she couldn't see much out of them, either. Biting her bottom lip, she felt a blackness envelope her. Mika turned to find Safi had passed out. Probably the tension, he thought, or weeks of not eating properly.

As they drew up to the curb he called one of the doormen to help carry Safi into the building. The movement obviously brought her round and they managed to get her to the apartment on foot.

Once inside the apartment, Safi ran to the toilet and retched until her stomach ached. The bilious hot feeling gone, she washed her face with cold water. Oh my God, where was her bag? Had she left it in the limo? She felt ill all over again. She rushed to the living room to find Mika sitting with her bag; he had had the good sense to take it.

Together they sat at the dining room table, opened the folded paper and smoothed it out. It read like any normal letter from a loved one, but after the first few words they immediately realised that it was a coded message. They scrutinised each word, quickly realising that every third line was in a different language. Safi knew Sasha was able to speak at least five languages; it did not surprise her that he had integrated Italian, German and even Cantonese into the letter.

'How are you going to decode this without having someone familiar with Chinese decipher the letter?' Safi asked. Then she realised something. It's not only Chinese, but Japanese too.'

The English, on the other hand, was pretty straightforward. Sasha was being well treated – that was a relief. He was missing them. He had no idea when they would release him. Nothing had been asked for, which meant that he did not know what to offer them in return for his release, or even when it would become apparent what they were after. He had been fortunate to befriend an officer who had studied with him in the States and was now working for the legal department at the holding cell where he was under civil arrest.

He hoped he would be granted bail, once they decided how to proceed with his case. Another inmate had already been there six months and still had no idea why they had arrested him; his family were out of the country.

He hoped Safi would remain in the States. He loved her more than words could say; just the thought of seeing her and holding her was keeping him strong. He hoped she would stay positive and strong until he returned.

Safi tried to stop the tears welling up in her eyes but failed miserably. She felt her shoulders sagging, then her whole body started to shake as she sobbed uncontrollably. Feeling like a weak fool, she ran to the bedroom and threw herself on to the bed. She grabbed the pillow, punching it to rid herself of the utter hopeless anger that overcame her.

She heard the door close as Mika let himself out. Wanting to read the English part again, she dragged herself into the dining area, only to find that Mika and the letter had gone. Not having Sasha's words to read over and over again until she had them imprinted on her mind made her feel lonelier than ever. She had felt so hopeful and joyful for a moment, and now that hope and joy had gone along with Mika and the letter. More than anything, she felt exhausted. She undressed, showered, put her clothes out for the next day. Her movements felt automated, as if on automatic pilot. It was as though she was someone else – or no one in particular. She crawled under the covers and lay in a stupor until sleep eventually crept up on her.

Mika was seated on one of the sofas near the elevator.

'I hope you are rested. It's tough, I know, you hang in there, Safi.' He was struggling to communicate with her, perhaps struggling to stay positive, too. He seemed exhausted himself. 'You see Sasha for sure. I believe not long.' But he did not sound convinced.

'I hope you are right, Mika,' she said, surprised at how her steady and forthright her voice was. Certainly, the sleep had done her good. She wasn't exactly back to old Safi, but she wasn't a zombie anymore, either. 'Not sure I can take much more of this skulduggery and intrigue. Not sure I am cut out for that kind of life.'

'I take letter to London. I leave tonight. Alexi, Kolya and I will be working to release Sasha. Please eat, yes? Smile, be with family, enjoy life.'

Easier said than done she thought as the elevator doors opened. She stepped inside, head held high, thinking how unsteady she had been on her feet only hours before. As the doors slid shut she saw Mika walking off. A serious expression had replaced his former show of bravado, for her sake no doubt. She knew now for sure that she would never know what took place behind the scenes, but she didn't really care if that meant Sasha coming home to her soon.

Mika walked into Alexi's office the next morning to be greeted by two Russian interpreters waiting to decipher the languages. They sat over the letter, translating the languages into Russian. At first, as the seemingly random words were translated, it did not make a whole lot of sense to Alexi and Mika. They waited patiently until it had all been written down, hoping that somewhere in these random words would be a message from Sasha. Having done their job, the translators departed, leaving father and son alone to work on the letter. If they were not able to find what it was Sasha had planted amongst the random languages, they would have to bring someone else in to try and crack his riddle.

In between many coffee breaks they worked on the letter late into the night. Even Valentina tried to figure out some system or link between the words or the different languages. But whatever they came up with did not apply to anything that was a valid explanation for holding Sasha, or a name of a person or persons they could deal with, or someone the authorities might want in return for Sasha's release.

Disillusioned they retired for the night. Mika took himself off to one of the many gambling clubs he enjoyed when in London. He belonged to a private club where he dined amongst Russian acquaintances, many now living outside of Russia, but no one ever knew who was spying on whom. The Kremlin was up to its old tricks; no one knew whose side anyone was on. The only difference was that now they were free to travel; but some were still in the deep pockets of the authoritarian establishment. For perks that included belonging to private clubs, they reported back whatever they deemed valuable, in and outside of Russia. Mika had his own reasons for making himself visible to the spies. He needed to find some way to make contact with whoever had allowed that letter to leave the holding cell. It was a sure sign there was an opening for negotiation.

He joined some old friends for good conversation, indulging in the finest caviar, many shots of the best vodka, and a meal to make one's tastebuds die and go to heaven, not to mention the beautiful women in the club. One of the finest Russian chefs in the world worked at the club: another reason Mika chose to put up with the new Russia and its many spies. Everyone's palm was greased and many found themselves enticed by the generous package that came with being in a foreign land while helping the mother country. After all, it was their motherland, once a

Russian always a Russian, and the Kremlin propaganda machine worked well even outside of the country. They were, after all, living in the digital age.

The expats all watched Russian TV in their homes, a sure way to keep them connected to whatever slant they wished to put on any political view outside of its borders. Most left to get away from the New Russia, but once living outside of its borders they reverted to believing all the propaganda they had run away from in the first place. As he retired to smoke a Cuban cigar in the smoking room with a few choice people, Mika thought human nature a strange thing. These were people he knew he could rely on to point him in the right direction, contacts in the right places who had always paid off over the years with the Kremlin and their worker bees.

He did not have to elaborate: everyone knew what had happened to the Rubicov family. It had happened to a number of oligarchs: when they sold up and left Russia with their assets, the State punished them in whatever way it could.; But in this instance the authorities had imprisoned a family member, everyone's worst nightmare. Those in the know were only too happy to help their comrade loosen the authorities' grip on Mika's brother. They promised to whisper in the right ears, to put pressure on those who had the power to release Sasha. But Mika wanted contacts; he did not want these influencers meddling in Rubicov affairs. Neither did he want to owe anyone on this side of the world any favours. Mika was critically aware that the situation could become even worse for Sasha if he, Mika, handled it badly from his end. The authorities would entrench their hold on Sasha, in a bid to increase leverage, they could prolong his stay, and who knew how long that would take. The Kremlin worked from the top down and they seemed to have Russia in their grip for the foreseeable future.

He needed someone expert at solving riddles or codes. In this environment it was easier to put out the word. The expats had networks that were not paid a great deal and he hoped the thought of extra money would bring someone out of the woodwork. He left a few contact numbers and retired for the night hoping his hours at the club had not been entirely in vain. Certainly, he had enjoyed himself – possibly too much. He began to feel a little guilty, putting his feet up in such luxurious circumstances while his brother was thousands of miles away, in a Russian prison, in God knows what condition. Maybe it wasn't guilt, but the aftereffects of too much cigar smoke and too many shots of vodka. He shook his head, as if to rid himself of the ill feelings, stood up and left. He could easily have gone home with a number of beauties, but he did not want to be distracted from the job of getting Sasha released from prison. Besides, several of the stunners were more than likely spies, very good at their jobs; few who became involved with them would ever know their true profession, while the spy in question would, of course, know everything important about their lover: his telephone and bank account numbers, his deepest secrets, his influence and aspirations, his political connections, how to seduce him and also how to destroy him.

As he was collecting his coat from the hat-check girl, a brunette he had been chatting to made her way towards him. Without a word she bent over to kiss him on both cheeks, pressing something into his palm as he did so. The Rolls-Royce was waiting across the road with Kolya at the wheel; one of many parked near the club with drivers waiting.

Mika opened his palm to find a business card. About to discard it, thinking it was the brunette's contact number, he noticed the name of a computer company with both a London and Russian address. Placing the card into his wallet, he decided that it may be worth trying to call the following morning.

Mika called the London number the next day, only to be greeted by a recorded message and the sound of a beep. Strange. What sort of company was this? He hesitated before leaving his throwaway cell number, hoping he wasn't being led up a blind alley.

Alexi had work-related issues to deal with and Valentina was with her charges from the ballet school. Kolya persuaded Mika to accompany him while he did some investigating. He took the unusual step of suggesting Mika dress down. They stopped at a coffee shop Kolya frequented, where he met interesting people who had contacts with many underground groups, working against the present Russian authorities. Kolya found out many things from these contacts, information few others knew. Mika trusted Kolya with his life, and was happy to follow any lead that could help with Sasha's release.

If Mika and Kolya had some idea where Sasha was being held, or to what extent his incarceration could be negotiated, and with whom, it would make their strategy for Sasha's release less complicated. As they walked into what Mika could only describe as an immigrant workers' café, filled with Eastern Europeans. Kolya greeted two Eastern European men at a corner table at the back of the café. A moment later, Kolya gestured to Mika and he made his way over. Once at the table, with hot tea and buns, the conversation took on a level of disclosure Mika had never been aware of. He was learning about a powerful network, 'Thieves in Law' an notorious mobster elite, became powerful during Stalin's reign. Russians and Eastern Europeans, but, as it happened, they were not happy to reveal much. Mika's proletarian disguise did not fool them; they considered him an enemy. Kolya's no-nonsense and entirely authentic presence helped. No explaining was necessary; these men with their tattoo codes, had he was learning, a fearsome reputation. Mika had had dealings with a certain element of the underworld, but had never come face to face with any of these mythical characters before now. He knew they had spies everywhere in all of the prisons, networks of informants, a state within a state, much like the Italian mafia. They understood how the prison system worked: many of them had been guests of the worst prisons in Russia. Some were wardens, others officers even KGB, many were students who had run afoul of the law. The criminal element was another side they harnessed for their own benefit, and so far, the Kleptocracy had persisted in Russia.

Kolya had explained that any 'favour' they did you would leave you in their debt, they expected favours in return. Mika was desperate enough to be prepared to take his chances. Kolya filled the men in on Sasha's arrest and where they believed he was being held. The clandestine phone call, resulting in the letter with a hidden message, no one had yet deciphered.

The younger of the two men, wiry a long scar running down the side of his cheek running into his throat with a shaved head, asked to see the letter, A thin high, pitched strangled voice, 'You show letter.'

Mika handed it over to the skinhead, he would not want to meet on a dark night.

'Translation,' he said, looking at Mika threateningly.

Mika looked embarrassed; in his haste, he had given the man the original letter. Mika exchanged it for the interpreter's version, then watched as the two men, the second man was presentable in contrast to the wiry tattooed skinhead, more personable jowly with beady eyes and heavy brows, now, both in total concentration, took a pile of serviettes and wrote down letters in a row. Some letters they scratched out; the remaining letters they broke up into three lines, which they played around with until, to Mika's amazement, a sentence started to appear.

'How on earth did you work that out so quickly?' Mika asked.

'We have seen this code before,' the skinhead said in his strangled thin voice. 'It's a tricky one that many use in prison to get messages out. The person who carried this message out for your brother must have encrypted the code for him. It's not usually in many languages. Now that it's in Russian, we help.'

They continued to work on the words until a full sentence appeared. Drawing in his breath, the skinhead did not mince his words.

'Your brother's going to grow old in prison unless Putin drops dead or is no longer Tsar Putin.'

The older Russian continued. 'The charge is embezzlement, company fraud, stolen antiquities, slander of a government official, and corrupting police and other high-ranking officials.' On and on it went, a list of concocted charges, not unlike those levelled in the Russia of old.

'My brother is not responsible for any of those charges,' Mika said. 'We have moved our assets out of Putin's greedy hands. However, he has taken control of our media company and other assets. This should be enough to please their small-minded treachery against our family.'

The two men shrugged.

'This is not new,' the skinhead said. 'That's how they operate. They take a hostage to punish the whole family. Your family are being made to pay for not paying enough taxes, getting away with a fortune. Your brother is suffering for your desertion.'

Mika knew this only too well; they paid more tax than was necessary. Still, it came as a shock to hear it so openly from these hard men of the streets. He was reluctant to ask if anything could be done to help Sasha; not only was he afraid of the answer, he was doubtful they cared what happened to an oligarch.

True, Mika could make it worth their while, and the many cogs in the network of these men would work on his family's behalf; but they could also make things far worse for Sasha if they chose to.

A look passed between Mika and Kolya, a silence fell over their hushed conversation. Kolya shook their hands; thanking them for their help, he slipped them his contact number and they made their way out of the café.

'Don't worry,' Kolya said, his voice still low, 'you will hear within the hour how much they want in exchange for the help, and what they will need in return for helping Sasha.'

'How will we know if they have been able to help him?' Mika asked.

'You have already had the kind of help they provide,' Kolya said. 'This meeting was set up by the person who dropped that message.'

Mika looked at Kolya and the penny dropped: while he was at the club, Kolya had been contacted by one of these men. It was probably one of the men driving a Rolls-Royce for another patron of the club.

'Why did you not tell me when you drove me home from the club?' Mika asked.

Kolya shook his head.

'You were pretty smashed. I thought it better to wait until you were more alert when we visited these men. They are quick to judge, and they are powerful in their own right. They are also dangerous to rub up the wrong way.'

They drove back to Mayfair in silence. Mika knew he had to convince Alexi to trust these men. He wondered whether he should share their opinion of Sasha's incarceration with Alexi.

He felt responsible for what had happened to Sasha. There was no question that Sasha had suffered because of Mika's carelessness and lack of concern during the negotiations. The family were given enough warnings, which they had stupidly ignored, thinking that it was impossible for anyone to derail a deal already completed.

Sasha was left to wrap up some minor part of the transactions that needed his signature.

No one imagined that selling to the Russian billionaire who worked for the government would anger the Ukrainians. Now Sasha was the fall guy, paying for his family's stupidity.

Skirmishes were raging between Russian forces and the Ukraine. The Ukrainians needed access to their gas lines, which Russia was holding them hostage. Until the climate between the two countries changed, there was not a person anywhere on the planet who could secure Sasha's release. It was a lost cause.

Their only hope was smuggling him out under some kind of subterfuge: an uprising in the part of the prison where he was being held, for example. But it would take planning and millions to grease enough palms to carry such a plan out, and even then, it was dangerous for Sasha; if caught he could be executed by the prison guards, to save their own lives in the subterfuge.

Alexi studied the napkin the underground forces working against the 'Putincratic' dictatorship in the new Russia had deciphered. No doubt they were being bankrolled by opposition forces outside Russia that he was not aware of.

Mika knew he would have to break the bad news to his father about Sasha's predicament. He knew, too, that Alexi was not ready to face the truth about his youngest son's situation.

Alexi's bravado completely vanished as his oldest son's words penetrated through the wall he had built up to protect not only himself but the rest of his family from the awful truth. Sasha might never get out, it was all his doing, he only had himself to blame.

With a heavy heart, Mika watched his father's reaction to the news. He was struggling to breathe, then clutching his heart. Mika grabbed the phone and dialled an emergency number, telling the operator his address, finding it impossible to keep the panic out of his voice. Alexi was now lying on the floor, with Kolya leaning over him and pressing down on his chest, trying to prevent him from passing out.

Kolya's cell phone rang but no one answered. Mika God don't let my father die. Mika called Valentina and somehow managed to leave a calm message for her to call him back immediately. What happened next happened quickly. The paramedics arrived and took over. Mika stood back, trying to assess the situation, trying to breathe. More than anything, he wanted to make sense of what was going on in front of him. His phone started ringing. It was Valentina, in a frenzy of worry, returning his call. But he did not pick up. For a moment he was frozen. Mika, the one who was always in control, had no control, not of this situation, not anymore. The strong one suddenly weakened, revealed as vulnerable, his powers gone. He turned to see the paramedics exchange glances. The look, it appeared, was extended to Mika. Alexi would be okay. Mika breathed again, breathed deeply, sat on a chair and took Valentina's call, diverting her journey to the London clinic, his father's choice of hospital.

Mika did not hesitate to pay for the services of the men who helped decipher the code, and he instructed Kolya to deal with any further suggestions from them as to Sasha's dilemma. He needed to be by his father's side; there was nothing more they could do to help Sasha right now. It was an awful situation, but they could not afford to be anything other than pragmatic. The time for idealism and cockeyed optimism was over.

Mika was relieved to find his father sitting up, albeit with umpteen tubes attached to his chest. By all accounts, it had not been a serious attack. Valentina, white as a sheet, was hovering over him, telling him in a trembling voice that his father would be okay, but that — her voice firming up now — he needed rest and less stress in his life.

Mika smiled apologetically, knowing the guilt and pain his father felt about his youngest son being punished for his business dealings. His head and heart hurt when he thought about updating the family on the hopelessness of Sasha's ordeal. How was he going to give Anna this terrible news! Safi would recover: she was young, energetic, resilient. Anna, he knew, would crumble: she had a troubled daughter she could not relate to locked up in a clinic, and now a son she adored (her favourite child) locked up in a Russian prison. This was too much for any mother to cope with.

Alexi leant back against the pillows in the hospital bed. He closed his eyes and allowed the chatter and noise to drift around him as he quietly sobbed. Seeing the tears roll down his cheeks, alarmed anew, Valentina was about to call the doctor.

He stopped her. 'Valentina, remain by his side, hold his hand,' Mika said softly, hoping his father would not hear.

'It was the shock of the attack, he needed to let it out.'

He had seen his father cry before – from joy, from anger, but never from a broken heart; even when dealing with Yvetta, his tears were more out of anger. This time it was from helplessness, guilt, and sorrow for his youngest son, who he loved with his whole being. Sasha had had his whole life ahead of him – to further the family's business, to start a family of his own, to be happy and successful in his own right, and to one day take Alexi's place at the head of Rubicov Enterprises. Now that life had been stolen by a country he loved. How could one love and hate one's country in equal measure? Perhaps if one separated nation and state, loving the former and hating the latter? No, it wasn't that easy, nation and state were too often indivisible. Not only did he love Russia, he sometimes hated himself for loving it! The pain he felt was unbearable.

They remained with Alexi late into the night, leaving only after the doctors decided to medicate, allowing him a peaceful night's sleep. It was agreed that Alexi would remain a few days for forced rest and observation before being allowed to return home.

Chapter 3

Safi had not heard from Mika in over three weeks. Her days continued in a blur of activity. She was grateful for the new Rubicov Gallery's first major show. Soon she hoped only a month away they would be opening their doors to the public with Janus's work. Ying, his, assistant relayed all of Janus's wishes: it was Ying who met with them at the gallery, and it was Ying who would curate the work according to the artist's wishes. Three-dimensional plans of the gallery space had to be sent before any negotiations were begun, and all of Janus's stipulations were to be met.

Zack and Safi worked in tandem to see that all of the artist's wishes were carried out to his specifications. Ying reported back when something did not meet with the artist's approval. Safi was relieved that Janus was the artist to open her gallery; it gave them ample time, not needing to turn over another exhibition after the initial three-month period.

Janus was a sought-after artist who had up to this point not allowed any of his work to be shown in small gallery spaces. It was a major coup for them to have Janus put his first show on at a brand-new gallery in the city.

It would bring the art critics to the gallery in their droves, and the public would surely follow. Janus chose to sell his work only to private collectors around the world. Ying worked to promote his work internationally. So far Safi and Zack had not figured out why Janus had suddenly opted for a gallery showing. But Safi did not want to question this aspect too much, grateful he had chosen her space for his work; it suited Safi at this point in time. She did not care whether Janus promoted his work in person; his absence – coupled with newspaper articles about his elusive nature and publicity-shy, hermit-like ways – would bring a certain mystery, which would in turn make his work more, rather than less, attractive to the public and art critics.

DuPont had been invaluable in his support. After their run-in with Fritzi, their relationship had turned a corner. They had fostered a working friendship with a deep mutual respect. Safi found she could share her fears about Sasha with DuPont; she knew he would keep her secrets and give her only his honest opinions. DuPont, in turn, was encouraging on all fronts. His assurances went a long way; he had faith in both Mika and Alexi to secure some kind of deal to release Sasha. He encouraged her to be patient, and kept her interest renewed in the art world, and in the gallery opening in particular.

Leonard and Fiona were stopping off in New York before they returned to England. Her father was cock a hoop about her move to Manhattan. Somehow, she could not bring herself to explain the scary situation with Sasha disappearance over a phone call; she wanted to wait until they were face to face.

Her folks would arrive in time for the celebrity opening, when the art critics would, she hoped, descend in their droves on the new Manhattan Rubicov gallery. The invitations were sent out to all who mattered in the art world: professional collectors, art lovers, and many hopefully with deep pockets who loved having first pick of any highly regarded artist.

Sitting opposite her folks at breakfast, Safi decided there was no better time to break the news of Sasha's incarceration. Her throat was suddenly dry and she swallowed nervously. It was the ideal time, she decided, the only time; once she left for the gallery there would be zero time. She needed to break the news to them now, wanting it off her chest so that she could concentrate on the evening ahead.

Coughing to clear the dryness, she sipped some water. She looked over the rim of the glass and, before any appropriate wording entered her mind, she blurted out, 'Sasha is being held by the Russians. They won't let him leave.'

She saw the shock in her father's eyes and the colour drain from her mother's face. Safi herself was trying so hard not to dissolve into a mess. These were her parents, she needed their love and support now more than ever. A part of her wanted to be strong; instead, she crumbled like a child whose heart had broken.

This was not a minor scrape her mommy and daddy could fix, nothing could be kissed better or wished away. She was an adult now, whatever that meant, even though she felt more helpless than ever. This time her heartbreak was major and she had no idea whether the scrape would ever heal.

Her father, a strong man always able to fix things, did not move from his seat. Instead, he stared at his daughter helplessly. It was her mother who took command of the situation. Taking her daughter's hand, she held it until her daughters' tears subsided. Fiona kept silent until she was calm enough to continue. Ever resolute, she decided there had to be an explanation.

Nothing could have prepared them for the incredulous story that unfolded. Sasha had been arrested with next to no recourse to the law, it seemed; a hopeless situation for Sasha, his family, and, most importantly of all, their daughter. Always critical of the new Russia, Leonard now seemed at a loss for words, his anger visible. Safi noticed his knuckles turning white as he balled his fist and his other hand shattering the thin stemmed wine glass.

Safi could see him struggle to keep his cool. His daughter was his priority, yet she had continued to forge ahead, opening a gallery and now her first major show. Safi could tell he had found a new respect for her fortitude under tough circumstances. There was nothing for it but to support her and the family; what else could one do?

They covered the same ground Safi had already been over a million times, something one needed to do before moving on. Both were adamant that she should continue working in Manhattan. Hearing of Alexi's heart attack, they decided to stop in London to visit him, wanting to offer him their full support.

Safi loved her parents for their stalwart attitude – it was so British, but that's exactly what everyone needed when things seemed hopeless. It would bring them closer together. Having everyone on board would make Sasha's absence less lonely, even for his family.

The evening turned out to be a resounding success. She could hardly move as people spilled out onto the pavements. She hoped that Janos's work would be in all the major broadsheets and her gallery would be on the map. Her parents were mixing happily with the high and mighty of New York society, including many stars Safi recognised. She couldn't put a name to any of the celebrities, apart from Polly, who made herself known to all and sundry, including Safi's parents. She knew Polly would mention the gallery in her column in *Vanity Fair*, amongst other high-end fashion magazines she freelanced for. Seeing Polly was a comfort and a joy. Always blunt and outspoken, Polly would be someone she could depend on, even use, if necessary, to publicise Sasha's predicament in the media.

The following month turned out to be a whirlwind of activity for the gallery. Janos's work was met with widespread critical acclaim, every painting sold. Many of his first-edition prints sold, too, and three large sculptures were under offer.

Ying became animated to the point of hysteria. Her conversations with Janus were alarmingly comical to watch; she would gesticulate wildly, bend over as if in pain, sliding down the wall until lying flat on the floor, the cell held a distance from her mouth, her answers in Chinese stage-whispers. No one understood what she was saying, but they gathered she was more than a little delighted at his success.

It turned out the show was Ying's idea. In fact, she had insisted on the show, threatening to leave if Janus did not agree to it. Janus, in turn, threatened to dispense with her services if the art critics panned his work. What resulted was a sort of Mexican standoff that ended amazingly well for everyone once the show's success became apparent. Safi knew that Zack would insist they visit with Janus after the show; much had to be discussed. Safi wanted to leave the excursion to Zack, but Janus insisted she accompany him. Still, Safi hoped to put it off for as long as possible, their previous visit had been less than welcoming.

The weeks dragged by with little news of Sasha. Everyone tried to keep Safi informed, including her parents, who reported that Alexi, though back home now, was not yet back to full health. Sasha's situation was an obvious strain for the whole family. Fiona was more forthcoming with her observations than Leonard. From Fiona, Safi learnt that Anna was a complete mess; her husband, the psychiatrist, had been keeping her under sedation. Mika was the only one who helped Safi's parents understand the situation. . Fiona went on to say that she was able to tell from Mika's grave attitude that it would be a very long time before they were able to secure Sasha's release – perhaps years. For perhaps the first time, Fiona was reluctant to be optimistic for her daughter.

Safi could tell that her mother did not want to give her false hope for the future. In her heart she was beginning to understand that Sasha may never be set free. It was a thought she tried without success to put aside. But the more she learnt and read of others who had been in similar positions, the less confidence she had of ever being with Sasha again.

At times she rallied, buoyed by strange surges of optimism that disappeared almost as quickly as they appeared, believing Sasha would beat the system. On other days she flagged, sinking into the depths of despair. She felt her emptiness and hopelessness like a noose around her neck. She felt paralysed, petrified, even during working hours. Often her concentration was shattered, though she tried to push on, be positive, pragmatic, resilient, resolute. Be strong, for her parents, for the Rubicov family, for Sasha, for herself. But being strong only got you so far.

Dan and Dax gave her the space to grieve. Pete would sit with Safi at the bar for hours, never saying a word. His quiet support gave her strength. After all, what was there to say, or do? They were long past 'It's going to be okay.' Everyone knew that no, it was not going to be okay, not by a long shot. Appreciating this fact, and not indulging in optimistic nonsense, helped a little. Nothing would ever be okay again, Safi thought. No one had any clever answers, least of all Sasha's family, who she believed had gone down every avenue of negotiation without success.

Mika had returned to New York to give Safi the family's blessing to continue managing the gallery as if it was her own; she had their full backing financially.

Mika brought Safi's future into sharp focus; no one else had broached the subject before. Mika was more practical and technical than others in the family, and he had a no-nonsense approach that Safi appreciated. His tough nature cut through so much of the euphemistic awkwardness she had grown used to from others. It was not that he was insensitive, just that he valued practicality above all else. She appreciated his efficiency, and his candour. She had not been ready to accept advice, yet here was Mika, Sasha's older brother, giving her full permission to form other relationships, to live her life, and not to allow Sasha's premature exit from her life to hold her back if she met someone in the near future. The family would understand, Mika informed her.

The gallery would remain in her hands. Whatever transpired the family would be there for her. She had become part of their family and they always supported their own. It should have been an awkward conversation, and yet it felt organic, even refreshing in its honesty. She appreciated that he had taken the time to speak to her, and that the family appeared to value her health and happiness. That said, Safi was still shocked at his words. She had no intention of moving on., she would wait for Sasha no matter what or how long it took. She loved him. She stared at Mika, anger welling up inside her. How could he be so disloyal to his brother? Did he not understand how important it was for them to show their support?

'Mika,' she said, 'I can't believe you are saying this to me. I love Sasha. I could never move on until he was free.'

Mika sat for a long-time, head bent. When he eventually looked up his mouth was thin and narrow, his eyes misty.

'Safi, it is my duty to you as family to give you permission to live your life. Sasha would not want you to be a 'Black Widow'. Sitting around waiting for him ... it may never happen. He may never be free. It's something we all have to face. Hope is good, but living life is better. You are young. Please believe me when I say we understand your loyalty to

Sasha.' He took her hand. 'Promise me you won't waste your life. If he is released in a few years, it will work out. If not you must move forward.'

They sat in stony silence. It was as if Mika had decided that Safi already existed outside of the family, that he had written her – and possibly Sasha as well – off. What, Safi wondered, was he not telling her? She could not fathom his attitude. Was he so sure Sasha would never get out? Was she the only one under some sort of illusion? Was there really no hope at all? It was too horrible to even contemplate.

Shaking her head, tears flowing freely down her cheeks, she stood and reached out to hug Mika. They clung to one another, both allowing the moment to absorb their pain. Mika picked up his briefcase, turned, and walked out. Safi watched him disappear from view. Falling back into her seat, she sat looking into space for a long time. Then, gathering her strength, she ventured back into the gallery. The only solace she had was to build on the gallery's success.

Mika ran every avenue past his father, but Alexi met each challenge with less and less hope. They had few bargaining chips to offer the Russian government. All contacts previously in their favour were now completely out of reach. The only avenue open to them was the underground movements.

Alexi was reluctant to put Sasha's life at risk. Feedback from inside the prison was alarming. Sasha could not be found in the system; he had disappeared. All enquiries had come up with nothing. No trace of a transfer had been noted; there was little anyone could do until he showed up somewhere in the Russian prison system.

Mika returned with Kolya to Florida. His family were slowly falling apart over Sasha's disappearance. Alexi had become a shadow of his former self; a cocktail of anti-depressants kept him from plunging into total depression. He barely managed his day-to-day business dealings. The restaurants were running smoothly, thanks to family support. The Rubicovs' major businesses were in the hands of managers, lawyers, and accountants. Head of companies were strongly advised to keep the family updated, and Mika tried to play as large a role as possible in anything, though this was clearly not a viable position. Mika was stretched thin enough as it was. Alexi had not attended board meetings for some time.

It was up to Mika to keep the whole machine running. The family had been strongly advised to consider offloading many of their assets, streamlining their businesses, and keeping only those the family could comfortably maintain.

At first, Anna had been a formidable captain of industry, keeping everything ticking over smoothly. The family had chosen Sasha to helm Rubicov Industries; with him gone, they were left without an anchor. Sasha had been groomed to take over from Anna. No longer would there be a Rubicov in control; neither Alexi nor Anna had the energy to return to the helm. Mika had built up a formidable business of his own; he was a natural trouble-shooter and an international lawyer in his own right, who the family employed to ward off hostile takeovers or unforeseen legal matters.

Alexi felt the need to visit his daughter at the Swiss clinic. The director had not allowed him to speak with Yvetta, but he was able to observe her day-to-day routine and found that his daughter had sadly become institutionalised, living a life controlled by her visits to various therapists and doctors treating her. Yvetta seemed content or perhaps that was merely all of the medication: not happiness but a subdued and aimless numbness that approximated it in some ways. She appeared happy to participate in her new life, if one could call it a life.

Alexi left the clinic disheartened to discover that it was up to him whether to bring Yvetta's treatment at the clinic to an end. In the same breath, he was told that it was strongly against the clinic's advice to release her into normal life. As a compromise, they recommended a half-way house. They did not feel she would be ready for a full transition for a number of years. An overpowering sadness enveloped Alexi; both of his children were out of his reach and beyond his help. Perhaps their helplessness was contagious – for he felt helplessness now, too. It was a completely debilitating feeling. With a heavy heart he boarded his plane and flew to see Anna; both wanted to discuss their children. Alexi needed to reconnect with Anna. He hoped their shared history would bring them both the kind of comfort neither of their partners were able to provide them.

Anna was sitting on the terrace overlooking the aquamarine ocean. A peach haze of Cannes's clay roofs spread out below, bougainvillea in a profusion of pinks and purples cascading over villa walls. In spite of her broken heart, Anna looked wonderful, better than he had seen her in years. She had lost a considerable amount of weight. This suited her, she looked at least ten years younger than when he had last seen her. Her hair had been styled into a soft bob swept off her forehead, giving her an elegant air of sophistication, he knew she did not feel. She looked relaxed in a white linen caftan. He noticed she had indulged in a pedicure, something she never bothered with in days gone by. Her sandals lay beside her lounger. She had a cigarette in one hand and a drink in the other. Through the veneer of relaxed sophistication, he was aware of her vulnerability. The sadness that lay behind her dark glasses was easy to see.

Anna's hands shook visibly as Alexi took them in his. As he pulled her into one of his bear hugs, old feelings of wanting to protect her resurfaced. He had to check himself; she was no longer his to protect. She was happily married to Bernard, and (Alexi had to admit) Anna had thrived under his loving care. Anna deserved to be happy in her retirement. It saddened Alexi that life had been so unfair to her. No amount of relaxed luxury in the South of France would be able to take away her pain.

Bernard had retired to his office, leaving them alone to discuss the children and their business empire. Bernard was able to observe them from the window, and, with his keen psychiatrist's eye, noticed Alexi and Anna's comfortable familiarity. He scolded himself for feeling pangs of jealously, but did even this in a wry manner. He knew jealousy was a natural emotion, and it pleased him that he was still able to have such strong feelings at his stage of life.

Alexi and Anna sat looking at the beautiful vista. History allowed them the privilege and intimacy of not having to speak. They would only speak again when they were ready to broach the fear they held in their hearts for Yvetta and Sasha.

Some time passed before Anna quietly asked after Yvetta. She listened with sadness as Alexi recounted his meeting with the board of physiologists and nursing staff. He tried to make it optimistic – after all, Yvetta was, by all accounts, responding. She was no longer fighting rebelliously against everything that did not suit her state of mind. Alexi and Anna agreed to revisit the situation in the months ahead, with a view to moving Yvetta to a less secure, open environment to see whether she was capable of coping without the strictures of the clinic. They left what had become the most severe situation until last to discuss.

Sasha's situation brought on uncontrollable tears. First, Anna quietly sobbed, then Alexi found his eyes welling up. Neither knew how to resolve their son's predicament. Alexi informed her that Mika was liaising with the underworld, the only avenue open to them. Until they found where Sasha was being held there was nothing anyone could do. The establishment had closed all avenues of negotiation, letting the Rubicovs know there was no longer an opening to negotiate. The family no longer had any leverage, or anything of value to offer. The State had taken what they wanted. Putin would not forgive them for working with the Ukrainians; the door was shut and Sasha was the price to pay for their disloyalty to the State.

Alexi and Anna had always met life's challenges head-on and overcome many obstacles; yet the challenge they faced with their children was beating them into submission. They felt, perhaps for the first time in their lives, defeated.

Both were used to giving orders and to making things happen. Yet here they sat now, utterly helpless, like babies, crying instead of beating their chests to get things done, the way they had done in the past. This was new to them, and too horrible to contemplate. They had no idea what – if anything – to do next.

After a light dinner, Alexi bid them a warm farewell and resolved to keep in touch more often. He promised to visit with Valentina and Marina, who was now entering her teenage years and would love being in such a glamorous beach environment, no doubt turning every young French boy's head. Alexi and Anna shook their heads in mock horror at the thought. Marina was Alexi's great pride and Anna was still her doting aunt Anna. Marina was the bright light of the future, Alexi realised, where so much of the present and the past, he now had to concede, appeared in the process of failing. Perhaps Marina could restore their equilibrium and faith in the strength of the Rubicov ability to rise above adversity into the light once more. Alexi hoped so. God knows he had tried everything to lessen his and the family's pain.

Chapter 4

Dax and Dan brought their beautiful baby girl home from the hospital. Safi had never witnessed prouder parents. Dax's family took control, assisting and giving advice, when and where it wasn't needed.

The surrogate had completely divorced herself from any connection with the baby. She felt her job was done carrying the baby to full term. She had provided the nourishment and was the incubator. Now the little bundle was their responsibility.

The surrogacy had allowed her to buy an apartment in Manhattan, something she would never have managed on her own. Fully furnished and in a good area, it was heaven. She thanked that baby every day for giving her shelter for the rest of her life, with no mortgage hanging over her head. Dan was the only one who knew her situation: it would not affect the foetus, but in years to come her eyesight would deteriorate, rendering her incapable of working. Now she had a secure environment she could familiarise herself with in every way.

The baby-naming was a great secret. No one had the slightest idea who she would be named after. Everyone stood around waiting with bated breath for the names to be announced, champagne glasses aloft. Dan and Dax had organised a catered brunch with family and friends in attendance for the big day.

Safi was not surprised when 'Rachel' was announced, named after Rupert, who would have been the proudest granddad ever. Safi was, however, completely taken by surprise when 'Saffron' was announced as the baby's second name. It was such a huge honour. In addition to this, she had become the baby's godmother, a responsibility she took very seriously. Shopping would obviously play a major part in her duties; the thought thrilled her more than she imagined it would. Safi had never given having babies much thought; it just was not on her horizon. But now she felt a pang of sadness, perhaps, who knows, she might have had children with Sasha; now she'd never know. All of a sudden, she felt emotional again, and here in the most joyous of occasions. What might have been, what would never be, tore at her now. A whole life, perhaps even family, denied her. And why? She still did not fully understand. And not understanding was the worst punishment of all.

Bruno had passed on a few months before Rachel Saffron was born, Rachel more than filled the huge gap Bruno had left behind. Safi had already witnessed the lavish gifts showered on Rachel the day she arrived home to a nursery fit for a princess. She would wake up to her own fairyland painted by her daddy's hand with loving care. It was a stunning piece of work: the gallery had superimposed it onto a print for sale in their collection, of Dax work.

Safi found her days running blindly from one to the next. She kept herself occupied from morning to late in the evenings, when she would collapse into bed, only to repeat the same routine the following day. The gallery quickly made a name for itself, growing from strength to strength under Safi's relentless, gruelling schedule on behalf of the artists she represented and the amount of time she gave to promoting their work at home and abroad. DuPont held true to his word, becoming an invaluable friend and supporting Safi and the gallery whenever he was able.

They seldom discussed Sasha. Sometimes it seemed to her that Sasha was already dead – he may as well have been, since only his absence loomed large. His ghost overshadowed her life, no amount of encouragement from DuPont or the two D's managed to lift the sadness from her soul. She attended social functions with little interest (she would not have attended if it was not for business) and had shown no sign of needing to date or socialise.

Rachel added genuine comfort to her weekends. Safi loved spending time with the two D's, who were doting parents. Sunday brunches were no longer quiet affairs – they included a howling baby, after all – yet it brought Safi into focus. Babies made sure they were the centre of attention, and all three of them loved everything Rachel did. Safi thought she was growing into the most adorable baby she had ever seen, and there were endless arguments about who she resembled most.

Shopping would never be the same again; she could not avoid a toy store or a baby shop. Rachel's wardrobe, she was sure, had to be the envy of every little princess on the block.

Safi resented a weekend away from Rachel and the two D's. Zack had managed to delay their visit to Janus by a few months and it was no longer avoidable. Zack hired a car to drive them to Janus's studio. Once out of New York the lush forests along the way were, she had to admit, beautiful. Apart from going to the park with the two D's and Rachel, it had been a long time since she had been anywhere near nature. She liked routine, it gave her little time for self-indulgence or self-pity.

News from Mika came less often now. No one had been able to trace where Sasha was being held; his family were resigned to a long wait before the authorities would divulge anything to their lawyers. Endless avenues had been pursued, even diplomatic channels had been tried, but all had ended in stalemate. The Russians maintained a steady denial of his incarceration in their system; no one seemed to know where Sasha Rubicov had disappeared to. He had vanished into the ether, and without a person or a body nothing could be proved or done. What he left behind was an emotional void and helpless, shapeless sadness that escaped no one in his family. Indeed, the void appeared to grow bigger, the odds of Sasha reuniting with his family becoming ever more, slight, the shared sense of grief and doubt becoming deeper, as did an uncanny sense of resignation and removal, as though everyone must, quite naturally and understandably, move on with their life, the notion that Sasha had been left alone for good.

Safi's parents had maintained a frequent dialogue with Alexi; it seemed Leonard had become a confidant, someone Alexi felt safe unburdening his heart to. She was pleased that her father could help in this small way, at least. For her part, Safi tried hard to stay in touch with Sasha's parents, and even visited on occasion when in the UK for business trips. She found that Alexi and Valentina had made Marina the centre of their universe, and they had started visiting Anna in Cannes during the summer months.

Marina now lived in the suite Safi had shared with Sasha; it had become a teenage haven. Safi was relieved to have the guestroom downstairs, far away from memories that she knew were still raw and that were likely to upset her for hours.

Zack parked the car in the front drive, now covered with spring blossoms. Safi remembered that it was fall on their last visit. The blossoms were prettier, the carpet of pale pinks softer, less dramatic. Ying must have heard the tires on the gravel drive for she was waiting at the front door. Ying herself was a picture of happiness, and quite welcoming, even charming, chatting away about the show, obviously something she was proud of. Safi wondered whether their welcome from Janus would be warmer this time. She caught Zack's expression when he noticed the spread on the long wooden kitchen table. Ying led them over.

'This is for you,' Ying said, 'please sit. Janus will be joining us very soon, yes. He is on a call, a buyer in Germany.'

Ying poured coffee and filled their glasses with fresh orange juice. The spread on the table looked delicious. It had been a long drive. Safi hadn't realised quite how exhausted she was. They were invited to start eating rather than to wait for Janus. Zack did not need a second invitation; the aroma of fresh coffee and bread was enough to make him tuck into a selection of cheeses, bottled jams, and thinly cut hams. Ying ladled mixed berries into a bowl for Safi, who had to admit that this was a major improvement from the last visit.

Zack was on to his second thickly-cut slice of bread and ham when Janus joined them, amiable and welcoming, quite a different person from the dark, disagreeable man they had encountered the first time.

The conversation remained about the Manhattan show, Janus's first in any gallery; it was evident that his confidence had undergone a major boost after the critics rave reviews. His deep-set, piercing blue eyes never left Safi. She became aware of his attention: it was direct, never underhanded, but it was definitely on her. He directed his questions to her, too: he wanted to know how her gallery was doing, he wanted to know whether she was ready for another Janus show. Would it be good for her gallery to have another show in the same year? he asked. Would that even be possible? And on and on it went, the questions multiplying, the gaze seeming to intensify, until Safi found she was unable to hold her distance any longer. His enthusiasm was infectious and had managed to grab her attention and help her relax. With the exception of her time spent with her goddaughter, she had not felt this carefree in a while. But this feeling was very different – it was …

Well, she didn't quite know what *this* was. She didn't want to give it too much thought. She even found she was enjoying his company; he had a quick wit that she had not noticed on their first visit. She also noticed he didn't flirt; his was a genuine interest in her gallery. His gaze was steady, like his hard-crafted body. She tried not to notice that Janus was a very attractive man. At least six foot, broad-shouldered with rugged, tanned features, like a cowboy but with more sophistication.

Zack, now full and bored of being ignored, asked to see the studio and Janus's latest work. To their surprise, Janus eagerly ushered them into the sanctum of his world.

Safi and Zack were greeted by sculptures of wood and glass, four in all, a mixture of skilled craft turned into fine art by the immense scale. The scale of the work gave the viewer the ability to draw their eye upwards, while at the same time becoming aware of the materials married together. Each supported the other, yet neither overpowered the other; they were interdependent but worked as a whole.

Safi and Zack walked around the sculptures while Janus remained in his office. He observed their body language from a distance. Safi could feel his eyes on her again, a hot glance that seemed to get hotter still. She did not mind; it was pleasing that he trusted her.

Zack was the first to speak. 'They speak for themselves in form strength and beauty, no explanation is necessary, quite exhilarating.' Safi nodded. 'These are works for museums Janus, not galleries, wouldn't you agree?'

Janus stood slightly apart from them, allowing some distance between himself and his work.

'Yes, they have been taken up by the Serpentine Gallery in London. One of their patrons is a good client of mine.'

Zack was speechless: he could see the sculptures working in the space perfectly, but why were they even here if Janus did not need them any longer? Obviously, he had made fantastic contacts since his gallery showing.

'I can see the questioning bewilderment in your faces,' Janus said, 'and yes, you are right, things have changed for me in a huge way, thanks to your show and the favourable and invaluable response I received. But I don't want a show of my paintings or prints in any space, I will only allow them to be shown in your gallery, Safi.'

'Great,' Safi said, nodding in agreement with Zack, 'we would be thrilled to have you show at the gallery. I will get my assistant to make all the arrangements with Ying. When were you planning this for? Have you any paintings to show us yet?'

'Many paintings that have not seen the light of day,' Janus said. 'Now I am prepared to show them. Let's see what the critics will make of them.'

'Can we see them?'

'Maybe another time. I have kept you long enough. Ying will be in touch.' He walked them out of the studio. It was obvious from his determined manner that he was not yet prepared to show them his paintings. He extended his hand in farewell. They had been dismissed. There it was again, that slightly amused lopsided smile directed at Safi as he walked off.

They drove to the city in silence. Neither were ready to voice their thoughts. Zack hoped Safi would open the conversation. He knew things were hard for her. It wouldn't be fair to tease her about Janus obvious interest in her, at least not until she had moved on.

She knew Zack would expect her to give an opinion of their visit, a rundown of the day's events, of which there were plenty. But her mind was empty, stuck like a broken record repeating itself at regular intervals, the needle not being able to move on. Her emotions were telling a different story, one of complete turmoil.

Dormant little sparks seemed to be reigniting deep down, feelings she had not thought were possible since Sasha's disappearance. She had not once experienced any sexual stirring, yet here she sat, feeling the familiar old excitement she knew usually ended up with her wanting more. It was a feeling she used to love it gave her pleasure like food, only better but she had lost desire for both.

She glanced at Zack. He was gay, yet he must have picked up on the chemistry that was flying around, hitting the walls every time Janus directed his gaze on her. Or maybe he had done nothing of the sort. Perhaps she was going mad from lack of interest in any masculine company.

'Zack,' Safi began tentatively, finding her way into a sentence that, even now, she did not know if she could articulate, 'besides Janus's work, did you notice anything else going on?'

Zack smiled. 'You mean all that sexual chemistry flying about dangerously heating up the ozone layer?'

'I am confused,' she said, trying hard now not to sound like a schoolgirl, suddenly sounding strange, even to herself, 'was it coming only from Janus, though?'

'Maybe at first, Safi, but I think the man got to you. There were sparks flying both ways, for sure. Let's face it, that man is all man, even in my book. No one could ignore his attention. He was not fooling about, he was sending you a serious message.'

'Unprofessional of me to encourage him though,' Safi said, trying to retain her professional perspective once again, trying to tidy her voice of emotion, flatten it, tighten it, perhaps give it a rhetorical bent, 'don't you think? Also, I have no interest in any relationship. I thought I was all shut down.'

'Maybe but you are human, right?'

Safi smiled weakly. She could tell Zach did not quite know how to respond, or which tone to assume. 'It seems so; his work did not disappoint, either.' It was good to regain a professional footing, no matter how clumsily. She still felt flustered though. Still, she felt comfortable around Zack and was grateful for his companionship and understanding.

'Never has, that's why I insisted on introducing you. He sure has changed. Maybe you will be the one to persuade him to face the public.'

'Maybe,' Safi said slowly, 'but I am not ready to open that side of my life yet – the feeling side. Sasha could walk back into my life tomorrow,' she did not look at Zack as she said this, in case he registered his disbelief, no matter how subtly, 'we just don't know, it's a waiting game, and I'm not giving up, not yet anyway.'

Zack shook his head. She was in a bloody tough position. He was not sure he would be coping as well in the same situation; indeed, it was difficult to fully comprehend what she was going through. He knew one thing for sure: he respected her loyalty. They changed the subject once again, leaving the white elephant in the room to fester in her thoughts.

A month after their visit to Janus, Ying called to arrange for Safi to visit the storage yard where Janus stored most of his collection that had not been seen by the public. Late one Monday, when most of the galleries were shut to the public, Safi and a new assistant, Greta, travelled to Brooklyn, where the storage facility was located. Safi had not expected to hear from Janus: he was not the chatty type, nor was he the kind of man to pursue her – yet deep down she hoped he would follow up on their visit with a personal invitation to view his work for their gallery; yet no personal invitation had been forthcoming.

Sasha's family had given her their blessing to continue with life, yet she had been reluctant to engage that part of her existence. She needed to come to terms with losing Sasha – but how could she when she knew he was somewhere out there helpless and alone? It seemed heartless to ignore his plight, while she indulged in being free to enjoy her life.

What if he walked into the gallery tomorrow or next week and she had taken up with someone – how on earth would he feel? how would she be able to look him in the eye and not see her betrayal of him? Perhaps she needed more time. What she knew for sure was that she needed to speak to someone. She also needed to speak to Sasha's family again. Was there something they were not sharing with her? She could not shake the feeling that this was the case.

Safi looked up from her laptop as Greta pulled up in front of the entrance gates to a huge complex of storage buildings. An official-looking man with a clipboard stood by the driver's window, checking them on his list of visitors. They watched as his hand ran down the list of names; he ticked them off and looked around the inside of the car. Satisfied that the car contained no contraband, he barked a command in his earpiece and the gates slowly opened. Inside a golf cart waited. Greta parked the car and they jumped in the golf cart, which whizzed them past one corrugated storage unit after another. The units resembled an army barracks, each numbered for identification. Safi rode in wonder, imagining what treasures these units held that made this facility so closely guarded.

The buggy stopped unceremoniously outside one of the units, dropped them off, and was gone; dust kicked up behind the cart as the driver chugged away from them into the distance.

'How will he know to pick us up?' Greta asked, in her loud sounding Queens nasal twang.

'I have a number to call when we are done here,' Safi said, smiling but irritated at having to explain everything to this assistant, who appeared more inexperienced than even Safi had ever been. 'I guess they will send someone to take us back.'

Safi punched the numbers she had been given on the keypad at the steel door. She hoped it wasn't a black cavernous space inside, allowing them no light to view the work.

The door slid open on tracks easily and the two women stepped into natural light from a huge skylight that ran the length of the building. Along the trusses above were downlights illuminating every aisle, all of which were numbered and dated.

Greta was new at the gallery, but Safi needed her to be on the ball; there was no way they would be able to find what they were looking for if the correct paperwork was not at hand. Greta leafed through her pages to find a date corresponding to an aisle. They walked along the rows, in awe of the work half-hidden here. In each row canvases were packed, one canvas larger than the other.

Curiosity getting the better of them, they started pulling out random canvases. It obviously was not all Janus's work – he was himself an avid collector of art. They recognised many well-known artists, among them Picassos, more than one huge Miro; not only paintings but wall tapestries, stunning works. Many of the artists that were unknown to Safi were on rollers, covered for protection, with just photographs on the outside to signify the contents.

Not only did Janus collect works of art, he appeared to be an avid collector of classic cars. In a wide area at the end of the cavernous space stood a whole row of shining beautiful machines.

'This place is like a museum,' Safi said.

If all this belonged to Janus, he had passions she knew nothing about. In fact, she had to admit that she didn't know the man at all. He kept on revealing himself in the most bizarre ways. She did not know what to make of his collection, it would take days to see it all. Huge

Chinese pots glazed in pale greens sat on shelving. Rows of tiny cylindrical shapes in paper thin white porcelain were in display cabinets. Installation's all priceless, all collectables, Edmund De Waal came to mind, the famous potter and author of *The Hare with the Amber Eyes*.

Greta gave a two-finger whistle, to attract Safi's attention (it was too cavernous to shout here), waving her over – she must have found what they were searching for. Greta was a bit rough around the edges, but she came with an enviable CV and recommendation, from Zack as a high-energy, capable right-hand person with a sharp mind and a straight-talking manner.

As they pulled out canvas after canvas to view the work, they became aware of footsteps. Safi stepped out into the aisles to see whether she could place where the steps were coming from – but it was almost impossible. They had lost track of time. Perhaps the place was closing and the buggy driver had come in search of them.

'Greta, whistle,' Safi instructed, 'shouting is pointless.'

Greta put her two fingers in her mouth. They heard the whistle bounce back at them – or did it? No, wait, there it was again, someone was whistling back!

Both stepped into the passage waiting for the whistler to approach; he obviously knew they were there. The footsteps had vanished; instead they now heard the whine of the buggy going from aisle to aisle, searching for them. Safi decided to stand at the intersection to make them more visible, the buggy was now coming towards them halfway down the main aisle. Safi knew it was Janus driving. with the tiny figure of Ying sitting beside him, a delicate little bird alongside his statuesque presence.

'Hey!' Safi was immediately aware of Greta's mouth dropping open at the sight of Janus in his worn pale blue jeans, white T-shirt, and cowboy boots. He jumped off the buggy to greet them.

'He sure is an improvement from our last driver,' Greta said, sounding even more blunt and unrefined than usual, 'more like a movie star.' Elbowing her to shut up, Safi introduced Janus to Greta, who stared in disbelief, all professionalism suddenly out of the window.

'Oh my God, and you paint,' Greta said rudely.

Not amused, Janus leaned down to hug Safi, who looked as if the ground would swallow her up with embarrassment. Janus thought of himself as a serious artist; Greta was treating him like a piece of meat.

Ying immediately stepped in, leading Greta away from the spot and engaging her in gallery talk. Janus smiled wryly shaking his head.

'She works for you?'

Safi smiled. 'Maybe not for long.'

Janus pulled out painting after painting, enthusiastically explaining how he saw them hung in the Rubicov Gallery space and why he wanted his earlier work to be shown. He now had the confidence to take whatever came at him, he said; it was time to stand by his work, old and new. Safi could tell that his earlier work was rougher and less resolved, yet it had the same energy and depth, leaving the viewer wanting more. She liked them and told him so.

Safi and Janus continued their conversation on the buggy ride to the gate after dropping off Ming and Greta at the exit of the warehouse, where another buggy was waiting. Outside the fading daylight was a reminder of how time had flown by while viewing some of the spectacular works sequestered from public view.

She had never said anything about his work, always stood by silently while Zack did the speaking. Janus took her hand in his and looked directly into her eyes, after dropping off the two assistants.

'What made you come all this way? I am sure we could have saved you the trip'?

'I understand Ying is the expert at relating all your wishes?' In her own way, Safi was quietly asking whether Ying was Janus's lover. No one seemed to understand Ying's position in Janus's life; Safi hoped this would give him an opening to explain.

Janus put his hand lightly on Safi's arm to get her attention, as they sped across the tarmac towards the exit gate where the cars were parked.

'Ying is my sergeant major, my right-hand man; we work well together. She understands me and I understand her mild Asperger's. You might not notice due to her Chinese mannerisms, but she finds it hard to communicate with others unless she is dealing with art or organising my works, which she is a genius at.'

Safi had wondered why Ying's movements were a little stilted, but had never given it much thought – after all, there were plenty of oddball personalities in the art world. And Ying was nothing but efficient at her job, a 'genius' as Janus put it.

'Now Safi, will you give me the honour of taking you out for dinner? I for one am starving, and you look as if you could do with a good meal.'

Safi nodded; she seldom ate much of anything these days She rejected all invitations in the evening, preferring to work until the early hours, then falling into bed exhausted at the end of a day: this left little time for reflection, which was the point.

DuPont had given up trying to get her out; she did not have the will or energy to socialise.

They found a small Italian in her neighbourhood with traditional red-checked tablecloths. They sat in two separate banquettes. She let Janus order. It was nice, for once, not having to worry about making a choice. She had enough other worries in her life right now. They shared a thin crust pizza with mozzarella and artichokes for starters, then a traditional spaghetti with meatballs in tomato sauce, crusty bread and cheap red wine. She was ravenous and found she loved sharing a meal; it was a delightful change from her nights alone, having a bite to eat – and seldom more than that – alone.

When she was alone at home, she was always reminded of Sasha and her problems and the emptiness inside her and around her – those feelings and fears seldom left her alone. But now, with another person, in a bright and crowded restaurant, she felt safe and cosy for the first time in a long while. She felt almost – *almost* – like old Safi again. She had a sense of what she was missing – joviality, companionship, connection – and she realised that it was a significant part of herself. And still, even now, with *him*, she could not help but talk about Sasha.

Janus listened to Safi tell her story about Sasha. He was heartbroken for them, but he had had dealings in the past with the Russians and nothing she told him came as a surprise. Sasha would be lucky to see the light of day, Janus said, they could make him disappear if they wished without a trace. Janus stressed what Safi already knew: that Sasha was payback for his family's disloyalty to Putin's autocratic regime.

Safi felt a thousand times better for having unloaded her burden with someone other than family; Janus's opinion was unrelated and unencumbered by emotion. She valued his input; he seemed wise, even familiar, in his understanding of Sasha's predicament.

'I will let you in on a well-kept secret, Safi,' Janus said. 'My actual job is in artificial intelligence, so I am well aware of how the Russians operate. In fact, I lived in St. Petersburg for two years during one of my fact-finding missions, it might surprise you to know that I actually know Mika Rubicov well.'

Safi was shocked; she had no idea he knew the Rubicov family.

'Did you know Sasha?' she asked.

Janus shook his head no. 'Only Mika. We have had business dealings in the past. He is one of the good guys.'

'May I ask what business you were in, in intelligence?'

'Ah well, that's complicated. I have my own business in surveillance and electronics of all kinds. I have for many years been developing components for governments to use in the military. Art is my way of relaxing, removing myself from the crazy realities of life.'

She stared at Janus for a long time. He allowed her to absorb what he had just divulged. He could see her mind ticking over and knew the question that would eventually come; he was ready for it.

Safi lifted her eyes to meet his.

'Janus, can you help Sasha in any way?'

Janus leaned forward. 'Because it's you – and because I respect Mika – I will try. But I must warn you not to hold out too much hope; it won't be a walk in the park.'

Despite these words, Safi felt excited for the first time in a long while. She felt elated, even happy, here was someone who may, just may, have the ability to help Sasha, even if it was to locate where he was in the system. Safi rose and sat next to Janus; she needed a hug so badly, and he understood. Indeed, it appeared, at that moment, that he understood everything.

Taking her in his arms, he allowed her to hold onto him. He could feel her bones through her clothes. The girl was literally fading away with worry and grief. He decided in that moment he would do anything to help her.

Janus walked Safi back to her apartment. There was an unspoken agreement that they would be sharing this human drama together.

She wanted Janus to stay over, but it was no longer possible; sex would make everything impossibly complicated right now, and it did not seem appropriate. Her relationship with Janus was suddenly much more complex, and she badly needed his help.

Suddenly he had become very important to the Rubicov family; it would be both stupid and reckless to complicate things further if they became intimate as well. Or would it?

He stood with her in front of her building. They were both speechless for a moment. She leaned in towards him; he held her close and kissed her lightly on the forehead.

'Sleep, it's an order. We have a rough ride ahead of us. We will be working more closely than ever on the show, and finding your Rubicov.'

He waited until she was safely in the building before walking away.

Janus would have to contact Mika. He was surprised Mika had not been in touch; maybe he believed the media spiel about Janus's 'new life' in the art world. To some degree it was true, but Janus had never completely stayed out of the intelligence game: his companies were doing just fine without him, while he indulged his passion to create something with his hands.

Silicon Valley had never fulfilled him, but it gave him choices, and one of those choices was to drop out for a while. He had never dreamt his work would find notoriety or even sell. Of course, he still dipped his toes into intelligence work, finding out what other agencies were up to. No longer the old cloak and dagger, international espionage was a whole different game now: stealing secrets, exposing deals, trapping terrorists, all done through technology, a much cleaner, more efficient and (if done right) undetectable way of finding out what was going on in a world that was getting crazier by the day.

The Iron Curtain certainly made it easier to know who your enemies were; today's bad guy was more ambiguous, less transparent therefore the dangers were tenfold in comparison. The global order, right and wrong, left and right, east and west, were no longer quite so black-and-white. Shades of grey were the game's true colours, and made everything more complex. The new code was an electronic one, a language and network of algorithms; strings of endless and invisible digits. Today's James Bond more closely resembled a bespectacled young person behind a computer screen, wiretapping, hacking, coding – setting passwords and breaking them – keenly studying screens beyond their screen.

Mika, it appeared was not altogether up-to-date on basic intelligence. For one thing, he was not aware that his old American intelligence acquaintance Jan was the same Janus whose works had recently been shown (too much acclaim) at his family's Rubicov gallery He had read and heard in the tech papers that Jan had dropped from circulation to indulge his passion. When Mika picked up Jan's call and heard his voice, he knew things had changed. Jan was back in the intelligence game and Mika felt relieved. His friend Jan had proved his worth in the past giving Mika valuable information he would otherwise not have had, on a number of occasions, helping the Rubicovs steer their vast interests in the right direction.

Janus used a non-traceable cell. He only used his Christian name when promoting his art. In the intelligence world he was Jan Jenks from GeoWorks. He wondered whether Mika had connected him with his showing at the Rubicov gallery.

When Ying brought to his attention the new gallery in Manhattan, Janus considered a show, knowing he could work with the Rubicovs. Still, he wasn't sure. But then he met the beautiful Saffron and had to become involved. Who knew where this would lead – but he was itching to find out. He loved nothing better than a challenge; another code to break.

Mika's leads had run into countless dead ends. Finding Sasha had become almost impossible without contacts on the ground in Russia. The Rubicovs were now persona non grata and most had left. His contacts with the government departments had run dry. Frustration was not one of Mika's vices. Instead, his habit was to chip away at a problem until something turned up – which inevitably it did. That was what happened when he received the call from Jan Jenks.

Mika met with Janus close to his home in upstate New York. They went bird-spotting, a popular pastime in Janus's neck of the woods.

The Rubicov Empire had many different businesses under its umbrella. One was a technology company, and they had used GeoWorks on many occasions to clarify deals made with the United States outside of Russia. The technology company had been sold off with many of the Rubicovs other assets when the family consolidated and moved their major holdings abroad.

Mika briefed Janus with a few more details than Safi could provide, but the basic story remained the same. Sasha had been squirreled away by the Russians; no one had found him in the prison system. Janus agreed that if the Russian mafia and underground gangs could not track him down, it was a worrying situation.

He was either dead or they were holding him outside the system, somewhere he could not be easily found, for reasons they had not yet established. It was obvious the Russians involved were not ready to do a deal, perhaps they would in time, when it suited them. Until then … what?

Janus would alert his company to watch for any movement. It would have to be done sensitively; if the Russians got wind of the investigation, it would make Sasha's release more complicated to negotiate. The stakes could then become impossible for both sides. The game may have changed but the Russians remained master poker players, brilliant at infiltrating companies and government computers, not to mention putting out all kinds of fake messages sucked up by an unsuspecting public.

Mika briefed Alexi on Jan Jenks's involvement and warned him that moving too swiftly could damage their chances. They had no options left open to them; the family no longer had any influence in Russia. What they therefore needed was an outside contact who could manipulate the system to work in their favour. The Russians were very proficient at hiding what they did not want found, blaming those beyond their own borders if the finger of blame was pointed in their direction.

Alexi needed to make sure that Safi put Janus's work at the top of her agenda. The gallery was a perfect foil to keep Janus's identity and the gallery separate. The gallery in Moscow no longer showed foreign artists, but still sold their prints and books. They would promote Janus's work and wait to see if the authorities made any objections. If the authorities ignored the gallery representing foreign artists' books and prints, it may mean they had not connected Janus with Jan Jenks or GeoWorks.

Safi was in contact with Ilona at the Moscow gallery. For some time after the Rubicovs had left Russia, Ilona had been harassed by the authorities. They only allowed the gallery to promote and sell local home-grown artists. Most of the family's collection of artefacts had been sold and the proceeds taken by various Russian art foundations. This seemed to have put a stop to further involvement by the authorities, and Ilona continued to run the gallery unchallenged.

Ilona had worked for the gallery since its inception with Yvetta. When Fritzi joined the team, they built up the German-Russian side of the gallery. Under Safi's direction, the gallery introduced British and American artists and brought the gallery into popular focus. Ilona was delighted to promote American artists once more, even if it was only printed editions of their work and published art books.

Ilona promised to let Safi know whether the gallery received any adverse attention from the authorities – but, she said, she very much doubted that would be the case. In fact, she had built a good relationship with the authorities while they worked together to sell off the Rubicov collection. Ilona was untarnished by the Rubicovs decision to move their businesses out of Russia, leaving behind the gallery. The art foundation had intimated that they encouraged Russian involvement in art around the globe; if the Rubicov name was promoted elsewhere, it seemed to suit them: part of the sales made at the Russian gallery went into the foundation's coffers. Having the gallery promoted in America made it popular with both clientele in Moscow and foreign buyers, which in turn made the foundation money.

Alexi and Mika passed the information on about Janus's prints being sold in the Moscow gallery; if the authorities made a connection, the family would know. Janus Jenks is a known AI operative to the Russians, they would not want him being involved with the Rubicovs in any way if they were hiding Sasha or had taken him out.

Sitting in a cab feelings of desolation enveloped Safi. Sunday was a day she used to enjoy – a day of rest and relaxation, of family and friends, of idleness and even indulgence. Now she found it a day she needed to fill until she could return to work at the gallery, to the relief of discipline and distraction, of paperwork and telephone calls. Tears of hopeless sadness took hold; her heart ached with a loneliness she had never before experienced.

The two D's and Pete had arranged to meet with her for brunch at Pete's Bar. It was something she would in the past have adored – they were the best company and the kindest friends anyone could have, yet here she was with a vision of endless days of blackness ahead and no one special to share her life with. In this mood, it was hard to appreciate anyone or anything. She wondered if her depression was contagious – if other people felt it, too. Shit, she was pathetic, drivelling in self-pity.

Months had come and gone without a sign of Sasha; all leads had come to nought. According to Mika, even Janus had not picked up a lead. Safi had not spoken or seen Janus, who, had been in London to finalise his show and had made several trips to LA (according to Ying), and had also popped in to the Rubicov gallery in Moscow (according to Ilona). All of this had given Safi hope, yet she had not heard a word since speaking with Mika, who kindly kept her updated.

She paid the cab at the corner of her block, and on a whim decided to pick up a coffee and muffin at the local coffee shop. Many people were out on the streets enjoying the cooler weather. Engaging in light conversation might be just what she needed. She tried a new place with scattered sofas and armchairs; tables with comfortable chairs were spread out beyond the long counter. Waiting to order her coffee and muffin gave her a few moments to focus on the scene and decide if she wanted to stay. She made her way over to an armchair and settled down to people-watch. She noticed cowboy boots extending beyond a pillar; she wanted to see who they belonged to. She edged forward, knocking her muffin off the table in the process. Sadly, no one familiar belonged to the boots. She felt ridiculously needy for company, any company.

It was well after midnight yet here she sat, looking for someone to chat with. How sad had she become? It was time to move on with her life or else she would go nuts. But could she move on? When? How? With whom?

Opening the local paper, she scanned the gossip pages. A pair of sockless loafers belonging to muscular legs in faded denim shorts had taken the seat beside her. Safi looked up and found she was staring straight at Janus, his mischievous eyes penetrating directly into hers. Too shocked to speak but not too shocked to notice his open linen shirt over a white t shirt. He looked tanned, relaxed, refreshed, at ease. Her heart did a double somersault. There was no mistaking Janus; he had the ability to remind her that she was still alive. Smiling weakly, she extended a hand.

'You have no idea how happy I am to see you,' she said, 'I know you are not a mirage or a figment of my sad imagination. I am holding your hand and it feels wonderfully real.'

'In case you were wondering how I knew you were here, I spoke to your doorman and he noticed you come in here. I have been waiting for you to come home all evening. He told me earlier in the evening that he called you a cab to take you to the opera, so I knew you'd be home round midnight.'

'Did you grease his palm to get all that out of him?' Safi said. Janus smiled. Safi realised she had never seen him laugh.

'Something like that.'

'Have you come with news?' she asked.

'Not as much as I hoped, but yes, some. Should we go somewhere more private to talk?'

Safi was relieved she never took Mika up on the offer to stay in Sasha's apartment. Still, she remained in the same building; the family had given her an apartment that was not on the family floor. It was smaller with less impressive views from lower down, but it was spacious and luxuriously furnished, and she was grateful for it. It was an apartment used for special guests of the family, or for when family members flew over for sudden engagements. Safi and Janus settled down in the swing chairs, facing a bay window off the kitchen that overlooked the cab-lined streets below. There was a small, immaculate and largely untouched eating area for two. It was here that Safi ate – or rather did not eat – her few lonely meals. Putting the coffee down on the table between them, Janus began to relate his findings.

'You know, Safi, I have been involved with many investigations involving information of the highest sensitivity. But this investigation has been especially baffling. We have been down every known avenue, spoken to our sources on the ground.' He paused for a moment, gripped his coffee cup again but did not drink from it. His voice, always soft, became lower still. He looked at her deeply with his frank, penetrating gaze. On the occasions when we cannot extract what we need from our sources, we employ other methods.' Suddenly, Safi looked at him in a new light. Who was he exactly?

'You don't mean torture, do you?'

Illuminated by the window, by the flashing yellow cabs below, by the infinite lights of the insomniac city, a shadow of a smile crossed his face. 'No, not exactly,' he said, after some thought, 'it's a bit more sophisticated than that. She did not understand what he meant, but then – as so often these last few months – she felt that so much that was taking place around her was incomprehensible.

'We were reliably informed by more than one source that Sasha was released just before the Sochi Olympics. The authorities were avoiding unwanted media scandals during the Games. It is believed – but not confirmed – that Sasha is amongst those set free, without a trial.'

'But where is he then?'

'That is the million-dollar question: where do we go from here? I have met with Alexi and Mika in London. We have decided to open another avenue of investigation with Kolya's help. We suspect there might be someone working closely with an unknown group of Russians to bring the Rubicov family down. They have tried to disrupt the Rubicov businesses a few times: once in Moscow, then in London, and here in New York.'

Safi's eyes widened with shock. 'You can't possibly be talking about Fritzi. Surely, she's in jail for fraud. She is wanted in Russia, in the UK, and goodness knows where else. I can't believe she is able to organise Sasha's disappearance from an American prison cell!'

Janus shook his head in agreement. 'We covered that ground. Yes, Fritzi is still being held, but she is soon up for parole. They cannot hold her indefinitely. We are going to find out who she is working for. It seems she might have had orders to set a trap – or to make life as difficult for Sasha's family as possible.'

'In that case you believe Sasha might have been kidnapped or worse, but no one has contacted Sasha's family yet with a ransom, they have let us believe he was being held by the Russians?'

'Agree again, in one way it's good that he is no longer being held by the Russians in another, it has put a completely different slant on our investigation. The information may now be spread over three different continents that means our search has widened and has to go deeper into little known territory. Once we have an anchor we will make more progress.'

Safi sat in silence for a long time. The news was overwhelming; she did not know how to digest what Janus had just told her. Was it possible he had been kidnapped or perhaps killed? But why had there been no word? Surely the kidnaper or perpetrator would want Alexi to know.

'None of this makes any sense to me,' Safi said, 'none at all, why haven't they in some way let Alexi or Mika know that they have taken Sasha, surely they would want them to know?'

'Yes we have come to the same conclusion, unless something went very wrong and they hope the Russians will look like the culprits, they may have changed tact, we just do not know at this stage, but we will. We have managed to uncover that he is no longer in Russia or being held by the authorities. We will get a lead and when we do it won't be long before the whole business unravels. The thing is, we have no idea where it may end, or what we may uncover.'

Safi nodded, Janus could tell that she wasn't able to take in much more, he took the coffee cups to the kitchen area helped Safi up and sent her off to bed.

'I will see you tomorrow try and get some sleep, we can meet for brunch.'

'I am meeting the two D's at Pete Bar for brunch, won't you come? Please come.'

She knew he hated having to chitchat with people he did not know. Janus could tell it was important to her, they were her family in New York; he would make an exception.

'Okay you call when you are ready and I'll pick you up.'

'No.'

Janus tried to fathom what she meant by 'No.' She sounded so insistent, almost desperate.

Safi was too tired to explain, instead she took his hand and led him to the spare room. 'Please stay, I don't want to be alone.'

A little taken aback but his voice still steady, he said, 'Okay, Safi, you are exhausted I will bed down in the spare room. Off you go before you drop on the spot.'

Janus dropped his rucksack on the bed, sat down brushing his fingers through his hair, not sure where this was heading, he was not about to take advantage of her. Closing his door, he noticed with relief that Safi's door was shut. He adjusted the AC, pulled out his work cell, answered calls from around the globe, and eventually dropped off.

Safi woke with a start not knowing where she was momentarily then her thoughts filled with Janus. Had he stayed? Pulling on her sweats, she tiptoed to the spare room to check. The shower was in full flow.

Safi dressed in white jeans, flats, and black T-shirt. Her freshly washed hair hanging in damp strands down her back took his breath away. She was one of the most naturally beautiful, feminine girls he had ever seen.

Her soft brown eyes bore into him questioningly. He said, 'I haven't changed my mind about brunch, though I will probably leave early. I have to bike back, things to take care of.'

Nodding she followed Janus out of the apartment, donning the helmet he passed to her. Jumping on the back of his bike, memories of Dax bike flooded back, so much had happened to all of them since her arrival in Manhattan.

Chapter 5

Holding onto Janus was a stark reminder of what she so longed for, and how alone she felt without Sasha. The smell of his skin, freshly shampooed hair, and physical strength were more comforting than she liked to admit. Her eyes fell on his hands as they gripped the handles of the bike. He was so different to Sasha: both were handsome, certainly, yet she became aware of Janus's powerful aura. He did not have Sasha's feminine side to his persona. Everything about him made him stand out: he was a head-turner; both men and woman were aware of his presence. Safi noticed how people stared. He had an animal attraction, a masculine strength that she had not encountered before. Janus had a relaxed confident aura, yet he shied away from people, preferring his own company.

She wondered whether he used his charisma the way some beautiful women did – to make sure they got what they wanted. Somehow she doubted it; he hated attention and he never encouraged it.

Zack had noticed how he had singled Safi out; indeed, it was hard to ignore. When they went to view his work, Janus had made it quite clear that he was focusing his undivided attention on her.

Confused by the turn of events, Safi wondered whether Janus had known about Sasha's disappearance all along and wanted to gauge her state of mind before he took an interest. Had he discussed it with Mika before she and Zack had been summoned to his studio the first time? Her thoughts trailed off as they parked the bike outside Pete's place. She warned the athletic Janus of the six flights, then laughed as he made light work of them while she struggled to catch her breath.

Pete had changed the décor; he had finally abandoned the dishevelled, masculine, shabby chic look Dan and Dax favoured. Instead, Rene and Pete had gone for an aura of Southern charm from Pete's New Olean days. The loft now had a distinctly French feel. Teak wooden shutters and faded floral sofas mixed with black-and-white-striped upholstered armchairs. The only piece left in place was the solid wooden dining table, now highly polished and surrounded by mixed-fabric French dining chairs. The whole place had a casual elegance that no one for a moment thought Pete would favour.

As they entered, Janus's presence diverted everyone's attention from the décor. Dax, with little Rachel in his arms, was the first to greet them. Dax wanted to draw Janus into shared, work-related issues, but Pete hijacked the conversation, and everyone's interest in Janus turned to the spread laid out on the refectory table and their now growling stomachs.

Safi found her appetite returning for the first time in months. The relaxed atmosphere and easy conversation seemed to unwind Janus, too; she noticed that his edginess was less evident. His plate was piled high with a mixture of dishes: Southern-fried chicken, grits, eggs, and even bagels and lox (a combination that could only bring a smile to everyone's face). Janus seemed totally unaware of his eccentric taste; he was his own man even with his choice of food.

After the meal and some small talk, he made his farewell, leaving Safi to weather the questions coming at her from all sides. The truth was that Janus made her feel alive again; she liked and trusted this man and was happy she was not totally devoid of feeling after all. She had begun to worry that not only would she never love again, but that she would never properly live again, either. Enough with being a ghostly presence, a kind of grieving widow in training. Or, worse, not being anything at all – numb all over, a shell of herself. Surely her friends were tired of this Safi. Certainly, she was tired of it herself. She was prepared to accept things were happening, even if she wasn't quite sure how to articulate it, even to those closest to her. Janus had left his larger-than-life impression on everyone. Smiling, she shyly acknowledged his charisma and movie-star looks.

They had picked up, too, that Janus was more than the sum of his looks; he had a quiet inner strength they all recognised and respected. He had not told her to keep quiet about the latest findings and Safi found she needed to open up. After all, this was her family and she had been withholding for too long and needed to unburden herself.

Pete was the first to expel his breath. He managed to say what others were feeling. 'Janus is what you need now. Not only as an artist for the gallery, or to help with finding Sasha. You need this man to help you heal. I, for one, like the dude.'

Janus lived up to his reputation as an artist and now a man of many talents, someone they thought Safi needed in her life. She left the loft with a spring in her step. Things were moving, she thought, in the right direction: information, good fortune. With luck there seemed a chance Sasha could survive this awful thing that had happened to him.

Janus bike turned towards JFK. He was needed in LA. Sensitive information had come to his attention during the night. As he boarded the plane he sent Ying instructions to deal with his show in London and to liaise with the Rubicov Gallery in Manhattan about the work to go into his next show.

Besides his art, he enjoyed nothing more than to be back in the field, even though this time it wasn't related to computer espionage or to any government agency. Sasha's disappearance was educating him and giving him an insight into another theft he had never dealt with. Art theft was of interest to him; he read about the thefts of priceless paintings but had never been summoned to follow any leads. It wasn't his area of expertise, yet here was an opportunity to uncover something he had an interest in. Besides assisting the Rubicov family and Saffron, he was eager to uncover what had happened to Sasha Rubicov.

Janus went undercover. No longer using his cell phone or computer, he chose to direct all of his communications through his company; they knew how to deal with personal calls to his cell and mail on his various laptops. He would be going underground, but his people would alert him to any emergency needing attention. Information would be coming in through another method employed during such a highly sensitive time. Today's information game had no borders; it had become an open highway, where everyone spied on everyone else. Janus considered his business the best in the world at doing exactly that: keeping tabs, piecing together the puzzles of clandestine activity around the globe; having eyes on the ground, in the sky, and everywhere else as well.

Six weeks had gone by since Safi had seen or heard from Janus or Mika. She had tried to contact them without success. The only person she was able to speak with at length was Alexi, who, as usual, indulged her concerns with ample sweeteners to keep her from becoming over anxious or paranoid. She began to wonder whether he was as much in the dark as her. Perhaps, rather than (as she always suspected) being overly diplomatic and sensitive with her, he himself knew very little. Certainly she noticed that even his famous pragmatism had worn thin. He was beginning to look very old.

Unlike Sasha, Safi was not family, yet all the same Alexi depended on her. He encouraged her to accept the gallery offer in New York. Recently he was showing more interest in both the Russian and Manhattan galleries. The accounts were now run separately, yet the galleries liaised and advertised each other; exhibitions in one gallery were screened in the other.

Finding the idea strange at first, Safi warmed to bringing the Moscow gallery into the forefront for New York buyers, and vice versa. The catalogues of either exhibition could be bought in both galleries, and the two websites easily shared content when appropriate. She supposed this enabled the Moscow gallery to share in the foreign artists they were no longer able to show. Ilona had managed to have the authorities lift their restrictions on the gallery. After Fritzi's disappearance, the authorities had once more clamped down on the gallery's overseas dealings. Now that Fritzi had been apprehended by the US authorities for fraud, the Russians had lifted some of the gallery's restrictions once more, and Ilona and Alexi were taking full advantage.

Safi found it hard to believe that more than a year had elapsed since Sasha's disappearance. She had heard through DuPont that Fritzi was up for parole for good behaviour; no one expected she would be released before she had served her three years. The family expected her to be returned to the Russian authorities once her sentence had been served.

Safi had not given Fritzi much thought since Sasha's disappearance. However, now that DuPont had alerted Safi to the possibility of Fritzi's release, it was difficult not to go back over everything that had happened to Sasha's family since her involvement with Yvetta.

Fritzi, it appeared, had an impressive ability to organise events in and out of prison; her list of contacts in the underworld seemed to be endless. Who was she working for and what was her ultimate goal while working with Yvetta and her family?

Safi had thought endlessly about events leading up to Sasha's disappearance. He must have been kidnapped; no other explanation made any sense. Janus had put the idea into her head and she could not get rid of her suspicions.

She wondered whether Yvetta was as crazy as her family believed; or was it engineered by Fritzi to have Yvetta sabotage her own family? But what did she have to gain by doing so? She was running a smuggling ring from the safety of the Rubicov gallery as subterfuge.

Safi went over and over every event she knew about that had been engineered by Fritzi. The more she thought it through, the more she became convinced that Fritzi had engineered Sasha's disappearance. But why?

She called DuPont to sound him out. He was the only other person she knew who would indulge her paranoia about Fritzi. She wondered whether Fritzi knew where Sasha was. Safi thought about paying Fritzi a visit.

DuPont enquired through his lawyers whether it was possible to get a visitors' permit to speak to Fritzi; he would then get back to Safi with the news. She did not want to go through her own legal team; she did not want Mika or Alexi to know she was doing some digging of her own, lest she tramp on anyone's toes.

The absence of any news had unnerved her. It seemed that all news about Janus was in lockdown; no one knew how to contact him – he had fallen off the radar. Ying gave no information, either; she would only discuss Janus's art show with Safi.

Alexi had been slightly more forthcoming about Mika's movements and why he had not contacted Safi in the last few weeks.

Safi thought Alexi less withdrawn. Her father, a regular visitor, had also noticed a marked improvement in Alexi. Safi wondered whether this had been because he knew something about Sasha's disappearance, or whether the heart attack he had suffered was now behind him and that his health had improved.

She found the whole waiting game frustrating. She wanted to be involved, everyone expected her to sit idly by and wait for news, entirely passive, at the mercy of everyone else – well, she no longer wanted to do that. It was time to take matters into her own hands.

DuPont came back with encouraging news: it would take a while to get a visiting permit, but he was sure they would grant one. He suggested Safi allow one of the young lawyers from the firm to accompany her.

Early one morning, several days after news of the visitor's permit came through, Safi met with a young legal eagle in a navy suit with Harry Potter, tortoise shell glasses. They drove out to the prison, crossing a suspended bridge that made the tires thump over the suspension grooves below them, waking her up from her anxious pent up feeling about coming face to face with Fritzi. Oliver tried to engage her in conversation but tailed off as she stared out of the side window and he thoughtfully respected her lapse into silence.

On arrival, she followed Oliver who lead them through the prison procedure passing through stark intimidating official security gates and checks until she was shown into the room where she was allowed to speak to Fritzi on her own. Safi sat on a wooden chair behind a small square wood table bolted to the floor, in this stark room facing the metal door, wondering whether she would recognise Fritzi after such a long time, the starkness of the place was heightened by the intense drama about to unfold, facing Fritzi by herself. Had she ever really seen the real Fritzi? Fritzi seemed to have so many different disguises and personalities. At this point, after years of concealment and reinvention, did she even know who she really was?

She sat in concentration going over her strategy, the approach she thought would work best, and an alternative if Fritzi failed to co-operate. She looked up as the warden walked in with a lanky red head she did not recognise. Safi was about to protest that this was the wrong prisoner when Fritzi gave a smile she would have known anywhere. The warden in her pressed khaki pants and white shirt stood against the wall with a frozen expression. Oliver would enter half way through as planned, to give Safi a chance to connect with Fritzi on her own.

'Ach, so a visit from the English Rose, du bist schon Liebling Safi.' ('You are beautiful, darling Safi.') Safi did not know German well, but she understood that Fritzi was flirting with her. This was a good start; she would flirt back, see if that worked in her favour, too.

Smiling broadly, she waved a hand for Fritzi to sit down opposite her. 'Wow,' Safi said, 'I would never have recognised you. But then you are a master at disguise. Red hair must surely be your natural colour, it suits you and you look well.'

Fritzi's slightly slanted green eyes fell on Safi. They stared at one another until Fritzi's eyes creased into cruel slits, her lips drawn into a thin line.

'Was willst du, what do you want?'

Trying not to look unnerved, Safi said, 'I want to know what I can offer you, Fritzi. that will encourage you to give me some information. There must be something we can help each other with, that could benefit both of us?' 'Ah you come with a bargaining chip. Good, take off your clothes. I would love to lick you where your Schatzchen has not been for a long time.

Taken aback at Fritzi's brazen crudeness, Safi decided to call her bluff. After all, she had nothing to gain by being offended, and would surely be playing into the other woman's hands. 'Okay, and what do I get in return?'

Fritzi leaned forward. 'Du hast mich.' ('You have me.')

Laughing in spite of herself, Safi tried to humour Fritzi. She needed to get out of this game, none of her formulated questions were working. She decided to try answering in French; it might also confuse the guard listening.

'Je veux Sasha, Fritzi, pouvez – vous aider.'('I want Sasha, can you help?')

'Ah, well, your lover ran out on you, Ja? Maybe woman are more faithful?'

'Something like that, yes.'

'By the same token where is Yvetta?'

Safi was not expecting that. 'Perhaps I could find out if you helped me?'

Fritzi's head fell back as she laughed; then she brought her eyes in line with Safi's. There was no mistaking the venom she was conveying, yet Safi was not sure whether it was general venom generally, or venom for Safi alone. She decided to go with general venom. After all, what had she ever done to Fritzi? She hadn't even interacted with Fritzi, on a purely personal level, for as long as she had today. And yet for as long as she had known Sasha, she had heard about Fritzi plotting this and plotting that. Well, maybe it was time for Safi to plot something, too.

'I am sorry about Yvetta. I thought you would understand. Aren't we both in the same boat?' She feared she might have touched a nerve. Fritzi was not expecting an ally. But then rapidly changing roles and sweeping the rug out from under the other person's preconceptions was part of good strategy.

'Klugscheiber.' Safi intimated ignorance. 'Carte a puce.' ('Smartarse.')

'No, it's true. I am only saying what's true, Fritzi. I am not playing a clever hand or being a smartarse at all. We both have lost the people we love, and through no fault of our own. Maybe we have more in common than you think. Think about it?'

She noticed Fritzi seemed to give this some thought before answering. Safi crossed her fingers under the table and waited. The shutter went up and the warder informed them that there were five minutes left.

The sign for Oliver to join them.

'Can you help, Fritzi, with any information?'

'Come back and visit me again, but bring me something.'

Once outside the high-wired security complex, on the drive back to Manhattan, the conversation with Fritzi repeating in her brain, sounding like an alarm warning going off, over and over again. Oliver was a comfort he knew the ropes and eased her nerves entering into a world she found scary and had no experience of, he did not insist on playing the big lawyer role, thankfully at this stage she did not want to antagonise Fritzi, she wanted information. and it allowed Safi time to digest and dissect the truth behind the games Fritzi played.

'We will have to return with bate next visit, I hope you will help me again Oliver it's been a comfort having you show me the ropes, I would not have had the confidence to see this through on my own, so thanks'

Behind Fritzi's façade of ignorance and sexual allure, it was obvious she knew something about Sasha. But what? She was not prepared to share unless there was a payoff, of which finding Yvetta was one.

The question Safi asked herself (and which she did not feel in a position to answer): was it worth it to the Rubicov family to exchange that information? Did Fritzi know where Sasha was? Or was she faking? Had someone tipped her off that he had gone missing? Why else would Fritzi intimate that she would satisfy Safi's needs since Sasha couldn't.

Safi was only prepared to share her conversation with Fritzi with two people: Janus and DuPont. DuPont would be her first port of call; after all, he had helped her organise the visit and would want to know how it went. Safi asked the lawyer to drop her off at DuPont's offices.

Having called ahead DuPont was waiting for her at the elevators as the doors opened, handing her a glass of wine.

'Drink, it will steady your nerves and help you think clearly.'

Grateful for the alcohol trickling warmly down her throat, feeling lightheaded already, Safi walked over to the bar and picked up a handful of crisps, olives, and nuts, which she threw into her mouth. She hadn't realised how hungry she was. She had been so focused on the visit with Fritzi that she had barely paid attention to anything else, and now she felt shaky and exhausted. DuPont waited until she was able to talk; she needed to fill a cavernous space in her stomach, and her emotions clearly needed to catch up with her before she felt able to critically assess her meeting with Fritzi.

DuPont listened in silence. His attitude to sex was thankfully European and very Gallic, he was more interested in decoding Fritzi's wordplay than her sexual appetite.

'I agree with you,' he said when Safi had finished talking, 'she needs something in return before she is willing to give us anything she might know. It's definitely worth a return visit, and I do believe that it should be you who returns, not someone else. She clearly likes you.'

'Why do you think that?'

'Well, you are both in the same situation. You were very clever to appeal to her ego, making her feel part of your drama.'

'Thank you for that. I was not sure I would be able to hold my own. Fritzi is not an easy customer. She is passive aggressive in a suggestive way, but I played along until I noticed she had given me a golden opportunity to appeal to her with the situation we both face. She with the sister, me with the brother, both outsiders who have invested so much of ourselves personally and with the gallery. We have both been deprived of the people we love. I needed her to feel that we were both up against the Rubicovs, to get her on side.'

'I am impressed – I think Alexi and Janus will be, too. Are you going to discuss this with them before you return to see her again?'

'I went without consulting either Alexi or Mika, but I owe them an explanation. Perhaps they will see it my way, hopefully give me something to work with as a bargaining chip to gain her trust.' It was a long shot but Fritzi has in the past shown her considerable skill at subterfuge.

Was Safi wrong in her suspicion? Did Fritzi not know more than she was letting on? Of course it was in Fritzi's interest to pretend that she knew something – anything – of interest, but perhaps this was just another one of her lies, to bargain for what she needed, without having anything of importance for them to go on? Fritzi they all knew loved

Yvetta, that was their bargaining chip but would the Rubicovs play her game?

'Can I call Alexi from your office, please. I need some moral support. I'm nervous that they might not appreciate my meddling in this sensitive investigation.'

DuPont poured her a shot of vodka for Dutch courage before she called Alexi.

He then watched her expression to read Alexi's reaction, as she related her news and thoughts over the line. Despite the vodka, Safi was clearly still nervous, prevaricating, shifting in her chair, glancing at DuPont, away from DuPont, looking at everything in the office, and at nothing at all. She was stalling. DuPont suspected it was hard to convey Fritzi's crudeness to the older man over the phone.

Safi looked up, catching DuPont's expression, but this time her eyes were steady and there was a resolute expression on her face. She cleared her throat and launched into a blow-by-blow account of her meeting with Fritzi.

Alexi was clearly ruminating all over again on Fritzi's devastating influence over his daughter, not to mention the chaos she had caused in London and the assault on his wife, Valentina.

She held the phone away as his Russian response towards Fritzi exploded over the line. Finally, thankfully, his anger dissolved into a cool, cutting response.

She stared at the phone, realising it had gone dead and replaced the receiver.

'Alexi will get back to me. I am not to do anything, not to contact Fritzi until he has given me poison to take back as a bargaining chip, that will be her final card in a hand she has held for far too long.'

'Do you think he means that literally?'

'If it were me, no. But it's Alexi. He is Russian and emotionally Shakespearian in his response to love, hate, vengeance and payback. I have no doubt it will be the last hand she plays though.'

Six weeks passed without a word from anyone. Her calls were not answered by either Alexi or Janus; her efforts to contact them fell on deaf ears. She began to find the whole thing unnerving; why was everyone stonewalling her efforts to help? And she had begun to feel better about everything finally – foolishly, perhaps. Now she felt desperately alone all over again, hating herself for having false hope, for trusting anyone, for being naïve, for being optimistic, for being resolute, all of the qualities she had once prided herself on. She tried to throw herself back into her work for the gallery, but that wasn't easy, either. She was unfocused, spinning in slow circles from one painful realisation to the next. DuPont tried to encourage Safi to be patient, but as the days and weeks passed without word, she considered taking things into her own hands.

So many implausible plans passed through her mind, came to nothing, turned eventually to further disappointment, depression, self-doubt. Sitting day after day in the small office in the gallery, working late into the night, often just staring into her laptop screen, was not helping to bring relief; only frustration and desolate sadness. After another long day without news, she picked up her briefcase to return to the loneliness of her apartment, her only relief was working on a plan to ensnare Fritzi into their game.

Stepping onto the sidewalk, a fresh September breeze clearing her mind, she felt slightly less lethargic about walking the twelve blocks to her building. Exercise had its benefits, it blew the cobwebs away, perhaps she'd even stop off for a glass of wine, it might help her notice that life went on.

Three blocks later a black limo with tinted windows caught her eye. It stopped along the kerb. Crossing the road, Safi tried to catch sight of the person getting out of the limo, but a fire engine, siren blaring, flew by, blocking her view.

She felt her stomach lurch. Drama, she thought, there was so much drama in the world, and it was good to remember that not all of it revolved around Sasha and herself. Still, she found that she was shaking. But why? Anxious not to appear nervous, she decided to stop off at an outdoor café; her paranoia was getting the better of her. She could do with company right now. Perhaps that had been her problem this last lonely year – being so stubbornly alone. Finding a table, she ordered a glass of wine and settled back to people-watch.

As the waiter put down her wine, a familiar voice said, 'Another one of those please, thanks.'

The waiter obscured the person, but the shoes gave Janus away; he always wore cowboy boots in Manhattan.

'I knew that limo was following me,' Safi said. 'That was you, right.' She let her anxiety subside into relief. 'You have no idea how glad I am to see you. I have been going quietly nuts waiting for someone, anyone, to contact me with some news. Any news will do. Please tell me you have discovered something, being away all this time.'

Janus took her hand firmly in his as they quietly sipped their wine. Only when the tension in her hand relaxed, did he indicate that they would speak later.

'I'm starving and you?' he said. It wasn't quite what she wanted him to tell her, but his words came as a relief nonetheless. She knew Janus would not budge until he saw her eat a decent meal. Having company was blissful (especially company as attractive as his), she hated eating alone, which was far too often. Now that he mentioned it, she realised that she was indeed starving – and for more than just food.

Chapter 6

Preferring to walk the ten blocks in silence, Janus insisted on carrying her briefcase, while Safi took the arm he offered. Feeling lightheaded, elated at having him back in her life, she pinched her leg to make sure she wasn't daydreaming. Indeed, she had had a few daydreams about him recently. She looked at him guiltily and wondered whether he was aware of her attraction. God she hoped not, she did not want him to think she was being disloyal (she despised disloyalty in others, why wouldn't he? she regretted her dalliance with DuPont, but that was water under the bridge and she was much younger then).

On the other hand, this man was an expert at intelligence, intuition, suspicion – of course he knew that she was attracted to him. How could he not know?

The elevator ride up to her apartment was excruciating. Having Janus in such close proximity diverted her thoughts. Hearing his findings, she hoped would bring her back into sharp focus. The espresso machine would give her time to concentrate her mind before hearing Janus's news.

She watched him going through his messages as he sat in the swivel chair he had occupied during their last conversation about Sasha. She watched the cabs snake slowly through the traffic down below, usually a mesmerising scene, but now she felt like darkening the windows. She had had enough of the outside world. She had started to hate that view, it reminded her the apartment was her prison, no longer a refuge.

Janus placed his coffee on the table between the chairs, waiting for Safi to be seated before they started their discussion. But she stood undecided behind her chair. She was tired of being the passive party, she realised, tired of everyone else giving her news, or making the rules. Tired of waiting. Tired of being disappointed and dejected. Tired of being at the mercy of others. She wanted so badly, just once, to be in control. But then control, she realised now, was largely an illusion. Who was truly in control? Even in this city. Especially in this city. It was so easy to lose yourself, for better and worse, to forget who you were, to become someone else. She wished she could reset her life, but it was easier said than done. She had connections now, ties to a past that felt more like a noose around her neck than anything else, an albatross, an anchor, a weight pulling her down.

'Something wrong?' Janus asked.

Shaking her head, she smiled thinly. 'Would you mind if the chairs faced inwards? For some reason I am finding the view outside distracting at the moment.'

They adjusted their chairs.

'Better?'

'I know it's silly, but that's me right now. Totally off the wall'

'Would you prefer it if we left this until tomorrow?'

'No, I can't wait a minute longer. Absolutely any news would do right now. It's the lack of hearing absolutely anything that's driving me insane.'

'Let's start with your visit to Fritzi. I would like to hear it from you, word for word, if you can remember. It would help piece together quite a bit of my recent information.'

Recent information. Just those two words cheered her up enormously, gave her hope.

Janus listened with interest, and she noticed his eyebrows raised as she reiterated the sexual innuendo Fritzi so obviously used as a tool to unnerve Safi. He seemed impressed by how Safi had handled this moment with Fritzi, how she had kept her cool, and not fanned out the flames of a suggestion that could perhaps provide some leverage down the line.

He looked up sharply as she repeated Fritzi's response to Safi's suggestions that the two women, with their Rubicov connections, were in similar positions. Her sincerity about them both being used and dispatched by the Rubicovs.

'I think you might have found a weakness by allying yourself in that way, as two women exploited and betrayed by the same family,' Janus said slowly. 'It was a risky but clever move on your part. We will have to wait and see how she responds on your return visit.'

Safi felt elated for the first time since Sasha's disappearance: she was a serious asset, they were considering including her. She wasn't leaving her thoughts to fester wildly, imagining Sasha suffering while she continued her life in comfort. She was wrong to believe that she was always passive – no, she decided now, in her own way she had been decisive, assertive, taken things into her own hands. Recent developments were because of moves that she alone had made – and they felt positive. At least something was happening.

If Sasha was found, Safi would be able to look him in the face.

She became animated once more, rather than the despondent young woman he had seen walking along the pavement. She resembled a waif, thin, possibly anorexic, and he wondered when last she had had a decent meal. The beauty he had seen so long ago was disappearing before his eyes. This pained him a great deal. To see someone so beautiful have that beauty cruelly snuffed out, and by forces beyond their control. Was love really a sin? Why else were so many punished for it? They sat in silence for some time, both in their own thoughts.

'It has taken longer that I would have thought to collate all the information, since Sasha's disappearance,' he said, surprising her with the renewed formality of his tone, 'then to analyse what we had. We have nothing conclusive. What we have pieced together you will find unsettling, even inconceivable. I have been over this many times with Alexi and Mika. The only thing that makes any sense at this point,' he paused, searching for words, 'and perhaps it makes no sense …'

He stopped suddenly, just as she felt he was about to tell her something substantive.

'What?' she said suddenly, not able to take it anymore.

'There is a possibility that Sasha may have – for some reason we don't know – gone to ground.'

She sat up now, suddenly angry, dizzy, trying to control her tone. This was not what she had expected to hear.

Sasha may have for some reasons we don't yet know, gone to ground, why we do not yet know?

'There is no way Sasha would not contact his family. If he wasn't held captive, they must have threatened his life, if not his family.'

'Well, yes and no.'

'What do you mean?' For the first time, she had lost her cool with him. She had to resist the urge to shout. She was done with the innuendo, with the piecemeal information, with the secrecy, with the codes, with the games. She was done with all of it – even, in that moment, with Janus and his silences and his formality and his constantly withholding information from her. Her eyes flashed fire.

'The Russian authorities may be using Sasha. Perhaps they released him with the proviso that he infiltrates a criminal organization that deals in stealing assets. . This organisation had more success than the Russians are willing to admit. After all, powerful businessmen and politicians are involved some connected to organised crime.'

'I can't imagine Sasha agreed willingly to anything like this, but I'm being foolish I know for freedom anyone would agree with anything offered.'

'He might not have had a choice.'

She put her head in her hands. The room was spinning. She wanted it all to be over, but – she realised now – it would never end, any of it. It would just go on and on until there was nothing left for anyone but emptiness and grief and regret.

'Why would it be of benefit if I saw Fritzi again?' she asked. 'She couldn't know about any of this.'

'We think she was working for someone who was determined to undermine the Rubicov influence in Moscow.'

'Surely sabotaging the Rubicov family personally wouldn't undermine their business empire?'

'If you are referring to the attack in London, we are no longer sure that was Fritzi's idea. But it did undermine Anna to have her daughter attacking her in her own home; Valentina's attack in London has affected Alexi's health. With Sasha's arrest and disappearance, one sees a definite pattern to all this. These incidents have shaken the family to its core. The sale of their media empire was undervalued after the most popular programs were dropped due to political shenanigans.

'After the theft of the priceless artefacts, the Moscow gallery lost its support from the government agencies to show and import foreign work. The restaurant was attacked on a number of occasions, both in Moscow and in London. The gas negotiations have not gone smoothly, resulting in Sasha's detention. The gambling side of the business was investigated after a politician was found to owe a great deal of roubles. That last incident has so far not found to be connected. All the same, when viewed cumulatively, this very strongly seems to be a concerted attempt at sabotage.'

'It has to be sabotage,' Safi said. 'It's the only explanation that makes any sense. When you put all the pieces together.'

'Systematic sabotage.'

'Alexi took decades constructing one of the world's most valuable companies, and they tried to destroy it in a matter of months. Like dominoes, one after the other, until there was nothing left but dust.' She got up from her chair, moved to the window, returned to her chair. 'Fritzi won't play ball if I don't go to my next visit with something that's to her advantage.'

'First you need to receive a date for the second visitation to the jail. Then Mika will put some checks and balances in place at the clinic where Yvetta is being treated. We hope that Fritzi will try and verify that the information we give her is correct. We will try and gauge from Fritzi's attitude whether she has accepted the information,'

'What is the next move once she has accepted the information as correct?'

'Fritzi might want to negotiate further. I doubt whether she will play ball that easily. She knows better than that. She is up for parole in the next few months. If that is granted, she will want safe passage out of the USA. We will have to wait until then. She has contacts all over the world; it's possible she might vanish without a lead.'

'Won't Yvetta be in danger if Fritzi leaves the USA?'

'Alexi has arranged for her to be moved to another facility, once Fritzi is on the move. We are hoping Fritzi will give us a solid lead. She may double-cross us, but that's the chance we have to take.'

Safi sat for a while digesting the information. There was so much riding on her visit to Fritzi. If Fritzi's information was a ruse to strengthen her (and whatever organisation she was working with') hold over the Rubicov family, it would be an endless game of Russian Roulette. Until one side or the other got the upper hand. The truth was, whoever was holding Sasha already had the upper hand.

So far, they had not played their hand; visibly none of the Rubicov companies had reported anything untoward for a long time. The gas pipeline exchange into Russian hands was not yet complete, not all the pipelines had been sold off, some of the contracts had to be completed before they changed hands, according to Janus it had not been sabotaged yet. The family were on high alert, including at the New York Gallery, for any signs of sabotage or interference.

'I am going to be a total wreck when I next visit Fritzi,' Safi said, 'knowing how much we are depending on a sign of weakness to exploit. I mean, I'm the weaker one. She is a very smart operator, yet she has been caught out on a number of occasions by her overblown ego, trying to outsmart who ever she is dealing with.'

'You are not weak, Safi,' Janus said. 'You are actually incredibly strong.' Janus stood stretching his tall frame, obviously tired.

'Do you mean that?' Safi asked, suddenly tired herself.

'I wouldn't say it if I didn't. Hopefully Fritzi will walk into her own trap. It seems like you have a keen sense of her psychology.'

'I don't,' Safi said. 'She is a riddle.'

'Everyone is. You just have to figure out how to crack the code.'

'Am I a riddle?' Safi said suddenly. 'What's my code?'

Picking up his rucksack, pointedly avoiding the question, he leaned over to kiss Safi on the cheek. But she turned her face round and his kiss fell on her lips. Taken aback he tried to apologise, but Safi continued to kiss him, her actions were deliberate, she felt alive and excited after months of being on her own. She needed Janus, needed to tell him that he had long ago cracked her code.

Holding onto his hand, not letting go, forcing Janus to pull her up towards him, Safi softly touched his face, running her fingers through his hair, while holding his other hand behind her. Janus stood in Safi's soft embrace. She could tell he had conflicting feelings, yet she was determined to stand her ground until he relented into her embrace. Closing her eyes, standing on tiptoes, she found his lips responding to her advances.

Janus parted her lips, kissing Safi hard on the mouth. He drew her into him, enfolding her frail body into his arms, holding her close, aware of her beating heart against his ribs. Her breath was shallow as her chest heaved with emotion. Weakening her grip, she fell against Janus for support. Her lips still lingering on his, scared to separate in case he should change his mind.

Safi tried to ignore the lump forming in her throat as the tears welled up in her eyes. Janus gently brushed them away with his hand, the other hand supporting her as they walked together to the bedroom. Leaning in towards him, she felt safe for the first time since she moved to Moscow with Sasha. So much had happened since her decision to become engaged to Sasha, her life a continuous roller coaster of emotions and events. She felt whipped about, never having time to breathe. She was so very tired of not knowing, living on a cliff edge, now she just wanted to breathe, to be.

The early morning light threw a beam of sunshine onto Janus's blond hair as he lay sleeping. She stretched out her hand, lightly brushing his hair out of his eyes, not wanting to wake him. Janus opened one eye. Smiling, she curled into him as he drew her close, kissing her forehead, then her eyes, lips, and chin. He kept going, travelling down until she gasped with pleasure as the tension left her body. Janus was a gentle lover and caring. He gently coaxed her into orgasm. She yielded to him completely and knew she would for ever.

Safi felt she was in love for the very first time in her life, she knew with every inch of her being that she was in love with this man. There was no part of her that did not want him completely. She had never felt this way before, not even when she thought she loved Sasha; this was different she was completely and utterly in love with Janus. She loved Sasha but that seemed to be years ago now, when she felt young carefree and adventurous and reckless, had she grown up, she hoped so.

They made love again tenderly, then with a ravenous urgency she had not felt before. She clung onto him, wanting to give every inch of herself with wanton abandon, not caring how needy she might appear to him. All Safi wanted was for him to love her back, however long it took.

Safi collapsed on top of Janus for the second time. He lifted her chin, looking into her eyes. Janus saw what he felt: Safi's raw love staring back at him. There was no guile in her love, it was laid bare and he felt a deep protective well open up inside his chest, an emotion he had not allowed himself to feel before. He loved this girl and he was going to marry her before the year was out. She made him feel whole; no one else had ever loved him just for himself. It had always been about his looks, but not really who he was. Safi loved in spite of the trappings, she felt his reluctance to commit and understood his yearning for privacy above all else, and he worshipped her for it. Perhaps she had cracked his code, too.

The apartment above had a direct view into Safi's bedroom. The man with the binoculars bit his lip as he watched Janus in bed with Safi. It was over. She had fallen for his colleague and friend Janus. Most women fell for Janus, maybe this time, Mika hoped, Janus would return the favour. She deserved to be happy. He did not hold her responsible for falling in love with another man. How could he? Safi had been alone for over a year – and during that time she had been nothing but supportive to their family, especially to his father, Alexi. Since his return to Manhattan eight days ago, Mika had been keeping watch over Safi. He knew that she was hanging on by a thread, returning home to an empty apartment, rail-thin and miserable.

Kolya had briefed him about all of Sasha's activities. Mika loved his younger brother, but he was not an angel. Nor a devil like Yvetta, thank God. Sasha had empathy. Yvetta was a dangerous narcissist. He could not label his little brother Sasha with any of those demons, but he knew Sasha to be ruthless with women, and he had on occasion shown a dark side even with Safi, treating her badly.

Over the months, Mika wondered whether Sasha had made a deal with their enemies. The more Mika found out about the people involved with Sasha's abduction, the more he doubted his brother's innocence in the whole awful affair. So far, he had not confided his thoughts to Alexi or Anna; it wouldn't bode well coming from him. Sasha was, after all, the favourite child. His parents had suffered far too much already.

Another possibility was his brother may have made a deal, but who with? Mika did not yet know. It could be with the government or the mafia. Sasha would have much to explain when he eventually showed his hand. Mika prayed for his innocence; it would make the end result less painful when everything came to a head, which he believed it would, in time.

Meanwhile, they would play the Fritzi card and see where she led them. Whatever the outcome, it would reveal if Fritzi had a hand in the whole affair. She had become a deadly adversary for far too long, they needed to put an end to her involvement with the Rubicov family, once and for all.

Sitting opposite Safi at breakfast the following morning, Janus reflected on her rare English beauty. Her reserved manner amused him, although he found it enticing and attractive, too. She would not exploit him, he decided; she had integrity, which in the art world was to be valued. Most people in this world were charlatans, only interested in their own profits. Ying had warmed to Safi, a rare occurrence. She encouraged him to trust Safi, admonishing him for not inviting them back to view his work when they first made the journey to his studio. He had felt an attraction when he first laid eyes on her, and told Ying to invite Safi back for another viewing. He would speak to Mika to find out about Safi and the gallery.

On Safi's return visit, after the success of his first show, he unabashedly and openly flirted with her, making it clear that he was interested. Time was on his side. He realised, of course, that Safi's life was complicated – how complicated he only found out later. Safi, then Mika, drew Janus into their lives, reawakening a side of the business he had left behind in California. His employees in the intelligence game were surprised to see him return to the field.

Falling in love had been off his radar, it was too complicated, in his business, he did not have the time or the luxury. It was far better to satisfy an attraction by seducing whoever he happened to feel that way about at the time.

Yet the more he learnt about Safi's involvement with the Rubicov family, the more he admired her grit and loyalty. She had a vulnerable side, even though accomplished and, it was he found hard to resist; it had caught him off guard and was difficult to ignore.

As he became more embroiled in her drama, he found he was falling in love. Safi had opened herself up to heartbreak and disappointment. The Rubicovs were renowned for their ruthless business dealings. It surprised him that they had trusted a foreigner. She was obviously special. Certainly, she had proved her loyalty to Sasha's family, who she had not yet married into, he could not help wondering why.

He suspected the family were exploiting her value; if she had no value, they would have offloaded her when Sasha disappeared. There had to be a reason they were continuing the relationship with her, not only through the gallery but by encouraging her to remain involved with Sasha, Mika had fairly not warned him off but all the same, it was in his line of work to examine every angle, apply critical thinking to all sides of the situation, objectivity was paramount for a clear assessment of the issues.

Janus had been trying to locate Sasha for a long time now – and with little success. What he had heard on the street and in the intelligence, world was that Sasha had double--crossed his own family in a deal his father had entrusted him with. It was a dangerous game to be playing. He did not want Safi caught up in a family feud she knew little about, leaving her emotionally adrift and estranged from the people she had put her trust in.

Mika had given Sasha the benefit of the doubt, but it had become obvious that whoever was sabotaging his family had inside knowledge. Such sensitive information about the Rubicov empire pointed to one of their own. The finger of guilt was starting to point in Sasha's direction.

Finding who his younger brother was figuratively in bed with, why they proved to be more important to him than his own family, was going to be the hardest thing Mika had ever done.

The lawyers and executives in the Rubicov organisation wanted to step up the investigation into the instances of systematic sabotage; if the company did not appear strong it was a problem for Alexi and his family.

The company's standing in the Russian business community was important in a society that thrived on strength. The lawyers felt they were now dealing from a weakened standpoint in the eyes of their competitors, not to mention the government, who were trying to undermine them at every step. All this put untold pressure on Mika to help his father through the most difficult time in the history of their company. Alexi had launched them into the rarefied world of double dealing and intrigue. Russians were used to playing for high stakes, yet it had come at the worst time for Alexi, who was depending on his youngest son, while recovering from his heart attack.

The repeated personal attacks on his family had undoubtedly weakened his father's usual resolve to fight back with equal measure. Alexi had never buckled under pressure; he relished the rough-and-tumble of business and politics in his country.

He had managed to keep the key positions in the family with very few nonfamily members heading up any of their companies. Technology enabled him to attend most board meetings, even if not personally present. Alexi liked to keep a close eye over his empire, no one was allowed to forget who was at the helm of the ship, and Anna was the hand that kept everything running smoothly. Now both had become disengaged from the everyday running of the company; Sasha had left them anchorless.

Sasha had been groomed to take over from Anna and Alexi. But Sasha had been taken out of the equation, and the family had no choice but to become involved once more with the everyday minutiae which had impacted on Alexi's concentration on getting his health and his family affairs in order.

There had been rumours of sabotage since Sasha's disappearance; some were manoeuvring to oust Sasha from his position. The instability Sasha's absence caused at board meetings was evident to all. Whoever was responsible for Sasha's disappearance had been successful.

Alexi was beginning to resent his son's absence, and thoughts he tried to ignore were creeping into his mind. After his heart attack, the doctors had forbidden Alexi from travelling for a number of months.

Now he had their permission to fly again. He chartered his private jet to fly him across the Atlantic to meet with Janus and Mika in Florida; while there he would take advantage of the Florida climate, compared to the damp English weather at home. While at Mika's villa he'd watch how the investigation was unfolding.

Safi did not recognise the number calling her cell. She found the uncertainty unsettling. After all, she had long imagined a call just like this one with Sasha's voice on the other end. Answering with hesitation she said, 'Safi.'

'Hello, it's Alexi. I am with Mika. You fly tomorrow to see me?' Alexi did not do small talk.

'You mean to London?'

'Neit, to South Beach. I visit Mika here in Florida.'

'Oh, okay, should I fly to Miami or Fort Lauderdale?'

'Mika booked flight 8am, JFK-Fort Lauderdale. He sends Kolya.'

The cell went dead in her hand, Janus had returned to upstate New York, he was completing arrangements for his London show with Ying.

She would take this opportunity to speak with Alexi. He needed to know things had changed between her and Sasha.

Climbing into the Range Rover with Kolya brought back memories of her time in Moscow with Sasha, when things were not going well. She realised she had no need to feel guilty about loving Janus; it had simply happened – organically and rather wonderfully – she had not planned it that way. She hoped if Sasha was alive he would forgive her, she was not going to allow guilt to override being happy again, being miserable was 'doggone awful,' as Pete would say. She was done with moping about being miserable. Her life was worth more than that.

If Alexi sacked her she would deal with the consequences, Kolya peered sideways at Safi but she did not stop smiling. It felt good to feel alive again.

'Safi feel better. Good, maybe get fat again, da.'

She could not help laughing. 'Not fat, thanks, Kolya, but maybe a little fatter than I am now.'

Shaking his head he showed agreement,

'Da, okay, a little fatter.' There was a short silence. 'Alexi sick man. Sasha make problem for family.'

Safi remained quiet, trying to work out what Kolya meant. 'Trouble?'

'You speak family, da.'

The cool interior of Mika's Floridian mansion with its high ceilings, vast spaces, and winding pale pink marble staircase took her breath away – and that was only the entrance. She was greeted by a manservant who led her out onto a magnificent outdoor covered terrace with roped back, striped black-and-white canvas curtains allowing a view of a turquoise-bottomed pool. A spray of fine mist and the overhead fans kept the humidity under control. Alexi was in the pool swimming lengths. The manservant waited at the end of the pool with a towelling gown. As Alexi stepped out of the pool she noticed he didn't look quite as formidable without his extra weight. Eyes hidden by dark glasses, he took Safi in with a cursory glance, and barked something in Russian at the servant, who disappeared with a nod.

It was not difficult to work out that Alexi had ordered lunch. It appeared that everyone was worried about her weight loss. Alexi sat in the high-backed cane chair next to Safi, his glass of iced water on the turquoise Tuscan tiled table. He patted her hand lying on the table with his one hand, while drinking his water with the other. Stretching, he took a mango from the overflowing fruit bowl on the table. She watched as Alexi expertly peeled the mango, putting each slice on a side plate next to her, indicating she eat each slice as he peeled the next one. The mango was sweet and delicious. She had forgotten how delicious mangos were – and messy. Without a smile on his face Alexi opened a cloth napkin and handed it to Safi.

Sitting back, he watched as she finished off the mango. She hoped he would speak now that she had eaten, but no, a servant arrived with a table setting for two, soon followed by a tray with a fresh Thai noodle tuna salad.

'Eat, it's quite delicious,' Alexi said, pointing at the tray.

He wasn't kidding; the salad was amazing. Fresh pieces of Ahi tuna melted in her mouth. Alexi obviously approved, shaking his head she saw a slight smile on his face for the first time in a long, long while.

'We both need to put some fat on our bones,' he said, 'this business has been stressful. You are a good person. I want you to know as a father, I bless you – and your family as well. We love them, your father has been a wonderful friend. I do not take that lightly.' He leaned forward, shifted his chair slightly. 'Now we speak seriously about our problems?'

You visited Fritzi in jail. You do not have to repeat her sick mind. I find her a disgusting human being. Mika and Janus will brief you before you visit again, I hope she gives us a lead. We will make it worthwhile for her to play ball. I think it is in her interest. Big time, as they say here.'

'Alexi,' Safi said, 'do you think Sasha is okay after all this time?'

It was a difficult question to ask, and couldn't be an easy question to answer. Staring into space, Alexi's mouth took on a hard line, his voice had an edge Safi had never heard before. It was chilling.

'Safi, what happened I cannot explain. My son perhaps not be innocent in this matter. Kolya and Mika fill me in. I must tell you, Sasha not deserve you. They briefed me on my son's behaviour. His philandering, even his drunken attack. I am sad, I am devastated. I knew none of this until recently. It has broken my heart. Like all parents, I wonder what I did to deserve such children. But he is my son and I will find him. After that I do not know…'

'Philandering! What on earth do you mean Alexi?'

Safi sat in stunned silence, trying to work out what Alexi had just told her. When did Sasha cheat? She felt terrible anger welling up that she could not contain. Jumping out of her seat with clenched fists, she ran indoors, tears streaming down her cheeks. Not knowing where to go, she ran to the entrance and out of the front door, but the suffocating heat hit her like a wall, forcing her back indoors.

Finding a bathroom, Safi shut the door and curled up on the cool tiles. Everything she had experienced with Sasha over the years began to make sense: his absence late into the night; leaving her alone in the dead of winter with nothing to do, but wait for him to come home. And how she had waited for him this last year, waited patiently, loyally – never cheating, just waiting, unable to concentrate on anything, giving up her life for him, a nervous wreck. For him! Who had, it now seemed, thought nothing of betraying her (and perhaps his family) at every opportunity.

His off-the-wall lovemaking in weird places she had found so exciting. but now she felt sickened by her own willingness to play along. The danger, the risk of being caught he was turned on by.

Safi had to admit she had bought into that heightened sexual aphrodisiac he so loved: she chose to believe it was she who was sexually, always looking for excitement.

True, she could not blame Sasha only: they had both cheated. Yet she felt anger at the lies he so easily told, taking her in completely with his excuses. So many nights alone, so many instances she now recalled with clarity, made her blood boil. Even when he came to New York after his drug-induced, aggressive lovemaking, turning something beautiful into something ugly, she was willing to forgive him, who was he, did she ever really know? It was all an horrendous mess. Alexi said he had not known until recently about his son's behaviour towards her and, she believed him but what about Kolya or Mika, did they know, she wondered, their loyalty and male loyalty came first in matters of fidelity. Everything she read always said the person being cheated, was the last to know.

Safi rose slowly, washed and dried her face, she glanced fleetingly at the person staring back at her in the mirror, older and wiser she hoped, than the young gullible girl who fell in love with an ideal and a person she now found difficult to continue feeling unquestioning loyalty and love for, yet there was still a part of her that adored Sasha, still had feelings for him, she could not deny it. She unlocked the bathroom door. It was time to go. Alexi deserved better, two of his children a disappointment.

She found Alexi at the table as he saw Safi he pretended to be strong, yet she saw his suffering, she longed to hug him. Alexi was patriarchal and tough but he was a genuinely kind man, Safi felt badly for him.

Looking over at him as she sat down, Safi felt a surge of affection. He and Anna had been so kind to her over the years, like surrogate parents, always concerned for her wellbeing. She could never think them responsible for Sasha's behaviour.

Leaning over nervously, Safi put her hand on Alexi's arm. She was scared he would reject her attempt at empathy. He was a proud man and Russian, it was not something he would like from a slip of a girl like her, but Alexi grabbed her hand and held it tightly.

'Since my heart attack I find I am not so proud or stubborn. I am a softy. Thank you, Safi.'

Safi recalled how her father had found Rupert a much easier man to get along with after his heart attack; she remembered how he had softened towards Dax and Daniel.

'Are you alright, Safi? Sorry you upset but I thought you should know truth.'

'Lots of things make sense now, Alexi. I have met someone and I think I am in love again It has only just happened, but I realised I have feelings for Janus. I loved Sasha and would go to the ends of the earth for him, and still will, because I can't just shut down my heart, but I'm hurt, angry and confused about Sasha's behaviour and my own gullibility.'

Alexi nodded, yet did not speak. He was processing what she had just told him. Was it a mistake to be so open and honest?

'This good news. Maybe give heart too quickly, Safi, I do not want you hurt, you deserve good man.'

She understood his concern for her emotional wellbeing. Once she fell she gave everything, as she had with Sasha (which Alexi knew only too well); this time she knew it was going to be different. Janus made her feel safe. Sasha, though eleven years older than her, was a boy in so many ways. Janus had lived a different life. She was prepared to take the chance – what else was there, no one really knew ever, did they, but she was getting ahead of herself, Janus wasn't yet hers to have, was he?

'I feel happy for the first time in a long, long time,' she said. 'It has taken me a while to admit that I had feelings for Janus. I had closed myself off to all feeling. Alexi, I couldn't go on much longer without having a complete breakdown. Janus came into my life just at the right time. He managed to bring me back to life – to *save* my life. It just happened, really, neither of us were looking. We have similar interests in the art world, and he gets that I love him for who he is on the inside, not only the outside. He is a startlingly handsome man, it has made him untrusting and shy.'

'This is good talk,' Alexi said softly. 'I like very much to remain friends with your family, good people. I hope possible when this is over.'

Safi shook her head in agreement. She felt the same way, though not sure what the future held. Somewhere inside she felt she needed to keep a part of herself protected from the Rubicov family, they were incredibly rich and powerful and used to getting their own way. And she had noticed how bad things happened to those who got too involved with the family.

'Mika work with Janus. Mika happy for you, too. Janus special man.' Alexi, I was wondering, you said in your call that we were having a meeting. Who are we having the meeting with?'

'Ah yes, dinner, they come 8pm.'

'Would you mind if I freshened up before dinner'?

Safi was shown to the guest room overlooking the pool. A member of the household staff had unpacked her few items of clothing. She took a shower, the pool though beautiful did not appeal to her, the humidity wasn't her cup of tea. Manhattan was bad enough during the summer months. She turned the tap, feeling the warm water rain down over her. Wrapping one fluffy towel round her head, the other enveloping her body, she sat on the edge of the bath, recapping her conversation with Alexi. She noticed a towelling gown and snuggled into it. Then she dropped onto the bed and drifted off.

She woke to the sound of a soft rapping at the door. She looked at her watch to discover she had slept for three hours straight. It was almost

8; the others must be waiting for her downstairs. Opening the door she found one of the servants with a jug of iced tea, a glass filled with orange slices, and a sprig of mint on a tray.

Standing aside Safi watched the servant place the tray on a side table. Turning to leave she handed Safi a note. Sipping the iced tea she opened the note with her other hand.

'We look forward to seeing you at dinner 8.30 sharp in the main dining room, smart casual will do, Mika.'

She decided on a newly bought green turquoise-patterned wrap dress from DVF and casual blue suede slingbacks with a Hermes tan clutch. She made her way down the grand pink marble stair case. The Florida water and high humidity had added a slight curl to her normally straight hair. Checking in a hall mirror on the way down the stairs, she decided she liked the softness of a wilder look.

Safi found everyone awaiting her arrival; drinks in hand, they all looked so tanned and relaxed. Mika welcomed her to his home with a glass of pink champagne then hugged her warmly.

'Welcome to my Floridian Pink Palace. I hope you like?'

Safi's eyes locked with Janus as she answered Mika.

'Lovely, Mika, it's really stunning.'

He guided her over to a seat between himself and Janus. Once seated, he made a toast. 'To beauty.'

Janus bent over to kiss Safi on the cheek,

'You look and smell amazing.'

'First eat, drink; after, we go study to discuss matters.'

Safi wondered how they were going to concentrate on matters when Alexi and Mika insisted on vodka shots between each course. She noticed Kolya seated at the table. He was no longer only the driver or security guard; he had joined the inner circle of the Rubicov family, honoured with a seat at their table.

Kolya looked comfortable with his new position. She was pleased for him, he deserved to be treated well. The Rubicov family were lucky to have him, he was skilful and trustworthy.

Alexi brought the dinner to an end with cognac and cigars. Then he led the way towards the study, drink and cigar in hand.

The study was more an elegant, smaller sitting room than a study, with large sofas and armchairs. Two TV screens were set into hand-built units, a high polished black desk faced a bank of patio doors that opened onto a massive terrace overlooking the coastal waters.

Mika opened the patio doors leading out to the terrace. A cool breeze blew in from the coastal waters lapping up to the edge of steps, leading down to a wooden jetty. Safi drew in her breath at the opulent scene. Below the steps two boats were moored: one an elongated speedboat, the other a large canopied yacht.

These were Mika's 'South Beach toys,' as he liked to call them. A boathouse further down the jetty no doubt housed another toy. There was ample terrace furniture in pale greys, very different from the pool furniture.

Janus took her hand as they walked along the terrace. Safi noticed a giant chessboard with tall pieces on the lawn below. The whole scene was one of relaxed entertainment, just what one would expect a moneyed person to have along the waterfront.

Back indoors oversized sofas and armchairs were upholstered in heavily woven fabric adorned in colourful exotic birds and palm trees, with heavily fringed leopard-print cushions. The furniture was dark wood with Floridian monkeys dressed as Blackmore's supporting fringed lamp shades. The whole ambience gave one a comfortable, rich feeling. It wasn't exclusively a man's room, it had East Coast whimsy added by the monkey lampshades, and ornate Ottomans in stripes with colourful legs, old Floridian charm to a tee.

They had crossed over a bridge to get to Mika's island, and she had to admit that it was heavenly; the homes along the coastal waters were magnificent.

Anna's home in Cannes had quiet European elegance, Mika's was unabashed opulence. She would not say no to either, each had something to offer that was hard to reject after living in a concrete jungle like Manhattan.

They reluctantly returned indoors; mosquitoes were harvesting on exposed areas and the light was fading. Everyone settled. Mika switched on a monitor to view footage obtained from Janus. Safi gasped as she recognised Sasha clearly gesticulating; the footage was grainy yet one could grasp that a container was being unloaded at a dockyard.

Mika enlarged the date the drone had taken the footage. Rising to get a clearer view of the dates, she found it hard to comprehend. It had been taken only a fortnight ago, which meant Sasha was alive and well. But where?

She asked Mika whether he could stop the footage where Sasha could be seen. She remained rooted in front of the screen as it zeroed in on Sasha (even if the image – now enlarged – was grainy, there was no mistaking it was Sasha, albeit dressed in worker's clothes. The sartorial Sasha now resembled a Russian dock worker, doubtlessly still in charge.

Lost for words, Safi took her seat and waited to hear what Alexi and Mika made of the footage. She was too shocked to make head or tail out of it. Janus spoke first; he had obviously studied the images and, had information the others did not.

'This footage was taken at a small fishing harbour on the Ukraine coastline bordering Russia. We have established that much. It's the only evidence we have right now that Sasha's alive.'

It was the first time Alexi, Mika, and Kolya had viewed this footage. Alexi dabbed his eyes, for him to see his son well after believing him to be dead, was an obvious relief.

More information was needed to establish whether Sasha was a captive or in charge of information – but, after so many months of false starts and empty leads, this was a start.

'I wonder whether there is any point in talking to Fritzi now that we have seen this footage,' Safi said. 'Surely she wouldn't k now anything about what we have witnessed?'

Mika looked up. 'Perhaps but we are not prepared to take that chance. Fritzi has been involved with smuggling for a very long time and may know something that could prove helpful.'

Janus did not believe Fritzi would cooperate easily with their plan. Behind her playfulness a master operator was at work; one never knew where her games were leading.

'Fritzi obviously wants Yvetta,' Janus said, 'and believes she has information about her arrest in France by the Russians. If we give her access to that information, she may show her hand – but she will have to offer up something equally valuable, so we will have to wait until you meet with her.'

Janus was prepping Safi, giving her confidence on how to approach Fritzi.

'When you next visit I will be with you. Fritzi does not know me, she will believe I am part of your legal team. I will observe her reactions, to gauge whether she is worth pursuing for further information.'

Janus looked at his watch.

'I am flying to LA shortly. Would you walk me to the car, Safi?'

A fine drizzle was falling but the humidity was still suffocating. Janus explained Safi's queries about the footage at the harbour.

'A photo of Sasha was sent via satellite. Most footage for agencies are highly classified or sent by drones. We can operate them from the

States without giving our investigation away into their activities, so they won't have any suspicions.'

Sasha being alive yet out of contact made being with Janus emotionally confusing. 'I have conflicting emotions seeing him alive. I've been in such turmoil, one moment I'm afraid for him, the next I'm angry, especially after my talk with Alexi, I've been such a fool'

Janus held Safi tight. 'It's only natural that you still have feelings for Sasha. Emotions are not like a tap that can be switched on and off at will – or, for that matter, can be strictly controlled by a timer. You have been through a great deal of trauma, Safi. You owe it to yourself to recover, to heal. You will fully move on in your own time, when you – and only *you* – are ready. You are a very loyal person, Safi. Perhaps it's loyalty you are experiencing.'

Smiling weakly, she leaned into him. 'I will be pleased when this gets resolved. I feel as if my life is on hold.'

'Not to me.'

'No, not to you, though loyalty has got a lot to do with these conflicting feelings. I feel I will be able to start a new chapter once I have terminated my relationship with Sasha.'

'Perhaps he has already done so. It appears he has started a new chapter in his life.'

'Even so I need to feel totally free to start mine, no unknowns lurking in the background.'

'I will see you in NY. In a day or so we may know more.'

A soft embrace and lingering kiss left Safi with no doubts who she wanted, yet here she was still attached to Sasha through his family – and now Janus was involved too. Stepping away was becoming tougher by the day.

Janus had returned to New York and Safi had received notice from the lawyers with a date to visit Fritzi. Janus picked her up from the gallery. He wore a dark charcoal suit and tie, with thin gold-rimmed glasses. She had never seen him in formal clothes. With a weathered old brown briefcase he resembled a legal eagle, albeit a devastatingly handsome one. Her knees buckled as she rose to meet him.

She had chosen to wear a fitted, tailored black skirt-suit with a crisp white shirt, buttons open just enough to show her breastbone. Fritzi might find that hard to ignore, or when the skirt rode up over Safi's crossed legs during their meeting.

Safi was prepared to play along with the flirtatious games Fritzi loved and lived for.

'Okay, I think we are ready to out play Fritzi at her own games,' Janus said.

Janus briefed her on the journey: Safi was to offer Fritzi what she claimed she wanted in return for information. If the information checked out, Fritzi would be given Yvetta's contact details. Fritzi would reject the offer, Janus was sure, but she wouldn't reject receiving updated footage of Yvetta, or a message from Yvetta personally.

'First we will tempt her with footage of Yvetta,' Janus explained. 'Then we will hold back the personal message until she has agreed to disclose information. Once we have got her hooked, we will show her a message recorded by a therapist at the clinic and, doctored by us Highly unprofessional and illegal, but we are playing for high stakes. The espionage game works around legal parameters, not within them. If you are going to play safe and nice, you shouldn't play at all – because everyone else plays a brutal game, with no set rules, all the time. Fritzi plays a mean game of poker. I intend to beat her! Once we gauge her reaction, I will either nod my approval, or we will leave abruptly, indicating that we are not prepared to share further information unless she gives us something concrete in our search for Sasha, or what he might be up to I am a lawyer, don't forget that. She will catch on if we do not play this part well. We need to avoid saying too much, I hope to tempt her with emotive, familiar footage. She may have an emotional lapse, it could result in further cracks in that armour she has built so solidly and shrewdly over the years. Frankly, it's a long shot, but at this point it's all we have to temp her to cooperate now.'

Janus was familiar with the prison-system procedure of checking everything in and going through the security checks. This all took time, and many questions were asked, before the footage was released back for them for use. Janus remained patient and relaxed throughout the questioning.

'That was close, they might have confiscated the footage and, we would have been sunk,' Safi said.

'Mostly they are worried about arms and drugs,' Janus said. 'This was just a formality.'

They were shown into a different room from the original small one Safi had experienced on her last visit. A different female prison warden accompanied Fritzi. Janus had a few words with the warden, who agreed to stand outside the door for the duration of their visit.

A low whistle escaped Fritzi when Safi and Janus entered. 'Oh la Meine Damen und Herren was fur ein Fest fur die Augen die Sie machen.' (Translated by Janus, for Safi's benefit: 'I take it you understood the ooh la? My lady and gentleman, what a feast for my eyes you make.' 'Ah ok you understand German,' Fritzi said, ;even better, we can talk privately, just the two of us. I would like this, how beautiful you are, pity you are so loyal to Sasha, Safi Liebling.'

Janus now understood what Safi meant: Fritzi had a tall elegant powerful charismatic presence and she knew how to use it to her advantage. She played with people like a cat played with a mouse before it pounced.

'Safi, meine Schatzi you are losing your glow we need to find your Sasha sie sind so dunn.'

'Yes, Fritzi, I know,' Safi said, 'can you help?'

Leaning over, Fritzi put her hand lightly on Safi's knee. Safi did not move and hoped Janus would not interfere either.

'Sasha is not such an angel, ja? Feigning innocence.'

'What on earth do you mean?' Safi asked.

'You have what I want. maybe we can play this game – if I get what I want, ja?'

Janus opened the computer. This was his opening to see how she reacted to the footage. Turning the computer to face Fritzi, he played the footage of Yvetta walking in the gardens of the clinic, she looked happy and carefree.

Watching closely, Janus noted Fritzi's face drain of colour, her face had taken on a softer expression, one of obvious affection. For a moment, she was a different person. Fritzi, who cared for almost no one but herself, really did appear to love Yvetta. And then she adjusted to the situation once more, shifted back into her other identity, as the battle-hardened, vivacious, all-powerful Fritzi. Janus thought they had partly succeeded.

Addressing her for the first time he said, 'We have more footage you may value highly: a personal message from Yvetta. Are we going to deal, or is this not of interest to you?'

'What do you want?'

Turning the computer to face her once more, he ran the footage of Sasha at the small harbour on the Ukraine coastline offloading a tanker into waiting trucks.

She studied the footage for a while, asking him to repeat it numerous times; something had obviously caught her attention.

Eventually she asked for part of the footage to be frozen and enlarged. Studying the images she turned the screen to face Safi and

Janus. She pointed out a name on the tanker. Why hadn't they noticed this before? Admonishing himself for the obvious error, wanting her to believe him a lawyer rather than a spy, Janus feigned disinterest unless she had something to share. Fritzi made a noise to indicate they were 'dummkopf' stupid.

'Did you not notice it's an Italian tanker, ja? Mafia!'

'How can you be so sure?'

Lying back in her seat, legs stretched out in front of her, Fritzi observed them closely, trying to see what her options were. To disclose her sources would be suicide, Janus figured, yet she needed to trade information to get what she needed.

'Okay, I give you information?'

Janus shook his head. 'Not so fast, we need a name or number to contact, someone who can shed some more light on this footage.'

'Ok, if I get what I want, I will give you a contact number.'

'Good. If that works out we will give you the information you want.'

Not waiting for her reply, Janus turned the footage to face Fritzi.

Yvetta was talking, a voice Fritzi had not heard for a long time but which pierced her emotions deeply nonetheless. She spoke Russian; Janus did not want her to doubt that the message was genuine.

The message had been interpreted by Mika, but Fritzi did not need to know this.

In reality, Yvetta had been acting out her feelings to a therapist, not speaking directly to Fritzi. But Janus had cut the therapist out of the picture, making it appear she was talking to Fritzi directly, which she was in a way.

The message was emotive. Yvetta wanted Fritzi to know she had not double-crossed her, she had been kidnapped. She was accusing Fritzi of letting her down, of running out on her. She would forgive her, but never wanted to see her again, it was over between them, she needed people she could rely on, trust in her life, and Fritzi had proved otherwise.

The screen went blank. Her expression was impossible to scrutinize, but her body language told another story. Her hands began to shake uncontrollably, her breathing had become shallow, all colour had drained from Fritzi's face.

Worried she may have a fit, Janus stood to call the warden. Shocked at her distress, Safi pushed a glass of water towards her.

The warden entered but Fritzi had managed to control her emotions or anger, whichever it was. She left the room with the warden, not looking back as the door closed behind her. A folded piece of paper lay on the table.

'She was definitely shocked to hear Yvetta,' Safi said. 'I hope this works in our favour at our next meeting.'

Janus spoke only when they were ten miles away from the prison complex.

'We had what I would call a damn good result, all in all. I think she will sing like a bird the next time we meet, that last footage shook her up pretty good.'

'What was in the folded paper you put in your briefcase?'

'I hope a contact number.'

Chapter 7

Janus had barely been back in Manhattan for a day before leaving once more, this time for LA. This time he had what he wanted – a contact number. This would, Safi hoped, allow them to investigate and open some solid new leads. Mika would fly out with Janus; they had agreed to work as a team. Alexi had taken to calling Safi periodically to catch up on the gallery and to give her updated information. He had remained in Florida, having persuaded Valentina and Marina to join him at Mika's home; neither had visited before. She thought Marina would prefer the South Beach scene, which was a little hipper than Cannes, especially the shopping.

For the first time in a while, Safi's life was a little less in limbo. Having Janus in her life had made waking up in the morning enjoyable once more. New days to compliment her new life. She was starting to feel her zest for life returning, yet in her subconscious unease still lurked.

She wondered whether Janus would visit Fritzi without her; the woman freaked Safi out. She never knew what she was planning behind those come-to-bed eyes, the ambiguity and double-entendres in her laconic humour.

DuPont had been round to catch up on progress with Fritzi. Her demise would greatly please him; her release from jail, on the other hand, would not.

Since their collaboration, when Fritzi had tried to involve him in her double-dealing and very nearly ruined his hard-earned reputation, Safi had found it easy to unburden herself to DuPont. Safi had become an equal in his world, no longer a pretty face he could seduce to satisfy his Gallic masculinity. It was a great asset having DuPont to work with, he was a smooth operator with great resources in the art establishment, which she had needed in her first months establishing the Rubicov galleries as serious contenders in Moscow and on the East Coast art scene. The galleries had once more become a worldwide trader in the arts.

Through DuPont's guidance she had over the years learnt her craft. Even more cynical observers of the art world had to concede that she was good at what she did. Her reputation, and her skills, gave her leverage with the Rubicov family; without successful exhibitions under her belt both in Moscow and in Manhattan, she doubted they would have retained her services with the gallery.

Yvetta had invested huge expenditure on space at Frieze and Art Basil, but due to her collaboration with Fritzi had not been able to complete her business contracts, and the gallery had not been invited back.

In taking over the gallery, Safi found she had to re-engage with the art establishment to carry the reputation of the gallery forward. Opening in Manhattan had helped her do just that.

Opening their doors with a major show had catapulted her and the gallery into a rarefied position, Safi found the Rubicov gallery was now invited to show at many major exhibitions round the world. After the Russian authority's interference with the gallery, when Safi began to fade from the scene, declining invitations, DuPont found his reputation once again hanging in the balance. Rumours had started to circulate about the gallery and he needed to avoid being seen as a front for it. He could not afford to fall from grace once more.

Having regained her spirit and zest for life, with a new love in her life, DuPont was sure Safi would flourish once again. Love and sex, after all, were the food of life; no wonder she had lost her appetite for life after all she had been through. Thank goodness for Janus, DuPont must remember to thank him for awakening his English Rose once more; he believed they had great things to achieve together in the art world, after all Europeans had a sophisticated attitude to relationships, life was complicated enough without complications in this regard.

Having found her sense of humour once more, Safi had laughed at DuPont's description, of as he named it, 'The Rubicov Saga.'

'No disrespect meant,' he told Safi, in his usual genteel, convivial, and wry, sophisticated, knowing manner, 'but they are in the habit of inviting more trouble than necessary. As far as he was concerned – and he was mortified to learn of her loss, a terrible situation for someone so young and vital to endure – Safi's position being so beholden to Sasha's family, with all of the responsibility and the politics implied, it did not seem right. In his inimitable fashion, DuPont continued to give his opinion.

'If the gallery had failed, they would not have thanked you. If Sasha is not found and you have taken up with Janus, it could turn the family against you. We must make a success of the gallery, you do not think, Chérie?'

Certainly, in his own sophisticated way, DuPont's charm masked a form of cajolement. It was in his interest to keep Safi invested in the gallery, and the gallery a success. For DuPont, despite his gentlemanly appearances, was as self-serving as everyone else in the business.

She had never thought of it that way; having been devastated by the events of Sasha's disappearance, she understood DuPont's concerns for the gallery, but she did not agree with his observations.

'I am pleased to say you are very far off the mark about the Rubicov family, thank goodness,' Safi said. 'They have given me their blessing with Janus, and do not expect me to wait indefinitely for Sasha before getting on with my life. Alexi and Mika have not said a word about the gallery, in fact I have something else to tell you.' She paused, carefully considered her words. 'Don't ask me to elaborate, but it seems we have a lead in Sasha's disappearance. All I can tell you is that nothing is as we imagined it to be.'

DuPont looked at her hungrily, but this time it was not a sexual hunger, but rather a hunger for information, an intense need to know all that was going on – and a frustration at being kept in the dark, even if he understood the need for secrecy. 'We will have to wait for further information before we have any answers to the *saga*, as you so aptly call it.' There was suddenly a turn in her voice, a note of quiet annoyance, even a snarl. 'I am surprised you did not call it the "Safi Saga," since you feel I have allowed the gallery to suffer because of my feelings of despair and loss, since I am apparently incapable of dealing with the situation.'

'Oh, Chérie, please, I did not mean to sound harsh,' DuPont said, his tone changing, softening, his handsome face shifting back to its familiar seductive expression, becomingly expertly placating now, eager to soothe and coerce and take control again. She revered DuPont's knowledge and expertise, but she knew him well enough to know his enormous reserves of bullshit, too. 'It was just that I was so terribly worried for you and all that hard work you have invested to make this venture of yours a success.' The tone – and the face – changed again. 'You know I see you as my protégé. I have the greatest respect for your strength of character in this whole sad affair, believe me.'

'I know that you in part, have contributed to our success,' Safi said, 'and I understand your concerns. But it will be okay. I promise I am back to my old self. You will be pleased to hear, I have my appetite back.'

'Well, Chérie, sex will do that for you, Oui?'

'Oh, for God's sake, DuPont, can't you French think of anything other than sex?'

They both laughed, but Safi could tell that things were different between them and that he meant what he had promised: she was now a colleague he respected, he would no longer see her as a sexual object, not while they were working together anyway; he was French, after all; sex was his nation's *raison d'être*, was it not?

Safi worked late into the night for the next few weeks. She had fallen behind with her colleagues and needed to re-establish contact, appear at their gatherings and parties, and be part of the art scene in Manhattan. To be seen was important, she thankfully had DuPont to escort her or keep her buoyant at the events, fielding the questions she could not answer and rumours circulating about Sasha or her sudden absence from the Manhattan social scene.

Alexi had flown to New York with his family to attend a party Safi was throwing at the gallery. It had been their first visit to the gallery since its opening over a year ago. Janus's drawings and screen prints and editions were on show. He was still the gallery's major artist since their opening, which suited both Safi and the Rubicov family. Valentina – typically Russian, tall, and elegantly dressed – turned quite a number of heads; as did Marina, who was no longer a gangly child, but a stunningly beautiful teenager blossoming into a beautiful woman.

Alexi for once was reaping pleasure, and Safi was pleased to see him so proud of his wife and daughter. She managed to introduce him to all the major players. Being proficient in art speak, he was able to hold his own; most were more impressed by his vast wealth rather than his ability to converse in the arts.

Safi noticed that Valentina had found a soulmate in the ballet world and they spent most of the evening comparing ballet companies. Marina tagged along, not without admiring glances from many of the younger men. It was not going to be long before she flew the nest; Safi thought that it would be tough for Alexi and Valentina when they were alone once more. She remembered how her own parents had suffered when she left for Manhattan, followed by Jake to Australia.

Jake's move had given her parents a wonderful opportunity to travel, and he had persuaded them to buy a small place of their own in Melbourne, along the beach in one of the older suburbs. Fiona, to Safi's surprise, loved it.

'Not the same as being in Brighton,' she had informed Safi, 'but it's Australia, after all, bound to be different.' Fiona had even begun to pronounce *Australia* like an Australian. Safi smiled every time she thought of her mum as an Aussie. Jake and his fiancé were finding a date for their wedding. Relieved that things were still a way off, Safi hoped to have some good news of her own.

Smiling, Safi turned to Polly. 'What would I have done, both professionally and personally, if Janus had not arrived in my life when he did?'

'I think we need to get back to the 'Rubicov Saga,' Polly said, her still chipper voice shifting slightly to a more professional tone, 'my readers will want to know the outcome – and so do I. The real reason behind the disappearance and what happened next.'

Polly's intermittent questions as the revelations of her life unfolded even those she thought and relived but did not divulge for her article in the glossy magazine, her steady gaze and kindly, knowing face, kept Safi from going off on a tangent. She was right, they needed to continue with the 'Rubicov Saga.'

'Just a moment, Polly, I need to do this before we continue,' Safi said, signing the bottom of the page with a flourish.

The contact number from Fritzi was run through analyses at Janus's headquarters in LA. The number threw up a new country every few days, as it passed through different satellite cell phone connections. Calls to the number they were feeding into the computers were being flagged and tracked but very few were being returned. Watching the screen Mika recognised the one number as it threw up connections on Janus's huge data base in LA. Shocked at the conversation typed up on the screens, he asked for the conversations to be voice transmitted. He did not believe it possible, yet there it was on the screen, unless the cell had been stolen.

There was no mistaking the voice identification: even if not clear, it was definitely his sister Yvetta's manner of speaking, she had an inflection in her speech that was unmistakable, left over from a lisp not quite eradicated by elocution, how had she managed to call out? Patients in the clinic were forbidden to use mobile phones (they were confiscated on arrival); all calls were monitored by the staff from land lines., the Swiss Clinic did not encourage visitors and very few in the first year got to see their relatives, not even Alexi had yet spoken with Yvetta.

Mika did not care what time it was in Switzerland, he would get to the bottom of this. He called the psychiatrist who oversaw the exclusive sanatorium; he needed an explanation. Fortunately, the staff were still on the premises, in a meeting running late into the night.

'It's Mika Rubicov,' he said, and then paused for a second so that the name would register. 'I would like to know why my sister, Yvetta, has been allowed to call out on a cell phone?'

'Good evening, Herr Rubicov, yes, well,' in a surprised, hesitant voice, 'unfortunately it has only come to our notice in the last few hours. Your sister has managed to persuade someone to give her a cell phone.'

'A staff member no doubt gave her a phone?' Mika said. 'Why? On whose authority?'

'This is not clear yet, we are in a meeting about this very occurrence, it's most irregular.'

'But how on earth could this happen?' Mika was struggling to control his anger, knowing it would hardly be helpful in this moment, and that any kind of perceived antagonism or hostility would be counterproductive. Surely you have checks and balances in place to ensure that you are aware which patients have access to the outside world – and when.'

'We have tracked a staff member down,' she said unhelpfully, 'he is on his way over here. We will be able to update you when we have more information.'

'Have you spoken with my sister?'

'Yes.'

'Well?'

'Yvetta was only prepared to name an outside source, we are investigating this breech very seriously.'

'Well, I doubt it's a clinician she works with. My sister is a clever woman, but then I'm sure you know that already. I doubt you will receive the truth from her. 'I will be there tomorrow. Please do not inform her I am coming.'

'But this is against our rules as you know we only allow patients to see relatives after one year depending on their progress.'

Mika had to reign in his temper; he had to have their cooperation to discover who she was talking to. *The rules*, he wanted to say, *since when do you care about the rules? I thought the rules were that patients didn't have access to cell phones. What about those rules?*

'This is matter of life or death. I have a question that only she can answer.'

'Very well, Herr Rubicov, but a member of staff will have to be present when you speak to Yvetta. She is still under our supervision.'

Mika was not prepared to argue over the phone, he had more productive uses for his time. The jet was waiting for them at the airport.

Janus had sent one of his field men with Mika to assist in undercover work. An expert in cyberspace and AI technology, with contacts around the world, they could track almost anything anywhere on the globe in a matter of minutes.

Yvetta walked in with a member of staff, shock registered in her eyes, when she saw Mika, who only showed up when there was trouble. Of all her family members she feared him the most.

Defiant as always, Yvetta put on a brave face. They had locked her up on this mountain, she was going to get her revenge one way or another, no one was going to stop her. After all, no one in the family was as smart or as cunning or as forward-thinking as her. They were not the only ones with contacts.

'Who have you been speaking to, Yvetta?'

She sat demurely staring straight ahead.

'Yvetta?'

If silence was golden, then she was, right now, the richest person in the world.

'We can sit here all day, Yvetta, but you are going to speak to me one way or another. I signed you into this sanatorium and I can sign you out and take you with me. Or put you in another institution altogether – one a lot worse than this. It's your choice.'

Still Yvetta did not speak. She sat with her head held high arrogant behaviour Mika was used to in his sister, but her hands folding and unfolding told another story.

'Have it your way,' Mika said. 'You always do, anyway. You have caused trouble – this much I know. Who are you working with, Yvetta?'

Still no response.

'Yvetta, I am losing my patience. Must I count to ten? Remember when we were children, what daddy would do when we wouldn't listen. He would count to ten. And then, if we still didn't listen, do you remember what he would do?'

Yvetta flinched – the memory clearly smarting, her expression more distant now, as though she had travelled back to her childhood, lost herself for a moment. She readjusted, gave Mika a hard, unforgiving look. But still she said nothing.

'One...' Mika began.

She smiled at him, daring him to continue.

He continued. 'Two... Three ... Four... I have a lot of time, Yvetta. So do you. You might spend the rest of your life in this place. Five ... Six ...' He rapped out a rhythm on his knee. 'Seven... Eight...'

She spat out her answer. 'Why don't you speak to Sasha and the politicians he has been working with. Or speak to Ringo, or my cousins; maybe to Ilona at the gallery. Why speak to me? What do I know? I know nothing and I am nothing – that's why you locked me up here, right? Here, in this nothing place with this nothingness. Why talk to me? You won't stop punishing me, abusing me. And for what? For *nothing*. What can I do locked up here? Think about it for a moment. You always think you are so intelligent, so good at strategy – but are you really? Really? Where has your strategy got you? Now think about *that*.'

'What are you talking about, Yvetta? You are very good at changing the subject, which makes me think you do indeed know. I ask again, who were you talking to on that cell – and why?'

Against his better judgement, Mika decided to have her discharged under his supervision. He needed to have her in a confined space alone; they would threaten her physically Yvetta loved exercise, they would deny her one thing at a time, if needed.

'Well, seems you will have to be discharged into my custody. Unless, that is, you start to talk.'

'Still a bully, Mika, after all these years. A small man who likes to pretend that he is big. Count to ten again, Mika, maybe you can grow up in that time. Still afraid of daddy, still desperate for approval, not yet your own man. Still a boy.'

'You have already destroyed our family,' Mika said slowly, 'but you can't destroy me personally.'

Yvetta stood, walked over to her brother, bent as if to kiss him, then spat in his face. She lifted her hand to strike, but Mika caught her hand in mid-strike; the assistant called for help while restraining Yvetta. Yvetta had not improved in all the time she had been under psychiatric care – that much was obvious. Mika wondered, and not for the first time, if anything could help her, or was she beyond help entirely, a lost cause, a dead end, incurable, unfathomable, impossible to be around.

There was so much love in his family for his sister (despite what she thought, Mika had always suspected that Yvetta, the only girl in the family, had for a long time been his father's favourite; indeed perhaps he had spoiled her too much, not disciplined her enough, not counted to ten in her presence nearly enough, let her get away with everything all the time), yet she had spurned them all, alienated everyone, until everyone turned away from her – everyone, that was, apart from Sasha, his father, and Mika.

If only she knew how faithful and sensitive and longsuffering, they had been – and where had it got them? If only, Mika now reflected, every time he had been patient and pleasant with Yvetta (treating her like an invalid, treating her like a child, treating her like she treated herself, like she was in some way special), he had punished her instead? Would things be different now? Probably not. Yvetta was nothing if not stubborn – all of the Rubicovs were. This was their great gift and also their biggest failing, what had taken them so high and what now threatened to destroy them. Now she was pushing them away, too. Her irrational mindset towards her family was hard to fathom, what more could they do to help her? *Nothing*. You could not reason with an unreasonable person, nor explain to an insane person that they were in fact insane. Attempting to do this was merely to humour them, and to waste your own time. And, unlike Yvetta, Mika had very little time on his hands.

He felt the full force of his exhaustion. The problems with the business, the problem with Sasha, and now Yvetta again… always Yvetta, always a problem. He was tired of her. She had obstructed the family for so long and to such a great degree these last few years, taken up so much of his time, depleted him.

Mika felt saddened by the events unfolding, Yvetta was dangerous. He had to protect his family; they could no longer indulge her vengeance against people who loved and protected her. They had to treat her for what she was – a serious threat. Kid gloves were no longer an option; something far heavier was called for.

Her thoughts were so irrational, she twisted every event to suit her own reality, and no one could reason with her when she was on a destructive path. Mika had witnessed it too many times in the past; she would harness all of her power to achieve her objectives, to play out the only reality she believed to be true – and he had no idea what those objectives were right now. He doubted the people she mentioned had any information, it was a ruse to get rid of him, to send him on a wild goose chase, but was it safe to have her released? Was he making a mistake? It hardly appeared that she was safe in the clinic, after all of this time. He saw no other option. Mika liked to pretend that he was resolute, confident in his decisions, but this time he was not confident at all. Maybe Yvetta had been right, he was a boy pretending to be a man, still very much under his father's enormous and ever-shifting thumb. Yvetta knew how to hurt him, which buttons to press – that was for sure. He told himself not to let her words get under his skin, but it was easier said than done. Her skin was his skin, they were blood, the same family, but they approached that family dynamic with different aims.

After Yvetta had been removed, he made his way to the office to organise for her release into his custody.

'This is most unusual, Herr Rubicov, she is not well, we need to help her. She's already come so far–' He looked at the administrator doubtfully.

'Really, I do not see any evidence of improvement in my sister in all the months she has been here. She is obviously pulling the wool over your eyes, doing what you ask, with no real improvement in her mindset. That is patently obvious–'

'Obvious to you, perhaps. But if you just meet with some of our staff and they can tell you how.'

'I've seen enough, thank you,' Mika said with a tone of finality. He made to stand.

'We can only work with what she chooses to share,' the voice now sharper, less flexible or forgiving, as though conceding a kind of defeat but wanting to lash out – within the limits the cosy confines of the clinic allowed – nonetheless. A grim smile accompanied the words. Grim *and* efficient, efficient above all else. It's a very long process. There is no quick fix.'

'Clearly there is no *quick fix*. But from the amount of time Yvetta has been here, there does not seem to be a *slow* fix, either.' The administrator fixed him with her eyes. She did not at all like him – this much was clear. He softened his tone, tried a different tack. 'Look, maybe she should stay longer, but for my family's safety I want her released into my custody. More than that I can't explain. There is no solution but to question my sister elsewhere.'

'You are operating under the assumption that she does not want to be taken out of the clinic,' the woman said, 'but maybe this is actually what she wants.'

'I don't understand,' Mika said. He had, indeed, been operating under this assumption.

'Perhaps she has engineered this matter. Have you thought of this?'

'What are you getting at?'

'You say she is clever, yes, well maybe she is manipulating the situation to get out of the clinic.'

Or maybe the woman was pushing this interpretation onto him as a way to keep Yvetta in the clinic. He felt manipulated from every end, not sure who to believe – it was like being back in Russia.

Still, Mika had to admit that he had considered this point. He thought he was up to speed with Yvetta's tricks, but he was in fact always a step or so behind. There seemed no end to her deviousness. And yet too often he found himself giving her the benefit of the doubt. Why?

It occurred to him that Fritzi had put Yvetta up to this, one of her many clever mind games, possibly resulting in Yvetta's release. Or perhaps Yvetta had thought of it herself – it was too easy and convenient to always blame Fritzi for Yvetta's duplicity. Yvetta was enough of a devil on her own, and she was certainly shrewd and fiercely intelligent, attuned to her own set of dark arts. Until he had some proof to the contrary, until he knew for sure what was going on, he allowed the director of the clinic the benefit of the doubt. She would have to stay here until he had more information and time to consider what action to take with his sister.

'I will be back tomorrow. If you have any further information, you have my contact number.'

Ron was waiting for him with his computer and the bag of tricks he never travelled without when away from his LA headquarters. These tools allowed him immediate unfettered access to pretty much every person and device everywhere. Mika needed fresh air to clear his brain. He was still struggling to process his meeting with Yvetta. Confused and hungry, he invited Ron to dinner at a Swiss restaurant the reception desk at the cosy Inn had recommended. Ron a computer geek tall and lanky with a baby face, spoke of communication developments that he himself had engineered, developments not yet used in the field. He had several patents out and grand plans. He was going to take over the world – but first he was going to wiretap it. He smiled innocently as he told Mika all of this. The communication game was a fast-moving business, and they had to remain one step ahead of rival agencies in his field, it was a cat-and-mouse game. A duplicitous, cat-and-mouse game within a much larger world of duplicity and games. The mirror world of espionage seemed endless indeed. There were worlds within worlds, and none of them were innocent or unspoiled.

Businesses and governments liked to keep ahead of the game, too: for some it was survival. For the hypercompetitive in Ron's case, it was outsmarting other geeks in the cyberspace race.

Mika's cell pinged. Leaving the table, he decided to take the call outdoors. The view was spectacular; the Swiss mountain air sharp enough to clear his mind. Just what the doctor ordered, he said to himself, taking a deep breath. Then he answered the call.

'Mr Rubicov, I am calling from the clinic. We have not spoken before. Can we meet this evening?'

'Come to the Inn,' Mika said, 'I will be back there in 15 minutes.'

A tall, nervous young man with wire-frame glasses and a full-length fur hooded khaki puffer jacket was waiting at the entrance for Mika and Ron. Cold vapour escaped as he spoke.

'Herr Rubicov, I am Guido Munti, an employee at the Sanatorium in a managerial position, you understand, I am in charge of all comings and goings, you see' Guido had a Romanish accent he was an Italian Swiss, the accent was softer than German Swiss.

Mika led him to a small alcove with a burning log-fire, near one of the sitting rooms where they could not be overheard. Mika asked Ron to accompany him.

'We may have found the information of how your sister was able to get hold of a cell phone,' the man said. In a nervous manner, eyes downcast apologetically.

'I'm waiting,' Mika said. Surprised at his own curtness but he was tired of excuses.

'Well,' the man leaned forward, clasping his hands together, clearly displeased by Mika's curt response but not wanting to inflame him further, 'we had a delegation of medics visiting from Italy and Germany recently. Some of that team had access to the patients during recreation. We are sure the cell phone was passed onto your sister by one of the delegation. The staff recalls your sister having an animated conversation with one of the delegation, while another was seated next to her in the gardens.'

'Anything else?' Mika did not mean to sound curt, but he was eager to learn all there was as fast as possible, so he could address the situation and figure out a way forward.

The man shifted uncomfortably. Perhaps it wasn't Mika's tone that had bothered him. 'It has come to our attention that one of the delegates was not on our list.'

'From which country?'

'Germany.'

Mika felt it in his gut – he knew where this was going already. 'Male or female?'

Fumbling in his pocket of his puffer jacket he brought out a sheet of notes to study.

'Female.'

He felt his heart beat in confirmation of his own suspicion – his worst fear, really – followed by a flash of anger. 'I will return in the morning, please see that my sister is ready to leave your clinic. She is no longer safe there.'

'You will not reconsider?'

Mika dismissed his comments – and, in a way, the man himself – making it clear he was no longer interested in what the clinic had to say. The young man had been dismissed to return to his superiors with the unfavourable outcome, an outcome they were hoping to avoid: the Swiss never liked to lose money.

Mika decided that before he moved Yvetta to another facility, he had to interrogate her. Under duress, in this situation, on the defensive and perhaps fully paranoid, her narcissistic nature would kick in. If she thought she could get what she wanted, she would be open to negotiation, and may even reveal whatever information she had. She clearly wanted to live in open society, and to reclaim her title as a kind of princess, her status and influence and all the trappings that came from extreme wealth.

Mika had never found it easy dealing with perceived political threats or the real thing. They had dealt with the real threat but the threat had not evaporated entirely, it remained lurking over their staff, and much smaller slimmed down skeleton companies including the Rubicov Art Galleries and, restaurants. and if they were perceived as the enemy of the state, dark forces, whether living in Russia or abroad, remained, powerful and had a long reach.

Sasha was involved in some kind of deal, what he was doing had not yet come to light, but Mika felt confident that it would. Mika dreaded the course of action his father would take, and doubted he would agree with those actions. Somehow a fissure had opened in their closely-knit business empire. It was undermining and crippling his father, who Mika respected and loved like no one else. He would protect his father at any cost, no matter who was involved.

With this in mind he had Yvetta removed from the clinic to a safe house not far from his mother's home in the South of France. If necessary, he would be able to call on Maurice, his mother's partner, a psychiatrist worthy of his esteemed reputation, and not at all like some Mika had met recently, none having had any success with Yvetta.

Mika had not thought through exactly how to deal with Yvetta. He felt it wise to speak with Maurice before he tackled the problem.

With Yvetta safely under lock and key, he drove to his mother's villa in Cannes. Anna was always thrilled to see her children, yet she knew a visit from Mika meant there was a problem in the family, and she dreaded any unfavourable news concerning Sasha.

'We miss Alexi and the family being over here in the summer,' she informed Mika. 'I am sure they are having a wonderful time in Florida, luxuriating in your incredible home during their summer break. So why are you here?'

Mika admired his mother's shrewdness – and, indeed, her gentleness. He felt grateful for both of his parents' love and support. Still, he did not want his mother to know about Yvetta.

'It's Maurice I have come to see. I need some professional advice. The company have a few delicate, unresolved personnel issues to handle with our staff – dealing with them in England can be complicated. Maurice might be able to give me some watertight solutions the employment rules cannot find fault with.' Since Maurice's marriage, to his mother he had shown to be expert in a number of issues relating to family and, with staff issues once the companies were devalued and broken up to please the Russian authorities.

'But Mika, Maurice is Russian.'

'True, Anna,' Maurice helpfully put in, 'but you forget that I have an international education. Situations crop up with my clients around the world, so I might be able to guide Mika in what is permissible.' Pushing back his chair from the patio table as he rose to show Mika into his study from where he had watched Anna and Alexi not so long ago discuss their family issues.

'You could not do this over a phone call?'

The only person in the family more suspicious than Anna, Mika decided, was Mika himself.

'I could have, Mother, but I had other business to attend in Europe, so here I am. Oh, and I wanted to see you, too.'

She gave him a hard look to signify she wasn't buying it. Mika and Maurice retired to his study. He was relieved that his mother had not questioned him further; the story sounded unlikely even to him. Perhaps he was losing his touch making up nonsensical excuses on the fly. Mika worried that he was losing his touch in other ways as well. Neither of them wanted to upset Anna. Having studied Relational Ethics and Psychology before majoring in Psychiatry at the LSE in London, Maurice was used to helping international clients with legal issues. Mika was hoping that together they would be able to persuade his sister to come clean of any inside knowledge, without much of a struggle or fight.

Maurice was the first to meet with Yvetta after her departure from the clinic. He had read her case history and had worked with patients with similar personality disorders. Personality disorders were undeniably hard to treat (and some patients could not be treated at all). However, Maurice had known successful cases, but the mind had to be significantly rewired to achieve this improved outlook. Long sessions were required from a very young age (which was easier said than done, since personality disorders often only manifested themselves – or at least became identifiable to professionals – in later life, from adolescence onwards. Yvetta unfortunately had no such early intervention.

Maurice informed Mika that something a person with a personality disorder valued more than themselves had to be taken away in order for them to change their mindset – or something had to occur that threatened their way of life. The former had already been tried; finding the latter would be guesswork on Maurice's part.

Yvetta viewed Maurice, a Russian she did not know with suspicion. With his non-aggressive, fatherly manner, Maurice found that most of his patients, before he retired from practice and moved with Anna, Yvetta's estranged mother, to the South of France, came to trust him after a time (indeed, he had had great success in his field). But now he had to rely solely on his manner, having very little time, to find out whether Yvetta had any knowledge of her brother Sasha's disappearance, through her contact with Fritzi, the reason her brother had removed her from the Swiss Clinic. Yvetta had no interest in her family so she would not know that Anna, her mother had remarried, in fact she did not want Anna's name to be uttered in her presence.

The relaxed surroundings Mika had provided made the meeting less formal, and Maurice would behave as the guest Yvetta took him for. He was there to visit with Mika after all not Yvetta, she was entertaining him while Mika was detained for a while on a business call. They discussed art, one of Maurice's favourite subjects; fortunately, the room had a few select pieces, which made introducing the subject natural. 'Those Yves Klein blue prints are delightful in this Mediterranean setting, don't you think?'

He noticed Yvetta come alive, even animated, when discussing art. It was an area she felt at home in, confident of who she was. He allowed her to elaborate while listening and watching her closely, subtly diverting the conversation to another topic without antagonizing her. It was best not to challenge her, but instead help her to come to her own conclusions. Then he would politely ask whether it was permissible to offer an opinion on the subject, Yvetta would take this into consideration, without in any way taking it as a criticism of her knowledge.

Maurice had forbidden any interruption while he was with Yvetta, Mika had to stay out of sight still on a business call as far as Yvetta was concerned. This was her time to open up – and she would have to do just that, if they were to get anywhere at all in such a short time frame.

Yvetta was clearly enjoying her interlude with a stranger who did not know her past, happy to be out of the clinic after such a long period of interment. Pleased with his progress, Maurice allowed her to believe he was just a guest who was visiting, her brother an old Russian acquaintance, for a catch up like all expats liked to do.

To his surprise she entertained him with various scenarios that happened in the art market, allowing Maurice to feign great interest in the unlawful side, asking for her knowledge on such dealings in the Art Market. 'How can one protect the buyer from these forgeries and the lucrative Art theft market?'

Yvetta was in her element she loved nothing more than to impart her considerable knowledge, it had been a long time since she had enjoyed a conversation about the arts and Maurice encouraged her to indulge in her topic.

She did not react to him with suspicion; having been away from her much-loved profession for so long, she was obviously keen to practice her knowledge once more with someone who had a genuine interest in art (and Maurice did, but not for the reasons Yvetta believed).

Maurice was fascinated. Yvetta's knowledge was all consuming and truly impressive; she was lost in her subject. He did not want to divulge knowledge of her past (that would give the game away, break her reverie and cause her to reassess everything about this encounter), rather he needed her to divulge this information on her own, draw her out about who she was, where she had worked, giving her back her lost self. Enabling her to find that lost self, the self she admired, trusted, and loved. From there, he could begin the process of exploring her psyche. But he needed her help, and trust, to do so.

He hoped he might be able to use her passion for her work, the one thing she wanted back in her life more than anything (more even than Fritzi): was her gallery and her profession.

Yvetta suddenly became very quiet looking off into the distance out to the blue azure waters a beautiful sight, he was sure after the frozen mountaintop sanatorium, she had been locked away in. Maurice allowed her space to absorb her own revelation, he wasn't part of her past anger, the hate she felt for those who had abandoned her, those who did not understand where she was coming from. He did not want her to revert to her irrational reality. She wanted back what was hers, what she loved and understood. He could tell Yvetta was struggling to come to terms with what was dear to her, what she had lost, her profession and her gallery. She might now speak to Mika again, as long as he did not antagonize her; she might just find her own way to gain what she most wanted back. If Maurice could keep this thought, this goal, uppermost in her mind, she might reach out and grab what was left of her former life in the art world, winning her gallery back.

Mika returned and, Maurice bid Yvettta farewell until they met again, perhaps to continue their discussion of the arts he so much enjoyed in her charming company. Maurice left Yvetta to enjoy her lunch, thanking her again for the interesting conversation and bidding her a fond farewell. His task had been easier than anticipated. Now he would have to run his idea past Mika's, who would have to put his past prejudices on hold if he wanted his sister to cooperate. Mika would have to become objective rather than remain subjective, which was no easy task, untangling all of his previous prejudices and experiences about Yvetta, decades of ill will, and separating them from the now, the reality and immediacy of the task, working together for the greater good, to find Sasha. The thing about Yvetta's version of reality, Maurice would have to stress, was that it was, to her, the truth. It was not a lie or series of lies that she was propagating, but a 'truth' so deeply entrenched in herself and her identity that she was incapable of seeing another side. Instead of being hostile to her condition, one could attempt to empathise with her, if not exactly agreeing with her outlook than understanding how and why she thought the way she did. In other words, live in her world, for a moment, and perhaps a kind of compromise, or at least détente, could emerge.

Perhaps they could work together to achieve different goals. Instead of approaching Yvetta as a devastating influence, a kind of plague, a lost cause, think of dealings with her as just another business proposition. In place of family passion try out Alexi's old-fashioned pragmatism once again. Approach the old problem of Yvetta from a new angle. Cooperate with her without destroying (or devaluing) her reality of the truth as she saw it, not an easy task for a brother without becoming overly emotive in the process.

Maurice briefed Mika on his session with Yvetta. Having had a wire fitted proved to be genius, something he would never have been able to do, but now he was an ordinary citizen no longer part of his esteemed profession, it became permissible and, he wanted above all to help Anna find her beloved youngest son Sasha.

Maurice was able to play the entire conversation to Mika. The recording enabled Mika to gain insight and knowledge of his sister's passion and love of the arts and that her gallery was her lifeblood, and hoped something they could take advantage of. Maurice could tell that Mika's reaction to his sisters' normal conversation and passion for the arts, had come not as a shock, he knew her profession was in the arts, but as a reminder that beneath the Yvetta he knew, there was another Yvetta, one he wished was his sister, the one he could now hear discussing a topic she loved.

Mika shook his head. 'This is the Yvetta we all love where did she go, I wonder, it's a tragedy and, for Anna and my father especially.'

Both Mika and Maurice were aware of Yvetta's intuitive and pathological distrust (in this instance, certainly not unfounded), of her irrational mindset. If any of this came into play, they would not be able to gain the knowledge they required. If she began to suspect them, she would pull away, resort to her old games, and everything they had accomplished to that point would unravel, and perhaps even rebound to Yvetta's benefit.

They would be playing for the highest of stakes now (a human life) that, if misinterpreted by Yvetta, could come crashing down on top of them with the slightest disapproving eye contact on Mika's part.

Mika replayed the tape discussing various avenues with Maurice. After an exhaustive discussion (encompassing the ethical foundation of the psychiatric practise, the intricate and defiantly unethical espionage business, and also where – if anywhere – these two very different points of view met), they opted for an earpiece for Mika, who would follow Maurice's questions and conversation. This was the only way Mika felt he would be able to give the impression of genuine objectivity without losing his temper with his sister.

Mika found Yvetta on the terrace enjoying the sunset. He had been fortunate to find a secluded villa overlooking the Mediterranean hills near Saint Tropez. The villa included a helipad, a stroke of luck that Mika (optimistic for the first time in a long while, and relishing the feeling since leaving behind all his previous Russian contacts) hoped his luck would continue. He offered Yvetta a glass of white wine. It was the first, time brother and sister had been alone like this, in a relaxed environment, without an outburst or crisis, for many years. But here they were, in the cool air, together, and he tried in his way to enjoy the moment, overlook the upheaval of so many years, start again – or even go back to the beginning, when they were very young, innocent children. But then children were hardly innocent, and Mika and Yvetta had never been close, never shared an idealised sibling bond, always been apart, even before Yvetta's condition became entrenched when she was in adolescence. There was no ideal to hold onto. Still, a game that ended in a stalemate (though uniquely frustrating) was still preferable to an outright loss. And, who knows, the next game might be a win.

Yvetta accepted his offer of wine. He knew it was best to treat Yvetta respectfully (if not affectionately; she distrusted affection and thus was largely unfamiliar with it), to make this moment as social and enjoyable as possible, allow her to feel safe. He kept reminding himself to forget his reflexively aggressive attitude, to keep his cool – and hers. If he so much as raised his voice to her, it would create a domino effect stretching and spiralling all the way back to their childhood, and knocking down everything, certainly the last hope of finding Sasha. Signify to her a new start. That was what Maurice had advised. Everyone wants the promise of a fresh start, a new beginning, a second chance. *But this is her last chance*, Mika said to himself under his breath. He laughed at the illogicality of it, it was so obvious she would, sooner or later, return to her old ways.

Everyone would. The Rubicovs were nothing if not slaves to their character, and their fate. And ultimately, this was what they did have in common: they were both Rubicovs, and knew the pain, the burden, perhaps even the glory of what this meant. His ideal was to build the family up even further; hers appeared to be to destroy it. But were these ideals really so different? She needed to trust him, feel he was there as her saviour, rather than the big brother she feared whenever there was trouble in their family.

Seated together on a long white-washed outdoor sofa, Mika turned to face Yvetta. She looked fragile, her petite frame dressed in green harem trousers, studded Roman sandals, and a loose-fitting silk top. Of course, none of this hid her gaunt, hollow cheekbones, her obvious and significant weight loss, and her sickly appearance. He wondered whether she was bulimic. Still, he marvelled at her beauty. Her haughty posture (almost impossibly impervious, imperious, aristocratic) and long elegant neck made up for her short stature. Somehow his sister had the ability to exhume confidence, even power. As she turned her green eyes flashed at him, narrowing in what could be construed as a questioning – or was it accusing – manner. He was not sure. All he knew is that he did not want those eyes to turn away from him, to shut him out once again, something she often did when insecure, with an arrogance that was impossible to penetrate once it set in. As a child, she was always the winner of their staring contests; but when she looked away, she could look away for ever, sometimes not so much as greeting you for years. You never knew the reasons for the slights, for the indifference and the obvious hostility. You may as well be dead to her.

They sat in silence, overlooking the hills towards the sea where the sun was slowly dipping behind the horizon. It would soon be dark, the outdoor lights would come on, and they would be called in for dinner.

Mika had insisted on the earpiece. It would give him time to adopt a relaxed manner, expertly engineer a gentle and unthreatening mood, before he began what now appeared more difficult than he had imagined, in theory anyway it seemed possible to pull off. It had been a while since he had been in a social environment with her, one of complete relaxation, free of recrimination and regret, and he needed her to feel comfortable before he switched over to Maurice's questions.

'You met one of my old friends and a client this afternoon,' Mika began, his voice even, gentler than usual, 'he was very impressed by your knowledge of the art world and enjoyed your company. Thank you for entertaining him. I was indisposed at the time and am grateful to you for keeping him from leaving before I had time to meet with him.'

He could tell Yvetta did not quite know how to respond. She was still wary and knew this was all about Sasha's disappearance and, Fritzi's ingenious method of staying in contact with her while at her mountain top prison, his kindness now had ulterior motives, but two could play that game and she had her ulterior motives too. Maurice could unfortunately not judge her expressions or her body language. Nervous in case he said the wrong thing, he waited for Yvetta to speak first. Maurice had advised him to give her as much time as she needed to respond, not to interrupt her thought patterns (in any case, an interruption from Mika could be seen as disapproving even aggression on his part, Mika attempting to take control, and might backfire on them, or at least inhibit her thoughts – and her trust), to give her room to gain confidence around him.

Mika twirled his glass and watching the red liquid swilling around. He savoured the taste of the wine, trying to take the energy away from whatever remained of his own antagonism, trying to feel as light as the air around them, open to any possibility, waiting patiently for his sister to speak.

'Yes,' she said. 'He reminded me how much I miss that world – *my* world and *my* gallery.'

Her use of the possessive was no accident. After so long being denied so much, at the mercy of others, she was asserting her independence again. She was saying that the gallery, in particular, belonged to her. And not Safi.

Maurice came through Mika's earpiece in a whisper. 'Shake your head in acknowledgement, don't say a word.'

Yvetta turned to face him. Her large green eyes on his face tried to decipher his expression. He wished Maurice could see her body language; it felt to Mika every bit as important as what she might say.

If they moved indoors to the main seating area, Maurice hoped to find a location outdoors and out of sight, where he could see Yvetta through the shutters from the terrace.

'This wine was so delicious. I need another. Can I get you one? Or perhaps we can go indoors, it will be dark soon?'

To his surprise, Yvetta rose, smiled, and placed her wine glass in his hand for a refill, she was playing along he could see that, good there was obviously something she wanted it would keep her usual unpredictability reigned in, he allowed her to walk ahead into the lounge (symbolically taking charge, which is what he knew she longed to do) while he moved up the terrace to enter at the door near the bar. This position allowed him to speak (unseen by Yvetta) to Maurice, and to pull open the slats of the shuttered doors that led onto the terrace.

Yvetta acquiesced to Mika's suggestion (it seemed they were both on their best behaviour; both of them inhabiting and shifting roles and positions, changing shape and attitude to form some sort of future compromise, the exact nature of which perhaps neither of them was yet aware of; losing purchase to gain leverage – or vice versa, moving rapidly to a dance that was unfamiliar to both of them) and took their seats facing the terrace with refilled glasses. It felt good to seat Yvetta, for once; Yvetta who was so used to pulling strings and arranging the seating for the dinner parties that had once been such a large part of her life, to making people her puppets, to being utterly in control. He took the armchair opposite, sitting slowly, trying to steady his mounting anxiety, for the next part of this game for information to unfold.

He realised that their previous, meeting when she threatened him, with violence had not made the slightest difference to her; that was then, this was now. She lived moment to moment, never responsible for her actions, caring nothing for all of those caught in the crossfire. She was now another Yvetta – blameless, luminous – and he had to accept this without reminding her of any incidents of the past, which would surely only poison the present moment and make everything untenable. Just go with the flow, he said to himself, still swilling his wine. He took a long sip, gave her an even look.

'I want my gallery back and I want my life back.'

Mika hoped Maurice was watching. He wasn't expecting this – not yet, anyway. Her body language had become one of aggressive entitlement. This meant that he needed Maurice to guide him. It was a dangerous moment and could blow up in his face if he answered in a manner that contradicted (or even challenged) her needs. He took another sip, waiting for Maurice to speak.

'Do not say a word,' Maurice said, 'let's see if she has more to add. Don't obstruct or impede. Let her lead. Give her space and do not challenge her with your body language, either.'

Not saying a word Mika tried to appear open to her suggestion. Yvetta was watching him closely for any reaction. When she found none she leaned forward, touched his arm lightly with her hand.

'I want my gallery back,' she said again. Her voice was softer now, perhaps she took his silence as a form of tacit encouragement.

Maurice better play this well, Mika thought, because I would like to give her a piece of my mind. He was suddenly angry again, reminded of the obnoxious, entitled, imperious Yvetta. So much for objectivity, he thought. When it came to family, objectivity was as much an illusion as that photo of the Loch Ness Monster.

How dare she make these demands, he thought, reverting very quickly to his old, impolite self, as she reverted to hers. She has never given anyone anything in return, not one iota of gratitude or remorse. Nothing – or no one – bothered her. She revolved around herself and her needs and her enormous, unfathomable ego the way the earth revolved around the sun. They all loved her, yet here she sat, after all this time, not a guilty bone in her body, no remorse for what she had done to Anna or Alexi, only interested in what she wants, demanding and entitled and impossible to the end. The bitter end, he suddenly thought. He remembered her as a child again, staring him down, unblinking, impervious, cold, she had no empathy for anyone but herself.

'Hmm, yes,' he said slowly, thinking of something more substantial to say.

'I worked hard. It was my life.'

'Yes.' He shook his head in agreement

No one was arguing with her, he could tell she was struggling with his apparent lack of contradiction, the fact that he wasn't fighting back. He wasn't agreeing with her, exactly, but he wasn't denying anything, either. What he was doing was confusing her – and this seemed, in its way, worse than an outright denial, a simple *no*. Not knowing where she stood, so to speak, she shifted in her seat.

Mika looked down at his drink. He did not want to look at Yvetta in case she read something in his expression that she did not like.

'What do you want from me?' Her tone was accusing, aggressive; she was not asking, she was demanding to know.

'I understand. I hear you, Yvetta.'

'Do you? You're not responding to me. You are barely looking at me. What is this, anyway?' She looked around her with disgust. Her face, previously relaxed, looked suspicious, even alarmed. She gestured to the beauty around her as if to cast aspersions on it.

'You take me out of the clinic and bring me here. Why? For what? Do you think I'm stupid, Mika?'

'No, of course not. You are many things, but you are not stupid.'

'Many things,' she said in a tone of extreme indifference. 'Ah yes, many things. We are all many things, Mika. Even you are many things. Some are good, many are bad.'

'We are not here to talk about me, Yvetta.' He knew he had already lost control. This was going horribly wrong. And still Maurice did not speak.

'And why are we here?' But he did not respond. 'It's my life and it's my reality.'

'Yes,' Mika said slowly, 'I understand that it's your reality. Would you mind if I told you *my* reality of the situation we are facing at the moment?'

She sat staring at him for some time, weighing up whether she wanted to hear his reality, she did not have the slightest interest. (Reflecting on the silence from the earpiece, Mika decided that Maurice wanted to keep her focused on her needs.)

'Ah, yes, of course,' Yvetta said, 'and now we finally come to it, the reason I'm here. This,' again she gestured to her surroundings, 'wherever this is. Your situation. And what you want from me. It's all about you,' she said, somewhat absurdly, because it was always all about her.

'You want your life back,' Mika said, 'I understand.'

'Tell me then? Since it appears that we are very much on your schedule, Mika, perhaps I could advise you to hurry the fuck up.'

He took a deep breath, tried hard to keep himself from smashing his glass of wine on the ground and leaping at Yvetta in rage. He looked through her, past her, to the magnificent view. But still no inner peace. Not quite.

'I would like to help you live your reality,' he said. 'Believe me, Yvetta, nothing would please me more than to give you the gallery back.'

'Well, what's stopping you?'

'It's complicated.'

It's complicated. A stupid, meaningless answer from someone thoroughly unprepared. Him, he was the one out of his depth here. Not Yvetta, who was in control and, in her own dispassionate, ice-cold way, enjoying every moment. Every moment of making him squirm. *What is this?* She saw right through him. She wasn't playing his game – he was playing hers. He was losing once again. Fuck, he needed to get this over with, he could not stand it any longer, it was not how he went about his business. He was sick of her being in control, sick of appeasing her, sick of giving her more of his attention than she deserved, sick of her obvious lack of respect for him, of her goddamn annoying imperious attitude, of having to look at her face – the face of someone who had ruined so many others faces, so many other lives, caused so much damage in his family, which was also her family – sick of everything about her. He couldn't wait to get back to not having to see her for months on end, her comfortably locked away somewhere, in her own miserable, delusional little world, of which she was evidently the queen.

If this was a man, Mika decided, he would have got to the point by now, whether he was nuts or not. Hell, if this was a man, Mika might have stood up and walked off, sick and tired of having his time wasted. But no… this was not a man. And it was not anybody else, either. It was his sister. And she was on her planet, which was not a place he ever wanted to visit.

Maurice could tell Mika was becoming frustrated with the slow progress.

'Terminate the discussion,' he said finally. 'Let her think about it overnight. I am sure by tomorrow morning she will be ready to barter for what she wants.'

'I have to go out for dinner,' Mika said. 'We can continue our talk tomorrow if you wish. I will be here for breakfast at nine.'

Mika stood kissed his sister on both cheeks. He would be glad to get away from her. 'Enjoy your dinner.'

He retreated from the room as quickly as possible, and met Maurice in the underground garage.

'Well,' Maurice said, 'that went rather well. To get what she wants she may decide to cooperate.'

'You think it went well?' Mika said in disbelief.

'It may not seem like that to you,' Maurice said, 'and certainly not in the moment, but …' he decided to change tack. 'You have to have patience.'

'I am not sure I have the patience to indulge my sister's warped entitled mind. You have to understand, Maurice, with my sister we have all had patience for thirty years. How much patience can we have? And how much can she be allowed to get away with? She ignores her past criminal actions and abusive behaviour. Our family have loved and cherished her from birth. And for that we get no end of punishment.'

He was getting worked up again – and for what? His anger was a sort of victory for Yvetta. He wasn't about to see her win. Not again. Not this time.

Maurice nodded in agreement. 'I have dealt with many families, all of them with children they have cherished and loved; children who have become abusive. Most of these children when young and with intervention can have a mind shift but in Yvetta's case, I must admit, as you well know, it has sadly not been the case.'

'Oh, I know,' Mika said, trying to ease the edge of irritation in his voice. It was as though, remaining calm so long with the infuriating Yvetta, he was not taking his frustration out on Maurice – Maurice who had gone out of his way to help him. 'Believe me, I know.' He suddenly regretted his bullying tone. 'Thank you so much for all of your help,' he said, by way of an apology. 'I'm sorry if I come across as hot-headed sometimes. All of the Rubicov men are. Some of the women, too.'

Maurice smiled softly and, with an appropriate gentleness in his tone, said, 'Your mother, by contrast, is so calm.'

'Oh, I know. She kept us all sane and in line for most of our lives. She was the yin to my father's yang.' But he stopped, feeling this line of conversation was inappropriate with his mother's new lover. 'And she was always so loving to Yvetta. Too loving, perhaps. That's why when Yvetta orchestrated an attack on her own mot–'

But Mika did not finish his sentence. He had had quite enough of Yvetta for one day. Even talking about her tired and angered him. Besides, Maurice, having read Yvetta's files and knowing everything about Anna, was only too familiar with the attack on his partner.

Maurice gave Mika his usual gentle, kindly, intelligent look. But Mika could see, too, that the other man was fatigued. After all, Maurice was no spring chicken, in his late seventies and Yvetta's antics could be exhausting even to someone of a younger age.

'I suggest you come straight to the point tomorrow morning,' he said, placing a surprisingly firm hand on Mika's shoulder, 'starting with the gallery, it must be pointed out that if Yvetta wants her gallery back and to live what she describes as her reality – which is a reality that, as I said, within the context of these negotiations, we have to acknowledge and accept, and never explicitly question or appear to condescend to – she will have to give something in return. She needs to understand that this is a negotiation, which is two sided; it is not a gift from you, nor is it unconditional, even if she thinks it should be, and she will.'

Mika found Yvetta helping herself to a hearty breakfast. The weather had taken a turn for the worst, which solved the problem for Maurice, they would not be eating out on the terrace today, he needed to be out on the terrace to have a vantage point without detection. With coffee and a croissant (but – alas – no welcome relief of wine this time), he waited for her to be seated before he began what he believed would be a very difficult morning. He did not expect Yvetta to be compliant, or to negotiate what she wanted without a fuss and histrionics he could do without.

After all these years, he knew Yvetta well, and what he knew was, outside of her hysteria and extreme narcissism, she was not at all predictable. In other words, he knew nothing about how she might behave. All he had to work with was an uneasy feeling. He tried for a smile, but it looked more like the kind of grimace that accompanies indigestion. He recalled Maurice advising him to come straight to the point. But for a long moment, uneasy and self-conscious, trying hard to regain some semblance of control over this situation he had (he thought!) engineered, his mind went blank.

'This is *my* reality of the situation, Yvetta,' he said when he regained his composure (but not before – he felt sure – she had seen, and taken register of, his momentary lapse into blankness), 'and before you interrupt, please allow me to finish.'

She looked up at Mika blankly – with a blankness to match his own of a moment before. Her face was impassive again, as it had been for so long in the clinic. It was as though the vigour and bile she had possessed in abundance just days before had faded absolutely. He noticed immediately that her whole demeanour had changed. He was not sure what exactly had changed since yesterday, but he sensed her mood had shifted considerably. Now she appeared to be arrogant and aloof. Or perhaps she was merely trying to throw him off his game. If so, mission accomplished, for he had lost any semblance of a game many, many moves ago.

'Are you feeling alright, Yvetta,' his gentle tone (borrowed, perhaps, from Maurice) was grating even to his ears, 'you appear to be disturbed. Has something upset you?'

Her eyes flashed distrust. Perhaps not knowing how to engage with him, she had evidently decided not to engage with him at all. She turned her head away, ignoring his query, and continued eating.

Mika wondered how someone could flip so easily from one moment to the next. One never knew where one stood with someone like Yvetta. Her mind went off on its own elaborate journey, mostly a destructive one. She was her own worst enemy. He reminded himself that he had limited time on his side; they needed any information they could get about Sasha. And he was determined to get it, no matter what Maurice thought about his methods.

Mika waited until Yvetta had finished her breakfast. He remained perfectly still, perhaps even imitating her motionless, upright, aristocratic posture, quietly observing her body language. Maurice had suggested that Mika wait until she indicated that he should begin.

'What do you want from me?' she finally said.

'We need any and all information you have about Sasha. If you do not share this information with me, I cannot give you what you want.'

'Ha, always the same. Everything has to be conditional in this family.'

He stared at her for a moment, listening to Maurice's reply, which he then repeated.

'Life is conditional,' Maurice (and then Mika) said, 'if you did not eat you would starve. If you did not drink you would die of thirst. In other words, even one's body stays alive conditionally; we need to feed it to have it do what we want, to remain alive.'

The statement, with its overarching sensibility, had thrown her off balance. She was not stupid, this was not a direct criticism of her statement – or of her. She tried to dismiss it, but he could tell her mind was in turmoil. She had expected him to disagree, to take her on directly, to give her some sort of ammunition to then fire off at him, to be bullying and adversarial even, to justify her hatred and therefore her hateful response. She was spoiling for a fight, to lay all responsibility at his door. She saw herself as the innocent party in their family, no one understood her needs, he had heard it all before.

She was searching for a way out and he was not going to give it to her.

'I have very little time, Yvetta, and Sasha might have even less. Whether you care for this family or not, I will reiterate my last statement. If you want your life and your gallery back, the only way you are going to achieve that is by telling us what you know.'

He did not expect what happened next. Yvetta's eyes rolled over, only the whites showing, she began pulling her hair, biting her arm, banging her head against the wall, screaming at him abusively. She began breaking down piecemeal, and then all at once. He began to fear that he had made a terrible mistake taking her out of the clinic. Or was this all a performance on her part?

'I hate you, I hate you all. You abandoned me, left me alone in that place. And now, when all I want is my life back, you threaten me. No one cares about me – I'm insignificant. *You hate me*,' she said again. And again. 'It's always darling Sasha, or Marina, or Valentina or wonder woman Anna, my heroic mother. Or someone else to replace me. Anyone other than me. And what about that bitch interloper who has taken over my life's work! That little whore. I am always seen as the bad one, everyone else counts but me.'

Maurice advised Mika to allow her to play out her tantrum; do not react, contradict or confront her, remain impassive until it subsides. Do not suggest she is to blame, or make any criticism of her situation now or in the past.

Yvetta was crying, yet Mika felt no sympathy. He had seen it all before. The only thing that had changed was that they were now older; too old for these antics, for this tantrum. More important things were on the line. He wanted this to be over; she was his sister, yet she never showed the slightest empathy for anyone in their family (which was precisely her criticism of everyone else; surely a form of psychological projection, perhaps the closest she ever came to ruthless self-awareness). No one heard from Yvetta unless she wanted something; everyone overlooked her ruthless, narcissistic character.

Mika had given up feeling pity for her – she had done too much damage for that. Now he felt nothing but anger for her. After all, she not only turned down all sincere offers of help, love, and affection, but made those who offered it suffer the consequences, punished them for it. Threw their love back at them, but somehow processed always to poison, always to hate. Everything was upside down in her world: love was hate, evil was good. She kept everyone who loved her at arm's length, until eventually they gave up trying to be there for her. Could you blame them?

'I am waiting, Yvetta. You might as well begin.'

Sinking onto the dining room chair, she struggled to breathe, fighting with her conflicting emotions. But Mika knew her narcissism and selfish nature would surface – after all, they were so central to her psyche, to who she was. He had no idea what would come next, but he hoped she would be able to throw some light on what they had seen of Sasha on that drone video.

Finally, through her sobs, her body relaxing somewhat, but refusing to look at him, she said, 'I have information, but it's third-hand, sent from Fritzi through her contacts.' She turned to make eye contact now, and there was something glib and pointed in her voice, a small, mean kind of triumph. 'They have been keeping me up to date since I arrived at the Swiss clinic.' She waited to see the shock register on Mika's face at her cleverness to outsmart them.

Maurice was quick to advise, 'Remain impassive.'

'Sasha was picked up by Fritzi's contacts,' she continued, perhaps disappointed by Mika's lack of reaction to her revelation about contact with Fritzi, now perhaps she was eager to deliver a proper shock, 'when he was released by the Russian authorities. The driver taking him to the airport was one of Fritzi's old Russian prison buddies.'

Again, she waited for his reaction; again none came. If she was annoyed, her face did not express it. Two could play at this game.

'The family jet remained at the airport when Sasha was arrested by the Russian authorities and was flown by Fritzi's contacts to a remote area. There, they persuaded Sasha to cooperate with their smuggling operations. They needed him to front their black-market gas and oil operations across the Russian border. They used him, the great Sasha Rubicov, to negotiate with people who would not doubt his credibility. Not so great anymore.'

Mika turned his computer to show Yvetta the drone video of Sasha and waited to see whether she had any further information.

'Those tankers are disguised by the mafia to export gas and oil to countries Russia is overcharging or withholding supplies from,' Yvetta continued. 'Sasha's presence makes the authorities believe the tankers are legitimate.'

Finally, Mika had what he wanted – well, the beginning of it. And he had also – thoroughly – run out of patience. How long had Yvetta known all of this? During how many long months when the family had assumed the worst. Sitting pretty in that expensive clinic with her criminal contacts.

'I need your contacts, everything.'

'No.'

'Yvetta do not make me do something you might regret.' And now he could no longer keep his tone even or relaxed. He was done being relaxed.

She took a small computer device out of her bra and belligerently handed it over to Mika.

'It's all there, everything Fritzi shared with me. Now can I leave this place?'

'Why would she share this sensitive information with you, Yvetta?'

He saw her turn her head in an arrogant, self-satisfied manner, letting him know that she and her lover had outsmarted him and the family. She was enjoying her moment. On some level, she had been planning and waiting for this moment – this revelation, this vindication, this revenge – for a long time.

'Don't act innocent, Mika. You are no better than any other criminal. When Fritzi found out you kidnapped me in Italy, locking me up ,lying to her about me, she swore that she would get her revenge. And she has – *we* have. She is no longer in jail, you won't stop her. She is at war with the Rubicovs and she has powerful allies. She is more powerful than ever, partly thanks to you. And you know what else, Mika,' she spat out, 'she will win. She will destroy everyone who ever tried to come between us. Even you. Especially you.'

Mika had arranged for his sister to be taken to a place she would never escape from or receive any information they were not informed of. He vowed that, this time, she would never be released or exposed to the outside world. He would not make that mistake again.

'Thank you, Yvetta, I suggest you go and get ready. My friend Maurice is picking you up. He lives in Nice. He will be here shortly to take you to the airport. From there you may go anywhere you choose. As for the galleries, you will have to be patient. The lawyers will have to prepare a contract for you to sign.'

She stared at Mika, not sure how to respond. 'But I have no pass port no money for a ticket.'

'No need. My jet is at the airport. You can tell the flight crew where you would like to go. They will give you a briefcase containing money – that should help you until you have your life together again.'

'How can I trust you?' she said.

'I'm afraid you have no option.'

Yvetta was flown back to Russia, where the authorities were waiting for her as arranged by Mika. Yvetta's information about the Russian mafia helped to reinstate his family name with those who mattered in power. The smuggling information freed the Rubicov family of their debt to the government imposed for negotiating with their enemies.

He would negotiate his sister's freedom when Sasha was safe and the smugglers had been caught, she was a Rubicov after all. Mika flew back to LA to meet with Janus. There he hoped they would be able to decipher the information Yvetta had given him. He needed to find Sasha before the Russians had a chance to put their boots on the ground; it was entirely possible that Sasha could be caught in the crossfire once the forces attempted to stop the next illegal tanker leaving Russian soil.

Ron had copied the stick for the Russian authorities, keeping the original to decode for landmarks and other sensitive information that would help them pinpoint where they were keeping Sasha. Ron's only hope was that Janus's men would be faster than the Russians at finding Sasha.

Chapter 8

Safi had returned to New York and her life had returned to relative normality – well, as normal as life could be in New York City. The gallery kept her busier than ever; she buried herself in the day to day running of the gallery, overseeing many of the decisions she had left to others while away.

The gallery in Moscow was free to do business as usual, and Ilona was excitedly organising new shows with Safi in New York for both galleries.

Ilona felt it was time to 'fess up about her love life with Ringo, who she knew Safi had worked with in Moscow and had befriended. Safi was pleased Ringo, who had moved up in the Rubicov organisation, had found someone like Ilona to date; they were both people she liked and trusted, and she could not say that about everyone she came into contact with during her time in Moscow.

The trust Alexi and Anna had in Safi's ability to run the gallery was not shared by everyone in the family, some of whom were openly hostile to Safi at family gatherings. In the past, she had experienced fleeting moments of anxiety – of not belonging, of being isolated and unwanted even – but with Sasha by her side, the family dared not put those hostile feelings into play. Things were different now that the obstacle of Sasha had been removed. She had noticed that when they gathered in small groups, she became overly sensitive to their unforgiving rudeness whenever she was present.

With hindsight they must have had a whale of a time laughing at her naïveté, surreptitiously knowing all about Sasha's reputation with women; everyone apart from her must have been aware of his philandering at the time. Maybe she had been wrong all along, misconstruing their dirty looks. Maybe they were in fact looking at her with pity, trying to warn her of something but not being able to express themselves.

Having Janus in her life helped, as did Alexi's honesty, yet she could not pretend she did not feel anger towards Sasha. Her life had become hell when he vanished, not knowing if he was alive or whether she would ever see him again. And then the revelation of his multiple betrayals, the fact that at least a part of their relationship was a sham, a ruse. Now she knew that he was alive and well, and (it seemed) with little to no concern for her or his family. It was beyond her comprehension that someone she loved unconditionally had turned out to be so untrustworthy. Her ability to make the right choices in love was at best doubtful, at worst disastrous, which did not give her much confidence for her future with Janus. What would she uncover, she wondered; was it worth embarking on another relationship when the last had turned out to be her undoing in so many ways?

Janus was in LA – at least she thought he was in LA; it was impossible to be sure. He had not called or contacted Safi in over a fortnight. She was beginning to doubt not only her feelings for him but her involvement with the Rubicovs. Paranoia was fast becoming her companion. Everything about her life since her involvement with Sasha and his family permeated into every aspect of her existence; even Janus was involved with the Rubicov family. Safi felt as if she were drowning in a Rubicov world she wanted her independence back and, she hated herself for thinking that had Sasha died it would have been easier to walk away and to mourn him, without guilt and, doubting her involvement with the Rubicovs!

Her trusted diary days, when she could work out her feelings by jotting down her problems, were long gone. Everyone she confided in when first arriving in Manhattan had moved on with their lives. Pete and Rene had moved in together. The two D's were completely besotted with Rachel and the last she heard they were trying for another. Sharing her paranoia about her life's choices felt embarrassing when everyone else was happily getting on with theirs.

Even the gallery could be returned to its rightful owner when the Rubicovs so chose, and where would she be then? She had seen how quickly even Sasha had been forgotten by larger society.

The only person Safi trusted with her paranoia was DuPont, who had strangely become her closest friend and business associate. DuPont's first name was Marcel, which was how he was known to his family and which he insisted Safi call him in the future, a sign of their growing closeness and mutual respect. Still, *Marcel* sounded alien to Safi after so many years of calling him by his surname.

Dare she continue to burden Marcel with her problems when they were hers alone to solve? No one could tell her what to do, but she needed an objective opinion, and he would be nothing but brutally honest.

DuPont met Safi for dinner at a small Italian close to her apartment. She was always happy to be in his company, she no longer worried about his intentions, they had passed that phase of their relationship. Instead he made her laugh at his ability to turn their waitress into a quivering mess with his French accent, charming her at every opportunity. He was flirtatious and entertaining to everyone. It was not until coffee that Safi unburdened her soul. DuPont sat back, contemplating Safi's 'paranoia,' as she called it. He was not sure 'paranoia' was the right word – after all, paranoia was, at heart, irrational, where Safi had every reason to feel the way she felt.

No, he did not think she was being neurotic. She had been to hell and back for such a young person; he admired her tenacity and loyalty, her self-restraint and self-respect. He did not think she knew how strong she was; how others would have crumbled at being confronted by half of her challenges. The youthful engaging beauty he had found so hard to resist when she embarked on her sexual adventures had long since disappeared. Now he saw a beautiful troubled young woman, carrying the world on her slight but shapely shoulders. Her youthful zest for life he had so loved was no longer present, and this made his heart feel heavy, too.

'*Chérie*, I believe time will solve your problems, but I think right now you should take a short break, no?'

Putting up his hand to stop her from protesting he suggested, 'Why not take a trip? Oui, your family are all in Melbourne. You have not been. It's a lovely city, what do you think?'

Safi had to admit it sounded tempting: she would be away from all her present concerns, away from New York, away from the Rubicov family, and, most of all, it would allow her to have space to get her mind sorted and she could immerse herself in Australian art and culture.

'What about the gallery?' Safi said. 'I have so much going on. The shows in London and Miami are coming up. We are working on new catalogues – you know, all the stuff that has to be sorted.'

He nodded his agreement, placed a hand on hers, but tenderly and fleetingly, rather than flirtatiously and heavily. 'Oui, but you have me, and you have a very good team, and you will not be out of touch Australia might be down under Cherie, but they have not dropped off yet.'

'I think you may have come up with a great idea,' Safi said. 'I will let them know as soon as I get home.'

She left DuPont feeling upbeat. Getting away from everything was just what she needed and seeing her family would be fantastic; they had not been together in such a long time. After all, who could set your mind at ease better than your own mother and father. She looked forward to meeting her brother's fiancé, too.

Two days later, after hurriedly leaving messages for everyone who mattered, Safi sat in the lounge at JFK. As the flight was called she closed her computer and boarded the long flight to LA, hoping Janus would have the time to see her before she boarded her next leg of the journey to Melbourne for a fortnight.

LAX had never been the best place to hang about, but seeing Janus would shorten the five-hour stopover. They met in one of the coffee shops in the departure terminal. Safi watched him as he made his way through the airport, noticing heads turn as he strode towards her. His quick, cool, long, easy strides. The way he moved, with such comfort and economy. He was a remarkably attractive man. She was aware of her pulse racing, of her heart beating loudly in her chest. When he noticed Safi his face lit up, and she knew in that moment that Janus was the man she wanted to spend the rest of her life with.

Enveloping Safi in his arms he held her close, she could feel his heart beating, too, against her breast.

'Will you come and live with me when this is all over, Safi?' he said. 'I do not want to spend one more moment away from you.'

They sat together at a coffee shop at the airport, talking and laughing. Janus would not let go of her hand, while he filled her in about recent events with Yvetta and Mika. His men were deconstructing the data they had received, and he did not think it would be long before they were able to locate where Sasha was, with pinpoint accuracy.

Safi boarded the plane to Melbourne, happy but more confused than ever about how she would deal with seeing Sasha. Like an airplane in a turbulent environment, her emotions were all over the place. Accepting the champagne on offer, she took two glasses, downed them, and put her head back, hoping sleep would come quickly to block all the thoughts racing wildly through her mind.

Yvetta was back in Moscow, on home soil, but not where she wanted to be, not at all. Once on the jet she gave instructions for the pilot to fly her to Berlin, where she hoped to meet Fritzi. Only when they landed did Yvetta have an inkling that she was not where she expected to be. As she dismounted, she saw a limousine with blacked-out windows waiting. No one would send a limo to pick her up in Berlin! She froze midway down the stairs, not sure what she ought to do. She tried to board the plane again, but the entrance was barred by Kolya. One look at Kolya's hard face and Yvetta knew she had lost everything Mika had promised her. Russia was the last place Fritzi would be able to reach her.

She sank onto a step, bewildered and scared, not knowing if the authorities would charge her for crimes, they were sure to fabricate. At that moment she felt overwhelming (but familiar, not uncomfortable) hatred for her family. Hatred, her old friend, welling inside of her, becoming larger and less containable by the moment. No one understood how lonely she was; they always abandoned her into the hands of strangers when she needed them most.

Yvetta curled up in a foetal position. She was picked up and carried to the waiting car, where Maurice was waiting for her in the back seat.

'Hello Yvetta,' Maurice said softly. It took her a moment to place him out of context, the last time she saw him was at Nice airport, when he dropped her off.

She stared up at him. 'Why you?'

'I am a psychiatrist and we are going to a private hospital just outside Moscow, where you will be quite safe and well cared for.'

'Why?'

'To keep you safe, of course, and to help you relate to the world around you with less confusion. You know, Yvetta, your family care so much for you – especially your mother, Anna; she talks of you each and every day.'

Yvetta's face changed, softened for a moment, before hardening up again, and looking angrier than ever.

'How do you know what my mother does?'

'I am your mother's husband, Yvetta, so I am part of your family now.'

'You deceived me. Why did you not say so when you first met me?'

'It's a long story, Yvetta, but you will be well taken care of. You have absolutely nothing to fear. It's a very comfortable environment, and very modern, not the old Russian sanatoriums of the past.'

Yvetta started to cry, confused and exhausted. She had nowhere to turn, no more cards to play. They would not let her go. All she wanted was to be free and to be with Fritzi. She did not understand why she was being banished from (and punished for) living her life in freedom like everyone else. She needed her life back, she needed her lover back, she needed her gallery back!

Maurice watched her face and body language as her emotions surfaced. He knew she was registering her predicament, not understanding why she was being held against her will. He felt sad for Yvetta, but he knew that once she was allowed to have her way she would revert to past destructive behaviours. He would not allow Anna's health to be destroyed by the unbalanced behaviour of her daughter; her son's disappearance was quite enough for her to deal with. He would take care of Yvetta; it was within his power to keep her safe from herself and her family. He reached out and took one of Yvetta's hands. She immediately withdrew it, and quite violently, but he had the reaction he needed to distract her. He had to stop her from lashing out in her despair. She did not know how to control her emotions, how to control herself, and of course had no regard for others.

'Being back on home soil will help, Yvetta,' Maurice said. 'It will enable you to meet likeminded young people. Many are from affluent homes, like you. Wait and see before you despair at not being allowed to do as you, please at this point in time. You will in time be allowed to do as you please, but not just yet. I promise you will get back what's rightfully yours. In time.'

Maurice deliberately stressed the future, the idea of a time beyond this time, a better time; the idea of possibility, improvement, repair. He was giving her hope – but she was pushing back.

'What do you know?'

'I know your mother and I know Alexi and Mika. They will keep what's yours safe for you. One day you will be able to step back into your galleries and continue your life in the world you love.'

She stared at Maurice. He was not sure she believed him, but he could tell she was calming down. Her thoughts were erratic, troubled, conflicting and often illogical. She felt lost – and in her hometown. The gallery was an anchor, something she felt familiar with, something she excelled at and that was a large part of her identity. She was able to keep her private and professional emotions apart, could function in her professional life where she was in charge, even accomplish great things. The gallery had always been a stabilizing influence in her otherwise unstable life. Maurice depended on her believing this was still possible when she managed to get her personal life together again. To take away the idea of the gallery, the possibility of the gallery, would be to destroy her entirely.

'We need to help stabilise your personal life before you are ready to embark further in your professional life,' Maurice said.

'But it's *my* life and *my* reality, not yours.'

'Yes, of course it's yours, Yvetta, and no one will take that away from you.'

'Then why am I going to this place?'

'Perhaps more than one reality could be possible without negating yours.'

Maurice had her attention now, he knew it would not last long and hoped they did not have long to travel before he had her settled safely. Some moments later he was relieved to notice she had closed her eyes behind her sunglasses. The whole experience must have been exhausting for her and he could tell by her even breathing that she had dozed off.

They were met at the car by uniformed porters very much like any five-star hotel, but Maurice knew they were highly trained therapists. The whole atmosphere was one of luxury, something he was extremely proud of having had a hand in creating.

The patients never felt they were being admitted to an institution. The reception was luxurious as were the gardens. Planters lined the entrance. Yvetta was signed in at the reception desk as at any hotel. A porter led her to a suite of rooms assigned to her. The only difference was getting past the guards at the gatehouse or the lake bordering the property. The vicinity was more secure than Fort Knox.

Maurice left Yvetta in the capable hands of his peers; her case history was in their hands, too. He was confident her treatment would be more advanced and in an environment, she would grow to love.

Alexi had never been keen on Yvetta remaining in Russia while the family lived elsewhere. Yvetta's crimes in Russia had also been a factor in their choice to keep her out of Moscow. Now that the family was once again in the clear, Yvetta's return was possible. With Mika's assurance Alexi had agreed placing her in the luxurious institution suggested by Maurice. An added favourable factor was that Fritzi would never enter Russia without being arrested, making Yvetta safe from her attempts to involve his daughter in her illegal schemes.

Alexi was relieved to have his daughter under Russian care. Maurice had become a trusted member of the family, and the family's improved status with the authorities on home soil gave him access to old contacts, without repercussions from those operating under the present regime.

The black cloud of doubt about Sasha's involvement in the gas link had been lifted, the authorities and the family now understood that Sasha had been kidnapped against his will. They were cautiously optimistic they would be able to rescue Sasha. Mika and Janus were working with the Russians, something he never imagined could happen but everyone had a vested interest in capturing the smugglers. Updated information gave a location close to the Ukraine border where skirmishes were a daily event. An operation was underway to apprehend those responsible for his son's capture and the illegal smuggling of Russian oil into foreign hands at below market value.

Alexi's greatest wish was to have his family together under one roof once more; perhaps he would be granted such a seemingly impossible wish in time. He imagined them having a family holiday in Cannes at Anna's villa; even Yvetta would be there with her two brothers, Mika and Sasha, and his own wonderful family, with his darling Marina enjoying the company of her siblings, getting to know them even better – but he was daydreaming.

This was how his children had grown up: family gatherings, always something to look forward to, uncles, aunts, brothers, sisters, and cousins. Always too much vodka, many arguments, but also trust and love for one another. He would never have imagined it would all fall apart so easily, Anna forever the matriarch had kept them together, but even she couldn't hold on through thick and thin. Once she became ill everything fell apart.

The family ethos was now hanging by a thread; they were now at each other's throats vying for control. Before his disappearance, Sasha had taken Anna and Alexi's place as the head of the organisation, giving Alexi the freedom to dabble in other interests. Mika had never been part of the everyday running of the Rubicov empire, he lived in St Petersburg and, his only interest was undercover work and, his law agency, Mika was his own man and Alexi respected and counted on his invaluable input at rocky times to steer the family out of danger. With Sasha gone, Alexi was drawn back to the boardroom to keep the family on the straight and narrow; someone had to be at the helm to guide them through this period of instability.

He liked a good fight (after all, he had fought – and won – more than his fair share), and it gave him reassurance for the future to have high achievers in the family, but he could not allow the Rubicov

Organisation to take its eye off the ball. No individual was more important than the organisation itself, an empire he and Anna had built from scratch. There was time for everyone to reach his or her potential as long as the empire grew at home and abroad; negative boardroom politics could be the beginning of a slippery slope to oblivion for the family, resulting in a nasty takeover he would not allow.

Alexi's presence at the board meeting, his mission to instil the company's ethos and core responsibility, would hopefully reignite what had obviously been ignored in the conflict of competitive, bullish egos. Without Sasha things had gone badly off-kilter; he would be banging a few heads together in the boardroom. Alexi had called a company meeting after he was briefed by Ringo, who had become his troubleshooter within the businesses since Anna's retirement and Sasha's disappearance.

After Anna's retirement Sasha had found Ringo's guidance invaluable and rewarded him as an honouree family member: the first non-family member to vote in an upper-echelon executive position. It was the Rubicovs' only option to have Ringo run their downscaled businesses after their hasty exit from Moscow, some of the younger Rubicov family had remained. Ringo had alerted both Alexi and Mika to the dangerous competitive vying within the family for Sasha's position. At the time, Alexi had not been able to handle this in person on Russian soil; now that he was back at the helm, and back in Russia, he expected company policy to be back on track.

Alexi walked into the familiar boardroom to find all family members present and counted for. Not all Rubicov assets had been offloaded when the organisation had embarked on their European venture; the Russian companies were consolidated into smaller, streamlined companies.

Since Sasha's disappearance, Russian business transactions had been scrutinised through government departments, which lost the organisation many millions.

Mika accompanied Alexi to the meeting, and he hoped his presence would avoid any disrespectful dissent from the younger members. Respect was not what it used to be, and Mika knew his father would not tolerate any unprofessional behaviour, family member or not.

Mika took up his position behind his father to watch the proceedings. Alexi sat in his usual position at the head of the conference table, scanning the familiar faces; some had inscrutable expressions, while others appeared tense and nervous.

After a greeting, Alexi began proceedings by answering the questioning faces turned towards him. Everyone wanted an update of recent developments about Sasha, whose arrest, and disappearance, had thrown so many aspects of the company's management into disarray. Alexi tried to assure them that the smugglers would be caught in the not-too-distant future.

Having their full attention he continued, 'I understand operating under a cloud has been extremely trying. For that reason, Ringo was put in charge. Some immediate family members have had to leave their motherland. If he had not been arrested, Sasha would have continued running the businesses from abroad during the fallout with the authorities, with Ringo as the company's figurehead in Russia and chief point of liaison.'

He sat back to scrutinise their expressions for any obvious displeasure, and he did not have to wait long.

Pasha was stocky and muscular in build with deep set eyes and, had always been as Alexi recalled, an arrogant rambunctiously unrestrained wild teenager, with a quick temper.

'Why should the family have to put up with a non-family member in charge?' Pasha said. 'We are more than capable of running the companies in your or Sasha's absence, without being watched over by a hawk.'

Nodding towards Ringo, who sat quietly watching the tsunami of hatred and venom towards him (much of it long pent-up) descend.

'Any other comments?' Alexi asked, hoping the answer would be 'no' but sadly knowing that in actuality this was the very beginning of a long and very bitter conversation.

'Yes.'

It was as though Pasha's question had slammed open a pen of hungry, angry bulls. He watched as the family members eagerly nodded to be heard. All had folders in front of them with the company mission, reminding them of the ethos he expected them to follow.

'I would like you to open the folders lying in front of each of you now,' Alexi said clearly, thankfully practised for such occasions, but trying harder than he thought he would have to keep his voice even and calm. 'Would you please read it out to me, Pasha, since you are the first to complain about having Ringo in charge.'

Pasha hesitated then read the page out loud. Alexi was disheartened to find the impassioned mission statement he and Anna had written at the company's founding had not penetrated their consciousness. In the new Russia the Socialist principals had left them unmoved. Everything was different now, he realised, it was all about position and money. The old family values were non-existent, and so was that sense of tradition, the company's legacy, and respect for those who had built the organisation from the ground up.

Pasha's indignant arrogance had everyone's attention once more. 'This is all fine when it's family. We are happy to follow your ethos to the letter for the Rubicov name, but not for an imposter.'

Alexi sat in silence for some time. The room, however, was anything but silent; there were murmurs and the bristling sound of papers being shuffled, and the static electricity of all of those suits with all of their folders and their phones. Still, Alexi had not expected such anger at Ringo's appointment. He had hoped the family would be grateful he had kept them safe from any government reprisals; yet here they sat spewing jealous insecurity instead. Mika banged his hand down loudly on the table next to his father's seat. He had had enough. He could tell his father's blood pressure was rising There was no mileage in allowing further dissent in the family ranks.

Alexi jumped at the unexpected intrusion into his thoughts, as did everyone around the table.

'Enough!' Mika yelled.

Alexi regained his composure.

'Mika, for God's sake, you nearly gave me a heart attack.'

'That's what I am trying to avoid,' Mika said, in his normal voice again. 'These little shits are too stupid to know when they are in good hands: yours and Ringo's.'

Now there really was complete silence in the room, before it was broken by a series of giggles around the table, which was soon followed by uproarious laughter. Alexi joined in the laughter, relaxing his scowl, finding the laughter infectious, realising Mika's intervention had defused the building tension. Mika joined in, too. The only person not laughing was Pasha.

All eyes were diverted in Pasha's direction as the others realised he had not seen the hilarity of the moment. As the laughter dissipated Pasha rose.

'I do not find this amusing at all,' Pasha said in his snide, self-righteous voice. 'The whole damn thing stinks of a setup. Especially Sasha – I do not believe he is an innocent in this smuggling ring, and I would not be surprised if he and Ringo cooked the whole thing up together.'

Shocked into silence, laughter now forgotten, all eyes turned to Alexi and Mika. Mika wanted to strangle his cousin, but had too much respect for his father to intervene directly. Instead, he bided his time, watching his father's reaction to the young upstart.

Alexi spoke very softly; everyone had to strain to hear. 'Pasha, first you question my ability to run my company. Now you have the temerity to question my son's innocence in this tragic affair. Is that right?'

Alexi's breath was short, both of his hands shook into fists, face now red with anger. He stood up slowly, but with the alert and aggressive posture of his youth, moving round the table towards Pasha. It had been a long time since Mika had seen his father this angry. Alexi closed in on Pasha and his hand shot out, striking Pasha across the mouth. Pasha staggered back and his hand flew to his bleeding mouth. White with rage, he pushed past Alexi disrespectfully, then stopped and turned around to face Alexi.

'Who are you to lift your hands to me, Uncle Alexi? With a daughter as mad as Yvetta and a son who screws anything that moves when he has a perfectly lovely woman working her arse off for this bloody family – another outsider taking over where a family member could have filled her shoes. And Ringo, who is he to lord it over the family? You tell me, who is he? It should have been me, I am next in line.'

Pasha stood his ground, staring at Alexi, waiting for the next blow to fly at him, almost willing him to strike.

Mika was as shocked at the audacity of his cousin as the others were. They all waited for the next move in this family drama that was unfolding in front of them.

What happened next no one could have foretold. Even after his illness Alexi was still an imposing figure with considerable girth. He grabbed Pasha by the pants and behind his neck, like one does with a child, and frog-marched him towards the conference room doors. But as he reached Mika he suddenly let go of Pasha, grabbing at his chest as he did so. Before anyone could move Alexi had collapsed on to the floor.

All chairs scraped back and everyone (taking a moment to comprehend what had happened) rushing to his aid. Mika pushed them aside as he bent over to massage his father's chest, both hands pressing down as he yelled for someone to call the emergency services and Alexi's own personal physician.

Pasha was forgotten in the drama unfolding; when Alexi let him go he had swung round to witness his uncle hitting the ground. For a moment he had not been sure how to react; but one look told him all he needed to know. Alexi was a goner and he needed to get out of there as fast as he could, before Mika and rest of his family turned on him.

The following fortnight went past in a haze. Alexi had not only suffered a fatal heart attack, but, unknown to the others, had hit his head on the porcelain tiles, missing the rug which lay under his body, causing severe internal bleeding, which had caused a simultaneous stroke. If his father had not died of the heart attack, he most definitely would have died of an embolism caused by hitting his head in the fall.

The family were gathered at his funeral in Moscow. The only members absent were Sasha and Yvetta (who refused to attend). Alexi's funeral was well attended by the high and mighty from Russian business and politics, and many others who respected him from around the world. The broadsheets in New York and newspapers in London covered his life's achievements and sudden death.

Safi stood with Janus, DuPont, and her family, all of them shellshocked at his departure from their lives. The shadow of his presence in their lives was never overbearing, but everyone who knew Alexi would miss the warmth of his personality, and the strength that emanated from his aura. He was a man of his word, a man one could rely on in adversity.

Safi found her eyes settling on Marina and Valentina, who were deathly pale, clasping hands as they watched Alexi's coffin sinking into the ground. She shivered and a cold hand seemed to stretch out and grasp her heart, goose bumps covering her body. Safi turned around involuntarily as if she felt Sasha's familiar presence. Searching the mourners for his face, she could not find it, yet Sasha was right there, she knew he was, she could feel his eyes boring down on her, feel his devastating sadness at his father's passing. Janus's arm instinctively drew her close, yet her stomach felt ice-cold. She could not shake the feeling that Sasha was there, amongst them, looking at her, yet knew it was impossible.

Chapter 9

Janus used surveillance drones to pinpoint the location the smugglers were thought to be in. He did this in conjunction with the Russian operatives, who were on the ground waiting to close in on the location, once the drone attacked the area they pin pointed as the smugglers location. The special ops team would enter the area to make sure the hit was successful and finish off the job. Perhaps it was fortunate that Alexi would never know that Sasha had not been found in the chaos after the drone attack. Russian special forces had gone in, arresting those escaping the scene and identifying those killed in the drone attack.

The area in the immediate vicinity had been swept clean, but Sasha had not been found amongst the dead bodies; Some of the bodies had been badly burnt and those remains had not been identified as yet in the aftermath of the attack. The worst scenario would be identifying Sasha's remains after the attack.

Safi had witnessed Anna's tragedy unfolding: she had lost Alexi, the father to her children; now she might soon find her son had been taken from her in a violent struggle with his captors, Safi hoped during the heat of the battle somehow Sasha had managed to escape.

The Russian authorities had deemed the mission a success; they had destroyed a feared underground smuggling ring within their borders. It could take months for the DNA results to be verified, if not years before any news on Sasha came to light. There was nothing anyone could do until the authorities notified the next of kin one way or another.

Safi had returned to the gallery in New York, continuing with everyday work issues, but her lifestyle had changed dramatically. She no longer lived in the Rubicov apartment building. Alexi's unexpected death meant that it would take months, perhaps even years, before the Rubicov companies were legally dealt with in his will. With no immediate word on Sasha, Mika would be at the helm of the business empire. Anna reluctantly stepped out of retirement to oversee many difficult decisions. Their lives were taken up with lawyers and complicated legalities.

Janus and Safi now shared an apartment in Manhattan. It was a welcome change to her solitary lifestyle, even if Janus only shared her living space a few days a week, it was a vast improvement from the debilitating loneliness she experienced since arriving in Manhattan to oversee the Rubicov Gallery.

She felt like a different person – or, more appropriately, her old self. She now spent wonderful weekends with Janus at his country home, walking his dogs through the forest of beautiful trees in his grounds. Safi had become an invaluable part of his team; together with Yin she encouraged Janus to concentrate exclusively on creating his art, leaving the two women to sort out the commercial side of his sculptures that were sought after around the world. The commercial side, never to his taste, became slightly less distasteful with Safi's help.

They had fallen into a comfortable pattern with Janus spending two days a week in Manhattan. He would work with the Rubicov galleries to promote his work with various companies, including a number of art institutions that considered him an artist they would support in their exhibitions. Even agreeing to the odd interview, Janus had emerged from his shell since meeting Safi.

From time-to-time Safi would accompany Janus to the West Coast, where he had business briefings to attend. Most decisions were left to his associates, but on occasion complicated matters arose that needed his personal input. The Rubicov Russian operation was one of those matters.

Several months had passed since Sasha's disappearance from the site of the drone attack; none of his remains were identified with those found. The Rubicov family had once more secured the services of Janus's company to track down any leads. At this point, the family wanted to know whether Sasha was dead or alive. Legal matters were becoming complicated and the family needed closure.

Mika and Anna requested a meeting with Safi and Janus in Florida on their return from the West Coast. The family wanted an update on the next stage of what was now being called Operation 'S.' Mika had not mentioned the legal ramifications of their visit, leaving it until their arrival.

They found Anna and Maurice under the covered patio at Mika's home, sipping ice tea. A pitcher of ice tea gleamed in the heat, a welcome thirst-quencher awaiting them after their journey from LA on a domestic commercial airline. She could tell already that the day would be a scorcher.

Mika had personally gone to collect Valentina and Marina. Joining them would be Yvetta, chaperoned by two members of staff from the Russian clinic, scheduled to arrive at noon.

The lawyers had insisted on Yvetta being present; the international lawyers working on the families behalf needed signatures. The assets, divided amongst Alexi's immediate offspring, were a complicated affair. The reading of Alexi's will and testament could not take place without the immediate family members present.

Sasha's portion of the will would be held aside until he had been contacted. The companies remained in the control of Mika and Anna until legalities for the businesses had been expedited thoroughly by the various legal teams.

Safi felt unsettled by the fact that Yvetta would be present. She had no idea how Yvetta would react to having her gallery run by an outsider, even more so since Sasha was no longer in Safi's life. The issues relating to the Rubicov galleries were legally complicated; Safi had no idea how it would affect her life; it had been and still was her only career.

Janus had been summoned by Mika and Anna because they realised the stumbling block Sasha's absence caused legally. Large sections of the will would have to remain un read until, further notice. They needed Janus's personal input to validate a legal clause in the proceedings, verifying the question of Sasha's absence as unresolved, as the case was still under investigation.

The dining room was filled with lawyers from various countries, who had arrived to help sort out the legal complications arising from Alexi's death. No one knew what preparations Alexi had made in case of such an unlikely event. Only Mika knew that his father had changed his will dramatically after his sudden heart attack.

A working breakfast had been set out on a long console, the dining room now becoming the boardroom. The family lawyers had decided it more convenient, and less stressful, for the family if the legal teams were assembled in one place.

Realising that the breakfast in the dining room was only meant for the legal eagles, Safi found her way onto the terrace, where the rest of the family were indulging in a full American breakfast.

Dietary concerns had gone out of the window she noticed: plates were piled high with pancakes, there was French toast, and maple syrup was liberally poured over everything. The only healthy food on Janus's plate was the small bowl of mixed berries he had on the side. Her own plate consisted of slightly healthier food: an egg-white omelette with bacon piled high on the side. Somehow, she could never say no to crispy apple-smoked American bacon.

Finding a spot between Janus and Mika, Safi glanced at the others breakfasting on the terrace. Anna and Maurice were sitting with Marina and Valentina; the only one's missing were Yvetta and the Russians who were to accompany her. Safi tried to shake free of her uneasy feeling at the thought of seeing Yvetta, distracted herself with her food, which was delicious. Amid the decency and relative quiet of those gathered around the table, Yvetta's absence loomed large.

Safi suspected she might not be the only one dreading Yvetta's arrival. Safi leaned over to fill up her glass with ice tea, her suddenly sweaty brow reflected in the pitcher. She forgot how hot it was in Florida. As she wiped her forehead with a cloth napkin, she heard the scrape of gravel and voices not too far away. She looked up to see heading in their direction from the garden Yvetta in jogging gear together with two burly Russians jogging alongside. Safi looked at Anna. For some reason she was worried for Anna's safety. She noticed Anna stiffen as Yvetta reached the terrace, where she paused to survey the scene. The two men kept close to her side, encouraging her to move forward towards the breakfast on offer, obviously hungry after their morning jog.

Nodding curtly to everyone, she did as they suggested. Safi tried hard not to stare but she could not take her eyes off Yvetta. She wondered whether she would engage her in conversation, and tried to gather her wits in case the trio joined them. She watched as Yvetta was steered to an empty table by her two body guards to eat their breakfast. Now, in spite of her anxiety about Yvetta, Safi felt oddly disappointed that they hadn't joined their table. She felt a flourish of belated bravado, of fraudulent grit, of misplaced courage

How she would have loved to give her a piece of her mind! How could she treat her lovely mother as if she did not exist – and, worse, in the past, degrade her like an animal; it was awful to watch. She couldn't imagine how it was for Anna; Safi felt devastated for her and the rest of the family. Not to mention Valentina, who had just lost her husband. Safi had almost forgotten the relationship to Marina; they were half-sisters, they had both lost their father. And Marina so very young, the apple of her father's eye, the joyful centre of so much of his late years, the light to counter all of the darkness, darkness that very much included Yvetta. Marina, Safi thought, in many ways the anti-Yvetta. Judging by Yvetta's behaviour towards her family one would never guess Alexi, who had recently died, was her father, or that anyone on the terrace were related to her. And yet Safi also felt odd flashes of guilt – after all, she had taken over Yvetta's position at the gallery, and along with it, perhaps, a part of her life.

The atmosphere on the terrace since her arrival was palpable; everyone, Safi thought, wanted to engage Yvetta; it had been such a long time since she had been at any family gathering. There was a strange combination of curiosity and contempt, the desire to confront Yvetta and the desire to destroy her. Safi wondered why she had not attended her father's funeral – she had not noticed her there, at least. Certainly, she would have been seated with the family in the chapel had she attended.

Mika put his hand gently over Safi's. 'I do not think it would be a good idea to engage Yvetta in conversation,' he said, 'she is still under therapy. We are trying to keep her on an even keel mentally. No one wants to be subjected to one of her vicious attacks.'

Safi nodded in agreement, embarrassed that her emotions were so obvious. 'I do feel guilty, you know, taking over the gallery in her absence.' Just expressing this out loud made her feel a little better. Mika gave her an understanding look, smiled softly.

'It was with Alexi's blessing and mine,' he said. 'Sasha believed in you and so did we.'

'Safi has been amazingly successful under the circumstances,' Janus said. 'It was with Safi's encouragement that I exhibited my work at the Rubicov Gallery in New York. That exhibition was a game-changer for me.'

'And for the gallery, too,' Mika said kindly.

But Safi was still preoccupied; the small talk hadn't helped. 'What happens if she approaches me?' she asked.

'It's not likely,' Mika said, his voice hard now, and she could see now for the first time how exhausted he appeared. There were fine lines around his eyes she had not noticed before; his brow, his face, was also lined. 'We will arrange it so that it does not happen.'

Looking up Safi noticed Yvetta being led away by the two men. Yvetta's body language was not easy to read, but she did notice Yvetta's expression of distaste as they disappeared through the patio doors.

Most of the day was taken up with legal matters. Safi was called into a room set aside by a legal team dealing with the galleries. To Safi's surprise Ilona had been flown over, arriving in time for the legal documents they both needed to sign. Safi and Ilona were both asked to read though the documents allowing them to continue running their respective galleries in the event of Alexi's death. It was what he wanted, the document stressed, but they were to sign an agreement to relinquish their positions if at any time Yvetta was to continue her rightful ownership of the galleries.

Pen poised, fingers shaking ever so slightly, Safi looked up before signing the documents.

'Just to make sure before I sign this document,' Safi said, 'I understand Yvetta is the rightful owner of the Moscow gallery, but I have, with the family's approval, started from scratch and successfully built up the reputation of the New York Rubicov Gallery. I just wondered whether that had any bearing on my signing this document, essentially agreeing to hand the gallery over. I mean, my position at the New York gallery did not precede me; I originated it. After all, Yvetta cannot return to a position that she never occupied to begin with.'

The lawyer stared at Safi. He had not expected any hiccup in the proceedings, having been led to understand that staff relinquishing their positions to a family member when the time arose was a matter of routine.

'This will have to be taken under advisement,' he said drily. 'I will contact you as soon as I can answer your questions from a legal standpoint. It should not take long as we have all the relevant parties here. Could I ask you to remain on the property until we have settled this matter?'

Safi agreed without signing and left Ilona to deal with her side of the agreement.

The matter in question should not have surprised her, but it was her life, she had put everything into that gallery and she was not going to relinquish it without knowing what future – if any – lay ahead for her and the Manhattan Rubicov Gallery. She owed that to Sasha and to Alexi, but mostly she owed it to herself.

It was close to two. The terrace was set for lunch. She looked for Janus but instead ran into Yvetta and her bodyguards. Not knowing how to relate to the situation, Safi nodded in Yvetta's direction, grabbed a salad, and found a seat. Her nerves shot, she couldn't taste a thing as she forked in what she thought was tuna. Safi found that her hand was still shaking. The meeting with the lawyers had unsettled her more than she could have imagined. In fact, she was incensed that she was expected to hand over her hard work to this woman who by all accounts had thrown away golden opportunities at every turn. Why should she not fight for her rights? She had built the Manhattan gallery from scratch, and the Moscow gallery had grown by leaps and bounds under her and DuPont's guidance; it had become a viable, profitable business for the Rubicovs, had it not?

Irrepressible anger surged through her and her mind shot off in all directions. She looked up and caught Yvetta staring right at her; this time Safi did not avert her eyes. They sat glaring at one another from a distance. Safi recalled what Sasha had once told her, that as children Yvetta had liked nothing better than to engage in a staring competition, to see who would blink first – and that Yvetta always won. Well, not this time, Safi thought.

Safi was ready to a stand her ground. Just let her say one word, she thought, freeing herself from the shackles of her anxiety, all the guilt and fear that held her back. I am ready, someone needs to tell her what an awful person she is, and if that someone had to be Safi, so be it! Yvetta appeared to increase the intensity of her gaze, moving forward ever so slightly, almost imperceptibly.

At that moment, Mika and Maurice walked out onto the terrace, realising what was about to happen. Mika nodded in the direction of his sister and Safi noticed the two burly men hastily exiting the terrace with Yvetta.

'Safi, I have spoken with the lawyers,' Mika said. 'The matter is under discussion. Please do not upset yourself. It will be settled. I promise you all will turn out well.'

'I am sorry, Mika, I know she is your sister – and Sasha's, but truly she does not deserve what is rightfully hers; not when I have built up those businesses and given everything, I have to make the New York gallery a success. I just cannot find it in me to sign away my whole career to your sister.'

Safi had not intended to get so worked up, to say so much so quickly. Mika looked at her gravely. Safi softened, looked almost awkward. Mika thought she was taken aback by her emotional outburst. Perhaps she thought she had overstepped the mark.

'This is unfortunate, Safi,' he said slowly. 'Yvetta is a Rubicov'

'By that you mean I am not?'

'Da, this is a fact, no?'

Safi stared at him intently, much as she had stared at Yvetta moments before. Her emotions were now slightly more under control. She did not want to anger Mika. Self-preservation set in. She needed to be very careful how she replied. It was easy to alienate Mika, not so easy to get on his good side again. She knew all of this because, in spite of his assertion, she was in fact part of the family, had been in the family for a long time – too long perhaps, she now thought.

She noticed Maurice wincing, his kindly face troubled; his expression brought her emotions into sharp focus.

'No, I am not a Rubicov, not anymore,' Safi said, speaking slowly so as not to get ahead of herself or let her emotions get the best of her, 'but I would have been. I never imagined any of this would happen to me, yet I have continued to support the family as if I were a Rubicov. I believe I deserve more – more than a legal signature on a piece of paper that will give away my hard-earned career to someone who does not deserve it, whenever it suits her – or the family – to take it from me.'

'Perhaps we should wait,' Mika said, his eyes cold and his face still tired – tired but tough – but his voice measured, even. 'Safi, say no more and neither will I, lest we both regret it. Sign the next set of documents, please. If not, we will have to part ways. But I am sure you will sign. It is in your interest to sign, wait and see.'

She knew he was being honest with her. After all, in spite of how she felt, technically, legally, she was not one of the family and therefore could not expect to own what was not rightfully hers. Still, even with this understanding, she found it no less difficult giving up something she loved.

A sad smile of agreement played around her mouth. She would read the documents. What bothered her was Mika's sudden coolness, as though he had written her off already, as though, with Sasha long gone and now Alexi too, Safi no longer meant anything anymore, was little more than a business transaction, like hundreds of other transactions the company negotiated every day, a small problem to be solved, disposable, immaterial. There was no affection here. She was, in the scheme of things, a very tiny part of a very large company; for Mika, just another issue to deal with, and no doubt expedite quickly so that he could move on to more important business. Anna aside, perhaps she had lost her real ties to the family. Perhaps it was indeed time to move on. She wondered if Mika had ever really liked her. She had always sensed a coolness from him, a feeling that maybe he didn't approve of Sasha's choice. True, they had become close at certain moments early on in Sasha's disappearance, but that closeness was over now too. Already she could feel that things were beginning to turn against her. Alexi had been nothing but pragmatic, and Mika was too – Safi's moment in the family appeared to be drawing to a close.

Safi sat opposite the lawyers again, this time with considerably more trepidation. A new document had been drafted and was ready for her signature. She struggled to concentrate, still feeling very emotional, her head all over the place, and wishing Janus was there for moral support. But ultimately, she realised, this was something she alone could decide. The lawyer explained the new clause that had been added to the document for her approval. Safi picked up the document to read the paragraph he had underlined for her. She sat forward, needing time to deliberate whether she had any choice or room for negotiation before agreeing to the family's terms.

She turned to a caveat added on the next page. The document they had asked her to sign was to assure them Safi would continue running the Rubicov gallery in Yvetta's absence. The new documents overleaf were only to be signed once Yvetta was ready to reassume her rightful position.

Safi had to sign to agree to this new caveat. No time or date had been stipulated. The agreement appeared to be open-ended. One other family signature together with Safi's would determine when it was returned to Yvetta.

Safi sat back again, staring at the lawyer. 'Am I understanding this document correctly?'

The lawyer shook his head in agreement.

'Yes, that is a new clause added to the original document. The only signature we need from you is the one that confirms you will continue running the gallery for the foreseeable future. Do you agree to the caveat?'

Safi left the office to find Janus. She felt wretched. She needed a drink – and a hug. Her head was about to come off. The stress and tension she felt was hideous. More than anything, she needed someone in her corner, someone who believed in her. She was beginning to doubt everything – including her own actions. Had she done the right thing? Should she have signed or not, it was an open, ended agreement, for her and, for Yvetta. Who she knew wanted her life back and, her galleries Was it the only avenue left open to her to leave everything she had worked so hard for by agreeing to this open- ended unsatisfactory agreement? It was not an ideal agreement for either of them. Safi wondered what she would walk away with in the end, when she agreed to sign that final document handing everything over to Yvetta. She was sure it would eventually happen but when?

Mika had consulted Maurice and one of the therapists at the clinic on the length of time it might take before Yvetta was ready to resume her responsibilities. Neither of them would give a specific timeframe, but they both agreed that knowing she would regain possession of her galleries as a member of the Rubicov family could only help in her treatment and her willingness to help herself. Mika had not been prepared for how strident Safi would be in her protest. He had underestimated Safi, and not for the first time either.

Her protest had resulted in the addition of the new caveat added to the original document. He hoped Safi would now see sense.

Alexi's immediate family – Mika, Anna, Valentina, and Marina – entered the office to consult with the lawyers. There were obviously papers Yvetta had to sign as a family member before the lawyers could carry out Alexi's wishes in his will.

Safi wondered whether Yvetta would comply, or whether the meeting would blow up in everyone's faces; she noticed the two burly men hanging around near the door in the event of trouble.

Janus and Maurice were on the terrace, deep in conversation. Seeing Safi they ended their discussion abruptly, eager to hear what Safi had to say, she had been very strident with Mika about her feelings about the gallery in Manhattan.

Maurice was obviously troubled about Anna having to be in the same room with Yvetta; she was known to strike out at her mother at the least provocation. Anna was fragile, but with Alexi gone she was responsible for the family overseeing the Rubicov holdings. Her responsibility for the family lay heavily on her now frail shoulders.

Not knowing whether Sasha was alive or dead while dealing with a daughter who was mentally unpredictable, verbally hostile and sometimes even physically aggressive could be the last straw for Anna. If Anna broke down, Mika would be solely in charge, at the helm of their empire, and finally in charge of the entire organisation, including aspects of the business he had never been fully involved with.

Mika had spent his life in St Petersburg, a more genteel city than bullish Moscow. Now, living in Florida suited him more than the frenetic Manhattan lifestyle. He had refused to remain in Manhattan indefinitely with his extended family to sort out the complicated mess they found themselves in after his father's death.

It was not viable for either Yvetta or Anna to be in Manhattan. He had argued for the meetings to be held in Florida, which was why the legal team had decamped from London and New York to his mansion in the Sunshine State. Mika had wanted to make the experience as stress-free as possible for his family, especially for Anna, who would be under immense strain. Yvetta was another concern; they wanted her under close supervision. Manhattan would have been a dangerous venue for the meeting, both Mika and his closest advisors agreed.

The lawyers had insisted on having Yvetta at the legal proceedings. Mika asked Maurice to help Anna prepare for a meeting with her wayward daughter. The last time Anna had seen Yvetta was at the clinic in America after her attack on their home in Moscow, which had resulted in his mother having a complete breakdown.

On her way to the bathroom, Safi peaked in to see how the meeting with Yvetta was proceeding. To her relief everything seemed to be under control. The family had been in the meeting for a long time; she was sure the meeting would adjourn soon.

While combing her hair and reapplying makeup she heard someone trying the door.

'I'm almost done, be out in a jiffy, sorry,' Safi said.

The house was crawling with people from the various legal offices; it was the second time Safi had tried the downstairs bathroom only to find it occupied. The latch on the door was not easy to open; as the lock gave, she felt the door being pushed from the outside. 'Oh, thanks,' Safi said, 'but I have managed to unlatch it.'

Opening the door she looked about for the person who had tried to help her. Instead, she felt someone push her hard. Safi stumbled back into the lavatory and the door was kicked shut behind her. She came face to face with Yvetta.

'You British bitch, you think I don't know what you're up to. I will kill you before I let you take my galleries, you bloodsucking whore.'

Lashing out she struck Safi across the face, then grabbed her by the throat.

'Always the innocent with your pretty smile and doe eyes, but underneath you are a thief, stealing what's mine. You're nothing but an imposter, cow.'

Her face was so close Safi could not move or breathe.

'You think I don't know you tried to seduce first my brother to get your hands on my gallery, then you try to seduce my girlfriend! Fritzi told me – she told me *everything*. I am not an idiot. I know all about your visits to the prison. Ha, you think you are so clever, you dumb bitch.'

Safi was struggling for air, trying to feel for something she could hit Yvetta with so she would let go of her throat. But she was pinned to the wall. The more she tried to shift, to breathe, to wriggle free, the tighter she was pinned, the harder it was to move. She felt dizzy, constricted, her throat tightening, blood rushing from her head.

Yvetta had her knee in Safi's groin, and one hand was now pressing down hard on her windpipe. Gasping, Safi tried to free her other hand from behind her back, where Yvetta had pinioned her against the wall. The only thing left for Safi to do was bang her free leg against the door, hoping it would alert someone. As she kicked the door aimlessly but insistently, pain shot up her foot, but she did not care, please someone hear. As if her prayers were answered someone started banging on the door.

'Go away, can't you see it's locked,' Yvetta shouted. But Safi kept banging. Then Yvetta swung her around, Safi lost purchase once again.

All went quiet but Yvetta's thumb was still pressed against her windpipe and she could feel her legs starting to buckle, her eyes were bulging and she wanted to pee, all she could hear was banging and thudding in her head, her legs relaxed, pain was gone for a moment and then intensified, and then everything went black. As if in a dream, she thought she could hear Yvetta's voice screaming, accusing her of taking Sasha away from her, something about her replacing Yvetta in her mother's affections, and on and on it went in her head. Breathe, she told herself, but that was easier said than done. The room spun around, circles within circles, kaleidoscopic patterns on the inside of her eyelids.

Opening her eyes Safi looked into a kind face, leaning over her, holding her wrist. She became aware of an oxygen mask over her face, tubes were hanging from a ceiling in a small space. She tried to talk but her throat was aching, her head still heavy and groggy, her eyes readjusting to what seemed like very bright light.

'Hi! Can you hear me?' a strange voice said.

Safi shook her head. There was a shifting, a rumbling, a reverberation. Flickers of further light from someplace else. Wait, where was she? They weren't in Mika's house anymore, of that she felt sure.

'I am Pete, a paramedic,' the voice spoke very slowly as though she was a small child, and the grip on her wrist intensified, and that felt tender and childlike too, 'you are in our truck. Don't worry, you are going to be okay. That was a close call though.'

Safi tried to talk but couldn't formulate any words. She wanted to close her eyes again, the air, the enclosed space, the light, everything around her felt very small. Instead of speech she tried to smile, but that seemed difficult too. You had to move your mouth in a funny position. A funny thing, a smile, if you thought about it for a moment, which very few people ever did. They didn't think at all, they just smiled, just like that, just like what? Pete, his name was Pete. How wonderful that Pete was saving her. She touched his arm, returned his touch.

'Yep, I'm real, honey,' his soft voice was strong and she felt for a moment that she was in love with him, though she hadn't yet seen his face, 'don't worry, just relax, your friends will see you at the hospital where the medical staff are waiting. You'll be as right as rain in a day or two.' As right as rain, she thought, what a lovely expression, like a smile. But why was rain so right? Why wasn't it? Everything was as it should be, absolutely right, she felt wonderful – wonderful – and then she closed her eyes and lost consciousness again.

She opened her eyes to find Janus, Mika, and Anna standing around her bed. There was a profusion of flowers everywhere, concerned eyes staring at her, an odd silence broken by occasional murmurs, soft voices.

Choked she could feel tears rolling down her cheeks. Why was there a drip in her arm?

'They decided to sedate you and the drip is in case you go into shock,' Anna said. Safi was surprised – she had not realised that she had articulated the thought. How? With what voice? But perhaps Anna had somehow intuited the question, much like Anna seemed to always intuit so much. She looked at Anna with gratitude and affection, even love. She felt filled up with love, or was that just from the sedative, whatever was in it? What a lovely feeling, yes, right as rain. Breathe. Smile. But then a flash of something else, something not so wonderful at all – not light, darkness. A flashback.

Safi croaked, 'Oh God, she tried to kill me.'

Anna now tearful said, 'I am so sorry, Safi, this terrible thing happens to you, my daughter…' At first it sounded like Anna was saying that Safi was her daughter, but then she realised she was talking about Yvetta, but she couldn't get the words out either. She choked.

'Yvetta not well, my fault, I am the mother.' She was having difficulty looking Safi in the eyes.

Safi tried to find Janus, she knew he was there, she felt his presence, she met his eyes. His mouth smiled but his eyes told another story; his usually tanned face was pale and his eyes were burning with anger. He stepped up to take her hand.

'Don't worry, I have been here all night.' All night? But she felt she had only been here for a few minutes. The room spun. Her sense of time, her sense of everything spun. Only Janus was a constant, she suddenly thought, and if, from certain angles, I see two of him, well, two is better than one. She tried to focus her eyes but she felt the strain in the dead centre of her head. 'The doctors say you'll have a sore throat for a while, and your voice won't be back to normal, either. They will let you go home tomorrow. Don't talk, rest your voice. Mika will fly us back to New York once you feel up to it.'

She was too exhausted to fully comprehend what he was saying. All she wanted to do was sleep. Probably the shock of it all.

Mika stood at the end of the bed; he looked mortified, clearly upset and shocked at what had happened. After all, he thought he had had everything under control – and not for the first time. And then what happened? Yvetta happened.

'You need never worry about Yvetta,' Mika said. 'She will never set foot outside her clinic in Russia, not while I am alive.' It pained him to say this, Safi could tell. The room was still spinning.

Safi nodded, closed her eyes, and drifted off again.

Safi was moved to Mika's home and Janus remained with her until she felt well enough to fly back to New York. He persuaded her to have a break from the gallery and to stay with him and Yin at his home upstate.

Everyone had left Mika's home, apart from Anna, who wanted a private meeting with Safi. Mika and Maurice had flown Yvetta to Russia before the authorities in Florida could question her. The Rubicovs looked after their own, not wanting any further complications or more mud against their (in some circles) already fairly filthy name. There were enough lawyers to cover over any legalities that arose with the authorities. The lawyers worked for the family after all, a whole team of them, it was their job to smooth things over in rough times, and besides they charged a pretty penny.

Safi had feared for Anna's safety, but she had never for one moment feared for her own.

Anna sat opposite Safi holding onto her hand for a long time before speaking. Was she giving Safi support, or was she seeking support from Safi? It wasn't clear. Perhaps both, Safi thought.

'Rubicov family broken,' Anna said, her words now broken too. She held up her hand so that Safi would not interrupt her. 'Sasha gone, Alexi gone, and Yvetta gone.' She touched her heart. 'You more daughter, Safi, to me than Yvetta.' Even the name *Yvetta* appeared hard for her to say. There was a pleading note in her voice now. 'Maybe still time to be family, I hope.'

Anna sat in quiet resignation.

'God punish me. I am mother, my fault. Maurice good man, he explains not my fault. But I am mother, always my fault for children, maybe work too hard.'

Safi smiled weakly, allowing Anna to get it all off her chest.

'Maybe you take galleries maybe not. Working not good for children. You not work long when you have children, da?'

It was a thought very far from Safi's mind, yet she understood Anna's advice, old-fashioned as it was, she understood her regretful reasoning.

'Anna,' Safi said slowly, 'I do not blame you for what happened. No one could have foreseen Yvetta's attack on me. I am fine now so please do not blame yourself.'

'You are a good person, why you not my daughter?'

Safi laughed 'We can pretend. I could be your goddaughter, someone you want as a daughter, and you can be like a special mother to me.' Anna laughed sadly. A sad laugh, Safi suddenly thought, a very Russian sound. As right as rain. But sometimes in Moscow it rained all the time. Now what was right about that?

'Da, that sounds okay, I accept.' Her words feigned a lightness, but her voice, her posture, her expression was still broken.

'I return to New York tomorrow,' Safi said, eager to get this awkward intimacy over with, 'and will let Mika know I am now officially your new goddaughter.'

'I stay here with Valentina and my beautiful Marina until Maurice returns from clinic in Moscow. Then we go back to our villa in Cannes.' Her voice became more severe all of a sudden. 'What will you do, Safi?'

Safi could feel Anna's genuine concern, her love. Maybe she was like her mother after all. Safi looked at Anna. Suddenly she wanted to confide in her; strangely, since the attack things seemed to be more in focus;

'I will tell you a secret,' Safi said. 'I loved Sasha with all my heart, but Janus saved me and I fell in love with him. I would so love to be married to Janus.'

'Da, you love him, he good man, you marry soon.'

'Oh, that means so much to me,' Safi said, trying to sit upright but not without great difficulty. Anna was still holding her hand. 'I am so sad about Sasha, so very sad, but something tells me he will one day walk through a door somewhere and say "Hello, I am back!"'

Anna smiled sadly, finally let go of her hand. 'I pray I alive when this happen.'

Safi and Janus sat on the private jet now back from depositing Yvetta in Russia and flying them home to New York.

Everyone objected to Safi returning to work until she was feeling better physically and fully recovered from the trauma she'd suffered. Besides a croaky throat and a bandaged ankle she was in pretty good shape – apart from her nerves, which were shot; she felt incredibly vulnerable.

'A little bird told me you want to be married,' Janus said. 'I was wondering whether you have found someone special yet to fill that spot?'

Safi felt suddenly awkward. 'Anna? I thought I could trust her. I should have known better; she is a Rubicov after all. Oh, that sounded awful, I'm sorry. I never meant to sound bitter.'

Janus came to sit on the footrest in front of her seat; taking her hand he popped the Coke can opener on her finger.

'I hope you were referring to me,' he said, 'because now you're officially engaged.'

Staring at the Coke can opener, she said, 'I always thought the man I married wouldn't be bling, but this will do perfectly' Safi stared at the coke can ring on her finger, was Janus joking or was he being serious, she wasn't at all sure. ' Janus I know you are trying to lighten the mood but are you being serious, it would be very cruel to tease me so mercilessly after what I've been through and I won't forgive you, if you are because I'm accepting your proposal even if it's being said in jest.'

Janus wanted to envelope Safi in his arms to make all her doubts and fears vanish but instead he kept a straight face and, said, 'It's been a while, let's seal the bling ring.'

Smiling he gently pulled Safi up from her seat, steering her to the back of the plane where they could enjoy their time alone, riding themselves of all the pressure of the past few days. Making love to Janus felt natural and perfect; he was a generous lover, something she valued after Sasha's wild games she had so stupidly found exciting – but that was then, this was now. She adored every bit of his amazing body, hands, and tongue exploring every inch of her.

Mika was pleased to have Maurice on the flight back to Moscow, where Yvetta would remain indefinitely at the clinic just outside the city. The doctors who had flown over to Florida with Yvetta discussed her condition and state of mind on the return flight while Yvetta slept a drug-induced sleep.

Shocked at his sister's violent behaviour towards Safi, Mika was determined to have her remain at the clinic for a very long time. She had sealed her own fate. Sadly, for too long and against his better judgement, he had been prepared to give her the benefit of the doubt. But it was no longer a possibility.

Mika had wanted a peaceful life in Florida; now he was left to oversee the Rubicov empire together with Anna, who he realised was no longer mentally or physically strong enough to fulfil this role, that he never, coveted he liked to be his own man, damn Sasha, now he'd be tied down by endless problems that came with running such a vast concern.

Maurice had helped him understand his mother's state of mind with his usual wise words

'Mika Anna can no longer take on the burden of responsibility of running Rubicov enterprises, she has given it her best years, but with Alexi gone and Sasha no longer around to take the helm, I'm afraid it's left to you now to decide where you take the company from here?'

He had no intention of losing another parent. Deciding to protect Anna from any further stress, he would reluctantly take sole responsibility for running the Rubicov Enterprises, for the time being until he could persuade the family to relinquish their shares and dissolve Rubicov enterprises.

He was his father's son and he would steer the business the only way he knew how, as a formidable ruler from the top down, like his father. He was not going to leave the family to squabble over the spoils after Alexi's death. There would have to be an updated company mission statement sent out to keep the older members from causing trouble. People like Pasha would want his head, too. He would employ a non-family member to weed out the dead wood in their bloated Moscow enterprises. He needed a trusted employee who knew the business inside out. Only one person came to mind and that was Ringo.

Ringo's promotion would cause much angst and anger among the younger family members in Moscow – the board meeting had offered a taste of that. After leaving Russia, Anna and Sasha had tried to get Alexi to streamline the companies. Alexi was more concerned with keeping the status quo and avoiding any further upset amongst the family. He was old-school for better and worse, and did not always move forward as quickly as he could have, sometimes stopping too long for deliberations and diplomacy, beholden to family and loyalties that were as cumbersome as they were often counterproductive, sometimes even too cautiously conservative, hemmed in by changing rules and regimes, not innovative enough.

The government in Russia never made it easy for them to run their affairs as they wished. With Anna's blessing, Mika would be the first Rubicov to cut loose the family deadwood that had been carried by Alexi for many years.

They would be well compensated, but it was time for many of the Rubicov extended family to stand on their own two feet. The company would no longer give jobs for life; it was time for a complete change in policy.

Anna and Mika had set up a fund to help grow new ideas, help set up fledgling companies for those who needed financial help to get their businesses off the ground. The Rubicov Organisation would be innovative at last: modern, mobile, streamlined, global.

Alexi had done this with Yvetta, under the Rubicov umbrella, when she had shown interest in the art world. They had set up other companies, too, but now new fledgling businesses would be carried by the family only for a period of time, after which they would be on their own.

Keeping in mind the board meeting resulting in Alexi's fatal heart attack, Mika had structured a different way of dealing with those who were to be offered a redundancy package. Pasha, one of the family's younger business graduates, would be the first to be given an opportunity to go out on his own.

Mika brought in a trouble-shooter from one of their British companies to deal with the delicate situation at home.

Mika gathered all senior family members at the Dacha. As they arrived, he met each individually, accepting their condolences; a few had been unable to attend his father's funeral, having been abroad at the time.

As expected, the new proposals were not received well by all; the meetings went on late into the night until agreement was reached and documents signed. Ringo had the go-ahead to start slimming down the companies, changing an old Russian culture to a new one. They were living in a technological age where spying was the order of the day. This meant Mika's business had come into its own outside of Russia; they would have to grow and compete in an even tougher business environment. He had every intention to compete in the new world – Janus had persuaded him a new way of business lay ahead. Janus was a valuable asset to their new life outside of Russia.

Mika would help streamline their operations and keep a close eye on the progress made, but had little appetite to remain as acting CEO with Anna as chairman for the foreseeable future in the old structure. They would encourage fresh talent into the Rubicov empire; many sections of the company had already been absorbed by diversifying and selling off their media empire in Russia; and other companies had been taken over by Putin's cronies, with little or no compensation. Alexi had felt this was a small price to pay to allow his family out of Russia with most of their assets in tact – until Sasha had been arrested, at least.

Chapter 10

Fritzi had been given her freedom from the United States penal system. Being a felon, she was never allowed back onto US soil. Fritzi had flown back to Berlin, found her way to a small Ukrainian town, and crossed over illegally onto Russian soil, with a new passports and identity to use on her new mission. While Janus's surveillance drones and the Russians were tracking the smugglers, Fritzi was on her way to the port where the illegal cargo ships were being filled with crude oil from pipelines that Fritzi thought were still owned by the Rubicov family.

By the time the Russians were onto the smugglers, the tankers were on their way to another port out of Russian jurisdiction. The special ops would not stop the smugglers, who intended to be gone before their position had been tracked, not knowing they had already been found.

In the ensuing confusion during and after the attack by the drones, Fritzi had slipped onto Russian soil and apprehended Sasha, secreting him out on one of the tankers carrying the contraband cargo.

Fritzi had been working with the Eastern Europeans and Ukrainian smugglers before leaving for the US to embark on an unfinished personal mission that had resulted in her arrest. Now she intended to finish that mission.

The moment she became free, Fritzi's contacts had her back in the field, sending her on a different mission. She was working with the same underground network of very rich, well-connected smugglers who moved and sold valuable commodities anywhere in the world for the right price.

She needed Sasha for her own purposes; the people she worked for only had use for him until his work for them was complete. Fritzi had successfully negotiated Sasha into her hands before they disposed of him, in the way she knew they would, not wanting to leave any loose ends.

As far as anyone knew, Sasha may have been killed by his captors, or killed in the attack on the smugglers' position. In reality, Sasha was unaware of the attack, having escaped with Fritzi only a few hours before the drones appeared.

Fritzi had saved his life twice now; he had mixed feelings about her intentions, but was happy to be alive. He agreed to her plan; being with Fritzi was a far safer option. If he kept his wits about him he would escape with his life intact.

Fritzi knew she was playing a dangerous game using her contacts for her own personal gain. She did not care; her objective was to free Yvetta from the clinic.

The Rubicovs were going to pay, not only for imprisoning Yvetta, but for ruining both of their lives. She had never stopped loving Yvetta. In spite of all the obstacles put in their path, they had managed to remain in touch throughout, planning their revenge. If that wasn't true love, what was?

She was aware that Sasha had been out of the loop since his arrest by the Russian authorities. She knew that he was kidnapped by her contacts to help them divert oil from the pipelines. Using Sasha to overcome obvious inconsistencies, drawing as little attention as possible to their illegal operation into the Ukraine and other Eastern European countries, stealing the oil enabled them to undercut the Russian government, making a hefty profit for themselves.

Being the CEO of the Rubicov Organisation, the authorities would not doubt his authenticity or instructions to divert the crude oil onto their tankers, heading out of Russian waters into Eastern Europe. The old Soviet satellites would not ask questions that undercut the Russians.

Fritzi had helped the smugglers identify Sasha, enabling them to apprehend him easily once he was released from the Russian authorities. Sasha walked straight into their trap, sending confused signals to his family, who still blamed the Russian authorities for holding him. By the time the family found he had been abducted against his will, the smugglers' operation would be well underway.

Sasha was unaware of his father's death. Fritzi decided it was to her advantage to keep the news from him. She had little tolerance for any weakness that might interfere with her objective, and a mourning son was one of them. If he found out she would feign ignorance; having been out of the loop herself, he might not doubt her.

After leaving the safety of the tanker, they made their way to another port along the Russian border, crossing over into Russia once more. Fritzi's objective was to reach Moscow undetected. Sasha would have access to fresh clothes, but she would give him no opportunity to contact his family. She would brief him of her plan to free Yvetta. The faster she set the plan into action, the less likely he was of trying to set a trap for her with the authorities.

Perfecting one of her disguises, she surprised Sasha in the kitchen of their family home, which had not yet been sold off; they owned so many properties, the family home would be the last in a long line of assets they had not yet unloaded.

She found Sasha in the kitchen, raiding a well-stocked pantry for food. Sasha had bypassed the keypad at the front entrance, instead taking her undetected through a side door that led to the underground garage and into the house. Fritzi was pleased to see the white Maserati and Anna's black Range Rover parked in the garage; they would need transport to arrive at the clinic.

Hearing a movement, Sasha swung around to find a man standing in the middle of the kitchen pointing a gun straight at him. For a moment he was taken in by Fritzi's new persona, but not her familiar body language.

'My God! Fritzi, you startled me for a moment. That's a pretty convincing getup.'

She had Sasha's clothes on, which perfectly fitted her thin tall frame. Her short red hair was now a brunette brush-cut. A false moustache and tortoise-shell retro glasses made her angular face appear more masculine. She strode towards him in a white shirt, a thin padded waistcoat hiding her small breasts and slim-fitting jeans, wearing her own masculine cowboy boots. The smart modern casual look finished by an American baseball cap.

'Let's hit the road,' she said.

In spite of himself, Sasha smiled. She had thought of everything. He doubted anyone would figure out she was a woman in disguise.

'This is how it's going down,' she began.

They sat at the long wooden table that brought back so many memories to Sasha, mostly of Safi. He wondered where she was at that moment, who she was with, and if she still managed the gallery in New York. He had every intention of tracking her down, even if, believing him dead, she had moved on, he was certain of one thing: her loyalty. He was sure she still loved him. Fritzi had refused to give him any information about his family or Safi. She had been incarcerated in an American jail, bluntly said she had other things to worry about. He knew she was a single-minded woman, with a formidable network of well-connected contacts. He knew, too, that she was dangerous.

Fritzi explained what would happen after they arrived at the clinic how they were going to arrive at the Clinic he. Sasha would disclose his relationship as a Rubicov and Yvetta's brother. He would sign the necessary papers for her release into his hands. Fritzi would portray an eminent doctor from Canada who had the necessary papers for Yvetta to be moved to a new facility in Montreal. Fritzi spoke fluent French. There were numbers for the Russian doctors to call in Quebec – there, 'doctors' would speak to their counterparts in Russia to verify the transfer of the patient.

Sasha stared at Fritzi. 'Who will they be calling in Montreal, Quebec?'

'That is no concern of yours,' Fritzi said. 'I have planned this for years and have thought of everything. If anything goes wrong I will deal with it. I have a weapon and I will use it, don't think I won't. If you want to get out of this alive, just follow my orders the same way you followed orders when you were being held by my people in that fishing port. This should be a walkover compared to your last assignment.'

'Allow me a few questions at least.'

She gave Sasha a fleeting glance.

'I told you I have been out of the loop. I have no information.'

Sasha nodded.

'I understand that. But perhaps now you can fill me in on a few things that have bothered me for quite some time. You have absolutely nothing to lose by telling me what I want to know.'

Fritzi shifted, intensified her gaze on him. Then, after a long moment, when he did not think she would respond at all, she said, 'Well?'

'First,' he said, gaining strength in his voice, 'could you tell me why you attacked my home and my mother. If you had not done that, none of this would have happened to Yvetta, or to you.'

He noticed Fritzi grimace; obviously the whole affair was not a successful or happy memory for her. She turned away from him.

'To be honest I was against it,' she said, 'but Yvetta wanted to repay your mother for her lack of support and distrust in me – and,' she glanced at Sasha again, 'for welcoming Safi into the family. Your sister was treated as an outsider when Safi was the imposter.'

He did not want to antagonise her so changed tact. He kept his voice soft and his gaze steady. 'How did your contacts know to apprehend me when I was released by the Russian authorities?'

Here he noticed her slim face plump up with a quiet arrogance at being able to pull off such a sophisticated plot even while in an American jail.

'It was easy,' and her voice had a glib tint now too, 'I needed them to get me out of that prison in America. For them to play ball I realised I needed to put up collateral, insurance, make it worth their while. They needed an updated image of you and had to be absolutely sure of your movements. My Russian contacts did the rest. Once my people had apprehended you, I had every confidence my freedom was assured – and I was right!'

Sasha shook his head in disbelief. She was an enigma. On the one hand, she bungled her personal affairs; on the other, she was a formidable go-between for those who needed information on a global scale.

No one had seen Sasha enter; the servants no longer remained on the property, but he was sure it was still maintained. If he crossed paths with the staff, it would not be long before his family would be alerted.

While in the pantry Sasha had left a note for whomever came to clean. If anything, further happened to him, at least they would know he had been released and had managed to get home.

If someone arrived while they were in the house, he hoped Fritzi would have a good explanation without resorting to violence, of which he had now seen enough to last him a lifetime.

Sasha backed the Range Rover out of the garage with Fritzi sitting beside him. He doubted this mission would succeed without his family or the authorities being alerted in the process.

'One more question: how are you going to get yourself and Yvetta out of this country?'

'That's where you, dearest brother, will be repaying your sister for all those years you deprived her of brotherly love.'

'What exactly do you have planned? I have very little confidence that this is going to succeed. If I am to help you both, perhaps you could enlighten me.'

She pointed the gun at his ribs.

'Just remember to follow my lead, use your wits, and keep any doubts safely tucked away in your head. This is all about confidence. You'll be surprised how easily people fall for a scam so keep your mouth shut.'

Sasha looked in his rear-view mirror; there had been an SUV on their tail for quite some time. He breathed. The last few years of his life had taught him to keep calm, be patient, and resign himself to fate. He had no control now. He felt Fritzi's warmth beside him and thought that, despite everything, it was not unpleasant. Soon he would be reunited with his sister – well, if this insane plan ever got that far. Or he'd be reunited with the prison system. No, that couldn't happen, he told himself.

He gained in speed, but kept his eyes on the SUV; it had gained in speed, too. It was like a chessboard, he thought, the clean geometry of the open road, the cross-stitching of the highway lines, the black Range Rover and the white SUV following it, gaining on it, waiting for its moment, waiting to pounce. Symmetry. Destiny. Strategy. The one who played the game the best was the one who survived, thrived, destroyed the opposition. But the SUV kept coming, its dull eyes staring, glinting. Still, he felt his hands shudder on the wheel – his heart shuddered, too. His game was no longer that good. He was rusty, worn-out, slow. In a way, over the last five years, he had become used to losing, to being used, used as leverage, as bait. His sheen had well and truly worn off and turned to dust. Worse, it had become a curse. What happens if he lost again? How much time did he still have?

'Look in your side mirror,' Sasha said, 'that SUV has been on our tail for quite some time.'

'Ah good yes,' Fritzi said, surprising him, 'those are the professional orderlies to transport Yvetta from the clinic safely to the plane waiting to take us to Canada.'

Indeed, Sasha could now see men in white coats sitting in the front of the SUV. Fritzi had obviously thought of everything. He shook his head but he could not help but be impressed, too.

'What plane are you referring to?'

'I have a plane ready. My contacts are paying for my services. Apart from assuring my early release from that American jail, it was my only other demand. My success in handing you to them on a silver platter has paid off richly. Do not underestimate me, Sasha. As I said, I have been organising this for a very long time.'

Fritzi herself left nothing to chance; whoever had managed to foil her plots in the past had done so only because she had not planned them exclusively, she had to depend on logistics and often on unknown foreign recruits to play their part. This endeavour, however, would, she was sure, go without a hitch. After all, she was the sole player in this role, and she knew her recruits had been in the field with them for many years; they were being paid handsomely. It was all up Sasha behaving, and she had no doubt he would; after all, Yvetta was his beloved younger sister – they had been very close in the past.

They arrived at the clinic gates. Fritzi, who was now driving, stopped to brief the two white-coated men in the white SUV.

She handed them a clipboard with papers attached, and watched as the gate orderly called to verify their arrival.

The orderly checked and counted the people in the cars and waved them through the gates, which opened slowly. Sasha noticed poles in the centre still blocking their path. Then, as the gates swung outwards, the silver poles went down, allowing them to continue up a tree-lined drive.

He glanced at Fritzi and found himself admiring her again. She was enjoying every moment; there was no evidence of fear or apprehension about her. She was in operational mode, a soldier going into battle, but he hoped not in for the kill.

They drove through manicured gardens with fountains on either side of a sweeping, circular drive, and drew up in front of steps leading to what could only be described as a very imposing private chateau.

Two smartly uniformed men ran down the steps to greet them, opening the doors for Fritzi and Sasha on either side of the Range Rover. They were led into a vast reception hall and offered refreshment as they waited to be seen in plush formal surroundings.

Sasha followed Fritzi's lead, ordering iced water, which promptly arrived on a silver tray. It tasted very cold – and very good. Delicious, in fact. While sipping from the glass, Sasha observed the people in the reception area: efficient staff going about their business. Fritzi and her clandestine crew were not attracting attention. An arrival like theirs was obviously a regular occurrence.

Striding towards them with a welcoming smile was a tall woman, elegantly dressed in a black suit, her grey hair cut in a severe bob. She carried a mini iPad, obviously her daily schedule.

Speaking in Russian she addressed them by name, checking to see whether she had the right information. Sasha rose as she called his name and noticed that Fritzi was called Dr Stoffenburg. Then, just like that, she switched to English as she led them down a long-carpeted corridor hung with watercolour landscapes of the gardens outside. They entered a small vestibule facing huge double doors. Here, they sat waiting to be summoned by whoever was sequestered behind the highly polished wooden doors.

Fritzi organised her briefcase and laptop holder ready for their first big challenge before anyone released Yvetta into their custody. Sasha wondered if this would be where Dr Stoffenburg would meet her Waterloo.

The same assistant entered to show them through the large doors into a boardroom where two men and a woman were seated behind a long conference table. All stood to greet them. Introducing themselves they took their seats, waiting expectantly to hear what Dr Stoffenburg had to say.

Fritzi no longer looked like a casual male assistant. Now she had transformed into a woman of his mother's age, soberly dressed in a tailored masculine trouser suit; instead of the brush-cut she now wore a dark wig coifed into a shoulder-length style.

Sasha watched with fascination as Dr Stoffenburg presented her case in a French accent. She referred to Sasha, referencing him as a family member. She handed over copies signed by what he could only imagine were his father and perhaps Mika, or perhaps it was his mother's signature. He could not be sure of anything anymore. They smiled at Sasha, acknowledging him, then huddled together to examine the documents.

Sitting back, catching only snippets of their conversation, he tried to observe them closely. Fritzi engaged him in conversation, executed an exceptional performance, an entirely different person, now wholly inhabiting Dr Stoffenburg, not a hint or shadow or iota of Fritzi, smiling placidly, almost passively, obviously putting on a relaxed front. Sasha noticed the three looking in their direction from time to time as they deliberated the highly unlikely request for Yvetta's release from their obviously first-class institution.

The woman cleared her throat to catch their attention. They were ready to discuss the request. Fritzi sat forward in her seat, hands on the table in front of her, a composed professional, ready for any question they may throw at her.

'You do understand, Mr Rubicov, your brother recently expressly stated that your sister had to remain here indefinitely, for the unforeseeable future.' She paused, gave Sasha an oddly intense look. 'We do not doubt these documents, but it is highly irregular and surprising, especially after her very recent return and violent behaviour while in America with your family. Dr Maurice Gottlieb, a founding member of this institution, insisted on her indefinite stay here with us for her own safety.'

Violent behaviour while in America with your family – all of this was news to Sasha. He wondered what had happened now.

Speaking in Russian, Sasha said, 'I wonder whether you would be kind enough to explain which attack you are referring to.'

'Yvetta physically attacked and almost killed an associate of your family while in America.'

Sasha was dumbfounded if not exactly surprised. He had been away for almost five years and was completely out of the loop. He had no idea what they were referring to. Fritzi, who had not anticipated recent family history to come out, quickly intercepted. Damage control was her first priority.

'Doctors, I am sure we do not want to distress Mr Rubicov any further. He is very lucky to be alive, only recently gaining his freedom from very dangerous men.'

She knew that Sasha would not know she was referring to his father's passing and hoped it would put a stop to it being referred to – or, for that matter, any other Rubicov family problems being addressed.

'Ah yes, yes, of course we understand,' the woman said, looking embarrassed.

'I do understand that you find this request for her release into our care highly irregular,' Fritzi continued. 'I wonder whether you could tell me how Yvetta has progressed since her return. You understand we are in the midst of a pioneering program, and the Rubicov family are very keen to have their daughter be a part of it. We have had some very favourable results. You can imagine that, under the circumstances, they would want to give Yvetta every opportunity to become well again.'

Putting up a hand Fritzi continued, 'Of course, once we have statistical success, we would be happy to share this new program of treatment with you. But unfortunately, at this point in time, it is still very much in the developmental stage and remains of a confidential nature.'

Dr Sukoff young and bespectacled now enquired 'May we ask how the Rubicov family were introduced to this new program of treatment?'

'Absolutely,' Fritzi said quickly, 'I am sure they would not mind me telling you that they have been more than generous in their financial grants to our institution in Quebec, where we have pioneered many new treatments in the advancement of mind and robotics engineering, in conjunction with McGill University. More than that I cannot divulge at this juncture.'

Sasha watched the faces behind the conference table. They were obviously very impressed and more than a little interested in the fabricated storyline Fritzi had just fed them. Now they were more inclined towards their own gain, rather than losing a very rich patient. Again, he admired the fluidity, the nimbleness, the intelligence of her performance. She was spectacular at subterfuge, the best con artist he had seen in action.

'Dr Stoffenburg,' Dr Maximoff, a grey bearded, mild-mannered older colleague, said, 'it has been a great pleasure to make you acquaintance and to learn of this new pioneering experiment with patients who have so far been very difficult to treat successfully. You will understand if we ask you to elaborate on how this treatment came into being?'

Fritzi gave this question some thought – or rather, she pretended to think, which was a skill in itself.

'I will try to give you an insight into our work,' she said finally, speaking slowly, her imagination just a few steps ahead of her words, clearly still fabricating on the fly, 'of course it will be at a very elementary level.' The others sat in anticipation, all ears. Even Sasha wondered what she would come up with.

'Together with the Japanese and the Israelis, we have conducted a number of experiments with robots and elderly patients. It has been quite astonishing to observe these patients respond and interact with the robots. We have taken it a few steps further along the line. Of course, it's much too early to have any conclusive results, but we are very confident in the new trials this far.'

'Wonderful,' Dr Galinov said, 'quite amazing. Absolutely we will release Yvetta for these new innovative trials, if this is what her family desire.'

'If I may suggest,' Fritzi said, now in full control, and began to unfold her plan, 'We have an SUV with skilled nurses to assist the patient. It would benefit Yvetta and her brother Sasha if she were sedated before we transfer her into the SUV, and then onto the plane waiting at the airport.'

'No problem, we will see to it straight away.'

'Thank you so very much for your cooperation,' Fritzi said. 'As soon as the trials are conclusive, we will share with you our research. Perhaps you will visit us soon?'

'We would most definitely arrange to do so, thank you.'

Hands were shaken and they left the room. The secretary ushered Sasha and Fritzi back to the reception area. Fritzi spoke briefly with the men waiting in the SUV, who were sitting in silence. After this, she entered the clinic again. Sasha was too shocked to speak. Fritzi continued to exist as Dr Stoffenburg.

The assistant requested they follow her. Suddenly suspicious (Sasha noticed that her tone briefly changed, an almost imperceptible flutter of anxiety across her sharp, otherwise affectless face), Fritzi said, 'Where are we going?'

'We will serve you lunch while the patient is being prepared for transport. It might take a while, you might want to relax. We will send for you once the patient has been transferred to the waiting SUV.'

This was obviously not on Fritzi's agenda: she understandably wanted the transfer to go as quickly as possible, avoiding any further anxiety or pitfalls.

'That is extremely kind,' Fritzi said smoothly, but Sasha thought he could still detect a hint of anxiety in her voice. 'How long do you suppose it will take for the staff to get the patient ready?'

'Usually an hour at least.' The assistant turned, as if to examine Dr Stoffenburg more closely, 'Is there a problem?'

'Well, there may be. Would you let the doctors know the plane has been given clearance to take off at 300hrs. Our arrival at the clinic in Canada needs to be at a reasonable time of day.'

Sasha stared at Fritzi, reassessing her anew. She appeared cool as a cucumber, but he knew she was worried. They took their seats in the restaurant – which actually looked like a restaurant, rather than the utilitarian, canteen feel of most eateries attached to clinics. They ordered coffee and food, which arrived in a matter of minutes. Everything here was clean, bright, prompt, professional.

Sasha watched as Fritzi bit nervously into her cream cheese and smoked salmon sandwich, while he tucked into French fries and a toasted BLT. He had forgotten how hungry he was. He recalled that he hadn't had time to raid the pantry in his family home before being apprehended by Fritzi.

The day was a blur – but then so much of the last few years had been, too. He had begun to feel like he was forever on the run – and felt exhausted. Wrung-out. Not a young man anymore. He finished his fries and wiped his fingers on a napkin. He looked at Fritzi. She was so close to success he almost felt sorry for her. What if something went wrong?

After all, it didn't appear to him that anyone could have planned this better.

Checking her watch intermittently, her sandwich unfinished, she stood exasperated at having to wait. Excusing herself, she left for the bathroom to refresh.

'I will be back,' Fritzi said. 'Do not try to be clever, it will not work. I will have you committed in a jiffy if you make as much as a peep. Believe me, once I have finished relating your mental instability after your abduction, you may never get out of here.'

He had little doubt she would do a good job of having him certified insane. Having witnessed her in action and more than once, he had no intention of testing her.

Fritzi returned to find Sasha standing with two uniformed men. The men had their backs to Fritzi, but Sasha could see her expression in the mirror on the wall and realised she had misinterpreted the scene in front of her. He swung round before she could respond and said, 'Dr Stoffenburg is back, gentlemen.'

'Dr Stoffenburg, said the uniformed orderly, all is ready for your departure.'

Sasha could visibly read her relief.

'Good, good, we are running out of time.'

Fritzi nodded to the orderlies, who were waiting next to the SUV, signing papers. Sasha was aching to see Yvetta; he had not seen her for years. But he knew it would not yet be possible; they needed to get out of there, fast.

Fritzi signed release papers and gave a last spiel to one of the doctors.

Sasha steered the big car down the long drive. As they passed through the gates Fritzi clapped her hands, as if to signify that she was Fritzi once again.

'Mein Got! That was the biggest high I have had in years, pull over in that lay-by now.'

The SUV pulled in behind them and Fritzi walked to the back of the truck to check on Yvetta. Sasha couldn't stay in the car another moment.

Yvetta was resting in the back of the truck, her eyes not focusing. She did not appear to recognise them. It was miraculous to see his sister. All the anger, all the hatred at past misdeeds, faded away, replaced by a love so warm he could feel it deep within him. The imperfection of the past replaced by the possibility of today. He knew now what it was to want to be reborn, to have another shot at life, to become someone else.

Why should his sister be any different from anyone else in this regard? Instinctively he wanted to enfold her in his arms, but Fritzi was already holding Yvetta.

'Hello, my libelling, we will be together now, all will be well.'

In the muddle of Yvetta's mind something must have registered. Yvetta tried to smile but her muscles did not want to work. She appeared exhausted, depleted, drugged. For the first time in many years, Sasha felt compassion for his sister. Yvetta had grasped that Fritzi had said something important.

Sasha took her in his arms and hugged her.

'Yvetta, it's me, Sasha,' he said softly but uneasily, unsure how she would react to his presence, or how much she knew about Fritzi's plan. 'I think your nightmare is over, darling. You are free to be with Fritzi once more.'

She stared at him, her eyes unfocused, then at Fritzi. To Sasha's surprise she closed her eyes and fell into a deep sleep.

Back in the Range Rover Sasha wiped tears from his eyes; it had been such a long time since he had held any of his loved ones, he was overcome with emotion.

'Where are you going to go with my sister?'

Fritzi had taken the wig off. Now looking her old self but still somehow ineffably stylish, she turned to answer him. Just then a loud bang. reverberated close by followed by a screech of tires. Fritzi grabbed for her wig, but it was now placed at a strange angle on her head, almost comical. If the shock had not frightened Sasha into a stunned paralysis he may have laughed. But even now, in his confusion, with a sense of mounting terror upon him, he knew not to laugh.

Behind them the SUV was swerving across the lanes into the central highway with cars speeding head-on towards them.

Fritzi screamed as she saw the driver trying to control the truck avoiding a tourist bus. They careered across the highway into a field beyond, coming to a sudden stop against a tree. Sasha pulled over. There was no way they could cross the highway on foot without being knocked down.

Fritzi grabbed her cell and called the driver, but his cell kept ringing.

'He must have been knocked out or something,' shouted Sasha, now scared for his sister.

'Shut up, idiot,' Fritzi said, 'let me think.'

For once she was at a loss for words and at the mercy of random chance. The bus had not stopped; the SUV was at an angle leaning to the side, its front crunched by the impact with the tree. Fritzi thought someone would call the police, something she did not want at any cost; it would result in her ending up in another jail cell, years of planning coming to nothing. If – no, *when* – the police found out who she was, she would be locked up for years.

'Drive until we find a gap,' Fritzi barked out. 'Make a U-turn, we must get to the truck before the traffic police arrive. Schnell, drive like the wind.'

A mile down the road they did an illegal U-turn meant for emergency vehicles only. Sasha yanked open the back of the truck to find Yvetta slumped at the side of the door, blood smeared across her forehead. He picked her up and carried her to the Range Rover, placing her on the back seat.

Fritzi grabbed the paperwork from the front seat of the SUV and jumped back into the passenger seat of the Range Rover next to Sasha.

'Schnell,' Fritzi screamed out, 'drive, *drive*, we want to be away before the police arrive.'

'What has happened to the men?' Sasha asked Fritzi

'They will be fine, just knocked out. Mein Gott, can anything else happen?' Fritzi said.

'Where am I driving to, Fritzi?' Sasha asked.

Fritzi was looking at Yvetta, slumped in the back seat. 'Stop when you can, I want to get into the back with Yvetta.'

'Drive towards Moscow.'

While Sasha concentrated on the road, he heard Fritzi speaking to Yvetta, coaxing her to open her eyes. Tears were rolling down Fritzi's cheeks. She took Yvetta's pulse, wiped the blood from the gash in her head with tissues. He had never seen Fritzi show vulnerability, certainly never seen anyone care for his sister with this degree of affection. He realised for the first time that this woman actually loved his sister.

Sasha heard her say the word 'blowout', she kept punching redial, she was obviously trying the SUV again.

'Have you called someone about the SUV?' Sasha asked.

'My contacts are on their way already. Those guys must be badly hurt, there's still no answer. It's only luck they weren't killed, when careering across that busy highway into oncoming traffic, I felt a pulse so they are not dead, for sure.!'

Sitting forward she passed Sasha the address of a private airfield where they were obviously meeting the plane she had mentioned.

'Where are you flying to with Yvetta?'

'Sorry, this time I am not sharing a thing with anyone. I want Yvetta to have rest and peace from her family; after that we will see. Oh meine Got, thank heavens, kleiner liebling, you are going to be okay.'

'What's happening with Yvetta?' asked Sasha.

'She has opened her eyes. Concentrate on your driving. I do not want to miss the turn-off to the airfield. How much longer?'

Sasha checked the arrow showing the route, the automated GPS, now on for the first time was getting on his nerves. He wanted to hear what Fritzi was saying. Watching her from time to time in the rear-view mirror, he now switched it back on to be told to make a legal U-turn; they had obviously missed the turn-off to the airfield.

'Argh!' Fritzi shouted. 'If I miss that plane, I swear I will shoot you on the spot.'

'Calm down,' he said sharply, surprising himself with his tone, 'we are only five minutes from the address.' After making a sharp U-turn in the road Sasha headed back.

'We have no room for error. They will not wait for ever.'

The plane was waiting with its steps down, and men were rushing to the Range Rover as Fritzi jumped out. She had changed out of her skirt suit and was dressed now in sartorially cool Fritzi attire: camouflage cargo pants, lace-up boots, skin-tight top, and Falstaff biker jacket with the label on her arm printed in gold. She looked the part, he had to give her that.

Yvetta was carried onto the plane. Fritzi had a few words with the men while Sasha waited as ordered.

Fritzi gave a signal from the top of the steps before disappearing inside. Sasha watched as the plane took off down the runway and into a blue sky – exactly where was anyone's guess; he doubted it was Canada.

He watched the metallic dot as it disappeared behind the clouds, not sure what to do next, confused, only now aware of his aimlessness and the emptiness around him. He found himself looking at nothing. What had just happened? And where did that leave him? And who was he, anyway, certainly not the Sasha that life had left behind? Someone else entirely.

Feeling paralysed with fear he remained motionless behind the driver's seat. He was beginning to gather together the threads of his freedom, but, for a long moment, at least, it was all too much to bear. For so long now he had been told what to do, where to go, ordered around, imprisoned, emasculated, oppressed. It was horrible to be a prisoner or a slave, but being free offered its own kind of hardship, the burden of choice.

For the first time in almost five years, he was free to do as he pleased. His mind was blank. He steadied himself only to find that he was shaking – with joy perhaps, or with fear. The hard, shrewd, quick-thinking Sasha had apparently been left behind, along with so much else. To begin again was no easy thing: where to start, who to contact, how to break the news of his return? What would he find had changed since his absence? He didn't want to think about it. As the light began to fade, he started up the car, allowing it to steer him to the only place he felt safe, back to his family home, somewhere he could hide out before he was launched back into a life, he no longer felt a part of.

It was dark by the time Sasha drove into the garage. He found his way into the house automatically, as though nothing had ever changed, as though he had been away five days rather than five years. He walked softly and easily along the passage, switching the familiar lights on. Making his way to the kitchen he suddenly came to an abrupt halt: why had the lights gone on? All appliances had been off on his arrival; either someone was in the house or they had found his note in the pantry.

Sitting calmly at the kitchen table, framed by the light, was a familiar figure. A little heavier, looking notably older around the face and jowls, with lines beneath his eyes that hadn't been there before, but familiar nonetheless. It was a man who looked oddly like his father, but it was not his father. It was Mika. The two men stared at one another, then Mika grabbed his little brother, hugging him tightly in disbelief. Both choked with emotion they slowly separated. Mika held Sasha at arm's length to take a better look at him.

'Scrawny as hell,' Mika muttered, as if to himself, then opening up his voice, and his arms again, 'are you okay?'

Sasha shook his head, too emotional and afraid to speak. What must Mika think of him? What would Sasha himself learn? Mika had got here too quickly, he must have been in Moscow already. Seeing his confusion Mika said, 'Old Yuri found your note. I had the jet turn around in mid-air. I read your note and saw the Range Rover was missing. The only thing to do was wait and see if you returned.'

Sasha was exhausted and had no idea where to start. He wanted to be alone to gather his strength before embarking on a debriefing, with Mika, not now anyway, he was exhausted, had not had a moment to gather his thoughts since Fritzi had secured his release from his captors, involving in her scheme to abduct Yvetta from the Moscow Clinic. He was not ready to admit he had betrayed his father's trust and the family's integrity. The suffering he caused his father and mother and Safi – it was impossible to explain, he wasn't ready, Mika would have to wait.

But Mika had waited so long already. Too long perhaps given his exhausted appearance. And Mika was viewing Sasha too, but with downcast eyes.

'You're shaking,' Mika said. Sasha had not been aware that he was shaking. It was as though when his brother had embraced him something had come loose within him, a spring had uncoiled, and had not tightened back up or stopped reverberating. 'And you're scrawny,' he said again, this time with confidence.

'I wish I could say the same about you,' Sasha said, feigning a cockiness that his voice and demeanour, to say nothing of his shakiness, betrayed. He wanted his relationship with his brother to go back to its old and easy manner, but he had to realise that, after all of this time, such a scenario was impossible. There was no going back to normal. Normal was a long time ago. Normal had perhaps never existed.

Slumping down in a chair he looked up at his brother beseechingly, hoping he would understand the improbable, the impossible, the unexplained, the long overdue.

'Okay, Sasha, take time,' Mika said slowly but with a note of agitation, perhaps even anger. Mika hated being made weak, and Sasha realised that his own absence, the family's loss, the lack of an explanation, had made Mika look weak. He had cost his brother, and the family, and would have to be forgiven. All of that would take time. In what ways he would be punished he did not know. Now that Mika was in control again, Sasha perhaps could not hope to easily regain all of the power he had long held and quickly lost. 'No one knows you are here but Yuri and me, so relax, we will talk tomorrow when you are ready. Until then, eat, clean up, shower, sleep.'

'In other words,' Sasha said, 'make myself at home.'

He wanted Mika to say it back to him, to acknowledge that this was, indeed, Sasha's home. But Mika did not respond.

Sasha took a piece of bread, stuffed some cheese inside, bit into it, and chewed until some energy flowed back into his body. He could not remember when he last ate. Mika poured a glass of milk laced with vodka, handed it to Sasha and watched his brother drink it down. Wiping his mouth with the back of his hand, Sasha smiled a thank-you with his eyes, then bade Mika goodnight.

'Yes,' Mika said finally, 'welcome home.'

Sasha took another thick slice of bread and cheese and disappeared but this time up the stairs to his old suite of rooms.

Mika stood alone in the kitchen and at a loss. He felt a sense of unease gnawing at him, an anxiety he couldn't explain, as though he was midway through a game of chess that everyone but himself knew he would lose. He had the hard lights of the kitchen on him, but he felt very much in the dark. He was a man who needed to be in control at all times, and he wasn't in control at all, he knew that much. There was so much ground to cover. Sasha had lost several years of life with family and friends; he had missed his own father's funeral. It was obvious he did not know that Alexi had passed away, a terrible shock for him to bear. Mika empathised with the guilt he must be experiencing, the sadness he would have to overcome, besides the demons that would no doubt haunt him from the past years spent in captivity and at the mercy of his captors. Janus through Russian intel and Mika's interpretation of events believed after the Russian's set him free Sasha was abducted against his will, it was something he had to believe and, it was what he told Alexi too, now he prayed it was true.

Having returned to Moscow without explanation, Mika had called family and various contacts with the only explanation he could think of, technical problems with the jet. He told them that he could only return once the problems were sorted; it would probably be another day or two before it would be safe to fly back, he had adlibbed.

He looked at his watch, deciding it was not too late to call the clinic. Had they managed to calm his sister after her attack on Safi? A part of him – an ever-shrinking part, to be sure – still felt it was possible for them to restore her state of mind. A practical person, his sister's madness was way beyond his understanding. He knew Maurice was attending to his mother and probably had not yet had time to enquire about Yvetta's wellbeing after the shocking behaviour she had displayed in Florida.

Mika got through to the clinic and listened to the update about Yvetta with increasing disbelief. His hands and voice began to shake. He was still shaking when he put down the telephone. He could not believe what he had been told: Yvetta had been handed over to a Dr Stoffenburg to attend a clinical trial in Quebec, and with her family's permission. There was no point wasting time over the phone. He left for the clinic to find out the details of this mysterious Dr Stoffenburg, dreading what he already surmised but still finding such a proposition hard to comprehend.

On his way to the clinic Mika called Maurice; he did not care what the time in France was, he needed to know the facts.

Maurice was as shocked as Mika had been to hear of Yvetta's release to a Canadian clinic he had never heard of. Incensed, confused, Maurice wondered how his fellow peers had fallen for such an obvious ruse. But Mika thought he knew – Fritzi was indeed a master at her craft.

All three doctors were there to meet Mika, in the same room they had met with Sasha and Dr Stoffenburg. Mika sat in fascinated silence as they related the whole scenario. Really, he wanted to smash the wooden table with his bare hands, but instead he nodded occasionally and suppressed the desire to scream.

'Did anyone think to check with myself or Dr Maurice Rheingold?'

'Of course, we would have done this if the documents had not been in order.'

'What documents are you referring to exactly?' Mika asked.

The doctor handed him a sheath of papers.

'Since your brother was in attendance, and gave us his full permission, we thought this meant the approval of the fa–' the doctor began.

'My brother?' Mika said. The surprise in his voice was such that one might think he did not have a brother at all.

'Yes, Sasha Rubicov.'

Mika scanned the signed papers and his eyes fell on Sasha's signature and the signature of a Dr Stoffenburg. They had signed a battery of documents for her release. They had also provided contacts for the Montreal clinic – a clinic which, Mika now felt fairly sure, did not actually exist – all signed by the mysterious Dr Stoffenburg.

'What did this Dr Stoffenburg look like exactly?'

'A tall, middle-aged French woman – and very persuasive about the new trials, which sound ground-breaking. We will be very disappointed if that is not the case.'

'I am afraid you have been hoodwinked by a very sophisticated con artist,' Mika said, handing back the paperwork and looking again at the wooden table in the corner, which he now dearly wished he had smashed to smithereens. 'Sadly my sister will have to pay a high price for that mistake, and I hope it will not result in another attack on someone else in our family.'

The three doctors looked crestfallen but said nothing. Their shocked faces and shameful expressions said enough. Mika was not sure whether they were shocked at being hoodwinked or having lost a very lucrative patient.

'Mr Rubicov, you must understand that your brother was here with Dr Stoffenburg or whoever this person is. We had no reason to disbelieve their explanation, or second-guess what we were being asked to do. Under the circumstances we were hoping to be included in these trials –'

Mika cut her off. 'Doctor, I assure you that there are no trials. Or rather not in the sense of the word you had in mind.' He reflexively touched his hand to his brow. His headache was back.

'Did you not think to call to verify with me or Maurice? To check the authenticity of this supposed trial my sister was becoming a guinea pig for before you allowed her to leave?'

'You must understand this only took place this morning. The patient was discharged to Dr Stoffenburg's care. We would have done so within the day.' But Mika doubted even this was true. 'You understand the flight to Canada is a long one.'

'I very much doubt they have gone to Canada.'

'This is a very unfortunate business,' she said in a voice that almost quivered at one point. 'We would never have allowed a patient to leave without the support and verification of a family member. Which we thought we had. After all, your brother seemed to be very much in favour of this new treatment.'

'I understand. I am afraid my brother may have been here under duress, without any choice but to go along with this Dr Stoffenburg.'

'Is he safe, Mr. Rubicov? Have you seen him since this unfortunate state of affairs?'

'Yes, it appears that he is safe and free – perhaps because of this dreadful business, he was able to gain his freedom.'

It was time to have a reunion of sorts with Sasha, and find out everything that had happened in the last five years.

Mika returned to the house, still shaken by the temerity and ingenious manner in which Fritzi had managed to hoodwink her way into a secure institution, kidnapping his sister. He needed to debrief Sasha and find out everything that had happened since his disappearance. He also needed to ascertain how Sasha had escaped the attack on the smugglers' stronghold.

Mika knew that Fritzi had been released from her sentence. It was unfortunate that the Americans had allowed her to escape without trace, a failure on their part and an obvious coup for Fritzi, which she had, in her inimitable, advantageous, self-dealing manner, made full use of. No grass had grown under her feet since her release; where she was now was anyone's guess.

Mika called Janus to update him and their discussions continued into the small hours. He retired to bed exhausted, his brother and sister on his mind as he drifted off, only they were not the images of his brother and sister now, so unrecognisable from those of the past, but as they were in his childhood, gathering around him, pulling him this way and that in a dizzying whirl of colour and sound, a merry-go-round of now and then, old and new sensations as Yvetta and Sasha embraced him, teased him, clamoured and competed for his attention. He hoped Yvetta would survive from this and from the fallout after they tracked her down. He had no doubt she would put up a fight. He just hoped that they could catch her this time. He did not even want to think about what Yvetta had in mind for the family now – she would be angrier than ever and out for revenge.

Mika had cooked and laid out a full breakfast. Sipping his second cup of coffee, he checked the clock: it was almost noon and there had been no sign of Sasha. Not wanting to wait any longer, he made his way to his brother's rooms on the top floor. He rapped on the door. No response. He rapped again, this time louder; but the non-response was the same. His mind jumped to wild conclusions.

Relieved to find the bedroom blacked out, not being able to see, Mika pulled the curtains open. He found Sasha curled into a foetal position, the pillow shading his eyes from the light filtering in through the window.

Mika stood for a moment, not sure how to handle Sasha, who even in good times was never exactly passive or predictable.

Sitting on the edge of the bed for a few moments, observing Sasha, Mika hesitatingly made his way back to the door. As he pulled the door shut, he became aware of a soft but insistent noise.

Sasha had swung his legs over the bed. 'What time is it?'

'It's pretty late. Get showered and meet me in the kitchen. We have a lot of ground to cover.'

The breakfast did not go to waste. Sasha had double helpings of everything; a good sign as he had become skeletal.

'I know about Yvetta and Fritzi's involvement,' Mika began. Sasha frowned, his suddenly lined face creased further. He looked at his hands (they were lined, too), then up at Mika again. He looked surprised then tense, his emotions clearly all over the place.

'Sorry,' Sasha said finally, uneasily, searching for eye contact now.

'No need,' Mika said, trying to keep his voice calm, level, untroubled. 'Start from the beginning. I will ask questions, but I need facts, as many as you can recall.'

Sasha struggled at first – perhaps unintentionally, perhaps deliberately, giving himself time and space to figure out his options and where he currently stood with Mika– to recall the events as they had unfolded. His mind was still a blur, his body still felt heavy, uneasy. He had slept for hours but he still felt exhausted, weighed down by the events of the last few years, now so heavily embedded in his bones, in every fibre of his being, it now appeared. Would he, could he, ever return to being the old Sasha?

With Mika's prodding it was not long before everything came rushing back. Like all close-kept and deeply felt confidences, it was an emotional moment for both parties.

Mika became alarmed at the ease with which his brother had been taken hostage, once released by the Russian authorities, who had arrested him before he could fly out of Moscow to join his family in Europe. The brutality he suffered at the hands of the smugglers when he refused to co-operate. Sasha had been thrown into a damp, darkened room, starved and beaten until he agreed to divert the crude oil onto foreign nameless tankers heading back through the Black Sea into Eastern Europe and Italy. His two-month ordeal under Russian interrogation had been a walk in the park compared to his incarceration at the hands of his new ruthless captors.

It had taken almost a year to refine and perfect the documents needed before they were ready to release Sasha with the papers. They needed to make sure the paperwork would not be traced back to the smugglers before the crude oil was safely in the hold of the illegal tankers. Documents had been falsified in the past; Sasha's signature on all relevant papers gave authenticity to the new shipping orders. No one questioned the head of the enterprise when the orders came directly from a Rubicov. The smugglers remained glued to Sasha's every move. He had no means of communication with the outside world, they made sure of that. When visiting the refineries Sasha was accompanied by gunmen, always dressed in black and army fatigues. The workers were all under the impression they were following a government directive.

Mika began to realise the professionalism of the people his brother was forced to work with. He could tell from his years of intel work that his brother had little choice but to fall in with their plans, to live with them and become part of the operation, the smugglers became, in a way, his new family, the Rubicov family a thing of the distant past, unless of course when he had to exploit his family name. His life was constantly threatened at the least provocation.

Sasha had tried to slow the operation down from time to time. He was under no illusions, and knew he was too much of a liability to be given his freedom. He did not know their real identities, but he had heard enough to know that he would be disposed of once the operation was completed. One of the smugglers he believed was a doctor, or at least had medical training. After being integrated with the rest of the workers, Sasha had become ill, leaving him weak and unable to work for months; this caused arguments and unrest amongst the hierarchy within the smuggling syndicate. A smuggler called Giuseppe was brought in to care for him. Giuseppe spoke Russian with an Italian accent, but Sasha spoke fluent Italian and this enabled him to build up a relationship with the medic.

Sasha was given medication and extra rations by the medic, and when it became clear he was well once more and able to continue his job, Giuseppe stayed close, warning him when things were about to get rough.

Fritzi's arrival had been a complete surprise; the smugglers treated her with a high degree of respect, and Sasha was released to go with her without argument. Obviously, she had carried out her side of the agreement successfully. Sasha soon understood he had a greater chance of remaining alive with Fritzi.

Mika, in turn, feeling comfortable with his brother once again, briefed Sasha on the joint operation with the Russians and with Janus's surveillance agency. Mika knew it would not be long before Sasha came around to family matters; he would want to catch up on a life he was no longer a part of. He must suspect, too, that there would be unwelcome news on many fronts since his absence.

Not sure how to break Alexi's death, Mika opted for a longer version, hoping to prepare his brother for what was to come.

Sasha understood of course that his disappearance would have repercussions for his loved ones, especially for his father Alexi, who he knew would have found it difficult to control his anger. He knew, too, that Alexi would be frustrated at not being able to fix things in his usual manner, through sheer will of personality and endless contacts (many of which dried up or closed down along with the increased restrictions on the business in Russia). But Sasha had never imagined his father suffering a heart attack; he had never conceived of his father as fallible or weak. In fact, he had imagined his mother would have been the one to suffer most.

Mika continued to brief Sasha on the Russian side of their business and how his disappearance had brought about unrest within the family ranks; and his father's eventual decision to organise a boardroom meeting to quell the younger members of the family. He went on to explain Alexi's growing frustration and anger at the disrespect shown by his cousin Pasha.

After observing his brother closely, finding his state of mind satisfactory (if not entirely steadfast), Mika continued with what unfolded in the boardroom that day. He recounted to Sasha how Alexi had lost his temper (and he recounted the initial part of this with a surprising amount of humour, which was not free of its own kind of heartache), marching Pasha out by the seat of his pants, then collapsing, banging his head and simultaneously suffering a fatal heart attack.

Sasha did not react for what seemed a little too long; then he found his voice and muttered something inaudible. 'Gone.'

'Yes, Sasha, I am sad to break this to you, brother, but our father, Alexievich Ivan Sergei Rubicov, is no longer with us.'

He watched the colour drain from his brother's face, the now-frail face grim, the eyes half closed, then opening afresh, as though to remember where he was. He put his hand against his head, smoothed over his hair, but he found his voice.

'When was the funeral?'

'Almost a year now'

Sasha's head dropped, he covered his face with his hands and wept like a baby. Mika knew they had covered as much as he was able to take for one day; the rest would have to wait for another time.

'Continue, please,' Sasha said softly but firmly, 'what else do you need to tell me?' Nothing could be worse than missing my own father's funeral.' He stared at Mika, the way Yvetta used to stare, in one of her infernal childhood staring contests.

'Please, Sasha, this is enough for one day.'

'No, Mika I need to know, I must know!'

Mika had long ago made up his mind to give Safi the best possible reference when it came to discussing their relationship. His brother had not been an angel or faithful, and she had suffered a great deal after his disappearance, putting herself in harm's way on several occasions to uncover any clues to help find Sasha – and not only for her own peace of mind, but for the family's as well.

He told it straight, giving Sasha the details of Safi's loyalty to him her endurance and unwavering will to find him, while working day and night to make the New York gallery a success. But she was human, Mika added, and, someone had come into her life who had offered to help find him, and who shared her interests in the art world. It was inevitable that her unwavering loyalty to Sasha would falter. She had no way of knowing whether he was dead or alive – she was human, after all – and Mika told Sasha that he had given her his blessing (as had Alexi) to continue with her life. She was young and becoming ill waiting for news, like Sasha she was fading away, had become a ghost of her former self.

Janus had not only helped to locate Sasha, but saved Safi from a life of endless sadness, gave her back her zest for life, and brought her much happiness. He looked at Sasha sharply, making it clear he had no reason to feel hard done by. He praised Janus softly, in an even, temperate manner, but was careful not to overdo it and tip Sasha over into outright jealousy and rage.

Sasha nodded but the hard line of his mouth told a different story, of loss and anguish for his former life.

Mika continued to bring his brother up to date – although he had the sense that Sasha was no longer listening, still dwelling on his loss of Safi and perhaps all of the things he would have liked to have said to his father but now never could. But there was more news – there was always more news! Mika recounted what had happened with the reading of his father's will, and how Yvetta had, on learning of Safi's success with the galleries and understanding that she would never regain the galleries until she relinquished her war of abuse on her family and continue her clinical treatment. Mika told Sasha that Yvetta was informed that in time she would be able to reclaim what was rightfully hers, but until then Safi would legally be in charge. But this, of course, was a step too far for the vengeful and self-righteous Yvetta. The lawyers had Yvetta sign a document relinquishing control of the galleries until it was time to take her rightful ownership of them. In the event of Sasha's continued absence, only Safi's signature together with Mika's would enable Yvetta to reclaim the galleries.

He told of Yvetta's attack on Safi, nearly causing her death. Mika stressed that they owed Safi a great deal as a family for remaining loyal to the Rubicovs in the face of very difficult situations, endured over a number of years, starting with her engagement to Sasha. 'You chose a good girl,' Mika said, more than once, though he himself had initially had his reservations – not so much about Safi's loyalty, but about his younger brother's fidelity. On brother fronts, he now thought, he had been proven right. She had never wavered in her support for him, the family, or their trust in her to run the galleries as a successful business.

An expert poker player, Sasha knew when he was beaten; he did not have much to contribute where Safi was concerned. He had treated her shabbily and had only himself to blame. And perhaps, in a way, he had suffered in kind. He could not blame her for moving on, she deserved happiness, and Mika made it very clear that Sasha was not to do anything to spoil that for her. He spoke of what an asset she had been to the family, especially Alexi and Anna, who both adored her.

Sasha could not help wondering whether they would be married now if he had not been kidnapped. He remembered their excited discussions about wedding preparations: invitations, venues, flower arrangements, caterers. Safi's beautiful face lighting up, all that possibility, all that joy, all of it squandered, wasted, ruined. Yes, he thought now, he was sure they would have been married by now. But would he have made her happy? A different question altogether. And how long until she discovered one or other of his secrets, or one or other of his women? What then? Maybe she was better off without him. He had loved Safi because she was a good person and because when he was with her he felt like a good person, too. But he was not a good person. Maybe, in a weird way, his kidnapping had been a godsend – for her. And perhaps for him, too, he thought, trying to see a positive side to beginning his life all over again.

He scraped the chair back and stood for a while, stretching, flexing, leaning against the table for support.

'I will remain here in the house for now,' he said, turning to Mika. 'I need time, you understand.'

'Yes, but you must also understand there are documents you have to sign, and, although you have been completely exonerated by the Russian authorities you will in time need to sign and answer their queries too and, we need you to come back to work. The company here needs you. Ringo has been invaluable during your absence and will support you.'

He could tell Sasha was not in good shape and decided to leave him for the time being. He watched as his brother retired to his suite. Then he returned to the study to see to his own affairs; he needed to be back in the United States.

Safi knew nothing of Sasha's return. In fact, no one had been informed. Mika had to decide how to break the news to his family first. The first person he intended to talk to was his mother, Anna, and then perhaps his stepfather Maurice. On second thoughts, perhaps it was best to let Maurice, with his sensitivity and history of psychiatry, deal with his wife. Anna was frail, her state of mind had suffered a great deal since seeing Yvetta; it had been a painful experience to watch her daughter wilfully block her out. The only time Yvetta now acknowledged her mother was when they were in the company of lawyers. Anna found watching her daughter unravelling into an angry, dangerous, destructive human being too much to bear.

She would have loved to take Yvetta in her arms, hold her, sooth her, memories of the beautiful little girl flooding back into her mind – but none of this was possible for either of them, alas. Yvetta had gone too far to turn back; she had pushed her loved one's away, denying herself any possibility of being welcomed back.

Knowing this Mika hoped Sasha's return would go some way to restoring his mother's health: it had been a difficult period her daughter a lost soul, a son's disappearance, and then her lifelong friend and father of her children, gone.

Mika would break the news of Sasha's return to Safi when back on US soil; or perhaps he would leave it to his brother – after all, it was his choice in the end if he wanted her to know of his return. The Rubicovs (himself included) liked to play the field, but he felt Sasha might in future see things a little differently, his charm and carefree arrogance had taken a beating, he had lost a father he loved and, more than likely the woman of his dreams.

Usually pragmatic and sharp, though certainly tested over the last few years, Mika felt unsure of how to handle Sasha's return. In the end he opted to discuss Sasha's reappearance with Janus; together they would decide who should tell Safi of Sasha's return.

Then there was the matter of tracking down Yvetta; they had no idea where she and Fritzi had vanished to.

Chapter 11

Life for Safi had turned around dramatically. Now back at work she found her routine hectic but happy. Fully recovered from Yvetta's attack, Janus had reluctantly agreed to her moving back to Manhattan on her own, to run the gallery. They would only see each other on weekends, when she joined him at his home upstate.

Janus relinquished the running of his company to his employees, and instead spent uninterrupted hours in his studio. The only time he took away from working was when Safi arrived from Manhattan. Ying took full advantage of his time out of the studio on weekends to collate, photograph and diarise his work for future exhibitions.

Safi's life with Janus was a world away from her life with Sasha in Moscow, where she became paranoid about everything that went on around her, never knowing from day to day what Sasha or his family or the authorities would bring, her life lurching from one drama to the next. Her life was now tranquil in comparison. In his gentle, undemanding, empathic (yet ambitious and innovative manner), Janus brought order into her life without the day-to-day uncertainty she experienced with Sasha.

Dax and Dan (sometimes together with Pete and Rene) drove up for the odd Sunday's lunch, cooked by Janus. They spent a heavenly day catching up on news with long walks in the woods nearby, with the dogs (who quickly became almost as friendly as the owners).

Now that Rachel was almost three, the two D's were embarking on another surrogate pregnancy and madly excited about the baby boy joining their happy family.

Dax to everyone's surprise had returned to his studio, but now both D's were happy to put work aside at a respectable hour, blissful in their domesticity: no one more so than Dax, his dream had actually materialised into a midlife paunch, to everyone's amusement.

Being left out of the loop since her return to the gallery had become unsettling. Safi had continued with the day-to-day running of the gallery: arranged shows, and liaised closely with DuPont, who remained a constant support both as a friend and a colleague. She continued to work closely with Ilona, who ran the Moscow gallery. The banks continued to support both galleries, yet since Alexi's death they no longer had any contact with the Rubicovs.

Sadly, Sasha had not been found after the Russian operation. Mika had left for Russia yet months had gone by without any news.

Running the gallery remained Safi's only connection with the Rubicovs. Other than that, it seemed to Safi she was on her own to do as she pleased.

DuPont advised her to continue until she heard from the family one way or another, which he was sure she would in time. It appeared that the lawyers were in charge of the family's affairs in Sasha's absence. Other than that, Safi felt that she was operating within a vacuum, adrift, unmoored.

For now, happiness and contentment with Janus and her work life were enough to keep her feet planted firmly on the ground. She did not have any intention of throwing a curveball into her new-found love life with a man she felt safe with – not to mention their sexual chemistry, which was considerable and increasingly intense. She had stopped worrying about the admiring glances from other females: Janus was the least egotistical of all the guys she had ever met. According to Ying (very slowly, perhaps, becoming something of her confidante, though still wholly loyal to Janus), he had cultivated an air of the lone wolf– until he had met Safi, at least. In the ten years that Ying had known him, she told Safi that he had very little interest in cultivating a relationship with anyone. Safi was the first, Ying said, and Janus had wasted very little time in getting what he wanted. Janus did not do romance, and he certainly did not play games, or waste anyone's time, least of all his own. A relationship either worked or it did not, a bit like his art. Luckily for both Safi and Janus it worked.

Her visit to London and her family would have to go ahead without Janus. Her parents now shared their time between Melbourne and Brighton. The seasons suited them well, being away from England during the winters, while spending most of their time in Australia enjoying their alternate summer season.

The art fair she was attending happened to fall in the same month her parents packed up and left to be with Jake and his fiancé.

Safi knew her relationship with Sasha had put the fear of death into her parents, who no longer visited America since Rupert's death. She felt sure they were reluctant to divest energy in whoever else had come into her life since. Her brother Jake had a much less complicated lifestyle making it easier for them to relate with. Heck, Jake's lifestyle was almost aggressively relaxed, and had been for as long as she could remember.

Alexi Rubicov's untimely death and his family tragedy drew her parents in but had also taken its toll; the disappearance of Sasha and the abhorrent and unforgivable attack on Safi by Yvetta had understandably shaken them. All of this bad news and attendant anxiety and disapproval had left Safi with no alternative but to keep them out of the loop, lest they fret too much about her and complicate her life any further. More than anything, she hated lying to her parents, especially to her mother.

Leonard would have preferred Safi to return to the fold and join his advertising agency, but he now knew it was a pipe dream; Safi had carved out a profession in the art world, and a significant reputation to boot. There was no going back from that – nor should there be. A long-time agency man and copywriter, Leonard was inventive and forward-thinking, but he was also a realist and not without compassion.

Fiona was resigned to Safi's New York lifestyle, and saw her daughter continue to cut out a niche in the high-end, overhyped art world, which Safi knew they found exhausting (indeed, as Leonard often remarked, fashion, media, and advertising were a young person's game).

She had sadly accepted their attitude but looked forward to seeing them before they departed for down under for the rest of the year.

'Gorgeous ring, darling,' Fiona had said over Skype, 'when do you think you will be marrying Janus? you will let us know well in advance, won't you?'

Janus had replaced the Coke can ring with a heart-shaped emerald surrounded with diamonds. Safi adored it; it suited her long fingers perfectly and also her cat's eyes, as Janus loved to remind her.

'Yes, of course we will, Mother. But I hope you get the chance to know him more before the wedding.'

'That would be nice,' Fiona said, but her voice was oddly cold. 'Pity he could not accompany you this time.'

Safi did not want to show her feelings: her mother was bound to read more into to them than she needed to, and she was aware of her mother's offhand comment about him not travelling with her to England.

'I told you, Janus is working on another show. It's mayhem. Sadly, there was no chance he could travel with me, and I had to be here for the art fair, but also to catch you before you fly.' She tried to hide the note of irritation in her voice. She had no idea why she was lying; it was totally unnecessary and stupid. Her folks always brought the petulant little girl out in her; she never wanted to show them any weakness, she still needed their approval in all she did. And she supposed she had failed them these last few years, though through no fault of her own.

They would be devastated for her if they knew Janus did not want children; she wanted to avoid any mention of this until she had come to terms with it herself.

God, her love life was always so impossibly complicated; no wonder they preferred being Down Under with Jacob and his partner.

Safi had little time during the art fair to give her relationship with Janus any further thought – and that, she thought, was a good thing. She was starting to rely on DuPont more and more, not only for his support professionally, but because he was the only person who knew her history with Sasha, the Rubicovs, and Janus. She could keep no secrets from him, not now. He was intertwined with her life, something she felt immensely grateful for.

The London Art Fair had been financially profitable; the Chinese, Middle Easterners, and Russians were investing in art for their new homes abroad, and the Rubicov Gallery had the elegance, the integrity, the signature, stable, glamorous reputation these customers enjoyed.

DuPont worked closely with her gallery; it helped keep his clients' interest fresh. He had over many years built a formidable reputation amongst those who wanted to buy art. They used him to guide them, and he used the Rubicov Gallery (amongst others) to sell them what he recommended. It was a very profitable relationship: his clients always came through when a sale was sealed; they never reneged on a deal (something that often happened after the heat of the moment, when the initial flurry of electricity had subsided and cold hard reality had kicked in). Many suffered buyer's remorse after the initial excitement of making such a costly purchase, something most galleries experienced, DuPont had the confidence of the super-rich, invaluable to those he brought his buyers to.

Safi never ignored DuPont when he suggested a meeting. They had developed a father daughter relationship both trusted one another explicitly.

She had only a brief moment of hesitation to his request to extend her stay by a few days before returning to New York. DuPont had invited Safi to join him at one of his Middle Eastern client's private homes in Mayfair for dinner. This man was, he stressed to Safi, one of his most important clients, one no one in the art world could ignore.

The exterior was imposing set apart from the adjoining terraced apartments lining one of the most expensive roads in Mayfair. The gates slowly opening as they entered into the circular drive with lawns and potted palms. They were greeted by a butler, waiting under the portico of Doric columns in front of open double carved oak doors. Taking their coats, he showed them through to the inner sanctum to one of the many rooms of the prince's magnificent home. Safi stopped to study the masters adorning the vast passages, Vermeer's, and Rembrandt's and a breath -taking Turner amongst others, beneath stood classic Chinese chests adorned with priceless porcelain pottery, by Grayson Perry. The room they were shown into was decorated in heavy ornate silk Chinese curtains piled on the parquet floors covered by a massive yellow gold and black silk Persian rug. the walls were of a bright canary yellow that perfectly set the scene for the mixture of classic and contemporary furnishing, and black silk shaded gold lighting on the coffee tables, the ambience was opulent and extravagant and a delight to be in. The prince had a wonderful flair for decorative Baroque exuberance.

The prince had only two other male guests, seated at a long conventional glass dining table. She was the only woman amongst them. On introduction she became baffled by her inclusion. The other men were attached to the prince's entourage: one was quite young and elegantly attired in Western fashion; the other was a much older man in more traditional dress.

Safi did not know much about the Emirates, only that they were oil-wealthy with unstable political alliances and a modern façade. She remembered having read that women were not regarded as equal in their cultures. This was more reason for Safi's confusion at being included at the dinner.

The evening was pleasant enough; she was included in their conversation at every reasonable opportunity. All the same, she felt uncomfortable, aware of the underlying issue: why had she been invited with DuPont? Had the Prince insisted on her accompanying him, Safi found him to be modern and a perfect host. After a delicious dinner the prince asked Safi to accompany him, asking for her personal opinion on a matter very close to his heart.

He was not an unattractive man: a little overweight, true, yet he exhumed an air of authority and confidence in a quiet, unsettling way. Once he requested your attention, one could not refuse him.

Safi found herself alone with the prince in a small elevator that travelled down rather than up. He conducted light conversation about the meal prepared by his Swedish Michelin stared chef, who travelled the world with him, obviously a man of immense talent in culinary matters.

The prince liked his food to be sourced from where ever he was; it had to be fresh and organic. 'I enjoy good food,' he said again, although he did not need to make this point, as his stomach more than made it for him. Prince Charles was one of his closest friends, he continued; they saw eye-to-eye on fresh produce and how it was grown. Safi found the idea of this man and Prince Charles seeing eye-to-eye on anything, because of the disparity of their height. Still, she could not help but admit she was impressed. She was about to say as much when he said, 'Safi, I have learnt all there is to know about you. I make it my business to know as much as possible about whomever I choose to befriend, or do business with.'

'Why me?' She hadn't meant to say it – certainly not in such a curt and childish manner – but there it was. And he seemed to appreciate her candour. He smiled.

'Ah, the million-dollar question. Straight to the point. I like that. First let me show you something, then we can talk.'

He led her through a passage lined with Arabic art, into a room filled with white light from tiny pin point spots around the perimeter of the room. On the walls were hundreds of sketches, prints, and paintings on every surface imaginable. The artist had painted on pots, wood, paper, and canvas, including on surfaces Safi could not identify. The work was intricate, brilliantly detailed; veins rippled on the surface of plants, drops glistened with such reality one expected them to run off the surface at any moment. Awed, exploring one work after another, Safi lost all sense of time. Each subject had its own reality and luminosity. She found the prince in a chair, watching her intently, his hands folded over his stout belly. His surprisingly smooth, unlined face was set in stone, awaiting her verdict with uncharacteristic vulnerability in his handsome, quicksilver, questioning eyes.

'Well, what do you see and what do you think?'

For a moment she was lost for words, never having seen such perfection and detailed work before. It was almost as if the artist was part of his subject; the intensity of the work was breath-taking, yet there was a distinct vulnerability which captured and shattered the realism of the subject. There was something frantic in the manner in which the work presented itself, almost as if the artist was afraid the subject would disappear before the work was completed.

'Astonishing,' she said finally, finding her words – and her breath. 'Something in these works are very honest. They draw one in. I feel quite breathless from the experience.' She stepped back, breathed again, stepped forward once more. 'Overpowered, really, by seeing so many together. They dominate one's attention totally. Who is the artist? I have never seen these before anywhere.'

The prince nodded his head agreeing with her. 'Yes, they are powerful, and it's true that no one in the art world has seen them – besides you, that is,' he said, leaning forward, a conspiratorial, or perhaps lubricious, tone in his voice.

Safi felt honoured but also alarmed; she was not an expert. There were people in the art world far superior to her, with knowledge she could never possess. There were people who had been in this business longer than she had been alive. DuPont was amongst them. Why had he chosen her? Prince Musa, as he liked to be called, saw the confusion in her eyes.

'Yes, now we will have that talk. Come, we will join the others; they will think us rude and wonder where we have vanished to.' Was there a hint of innuendo, of flirtation, in his voice here, too? She couldn't tell, she was still too mesmerised by the art.

In the elevator ride up Prince Musa told her not to mention the work she had seen to anyone, that he would contact her to discuss the subject further.

Safi had no doubt that he meant what he requested, and she had no intention of dishonouring his wishes. It was obvious he was not to be taken lightly when he requested something from someone, he gave his trust to, and she was not about to take any chances, even though she would have loved DuPont's input.

Safi's hotel phone rang early the following morning. A polite voice requested her to meet Prince Musa at his private club in Mayfair; she was to come on her own.

On arrival she was greeted with great deference and shown though to a private wing of the club. This time none of his entourage was around. Prince Musa was on his own. He had a light lunch of exquisite sushi laid out on the table; standing to greet her (and suddenly he looked much taller, and even slimmer, than he had the evening before), he waved for her to be seated and dismissed the waiters.

'Thank you for coming, and thank you for delaying your trip home. Please allow me to explain. Once I have, you may ask me any questions you wish, I will not be offended. The work you saw last night was done by my youngest son, Faruk. He is 18 years old. Yes, I know it is hard to believe, but it's true. The reason he paints this way is not a mystery: he is an autistic savant, one of the few in the world who have been given this rare gift.'

There was a long pause. Safi was not sure he had finished she waited for him to continue to explain why he needed her presence in a matter that obviously pained him a great deal. As he had said before, and as she had seen for herself, Faruk's work was very close to his heart. There was a clatter of chopsticks, and she heard his voice again.

'You must understand the reason for my intrusion into your private life was of the utmost importance. I needed to know your character. Also, you are very beautiful; my son, you understand, has peculiarities, to say the least. One of them is his preference for the company of women, not men – not even for me, his father. He will only show or speak about his work to women. I need someone who can not only relate to him, but someone I know has a dependable, loyal character. Who better than you, Safi, and you are in the art world.'

He freed his fingers of chopsticks and held up his hand, 'I am not quite finished. What I need from you is simple. I need you to put my son's work in your gallery: not for sale, as such, but I believe he needs recognition. His work should be seen, even assessed, by the critics. I would like to open a museum where his work can be housed for my people; of course, I could do this without appraisal from the art world, but it would not have any value. I want my son's work to be of value to the wider world, you understand, like a Picasso or other great artists. I want his work to be recognised first.'

Safi was flabbergasted, not sure what he was expecting; she opted to remain silent until he asked for her opinion. She noticed that she hadn't touched her food. Indeed, it looked too delicately and deliciously prepared to eat.

He looked at her expectantly and indicated for her to speak when she was ready.

'I do not see a problem as such,' she said slowly, 'putting the work on show. The problem is that,' she picked up her chopsticks, just to have something to hold, the way in social gatherings a cigarette was little more than a prop, something to do with your hands so your mouth didn't overcompensate and say something stupid, 'other than…' She stopped, privately reprimanding herself again. She was a businesswoman and had been for some time. Who cared how esteemed this man was, or what talents his son exhibited? She placed the chopsticks on her plate again, leaned forward, made her voice firm. 'You do not want the work sold – a rather unusual proposition, I'm sure you'll agree.' She had meant for him to laugh at this, but he did not laugh. 'You do understand that the gallery does not belong to me. I have to make a profit from a show for the gallery – and for the artist.'

'Of course, yes,' he said, as though he had hardly heard her at all, 'the gallery's use will be handsomely rewarded, including all catalogues, invitations, and other such necessities, including a prestigious opening night that will be taken care of. If you have any doubts about my integrity, you can ask my friend DuPont.' And here, perhaps, his voice was a little snide, a little sour.

'No,' she said, 'no, of course, I have no doubts. I am in fact familiar with your philanthropy – and your esteem. And we have an incredible working relationship with DuPont.'

'As do I. The Rubicov gallery will be doing my family a great service; but without you I would not have chosen their gallery.'

'May I ask how you came to me in the first place?'

'I have been buying through DuPont for many years. He is a trusted friend,' he said, and there was a glint in his eye that could even have been mischievous, 'and when I recently purchased pieces from your gallery, I saw you, enquired about you, and the rest, as they say, is history. He gave her a disarming smile, reminiscent of his smile last night when he had first shown her the paintings, placed his chopsticks together, and said, 'I took it upon myself to have your life investigated for my purposes. I was lucky to find in you the character that I believe trustworthy for this very delicate proposition. I also feel certain that Faruk will like you. If you forge a good relationship with him, as he has with my daughters, he will be encouraged to paint from a fresh perspective, from a more sophisticated palette, as he grows older. He needs to have a mentor, someone who is in the art world, who he can relate to.'

'I am a little nervous of meeting Faruk. You understand I have absolutely no experience with autism.'

Prince Musa smiled. 'You ask the right questions from the outset. You prove me correct in my assessment of your character: you are a sincere person, someone I can trust with my son, who is so very dear to me and my family and my people. There is nothing to be hesitant about. He is what they call "high-functioning" and, in fact, quite pleasant. It's hard to realise when meeting him that he has autism, apart from his directness, that is. He has a strict routine he likes to keep at all times; if it's not adhered to it can become a problem.'

'When could I meet Faruk?'

Prince Musa gave her his winning smile again. 'You have already met him. He was at the dinner with us last night. The younger of the two men was Faruk; you may not have caught his name when introduced?'

'Oh, I would never have realised him to be autistic. He is very handsome. I did notice his intensity. For such a young person he seems very serious. I don't recall him speaking, apart from *yes* and *no*, that is.'

'Faruk does not often partake in conversation. He has learnt to attend small dinners with select guests; unfortunately, these events have to be meticulously planned around his routine. My cousin Omer was also in attendance. Faruk will only attend if my cousin is present; one of his characteristics, you see. I know he likes you because he did not take his eyes off you the whole evening. In his guarded way he was assessing you. He asked after you when you left, so you have won him over already.'

Safi recalled Faruk's interest in her, but she was used to young men being attentive and wondered at the time whether he was reluctant to speak to her in front of the older men. She also recalled him dropping something into her handbag, but had forgotten all about it until now. Fumbling in her bag she brought out a napkin, unfolded it, and gasped. It revealed a detailed drawing of her; every nuance and expression was captured in the sketch. It was unbelievable.

'How did he manage to do this without anyone noticing?' she asked, handing the sketch over to Prince Musa. The Prince smiled again, but this time it was a kindly, paternal, proud smile.

'He probably had it on his lap. You were sitting on the opposite side of the table, remember? It's one of the reasons he joins us at the table; we do not interfere with his drawing where ever he chooses to do it or when. If he gave you a drawing – and such a lovely drawing, too – it's a sure sign that he approves of you.'

Safi deposited the sketch back in her bag. 'This drawing shows his subject is more than inanimate objects, food, or plants.'

'We do not believe the likeness of the human form should be manifested in another form. Faruk has done this many times, of course, but we do not encourage it.'

'I do understand, but if he is to be recognised by the art world, perhaps it would help if all his work was viewed equally?'

Prince Musa remained quiet for a long time. He was no longer smiling. Safi began to regret the question, feared it was a stumbling block, or that she had inquired into a taboo.

'I have given this subject much thought. Of course, I have bought the work of many great artists – work where the human form has been the subject. But my people would not accept this art in my country, and certainly not from one of their own people. It would be disrespectful to their religious beliefs.'

Art and religious beliefs rarely meet with any lasting degree of harmony, Safi thought, although there were certainly near-miraculous exceptions. She thought of Rome and the renaissance and work of nativity and buoyancy and bliss and rebirth.

'I understand, yet it is a great pity for any artist to be restricted in his subject. I am sure you must understand this from an artistic viewpoint, having bought Modigliani and other great artists yourself.'

Shaking his head, Prince Musa agreed in principle only. Safi realised it was something she would have to deal with at a later date, if indeed it arose again. Or perhaps it simply wasn't her place. After all, her own upbringing and appreciation for art would have been very different from Faruk's. She could no more impose that on him, than he could his religious beliefs or dietary restrictions on her. In the world of belief – as in the world of art – there was surely enough space for everyone to co-exist – and still create great work.

'Will you consider working with Faruk?' the prince asked. 'Perhaps you could give him a show sometime in the future when you believe he is ready.'

Safi smiled. 'Yes, I would love to show Faruk's work. He deserves to be seen. But if I am to show his work, whom am I to say it is by.'

Prince Musa stood. He did this as he did everything – with a leisurely and unbothered elegance.

'We will discuss that at a later stage, shall we? You will never regret our association, Safi. My country will always be at your service, and you are always welcome as a dear friend of my family, now and in the future, do you understand?'

Safi nodded.

'I appreciate your gesture,' she said, 'truly I do, but I am doing it for Faruk. I hope it brings the kudos and recognition he deserves.'

Prince Musa pushed his chair back and took Safi by the hand.

'This is a French gesture of appreciation.'

He brushed his lips lightly over her hand.

'I believe mystery is never a bad thing, even in the art world.'

But Safi had had more than her fair share of mystery.

'That is very true,' she said, 'discretion will be uppermost in my mind. But I do need to share certain aspects of this show with my colleagues.'

Safi flew back first class a guest of the prince's airline. She enjoyed untold luxury, waited on hand and foot by his attentive staff. She learnt that his airline would be at her disposal on all their routes as their guest.

She could not wait to tell DuPont and Janus of her experience. It was something extraordinary; she hoped it would turn out well for the prince and his son – and for her as well.

Sasha remained cloistered in his family home, attended to by the staff who were exhilarated to have one of the Rubicov's back in residence. Having worked for the family for most of their lives. They had been pensioned off with a good package having worked for the family for most of their lives, but an idle life did not suit either the housekeeper or the older servants, and they made sure Sasha was undisturbed for as long as he wished.

Most of the family members were turned away; the only person Sasha reunited with was Anna, who flew out to Moscow to be with her son after believing him dead was a miracle. Anna had stopped being judgemental about her offspring and, being re united with her youngest son was all she needed holding him close to her heart to reassure herself he was indeed flesh and bone and not a figment of her imagination. The reasons behind all their misfortune was unimportant to Anna she had been through many Russian upheavals, to be safe and have her family safe was what counted for Anna.

Six weeks after his return, Sasha went back to work. Carrying out Mika and Anna's wishes, he met with each family member, encouraging them to develop their Independence, from the company, some had already put their ideas into practice; to Sasha and Ringo's surprise Pasha proved to be the most hesitant to fly the coop.

Sasha had little patience with Pasha's reluctance to make a go of his newfound freedom, recalling Mika's harrowing description of his father's anger at Pasha closely followed by his fatal heart attack, which sat heavily on Sasha's heart, something he was still trying to come to terms with. He had blamed his own incompetence at handling the oil and gas deal badly, but Mika had assured him that what had happened was in no way his fault, he was the family hostage the authorities punished for his families business ties outside Russia. Sasha did not hold his cousin responsible, but he was a Russian by birth and by character – and he was proud of being Russian, and, in fact, despite his many residences and friends in different countries, would choose to be born into no other nationality –

and he would not forget. Pasha's troublemaking had caused everyone pain and upheaval at an extremely trying time, for the family and the company.

If he did not take the opportunity he had been handed, the family would cut him loose and at a time and opportunity that would certainly surprise him (the Rubicovs were nothing if not stealthy, resilient, imaginative and, yes, occasionally even vengeful). There was no place for him at the Rubicov Organisation any longer; they would support him only as long as the contract allowed. He had proven himself not to be trustworthy, to be out only for himself, and, more even than incompetence or complicity or laziness, this was, in the eyes of the family, the worst sin of them all.

Sasha's first week back at the company, dealing with Pasha, was cathartic; he needed to carry out his father's wishes now more than ever. It felt good to be doing his father's work, to have the image of his father watching over him, nodding, smiling. To make his father proud again – and for the first time in a long while. He was surprised by the pleasure he got from this, and from getting back into the rigours and rituals of everyday work. Of no longer being a prisoner. Of being in control again. Of being a responsible member of the family – and society – once again. And of, slowly but steadily, with each passing day, being restored. The weight of those five years would be with him for a long time – he had no doubt (and conversations with Doctor Maurice had assured him of this, too) – but it felt good at least to work towards a better future, to try and put the past behind him, to fill his days up as much as possible and forget his yesterdays and concentrate on tomorrow.

The only stumbling block was returning to an empty house: knowing was one thing but forgetting was another; he yearned for Safi more than ever. The emptiness – that was something to get used to. It was everywhere, all-encompassing, obliterating, terrifying. This house where he had spent so much of his life, so familiar and yet suddenly utterly disconnected from himself and his past, as though he had never set foot in it before, silence reverberating around each room – silence and regret and pain – it was just another jail. But he had to press on. What choice did he have?

Remaking his life, starting again, was not easy – indeed, few things were more difficult. But he told himself he was a survivor, from a family of survivors, that he had survived infinite suffering and surprises thus far, often not knowing when he woke up if he would see through the day – and that helped a little. But just a little. The silence helped him think, too, and then it got too much and he switched on the television or listened to music that reminded him of his childhood, of better times. He tried to get in touch with his youthful self – but he failed at that, too. He felt demolished and alone. It was the first time in his life he had hated himself. He had always been so proud, pride had been such a distinctive feature of himself and his family, and now he had no more pride, not a shred, just self-doubt and guilt and grief.

While in captivity he concentrated only on surviving – surviving the pain, pushing past another day (one of God knew how many, endless and unbearable. Now that he was free he had no desire to return to his hedonistic ways. One good woman, he understood now, was a blessing – indeed, Safi had been more than he ever deserved. Perhaps he had known on some level that he had not deserved her; perhaps that was why he had treated her – and, by extension, himself – with such contempt. No, that wasn't the answer, he knew it in his heart. He had been a spoiled, ungrateful, entitled brat. But he hoped that had changed, too.

Sasha felt remorse, a sharp, stinging feeling – like physical pain. He recalled all of the times in jail he was pummelled in the stomach, kicked in the head, levelled to the ground. Not celebrated because he was a Rubicov but punished because he was one. What was in a name, anyway? Nothing, it turned out – nothing good, anyway. Beaten on the buttocks, smashed on the knees with a club. There was no end to the ingenuity of human pain. If every time one was beaten – beaten for no reason, beaten for being born in a certain country, with a certain name; beaten for crimes you had not committed, and for crimes you had no idea about, for sins you had not yet thought of committing – it was enough coins in a jar, then after these last few months Sasha must be one of the richest men alive. And yet he felt poorer than ever. Perhaps it was better to be born a bricklayer, and to live one's life like that – having children who one would train, in turn, to be bricklayers – than a Rubicov. Perhaps being rich, in fact, was the very worst thing in the world. He had suffered so much pain, he did not think he could suffer any more. And yet he hoped he was still strong. There seemed to be no end to human resilience, just like there was no end to the pain humans inflicted upon each other.

Sasha knew he did not deserve Safi, and certainly not her love. He had taken her for granted, lied to her, cheated on her, cheapened her, even resented her purely because she had loved him so much, been so trusting and affectionate of someone who deserved none of that. Could she not see how bad he was? How naïve was she? How cruel was he? Was she really that innocent? She was an angel, loving and loyal, she had supported him through every upheaval, and he had cheated at every opportunity, leaving her to fend for herself in a strange country (and what country could be stranger than Russia, in winter).

Sasha followed what was happening in her life, in order to feel close to her, to stay connected with her, albeit in a one-sided, elusive frustrating way. Knowing she was running the new Rubicov Gallery gave him the opportunity to be involved on some level. Keeping track of the galleries' finances without her knowing gave him control over a part of her life without her knowledge, and he was going to use it.

Ilona was his entre into Safi's life, she had been sworn to secrecy as had all those who knew of his return, when he was strong enough, before she found out he was not a ghost, he would, he hoped be able to enter her life once more. Janus was now in her life but Sasha conveniently over looked this fact, it was something he hadn't acknowledged fully, couldn't and wouldn't.

The New York gallery was showing a remarkable upswing in its profits. In a time when the art world was in flux and prices for up-and-comers in decline, the Rubicov Manhattan Gallery, with its fresh feel, new (at least to New York) name, and bold exhibits, was outperforming most of the major galleries. Why? He felt sure the reason was Safi and he felt no small flush of pride. And yet… well, he could hardly take credit for her virtues. He was just glad he had not brought her completely down with him. She was good because she was good – good in every way – and perhaps some of that goodness would one day rub off on him. But still he felt proud of her. He couldn't help it; didn't want to. He loved her still. Probably he had never stopped loving her. Who else had touched his life so much? He studied the Rubicov galleries' performance since it opened its doors and, was more than a little interested to know what had caused the upturn in the Rubicov Manhattan Gallery fortunes so dramatically. Of course, he thought, to a large degree, he already knew. he was in love with her again. Had he ever not been in love with her?

His only contact on a personal level with Safi was Ilona, who spoke with her on a daily basis. On a pretext to find out more, he visited the Moscow gallery as often as he could. Ilona was now involved romantically with Ringo so she learnt of his return soon after he went back to work.

On one occasion he was in Ilona's office while she was on a Skype call with Safi. Sasha stood out of sight, but he had a perfect view of Safi as she spoke excitedly (her infectious excitement – the one he had at first fallen in love with – had not wanted!) of the gallery's newest client.

Sasha's heart ached. He could feel his heart pounding, his hands sweating. She was more beautiful than he remembered. She was no longer a girl; she had matured into a stunning, confident, commanding woman. He was in love all over again. This was not the Safi he had left behind – this was a different Safi altogether. A brighter, bolder, even more self-possessed and beautiful Safi. Now, for once, in relation with the opposite sex, it was his turn to feel vulnerable, out of his depth, even shy. Safi sat behind her desk all Sasha could really see was her beautiful large brown eyes and new shorter chic hairstyle and, her cutting English accent he loved so much.

'Ilona, Safi does not know I have returned. Please do not make the mistake of telling her. Our lives have moved on, especially Safi's, as you know,' and here he gave Ilona an unusually knowing, and quite unsettling, intimate look, 'and I do not want to upset her. She will, in time, of course, learn of my return – but,' and here he made his voice harder, perhaps harder than he had intended it to be (after all, he needed to keep this girl on his side), his occasional bullying side shifting back into play and filling him with a surprising surge of not unpleasant power, 'it must come from me, do you understand?' The question was not necessary, his tone had relayed the severity of his concern. Perhaps too severely, for Ilona suddenly looked shocked – or perhaps that was at the shock of Sasha keeping his return from Safi after everything she had been through surely, she deserved to know?

Ilona knew better than to upset Sasha; she had heard how the younger Rubicov family members had been given their marching orders after Alexi's death. She was not family, she had no real leverage with which to bargain with (although she knew she had done a good job at, and with, the Moscow gallery), Safi was the closest person she had to someone in power to depend on, and Safi's power was in itself conditional and sequestered, which was why she was terrified of whatever new developments Sasha's return would bring to bear. Ilona felt constantly uneasy, and too anxious to confide in anyone other than Safi, who in any case was her superior and had significant problems of her own.

One thing was for sure, they would not be as generous with her package if she were asked to leave. And then what? What would she do?

All she loved was art, but now that Ringo was in her life things for her had changed too. Once she had felt art was worth more than money, more than anything) – and the art she loved she could scarcely afford. Art, the symmetry, the elegance, the abstraction and peculiar clarity, the indefinable and wonderful power of it all. If only more of life was just like that. Not mundane and peculiar and awkward, like this conversation with Sasha, she wondered whether he knew of her relationship with Ringo, his right- hand man, but it wasn't her place to inform him.

'I understand,' she said with a surprising curtness that she had not intended. But she was thinking what an upstanding person Safi was, and the rumours she had heard about how Sasha had mistreated her. Not that Safi was as good as gold – Ilona knew all about her brief affair with DuPont. She had read – and quite by accident – a text message between the two. It was written in a kind of code, but not a very good code, not very good at all. Relationships of the heart were all so obvious and predictable and painfully transparent from a certain perspective – not like good art at all. Ilona knew a great deal about a great deal, which perhaps made her more useful to the Rubicov Organisation than they themselves understood.

Sasha took a seat, swivelled in a self-conscious, rather boyish manner, affected a relaxed demeanour, trying to calm his mind down. He smiled at Ilona again, attempted to manufacture his old Sasha charm, trying to soften her up. He wondered if he had any of that old charm left, or if he even wanted to regain it? It seemed it had given him nothing but trouble – a great deal of pleasure, yes, but trouble, too, and often in equal measure. There was rarely the one without the other, especially with young Russian women. He realised suddenly that he did not know Ilona – Safi's right-hand woman – at all, had barely said two words to her up to now, always viewed her as an inferior, and a rather uptight and insipid one at that. But how well did he know Safi, for that matter?

(This was just another instance of his ignorance, his indifference, about Safi's professional life, which was to say, in a very real sense, he had been indifferent to almost everything about Safi's life, except perhaps how her life fit into his – and, ultimately, perhaps, it hadn't, or not very well. After all, even before he was arrested, they had grown apart. It was difficult to forget this when viewing Safi through this prism of so much absence, and so much love. But there had been so much pain, too.)

After five years in prison, in solitude, in captivity, the only person he knew was himself – and he could do without that kind of knowledge. He longed only to strip his identity, begin anew, become someone else entirely, only with Safi at his side. But Safi too had changed, wasn't the same Safi of his memory. All of this was easier said than done. It was clear that everything and everyone had changed – perhaps most especially himself. This office belonged to his family, and yet he felt alienated and alone in it, a stranger, part of nothing. He leaned forward in his chair, deliberately keeping his distance lest Ilona – seemingly so prudish, so prim, so buttoned-up – get the wrong idea, he sensed her unease at his presence.

'Can you fill me in on our new clients in Manhattan?' He looked at her eyes, aware that he was previously unaware what colour they were. 'I have been watching the spreadsheet go up and up. Who are these new-found mega rich clients?'

Her eyes were green. The colour of money. But pale and dull and ineffable.

'Well, it's quite a story – amazing, really.'

'Astonishing, if our finances are anything to go by,' he tried to transform his suspicion into genuine interest, but it wasn't always easy – after all, he was a man of appetites, and his appetite had not been fed for a long time. '*Amazing*,' he said, repeating her word, as though trying it out for the first time, interrogating it in his way, asking her for more. But she looked uneasy now. 'And you say his show caused quite a stir'? The critics and the broadsheets made all kinds of speculations about the artist, but no one appears to know who it is' – he gave Ilona his keen, ugly interrogative look again, 'am I correct about that?'

He waited a beat, but she did not respond. He swivelled again, attempted a revolution but pulled himself back at the last moment, his legs aching dully. *Dull*. He stared at her again, this girl he hardly knew. What he knew was that she was close to Safi – possibly knew everything about her – and he hated her for that. Green eyes. Dull eyes. A dull girl.

'Yes,' she said finally, and this time her voice was not shy but bold. Perhaps not dull at all. Safi valued her for a reason, he reckoned now. There was more to this girl than first appeared. He looked at her closer. He was now trying to make her uneasy, even fearful, but after years of having fear instilled in him by others, perhaps he had forgotten how to be fearful, too? Perhaps he was merely a joke of himself. Perhaps he was the dull one.

'Isn't that ridiculous,' he said, tempering his voice again, feeling sure all of a sudden that she was on to him, knew everything about him, even things he himself was not aware of, knew his tones, his gestures, his next moves, this dull-eyed, uneducated, untitled peasant girl, feeling his old entitlement return with a flourish (and how good that too felt after years of being little more than a serf! the power of wealth! The indescribable psychological wealth of being born rich, of carrying influence around with you like a weapon, of being someone special: a rich man with a title, not quite God but the closest thing this earthly world had to Him), glaring at her now, but smiling at the same time, trying to confuse her – or himself, for it was he who felt thoroughly, unforgivably confused, removed, resigned, outside of everything he thought he knew. 'How on earth have we made so much money if the artist did not sell any work?'

'Well, that is the incredible part,' she said with a brightness that surprised him, returning her smile, leaning forward, either affecting an attitude of unexpected informality or – was it possible! – flirting with him for the first time.

Amazing, he thought. *Incredible*. All of these big and shiny and – yes – wealthy words. Not the dour, depressing language of the Russian past – Russian tractors and famine and servitude and pain – but something new. Almost American. New York.

Ilona seemed to have opened up now, perhaps she responded to his surliness, his unpredictability, nothing better than an old-Russian attitude to bring a young person back to earth, however grudgingly. He tried to figure out how old she was. Thirty, perhaps? Not so young at all. It was Yvetta who had hired her, and who thought very highly of her, too. She had been through several iterations of the Rubicov family, and knew a great deal about it, which meant she knew a great deal about him. Perhaps it was time to find out about her, in turn.

'Since the show,' she said excitedly, and for a moment reminded him almost of a less pretty, more reserved, but efficient and energetic version of Safi, 'money has been pouring into the gallery. Someone from the rich Gulf States has been buying literally thousands of dollars' worth of art though the Rubicov gallery.'

Sasha sat in silence for a while – he felt suddenly exhausted (he hadn't regained his usual rigorous routine, this extended not only to work, but to women as well), then he asked if Ilona had a video of the show. She did indeed, and opened up a full-colour, cinema-quality screen on her computer with characteristic efficiency and speed. The screen, in the centre of the flat monitor, took up just a quarter of the monitor, but since the monitor was the size of the average artwork on display in the Rubicov Gallery, this did not matter.

Now comfortable in the leather swivel chair, from which he could somehow be both upright and at rest, Sasha watched the images of the exhibition not once but three times in a row, surprising Ilona with his perspicacity and the obsessiveness of his interest. The work was quite incredible, Sasha thought, and questioned Ilona further, now enjoying her company and beginning to see what Safi saw in her. The back story told by Safi to Ilona in itself was fantastic. Furthermore, if anyone could engage trust and loyalty in a client it was Safi. He was not at all surprised, only saddened that he had missed the occasion – and so many others.

He looked at Ilona again, this time perhaps a little too long. Her face was soft and round and not, as he had initially thought, unpretty. She had a keen, quick-witted nature about her, which was somehow lost by her more inhibited characteristics, her quiet, even, sometimes even affectless voice, her tendency towards shyness, her old-fashioned but nonetheless quite refreshing formality, her shrewd and obviously well-served tendency to think carefully before speaking. And her eyes were anything but dull, he now thought. They were bright and rather beautiful.

'Who is the client?' he asked.

'Prince Musa,' she said quickly, but not in an intimidated or even especially interested manner. After all, she dealt with people who dealt with people who dealt with the rich and famous all the time. 'From the Emirates.'

Sasha hadn't heard of him, which irritated him. Really he had been away a long time. Or maybe Prince Musa was a minor player. Or a pseudonym. Or someone standing in for another buyer. Whoever the buyer was he was obviously powerful. Sasha wondered whether Safi was aware of the dangers in capturing such a demanding client, especially a Middle Eastern one. But he recalled that Safi was no longer a novice in the game, and surrounded herself with seasoned players – like DuPont. DuPont, Sasha thought with a wince. He hadn't thought of that name for a long time, and hadn't missed thinking about it, either. That lubricious lothario long past his expiration date. With his fancy French – dressed up and overdone, like everything else about him (Americans were such suckers for foreign accents – even in some parts of New York City) – and infinite array of contacts. He dropped names the way people dropped twenty-dollar bills in private clubs. He wondered how – and in what way, exactly – DuPont had comforted Safi in Sasha's absence. Had he facilitated Safi's introduction to this Prince Musa? And what was DuPont's angle in all of this? DuPont always had an angle. Everyone in New York did.

He needed to know more about Prince Musa. Was he buying more than just art from the Rubicov Gallery? He knew it was no longer any of his business – he knew this, but he did not feel it, and the heart and the brain were entirely different organs, and often uniquely opposed – yet he felt the need to be protective of Safi. Or was *protection* the word?

'Well, I know that Safi has flown on their airline a number of times,' Ilona said, her characteristic reserve failing her for once – a victim of Sasha's charm (which really was sizeable, and palpable – she could understand it now, why the women fell for him: his even, intense gaze, the set of his mouth, his taut face and good chin, the occasional and always rewarding smile), suddenly wondering if she had said too much but not at all able to help herself, 'apparently she can use it whenever she wishes on any of their routes as their guest.' Ilona smiled back – not as practiced or as pretty, as vibrant and enticing and immediate, as Sasha's smile, but a valiant attempt nonetheless (born without a father, and into a family of women, she had never learnt how to flirt – working hard and moving up in the art world was her true passion; observing art her erotic joy), as she realised that getting on Sasha's good-side, supplying him with valuable information, as long as it did not directly betray Safi, may not be the worst thing in the world. After all, Sasha – not Safi – was part of the Rubicov Organisation, and helped to decide its operations and its fate.

After all, look at how Anna (and then Mika's) attachment to Ringo – like her an outsider – had elevated him to almost the highest echelon of the organisation. She admired Ringo and thought of him with a curious mixture of envy and affection, now love. She remembered how he had in the past, greeted her with his usual familiarity and jocularity, ,but since the Rubicov company problems manifested and Ringo became their lynch pin, they had bonded. Ringo communicated with Safi and Ilona which in turn brought Ringo into her life and she wasn't about to spoil that in any way for either of them, she would keep her personal life personal from Sasha.

Sasha leaned forward, stretched his arms out on the oak desk, rewarded her with another smile – this one deeper, more intimate, more meaningful somehow. He seemed to be telling her something – but what? Once Ilona started, it was not easy to stop. She felt simultaneously mischievous, ambitious, duplicitous, loyal, smart, dumb – to hell with it all! She felt she was cutting loose, putting everything on the line – and perhaps for the first time. And it felt good.

'DuPont says that Prince Musa has taken Safi into his inner circle,' she made a circle with the fingers of one hand, but still did not look away from Sasha's gaze, 'entrusting her with their youngest son, who apparently has taken a shine to her in a big way.'

'How old is the son?'

'Oh, a teenager,' Ilona said, after such a rush of excitement suddenly restraining herself, coming to her senses, realising that she was on the edge of going too far. She had to be careful: Sasha was obviously not over Safi, and teasing him was dangerous, Ringo had mentioned how insecure and tortured Sasha appeared since his return like treading water trying to find his footing. This much was evident in everything from his body language to his misplaced (and surprisingly sloppy) attempt to flirt with her, from the way he said Safi's name, the frequency, the tone, the echo of it afterwards. She wondered why Safi had not been told of his escape and return; she felt it very unfair, knowing how loyal Safi had been, and still was, to the Rubicov's. What Safi had gone through – Ilona couldn't even imagine how it must have felt, and yet Safi rarely confided in her, always kept things professional, spoke about work – her resilience, diligence, intelligence, resolve.

Noting her sudden reticence, stiffening in the chair, a barely suppressed flash of anger in him now, feeling this meeting (or whatever it was) was long past over, Sasha said in a firm tone, commanding but not angry, reasserting his hierarchy after playing her peer,

'I want to be informed of all dealings Safi has with this Middle Eastern prince in future. I want to know when and where she travels with him, and about all large acquisitions bought through the gallery.' There was no doubt in his tone – he was deadly serious, and he was in charge once again. Perhaps the old Sasha was back.

Anna and Mika were not happy with Sasha's decision not to immediately inform Safi of his return. Mika had not confided in Janus of Sasha's return, he respected his brother's request for time and privacy to come to terms with what had happened. After all, despite their differences over the years, he had his brother's best interest at heart. He was firmly of the opinion that until anyone had, God forbid, been through what Sasha had been through, they didn't have a right to dictate the terms of Sasha's re-introduction into society. And God forbid, if things had turned out differently, it could have been him in prison rather than Sasha; those lost years would have been his. Far from being a criminal, he now understood, after hearing Sasha's full account, Sasha had done the entire family an invaluable service: he had suffered for them all. It was time now to repay the favour, and allow him the luxury, indulgence, and sensitivity of a smooth landing, so to speak. He had no doubt it would take time. Allow him to settle into work, regain his footing, adjust to what was new and what was lost (Alexi most of all), an environment changed in some ways inviolably, not just in Russia but globally as well, gain his confidence, his independence, his authority back at the helm of an organisation which could flourish even further with the nightmares of the last few years behind it. His private life was, after all, his own business. How he planned to conduct it was his affair. Mika could only help so much. Indeed, he felt that when it came to Safi he had already helped too much. It was time for Mika to step away, and to return to his own past life. The madness, he hoped, was finally over.

Marina was now studying journalism and had grown into a stunning young woman. She visited on occasion, staying with Sasha at their family home in Moscow. Valentina mostly visited St Petersburg, her home town with Marina to visit, her mother, but had managed to secure Marina an in-depth interview with the Bolshoi Ballet company in Moscow. Valentina had inherited Alexi's considerable personal fortune. Valentina had never had an interest in the Rubicov business (which was, in fact, one of the aspects Alexi had loved most about her: she truly – truly – wasn't interested in wealth; this was not to say that some of her tastes did not run, quite naturally, to the ostentatious and antique, but that no one could ever call her a gold-digger, a meddler, or a kingpin-in-waiting). She had maintained her distance following her own interest throughout their marriage. Sasha loved having his younger sister Marina around – her vitality, her optimism, her youth – she boosted his morale and kept him from moping around when not at work.

Once his friends learnt of his return, they had tried but given up trying to include him in their social lives, and for the most part Sasha had put them on hold, neglected their calls, ignored or postponed their visits, even pushed them away. He needed time to adjust, yet months had gone by and still he showed little if no interest in his friends or his past life. Old girlfriends called, tried to visit, draw him out, tempt him into bed, seduce him anew, regale him with anecdotes about their past or incidents from the years he missed, to little avail.

Right now, though, only two people mattered to him – the presence of his sister and the absence of Safi. Marina's visits spurred him, re-energised and filled him with optimism, the optimism he himself had been so filled with years before. She was the antidote to all that was bad or stale or sordid or cruel in his world. She was his shining sun. He made the effort to entertain her, taking her to the theatre, which slowly reengaged him with his social life once more. Introducing his little sister Marina to Moscow reminded him of his early years in the city with Safi, schooling her and spoiling her, enchanted evenings of laughter and vodka and fun. It was nice to have a young person under his wing. Since his return to Moscow, he was full of regret, kept running through in his life all the options he had once had, all the choices he had made, and the mistakes, too. Perhaps he should have had a child. Perhaps he still should.

But with whom? Imagine bringing a bright, buoyant, innocent boy or girl into the Rubicov family, which meant the Rubicov Organisation (for there was little difference anymore), with all the dangers, corruption, and complicity that entailed? Alexi Rubicov had made the Rubicov family business – and that same family business, with all of its complications, its corner-cutting and political gladhanding, its attendant stress and strife (normal people didn't know how hard it was to be filthy rich; if they had any inkling of its pressure, they may be happy with their lot), had also killed him. No, to be part of the Rubicov clan was to be always close to trouble, and trouble was one thing Sasha had had enough of. In jail he had had time to think all of this through. In jail, at certain moments, all he was to his captors was a Rubicov, and, at other moments, he was nothing at all, subhuman, vermin, scum.

Too much money, too much trouble. It was better to have less of both, and to keep your interaction with innocent people to a minimum. Safi, he reflected now, was lucky to have her freedom, to have returned to a relatively normal life. How normal. Well, he needed to investigate that further – he couldn't stop thinking about her, even though he knew he shouldn't. He knew he should never re-enter her life, but what one knows and what one wants are two different things.

Tania, an old girlfriend, from a life time before Safi had returned to Moscow from working abroad, re-entered his life. Sasha had dated her on occasion. For ever the playboy, he had never given her serious thought. Now she was a permanent fixture in his life, he found himself going out with her two or three times a week, sometimes more. He found being involved helped heal the hole Safi had left. Tania was very different from Safi, of course – but in this case, that was a good thing, she was blonde and petite and had a no-nonsense blunt personality, she did not do small talk. Still, she made him realise how much he missed Safi, and being intimately connected to another human being.

Tania was vivacious, fun, alert and informed on the Moscow social scene, familiar with all of the clubs and all of the major players, on first-name basis with bouncers and moguls alike, used to being on the arms – and laps – of famous men, and, in her own way, exceedingly charming, though in a somewhat jaded, knowing way. Not only was Tania the opposite of Marina, but Sasha wouldn't dream of introducing the two women.

Tania was ready for anything he offered – she spoke three languages, but 'no' didn't appear to be in the vocabulary of any of them. And yet, in bed, she was, if not restrained (no, she was never that), oddly uninteresting, lacking real passion, perhaps. Even though Sasha hadn't been with a woman in his own social circle for years. He and Tania quickly fell back into a familiar, if mild and modulated rhythm – it wasn't exactly exciting, but it wasn't mechanical, either; it was just serviceable and that was enough. He still thought too much about Safi, even when he was with Tania. Sometimes his expression would go blank, he would stop speaking at a dinner table or cocktail party, and Tania would wonder why – what was (or wasn't) he thinking about? How much he must have suffered in the years since she had seen him last. And yet she rarely asked because she did not want to be confronted with his truth, to hear his sadness, to give him fresh pain. No, what Tania wanted was to have fun with him and to bring him back to life. And in this she partially succeeded. Tania didn't do depth, she didn't do philosophy or profundity, she did *fun* – and she did it very, very well. If Tania had a philosophy at all, it would be what used to be called hedonism but was now more widely referred to as being young and free. Sex with Tania was just sex, Sasha had little interest in his former lifestyle of wild sex parties and drugs.

The drug scene bored him and didn't even work all that well on him anymore. What he wanted was contemplation, relaxation, and, yes, freedom – freedom from guilt and pain and self-doubt and self-hatred. Freedom from other people, and from himself. Besides, he was no longer young (Tania had been surprised one night when he announced he was tired shortly after midnight – was this the same Sasha of long ago? evidently no), although not yet old. He was beginning to feel different – not tired, just different, resigned to his life and his position in both the company and the city, less irresponsible, more mature. When Tania wasn't sitting on his lap, she was twisting his arm. Have another line of coke? No thanks, I'd prefer a cup of coffee and a waiting car to take me home.

Safi was never far from his thoughts. She hovered in the back of his mind, and he thought of her especially when he was out with other women, sometimes unconsciously comparing them to her. Once or twice, in a crowded club, he thought he saw Safi, felt a shudder move through him like a chill, like a drug. The way that women wore her hair, a sudden movement, a laugh, a bare elbow. But no, Safi was far from Russia, and thank God for that. She would never be coming back. He saw his past with her in an almost loop, the sublime moments – late nights in luxurious hotels, late mornings in bed, breakfast and lovemaking and idle chatter and more lovemaking – but also the bad moments, the moments he had betrayed her, the lies, the late nights with other women in other hotels, the telephone calls cut short, the wounded feelings, the brutality and carelessness of unfaithfulness, the weird distances and half-sentences and the half-hearted and cursory attempts at atonement, of making up for the emptiness betrayal, even if the other partner didn't know what had happened. Well, they always knew, on some level, didn't they? He regretted every moment he cheated on her; every moment he purposely spent away from her. Now she wasn't in his life any longer, and he deserved it, and it hurt like hell. It hurt all the time and he couldn't deal with it any longer, he decided. He could never see her again. No. He had to see her. As soon as possible. He didn't have a choice. But was it fair to her? He had lied to her enough already. Enough betrayal, enough secrets, enough lies. Put everything on the table and if she never wanted to see him again then so be it. But at least give her the choice. She was a strong enough woman to decide for herself – that was why he had fallen in love with her, why he was still in love with her, because of her strength. He found it difficult to come to terms with his former lifestyle, which seemed so empty and, in some ways, even repellent, to reconcile himself with himself. Now, for the first time, he could look closely at himself and recognise his shortcomings, and his sins. His selfishness, for one thing, typical of spoiled rich brats, but so tiresome and – surely – not so difficult to self-correct. His perceived superiority – what was that? It was as illusory as air. He was Sasha Rubicov of one of the wealthiest families in Russia, certainly, but he was also Sasha Rubicov who had been in jail, hiding out in a camp, beaten even beyond recognition. He was everyone and no one. There was nothing special about Sasha Rubicov. And he realised how lucky he was to be alive, and to make the most of what time he had left. He realised, too, his lack of empathy for the people he loved most; perhaps he was like his sister in some ways. He needed to work harder, be better, be more empathic and inclusive, like Safi. And he was determined to change.

No one had heard from Yvetta or Fritzi. All Mika's efforts to track them down had come to naught. The family would continue to follow every lead, of course. Sooner or later Yvetta would show her hand. One thing was for sure, no one was safe with Fritzi on the loose.

Sasha considered flying to New York, having a meeting with Safi and begging her forgiveness. He thought of every angle, but none were acceptable; nothing felt right. Ideas popped into his mind continuously, but he rejected each scenario out of hand; none were realistic.

The more he struggled with a plan of action, the less confidence he had of his chances to win her back.

His family were unhappy with his decision to keep Safi in the dark. Mika did not want her to hear from another source. The longer Sasha put it off, the more chance there was of Safi finding out from someone unrelated to the family. Mika gave Sasha an ultimatum: it was time for Sasha to either tell her himself, or Mika would discuss how to break the news to her with Janus, who she was still engaged to.

Marina was keen to visit Manhattan with Sasha, and to visit with Safi, who she had always had a bond with; she was throwing hints every moment she had. 'Come on, Sasha,' Marina would say, 'take some time off, especially now when I have a break from shadowing the Bolshoi Ballet Academy.' The Academy was on a well-earned break.

Sasha decided to take the chance; he no longer had an option. He had asked Ilona to make an appointment with Safi to meet him at the Bowery on the Upper East Side; the lounges were dark with private areas to meet someone, and there he would not feel on show. Jemma, the restaurant, was easy Italian if she agreed to have brunch, and he recalled that she had stayed at the Bowery with her family when they became engaged so many years ago now. Ilona was to tell Safi she was meeting a prospective client.

Sasha no longer had their plane, so he had his secretary reserve two first-class seats to JFK on Emirates, an airline he wanted to try, since Safi now flew as a guest. He found it interesting to experience their luxury cabins for himself.

Safi had enquired about the client and agreed to meet him at 9 before she started at the gallery, which opened at 10.30. Marina had a day shopping with one of her many friends from college who now lived in Manhattan, so Sasha was free to do as he pleased. They had arrived the day before and had settled into his apartment. Sasha arrived at the

Bowery early. Manhattan felt so familiar as if he'd never left, the frenetic pace and jumble of storefronts all a welcome aphrodisiac as he briskly walked the blocks taking in the smells and sights. On arrival at the Bowery, he ordered coffee, and settled down to read the papers – but found it almost impossible to concentrate. He kept checking at the reception desk, reminding them where he was seated when his guest arrived.

The long dark shabby-chic seating areas were deserted apart from one other guest reading the papers near an alcove with a roaring log fire. Sasha had chosen deep leather seats near the reception obscured by palm trees. He looked up and saw a tall elegant woman looking around. With a shock he realised it was Safi: she now had shoulder-length hair swept away from her forehead. He had not recognised her at first glance. She swung round as he rose up; for a moment they stared at one another. Neither moved.

Safi put her hand to her mouth to stifle the sound that escaped as she realised the man standing across from her was Sasha. Finding his legs wobbly, his mind a blur, the moment stretched unbearably taut, then exploded as he walked slowly towards her. Not sure how she would react, he enveloped her in his arms. For a moment she collapsed into him; both had tears running down their cheeks. Gathering a semblance of decorum, she stood back to look at him. He had changed. Gone was any sign of his youthful charm and easy smile; instead, she was staring at a more serious version of the young man she had once been engaged to.

She followed Sasha to the seating area, still too bemused to know what to think. They sat staring at one another, thoughts racing through their minds. The choice of venue had not gone unnoticed by Safi and, it brought back painful memories of their earlier relationship; the beginning of their turbulent love life; leading to Sasha's disappearance, an absence which had consumed and eclipsed so much of her life these last few years. Where to begin when so much had happened?

'I guess you chose this hotel for a reason,' she said, 'since it's where my family stayed when we got engaged.'

'Yes and no,' he said, suddenly flummoxed by the complexity of what was supposed to be a simple response. He certainly had not meant to make their reunion *more* complicated. 'Yes because it was familiar. And no because I could not think where else to meet. It just seemed right.'

Safi had to agree it was the perfect place to meet; it felt familiar to her, too.

'How are you. Sasha?'

'Physically I am fine. So much has happened to me and to you. It's tough to come to terms with how much my life changed in a split second. One moment I was free, my life was my own. And the next moment, well I wasn't free at all!'

'What happened? I know the government apprehended you. But after they released you, these people just kidnapped you in broad daylight?'

'Fritzi helped them,' Sasha said. 'You know that, don't you?'

'I did not know that,' Safi said. 'She was in jail here, you know. How on earth was she involved exactly?'

Safi listened with astonishment as Sasha related what had happened to him, and how Fritzi had helped him escape with the purpose of masterminding Yvetta's release from the psychiatric institution.

'Safi, I was thoughtless and stupid, a fool. I deserved to lose you. I wonder whether you can forgive my behaviour towards you in Russia. It was more than thoughtless – it was cruel to leave you alone in a strange country the way I did.'

He could tell from her expression that she knew about his wild philandering, his cocaine habit and his drinking, while she sat alone day after day in the apartment.

Safi could tell he was suffering, but she could not bring herself to forgive him out of hand. He had suffered terribly, but so had she.

'Yvetta warned me you were not the perfect angel, as she liked to refer to you. I never believed her though, because she wasn't exactly trustworthy where reality was concerned.'

'How long have you been free?' She looked at him closer as though realising something. The once familiar but now curiously distant face becoming familiar again. 'Does everyone know but me?'

Sasha sat for what seemed like ages, staring at Safi; his thoughts were all over the place; his emotions were not under control. Internally, he was experiencing something he had not bargained for; he was still very much in love with Safi.

'Again, I am sorry. I needed time to heal and to get my head together, before I had the strength to face you to tell you myself. I just wasn't ready before. I had to come to terms with so much loss.'

'Yes,' Safi said, nodding. She remembered his father's passing with a shudder. 'I am so sorry about Alexi; it was such a shock.'

She could hear a tremor in his voice, looked up to see him shaking slightly. It was so terribly difficult to be angry with Sasha. As much as she tried, she could not bring herself to condemn him for his past behaviour.

'When we were at his funeral,' she said slowly, remembering everything again as though from a fresh perspective, 'I had this unbelievably strong premonition that you were there. But now I know it was my imagination getting the better of me – or wishful thinking perhaps.'

Sasha stared at her for a long time before he spoke.

'You know, losing my father, facing death almost every day while in captivity, then dealing with Fritzi and Yvetta – finding out I had lost you, too, on top of that – you, my strongest ally and greatest blessing, my love – was overwhelming. When you were in my life I had everything. When I lost you I lost everything. I wasn't sure how to cope at first – actually, I'm pretty sure I didn't cope at all.; Facing my demons made me realise that I never knew what I had – or that I was the luckiest man alive – until I lost the people I loved. I love you, Safi. I can't pretend I don't. Just being near you is enough for me right now.'

Safi looked startled. Sasha looked closely at Safi and, once again, but also for the first time in so many years at those beautiful long-lashes fluttering in surprise, he closed his eyes, every day he was away from her, was torture. She had not expected Sasha to be so honest about his feelings. She felt confused, felt that perhaps he had too much power over her – deliciously so – like the first time she ever saw him, at the Rubicov restaurants opening party, herself newly arrived in New York. Being with him seemed so natural, rekindled feelings she did not know she still felt.

'Sasha, you know I am engaged to Janus.'

'I know,' he said, finding his voice, speaking firmly now for the first time, his confidence growing with each word, 'yet I find it hard to believe you love someone else. I do respect that you do. Yet you are so close to me every day. I have been following your progress with the Manhattan gallery through Ilona. Please don't be upset with her, she was sworn to secrecy.'

'Then you must know that we are now one of the most respected galleries in Manhattan and around the world. And financially successful, too.'

'Ah yes, the prince from the Emirates.'

'Ilona obviously filled you in.'

'No, but maybe you could. I obviously took an interest when the profits kept increasing. He has spent literally millions.'

For a moment Safi felt protective towards the prince and his son, but then she realised Sasha was entitled to know the backstory; after all, it was a Rubicov Gallery; she was only an employee, one of thousands. If she were honest with herself, she had very little claim on the gallery; it still belonged to a Rubicov; bore the Rubicov family name.

'Yes, you are entitled to know, but let's discuss business another time, maybe at the gallery.'

Sasha was playing for time; he wanted to keep Safi from leaving, but cared little about the prince and his autistic son. Any gallery would kill for a client like Prince Musa Alif Abdullah Rani. A background check had been done, of course; there was nothing more to learn about the oil-rich little state in the desert; far be it from him to make waves when they had such a rich collector.

They both sat in silence for a few moments, each in their own thoughts; neither wanted to upset the other, but Safi knew she would have to leave shortly. The dim oppressive lighting in the lounge was getting to her; she needed fresh air to clear her mind. The shock of seeing Sasha had left her reeling; a brisk walk would help.

'Sasha, this has been quite a shock to my system. I am struggling to cope with my feelings. Perhaps we could see one another again tomorrow at the gallery.'

Standing she smoothed down her skirt and leaned over as he stood to hug her. She could feel his heart beating – or, wait, was that her own heart she could hear? She quickly disengaged from his embrace and pecked him lightly on the cheek, but Sasha turned his face and she felt his soft lips brush hers. A frisson of electricity shot through her. The feeling scared her and she moved away.

'Let's meet for brunch tomorrow near the gallery? Sasha requested

Sasha sank back into the leather armchair. Safi might have left, yet to him she was still present: her perfume filled his senses as did her touch, which he could still feel burning into his lips. He knew without a doubt that he still had an effect on her, as she had on him. There was no way in the world he was not going to fight to get her back.

His time in Moscow had gone well, he no longer feared the government, he was their golden boy Since the capture of the smugglers who he hoped were rotting in a Russian jail, his time in Moscow was healing; and, Ringo had once more proved his worth and together they had streamlined the company's Russian enterprises, finally modernising and innovating the company, while also cutting off a lot of dead weight. Some of the younger family members were successfully forging ahead with their own ideas. Sasha felt good about all of this. At last, he felt he could relax. It was time to visit Mika in Florida then fly to France to visit with his mother.

Sasha called his sister Marina – with seeing Safi so much on his mind, he felt he had neglected her. Hopefully her friend had shown her a good time and taken her to shops – that mattered at Marina's age. He would make it up to her. They would eat out at one of Manhattan's chic restaurants, giving her a chance to wear one of her new outfits.

Back at the apartment he called down to the restaurant to enquire where he should take a teenager for dinner. He felt that his old haunts were more than likely no longer cool or in existence. But maybe that was a good thing. Start afresh! See the city as Marina saw it, through innocent eyes. Marina deserved to be spoilt; she missed their father as much, if not more, than Sasha.

Valentina had become totally engrossed in the world of ballet. Sasha had heard that she had taken up with one of the directors of a Danish ballet school. He could not blame her; she was still young and attractive and independent of means. Marina would be starting university after her gap year, which left Valentina facing a very empty life after Alexi's death. She had always been a pragmatic woman and a wonderful wife to his father; he wished her happiness.

'Oh, mama, stop fretting,' Sasha heard his baby sister gigging on the telephone, 'Sasha has been great. I have had the most fantastic day shopping. It's so incredibly cool here. We are going out to one of the hippest places in town, and I am wearing one of my new dresses. Don't worry, I am sure Sasha won't let me go out in something less than spectacular.'

With her own ineffable energy and the optimism of the attractive teenager, Marina was a welcome distraction from his thoughts and she would keep them filled with her chatter over dinner, until he met Safi for brunch the following morning.

Safi's cell rang incessantly throughout her fifteen block walk back to the gallery from the Bowery. She was in her own world. Eventually she glanced at the calls and noted four from Janus, who had also left a string of messages. She turned the cell to silent, feeling relief as she did so. She just could not cope with anything or anyone right now: her head was throbbing, her heart was aching, and she had a tension headache. The only person she wanted to talk with was DuPont: he would listen without judgement, give her the opportunity to vent her emotions, and help her find what her heart, not her head, was screaming.

She sent him a text to see if he was free; she needed his undivided attention (she did not want to share him with his usual business contacts around the globe).

Finding work impossible she sat at her desk in a daze, her thoughts returned repeatedly to Sasha. What a shock to see him again in the flesh – it was a possibility she had buried deep down, tired of being wounded, disappointed, over and over. The hope she had once held had died after Alexi's death and the drone attack. She had moved on, finally, reluctantly. What choice had she had? She waited impatiently for DuPont to reply. There was no way she could spend a night on her own, and going back to Janus was not an option, either – it was much too far.

Janus had the usual brief conversation when she returned his call, he allowed himself only a limited time for small talk, his work engulfed every waking moment. She was thankful for their shared weekends, she had not mentioned Sasha it would have to wait for the weekend, she wondered whether he knew that Sasha was alive; everyone else seemed to but her?

Safi tried DuPont again; he was not picking up her calls. She must have left dozens of messages, where the hell was, he? She tried to remember if he had gone out of town but couldn't. A customer came into the gallery interested in something particular usually Safi liked to deal with celebrities when they were shopping for art. She had the knack of helping them make a decision, even allowing them to live with a painting or sculpture for a few days, sending someone round to install or hang it, in most cases they never returned the work. As she walked into the gallery to engage with the customer, she noticed the long-awaited answer from DuPont and was relieved he had suggested meeting her at their usual small Italian neighbourhood hangout a perfect place to pour out her heart.

The celeb took up the rest of the afternoon and as usual left having arranged for a painting to be installed in his New York loft, to be decided, it would be a sure thing they usually found it hard to part with a piece of art once in their own space. She never encouraged work that sat uncomfortably with their tastes, they had to live with it after all, it had to please them not impress their friends, which was often a reason for an expensive purchase.

DuPont was waiting at the bar; one look at Safi told him she had something important on her mind. He ordered a peach Bellini, watched her down it, and asked for another to be brought to the table. Safi leaned over conspiratorially and said, 'Sasha is alive. I saw him this morning.'

'You *saw* him?

'We met – at the Bowery, of all places.'

But DuPont was strangely silent now. It took Safi a moment to register his expression, his surprise – or, actually, lack thereof.

DuPont sat in silence it took Safi a moment to collect her thoughts,

'Oh my God, you knew he was alive,' Safi said, 'you *knew*; everyone knew but me. How could you not tell me! Why did you not tell me, for God's sake! Didn't I deserve to know? After all this time! What is this conspiracy of silence all about?'

'Ilona told me Sasha came to her in Moscow, asking her questions she could not answer. She asked him to speak with me directly, to explain the hike in your figures at the gallery. The fortune the Rubicov Manhattan Gallery was bringing in was extraordinary; there was no way it would not cause a stir.'

She shook her head.

'Yes, but why not me, why you? Oh, I know the answer to that, but I can't deal with my emotions or my thoughts, they are all over the place. I have tried to be pragmatic, but I can't. I have no idea how to handle this, it's churning up all kinds of unfinished emotions. I haven't even told Janus that we've met. I suppose he knows Sasha is alive, too?'

'I have no idea what he knows. I presume through Mika he must know.'

'A part of me is trying to understand the secrecy but I can't pretend not to feel anger at being kept in the dark for so long about someone who I love.'

Tears had welled up in her eyes and she brushed them away with a napkin. The waiter was asking her a question, far off she heard DuPont answer for her, her mind went blank. She became frightened feeling her equilibrium upside down; gone was her settled existence.

'Safi we have been here before haven't we, *chérie*?'

'What do you mean exactly?'

He could tell she was irritated by this remark, nevertheless he was determined to make her examine her feelings; she needed to work out what it was that attracted her to Sasha before turning her life upside down yet again.

'I mean just that, you tend to lose all perspective on reality when Sasha steps back into the picture after breakups, fall outs and do not forget your tryst with me, what was that about if you were so much in love, something about him turns your otherwise sensible self-upside down, don't you agree?'

'You have a point he brings out a disagreeable side in my nature not only that I feel incredibly alive when I am with him, the chemistry is still there, but I am not sure if that's love, what do you think?'

'Ah, the million-dollar question, what do you want stability or chemistry?'

'I have stability with Janus but I will always be second, his work comes first, he does not want a family but I do, it's not all plain sailing?'

'When did you realise this, you have not said anything'?

'I know, I wondered whether he would change his mind, but knowing Janus he won't. I was trying to ignore my own feelings to please him, why on earth do I do this? I did the same with Sasha, I ignored the signs of his philandering and rotten behaviour towards me. I threw myself into the Rubicov gallery found a way of belonging to the Muscovite society that Sasha moved in, even though I succeeded he still continued to string me along. I was just another conquest even though he was supposed to love me, we were engaged for goodness sake. He wanted to marry me! Go figure, as the American's love to say!'

'Do you mind if we leave seduction out of this conversation where we're concerned, we enjoyed it while it lasted, but haven't we gone past that now in our friendship?'

'We?' he said, smiling. 'Cheri, we have, I love you, you know this right?'

'And I love you, but no longer as a lover or, you me?'

DuPont laughed took the back of her hand and kissed it, looked her in the eye mischievously.

'You are such an innocent, you are beautiful, intelligent and wonderful company when not being a cry baby, what's not to love?'

'Ah now you are teasing me stop it immediately, I am not in the mood for your French charm I have a genuine problem and, difficult choices to make. I need you to be serious with me what do I do?'

'Ah well, not so easy, oui? As a Frenchman the operative word is 'love' you are English so you think too much, get lost in that psychobabble drama, I would prefer you to lose yourself in making love.'

'DuPont are you suggesting I cheat on Janus?'

Laughing he said, 'Am I so repulsive?'

'No, but it's not about you.'

'Sadly.'

'You were devastated about Sasha in a deep depression, it took Janus to bring you out of. Now Sasha has appeared on the scene again and you are once more lost, no? I have given you my suggestion, do what your heart and emotions dictate and deal with what happens after?'

'I don't know, I will be with Janus this weekend perhaps knowing Sasha is back will resolve our relationship one way or another, we seem to be stuck in a stale mate at the moment and, if we can get past that, I may know what I want.'

DuPont nodded, paid the bill and left. Safi hugged him goodbye. 'Thank you for putting up with me, I do love you.'

'Oui, oui, goodnight, *chérie*.'

Sasha was sitting at a window table watching as she crossed the road, standing as she entered. His features tense with nervous apprehension, the tension broken by a waiter filling their mugs with coffee as he swept off to another table Sasha leaned over to kiss Safi hello on both cheeks.

The softness of his lips on her cheek sent spasms of electricity through her body and as he reached for the other side she turned her face towards him, his lips brushed hers, their eyes locked and, in that moment, volumes were spoken without a word passing between them. The silence continued yet the tension had evaporated, they both knew what would happen next or would it, neither spoke too frightened to break the spell.

Safi looked up at the waiter relieved he had returned to take their order forcing them back to reality.

Alone once more Sasha leaned across the table grasping Safi's hands in his. 'Say something, please?'

'It's too hard, Sasha, the whole situation is just unbearable.'

'Because you are engaged to Janus?'

She nodded. 'And so much more much, much more.'

'Trusting me again, I know, why should you?'

She nodded, 'I deserve everything you throw at me nothing you say could make me hate myself more than I do, for putting you through such hell, yet deep inside I believe in us, that we'll be okay if we can move forward from this?'

The breakfast arrived and they ate in silence, both in their own thoughts from time to time their eyes met, the space between them evaporating with physical desire it was palpable every fibre in their bodies were on fire. If they touched it was over their longing painfully obvious yet both were reluctant to be the first.

The bus boy returned to fetch their plates, the waiter followed with the bill, both reached out to grab it and it was over, Sasha threw bills on the table, they grabbed their coats and ran for the door. Sasha was holding onto her hand and hailed a cab with the other, once inside they kissed passionately.

'Come to my place, I don't want old memories to come between us'

A toddler and mum were in the elevator with them, Safi found herself staring at the toddler not thinking she leant into Sasha, somehow seeing the toddler had made everything in her mind crystal clear, she wanted to be a mom, she knew that now, what ever happened she could not marry Janus.

Once inside the apartment they fell onto the bed, their tongues touching felt so sensuous both shuddered with the intensity of their embrace. Slowly Sasha moved his tongue down her neck lifted her silk shirt, found her nipples circling his tongue lightly on her erect nipples, Safi's mind exploded with desire, her body felt alive with longing. Sasha had pulled her skirt above her waist, ripped her panties, sinking his tongue into her. She had never before felt such intensity. Exploding with that intensity, her whole body lifted off the bed, and she arched her back with the tension of her orgasm.

He entered pushing deep inside pressing his body hard against her as they both came together. They clung together for what seemed ages Sasha stared at Safi hardly believing it wasn't a dream pinching her bum, yelping she jumped on top of him kissing him relentlessly, both finding it hard to comprehend after so long that they were once more together and in each other's arms. They made love repeatedly collapsing with exhaustion as their bodies shook with each rhythmic throbbing release.

Safi thought what she had just had was a religious experience, she had never felt at one with another human being before and it was so incredibly wonderful. She knew he had, had the same experience unabashed tears were running down his cheeks. She lay her head onto his chest his heart was pounding into her ears and for the first time since knowing he was alive, she became aware how precious it was to have him back in her life again. They had a second chance to be together again.

Part II
Chapter 12

Dawn light filtered in through the mosquito nets covering the four-poster bed; twisted crisp white sheets barely covered the long brown legs stretched out beside her. She lay for a while enjoying the sounds of the bush breaking the silence of the day to come: hot, dry and dusty. She waited knowing it would come at any moment to wake them for another exhilarating day: that daily knock on the door at exactly 4am. Breakfast laid out on a long black mahogany table overlooking the dry arid Namib desert. If she squinted, she could just make out the outline of a buck or zebra at a shallow, fast-drying drinking hole in the hazy distance.

Six months had passed since they arrived in this heavenly country far away from a life she no longer owned or wanted. A truck waited at the tiny airport where English, German, and a spattering of a language she learnt was not Dutch, but Afrikaans was spoken. Nico, their driver, spoke all three fluently to whomever addressed him in any one of the three languages.

He tossed their few belongings into the back of the pickup truck covered with a dusty canvas tarpaulin. As they covered the endless dusty road ahead, his pleasant voice lulled them with his impressive knowledge about every bush and tree. The only contact with the outside world was the old-fashioned walkie-talkie crackling into life intermittently. Each person became trapped in their own spiritual stillness as the landscape changed from shrub to lunar rock formations.

The miles were only broken occasionally, an oasis in the middle of nowhere along the endless journey to the Skeleton Coast, where Fritzi's uncle owned a five-star lodge popular with mostly foreigners, many of them German.

Yvetta and Fritzi intended staying only a few days before setting off on their own adventures in Namibia, what (before the country's independence in 1990) had been the old South West Africa, a German colony bordering South Africa and Angola now their new temporary home.

Sossusvlei was an oasis they both returned to so Yvetta could ski down the formidably high sand dunes and trek into the desert in an open Jeep in order to fly over the landscape with Andre the Frenchman in his air balloon at the crack of dawn. Today was another of those wonderful days when she would look down over the endless veld, watching sand elephants trekking or lone zebra running with buck looking for food and water. One could not imagine how they survived, but each year the rains came and the desert bloomed and filled with water for only a short period – to Yvetta this was heaven on earth.

Fritzi marvelled at how communing with nature had healed Yvetta from her nightmare, being locked away in clinic after clinic, each more terrifying than the next, a hostage to her family's oppressive indifference. She was happy to indulge her darling Shatzi in anything her heart desired: she had never seen her happier. Yvetta had not suffered one episode since leaving Russia and her hateful Rubicov family or their vast business empire.

They had found the most incredible home in the colonial coastal town of Swakopmund, close to Walvis Bay, one a German Colonial town the other British Colonial, with endless beaches and madly dangerous sporting pursuits. Here being German went unnoticed; one could melt into the indigenous population without much fuss from anyone, tourist or inhabitant.

Ships from Russia often sailed through on their way to the Cape, so even Yvetta's slight Russian accent went without comment. It was a perfect haven to escape to.

They travelled to the Etosha National Park close to the Skeleton Coast bordering Angola, no longer a battlefield between the South Africans and the communists. Flying over the Etosha Pan was a turning point in Yvetta's state of mind, she left her torturous memories of Russia and her family far behind, revelling in the wild life stretching out in the endless lush escarpment below. Sleeping in the open bush, washing in streams along the way became her saviour; as far as Fritzi was concerned, they could remain here for ever.

Yvetta was happy their relationship had gone from strength to strength: it was bliss not to be hounded by the authorities, but she knew the time would arrive when she could no longer allow sleeping dogs to lie, before they hunted them down, she would have to strike to protect her liebling, Yvetta.

The plane that flew them to Johannesburg from Moscow allowed Yvetta to come around from the drugs they had pumped into her body.

Yvetta continued to be suspicious, and it took Fritzi most of the journey to ensure her that she was safe.

Once in Jo'burg, Yvetta, still furtive around authority, became more relaxed on the next leg of their journey to Windhoek in Namibia. Nico and their endless road trip through the changing landscape had convinced Yvetta she was genuinely free from being taken to another clinic.

Nico answered her questions about the lodge, with the patience one allows from a first-time tourist, who he knew doubted a small African country like Namibia could have first-world comfort with unimaginable luxury to offer. By the time they reached the lodge it was dawn; Dieter, her uncle, had put on the same welcome he would for paying guests.

Standing beside him were some of the staff in their African dress. They were greeted warmly with an African ditty, ice-cold face towels, and a mixture of lemon and lime iced drinks to cool their thirst from the dusty road trip.

Dieter showed them to their own private lodge, an oasis looking over the desert with bare floor boards covered in rugs. Their double bed faced a bank of windows looking over the dry veld beyond. The glassed-in shower hung over the edge of the veld, allowing views over the endless desert plains. To cool themselves after a hot day travelling the dusty desert plains was a small patio with an ice-cold dipping pool.

Yvetta's delight was now infectious. Gone was her anxious exhaustion from the long trip; she opened the shutters to reveal the most stunning view from a bed that sat in the centre of the room. She jumped on the bed and screamed her delight to no one in particular but a lazy curious ostrich that ambled past the open windows, wondering what all the fuss was about. He peeked inside, huge eyes stuck on a small head at the end of his long neck; both women became hysterical with laughter, felt like children again, reborn.

Namibia, from its very first experience, continued to feed Yvetta's soul. There was no doubt Fritzi had made the best decision for the only person she had ever loved. The evenings were spent reacquainting herself with her uncle and his partner Frieda, who turned out to be a homely, kind, generous woman, someone Yvetta immediately warmed to. By the time they made their way back to their lodge with a torch, it was freezing cold as only the desert could be. Inside their lodge the fire would be crackling in the grate until it burned out long after they had made love and fallen into a peaceful sleep, warmed by the wine and the flames of the fire.

The four days at the lodge came to a blissful end. It was a wonderful introduction to what lay ahead. A small plane flew them back to civilization, and their hunt began for a home in one of the coastal towns recommended by Dieter.

Once settled, Fritzi, not one to rest on her laurels when profitable opportunity presented itself, reopened a tiny, run-down gallery and set Yvetta to work, hoping to rekindle her interest in a profession she had not been involved with for quite some time. At first Yvetta baulked at the idea, but once Fritzi introduced her to the old German Jewish gentleman who had owned the gallery she became caught up in his immense knowledge and found her own considerable experience helped him rekindle his hunger for finding new artists, amongst the many working along the coast. They soon fell into a routine, taking breaks to travel and explore the stunning wildlife Namibia offered.

With Hans's guidance, the gallery was building up a small collection of interesting work. Yvetta relished her trips with him to view work, meeting the artists they chose to represent. Hans encouraged her to look closely at the African artists who were not influenced by European art but found their own style. They found tourists were drawn to the work and the small gallery started to become known on the tourist route.

Fritzi kept in touch through an untraceable account she set up on her laptop. Her life became unhampered by her commitments to anyone but herself and Yvetta. She took on light investigative work for her contacts, only contacting them when she had something of interest. An anonymous, tax-free account was set up to receive any payments due to her, with no possible links.

They found their social life in the small community became one of endless invitations to private homes for early evening sundowners, or meeting acquaintances at restaurants. Where ever they went people stopped to chat amiably, no one was interested in their past lives, only what they had to offer in terms of their bohemian lifestyle, personality, and company; it was a perfect stress-free existence from their past. The gay community was well established here, and Fritzi and Yvetta found their relationship easily accepted.

It became evident that Yvetta wanted to explore her newfound love of children and babies. The opportunity fell into the couple's lap unexpectedly after they employed someone to clean house who then insisted, they needed a gardener and a cook. Although the Herero tribe were used to role-reversal through modernity, which had been absorbed into their long-practiced cultural ways, the cooking remained a male preserve.

Not only did the Herero staff take over the running of Fritzi and Yvetta's home on many occasions, they brought their babies, having no other place to leave them. The much-loved African practice of working with a baby tied in a blanket on one's back still remained, so it was easy for Yvetta to become involved with the lives of their staff, and the two women helped where they could.

A toddler would often accompany the cook. It wasn't long before the child accompanied Yvetta on shopping trips, returning with not only toys but new clothes. Some of their problems she learnt were insurmountable on their meagre wages. The staff, therefore, became a fixture. Six months turned into a year, allowing Yvetta to explore a part of her nature she had never known existed.

With Fritzi's help and encouragement, Yvetta took over the care of the children and provided for their needs with a nursery school for the toddler. The housekeeper and gardener moved into small empty quarters on the property with their baby. The four-year-old had lost his mother, and the cook found himself a single parent. Until he worked for Yvetta and Fritzi he had struggled to find work, having nowhere to leave his son.

Fritzi found his German impeccable and they both loved his cooking. The child was amusing and fun to have around, but it became alarmingly obvious that travelling to work each day was an ordeal for them, and it did not take long before the cook's small family became a permanent fixture in their home.

The large-walled property had been on the market for a very long time before Fritzi found it. They both immediately warmed to its ranch-style with closed-in, surrounding balconies. There were three complete suites, one at the back of the house large enough for the cook. The suites all opened up onto the closed-in balconies leading out onto the garden, which made it ideal for any guest to keep their quarters private without intruding.

With the convenient living arrangements their lives became one of comfortable domesticity, something neither woman had ever experienced. Yvetta would turn up at the gallery at odd times, having entrusted Hans to run the small business with his previous staff, now free of ownership he loved having something to do besides sitting at home.

Hans' well-earned retirement did not suit his temperament. That was when the two rich girls from Europe came into his life unexpectedly, saving him from self-imposed boredom. He was happy to do whatever they asked of him; anything was preferable to empty hours without his lifelong partner, Rosa, who had recently passed. They were to spend their declining years enjoying pursuits neither had made time for while active in business.

Hans and Rosa had not had a family and most of their friends had long since left Namibia, leaving them accustomed to transient friendships, easily formed through their gallery dealings. Hans kept his thoughts about Yvetta and Fritzi to himself, never entertaining others with gossip when asked on occasion, believing he would know their history. He understood the small-town's need to know was more from One-upmanship than curiosity, something to regale their friends with over a meal. Tourists had little interest in the attractive Russian or the charismatic German, who often popped into the gallery for short periods of time to chat or work. Until he noticed a young man hanging around the gallery for more than a few days.

At first, he did not give the man a second thought, thinking him a tourist browsing, looking for something to buy. That was until his staff noticed the man sitting in coffee shops day after day, always facing the gallery, taking notes of the comings and goings of Yvetta and Fritzi. Not wanting to jump to conclusions, Hans decided he would confront the young man the next time he ventured into the gallery, find out who he was, or, what he was up to, before alerting either of his new-found friends; he had become very fond of both women.

It became patently obvious the stranger did not want either of the women to observe his interest, never entering the gallery during either woman's visits, keeping up his vigil from a distance only.

Hans noticed he had a particular interest in collage and photography. Using this as his front to befriend the man, Hans began a series of light-hearted conversations every time he entered the gallery. He noticed the man spoke English with a slight Russian accent, and wondered whether he had some attachment to Yvetta, whose accent was similar. He also noted that his visits to the gallery were in the mornings; the man had clearly worked out that both women only came in towards noon, or later in the day.

On further reflection, Hans was convinced it was Yvetta the young man had an interest in. The man's reluctance to approach the two women became clear when Fritzi turned up one morning out of the blue while he was in the gallery. Hans noticed him hiding from view behind a large canvas, then disappearing into the toilets when another person entered the gallery. Once the coast was clear, he left in a rush and decided to sit on the information.

What happened next turned out to be more interesting than Han's had imagined. Fritzi had arranged a fortnight-long business trip to Germany, taking with her a number of interesting Local Namibian prints from various artists to promote, he noted that Forbidden love and false idols by Chris Snyman was one of her chosen prints. Fritzi requested Hans keep an eye on Yvetta. Fritzi said that she wanted to be kept up to date on anything Hans might find worrying, and explained that Yvetta was an innocent who needed looking after.

The morning Fritzi had waltzed in uncharacteristically to announce her trip, asking for the chosen prints to be packed and dropped off at her home, the young man did not return later that day, obviously not wanting to be found spying on them.

But the following morning Hans noticed the young man back in the gallery; this time he actually chose a number of paintings and prints, paying in cash, and asking for them to be shipped to an address in New York. In the course of conversation, Hans tried to find out whether the young man knew either of the owners of the gallery. This turned out to be exactly the right question.

'No, I thought you were the owner,' the young man replied.

'Ah, well, I was, but I have sold it since.'

'I see. May I ask who the new owners are?'

'Well, yes, Yvetta Rubicov is the new owner.'

'The woman who was in the gallery yesterday, is that the new owner?'

'Oh no, but they are a couple, you see.'

'I overheard her saying that she was leaving for Germany,' the young man said, 'is that correct?'

'May I ask why you want to know?'

The man hesitated for a few seconds.

'Can we speak privately, do you think?'

Hans took him into a small office and closed the door. He hadn't noticed any likeness but there was most definitely a haughty mannerism not unlike Yvetta's but less arrogant, his manner had a natural elegance carried in those who are comfortable with their, heritage or wealth, Han's had many years observing others passing through his gallery, and found he was often spot on in his assessments.

'I am Sasha Rubicov,' the man said, 'Yvetta's brother.' On second thoughts now that he knew the relationship, there were similarities but the brother was handsome, while Yvetta was elfin and pretty her haughtiness never far from the surface.

'I have noticed you hanging around,' Hans said quietly, 'and became aware of your reluctance to be seen.'

'It's a long, complicated story. Let's just say that my family have my sister's best interests at heart. It has taken a long time for me to track her down. To be honest, I do not want to upset her. Do you think you could shed some light on her wellbeing for me? You seem to be a person I can trust.'

Hans sat in thought for a few moments, digesting the information he had just heard. He liked the *girls*, as he had begun to refer to them; but family was family. the Rubicov brother appeared only interested in his sister's wellbeing, no more, so what was the harm?

'How much longer will you be here in Namibia?' Hans asked.

'I plan to fly out tomorrow, so you see it's imperative that I have at least some news to relate to the family – especially to my mother – when I return.'

Hans nodded. 'I have the shop to run. Could you stop by my home this evening at 7 where we can speak in private?'

Sasha left with the address in his pocket. He was positive he could trust Hans to keep his visit quiet, but he knew Hans would want some further information. Sasha decided that he would satisfy Hans' curiosity with a love story. A love story always helps to capture the imagination, without too much elaboration, Sasha thought. The thought itself stirred him, made him smile. It felt good to smile, something he had not done too often lately.

Punctually, at seven o'clock, Sasha stood outside a modern beach house with a neat garden out front he looked up as the glass door slid open to reveal a home straight out of an early modernist period. Inside, every piece of furniture was an authentic classic, from the Mies Van Der Rohe chairs to the Barcelona coffee tables, comfortable Eames chairs, and Saarinen Tulip dining table surrounded by Louis Ghost Chairs. It was hard-edged, yet the floor-to-ceiling paintings and prints, and Persian rugs scattered on the wood floor, softened the look. It suited Hans, Sasha thought, he projected a modern image that sat well with architects or gallerists, with short cropped grey hair and frameless round glasses.

The two men settled opposite one another in a pair of animal-print Le Corbusier chairs overlooking a sloping, well-tended, walled cactus garden softened only by the long floor-to-ceiling drapes neatly folded into a corner with large canvas awnings overhanging the patio.

Drink in hand, Hans sat expectantly waiting for Sasha to begin. Hans had done some research of his own on the Rubicov family, and was shocked to find they were billionaire oligarchs, as they were now called in Russia, with huge resources. He wondered, with all of the resources at their disposal, why it had taken so long to track down a family member, and why the brother had flown all this way in secret. He reflected that perhaps Yvetta's desire not to be found had decided their settling in Namibia, in a most far-flung and removed location. Yes, he thought, this made some sense. He had wondered why two women so obviously well-travelled, and with considerable money at their disposal, had chosen to settle here. And yet he had not thought too long on this: the expat community in Namibia attracted its fair share of eccentrics, from those running away from something in Europe, eager to reinvent themselves or begin their life anew, to those drawn in by the wildness of the desert or the warmth of the locale. And yes, there were very wealthy people amongst these expats. After all, Hans reflected, the wealthy needed to escape, to become anonymous, just as much (if not more) than people of less ample means.

Sasha swivelled his drink, savouring the Van der Ham, an old South African brandy he had never before tasted; it slipped down easily, warming him.

'First, before I begin,' Sasha began slowly, 'I want your word that you will not mention my visit to either Yvetta or Fritzi. What I am about to tell you, my story, hopefully will persuade you from doing so.'

Hans waited for the story before promising anything. He sat elegantly but somewhat uneasily, with a sense of expectation he was not sure he liked, but which felt exciting nonetheless. He felt, all of a sudden, like a much younger man. Adventure and surprise had been scarce in his life of late, perhaps he could do more with both elements. His life, he thought, had become too restrained, too controlled, too self-contained. He knew when he met the girls that they would shake up his life in some way, he just wasn't sure how.

He looked at Sasha and thought how he looked nothing like his sister, Yvetta. And yet there were certain similarities in speech and mannerism, a directness in the gaze, an arrogance perhaps, a fierce and somewhat frightening pride, an aristocratic air. The aura that great wealth bestows upon one: self-satisfied, self-contained. Not happy, exactly, but certain of oneself and one's place in the world.

'I must tell you,' Hans said, 'I like the girls, as I like to call them. They have given me a semblance of my old life back since my dear wife passed. I was a struggling old man who had lost interest. Now I do not have to worry about the finances of the gallery, I can just enjoy it once more.'

'I understand,' Sasha said, finishing his last, cherished sip of the brandy, feeling warmed by the drink and the old man's company, his even gaze and sensitive tone. He thought he could understand why his sister and Fritzi had taken a shine to the old man. 'Please know that none of that will change. Yvetta had her own gallery in Moscow, a very successful one, in fact. We are still running it, and we now have opened another gallery in New York, too, also extremely successful.' He thought about Safi for a moment – so far away in Manhattan, a place so unlike the barren desert wilderness of Namibia – and smiled at her success with the gallery. 'She is an old hand at this.'

He paused, took a breath, wishing Hans would offer to refill his glass, but he needed to be clear headed and alert. He didn't like to talk about Yvetta, but he had no choice but to talk about her now. He was an intensely private person, but he was aware of the pressure of time. He wanted to resolve this matter and fly off again – to Safi, to the familiar noise and bustle of New York. After all these days in Namibia, he still felt lost. Feeling lost meant feeling powerless, something that reminded him too much of jail. Strange how the most open spaces often imprisoned one. Namibia felt endless and impenetrable, its desert a puzzle, a riddle he couldn't solve.

'In a nutshell it's a love story, one that my family do not approve of. That disapproval has had unfortunate consequences for my sister. He paused again, trying to express himself as diplomatically as possible. She has chosen her lover over her family and her business.' For some reason, he thought about Safi again. 'I must say that is really something. I understand her choice completely, and I respect it. You have my word that I will not shatter their secret hideaway.'

'Thank you. As I reiterated, all we want is to know that she is safe, happy, and well. Hans, that is where you can be of great service to us. If I may ask, can you let me know from time to time how she is and what they are up to, for Yvetta's benefit and for my mother's as well. She is sick with worry. It's a very delicate matter, you understand, that's why I had to fly over and see for myself.'

Hans was satisfied. They exchanged email addresses and numbers. He promised to keep Sasha informed: it seemed easy enough, and he would not be upsetting the lovebirds, who, Sasha had stressed, were to be left alone to get on with their lives here in Namibia, which suited Hans perfectly. If more was needed from him, Hans decided, he would ask to be paid for his services. In his old age, money would go a long way to making him feel secure. After all, he had no one to rely on in his declining years, with Rosa now gone. And besides, from what Hans had learned about Yvetta and from his research of the family on the internet, the Rubicovs had no shortage of money.

Sasha flew out early the following morning, sad not to have contacted his sister directly, but knew better than to alarm them in any way, for the moment things were calm. But the purpose of this mission was to determine where she was, and to keep a close watch on Fritzi, who the family did not trust and with good reason. His own life had taken a dramatic U-turn, and in many ways he felt reborn. Yvetta, he thought, deserved a second chance at life, too.

Sasha relished this new chapter of his life with every fibre in his body. He had learnt the hard way to appreciate what he had so nearly thrown away; it was almost impossible to believe Safi was once more part of his life.

Just before he flew out to Namibia on this mission to find his errant sister after receiving information of her whereabouts from the investigators, he had spent a night of passionate lovemaking with the love of his life. He had been reluctant to leave for Florida, knowing his news of a reunion with Safi would more than likely not please either Mika or his mother. They held Safi in high esteem. As the family detested Fritzi, they adored Safi, who was, in so many ways, her polar opposite. Having left Safi for so long while he was imprisoned and afterwards, Sasha never wanted to leave her again.

Kolya picked them up from the airport. Marina was still in New York, seeing family, and she accompanied Sasha to Florida on his return from Namibia. As Kolya drove up the palm-lined drive and coming to a stop under the impressive pillared portico of Mika's mansion, Sasha was reminded how much had changed since his time in the wilderness, during his kidnapping. If Namibia had been a desert, prison was a desert too.

As he stepped from the limo he was greeted with love and warmth by everyone who mattered most to him. Anna, her husband Maurice, and his brother were there to welcome him and Marina. This was his family now, the people who kept him going after the darkest time of his life had ended. Marina threw her arms round Anna. Not expecting Anna to be in America, she jabbered away excitedly about her time in Manhattan with Sasha as they stepped into Mika's impressive Floridian mansion on the edge of the coastal waters.

Mika did not waste time in briefing Sasha about their sister's new home in Africa. 'I want you to make this journey, Sasha. It's important not to make waves. We need only to establish if they have set down roots. My hope is that you will be able to get a contact to pass on any valuable information about Yvetta and Fritzi's new life, and especially Fritzi's movements. This kind of information would go a long way to keeping her from causing any surprise attacks on our family. Find out as much as possible and leave without them knowing you were there, if possible.'

While discussing Yvetta Sasha decided to come clean about his renewed relationship with Safi. Mika stared at him in disbelief.

'My God! Why has she returned to you now, after all the pain you have caused her?'

Sasha was shocked at his brother's reaction.

'Sorry,' Mika said, not sounding sorry at all, 'but you have to admit this family have put that poor girl through hell.'

Sitting in silence for a while contemplating his response, Sasha no longer found it easy to make flippant comments in his defence. 'I know Safi has been loyal to this family throughout her relationship with me,' Sasha said, 'and that her love was a comfort to Alexi and Anna during my ordeal in Russia. And yes, of course, she suffered a devastating loss, too.' He tried to keep his growing annoyance out of his tone. He did not feel he had to explain himself to his older brother, not now, not ever. 'I am aware of all this, but all the same, Safi and I are not sure what happened when we met: call it chemistry, or maybe it's really true love, whatever that may be. The point is, if she'll have me back, I am never letting her go again.'

'Does Janus know of this yet?' Mika asked.

'I have not spoken to Safi yet, but I believe she is spending the weekend with Janus while I am here. She did not want me to contact her while she was there, but I am about to call her, so we will know soon.' Sasha had his doubts once Safi saw Janus would she change her mind, he wasn't going to go there, it was a possibility he did not want to contemplate.

Mika was dumbfounded. Life certainly had a strange way of turning everything on its head. He never ceased to be surprised by the choices people made.

'We have gallery business to discuss,' Mika said, 'and one of our most generous clients has made some unexpected requests. So when you speak with her please ask her to fly over; we would love to see her.'

Sasha smiled. Mika knew how to phrase an invitation so it could not be declined, but he understood his brother wanted to hear the latest turn of events from Safi. Mika had been Safi's protector from afar for a very long time; he had a vested interest in her wellbeing. Sasha had to remember that he wasn't the only one who had enormous love for Safi – most of his family did, too. It wasn't the same kind of love, he thought protectively, but it was still love, strong, undying affection.

He flew out of Florida after only spending one night with Mika and Anna; he wanted to be back when Safi returned to New York. The following day, Sasha left for Namibia. This left Safi two days before she drove upstate to speak to Janus. Sasha had made it his business to find out Safi's movements. He knew she normally only returned to Manhattan on the Tuesday, which brought him back to the States almost at the same time as Safi returned to New York.

He closed the door to his room, found a comfortable chair near the window looking out onto the coastal waters, and dialled her number three times before he managed to stop his hand from shaking. Would she pick up straight away or would he have to wait? God knows he had waited long enough. The buzzing in his temples blurred his vision as he waited for the ring to be answered. As it rang Sasha realised, he was probably too exhausted to talk, to formulate words – the right words, anyway. He needed sleep; he was suffering from jet lag. The tension became unbearable and he rang off without leaving a message.

He lay back in the recliner, allowing the cool breeze from the coastal waters to blow in through his patio doors. He put his head back and closed his eyes. There were so many questions in his mind – altogether too many questions for such an exhausted, emotional state. Would Safi have had time to reassess their passionate reunion? What would her findings be, her final decision? The last few years had humbled Sasha, but he was still a fighter, he wasn't used to losing.

Perhaps Mika was right; their family had put her through enough. It was time to let Safi go – an unthinkable thought that Sasha almost instantly rejected. He had not contemplated rejection, and did not know how he would deal with his emotions if she had changed her mind. Being rejected was foreign to him, almost as foreign as the deserts of Namibia. Until recently, his whole life had been a celebration of success. But now what? Everything was different now. The uncertainty was worse even than the possible rejection. The not-knowing was killing him. Falling into a troubled sleep he woke to a distant ringing, grabbed for his cell, and answered apprehensively.

'Hi.'

'Safi, hi, you okay?'

'Yes and no,' Safi said. he was aware of the quiver in her voice as she spoke.

'Oh! Is that good or bad?'

'Sad.'

He could hear her breathing heavily, faltering as she tried to relate what had transpired. 'Are you okay to speak right now?' Sasha said. 'Mika has asked me to tell you to fly down. He wants to discuss the gallery and one of your clients. Perhaps you'd prefer to wait until we see each other?'

'Oh, no, I couldn't possibly do that.'

'Do you mean fly down?'

'No, no speak later.'

They were both clinging on but the gulf that had appeared between them was not healed and patently raw, it was hard now but they would he knew with certainty and, the tenderness he felt for her in his heart be revived if she opened her heart to him once more.

There was a long pause. Sasha could feel his hand sweating. He changed hands while he wiped his clammy hand. He returned the phone to his ear, just as Safi was speaking again.

'I spoke with Janus,' Safi said softly, uneasily.

'Yes, how was that?' It was as if Sasha's voice did not belong to him.

'Oh Sasha, I am in a terrible state, really terrible.'

She began to cry and Sasha felt weak; he wanted to reach over the phone through the miles to comfort her. Struggling for the right words, not knowing what was to come, he made feeble noises of comfort to let her know he understood, empathised with her.

'Janus was devastated, angry and hurt,' Safi began uneasily, 'though he understood, had known for a while that things were not right.' Normally so articulate a speaker, with unusual clarity, Safi couldn't find the words now, they seemed elusive, far away, like Sasha himself. She felt surrounded by awkward silences and half-finished thoughts. Why did everything have to be so difficult? she thought. 'But he did not expect you to come back into my life, and was visibly shocked that we had resumed our relationship. He...' She faltered, trying to stop her tears. 'Janus had made such an effort to heal our rift. He put all of his work aside for me. He had booked a table at a restaurant to rekindle the gap that was growing between us, but it was over.'

She gulped. 'I think he knew before I told him about us, that it was over.'

Sasha's hand tightened on the cell; he closed his eyes in prayer. Had he just heard her say 'us'? He held his breath waiting for her to continue.

'Janus knew I could not foresee a future without a family of my own. Oh, Sasha, how could this have happened to us? I know now that I never really stopped loving you.'

Tears were flowing down both their cheeks, though neither could see the other – still, they could feel the emotional bond, the connection. The intimacy had returned, too. Sasha felt unbearably happy.

The electricity across the wire was almost static with emotion.

'You have no idea how happy I am to hear you say those words, Safi.'

'Should I get on a plane tonight? I could try and get the last flight out.'

He stared at the bed longingly but instead dropped his head back against the armchair. His feet stretched out and he drifted off into a restful, exhausted sleep, needing to be alert when Safi arrived from New York. They would face everyone together as a couple once more the following morning. He felt the intense happiness still, a warmth in his chest, in his heart, even while he slept.

Grabbing his cell he switched off the alarm and checked to see how long he had been sleeping. Three hours had vanished since he finished his call with Safi; she would be landing in an hour.

Dragging his aching body to the shower, he pulled on black sweatpants and a black T-shirt, and left the confines of his bedroom for the grandeur of his brother's many comfortable rooms that he had only glanced at on his arrival. He knew Mika would have staff on duty at all times, service and security was always a high priority wherever he was. Sure enough, as Sasha stepped into the cavernous entrance hall at the bottom of the marble staircase, he was greeted by a manservant. Sasha was surprised to find him a Latina; Mika mostly employed Russians.

After a guided tour he settled in the study to await Safi's arrival. Miguel had orders to bring her through as soon as she arrived. Although Sasha hoped to hear the front door it was safer to have Miguel meet the cab in case he nodded off.

Annoyingly brushing away an irritation, he found a hand hovering over his eyes. Sasha shot up. Knocking Safi off-balance, he grabbed her as she was about to fall and pulled her onto the sofa he had been snoozing on. Her eyes were only inches away; they lay staring at one another, each reading a history of past and present with a hint of a new beginning neither wanted to waste on mistakes. The present was what mattered now and a future together.

Breakfast was crazy; no one quite knew how to react to Sasha and Safi's newfound happiness. Having only recently found Sasha, Anna wanted his undivided attention, Marina wanted everyone's attention, and Mika appeared to be completely lost for words.

Chapter 13

Fritzi arrived in Switzerland dressed appropriately for a meeting at her bank. She was attired elegantly in a dark Armani suit and a long-fringed silk scarf which swung with her long strides, now slightly curtailed by heels. She carried a tan calf Gucci briefcase, and her expression was hidden by mirrored sunglasses. Fritzi was done with hiding. Not expecting anyone to know her, she was enjoying playing a rich bitch; it would be fun being waited on, even if only by Swiss gnomes.

She had not been to check up on the millions of euros safely hidden from authorities around the globe. No one knew her real name. she had a code for her most valuable possessions in the vault. She was enjoying a role she seldom had the opportunity to play.

As she swung through the glass doors she was escorted to a private room, the plush office of a very elegant, bespectacled Swiss German banker, who oozed manners and charm – as much charm as one could rightly expect from the Swiss, which was not much. All the same, Fritzi was going to enjoy this meeting, it was long overdue. Charm was low on her list, yet the man behind the desk seemed to be expecting some response.

He complimented her on her style, her beauty, and offered her a refreshment. Opening the ledger on his desk, he pushed it over for Fritzi to read.

At first the numbers blurred as she focused on the actual sum. Then she paled. Was there some mistake? No wonder this man was pandering to her; if this was actually her account, she was a very, very wealthy woman indeed. She was a billionaire!

Fritzi sat back, crossed her legs, took a sip from the crystal water glass, and spoke in a soft German accent tinged with American.

Herr Stoffel listened intently as she gave instructions. She opened her briefcase took out a ledger, and ran through some of the figures. She asked pointed questions, absorbed the answers, leaned forward, and stared intently at Herr Stoffel.

'You say the last payment was made only six weeks ago,' she said.

Herr Stoffel nodded. 'Exactly six weeks to the day.'

Fritzi leaned over the ledger once more. The sum paid into her account in the last six weeks exceeded all expectations; it had raised her account into the stratosphere. She was not aware of any transactions to warrant such a huge sum. Was there a job she was being paid for she had not yet been notified of?

Perhaps, but she doubted anyone would pay before a job was completed. Having been in an American jail, she had not fully negotiated for the abduction of Sasha. So why had they transferred so much into her account?

Were her unknown contacts using her to launder money? It was the only answer she could think of. They only ever negotiated through the dark web and, then only through various sub divided layers before it eventually arrived in her in box in a coded number, that changed every six weeks.

She did not want to show any sign of agitation or doubt, certainly not in front of Herr Stoffel. The best way to deal with bankers was to be in command at all times. She shot off some more demands, transferring the bulk of her own money into another account, signed, and left without a backward glance. She sailed out of the bank and caught the first flight back to Namibia the following day.

The further she was from that money, the safer she felt. It was only a matter of time before she was contacted, and she wanted to enjoy as much time with Yvetta as she could before she became involved with another international operation. If they came to her with a job, she could not refuse. It was obvious whoever had put that money into her Swiss account would be wanting something very important in return.

Fritzi refused to open her computer until she reached the safety of Yvetta's arms, convinced there would be something waiting there to wreck her peaceful life. She was happy to be away from the usual lawlessness that she had once not only enjoyed but thrived upon.

Somehow having that amount of money made her realise how liberating her choices would be, but this was only true if it were truly hers to spend as she wished. However, she knew if she were to touch one euro over her own few million, she wouldn't live to tell the tale, and whoever else she was involved with would be killed too. She had to protect Yvetta at all costs.

For the first time in years, Fritzi's know-it-all persona felt vulnerable. Perhaps her persona had vanished with those millions that suddenly morphed into a hundreds of millions. Much to her surprise, she was completely unnerved by what she found in her Swiss account.

Yvetta had been happily playing house while Fritzi was away. Hans had taken wonderful care of her, as had there many other friends since their arrival in this strange place. Well, it wasn't strange anymore – now it was home. She found she missed the damp, concentrated, strangely refreshing heat of Namibia while she was away from it. But the idea of the money in her account had begun to oppress her. It was a dreamlike amount of money, but it could be the stuff of nightmares, too. After all, she knew some major players in the underworld who wouldn't blink an eye at cold-blooded murder or targeted assassination.

Perhaps it was time to travel, another safari, lose themselves in the Namib desert. She would be out of contact with technology – a rarity in this day and age, a godsend. Technology today was ubiquitous, it was all-encompassing, it was oppressive; it was enough. If you tried to lose yourself, Fritzi thought, technology would find you, even if you did not want to be found. She wanted to be alone in the wilderness – alone with Yvetta, that is. They could go on another walking safari deep into the bundu. Spending a few nights sleeping under the stars might help her face whatever was coming her way; she had a dreadful premonition it was not going to be good.

Long days hiking and nights spent under the stars in the wild allowed Fritzi to unload her fears. She returned home rested, renewed, and ready to take action. She opened the private mail only she could access, and scanned through her messages, not finding anything untoward. There were, of course, the usual offer of small contracts for her to undertake – but nothing enormous, nothing suspicious. No red flags. She sat staring at her screen wondering where to start searching. Who could she trust with information? She had many contacts in the underworld, but how many of them were entirely trustworthy? She was on friendly terms with some of these people, but friends with none. You couldn't trust a criminal, after all. Certainly, there was honour among thieves, but not when a billion dollars was involved. The higher the stakes, the less honourable the intentions. It was a delicate matter trying to get a lead. She did not need others to get wind of her sudden elevation in wealth; it would hugely change her relationship with her network, perhaps even jeopardise her safety and Yvetta's. After all, even in faraway Namibia she wasn't as anonymous as she would like. There was Yvetta's gallery, there were new customers, new friends, a whole new trail.

Fritzi decided she would start putting feelers out for any information on banking irregularities that may have come to light in the last six weeks. She would give each contact the same answer, saying she had been approached for this information and was investigating a source.

She sent out the request and closed down her private account. Until she had wind of something concrete, she would not be taking on any work.

Yvetta was totally absorbed running her gallery with Hans. The gallery had become well respected in the short time they had owned it. Fritzi was enormously proud of Yvetta – whatever she turned her considerable skills to quickly became a success. The couple's staff and extended family were absorbed in their everyday lives; the youngest was at a nursery school and the older child had been enrolled into a primary school, freeing their parents of a financial burden they could never have afforded. Their loyalty to their employer was without question; together they worked to protect Yvetta, who they now realised was frail of temperament and prone to overreaction. They made allowances for her outbursts while Fritzi was away, during disruptions that only Fritzi knew how to manage. It was a steep learning curve for the staff, who soon realised Fritzi was the stronger of the two and looked towards her for guidance in all things when Yvetta was away from the house.

The one thing Fritzi needed now was staff loyalty: she warned them not to discuss their affairs out of the home, with other staff. Fritzi felt confident the staff would not give up their security for a few moments of tittle-tattle. More importantly, she needed the staff to report any stranger asking questions about them; she stressed that they were to report only to her, immediately.

It was almost impossible to hide in today's world, but she needed Yvetta to feel safe and she had accomplished that for the time being. The Rubicovs, she was sure, had no idea where Yvetta was… yet. But she also knew that it was just a matter of time before the family tracked them down. Hopefully by being cautious and lying low when necessary, the two women could buy themselves some extra time.

The weeks that followed were void of leads from her contacts. She was beginning to wonder whether the fortune in her account could actually be her own, when she noticed unopened mail. The email was encrypted and there was no way to reply to it. Fritzi thought it could only be a hacker paid to find out what she so badly needed to know about those millions sitting in her Swiss account. Reading the email made Fritzi's hair stand on end and sent cold shivers down her spine. Someone had somehow broken her banking co-ordinates. It was one thing when she had money wired into her account, but it was another to have her private banking code at a Swiss bank hacked. In the last six weeks, money had been transferred into her account by an unknown source, not only could they deposit, they could clean out her whole account. Fritzi mouthed the email to make sure she was focusing, 'Codes of this numbered account now belongs to an unknown source to play with at will, no feed yet to break into unknown sources encryption.'

She had been wise to move her own money into another account, now she would move her money to a new tax haven and leave what she did not own in the Swiss bank, while following its trajectory. She did not have all her eggs in one basket, as the English like to say, but all the same it was a very, very large basket, and whoever was messing with her wanted her to know that. She could do virtually nothing until they made contact.

Whatever they wanted had to be a life-and-death situation; why else would they deposit millions in her name? What did they want? The question was eating at her every moment of every day that passed without answers. She found herself distracted in her daily life, thinking only of the huge amount in her bank account. She wished they would show their hand.

Sasha had briefed Mika about his trip to Namibia and that he had managed to bring Hans on side. Hans had been more than forthcoming about his sister's new life in Namibia, and was happy to pass on any information to Sasha. They discussed Yvetta's state of mind with Bernard, Anna's husband, and were relieved he thought the change of country and climate would be beneficial. Yvetta would act out eventually, Bernard said, it was a pattern that would manifest itself wherever she was. He was convinced she would return to her manipulative, destructive behaviour – the question was when?

The International Art fraud squad were working round the clock uncovering Fritzi's secrets he wanted every scrap of information they could gather from contacts to hidden assets and accounts. He passed the information onto Interpol, knowing they had her under surveillance. Many of the insurance companies and governments wanted to break the ring of smugglers Fritzi worked with around the globe. It was Sasha's mission to have her put away for life; she was a danger to his family, and he was not prepared to take any more chances.

His sister's wellbeing was important: they had discovered where she was, and had someone reporting any changes in her immediate situation. This gave them time before they decided on their next move. Yvetta was stable and being cared for, and, according to Hans, the new gallery was becoming quite the success. Sasha was not oblivious to the fact that there was much positive news, and that Yvetta was in a good state again, at last. The move to Namibia may yet turn out for the best, Sasha reflected, financially they could work something out with Hans as their permanent intermediate Yvetta may have found herself a safe haven. Locking her behind closed doors in clinics all over the world had never sat well with any of the family; everyone wanted Yvetta to be happy.

Anna had suffered their cruelty first-hand during the attack on their family home in Moscow, yet she wondered whether leaving the couple to get on with their lives in Namibia was the best option. She was prepared to forgive, but was under no illusions as to how dangerous her daughter could be. The attack on Safi right under the family's noses had been a stark reminder. Her sons were not prepared to take that chance again. Together, Yvetta and Fritzi, were a fatal combination. The operation the family were putting into action to apprehend Fritzi would have to be carefully orchestrated. Sasha hoped that Hans could be trusted to help with Yvetta when the time came to arrest Fritzi. There was no accounting for Yvetta's mental state once she realised that she had been apprehended by the authorities.

Mika and Sasha flew to meet the intelligence agents who were working with them in LA. Janus had instructed his team to be on board. Mika had not expected a warm reception from Janus, but to Mika's surprise he greeted them both without rancour. Janus was ever the professional, and even appeared to have a sense of humour about the situation.

'May the best man win?' Janus joked when seeing Sasha then on a more serious note.

'I have absolutely no intension of allowing Fritzi – or Yvetta, for that matter having another shot at hurting Safi.' He turned to Sasha, and his voice was firmer, sterner, and without humour now. 'You were not around when that happened.'

Sasha could feel his gut clenching, but let it go. Was this meant to hurt him? To tell him that Janus, rather than Sasha, had been there for Safi in recent years? Was someone as direct and professional as Janus also snidely passive-aggressive? No, Sasha thought, perhaps he was being oversensitive. Janus, after all, was on board to help not hinder the operation. Janus had never been anything other than professional, and had a considerable reputation in the intelligence community for a reason.

'Yes,' Sasha said, 'my sister has been unpredictable for many years. I am thankful you were all there to stop Yvetta in time; we know what she is capable of if provoked.'

They followed Janus into a vast, subterranean area where all computer banks were kept. On a wall were fixed huge screens that picked up every area and covered the globe, where all the cyber networks interconnected. The whole operation was astoundingly impressive; everyone who worked with Janus was an expert in their field. Sasha felt another small surge of relief.

If Fritzi took the bait, hopefully they would be able to watch from the control centre, but there were a few major links in the chain that would have to be ironed out before FBI operations could be activated, more than one agency was already involved.

A decoy had been laid, all Fritzi had to do was make contact with her network; finding her account bloated with money she had not deposited would have its benefits: she wouldn't dare touch the money for fear of being taken out by whoever had put it there. Operatives involved would be told that Fritzi had checked her account in Switzerland, where she discovered that she had become a multi-millionaire overnight.

The insurance intelligence agencies on board had all deposited fake money into Fritzi's account, with the purpose of unsettling her enough to contact the people she trusted most – her fellow criminals, connected to the highest levels of the underworld. These people had helped her out of two secure jails in the past, through a deep network of cells working across the continental line and in the wider world, including the United States. These were people they were hoping to snare in the net with Fritzi's unsolicited help.

If Fritzi followed the pattern they expected, she would shortly enter the co-ordinates that would hopefully help them break the code divulging who the main players in the world-wide smuggling ring were. Billions worth of treasures had passed through these people's hands, including priceless artworks that had never been recovered. Fritzi was a small fish in a huge pond, and now they were using her as bait to lure the main players. Everyone agreed that Fritzi was too big for her britches, but the truth was, in the scheme of things (and how Fritzi herself would hate to hear this), she was tiny indeed. If Fritzi's contacts got wind of any carelessness on her part they would neutralise her; before allowing that to occur, the intelligence agencies' intentions were to use her to maximum advantage. The sting had to be quick before the network closed ranks.

Mika spoke of their contact in Namibia who had come on side. Hans had not been given any details apart from keeping them updated on Yvetta and Fritzi on a weekly basis. He was being handsomely paid, giving him a comfortable pension in his retirement years, so would play ball. Mika added that Sasha had brought him onboard personally.

When the shit hit the fan, Hans would be notified to persuade Yvetta to travel on an art mission. This was only if their investigative sting took them to Namibia. Until then, they would slowly feed more into Fritzi's account, with the cooperation of the banks, who would notify her when funds were deposited.

Contacts were slowly being decoded around the globe. This was a top-secret investigation that was hellbent on succeeding, whatever the cost; these players had slipped through their net on too many occasions. The payoff would be a coup for the insurance companies, who had been vilified by their peers on other Intelligence missions around the globe.

They needed to keep Fritzi guessing without her becoming suspicious. She was their only lead, so much depended on how she decided to play this game. They knew she was a superb poker player; she had proved herself to be resilient to capture on more than one occasion.

Mika flew to Florida while Sasha flew to New York to be with Safi. The brothers had serious discussions about the Russian side of their businesses; both wanted to extricate themselves from Russia. Sasha no longer wanted to remain in a country where he had been subject to the whims, and indeed cruelty, of the government. They had sold off all of the TV franchises and were slowly selling off others, including the restaurants, which had been his father's last enterprise. A decision had still to be made about the galleries. The lawyers were constantly flying back and forth to the States to finalise the sale of one or another business in the Rubicov empire. Oil and gas were now tightly controlled by the government.

Anna had sole rights to many smaller enterprises that fell under the Rubicov umbrella in Russia. The family would naturally only offload these enterprises with a huge cut going to the government. There was no reason for Sasha to remain in Moscow, nor, after his imprisonment, would he agree to do so. Having Ringo in Russia would suffice. Once the company was floated on the open market, his shares would make him a very wealthy man.

Now that Safi was securely back in Sasha's life, they needed to consolidate their holdings, but the galleries were still to be decided. The family's legal team would assist the family in putting their holdings on the open market. Their employees were given shares. The extended family would be free to move to other continents, and all would have considerable wealth.

Alexi's restaurants, hotels, and apartments in London and abroad were formed into a separate holding company after his death and were sold off to a well-known Russian conglomerate. This left Valentina to live her life in comfort. Marina would never want for anything; she was well cared for by the sale of all the Rubicov assets. Their considerable property portfolio around the world would remain under Rubicov Holdings.

Safi and Sasha moved into a four-storey building close to Central Park. They had a civil ceremony with DuPont as their only witness. While their home was being decorated, they flew to Cannes, where Safi's and Sasha's families met for a wonderful, low-key wedding ceremony. They celebrated in a local restaurant overlooking the ocean. Bougainvillea drooped down the high walls, long tables with crisp white linen were decorated with beautiful fresh herbs and flowers, and champagne and wine flowed in abundance while the families feasted on local dishes especially prepared by an old friend, known as one of the best chefs in the area.

Safi's family had never met Janus, and had, had a close relationship with Alexi and Valentina, so seeing their daughter back with Sasha was where she belonged as far as they were concerned. Jake was settled in Melbourne too far to travel for a short affair and too caught up in his own life, which did not come as a surprise to anyone in Safi's immediate family, Jake was as always dismissive of conventional traditions.

Afterwards, the newlyweds flew to Mauritius for their honeymoon, then onto a game reserve in South Africa. Windhoek was a business stop before the couple flew back home, where Sasha had a meeting with Hans to finalise their plan to use Fritzi as an unwitting decoy to break into (and bust open) the smuggling ring.

They no longer kept secrets from one another: Sasha filled Safi in about Yvetta and her relationship with Fritzi, their attack on Anna and the family home. He told her, too, about Mika and Kolya's subsequent abduction of Yvetta, sending her off to a number of clinics to help with her mental state, and ensure that she could no longer interfere with the family. He informed Safi of Yvetta's escape from three of the clinics with Fritzi's help, and Fritz's involvement when he himself was abducted. Thus, he brought Safi up to date on what she had previously been in the dark about.

Everything once concealed from Safi was now brought into the open. She was truly one of the family now. Safi felt relieved by this new honesty and transparency, even while on some level she understood why Sasha had initially kept all of this from her. She had no idea what dangerous elements lurked in the family, and how her own life had been threatened too. She felt refreshed by his sudden honest – but afraid, too. Yvetta and Fritzi were a greater danger than she had ever understood.

She knew his family were concerned for their safety; Fritzi and Yvetta were ingenious at striking when they least expected, Sasha informed her. Fritzi was wanted by the authorities in many countries. Sasha could not tell Safi about the sting yet (still more secrets to keep from his beloved, but in this case, secrecy was paramount – for everyone's sake), but he filled her in on the reason why they had not yet arrested her. They were hoping she would lead them to her contacts before they arrested her.

Hans was perfectly placed to do the job. They felt him worthy of their trust, and he had not disappointed. Sasha had trusted the man from their first, impromptu meeting. They had no other contact as close to Fritzi and Yvetta . Fritzi had bought the small art gallery from him soon after arriving and putting down roots.

Safi felt sad for Yvetta; she wished she could share in the success of the galleries in New York and Russia. Still, Safi was aware that, with the recent breaking-up and selling-- off of all the Rubicov companies, it would not be long before the galleries would go the same way. Safi had discussed this fleetingly with Sasha, but he claimed that no decisions were yet made one way or the other. Safi was not sure whether she was ready to give up her life in the art world, but for now all of that was on hold anyway; she was happy and enjoying life, everything else would hopefully fall into place.

Her life had taken a strange turn; she had experienced an emotional rollercoaster ride with the Rubicov family, had thought her only connection to them would remain the galleries (and even then she worried that the galleries could be taken away from her at any moment, that her connection to them was tenuous). Marrying Sasha after he had taken advantage of her naïveté and youth seemed a stupid thing to do, yet the reality was very different. They were interlinked in so many ways through family and business. Almost in spite of herself, Safi had been shocked to find their chemistry reigniting, with a passion they found hard to ignore. Both had experienced tumultuous upheaval and change, yet here they were reunited and madly in love. She had a ring on her finger, had just spent a glorious uninterrupted honeymoon with the man she had thought would be her husband all those years ago. She thought back to when she had to beg her parents to allow her to leave with Sasha for Moscow. How long ago that was, how young she had been, and how different everything was back then. Life had a very strange way of making fools out of those who thought they knew what lay around the corner. Each had challenging experiences with massive amounts of luck thrown in; Safi hoped their luck would continue now that they were actually together again, against all odds, finally, wonderfully, as man and wife.

They arrived in Windhoek at dawn in the middle of a massive windstorm, booked into the same hotel he had stayed in on his last visit. Sasha did not want to hang around for longer than necessary, in case Fritzi got wind of their visit. The Windhoek hotel, made the meeting less fraught with exposure or the risk of being detected. Swakopmund, was even smaller by comparison.

Sasha met with Hans in his suite; it was the safest place to talk unhindered and unseen by anyone who might know Hans. Windhoek was a very small community, and neither man wanted to draw attention to their meeting.

Safi would have liked to go on a sightseeing expedition, but Sasha thought it too risky. He had booked for the two of them to fly out the moment the travel agent called to give them the all-clear. So instead, she spent a heavenly few hours indulging at the hotel spa, enjoying the organic spa products, having a facial, massage, pedicure, and manicure. She was now ready to hit the ground running when she arrived back in Manhattan.

The girl doing her facial was German, as was most of the staff Safi encountered, apart from a stunning black girl who managed the salon. All facial treatments were in private, but the pedicure and manicure were in an open-planned section with many workstations and a row of foot baths.

Safi took her place at one of the nail workstations, sipping the ginger tea brought to her by one of the staff. Safi couldn't help listening to a heated conversation someone ahead of her was having on her cell phone at the foot spa. It was impossible not to listen to her speaking as the space was quite intimate. The woman on the phone had an incredibly familiar air and way of speaking that kept Safi's interest. Safi could not see her properly, only her back, while the manicurist was painting her toes.

'Ag, liebling,' the woman said in her familiar voice, 'not tonight. I won't be home until late from Windhoek, you know that, can't you arrange for Hans to come to the house tomorrow. Surely, he can put it off a day?'

Hans. Wasn't that the name of the contact Sasha was going to meet? The man who managed the art gallery with Yvetta and Fritzi. Safi felt a cold shiver down her spine, realising the voice behind her belonged to Fritzi. Safi flinched, turned her head away, tried to relax, struggling with the uneasy sensation in her stomach. Oh my God, this was dangerous, she recognised Fritzi's mannerisms, there was absolutely no mistake.

Not wanting to be noticed, she remained seated, tension running along her whole body, in lines that curved and cut. Obviously, she was waiting for Fritzi's manicurist to finish. If she left now, Fritzi may turn and recognise her. Safi's mind raced, came up a blank space filled only with anxiety. There was absolutely no way to explain why she was here, in Namibia. Shrewd, cynical, canny Fritzi would not see it as a coincidence. And who knows what she would do to Safi after that. Safi shivered again.

Her only option was to keep her head turned sideways, hoping to hide her face, loosening her tie-back and allowing her hair to fall free, obscuring her face, she continued paging through a fashion magazine. Hopefully Fritzi would walk past without giving her a glance.

The relaxing benefit of the massage and facial were now wasted, replaced with every fibre in her body on alert, waiting for a tap on her shoulder – or worse. This would make it impossible to avoid blowing Sasha's cover, or maybe even Hans'. Was Safi going to ruin the entire operation by literally doing nothing?

Seconds became excruciating hours, the manageress apologised for the staff shortage, offering Safi another refreshment. Not wanting to draw attention, afraid that one word out of her mouth might give her away, Safi just smiled and nodded, hoping the manageress would go away. Anxiety wasn't kind to her brain, her body, or her bladder, which desperately needed emptying.

Paralysed, not wanting to bump into Fritzi in the bathroom, she held on. Shit, she hoped Fritzi would leave soon, she couldn't take much more of this tension. Even if Fritzi were to leave, she might meet her in the elevator on the way up to the reception area. As they were in the basement there was only one way up to her room by lift. Another terrifying thought struck her like a fist: what if Fritzi had already noticed her but had decided to play dumb? What if Fritzi planned to wait for her and sabotage her later, when she was alone and away from all these inconvenient witnesses?

No, Safi, thought, she felt sure that Fritzi, still obviously distracted, had not seen her. But this was cold comfort; it was what *could* happen in the next few minutes that really rattled Safi. And the questions kept coming. Why was Fritzi here, surely, she must know that Hans was in Windhoek, too?

The whole scenario suddenly became suspicious. Could this Hans really be trusted? Perhaps he was playing a double game. How much did they know about this Hans, anyway? Sure, Sasha was paying him money to be an informant for the family, but Fritzi and Yvetta could pay him plenty of money, too. Besides, the two women had the benefit of bending his ear all the time, and could be very convincing. She knew that Sasha had found Hans to be trustworthy, but he had felt the same about those high-level Russian politicians who had sent him down the river. Sasha had been wrong before, he was only human, as was Safi. She had to get to Sasha to warn him.

Quickly, slyly, with only half her face turned, Safi checked to see how the manicurist was doing; it seemed she was almost complete. Fritzi would have to return to the manicurist to give her a tip, at which point it was highly likely that she would be doing Safi's manicure. If that happened the game was up. She had no options left but to leave.

Grabbing her handbag she briskly walked past the reception, luckily they were on calls; hopefully they would think she was going to the bathroom.

She decided to find the stairwell, there had to be one, every hotel had a way of escape in case of fire. Finding a set of double doors at the end of the passageway next to the lifts, she pushed through them. Her heart was still beating loudly, pounding twice as hard. Double beats, double doors. Who knew what would be on the other side? Relieved to find stairs, she climbed them two at a time, the flip-flops helped her grip. Reaching the reception area, she had no choice but to enter in order to take the lift up to her room. Hopefully wearing a towelling gown would not divert attention her way.

Still, she tried to cover up part of her face, not sure what – or who – could be waiting for her. Riding up to her floor she had another sudden realisation that almost knocked her off her feet, set her heart on fire again. What if the receptionist called out Safi's name, not being able to find her in the salon? If Fritzi heard her call 'Mrs Rubicov,' or even 'Safi,' her cover would be blown. After all, neither were common names. Safi would be busted without even being present.

She found Sasha on the bed, watching TV. She closed the door behind her, leaned against it to catch her breath. Her heart was still pounding, and her hands were shaking now, too.

'What's got into you,' Sasha said by way of a greeting. 'You look like you've seen a ghost.'

Her hand flew to her mouth. 'Fritzi! I've seen Fritzi.'

Sasha stood up. 'Where? Did she see you?'

'No, I made a run for it, but it was touch-and-go. She was having a manicure. I had to wait for her manicurist to finish, so I was a sitting duck, but she had her back to me.'

'That's bloody fortunate.'

'I know, but what if the receptionist calls my name, looking for me thinking, I am in the loo?'

They stared at one another. Safi ran for the phone, called down to reception, and asked them to give the spa her apologies for not waiting, hopefully it wasn't too late? But still Safi felt tremendously uneasy. What if Fritzi was standing at reception when they made the call, or even bumped into Hans? And could Hans really be trusted? Sasha seemed to think so, was not backing down on this.

Sasha called Hans, who picked up immediately. There was a pause as he listened to Sasha.

'Yes,' Hans said slowly. 'Hans this is unfortunate, I think it best you let us know if you bump into her. There is no reason you should not be in Windhoek, is there?'. Do they know of your visit here today?'

Safi could see the doubtful expression on Sasha's face and feared the worst. She tried to make out Hans' words on the other end, or at least his accent and manner of speaking, as if through this she could determine whether or not he could be trusted. But she could hear very little, and what she could make out was vague and uneasy, like the day itself.

Putting down the phone Sasha looked at Safi. She could tell he was trying to figure out if this was all a coincidence. Did Hans betray them? Safi knew Sasha well enough, in times of happiness but also in times of crisis, that she could read his mind. She tried to read it now, but saw only anxiety and alarm. Her heart was still beating irregularly, in time with his. Then the hotel phone rang and both their hearts exploded. The sound of the phone wrapped itself around the silence and pulled their throats taut. They jumped. Sasha picked it up, listened, then put it down. He dialled the reception and Safi listened as she heard him ask for security to be sent up to their suite immediately.

'That was the travel agent to let us know our flights would be taking off as scheduled tomorrow,' he informed Safi, sitting now on the edge of the bed, 'but I am not taking any chances.' The television was still on but Sasha had muted it. Safi tried to relax, but her heart had other ideas.

There was a knock on the door. Sasha opened his briefcase, took out a small handgun, and walked to the door. The gun was given to him by the FBI through Janus and according to them could not be detected, so far it hadn't and now was the time to use it if he had to.

'Who's there?'

'Security, sir.'

He opened the door with his gun at the ready. The security guard, a big, burly, black man who was also armed, put up his hands as if to say 'Whoa!' Sasha put the gun down as the man walked in.

Sasha briefed the security guard, then asked him to call in private security. Sasha wanted someone on guard until they flew back earlier than planned.

As the time ticked by and they were confined to remain in their suite, Safi could tell Sasha was never going to wait until morning for a regular BA flight.

He opened his cell, called Mika, waited until the call connected, a seemingly impossible amount of time that was really only a couple of seconds. the two brothers spoke for a few minutes. Safi watched Sasha intently, hoping to figure out what was happening.

As Sasha finished the call, she knew he had arranged to charter a private jet to fly them out earlier. He was still a Rubicov, after all, in charge of his own destiny once more by having all the choices that billions of dollars allowed one. Lots of money, lots of choices. But billions of dollars also attracted danger and unwanted elements. Being very rich, Safi sometimes thought, wasn't all it was cut out to be. The security guard had a car waiting for them in the underground car park which drove them to a private air field, where they boarded a chartered flight to Johannesburg, enabling them to connect with their regular BA flight out to London and home.

Hans had a steady flow of new people in the gallery on a daily basis. Recently he had noticed two American men frequenting the gallery. They had not bought anything, only shown interest in one or two pieces presumably for their home (where exactly that was he wasn't sure).

'Hi ya,' one of the Americans said, 'y'all have a wonderful little ole gallery. Chuck and I can't make up our little old minds.'

'That's okay,' Hans replied kindly, in the gentle manner that had earned him so many friends and devotees around town and made his gallery such a popular stop for locals and tourists alike, 'you take your time. Ask if you need advice, we ship all over the world. Where in the States would you be shipping to?'

'I'm a born-and-bred Texan, from down South. You been to the States?'

'New York a long time ago, when my dear wife was still alive.'

'I'm sorry to hear that,' the man replied, his voice no longer quite so brash.

'Are you gentlemen here for a while?' Hans asked.

'We on mining business, then some game hunting, then back home.'

Hans disliked hunters, but his soft, lined face wasn't one to show judgement. Besides, in this part of the world, it was difficult to avoid hunters. Hunters, in Hans' experience, were an inordinately boastful lot.

'Ah,' Hans said simply. He was used to Americans coming to Africa for big-game hunting. He did not approve, but it was hunting season, so he guessed they had a license. If they hadn't, they'd be in big trouble. The Namibian the government had tightened the laws on game hunting. Besides, you couldn't dislike Americans too much – they did wonders for the local economy, an economy that could use all the help it could get.

The next time Hans saw the two Americans they were chatting to Yvetta. Both had now bought a number of works to be shipped. He heard Yvetta talking with them, with unusual interest in her often-indifferent voice, about Russian politics, and her love of Africa. Hans, more and more curious about Yvetta and her motivations, couldn't help but eavesdrop. That was when he heard Chuck inviting Yvetta and Fritzi to join them for drinks at their hired villa on the beach. Chuck looked the quintessential statuesque Texan, while his sidekick resembled the old-fashioned brush cut military private eye type, he remembered from the movies from the 50 ties.

'We are having a little ole drinks party and would love to have you folks come by,' Chuck said.

As Hans walked over Chuck slapped him on the back. 'That invitation is open to you, too, Hans. You come by now, you hear?'

They had purchased a large number of painting and sculptures, it would be rude not to accept, Hans decided. Besides, it was always good to get to know people from other countries (it was too easy, in this small town, to get stuck in your own small circle of acquaintances), and perhaps they may have contacts in the art world in the States. Business wasn't about what you knew but who you knew, Hans told himself as he agreed to pop round to the villa at 7 the following evening.

Chuck and his partner-in-crime, Ethan, were scrambling their brains who else to invite to make their drinks party a memorable event. Not having been in Namibia long, they did not know anyone. Besides, they were having a tougher time socialising than they had in other countries with large expat communities (Spain, Italy, Mexico, Argentina, to name just a few places they had visited in recent years). They needed a rent-a-crowd, so Chuck spent the rest of the day writing out invites (a winningly old-fashioned thing to do, he thought with a smile), and calling on neighbours (a little Southern charm went a long way). Getting acquainted was always a good thing in a new neighbourhood, he thought as he dropped his invites. Certainly, it was very hot here, but then being from Texas Chuck was used to the heat – it made him feel at home, even.

Both wearing faded blue jeans, cowboy boots, and loose-hanging linen shirts, there was no mistaking who the Texans were amongst the party guests; only the Stetsons were missing.

Ethan noticed Fritzi immediately; she was hard to miss in any gathering. For a practiced eye like his, her mannerisms, which he had studied, were hard to ignore. She was a charismatic character, for sure: tall, lanky, and exquisite in her flamboyance, he felt relieved that the neighbours had turned up for free drinks, Texan chilli and Chimichangas, burritos by any other name. He made his way across to greet Hans and Yvetta, introducing himself and Chuck to Fritzi, then moving on expertly (after all, if he had done anything in his life it was host a lot of parties, almost all of them successful – for his purposes, at least), socialising among the other guests.

Chuck saw Hans move outdoors to take a call; he alerted Ethan, who moved to speak to a waiter close to the pool out on the patio, where a few of the dozen or so guests were seated at tables enjoying cocktails. Hans was standing behind a pillar, close enough for Ethan to hear his conversation with Fritzi.

He noted that Hans answered only in monosyllables, so unlike the man who, until very recently, had spoken so vigorously about the gallery and himself. He watched Hans shake his head, then look over to where Fritzi was standing with Yvetta. A crowd had gathered around the two women; Fritzi's charismatic personality drew people's interest where ever she was; she was a star around which others seemed desperate to orbit.

Hans turned to one of the waiters, downed a drink from a tray in one gulp, then made his excuses to his hosts and left.

Chuck followed from a distance. The days were hot but the nights often refreshingly cool. Hans obviously lived within walking distance of the beach. The German had made no further calls on his cell. Watching him from the pavement, Chuck waited a few moments; the German was clearly visible through the huge expanse of glass windows surrounding his home. Still, he had made no attempt to use his cell phone. Chuck watched him pour another drink from the drink's cabinet, then switch off the lights, leaving the front room in darkness.

Chuck immediately dialled Sasha in the States. Chuck wanted to check if Sasha had spoken to Hans as planned during the drinks evening, and to establish whether Hans had encountered any problems after their meeting in Windhoek with Fritzi. He was especially interested to establish whether she had seen Hans leave the hotel.

Both Chuck and Sasha agreed Hans would have alerted Fritzi about the call by now if he had double-crossed them. It was time to get serious, they would pay Hans a visit, make sure he knew what was at stake. Hans was about to get more involved in their sting on Fritzi and her network of smugglers than he perhaps was prepared to. But at this point he did not have a choice.

Hans opened his door to find Chuck and Ethan on his doorstep.

'Hey there, Hans, can we have a little ole word?' Chuck said, but his voice wasn't as friendly as before. He didn't sound so Southern all of a sudden, either.

'Sure,' Hans said, and his voice remained even, careful not to sound surprised, 'join me for a sundowner. It's that time of day here, a habit that's hard to break. I hope there wasn't a problem with the shipping of your artworks?'

'Nice place you got here,' Ethan said, ignoring the question.

'Yes,' Hans said, ever the diplomat, 'it's a passion. We were avid collectors of classic pieces, art and first editions, hence the overstuffed bookcases. The classic furniture are all originals.'

Poor old guy, Chuck thought, he's clearly still cut up about his wife's death. He mentions her often enough. He's clearly lonely. Maybe making him part of our plan will be doing him a favour in a way. It was easy for Chuck to go to great lengths to justify his actions – he had been doing it for years.

'Unfortunately,' Hans continued, 'I have no one to leave it all to, having had no children. A shame, really.' His voice became low. 'I mean, to die in comfort surrounded by the things we loved is morbid maybe.' He sounded very Germanic all of a sudden. 'All the same, it's something I have given much thought to'

'How old would you be, if I may ask?' Chuck said.

'Seventy-nine,' the German said with an odd smile. 'Getting up into the high numbers, but I still feel great.' He smoothed down his thinning hair, as if to emphasise this.

When they were all seated with drinks, Hans asked, 'Now what can I do for you both?'

Chuck spoke first. 'Fritzi is our bosses' concern,' he said, staring knowingly at Hans.

Since Hans offered no response, Chuck continued. 'Not only our bosses' concern, but the authorities around the globe, for that matter.'

'When you say *boss*,' the old man said slowly, 'do you mean Yvetta's brother, Sasha Rubicov?'

'Yes, you could say that,' Ethan volunteered, 'amongst others.'

'Who are you actually?' Hans said.

'You could say Intelligence,' Ethan said.

'CIA?'

'Close enough.'

'How do I fit in here?' Hans said. 'I thought the two women were happy young lovers, running away from family disapproval. I have been keeping Yvetta's brother up-to-date on his sister's wellbeing. To the best of my knowledge, that's all I was hired to do.' There was no longer any warmth in his voice. There was a shrewd look on his lined face now, and he appeared almost angry.

'It's slightly more complicated,' Ethan said. 'Fritzi and Yvetta are lovers, but Fritzi has been involved with international thefts from major collections. She is an arch criminal, an *ace* criminal. In her own way, she is a very dangerous person, although she may not seem like it. But if you can put her charm, which is of course considerable, aside… She is extremely good at what she does, and what she does is extremely bad. Some valuable works belonging to powerful organisations and countries have disappeared, you understand?'

Hans nodded that he did, indeed, understand. Still, he was not yet ready to commit. He felt deeply uneasy.

'She is involved up to her neck,' Ethan continued, 'works for this network of art thieves. But first we need to use her as bait, do you understand?'

This time, Hans was not sure that he did understand.

'I am still not sure where I fit in,' he said, and he suddenly felt the weight of these disclosures on his heart, on his head. 'Why don't you just apprehend Fritzi? After all, you know where she is. Why this charade'?

'Ah, that is where you come in, Hans,' Ethan put in. 'Why me?'

The old man looked and sounded very tired. It was time to cut to the chase.

'We are not quite ready to give Fritzi up,' Chuck said. 'She can be useful to us still.'

'And me?' Hans said. 'How can I be useful to you?'

'You are conveniently placed, and you have their trust. We need Fritzi as a decoy to flush out the main players. You must continue to inform us where Fritzi is at all times. Under no circumstances must you alert her in any way. This could be dangerous for Yvetta – and for you.'

'How so?'

'She is an extremely clever operator,' Chuck said. 'Slippery as an Eel when cornered.' He made a flapping motion with his right hand. 'Cunning as a fox. Here's where you come in, Hans, we would like you to put bugs in their home. We will make it very simple for you to place them when you next visit.'

'If I go along with this, what's in it for me?'

'Firstly, besides financial benefits, powerful people would be indebted to you. How you choose to make use of that, would be your business, of course, but you would be able to live comfortably anywhere in the world, if you so choose. If this sting is a success, that is.'

Hans was dumbfounded, wondering whether he was being hoodwinked into some elaborate hoax. He was old, lonely, and bored most of the time, this would add a generous dose of spice to his life and for next-to-no effort on his part. He could only stand to gain, could hardly refuse; at least he was on the right side of the law. At least he thought he was on the right side of the law – it was difficult to tell anymore. He felt dizzy from all the twists and turns since the two women had come into his life. What next?

'Okay, when do I do this job for you?' Hans said finally.

'Good chap, as my British counterparts would say, we knew we could depend on you.'

Chapter 14

Fritzi had come to trust and confide in Hans; he spoke German and reminded her of her past. Not that her past consisted of fond memories – that was why she was here, to rebuild her present and fine-tune her future, to give herself the life she so richly deserved, to reinvent herself once again. A new country, a new life. Turning the page, she thought, perhaps for the final time.

At least they had friends and kindly associates here, and she recognised this as an important first step in settling down into a new home. Hans, for example, was good to Yvetta and kept her out of mischief, which allowed Fritzi to get on with business unhindered. With Yvetta kept out of mischief, Fritzi could get up to mischief of her own. The two women's idea of mischief was often very different, of course, which was perhaps why they got along so well. Secrecy was something else that strengthened the relationship; Yvetta didn't know the things Fritzi got up to, and Fritzi liked it that way. Fritzi was always arguing for more honesty in their relationship, but then Fritzi was a great proponent of the 'do as I say, not as I do' philosophy. She had one set of standards for herself; one set for everyone else.

Still, when Fritzi gazed at you, when Fritzi *stayed* with you, she was undeniably special, and made you feel special, too. This attribute alone was worth more than diamonds and gold. That was why Fritzi, even when young and penniless, had felt undeniably and incalculably, rich. Her self-esteem was a Learjet upon which she travelled above the clouds. She knew she should be in the company of billionaires and famous artists, because deep down she felt, had always felt, that she too was a billionaire, deserving of high praise and infinite riches. Certainly, she illuminated Yvetta's often cloistered and unhappy world, something Hans himself had taken notice of.

Hans, too, evidently respected secrecy, gentility, diplomacy. Hans kept himself to himself, and who that self was was a mystery all on its own. He had an old-school tact – or detachment – that could be mistaken for respect, even affection. In fact, a still-grieving widower he was removed from everyone. Fritzi would love to dig into his life further, but had too much else on her mind right now. She was simply glad that Hans was around, and that she now had the time and space to attempt to sort out her life which had suddenly become impossibly complicated again. After months of solitude and simplicity, she was back inside the whirlwind – even if the threat to her had not yet fully shown itself – and, where usually she thrived on chaos and confusion, for the first time she wished only for quiet again. Perhaps even ever-young Fritzi was getting older and more staid. Or not.

If Fritzi asked Hans to take Yvetta on field trips with him, he never enquired why Fritzi wanted her out of the way. More importantly, Fritzi had sequestered Hans to keep a close eye on visitors to the gallery becoming too familiar with Yvetta. Fritzi wanted to be informed if anyone was inquiring about them; any questions, no matter how seemingly innocent, should be reported back to her. If Hans had any problems with this role, he did not express them. He was stoic as usual, going about his daily gallery business with a thin smile on his lined face.

Hans had not queried her requests; she figured he was happy to have sold his gallery, now working without hassles but working nonetheless. He needed something to occupy himself with, she thought, and especially to get his mind off his late wife and what must be, when he came home to it, a very empty house – well-furnished, certainly, but empty all the same. He had money in his bank account and a job to keep him busy. Though Fritzi had not expressed this to anyone, she suspected Hans was happier now than he had been when they first met. Somehow it felt good to have him as part of their lives and their world – he just fit in.

Lately she had noticed Hans visiting on a more regular basis, dropping in unannounced for drinks in the evenings. Once she found him playing on the floor with one of the servant's children; another time, with another child, he was throwing a ball in the garden. She figured he must be lonely, and had taken to treating both Fritzi and Yvetta and even their staff as extended family. However, now that she had problems overshadowing their peaceful existence in Swakopmund, she was not sure she wanted to encourage this kind of closeness.

It was a shame that her problems had followed her to Namibia; even though a popular holiday destination, the country had its benefits in more ways than she had imagined for her and Yvetta to continue their lives in peace. Namibia offered anonymity and great beauty – this place wasn't New York, London, or Berlin – but that was exactly what was so special about it. Everything had gone better than she could have imagined for them in Namibia, but she wondered for how much longer that would last. The email from the hacker signified that Fritzi's world was closing in on them once more, it was time to be on the alert. Fritzi reflected that a criminal past truly followed you around the world, whether you wanted it to or not. You only had a short amount of time in one place to truly be free, so you better enjoy that time and that place while you still could.

The hackers she employed on her behalf had come up with very little to explain why her Swiss bank account was suddenly overflowing with money, making her a very wealthy woman far beyond her dreams. Who would have thought having money could be a bad thing? But this mysterious money was keeping Fritzi up at night, tormenting her, driving her crazy. It was unnerving her in so many ways, and she hadn't yet settled on a solution. Was this what had been intended by the person or entity who deposited the money? Were they trying to drive her mad? If so, mission accomplished.

She wished she could rewind time to just a few weeks ago, and enjoy her old, untroubled Namibian life again. The money left her vulnerable to blackmail or worse – not knowing the true motivation was the worst punishment of all – they were hanging her out to dry, she would become expendable to her powerful contacts. For, even as Fritzi liked to believe (and portray herself) as powerful in her own rights, the truth was that she was very low down on the criminal food chain. She had very little real power, and what power she had was firmly in her own mind, her ego, her projection to others of herself.

But even her self-esteem wasn't what it once was – she felt rattled by her bank account, and by not knowing what was in store for her now.

For the first time in a long while, she was losing her cool. This was not to say that her life was entirely unravelling.

Her inbox was busier than ever, there were plenty of inquiries for her services under the different guises she had devised to be contacted through; surely if they were hanging her out to dry, the jobs would have slowly dried up by now? Or were these emails meant to confuse her further?

There were too many variables to check, and she wasn't getting a handle on any one of them. Every avenue she had tested and gone down had come up empty. Still, her instincts told a different story – something was up, but what? How could she plan or deal with a situation when she had little to go on apart from the money lying in her Swiss bank account? She hoped that Yvetta had not detected her newly anxious state. Yvetta tended to be unusually perceptive about Fritzi's many moods, and with each new mood there were a series of questions – questions Fritzi could not answer right now. No, she did not want Yvetta to know any of this.

It had been eight weeks since her return from Zurich; to her knowledge, no one had been in touch through any of her usual channels. Things were definitely too quiet; decisions had to be made one way or another. Perhaps another trip to Zurich was the answer?

Herr Stoffel was the only one who could shed any light on the deposit. He had to be pressured into action on her behalf; after all, he was sitting on her fortune. She was sure he would cooperate if she offered him a large-enough sweetener. He was only human, after all. It was the only avenue left open, persuading him in no uncertain terms to give her a clue about the funds residing in her account; she needed a lead to counter the attack she felt was coming.

Yvetta had become accepting of her partners comings and goings. Fritzi felt safe in the knowledge that Hans and the staff were around in her absence should anything happen during her travels away. She was suddenly a lot less certain of her life than she had been just a few months ago. Yvetta brought her stability, intimacy, affection; she had someone to come back to. So much in life was conditional, but Yvetta's love, at its purest, felt unconditional. Yvetta had changed Fritzi, who no longer took reckless chances, and had no need for subterfuge any longer.

Fritzi liked to think that they had changed each other, and for the better. Alexi Rubicov was dead, his sons were useless, toothless Oligarch's running away with their tails between their legs from Russia. As for Anna, she was no longer a force to be reckoned with, they had seen to that.

Fritzi was left free to concentrate on her business dealings, setting up meetings with contacts for the next big deal or heist. These contacts were deeply involved in the art world; many priceless antiquities were being sold to buyers wanting relics from wars in the Middle East, artefacts destroyed by terrorist fanatics; even prestigious museums were offering staggering sums for the smallest fragments.

They needed people like Fritzi and her people as go-betweens; in the end no one cared where the bulk of the money came from or went to, least of all her contacts, for whom it was all in a day's work.

Many were sent deep into the desert to secure fragments of these ancient historical relics. Statues, palaces, and religious icons were now peddled to the highest bidder in underground caves used as art markets away from drones or prying eyes.

Like in any other auction, the highest bidder walked away with some of the most priceless loot.

If the finger of suspicion fell on any untrustworthy infiltrator, they were dispatched by a desert law older than the antiquities they were offering. But Fritzi's contacts knew the ropes; they had been in dangerous situations all over the globe, working for some of the most high-profile secret establishments, prepared to pay almost anything for the smallest of these antiquities.

The network had to be protected at all costs from the slightest exposure, layer upon layer of protection was built in, to keep the syndicate safe. Many had tried and failed to break through over the years, but there were too many layers, and punishment for infiltration was too severe. You did not mess with the syndicate and live to tell the tale.

The syndicate included powerbrokers from many countries. Fritzi had her suspicions about some of these players; Rome perhaps was involved somewhere along the line, amongst many other brokers.

If the syndicate got the smallest whiff of danger, Fritzi would be instantly exposed to the darkest of forces. There was no doubt her life would be snuffed out immediately. Not that Fritzi, long steeped in the rules of the game and only too aware of her own position in the syndicate, would ever damage her own nest. The people she knew and worked with took no prisoners; many of her contacts had disappeared or died untimely deaths; she was going to make sure she was not on that hitlist.

If she became aware that something bad was coming, she would have to sound an alert in the right quarters. The ranks would close around international networks; it was her best chance of saving herself from being taken out. The syndicate had their people in every profession, every walk of life.

Her only problem was who to trust with the information about her sudden swollen coffers in a numbered Swiss account? This information could backfire on her – horribly.

Forces were at work beyond Fritzi's control; they had been put into motion by security agents across the globe. Government agencies and private players were working together to stop one of the darkest religious, political terror organisations that had ever entered the world stage from looting ancient sites for enormous profits to shore up their coffers and use the money to buy arms and take lives, and increase their reign of terror.

Some of these agencies were working for economic reasons, others for political and religious reasons, to protect liberty, democracy, and the safety of their own state, but all of them had the same agenda: to stop what they perceived to be an evil juggernaut from gaining any further foothold in what could become an accepted normality in an already dangerous and divided part of the world that could easily spill over into the West, destroying innocent lives. Looting was one of the organisation's most profitable side lines and, while the war was at its peak, there were many who would take advantage to buy their illegal medieval loot.

The Rubicovs' reasons in apprehending Fritzi remained personal. Their interest in Fritzi was purely one-dimensional: to rid their family of someone who had wreaked havoc for far too long, and to extricate Yvetta from Fritzi's world. If it meant providing others with an opportunity to apprehend Fritzi, so be it – as long as Fritzi did not bounce back (or defy the system that was containing her) anytime soon, as had happened last time.

Whoever managed to take her out would be doing the family a favour. The Rubicovs would provide all information to the authorities involved (and the family had now learnt that there were multiple authorities trying to bust open the scheme and arrest the players for many different reasons). Whatever game Fritzi was playing, or had become involved with, was catching up with her at last.

The danger for the family was in keeping Yvetta safe from being caught up in the midst of the sting that was being engineered by those involved in apprehending Fritzi. Trying to lure Fritzi into their net and getting her to reveal her sources, without alerting Fritzi's suspicions. Too often in the past Yvetta had become inextricably involved in Fritzi's machinations – which was no doubt in Fritzi's self-interest as well. From the family's perspective, it was impossible to make Yvetta see the truth about Fritzi, and they had long ago given up trying.

Hans was on a call with Sasha. Hans had installed the listening devices in Fritzi's office without suspicion, but he believed she was in a state of high alert. He had been asked by Fritzi to report any suspicious persons or activity; he informed Sasha that her behaviour had become more entrenched and odder since her return from Switzerland.

He told Sasha that Fritzi was apparently considering a trip to Europe in the next week. It was none of his business, Hans continued, but could they not apprehend her then, leaving Yvetta and himself out of the whole affair? This whole business was making him nervous.

Sasha gave it some thought. 'I will come back to you when I know more,' he said finally. 'It's a sound suggestion, Hans, but at the moment I'm afraid it's out of my hands.'

Hans did not like the sound of this. He was prepared to help, but all the cloak-and-dagger stuff was making him more than a bit anxious. If Sasha wasn't in control, who exactly was? How dangerous were these people, and to what degree was his own life in danger? He hadn't reckoned for any of this. He had intended to relax and retire, not a late-in-life career change as an undercover agent.

Yvetta had begun to behave erratically, especially since Fritzi's mood had changed to one of overprotective aggression. Fritzi's control of Yvetta's day to day excursions with the households extended family namely the children of their staff, had become, not only for their staff and, parents of the children but for anyone who witnessed Yvetta's affection and hold over their day to day lives, she had taken over as their mother, ignoring reality.

When taken to task about it, after Han's presumed the staff had requested Fritzi to intervene, on their behalf, Yvetta had thrown a tantrum Han's hadn't witnessed beforehand and, had left shaken to the chore realising Yvetta wasn't stable, beating her brow biting herself and, throwing whatever came to hand at the wall, kicking and screaming when Fritzi manhandled her into their bedroom locking the door.

He had not mentioned this fact to her brother and decided he would if she flared up into an uncontrollable rage again. They had lost one valuable member of staff as a result, of Yvetta's rudeness and Hans did not want the gallery to become the talk of the town for unfavourable reasons.

Word travelled fast here in the middle of nowhere, and if this incident happened more often, if the gallery developed a reputation for being unstable or unprofessional, there would be serious repercussions for the gallery that Hans had, for so long, poured his heart and soul into and, with his darling wife, the love of his life, built from scratch. How hard he and his wife had worked to make the gallery infinitely respectable, a name known outside of even Windhoek, perhaps known overseas as well. And how quickly, indeed, a reputation, built over many years, could be demolished. Hans hadn't been in the business for most of his life for nothing. He knew the way things worked – and, he thought, he knew *crazy* when he saw it. He was less and less comfortable with the way Fritzi and Yvetta's relationship was playing out, and how this was affecting the atmosphere of the gallery. They lived in a small community and bad news travelled like lightening. He found Yvetta to be particularly paranoid of late. They were all, even the cleaning staff, walking on eggshells around her at the gallery. She saw provocation in almost everything, picking on them for the least little thing.

Things between her and Fritzi were obviously fraught at the moment. Hans could guess why, but all the same he worried that the whole sordid affair might blow up in his face. Hans had had enough trouble in his life, he didn't want other people's trouble spilling onto him.

On the one hand, Fritzi wanted to take the money and run. But she knew only too well there was nowhere to hide. If she wired the money into some fabricated offshore company, whoever had had the ability to put it in her numbered account would track it, she was sure of that.

For all her clever schemes over the years this one was out smarting her – or was it? Was Fritzi, who outsmarted everyone all the time, who exploited and engineered, finally being taken for a ride? And where, precisely, was this scam taking her? Was she becoming slow and soft in the head now that she had found a safe haven for her and Yvetta? She had felt content, even happy until she found this shitload of money sitting in her numbered account.

Apart from allowing her to accesses it when and where she needed it, her account was of little value. The rest of her assets were in safety deposit boxes spread throughout the world. The new funds sitting in her account had to come from somewhere. Fritzi knew the Swiss authorities were now obliged to work with world authorities if any suspicions were to befall on one of their account holders. If there had been anything suggesting she was laundering money for some illegal purpose, she would have heard from the Swiss authorities by now, surely?

She had no way of proving where the money had come from, and therefore had no idea yet why it was there, or who wanted it there, or why. And what did Fritzi have to do with it all? She still didn't have a clue.

She had travelled down every avenue, trying not to alert suspicion, but had come up with nothing. It was driving her to distraction, waiting for them to show their hand. She wished she had something to go on, be it good or bad.

It was time for action, one way or another. Her hacker friends had not been able to trace where the funds had originated, which was odd. Her trusted contacts in the field came up with no answers, either. This only left Herr Stoffel at the Swiss bank to interrogate. She had no other options open to her.

She decided to drop Herr Stoffel an email about the funds and her next visit to discuss what to do with them.

Unknown to Fritzi, the intelligence agency working in LA were tracking her every move: each email she wrote was now on their screens, each contact she had was now open to securitisation; they were waiting for her to make a move before they made their countermove, avoiding any unnecessary suspicion.

Also unknown to Fritzi, Herr Stoffel was an intelligence agent put in place to start the ball rolling. So far they had leads to a new group of hackers who worked on the dark web following conversations once they broke into their suspects' computers. Fritzi's contacts had many firewalls, but the hackers they used at the intelligence bureau in LA were easily a match. Anything written to Fritzi could be traced back to other contacts, working down the line to whoever had been part of the conversation.

Herr Stoffel had been instructed to respond with an appointment when Fritzi arrived in Geneva or Zurich; either would be convenient for the bank.

They had not yet tracked down the movers and shakers in the network. From Fritzi's computer they were able to follow leads of well-known heists, including jobs they had not been alerted about, all lucrative, priceless, illegal art thefts.

The insurance companies felt they had enough to bring a charge that would put Fritzi away for a very long time, but they needed to keep Fritzi hooked until she led them to the top players and ringleaders.

They had to track down her contacts in the art world, alerting the smugglers what to steal; they were playing for high stakes. If they got lucky, the contacts would lead them to antiquities and priceless art stolen from museums and private collections through the years.

Fritzi would be handed over to the Russian authorities for absconding from one of their prisons, whatever happened she would not be able to fiddle her escape this time round; she was in their net and they were determined to catch more than just one small fish with her help.

The authorities felt sure that Fritzi would offer Herr Stoffel a sweetener for information. After all, she desperately needed to know who had wired the money into her account, and Herr Stoffel was the only person she knew who would be able to access the information for her.

The Swiss sky was ice blue and the snow hung heavily on the eves of the rooftops as, Fritzi walked into Herr Stoffel's office in Geneva, looking every bit the high-powered, sophisticated businesswoman, with that carefree air of those used to getting their own way. For his part, Herr Stoffel, ever the professional, a career intelligence agent, had long been expecting this moment. He could see the impatience and anxiety written all over her lean body, much as she tried to hide it and pretended to be happy to see him. Was the famously-always-calm-even-under-extreme-pressure Fritzi now finally showing her nerves? Or were these antics – deliberately slight and notable only to the practised eye – just another bluff in the endless poker game that was Fritzi's infamous life.

Pleasantries over, Fritzi wasted little time. 'I need a favour, Herr Stoffel,' Fritzi said, and gave him her smile reserved only for people who could advance her own life in some way, a smile that said she needed something important, and that only an important person, like the person she was currently speaking to, could provide this for her. A smile that would have melted hearts in a younger or less man (or woman). Her Stoffel returned the smile with an even gaze, but quietly held his ground. He wasn't going to help her out, he was going to make her work for this. He had heard she could be quite mesmerising, and he wanted to see for himself.

Fritzi leaned forward, let the silence stalk the room, enjoyed the sudden quiet, seemed to bask in it, making him wait, as though she alone was in power now – and perhaps she was. He smiled, let her have this moment, this imagined smile. 'For this favour,' she said, lowering her voice, but her smile and her direct gaze fixed on his, like a flag but not removing it, keeping both her smile and her body steady now, flicking a finger, snuffing out the silence like a candle flame, 'I am prepared to pay a very high price in money, or, perhaps valuable antiquities, or priceless art you may want for your private collection.'

Silence again as Herr Stoffel feigned surprise. He was good at this, was every bit as much as a practised actor as Fritzi. They should appear in a production together, he slyly thought. Indeed, as it happened, they were doing exactly that. He reflected on her flirtatious gestures, her studied spontaneity – it, too, was rehearsed. The only thing authentic about her, he reflected, was her utter lack of authenticity. He looked at her closer. No, who was he kidding, the smouldering lips, the lean arms and shapely legs, the way she seemed to be moving even in her stationary chair, coming closer to him, the sexual energy she manufactured out of thin air and used like a weapon, she was masterful. And thus, watching her was in itself a kind of master class. She was surely one of the best there was, and perhaps only hubris and bad luck had kept her from taking over the world.

'Ah well,' Her Stoffel said slowly, and he was smiling now, too. Her smile was infectious, as was her energy. Her Stoffel wasn't naturally a flirtatious man (he was happily and faithfully married, for one thing, and his oldest child wasn't too much younger than Fritzi), but he gave it his best, 'you know this is not usual, but tell me the favour, yes?'

He teased out the silence, then handed it over to her for closer inspection. But she surprised him by becoming suddenly abrupt.

Fritzi switched to her masterful role-playing. 'Well, it's extremely personal,' she said, and made a flustered gesture that should have been nominated for an Academy Award. Cool as a cucumber one moment and pretending to sweat the next, she really was a natural. 'I have no option, you understand, it is a very delicate situation.'

You understand, staring him in the eyes, appealing to his better nature, his best nature. As though only the two of them existed, not merely in the room, but in the world.

'Yes, I understand,' he said, enjoying the scene all of a sudden, 'please continue.'

'It's my grandfather and my father,' she said, a new note of tenderness in her voice, somewhere between sentimental and sympathetic, a quaver in her voice appearing like a line of strain between the eyes, 'you understand my grandfather was a terrible man, I am sad to say. I never tell anyone,' and she looked at him with unusual intimacy again, as though Herr Stoffel was meant to believe he was extremely special to be confided in by her, that he was, in fact, blessed, 'you see, he was a Nazi during the war and when the two Germanies split and the Berlin Wall went up, he conveniently became a Stasi, as did my father.'

Herr Stoffel was well-versed in Fritzi's file, and knew all of this to be true. Masterful again, just as he expected her to tell a lie, she stymied him by telling the truth. Now it was his turn to lean forward. He had stopped smiling. He no longer knew what was real or what wasn't. 'Yes,' he said simply. She looked back at him, took in his one-word answer, seemed somehow satisfied.

'Yes,' she repeated, and there was a new note of pride in her voice. She nodded. 'I do not want anything to do with them, but I do believe the large sum now in my account must be from my grandfather. He stole from innocent Jews, becoming a very rich old man way, beyond his dreams, through his years of terror.' Herr Stoffel stifled his desire to smile. Fritzi's grandfather had indeed been a Stasi and, by all accounts, an awful human being, but he had not become fabulously wealthy, even on the back of dead Jews. This was pure fabrication, but artful nonetheless. The old man had in fact died penniless, a drunk and a Jew-hater to the very end. Done in not just by Nazism and being on the losing side of an awful war, but then by communism, which he bought into wholeheartedly and which cost him everything. Evidently, the old man lacked his granddaughter's ingenuity, resilience, and finesse.

Herr Stoffel couldn't immediately say who was the less desirable character – grandfather or granddaughter – but one thing was for sure, they gave each other a run for their money. But that money wasn't in the billions – not by a long shot. He gave Fritzi a cursory glance, the equivalent of a raised eyebrow. Perhaps he was wrong to do even this, but she was talking fast now, perhaps flustered for real. Or maybe not. Who was he to say?

'I was his only living relative,' she continued, and suddenly she was looking away from him, at the bookshelf behind him, and above and behind that, out the window, at the snow that freshly covered the black tar of the road. *Pure as the driven snow*, Herr Stoffel considered the phrase while he looked at the utterly corrupt Fritzi who seemed at that moment to be as innocent, as vulnerable, as tangible and helpless as a new-born babe.

She paused, bit her lower lip, perhaps decided to reformulate or refine her story. Who knew what went on in that head of hers? Certainly not Fritzi herself, Herr Stoffel thought. And yet she was good company – he had to give her that. He hadn't been this entertained for some time. She would be a riotous entertainer if she wasn't a cold-blooded criminal capable of dark deeds. 'Even though we had no contact, he may have been able to find out my banking details, leaving his dirty money to me.' She crinkled up her taut, elegant, unlined face, made an appropriately dirty expression. For a moment, perhaps intentionally, she looked like a little girl. 'If this is the case,' the voice now was soft and low and little-girlish, too, 'I must know, you understand? I would then donate the funds to a charity of my choice. I could not possibly keep this money, knowing the horrendous things they did to innocent victims living during the war.' She fell silent again, as though exhausted, bowed her head. From some auditorium not far away, the crowd performed a standing ovation. Flowers were thrown while claps, cheers, tears, and chants of 'Encore!' echoed for miles.

Herr Stoffel sat in silence, too. She was one hell of an operator, he thought.

'I won't take too long,' he said finally, 'but you'll have to excuse me while I look into this for you. It is highly irregular, you understand, but under the circumstances we may be able to track the sender of the funds, or at least where the funds came from.'

'I would be more than grateful, you understand?' She gave him a meaningful smile.

'It would be my pleasure to present you with a gift, perhaps some art to hang on your walls?'

Herr Stoffel smiled benevolently, wondered if this 'gift' possibly included other things as well, and left Fritzi with a glass of iced water while he made contact with his superiors on how to proceed.

Fritzi looked up with an anxious expression as he entered, and this time her anxiety appeared authentic. She was no longer playing around. But then neither was he. They were close now. Herr Stoffel took the seat opposite her, now no longer sitting behind his desk.

'It may take a few hours,' he said softly, 'but I will most definitely do this for you.'

'You must call me Frieda, please. Now tell me, Herr Stoffel, how can I repay you? I like to settle my debts.'

A career thief who liked to settle her debts – this was amusing, thought Herr Stoffel, but he said only, 'Ag, nein, not necessary,' and then, wryly, a mischievous note in his voice, 'though I am partial to Picasso, especially from his Blue Period, the valuable older works.'

Fritzi smiled and winked. She had the uncomfortable feeling that she detected a note of self-amusement or insincerity in his voice, but she wasn't sure. She thought that Herr Stoffel was implacable, and this annoyed her: she liked her targets to be easy to operate, to manipulate, to read and to use. Herr Stoffel, on the other hand, would have made an excellent poker player, like herself. Still, she enjoyed nothing so much as a challenge. She could always manipulate young heterosexual men (and, for that matter, women), but men who were old, or gay, or both, it wasn't always that easy, although she had been known to work wonders in her time. But now she felt genuinely jumpy, eager to get this over with, get back on the plane, go home to Yvetta once again. She even missed that old fogey, Hans.

'We'll see,' she said slyly, on-form again and giving nothing away, a flash of fire in her eyes, 'perhaps a small antiquity, if not a Picasso.' Counter to her nature, she had acted deferential and sweet for too long, she was ready to assert her true self once again. She had given him enough, she thought; now she wanted something in return.

'I believe since the unrest in the Middle East they are not hard to come by,' Herr Stoffel said, who knew more about the subject than most, suddenly asserting himself too, but his voice still soft, gently probing, inquiring, 'if one knows the right people.'

'Yes, I have read about this,' she said airily, sounding tired, 'such a travesty.'

Herr Stoffel smiled. He was tired too. Time to end this meeting, or whatever it was. Both would no doubt leave thinking it a success. 'Let me have your contact details at your hotel,' he said, returning to his original discreet-but-professional tone, 'and I will call as soon as I have the information about your account.'

Fritzi scribbled down her cell number, shook Herr Stoffel's hand, and left with a spring in her step, knowing she as good as had the information in the bag.

All she needed was a hint as to the identity of her mysterious benefactor; after which she would have her contacts find all of the answers.

Herr Stoffel, the intelligence officer, had just acquired her work cell details, and sent them straight off to his associates.

They would delay the information she required for as long as it took them to find a foothold into her criminal network. For, despite her own pretensions and delusions of grandeur, Fritzi was a small fish in a large and rather poisonous pond. She may be a very shrewd, attractive fish, but that was all she was, one fish among many others, some with sharper teeth and even stronger wills. And some of them weren't fish at all – they were sharks. They would rip you to shreds if you so much as glanced their way. They could smell blood on the water, and they thrived on it. And when mere teeth would not do, they had other weapons at their disposal – guns, bombs. Herr Stoffel knew, too, that these fish fed on each other, and he wasn't about to lose Fritzi – not yet, at least. She was too valuable right now.

Her primary asset to him was not artwork or artefacts but information, solid leads, bigger fish. Through her the intelligence agencies would hopefully uncover numbers and networks, which they would then infiltrate with their own people. It would take time, but in the end they would find the stolen art and antiquities, tracing them back to sellers and buyers alike. Whichever art dealers were passing on information to the criminal networks, or helping to set up heists, would soon be set up themselves, exposed and imprisoned. Herr Stoffel could not wait for the ring to be busted wide open; he had been working on this case long enough. He was tired and wanted a rest and something other than art theft to be fixated on. He had long been fascinated both by the art world and the criminal world, but right now, he had had quite enough of both.

Fritzi would have to remain in Geneva until she secured the information she required. Herr Stoffel was a gentle and diplomatic man – too gentle, too diplomatic, Fritzi thought. She did not know what to make of him, which meant he wasn't an easy mark. And this irritated her. Who was playing whom? She suspected the banker might just try to brush her off with irrelevant information of little use to her. And if so, what recourse did she have? She needed him – he was the only source of information she had. She would stay here until she had some solid evidence to give her people in the hacking trade, who could then uncover the identity of her benefactor. After that, she would deal with the situation in her own way.

Herr Stoffel had been requested to accept Fritzi's offer of an antiquity or any major artwork she offered, it would be to their advantage to follow her dealings for any of these works if genuine. If possible, he would play hardball, extracting the artwork before he handed over any of the information she was seeking. The hope was that, even if she suspected something and didn't hand over an antiquity, they would have enough information from her computer and cell phone to infiltrate the network.

No matter how she decided to react, Fritzi would be apprehended, but only when she was no longer useful to the intelligence agencies, when she was expendable once again.

Herr Stoffel waited three days before making contact with Fritzi on her cell phone. She was to visit his Zurich office the following day, but he wanted to warn her that the information she had requested had not been easily obtained, and, considering how he had put himself out for her, he would most definitely want to be rewarded. After all, he stressed, he could suffer repercussions, his illegal disclosure could backfire on the bank – and on himself.

Fritzi had expected as much. She knew of no banker who would give anything for nothing, no matter how polite they pretended to be. All bankers were the same, greedy bastards. For this reason, she had organised with one of her many dealers in France to secure valuable small Picasso, and from her Middle Eastern colleagues she secured a tiny fragment of the butchered ancient ruins of Iraq. In their early days of murder and mayhem, Isis had flooded the black market with these fragments for a quick turnover of funds – funds that went to furthering their cause, thus producing more murder and mayhem. It was a vicious circle, but then this described the underground art market as well.

From Fritzi's perspective, it was a small price to pay to extricate herself from any knowledge of the funds she found in her private numbered account. She was desperate to keep her connections to the black market, and to those she had been doing very lucrative business with for many years. They would cut her off before she had the slightest inkling; it would not take long before they found her bloated body floating down a Swiss lake. Fritzi knew the game, had played it often enough. A player might have a long and impressive winning streak, but, as with any kind of gambling, it never lasted for ever. It always ended the same way: a gunshot, an 'accident,' an unexpected fall off a very high (albeit scenic) balcony, 'suicide' that wasn't anything of the sort. And when you lost one big bet, that was the end of it. There was no such thing as losing twice, not in this game, not in her line of work. Deep down, Fritzi knew the truth: there were no long-time winners in this profession; everyone lost in the end. The game ate the players; the pool swallowed the fish, large and small alike; the house always won. Large and small alike, they all went down, their stories illicit, untold, even their deaths a whisper, a rumour, an inconveniently honest report conveniently gone missing, a question mark dangling infinitely like a hangman's noose.

Janus's LA agency had made it blatantly clear to the hackers they employed that they had to tiptoe on this job, no leak was to be evident anywhere along the line. The agency was terrified that if it was discovered by the criminal network that they were being hacked, Fritzi would be terminated immediately, cutting off all her key contacts. In this event, everything they had accomplished on the case up to now would be for nought, the syndicate would become even more impenetrable, they would go dark, blotting out any leads the agency might have been able to infiltrate.

So a whiff of suspicion did not befall her, the Intelligence agencies would even allow Fritzi to escape her jailers to continue her dealings. It was a delicate operation, no one wanted to scare the big boys off; but it was not that easy to convince Mika or Sasha to allow their long-time nemesis to escape arrest. After all, despite their efforts to lock her away and to their considerable humiliation (a humiliation that, if the Rubicov brothers were honest, still burned like a wound), Fritzi had escaped countless times, outsmarting the family over and over again, attacking them repeatedly in one form or another. She was a danger to the family when she was free; and, even when she was imprisoned, she appeared always to be plotting something, desperate for vengeance, more evil than ever.

Persuading the Rubicovs to allow her escape yet again in order to catch a bigger fish was a bloody hard sell; short of murdering her, they wanted her gone from their lives forever, her unrelenting possessive hold on Yvetta had caused the family too much heartache.

Fritzi met with Mr. Stoffel at his Zurich office, carrying a small, valuable first-edition Picasso print and a fragment of an ancient Iraqi temple destroyed by those Isis maniacs in the Middle East, bad for everyone else but not for the art dealers she worked with, who were so adept at turning tragedy into good fortune. Sometimes, the difference between an art dealer and a war profiteer wasn't much more than semantic. Someone always benefited from war one way or another; money was always involved in any war. Almost everyone lost, but some people – the few, the lucky, the ruthless, the soulless, the utterly sociopathic – got filthy rich. The bigger and messier and uglier the war, the more money was spent, the richer some people got, while the majority of people in the war-torn country had to fight for their lives – or, if they were lucky, flee the country. Art was looted from the Jews in the Second World War; the authorities were still (even today!) trying to establish ownership, almost a century after the thefts. It was easy to steal, easy also to kill, but not so easy to reclaim what was rightfully yours, to fight for justice, and to win. All these decades later, the war in the Middle East was no different; theft was a major money-making machine. Down the millennia, rich pickings were the trade of any war, not to mention land (Europe, and much of the rest of the world, had been carved up and out of war), so Fritzi never felt the least bit guilty. In general, feelings of guilt were entirely foreign to Fritzi, who lived in the moment and operated entirely for herself and Yvetta, the only other person she had any affection for. Everyone else was expendable to Fritzi – and, Fritzi was only too aware – she herself was expendable to those high up in her organisation. Her trade placed the precious cargo in the ownership of the thieves, and Fritzi was damn good at subterfuge had no intention of retiring yet – or, perhaps, ever.

To her mind, she wasn't just a criminal, but a master criminal – not any old street artist but the real-deal, a kind of Picasso of the underworld. Crime wasn't so much her profession as her vocation. To deny the world her gifts would itself be a crime. At least this was how Fritzi reckoned and rationalised it in her more self-aggrandising and delusionary moments. Who but the criminal version of Picasso to handle the work of the other Picasso (himself often rumoured to be something of a charlatan, a chameleon, a cad). After all, it took a thief to catch a thief. That she had avoided long-term imprisonment up to now certainly spoke to her own superiority as a criminal, and the ineptitude of everyone else, to escape her captors.

Seated behind a beautiful oak desk, looking more rested than he had the other day, in a pinstripe suit, annoyingly neat and proper with not a hair out of place his square jaw set and, dull eyes fixed on what was pleasing him a faint smile on his thin lips, Herr Stoffel could not hide his delight at the marvellous small Picasso she offered up out of her large bag. He smiled more effusively than usual – a smile that was the equivalent of a wink, furtive, sneaky, clandestine – to signify that they were now working together, that her secret was now his, too, that this transaction and conversation was strictly private. He wanted to relay that what was going on here was highly confidential (i.e. highly unethical), but that they were in on this together. 'We can speak freely here,' he said, putting aside his smile and waving his hand to assure her that there were no cameras or offending equipment in his office. Perhaps this over compensatory gesture should have tipped her off; but it didn't. She smiled, too, as he waxed lyrical over every inch of the beautiful miniature antiquity. She had never seen this otherwise staid man so animated, so ecstatic. At times like this, Fritzi remembered why people went to such lengths, spent absurd amounts, even risked their own lives to get great works of art in their hands. Great art was life-affirming, more of a thrill than any drug on the market – and more expensive, too. Dizzy with ownership, he sat down in the leather armchair next to Fritzi.

'Do you have the provenance for these wonderful artworks?' His soft voice trembled a little.

Fritzi smiled knowingly. 'Well, of course, dear Mr Stoffel – Henrick, if I may call you that.' They were exchanging illicit material – art, information – it was time to put aside formalities and exist on more intimate terms. To assure him of this, her smile – in fact, her whole face – became altogether more intimate, as it had in their last meeting. 'But first we have to exchange as agreed, yes?'

This was the bit Stoffel was not looking forward to. The LA office had had trouble coming up with a clear solution to the problem that Fritzi's visit posed, and he would now have to muddle his way through until he heard word from LA on how precisely to proceed, further before allowing her to escape their clutches.

'Ja, Ja, of course,' he said, trying to keep his voice even and to retain the delighted tone of just a minute ago. But whatever delights had been in the air a moment ago – the gifts bestowed upon by the Picasso – were gone now, and a curious air of expectation and frustration replaced it. He could feel the electricity of Fritzi's impatience. He realised, not for the first time, that he was a little afraid of this strange and storied woman. 'But there was a slight hitch, you understand, the reason for the delay, you see.'

The surge of uneasy electricity increased, flexed itself, metastasised. Fritzi stared at Herr Stoffel, not liking what she was hearing, her hackles started to rise. She didn't know where her hackles were, exactly, but she knew she had a lot of them, more than most people. She could feel the hair prickling down her neck, her throat started to constrict, and she felt in her bag for the tiny Berretta, locking her fingers round the catch to release it. She knew to use it only in an emergency situation, if she needed to escape; to use it more liberally would have disastrous repercussions – would probably mean she would be arrested at the airport, if not before. Was she being played? Had she been a fool to come here, and to bring the artwork with her? She looked at him closely, as if to detect his true motives. More anxious than he would like to admit, but determined to remain calm, Herr Stoffel stared back. He smiled, but her face remained stone. The hackles were cutting off her blood supply, shooting towards her heart. She ran through her options in her head, but her head, heavy with hackles, was slow to respond. The grip of the gun, at least, felt comfortable, cool. How she wanted to draw it out, and point, and shoot.

How the presence of a gun changed everything, the mood of a room, its occupants. Not at all sure of her next move, she released the catch and pointed at Herr Stoffel's considerable midriff through the canvas of her large LV shoulder-bag. Herr Stoffel stared at the gun, surprised in spite of himself. He had not thought it would come to this, not so quickly. He had thought, for some reason, that Fritzi would have more class. Clearly he was wrong. Perhaps the intelligence agency had overestimated her gifts as an operator. Or perhaps not. After all, what was more persuasive than having a gun pointed right at you? Being gifted with a Picasso was one thing, but being threatened with a gun was something else entirely. But Herr Stoffel had been trained to operate smoothly under pressure. It was not the first time he had had a gun pointed at him (though it was the first time that his assailant had been so elegantly attired or attractive-looking), and, his retirement imminent, he hoped it would be the last. He was comforted, too, to know that, in spite of his assurances to Fritzi to the contrary, there were of course security cameras in his office. But was anyone watching? And how would the agency play this? When would they move in? How would *he* play it? Certainly, he had come up with a game plan for a moment such as this (he had been trained to prepare for anything and everything; to 'game out,' as the Americans put it, various circumstances and scenarios, so as to be on top of any situation), but right now he could not for the life of him recall what that game plan was. Having a gun pointed at you tended to scramble your brain – and your plans. He recalled a quote by the American boxer, Mike Tyson: 'Everyone has a plan, until they get punched in the mouth.' It didn't matter who you were, or how many times before you had been confronted with a gun, but being in such a situation levelled one. The other person was rarely present in those moments: it was just about you and the gun aimed at you. Just the two of them, the gun and him. Perhaps it would be easier to reason directly with the gun? Cut Fritzi out of the conversation. After all, right now, at least, she didn't seem in control of her emotions. And that was scary. She was glaring at him, flexing her hand with the gun in it, aiming now for his head.

'Come now, Herr Stoffel,' Fritzi said, her voice calmer now, 'we are both adults here.'

'Indeed,' he said, looking at her again, this time trying not to look at the gun, just at her. He could hear a clock ticking from somewhere down the hall. He waited for something to happen. Then he heard the gun, a click – perhaps she had switched the safety off. He nodded, handed over the paper with the co-ordinates from the account the money was wired from.

Fritzi stared at the combination of numbers and then shrugged, still holding the gun pointed at Stoffel's head. She lowered it to his midriff again. It was as though they were going around in a circle, doing some terrible, dangerous dance, the moves to which Herr Stoffel did not know. All he knew was that Fritzi was entirely in control.

'I see you understand the combination was run through our data,' he said, 'but it proved to bring up no conclusive place of origin. A place of origin was exactly what you required, yes?'

Fritzi nodded, flicking her eyes towards the door, wondering whether this was a trap. Had she ensnared herself, walked right into this trap? Could she have made it any easier for them? Perhaps she should train the gun on herself, due to her own stupidity? Was she her own worst enemy? Had she been an idiot to believe this money was placed in her account by her own sources? She thought she was beginning to see the light.

Ever attentive, Herr Stoffel watched her closely to see whether she was having doubts about the authenticity of their complicated ruse. He thought he glimpsed a slight flicker in her eyes, now harder than ever, as her tight mouth twisted (also very slightly). Her body erect, alert, primed to run – or to kill. Again, of course, he glanced at the protrusion in her purse, the unmistakeable gun-shape, now slowly being lowered on to her lap once more. Was it a reprieve? An impasse? A détente? A second – and final – chance? He did not know, and not knowing was in itself a kind of wound. But then Fritzi herself did not know what was next – they were unified in their ignorance of the precise motives of the other. His next sentence would either make or break their elaborate charade.

Stoffel held out another piece of folded paper and nodded for her to look at it. To placate her, he smiled, albeit uneasily, forcing his mouth into the shape of a smile, and gave another encouraging nod of his head.

Fritzi unfolded the paper, slowly, precisely. She felt his eyes on her – and not only his eyes, perhaps. Her eyes fell on three names; focusing, she saw that they were places.

Ireland. Panama. Lichtenstein.

He could tell she was confused, a line appearing between her usually smooth brows. She read the names again and again, but still no light went off in her head; they were just names on a piece of paper.

'Why these three countries?' she asked.

'Ah well, let this be our little secret.' he smiled cannily, trying to forget the bag, the gun. He wanted only to be in control again. But had he ever been in control with her? he wondered. 'I used a contact of my own to track down this information for you, and it seems the money was wired from three different locations.'

Fritzi was no longer sure of Herr Stoffel's role in this investigation; she was more confused than ever. Perhaps she had read the earlier signs badly. Still not completely sure, she hesitated before making her decision.

'You have come through for me, Herr Stoffel, yet I have an uneasy feeling about the countries written on this piece of paper,' her voice was stern, but she lowered the bag so that it sat on her lap again, out of range of the man sitting across the desk from her. Herr Stoffel exhaled, but silently. More investigation will have to be done to minimise this uncertainty, you understand?'

He waited for her to continue, watching for any signs of distrust. But she did not speak. She seemed to still be deeply in thought.

'What will you do then?' he finally asked.

'I will fly to Lichtenstein tonight. When I have the information I seek, I will contact you about what I want done with the funds in the account.'

He nodded his understanding with a questioning expression on his face. 'I did my very best for you. Believe me, it was a highly irregular request.'

'You may keep the gifts as a token of my appreciation,' she said, her voice slow and soft. 'But let me warn you, Henrick Stoffel, if these cities do not throw any light on my request, I will not be pleased, and when I am not pleased, there is always a high price to pay.'

The agent believed her. He well knew from the case notes that she was not an enemy anyone would want to make in a hurry.

'In that case,' he said, 'let's hope they do.'

Janus's company Geospace in LA had established many leads through Fritzi's computer and cell, which they had been monitoring for the last few weeks.

Lichtenstein would throw up only leads Geospace had planted. Fritzi's efforts to find answers would result, they hoped, in her being careless with her sources, disclosing more information on the inner circle of a very sophisticated network. As she disclosed more information, Geospace would feed her more false leads to follow in order to find who had deposited the funds in her account and why.

The world's most lucrative art smuggling network had unwittingly opened a small window into their world, through one of their contacts. It would take very little for them to eliminate her if they were to smell a rat. Even though the Rubicov family would find her elimination beneficial, the intelligence agencies did not want this window into the criminal network's world to be shut down, at least not before a solid foothold into the network had been established. Once the agency's investigation was operational, and they were on their way to infiltrating and then apprehending the very heart and brains of the network, Fritzi would be handed over to the authorities for absconding from a Russian jail.

Chapter 15

Fritzi arrived in Lichtenstein, a small municipality she knew well. It would not take her long to track down what she was looking for; she had been given a contact by Herr Stoffel. Swiss bankers were used to dealing with highly sensitive money matters; it was what they did. After all, everyone wanted their finances to remain private from unwanted attention; Fritzi's benefactor certainly had his reasons.

She was met by an undercover officer in the hotel lounge, who had been notified of her arrival and briefed by both Herr Stoffel, the Swiss agent, and Janus's agency in LA. They were ready for any eventuality Fritzi might throw at them. Herr Stoffel had stressed to the agents how predictably unpredictable the fickle Fritzi was.

Heinrich Strum was a good-looking blond German who greeted Fritzi with polite, old-fashioned East German manners. He remained standing until she was seated. He signalled for a waiter, making polite conversation until their drinks arrived.

He could tell she was studying him closely (his notes had warned him that he would be observed, analysed, scrutinised silently), trying to get the measure of this new contact, a stranger who was helping her – or was he? She had to be absolutely sure. His background obviously made her uncomfortable, and she avoided any light conversation about her own East German roots. He obliged by getting straight down to business, knowing her time was limited. He was brisk but not abrupt, efficient at all times – and she respected that.

Heinrich Strum suggested they retire to the suite he used when on business in Lichtenstein.

'I assure you it's strictly a business arrangement,' he said, 'as you will see when we enter the suite. I have my secretary waiting and my assistant, who does all my computer legwork.'

Unknown to Fritzi, the secretary was a law enforcement agent from Moscow, and the young assistant an expert hacker working for the LA agency.

Fritzi was shown to a high-backed armchair in front of a huge mahogany desk. Heinrich took a seat behind the desk, on which his secretary had arranged all the papers they had prepared on Fritzi's case.

Speaking in a direct, methodical, always professional manner, Heinrich went through preliminary details, which he immediately sensed was what Fritzi wanted to hear. Very quickly, expertly, he relaxed her doubts about the whole operation. Coffee and a jug of fresh water were brought in by his assistant, who then joined them, introducing herself in a Southern drawl.

'Anything hiding won't be hiding long,' the young woman said, in a warm, immediately intimate voice that was almost the opposite of Heinrich's blunt, brisk, all-business tone, 'once I get going on this here baby.'

She introducing herself as Marylou, while plugging in her various technical devices behind the computer. Fritzi could tell that she did all of this – plugging, turning, typing, rebooting – expertly. Marylou's long pianist fingers were brisk and elegant on the keypad, modems, and mouses of the machines. There seemed an awful amount of devices – altogether too many – but she handled them very well. displaying her comfort in a world that increasingly belonged to the younger generation, it almost made her feel old and, she found her eyes fixated on her pony tail swinging from side to side as she fiddled to get everything prepared.

Heinrich, his secretary, and even his assistant shot various questions at Fritzi. At first, she was compliant, answering their questions. But after a certain amount of time, and a certain amount of questions, she began to sour on the whole procedure.

'Is this information really necessary for you to find the answers I am after?' Fritzi asked, finally breaking the spell of the rapid question-and-answer sentence, her soft, efficient voice relaxing back into its old, curt tone. 'I need the name of the person who deposited these funds into my private Swiss account. Nothing else.'

She gazed at the three faces around her, suddenly suspicious. After all, these people were complete strangers and she was entrusting them with a very private, very sticky situation. They could help her, but they could also make everything worse for her. She remembered Herr Stoffel – perhaps the terminally suspicious Fritzi had, for once, been too trusting.

'Yes, yes, we understand,' Marylou said softly, empathically, trying to counter Fritzi's obvious irritation with some Southern gentility – as they said in Texas, *You catch more flies with honey than with vinegar.* 'A nuisance to have your numbered account broken into. All the same,' and here it was difficult not to let a hint of snideness enter her tone, 'many have money taken out of their account, not added in. So, you can count yourself lucky in that respect.'

Fritzi stared at Marylou, her eyes unwavering, dull and then suddenly defiant. A very ugly expression on a very beautiful face.

'I see you have a point,' Fritzi said, 'but to me those unexpected funds in my account may cause problems I do not need, do you understand?'

The question was asked to no one in particular. Fritzi did not seem to be enjoying her good fortune, Marylou thought, considering the profile of the real Fritzi, as opposed to the face she had seen so often in photographs in the case file. If Marylou had begun to annoy Fritzi, the opposite was also true. You could indeed catch more flies with honey than with vinegar, Marylou thought, but you could catch even more with a fly swatter. The honeyed approach was, after all, getting them nowhere.

'We are beginning to, yes,' Marylou said, returning to the paperwork in front of her. 'Now, if you could answer one or two more questions, we may – if I am on the right track – give you the name you are after. It could take minutes or a few hours, but you will leave here with what you came for, I can assure you of that.'

Fritzi shifted in her chair. The chair was soft leather but, at that moment, oddly uncomfortable. Indeed, Fritzi was beginning to feel a general and unclassifiable discomfort. She wanted to be somewhere – anywhere – else. She was familiar with computers, but she did not have the knowledge these people had. How much information could she let them have without compromising her contacts? How did she know what was genuine tech-talk and what was gobbledygook? In other words, how did she know they weren't calling her bluff? She had a conflict of interest going on and she needed to think carefully before disclosing more than was healthy for her wellbeing. She couldn't help but feel that she had been drawn into a very elaborate trap. After all, she hardly knew these people she was talking to, and certainly did not know the people *they* could soon be talking to. Information was a form of currency, and word spread fast. It would not be long before the syndicate tracked down who had crossed the invisible line in the sand they had drawn.

With this in mind, she evaluated their new questions carefully. Given her information, what would these people be able to track, besides what Fritzi herself was after. She needed some form of surety.

'If I answer these questions I need assurances from you first,' Fritzi said bluntly.

They looked up at her quizzically, understanding her reluctance to comply with their request to help her, or why she was holding back important information.

'The information you require could compromise certain people I would rather not anger,' she continued. 'Therefore, I may have to abort this investigation.'

But at this point, Marylou thought, even Fritzi knew it was not smart to abort. The questions, their answers, the investigation – everything – was beyond her control. For once, Fritzi was out of her depth. But Fritzi wasn't the only one who appeared anxious. Heinrich was alarmed; they were so close now, had come so far. He needed to hold onto her trust; whatever happened after was irrelevant, right now they needed her to play ball. They had been trailing the syndicate for so long, invested so much in the investigation itself, he wasn't going to fail now, or be the one to tank the whole thing. He glanced at Marylou, who in turn shot Fritzi a look. Then Marylou turned the computer around so Fritzi could read her private numbered account on their screen.

Without Fritzi's knowledge, they had hacked into her bank account to show her how easy it was to access, and how they would be able to help her glean more information about her mysterious benefactor, but that that would only be possible if she furnished them with the information, they required from her.

Fritzi leaned in to check that it was indeed her account, that this wasn't an elaborate hoax. Determining that it was in fact her account, she drew in her breath sharply. Everyone else in the room could feel the sudden silence, the room turn with anxiety and despair. Shocked, Fritzi's hand flew to her mouth. 'Mein Gott, Verdammt.'

They all stared at the screen: the only thing visible was numbers – big numbers

'Is something wrong?' Marylou said.

'Ag guter Gott, you could say so,' Fritzi said, speaking and thinking quickly, 'there is another million dollars, and not wired in by me. This is very worrying, very.'

They stared back at her in mock alarm.

'All extremely irregular,' Marylou said.

Fritzi sat back for a moment in thought.

'Okay, I will give you that information. I need to know who is doing this'

'You can leave after,' Marylou continued, 'if you wish get some fresh air. We will call you when we have some news. Perhaps it's better than sitting here staring at the walls. Time may go faster if you have a change of scenery.'

Needing to clear her head, which felt as if it were about to explode, Fritzi agreed, collected her bag, threw on a jacket, and decided to go in search of a restaurant. Suddenly she felt ravenous, nerves always had that effect on her.

As the door closed behind Fritzi, the agents high-fived one another; they had extracted as much as they knew was possible from Fritzi. With luck the information would crack open a significant part of her syndicate to allow them to plant what they wanted, giving them valuable insight into their affairs, old and new.

After indulging in delicious food from the region – small dumplings topped with cheese and, for afters, some delicious apple strudel accompanied by a fine Austrian wine – she sat back to enjoy a few moments of peace before she had to return to unresolved problems: problems she had no idea how to tackle without these people. She hated relying on others, especially strangers. Anyone she did not intimately know (and even many of her intimate acquaintances) she did not implicitly trust. She was built that way, to distrust and deceive. Her dishonourable father and family had fostered this distrust within her.

Even when she found who had deposited the money, what was she to do? Waiting was an option she did not like very much. Much as she wasn't built to trust, she wasn't built to wait. She was impatient, restless, reckless, relentless. But wait she must – what choice did she have? She thought of all the cons she had participated in or even engineered – 'long cons,' they were called, where waiting was often the name of the game. The longer you hustled and assumed an identity and a ruse, the longer you wait, the more money you stood to gain. But this situation wasn't like those ones, where she was either in control or on the winning side. No, she had the distinct feeling that everything was out of control now, that she might just lose – but what she did not know. And not knowing was worst of all. She might have opened a larger can of worms than she could handle.

Perhaps she shouldn't' have come here at all. She had it good back in Namibia, why get on a plane, why tempt fate? But fate had come to her, it had knocked on her door, or rather made an appearance in her bank account. Of course, she wasn't in control, she realised when she finished her second glass of wine, her strings were being pulled like a puppet. It was all a set-up, from the start. And she had walked right into it – she who should have known better, the conner becoming the conned. Suddenly all she wanted to do was go home to Yvetta and to their idyllic life in Swakopmund, Namibia.

Scanning the restaurant, she noticed two men at a table, who she thought looked slightly familiar – one wore a hat, and a cold expression in his eyes, that she could swear she had seen before. The way he was not looking at her, looking around him at everything and everyone but her, made her think that perhaps she was his sole point of interest. She finished her wine, breathed, looked away, too. On second thoughts, she decided, she was getting paranoid. No one could have cottoned onto the information she had divulged so fast. That man with that hat and those eyes – it was just a hat (one of millions), just a pair of eyes – she was sure now that she had never seen him before. He was not concerned by her, so why should she be concerned about him? And if he did look at her from time to time, why not? That was not a crime. She was very beautiful, after all, and if she was someone else, she felt strongly that she would be in love with her (and, in a way, she was). She felt optimistic again, a wonderful feeling (was it the wine?), a warm, buoyant feeling in her stomach and in her head.

At the very moment she placed the empty wine glass down her cell phone buzzed. Quickly, expertly, giving the strange man with the hat a flirtatious, happy-go-lucky, fate-tempting wink, and the young waiter a nice tip, she was on her way out of the restaurant, back to the hotel suite to find out, she hoped, what she had come for.

Fritzi entered the suite to find that everything had changed. The three people she had trusted to find the information for her looked startled and shocked and scared out of their wits.

Marylou met her at the door, ushered her in, and sat her down at the screen. All three agents stood behind her. At first, she could not focus, then her account flashed up on the screen. She studied the margin with the final amount, but she only saw zeroes. Instead of her private numbered account being bloated with funds, she now saw a depleted, empty folder, signified by the round and complete blankness of the zeroes. Her heart stopped beating and her head went numb. Her account had been drained of all funds.

'This is a joke, ja?' Fritzi managed.

There was complete silence behind her. She turned, expecting an explanation, but faced expressions that were every bit as blank as the zeroes on the screen.

Fritzi felt her head spin and the contents in her stomach was in her throat. She grabbed for the trash can next to the desk, doubled over, and wretched out every morsel of dumplings and strudel, feeling the colour drain from her face and her legs go weak. Her body became ice-cold and so did her temper.

'What the fuck?' she demanded of everyone and no one. 'Where is that money? And where is my money I left in that account, *my* money. There is zero in the account, not even a pfennig, nothing! Have you stolen my money? Is that what you have been doing? Have I become a dummkopf after all these years? This is a fucking scam.'

Strum sat behind the desk in his chair and waited for Fritzi to calm down.

'We think the person who deposited those funds into your account may have been waiting for you to start searching for their identity. Once they saw movement, they withdrew all the funds in the account, including yours, I'm afraid, leaving it empty. We are so sorry, Fritzi, we think you have been scammed by the very best in the business.'

How could this be happening? She felt helpless to fight back. How did one fight back some faceless criminal? Where was she supposed to direct her wrath and who was she to target in restitution and revenge? Thank God she had spread her money around and her deposit boxes would be safe. She reminded herself that she was not destitute, but this was no small consolation. All the same it was a shock. She felt the numbness and weakness being replaced by anger, a great deal of anger, uncontrollable rage. She balled her fists and bit her lower lip and tried not to explode.

Then it hit her like a hammer: whoever had emptied her account may be from the syndicate. She was as good as finished, they had caught her in a web of her own making. If she had not inquired about the money, had left it alone, the funds might have been withdrawn, and she would never have known one way or the other; but at least she would have been safe from being taken out. Now, they would never trust her again. Much worse, her life would be in danger.

She heard a voice far off in her head, then realised it was Strum talking.

'Well, this shows us that your account has been compromised,' Strum said. 'We will trace the culprits, I assure you, at which point your money will be returned. The bank will not leave you destitute. Your own savings will be refunded, once this has been fully investigated. As for now, we need to terminate this investigation.'

There was a clipped note of finality in his voice as he said this last part. It was as though, investigation now over, Strum and his colleagues were done with Fritzi absolutely. But she was not done with them. Typical fucking banker, Fritzi thought, clean me out and tell me to piss off when the shit hits the fan. The investigation may be over, but the aftermath was only just beginning for Fritzi, she realised. She was still fuming, but now at least she had a target for her anger. She glared at Strum, and then behind him and around him, at the others, who sat there with the same slack expression.

Fritzi was exhausted all of a sudden, her anger flattened out and replaced with fatigue. All she wanted to do was crawl into her bed, take a sleeping pill, and fall into deep oblivion. She made her way down to the lobby to check in and pick up the keys to the room she had booked.

In the lobby she noticed the same two men from the restaurant, standing at the reception desk, picking up their keys. The taller of the men was still wearing his hat, still looking everywhere else but at her. She was much too tired to bother with them, whoever they were, but something about them made her feel uncomfortable.

She showered, doubled the dose of her insomnia medication and swallowed it with a small bottle of wine she had taken from the plane. She fell into the crisp white sheets, pulled the covers over her head, and switched off the bedside lamp. As her head hit the pillow, her mind blanked out and she dropped into la-la land.

Hours later, she was not sure when exactly, she tried to lift her head, then her arms, but nothing moved. She must have taken one hell of a dose of sleeping tablets. Her body felt heavy, almost as if she was strapped to her bed. She lay still for a few more moments, waiting for the fog in her brain to lift. A soft droning sound filled her mind. She waited for it to stop, but it was continuous, relentless. She could not place the sound at first, but after a while it became familiar. Slowly, blinking, still adjusting and in considerable discomfort, her eyes became aware of her surroundings.

Where the hell was she? The space she was in resembled an aircraft hold not a hotel room. She blinked again, tried to fix on the image around her. As her eyes took in her surroundings, she tried and failed to lift her arms and head once more. That was when it hit her that she was strapped into a gurney of some kind, positioned against the wall of a military-type aircraft.

Shaking with fear and still dizzy from the drugs, she wondered who her jailers were. She did not have to wait long. The two men she had seen in the restaurant and in the hotel, lobby were leaning over her, noticing she had woken up. They smiled. Fritzi closed her eyes, hoping that when she opened them again the men would be gone and she would be back in the hotel room, the whole thing a nightmare. But no, the taller man who was no longer wearing a hat was moving towards Fritzi, speaking to his companion, his cold eyes fixed on Fritzi. Russian they were speaking in Russian. And now the taller man addressed her in Russian, too.

'Good,' he said, 'you have woken up in time to learn that you are now in Russian police custody, and about to return to the most secure jail in the whole of Russia. You won't be escaping from this place, and if you do leave it will be in a coffin from overwork.'

She knew they would throw the book at her, a repeat offender. Even in her drugged state she knew she was fucked this time.

Fritzi stared at the two policemen. Now she recognised them; they had interrogated her once after a theft, assholes both of them. She had bluffed her way out of that one.

'Nowhere to go from here but to hell,' the other man said.

She turned her head to face the wall, then felt a jab in her upper arm as she passed out.

Chapter 16

News travelled fast. The Rubicov family were the first to learn of Fritzi's capture in Lichtenstein. Janus had called Mika in the early hours to give him the news; now they had to decide what the best course of action was to take with Yvetta.

On a conference call the following day, Mika and Sasha listened to their mother's feelings about their sister's future.

'All that matters is she is safe from herself and from hurting others,' Anna said. 'My love for Yvetta has not diminished with the years. I know she can't be that sweet little girl your father and I adored, but she has shown time and time again her lack of love and empathy for her own family. So I am leaving the decision to both of you. Whatever I decide won't be practical, and Yvetta needs to be looked after, and perhaps professional care.'

Yvetta's attitude to the family broke their mother's heart. They hoped that with Fritzi finally out of Yvetta's life for good, Anna would take more of an interest in her daughter's future, want her closer to home, childhood memories clouding his thinking. Still, after all Anna had suffered through, they certainly understood her reserve, the slow but steady hardening of her heart when it came to her daughter's affairs and state of mind. They recognised, too, that Anna was right: Yvetta needed professional care. It was becoming tiresome and difficult dealing with their sister, a responsibility neither Mika nor Sasha relished having to put in place yet again.

'Don't you want Yvetta closer to you, Mother?' Sasha inquired. Not being able to let go of his fond memories and closeness to his sister, away from home in the UK.

Mika found Sasha's continued support for Yvetta irksome, but then they were close as children and Sasha had been a hostage away from the family drama that was Yvetta, while they all became Yvetta's hostages.

'Sasha, darling, I appreciate your thoughts, but no I have no longer the strength or the will to deal with Yvetta. Let me know what you have decided. If there are any documents to sign, I will do so. Now I must go.'

The line went dead and it was left to Mika and Sasha to decide

'I think we should contact Hans and tell him the news about Fritzi,' Sasha said to Mika, 'find out what's happening and whether he thinks

Yvetta will be able to handle living in the house on her own for the foreseeable future, with the staff to care for her, until we have to make other arrangements, depending on her mental wellbeing.'

'Okay, Sasha,' Mika said firmly, 'you have dealt with Hans in the past. Perhaps you can call Namibia tomorrow. I will wait for an update.'

'She will have to be told that Fritzi won't be returning, which won't be an easy conversation. Who knows how she will react? It may well result in the course we decide for Yvetta's immediate future. We will have to think of a way to break that news. But, for now, let's hear what Hans has to say.'

They hung up and Sasha decided he did not want to be alone, he shut the door behind him, bought a coffee at Starbucks, and walked the six blocks to the gallery to be with Safi.

Looking up from her desk as he walked into her office, at that face she had learnt to read over time and love so dearly, Safi knew things had come to a head. Janus and Safi were still firm friends; having to work together made it sensible for both of them to put their personal feelings aside. Janus understood his own short-comings better than anyone else. He did not blame her for choosing someone who could love her with his undivided attention, and give her what she so badly needed: a family.

Sasha bent over to kiss Safi on the back of her neck. Laying his hands on her swollen belly, he swivelled her chair around to face him. She was glowing, six months pregnant with a little boy. He could not believe time had flown past so quickly; they had never been happier, or Safi more beautiful to him than she was now.

'I know about Fritzi, Janus just told me. I have just put the phone down as you walked in. She is on her way to a Russian jail. By all accounts, it's been a successful sting. Janus said she's provided – or they've uncovered – enough information to infiltrate the network she was working for. Well, that's the end of that,' Safi said, smiling. 'I can't believe it really. What's going to happen with Yvetta?'

Safi had hoped that Sasha would smile, too, but he looked troubled. Safi remembered how much stress and strain Yvetta had caused Sasha in his life. And Safi had felt Yvetta's wrath personally and close up.

'It's not an easy decision really,' Sasha said. 'What happens to Yvetta next depends on her state of mind and Hans's opinion about how she would fare if she remains in Namibia alone. Mika and I don't really know whether we want to have her locked up in some clinic again. We have to consider her own wellbeing, too – if she is happy, she won't make our lives quite so difficult. And it does seem that she has been happy out in Africa.'

They both sat in thought for a while. It was easy to forget all the awful things Yvetta had done in the past. Everyone had got on with their life; Fritzi was out of their lives, which made it easy to overlook Yvetta's unpredictable streak. The family anyway tended to blame Fritzi, rather conveniently and excessively, for all of Yvetta's recent misdeeds, giving Yvetta no small amount of cover. They would no longer have that luxury.

'You know, I feel the same way,' Safi said. 'Why not wait? Perhaps life in Namibia can give her some kind of stability. She has staff who care for her, and she has taken on a surrogate role caring for her staff's children. All that responsibility may be what she needs. The big question is, can she cope without Fritzi in her life?'

Sasha felt he had covered all the bases with his family, enough to have a meaningful conversation with Hans. He would then take it from there, let things ride for a while longer.

The main problem was how to break the news about Fritzi he was slowly adopting a view he had not previously considered: why tell her? Instead, allow time to pass, let Yvetta get used to the idea of not having Fritzi around. After all, according to Hans, Fritzi often went on jobs where communication with the outside world (even with Yvetta) remained infrequent for weeks, even months, on end. Yvetta had been alone without word on a number of occasions. The more Sasha thought about it, the more he liked the idea. Who knows, he thought, his sister might not merely adjust to not having Fritzi around, she might grow to genuinely enjoy it. He could only hope that it was just a matter of time that his sister would outgrow (or at least fall out of love with) the egomaniacal and exhausting Fritzi.

Sasha waited for Hans to be home before calling (Namibia being six hours ahead of New York worked out perfectly). Hans picked up on the second ring, Sasha could tell he had been waiting for the call.

'Hi, Hans, how are things with you?'

'Good man, good; what's news??

'Have you got your sundowner in hand? If so, take a good stiff shot; I have some interesting developments for you.'

Hans walked out to the patio and sat facing his pool, drink in hand, waiting for Sasha to fill him in. He hadn't had much excitement in his life, not until the Russians and those FBI agents arrived on his doorstep, that was.

'Fritzi has been taken into custody by the Russian authorities,' Sasha informed him.

'Bloody hell,' Hans said, 'what happened?'

Sasha could hear a sharp intake of breath on the other side. He filled Hans in on the details since Fritzi's arrival in Switzerland, and the sting.

'You are telling me the Russians put all these dollars into her account, then waited for her to fall for the bait?' Hans said, sounding amazed.

'Exactly.'

'Why didn't she just take the money and run?'

'The setup was too complicated, she was bamboozled, afraid to withdraw the money in case of reprisals from the criminal enterprise she worked with. Fritzi seems fearless, but it turns out that, like most people, she is in fact afraid of her bosses. In this instance, it seems she did not know who could have hacked into her private Swiss bank account, and deposited the huge sum without notifying her. They might have been laundering money through her account. The investigative agent thinks that she would not touch the money because she feared it was a trap set by the syndicate she worked for; they are a ruthless bunch, for sure. When her own hacker acquaintances turned up no lead, she tried to have the bank investigate. Which is exactly what they were hoping for. They took a chance, it worked. She divulged enough for them to hack into her criminal network. Then they pulled the plug, withdrawing all the funds, including her own, from the account, to show her the person or persons who had put the dollars into her account had obviously waited for her to act before making a move, like playing chess.'

'It must have given her one hell of a shock to see all that dosh disappear from her account,' Hans said, trying to think how he would react if his own bank account was flooded with mysterious cash. One could but dream!

'Believe me,' Sasha said, 'it did the job so well, they were able to remove her in a comatose state from her bed into a private jet the very same night.'

'How?'

'She had taken a large dose of sleeping medication before turning in – she was that rattled by the whole affair; the rest is history.'

'Well, well, I guess Fritzi won't be free for a long time, if ever. Do they still send people to Siberia?' Hans shivered thinking about it, something that was not easy to do in the warm Namibian afternoon sun.

'We hope so. She has escaped once before from a Siberian jail. She is a very clever operator, although not quite clever enough, it would now appear. This time she won't be escaping, that's for sure.'

But Hans was now thinking about the gallery and how Fritzi's arrest would affect his livelihood, and indeed his life. Excitement at hearing about Fritzi's fate was replaced by his own anxiety.

'Hans,' Sasha said, his tone a little different now, as though he intuited Hans' sudden insecurity and was easy to appease it, 'with Fritzi now out of the way, I would like to discuss my sister with you, and put our ideas past you. My family and I really respect your insight, and your input, and what you have done for us up till now. Your thoughts on the matter may help us decide how to move forward.'

As he had done with Mika earlier, Sasha discussed with Hans the pros and cons and various scenarios for Yvetta.

'I guess under the circumstances,' Hans said, I agree with your assessment: let Yvetta get used to the idea of living without Fritzi. The police inspector in this town is a close friend of mine. When Yvetta does become anxious about Fritzi's absence, he could pay her a visit with the news of her arrest.'

Sasha was happy with this suggestion, and, not for the first time, impressed by Hans' ingenuity, quick mind, and helpful nature.

'If you could organise for this to happen, we could let your friend have the case details from the Russians who were involved with the sting from the start. But allow it to take its natural course before we put that into action, to give Yvetta – and us – time.'

'I will keep you closely informed,' Hans said, not for the first time. 'I see Yvetta on a daily basis at the gallery. In fact, since Fritzi has been away, she has adopted me as a mentor and close friend.' Sasha was surprised at how happy he felt to hear this; Yvetta could do worse than a solid, compassionate friend like Hans. It was people like Hans, not Fritzi, whom Yvetta should be surrounding herself with, he thought. Yvetta had never had a good relationship with her own father, but there was something paternal about Hans, and he was far gentler and more empathic than Alexi had ever been. 'I often help with her new surrogate family; your sister has become very close to them, but also needs advice on a regular basis. I have to keep reminding her that the staff who work for her are the children's legal parents. Yvetta needs to discuss any changes to their lives with them. She cannot just do as she pleases.' Sasha smiled, knowing only too well how impossibly headstrong and imperious his sister was. No, he thought suddenly, he did not much miss having

Yvetta living close by. Faraway Namibia was just fine with him. 'At the moment that relationship is working out okay: the staff need her and she needs them.'

Until I hear from you again, Hans, we are eternally grateful for your updates and your services. I know we have a financial agreement, but if there is anything you need, please let us know.'

Hans no longer felt anxious about his role at the gallery. For as long as Yvetta stayed in town, he decided, the gallery would be operational, and Hans's job there would be secure. He had, in his own way, become indispensable – and not just to Yvetta, but to her brother, too.

'Ja, ja, understand, cheers until our next conversation,' he said, happy to get back to his drink and the sun still burning across the vast and endless horizon.

Fritzi had spent extended periods away from Yvetta before, though she had never before been without contact from her for more than three weeks. But eight weeks had now passed with no word from Fritzi, and Yvetta could not help but be concerned.

Hans tried to keep her grounded, reporting back to Sasha on a regular basis. Hans felt it was time for the police to inform Yvetta of Fritzi's fate; there wasn't much more he could do to allay Yvetta's fears.

After being filled in on Fritzi's case history by the Russian authorities, Inspector Gramman agreed to break the news gently to Yvetta. Hans had voiced to Gramman his concern for Yvetta's mental ability to cope with the whole truth straight off.

'Hello, Inspector Gramman, have you any news for me?' Yvetta inquired.

'Well, yes, I would like to make an appointment to visit you at home. I think that would be the best place for us to discuss the issue. Perhaps at the end of the day?'

'Why can't you tell me now?'

'It's complicated, and I have other appointments,' Gramman said, satisfying no one with his answer. 'Can we agree on six this evening?'

But now Yvetta was more anxious than ever. She felt sure something terrible had happened to Fritzi. But what? Unable to concentrate she moaned all day to Hans.

'Why the hell do I have to wait? He could have told me over the phone.'

On Hans's advice, Yvetta had been to speak to the inspector personally, to make enquiries of her own.

'I can't face this alone. Hans, will you be with me when he comes?'

'Yes, if it will help, of course.'

Inspector Gramman sat across from Yvetta, making occasional eye contact with Hans. The two men had already discussed how to break the news to Yvetta. His eye fell on the photographs on the desk: the two women clearly in love in many of the frames; more recent pictures of the staff and their children, taken with Yvetta and Fritzi as though they were all a family, prompted him to say, 'I can tell from your photos you have settled well into Namibian life.'

Yvetta followed his gaze, then acknowledged his interest with a smile on her lips, but there was no smile in her eyes. He decided it was time to get down to business; she had waited long enough.

He brought out a folder from his briefcase, opened it on his lap, and began to read from it to Yvetta.

'First we contacted the Swiss police to investigate whether Fritzi had been to Switzerland. What we discovered was that she had entered Switzerland on the 16 July. Leaving two days later for Lichtenstein from Geneva. She arrived in Lichtenstein on the 19 July. Now it gets interesting because the hotel in Lichtenstein have a record of her checking in but not checking out.'

'So, what does that mean?' Yvetta asked, her voice heavy with anxiety and anticipation. 'Is she still in Lichtenstein?'

'No, that is where the lead has gone dead, you understand?'

'No, I'm afraid I don't. So, you have no other information since Lichtenstein? Are you asking me to believe she has just vanished into thin air?'

'For now, it seems to be, I'm afraid, the case,' Inspector Gramman said wearily, his voice making it clear that whatever mistakes the Swiss police may have made could not be projected on to him. 'Until, that is, the Europeans get another lead. That is all I can report at this juncture, but they are still investigating. Something will turn up, or Fritzi may call, perhaps. And if she does call,' he gave her an earnest look, 'please let us know, so I can alert the Swiss authorities and they can abort the investigation.'

Inspector Gramman stood, shook hands with Hans, had a few further words, and tried to reassure Yvetta, who had sunk into an impenetrable fog. Gramman quickly realised that she was inconsolable. There was nothing left for him to do. He looked at Hans with regret and no small amount of sympathy. Hans saw him out and returned to Yvetta.

'Well, it's not conclusive,' Hans said slowly, 'but in a way that's good news.' He felt strongly that Yvetta wasn't listening to him, or was wilfully misinterpreting all his words. She was still sitting in the chair, glaring at him now. Or perhaps she was looking through him, at the photographs on the desk that Inspector Gramman had admired not so long ago. But everything was different now.

'Fritzi may be somewhere she cannot communicate from,' he continued gamely, trying to sound authentic and believable, worried now that Yvetta would be so broken that she could not easily be mended, least of all by him. He had begun to sweat. Blame it on the heat, he thought. One could never get used to the heat, no matter how long you lived here. 'Best to look on the positive side until we hear again. As Inspector Gramman said, you may get a call, then it will all be okay.' But the words felt hollow, empty, facile, even to him.

'I have a gut feeling about this, Hans. She is in business with some nasty people.' Her voice lowered and she said, 'We may never know what happened to her. To tell you the truth, before she left I found her in a weird mood, very secretive, even more so than usual. She was always on her computer, the one she kept for business. And other things were different about her as well. Sometimes she seemed almost in deep despair, but she never spoke about it, so I couldn't help her even if I wanted to. Then suddenly she left on one of her business trips. She knew I hated it when she went away without consulting me, not even telling me so much as where she was going, but my protestations were useless.'

'Best to be positive, let's not jump to conclusions,' he said flatly, 'something will turn up.'

Hans walked into the kitchen to speak to the cook. The staff were all sitting round the kitchen table having their dinner, a ritual they had established since living with Yvetta, who liked to share the evening meal with them (and Yvetta always kept in mind Anna's busy kitchen and well-fed staff, aspects of her childhood she genuinely enjoyed). The staff had very quickly and easily obliged, and a makeshift family unit had since been formed.

'Is Auntie Yvetta coming to eat? Aina said.

'She will be here soon,' Hans said. 'You eat up all your food like a good girl.'

He asked the cook to follow him out for a chat.

'I want you all to keep a close eye on Yvetta. She is very worried about Miss Fritzi. Tell the others. Until we hear from her, I am afraid Yvetta might need a lot of comfort from you all. Please keep me updated if you have any other concerns.'

The sun was setting slowly over Hans's patio. Sometimes he wondered why he chose to live here, and the sunsets reminded him. Evening. He calculated it would be lunchtime in New York, a place so different from where he lived that it may as well have been another planet. What a wide world, Hans suddenly thought, full of strange people and stranger quirks, incidents and coincidences. How had Fritzi and Yvetta found their way into his life? And now, what was happening now? He had been drawn to Namibia because it seemed a predictable, even dull, place, but life was now anything but predictable. He decided it was time to call New York.

'Hello.' Sasha answered on the first ring.

'It's Hans. Things are coming to a head here, too. I think not giving her the news right away about the arrest was the right way to go.'

'How did Yvetta take the news?'

'Well, that's the interesting bit. She told me about Fritzi being in a very bad way before she left for Switzerland, and that Fritzi had dangerous business associates. She said she had a really bad feeling about this whole thing!'

'Okay,' Sasha said, 'call me again when she hears the truth about Fritzi.'

'Sure. The staff will look after her. I have told them to give her extra attention, and to let me know if anything changes. They know she can be a little unpredictable,' Hans said diplomatically. 'They are used to dealing with her ups and downs by now'

'That's good to hear, thanks. Hans. As I said before, we are in your debt.'

'Ag, it's the least I can do. I do hope Yvetta remains here, Sasha. You know she is very settled in that house with the staff. By all accounts, she loves the life and the gallery. She may be okay.'

'I hope you are right, Hans.' Of course, it was in Hans's interest that Yvetta stayed in Namibia, something Sasha implicitly understood. 'Auf Wiedersehen.'

'Tschüss!'

Sasha knew Mika was undecided about Yvetta's future in Namibia. he wanted to take risk out of the equation, under the circumstances, a near-impossible proposition. Not trusting her unpredictable character and mental issues, they needed to discuss her future in depth.

Sasha's main concern was for his mother and for Safi, who he knew his sister resented with an unhinged, jealous hatred. She had shown what she was capable of without Fritzi as an influence. It was convenient for the family to have Fritzi as a scapegoat and excuse, to absolve his sister of her sins, but Fritzi was now gone, and they had to acknowledge the truth. His sister had attacked Safi, almost strangling her at his home during the reading of the will. Sasha had not witnessed that episode (and thus blamed himself for it occurring at all), but he had experienced similar behaviours in the past.

Even so he pitied Yvetta, who was, after all, and would always be, his sister. He wanted her to be happy, and decided it was time to adopt a softer approach. Things had not always been this way. Growing up with Yvetta, he had shared a bond with his sister; they had been close when at school in the UK. She was strong-willed, difficult at times. Once Fritzi became part of Yvetta's life, his sister became estranged from the family dynamic. It was hard to disagree with Mika's assessment of Yvetta. But Sasha had a somewhat different take on the situation, having himself been cut off from the family for years, experiencing the loss of loved ones, absence and loss, grief and guilt. If he could avoid the same fate for Yvetta he would try.

Hans had been a great ally and friend; he clearly needed the cash, and he had fallen in with all their plans. There was little reason for him to refuse to continue as their link to his sister. Sasha had begun to think of him as, if not a friend, than a warm acquaintance, and his information. Furthermore, the family could from time to time send over others to assess the situation without Yvetta's knowledge.

Safi had her doubts. Yvetta had a way of turning up and unbalancing everyone's equilibrium when least expected, everyone was, conveniently forgetting that Yvetta wanted her galleries first and foremost. And she had to consider not only her safety but her child's. Truth be known, she was petrified of Yvetta after her crazy attack at the reading of the will. Yvetta would she was sure to turn up like a bad penny when they least expected it, she couldn't help feeling anxious.

She tried to understand Sasha's compassion after all, it was his sister – but, by the same token, she was his wife. Sasha was being too warm hearted towards Yvetta for her liking.

'Sasha, I am sorry but I have to side with Mika's assessment of Yvetta. She is a loose cannon and I am not about to let her back into our lives, sorry but right now being pregnant I don't want her anywhere near me'

She could tell he was taken aback. He hunched his shoulders (an old-man gesture she thought he had inherited from his father) and, for the first time in a long while, turned his back to her. When he turned towards her again, his voice was softer than it had been all morning. 'Why doesn't she deserve a life? After all, she is so far away from us there is no need for concern.'

'Maybe the fact that she is far from us *is* the cause for concern,' Safi said. 'We won't know what she's doing… or plotting. I mean, you were not there when she almost succeeded in strangling me.' She knew, of course, that bringing this up was a low blow, something to put the argument firmly in her court. After all, he had described his devastation at not being able to protect her that day more than once, and, indeed, it haunted him still. Now she threw this back at him, and in a moment when he was only expressing care for his sister. Her voice softened, too, regretting her last remark, and she said, trying another tack, 'And I have our baby to think of now.'

'*We* have our baby to think of now,' he said, coming over to hug her, wrapping her fully and tenderly in his strong arms. 'I understand, of course,' he continued, still embracing her, his mouth by her ear, 'but tell me why should she travel from Namibia to New York to harm you. She does not even know we are married or living here?'

'How do you know she doesn't know?' Safi asked. 'Can you tell me that? Don't they have internet in Namibia? You investigate her all the time, you think she doesn't know how to investigate *you*?' He hadn't stopped holding her but was on the verge of turning away again when she said, 'You think I am being paranoid?'

'Maybe a tiny bit too cautious, yes,' he said diplomatically, sealing the diagnosis with a kiss on her forehead, which at that moment she thought not affectionate but irritating, even patronising.

'Well, okay,' Safi said, suddenly exhausted of the subject, deciding that no progress on this was possible right now, 'but let's find out what Mika says about letting Yvetta remain in Namibia for the foreseeable future, then we can discuss it again.' If Sasha infuriatingly wouldn't listen to reason from Safi, maybe he would from his older brother? Besides, with Fritzi out of the picture, what guarantee did the family have that Yvetta would stay put in Namibia? They were all operating on the narrowest of assumptions, and they were forgetting Yvetta wanted her galleries back, why wouldn't she make waves, now that Fritzi was out of her life?

They decided to wait until Yvetta had been given all the facts about Fritzi before making any concrete decisions.

A fortnight after he had given her the original information about Fritzi's last movements, Inspector Gramman decided to call at Yvetta, as agreed with Hans.

He had the detailed report for her now, and felt it was time to disclose all the information he had on Fritzi's disappearance to Yvetta. Hans was unwell, according to Yvetta: he had been having dizzy spells for the last week, and the doctor had told him to rest until the new blood pressure medication started to work.

Hans called to warn Gramman not to disclose the information without him being present, but the Inspector was of the opinion that they had sat on the information for long enough, he wanted the case closed.

'Well, I am not an invalid,' Hans said, impatiently, quite out of character, his mood had not improved with his new medication, can't you do it here at my place, then?'

'No, it would not seem proper, it should be on the premises where they both lived, I am sure Yvetta would be more comfortable in her own surroundings.'

'Okay, but I warn you she might not handle the news well. When she feels out of her depth, in a situation out of her control, she starts to spiral. When this happens, she becomes pretty wild, unpredictable,' Hans said, reflecting on the first few times he had seen her act out in this way, her personality changes absolutely in mere minutes, she became a fearsome monster, and how shocked he had been (indeed, he felt shocked anew each time she unravelled in this way). 'I highly advise you make sure the staff are around. She should feel that she is in as safe a space as possible. She should not be left on her own.'

Inspector Gramman sat facing Yvetta in the same office where he had given her the first part of their investigation on Fritzi. This time he accepted the cool drink offered by the kitchen staff on duty. He noticed the house was very quiet, the staff's kids who lived with Yvetta must still be in school.

Opening the folder, he looked up trying to gauge her state of mind, how best to relate what he had in the report, what to include and not to mention. Perhaps he should just read the whole report straight out; she appeared to be pretty composed. Maybe she suspected something bad was coming?

Yvetta sat in numb silence but in her heart, she knew but dreaded the truth, what if Fritzi was dead, she couldn't allow herself to think, or worse being tortured by who, she did not care to think, this was the end, she could feel that in her bones, the end of her being cherished and adored by Fritzi, her rock, her everything through dark times.

'Would you prefer the report read or for me to break the news in a less official capacity?'

She appeared undecided yet expectant; he did not want to shock her with hard facts. 'It seems, Yvetta, if I may call you that, Ms Rubicov?'

She shook her head in agreement. 'Yvetta's fine.'

'Well, Yvetta, I have no other way to say this: it appears the Russian authorities had set a very elaborate sting to capture Fritzi and it was successful.'

She stared at him for a few seconds. 'Are you telling me they have taken her to Russia?'

'Yes, it seems to be the case.'

'Oh my God, they will throw away the key. Oh my God, I will never see her again. Oh my God… Oh my God… No, no, no, this can't be happening. Those bastards…' She spoke until she could no longer speak, or no longer manufacture words that made any sense. Then she sputtered. Then she screamed.

Inspector Gramman sat bolt upright for a moment, then walked to the drinks' trolley and poured her a stiff brandy: it was the only thing that set the world back on kilter for him at bad moments, and he had had a few already tonight in anticipation of this very moment.

Standing in front of Yvetta, he put the tumbler in her hand, folded her fingers round the glass.

'Drink, this will help.'

He saw a wild look in her eyes, her mouth gaped, but he encouraged her to drink the brandy, waited to see what happened when it burned down her throat and hit her stomach, then her brain, hoping it would have the calming effect it did for him. After all, alcohol was more effective at breaking bad news than he could ever be.

'It's my fucking family,' she finally said, glowering, her cold hard eyes shining and her mouth set, lips a thin line now, set in determination, 'I am sure they set this sting up. Who else would know where to find her?'

Inspector Gramman did not know Yvetta's whole history, but Hans had told him enough to know she was estranged from her extraordinarily wealthy and (in Russia, at least) very famous family, although they continued to look out for her wellbeing.

'According to my report, they do not mention your family, Yvetta.'

'Well, it wouldn't, would it,' Yvetta shot back, 'since my family probably came up with that report.'

'I am afraid that it is impossible,' he simply said. 'This is a police report. It cannot be manipulated.'

She made a scoffing noise that sounded more like a dog barking. She looked mad, ready to hit out at something. He wished Hans was represented (Hans, who clearly knew the intricacies of this situation far better than him) were present, but continued nonetheless. After all, Gramman was a big boy and had been an inspector long enough – perhaps even too long. He was tired of his job, and of moments like these. Hans had warned him to keep her family out of the discussion.

'The report mentions other insurance companies hunting her down,' he continued, in a voice that was unnaturally calm, even strained. 'They were working together to do so. She broke out of a Russian jail, and there are other pending warrants out for her arrest in Russia for impersonating doctors from a Swiss clinic, a Canadian clinic, and breaking out a patient from a Moscow clinical institute.'

'Does it say the name of the patient?'

'Not to my knowledge, no.'

This bit of information seemed to calm her down. He figured it had to have been Yvetta Fritzi had sprung from that Moscow clinic; it was not difficult to put the pieces together.

'Anything else in that report I should know?' she said flatly. She seemed to be breathing normally now, and so he breathed as well.

'Only that there are a dozen or so outstanding warrants for her arrest from various countries. It seems Fritzi worked for a very secretive smuggling ring which deals in priceless art, museum antiques, and ancient relics from the Middle Eastern wars. For that reason, I do not think your family could have had anything to do with her arrest. It would have happened without their interference; after all, she managed to escape for a long time.'

Yvetta stared at Inspector Gramman; her eyes had become hooded slits, an arrogant elongated turn of her neck swivelled to face him.

'I need for you to leave now,' she said simply. 'I want to be alone, please see yourself out'

Inspector Gramman could tell by the tone in her voice she was about to blow.

He turned on his heel, stopped by the kitchen and asked the staff to keep a close watch on her, and shut the large double front doors behind him with relief. It was over, it was finally over. He could go home and have another brandy (or two) and enjoy an early night and a good sleep. At least he hoped it was over.

Standing on the veranda he tried to listen for any disturbance, ready to come to the staff's aid if needed. He took a larger-than-usual inhalation of the sharp evening air, and wondered whether Yvetta would remain in Namibia. If so, he would have to keep a close watch on this girlie, she was obviously not stable. And if she did leave, it would cost Hans his job at the gallery, he realised. Still, there were always consequences for everything, and it would not be the worst thing if Hans finally enjoyed his retirement. He had noticed the situation with Yvetta had given Hans a great deal of stress, and dizzy spells as well. No, it was healthier for Hans not to have Yvetta in his life. Healthier for Inspector Gramman, too.

As he opened his car door a black SUV flew past him, swerving as it bounced over the brow of a hill, disappearing like a bat out of hell in a cloud of dust. Yvetta, he thought. Hell, he could see the car swerving all over the road in the distance. He had no intention of going after her now.

He had better alert Hans, she was more than likely on her way to see him. Unfortunately, if that were the case, they would have to put off the briefing of his visit for another time.

The staff were relieved their children were at school; they did not want them scared witnessing aunty Yvetta's distress. Not knowing the full story, they assumed by the pictures swept onto the floor, then smashed into fragments by Yvetta stamping on the frames of photographs of Fritzi's face until the glass had turned into fine shreds of splinter.

Yvetta then moved down the passage to Fritzi's private office, the locked door of which she kicked open after using a sharp metal letter opener to the lock. The staff watched her from a safe distance. She did not appear to see them, so thoroughly involved was she in her own angst. Once inside she went about rummaging through Fritzi's desk drawers, smashing everything she could lift from the desk, including a computer, with a heavy rock-like object. Frothing at the mouth, pulling at her hair, biting herself, she dropped to the floor with a guttural howl. Before the staff could assist her, Yvetta sprang to her feet, grabbed her car keys, and ran past the bewildered and frightened staff, and out of the front door.

Shocked, they began clearing the mess, sweeping the glass, tidying before the children arrived from their schools. The cook, gardener, and the housekeeper congregated in the kitchen, all in shock.

'This is very bad, very bad.'

'Call Mr Hans,' the gardener advised, 'he will know what to do. I think she has gone there, you better warn him.'

They gathered round as the cook called Hans, trying to hear what he had to say. They shook their heads sadly all the while, spoke in whispers. Things had changed. They recognised the signs, had seen many strange things working for white people, but never anything like this. Yvetta was unlike any other white person they had worked for. This was a very bad day, maybe for all of them. It seemed their family security was in jeopardy. Perhaps they should leave before Yvetta returned; this house might not be a safe place for the kids any longer. Yvetta had spoken often of adopting the children, but what kind of mother would she make? She could not even look after herself! Often, it appeared that it was the children who mothered her. Without Fritzi, Yvetta would be very unstable. They had learnt to look to Fritzi for guidance in all things since moving in with them, and now that guidance was gone.

Hans' line was engaged, and so they went about their chores as usual, fetched the children from school, made dinner, then escaped to their private quarters to a long and uneasy night.

Hans had just finished a call when he heard incessant banging on his front door. Knowing immediately, it was Yvetta, he made his way to the door, not sure whether he had the strength to deal with her hysteria, wondering if he should call for reinforcement, or even pretend to not be home. No, that wouldn't work, she would bang on the door until she gained entry, and then God knows what she would do.

As it happened, Yvetta fell through the door, blood on her hands, her hair wild. Before he could think what to do next, she rushed past him onto the patio and threw herself into his pool fully clothed. At first he thought she was going to try to drown herself, but then she started to swim in lengths up and down the pool. He watched her standing on the edge, ready to jump in if she went under, but she kept going length after length until her arms stopped smashing through the water. Rechannelling her anger and energy into athletic activity, Hans thought, that was smart. That ought to wear her out in a good way, perhaps even give her a hit of endorphins. She floated until she reached the pool steps on the shallow side, exhausted and breathless.

Hans remained standing where he was on the opposite side, waiting for Yvetta to get her breath back, hoping she had spent her insane emotional anger with all that physical exercise. Just before Yvetta arrived, and after Hans had spoken with Gramman, the cook had managed to get through. But they did not have time to talk, as that was when Yvetta had begun knocking on his door. The cook did, however, alert him about her mindless trashing of Fritzi's belongings.

He watched her closely, decided it would be safe to fetch her something to drink, replacing the liquid she must have lost swimming all those lengths.

He placed the glass of juice on the edge of the pool along with a towel, sat down under the awning, and waited for her to join him having poured a much-needed drink for himself.

He had no intention of letting her go berserk in his home, but he doubted she had any energy left for that, or at least he hoped not.

He noticed she had stripped to her underwear, placed the towel round herself, gulped the juice down, and then stood momentarily undecided and thoroughly bewildered, as though she did not know where she was. She gave Hans a long hard look, as though reorienting herself. Then, meekly, with head down, she walked over and took a seat at the patio table.

'I guess you know all about Fritzi,' she said finally. 'I am sure Inspector Gramman filled you in?'

Hans shook his head, letting her do the talking. Anything he might say could spark an emotional outburst. She was not yet in a stable state, her eyes were still wild, her body still trembling slightly, either from the cold water or the evening's events.

'What do you think I should do now?'

He met her gaze, let her question hang in the air for a while

'What do you want?' Hans said. 'Are you happy here enough to remain'?

In a small voice he could hardly hear she replied, 'I think so, Hans, but I'm scared. Who will look after me? You know, Fritzi understood me, she took care of me, you understand.'

'Yes, yes, I do understand. It won't be easy, but you have the staff and you have me. That might 'not be the same as having Fritzi, but it may be enough until you feel stronger, yes?'

'And I have the gallery, don't I?'

'Of course, yes, that is your gallery, and you run it so incredibly well. What would I do without you? We need you there.'

This seemed to please Yvetta; he noticed her straighten up in the chair.

'You know I have other galleries, don't you?' she said.

Hans was not sure how to reply. He wanted to avoid any discussion of her family. She was sharp, any slip of his involvement could result in loss of trust and his credibility in her eyes, to say nothing of his job at the gallery.

'Do you want to talk about it?' he said.

'No,' she replied decisively.

He watched her face: thoughts were obviously racing through her mind as her expressions changed, but at least she wasn't shaking anymore. It was obvious she was struggling to come to terms with what had happened, she seemed devastated, a little girl abandoned before, who had once again lost her anchor.

He did not want to tell her what to do, but she looked exhausted, depleted of all emotion. He hadn't before seen her quite like this.

'My body aches,' she said.

'Do you want to go home, or sleep here perhaps until tomorrow?'

'Sleep here. I'm not sure I want to remain in that house without Fritzi.'

'That's not a problem, we can talk about the house in the morning.'

Hans stood. 'Come, follow me, let's get you to bed. Or are you hungry?'

Leading the way, speaking softly, he made her feel comfortable in the large guest room, decorated in soft African prints, mixed with faded florals by his dear wife Rosa. Closing the door behind him, Hans stood for a moment, not sure what to do next, then tiptoed down the stairs, locked up, made her a sandwich and left it outside her door, then went to his room to call Sasha.

It was a strange conversation, one he was not sure how to phrase, when asked whether he thought Yvetta could remain in Swakopmund.

'I will tell you my feelings, Sasha, she is in shock but the impression I got was she wanted very much to remain here. She trusts her surroundings, feels safe in our small community, and she has her staff, who will follow her to any home she chooses to live in – and of course the gallery and myself, quite an infrastructure, not to mention Inspector Gramman, who I know will keep an eye on her from now on. I can vouch for him, a good man and a friend.'

They spoke for a while longer, with Sasha promising to send someone to liaise with himself and Inspector Gramman before the family came to any decisions. Sasha stressed that he wanted everyday life to continue as normally as possible for Yvetta until the family decided whether Yvetta should remain in Namibia.

Not for the first time, Hans wasn't sure what exactly he had got himself involved with, but he felt happy to help young Yvetta and her brother. He liked them both, and he was sure the rest of their family would be upstanding people he would be proud to know. (After all, the Rubicov family had a good name in the international art world; Hans had checked up on this.)

No one could help having a wayward family member, a black sheep. Every family had a member that didn't quite fit in, for whatever reason. He wasn't privy to all the backstory, but he had the impression the family had Yvetta's best interest at heart. Whatever she had been up to with Fritzi had ended. This would be a fresh beginning for Yvetta, if her family left her to make some decisions for herself. A sense of renewal, of rebirth, of self-improvement and advancement.

Hans believed she needed a new beginning, and he would help her if he could. A new beginning for Yvetta – and for Hans as well. A better life. Who knew, maybe she could become the daughter he never had? He knew he was being a sentimental old fool, probably signs of getting soft in the head. But who cared? In for a penny, in for a pound, and that was another reason for his motivation. He was being well-rewarded, it gave him security, something that became more of a problem in old age. He had been horrified at how weak, how much of an old man, he had felt in recent days. Money meant security and security gave him choices. He liked the thought of being cared for by nursing staff at his beck and call, in his own home, surrounded by what he cherished and loved.

Since his dear wife's passing there had been no one to take on that mantle, and he had increasingly struggled financially, with a gallery that sometimes seemed more of a burden than a treasure chest. With extra funds he could employ help indefinitely, until he kicked the bucket, no smelly old municipal old-age home for him.

With that thought lingering in his mind, he swallowed his medication with the left-over whisky, switched off the light. Tomorrow would be another eventful day, just what the doctor ordered. All of this activity (which, just a few months ago, would have seemed unbelievable and absurd) was good for him; it gave him little time to dwell on his own silly problems. When he was not occupied with work, he was well on the way to becoming a hypochondriac, taking note of every ache and pain. For that reason, he had to keep busy, with work, with anything at all but his own ill-health.

He had always prided himself on a healthy lifestyle; after all, he still had a full head of hair, even though it had turned what he considered a stylish snowy white; on a good day, he resembled the Country and Western singer Kenny Rogers, a good-looking man, pity he did not have his talent for singing. He still did his morning exercises at the local Pilates studio, and could walk an 18-hole golf course on a hot African day; not bad for a 79-year-old fart. With that thought in mind he drifted off, a little tipple at bedtime always did the trick.

He woke with a start. Somewhere in the distance he could hear a soft knocking sound, scraped his head off the pillow to make sure he was hearing what his mind was sure of. Yes, someone was knocking on his door. Oh, right, Yvetta. Shit, he was becoming ridiculously forgetful, the poor girl, he needed to see if she was okay.

Pulling on his trunks he called out hoarsely, 'That you, Yvetta?'

The clock on his bedside table said 7:30. long past his usual beauty sleep. Hans prided himself on an early start, but since this blood pressure thing he was struggling, his routine had been off-kilter.

He swivelled the last dregs of the whisky left in the glass round his mouth, not his habit but he needed a kicker, stretched his body, his feet dangling over the edge, before attempting to put one foot in front of the other to open the door.

He found Yvetta curled up in the corner of his doorway. What the hell was she doing there? He bent over to check she was alive; her body appeared limp. Once he realised, she was physically okay, he leaned over and yanked her to a standing position, supporting her under her arms, half dragging her to the armchair in his room (how could someone so slim feel so heavy? this really was quite a workout), the closest place for both of them.

Once in the chair he dropped to his haunches by her side, suddenly exhausted and feeling old again.

'Now what's going on?' he asked.

'They have left.'

For a moment he wasn't sure who she was referring to, but then he noticed she was fully dressed.

'Have you been back to the house, Yvetta?'

Tears swelled in her eyes and dropped down her face silently. Then the dam burst. Tears flowed unchecked as she rocked back and forth in the chair; she seemed inconsolable. Hans stood back, assessing the situation. He decided to leave her to cry. There was little he could achieve by trying to console her, and besides he could already feel his dizziness returning. To wake up to such a sight was no help at all. She was obviously feeling sorry for herself. The staff buggering off brought home the loneliness she faced: no biological family, no Fritzi, and now no surrogate family, either.

Hans was all she had left. Not much to be consoled by. Overwhelming doubt grabbed at his gut. He wasn't equipped to handle Yvetta, and found he did not want to be solely responsible for the demons floating around in her brain on a daily basis. It upset him to have his tightly held routine upset in this manner. Once the morning had been tampered with, too often the whole day fell apart as well. It was rather like a stray thread on a jersey that, when pulled, led to a larger and irrevocable unravelling.

Had he taken on more than he could handle? Was this partnership, this relationship, even sustainable? It had seemed so yesterday, but then yesterday he had felt altogether more buoyant and optimistic. Today he was worn-out, and it was not yet eight o'clock in the morning. Yvetta took more dedication than he could muster right now; apart from the money, it was a huge responsibility, perhaps he was too quick to assure Sasha of her stability or his strength – or, for that matter, his own.

Hans picked up his cell and disappeared into the bathroom, switched on the shower, and called Inspector Gramman, not knowing who else to call.

They had a short conversation, after which he he switched off the shower and returned to find Yvetta was no longer there. Rushing out into the passage he found Yvetta in the guest room bed, curled into a foetal position facing the wall.

Hans closed the door and left the room. He stood in the passage, not quite sure what to do next. This babysitting was becoming a routine he didn't much like, since she had fallen over his threshold last night.

He needed to get some semblance of order back into his day. He walked into his room, shut his door, tried (with varying degrees of success) to forget about Yvetta, and continued with his daily routine. Dressed and ready for the day, he bounded down the steps to prepare breakfast, leaving a seeded loaf of bread out and some preserves for her; he wasn't going to wait around fretting.

Hans left for the gallery, determined to get on with his day by lunch. Gramman would have some news, and he would then check up on Yvetta; hopefully she would be in better shape. If not, he would have to contact Sasha and leave decisions to the family. Where was his wife when he needed her? She would never have allowed him to get this involved, that was the truth. She would not approve of Yvetta and her antics, not at all.

Gramman walked through the gallery door.

'I need you to come with me, Hans, there is something you need to see.'

Not sure what he was going to see, Hans decided it best to go along with his friend. He had been expecting something all day and here it was, he just hoped it wasn't his place they were going to see.

Following Gramman down the passage to Fritzi's office, he was met with the remains of Yvetta's tantrum: shards of glass were still all over the place as his shoes crunched over them. The staff had obviously tried to clean up, but she must have gone berserk again this morning when she found them gone.

The house had been trashed completely. The desk had been taken to with a hammer that lay discarded on the floor; further down the passage remnants of photos lay scattered on the ground, while Fritzi's study resembled a disaster zone. Yvetta had assaulted the book shelves and desk; even the windows were cracked as she had wielded the garden soil pick axe through everything; even the TV on the wall had been axed.

Shaking his head in disbelief, no wonder she was sleeping she must be totally wiped out from her orgy of violence, destroying whatever got in her way.

They made their way to the master bedroom. Here Hans stood aghast. How long had she been at this? And with what deranged pleasure had she conducted her wrath? The place was a minefield of torn clothing. Even the bed had been axed, bits of the headboard hanging off the wall; the most worrying was the blood stains on the bedding and rugs.

He hadn't noticed any injuries when he sat her in his armchair this morning.

He was almost too scared to ask, so he pointed instead.

'Fritzi kept white cockatoos. Poor little mites.'

Hans noticed the white feathers in the white bed linen for the first time.

In the kitchen he noticed the empty cage through the window on the back veranda. No room had escaped her anger at being abandoned, not even the kitchen cabinets, where smashed crockery lay everywhere.

In the staff quarters the beds had been hacked; she had become Superwoman in her frenzied state. Hans could not believe one person could do that much damage, it was beyond anyone's imagination. Last time he had seen her, she could barely get up off the floor. No wonder she had been so exhausted!

'I better get back to the house,' Hans said. 'God forbid she gets it into her head that I have abandoned her, too. Shit, do you think she has any strength left to do damage to my collection of classic furniture?'

'I tell you, Hans,' Gramman said when they were back in his car, 'I have never witnessed anything like this in all my years. She is completely fucked in the head, man, fucked.'

He had never heard Gramman swear like this, it was pretty outrageous. *Fucked in the head* was the only way to describe what he had just witnessed for himself – and even that seemed altogether too kind. Hans was still in shock.

Gramman put his foot down.

'To hell with the speed limit.'

'What are you going to do with her? We can't leave her to her own devises any longer.'

'Let's see what's up at your place first, then we call her family.'

'No wonder the bloody staff ran off, they must have known what she was capable of. Thank goodness those little kids did not get to witness her killing the birds; it's enough to give anyone nightmares.'

Not a sound met them as they walked through the door; the fresh loaf of bread he had left on the breakfast bar was untouched. They made their way up to the spare room cautiously, not sure what they might find. Hans pushed the door open gingerly; there was no Yvetta in the bed. Gramman moved to the shower room: the place was deserted. They continued searching the whole house, even under bushes in the garden, just in case, but Yvetta had vanished.

Gramman got on his cell and called for reinforcements to search the town and beaches, even to scour the sea for a body, who knew what she was capable of?

The only sign of Yvetta was her missing truck, but Gramman was sure it would not be long before they tracked it down.

'Do you think we should wait until we know where she is before calling Sasha?' Hans inquired.

'No, I need some answers.'

Before he had the opportunity to call Sasha, Gramman's cell buzzed, Hans waited to hear any news. Five hours had passed since he had seen the carnage at the house, which meant Yvetta was missing for 10 hours.

Gramman switched the cell off.

'They have found her truck on the road to the airport, which means she might have left Namibia. I will call the airline, they will know where she has flown; but where ever it is, she could be well on her way to that place by now.'

'Make that call to her brother now,' Hans said, thinking perhaps it was better if she had flown to another country, become someone else's problem, was long shot of them all. Still, he couldn't help but feel concerned for her. In spite of himself, he had formed a genuine attachment to her. He had thought that the attachment was mutual, but given the speed she had left, he had to wonder now. Perhaps she had never really cared about him at all.

Sasha and Mika were reviewing their options on Yvetta's future over a conference call; no consensus had been reached, neither wanted things to ride for longer with a stalemate. Sasha's cell phone buzzed. Noting it was from Hans, Sasha switched on the speaker so Mika could be part of the conversation.

Both remained in silent shock while Hans described the events after Fritzi's arrest had been disclosed to their sister, followed by the carnage they had found at Fritzi and Yvetta's rented home. Yvetta's wild rage taking a pick axe not only to the furnishings, but also, shockingly, to three beautiful cockatoos that had the misfortune to belong to Fritzi and which Yvetta therefore slaughtered, resulting in blood splattered over bedding and the master suite. Inspector Gramman related the investigation into her disappearance and the day's details, culminating in the most recent information on where Yvetta might be.

'It is now almost certain that Yvetta has left Namibia for Johannesburg, where she boarded a flight to London. There the trail has gone cold.'

There was a momentary pause, after which Inspector Gramman continued on a more personal note.

'I must be honest with you, I have not come across such wilful destructive behaviour. I am sad to say that your sister may be mentally deranged. I am sure they have a medical term for such behaviour, but here in Namibia we just call a spade a spade. She needs to be mentally assessed, and in my humble opinion, under supervision and away from the public, before she is given the opportunity to do any more harm. Now here's the thing, there is also the matter of the damage she has caused to the Miller's home. We have not yet contacted the family, but it will have to be done. They decamped to live in Cape Town to be near their kids and grandkids. I am sure they were thrilled to rent out their home so soon; goodness knows what they will think of the awful destruction to their 20-year-old family home.'

Neither Mika nor Sasha had uttered a word since Hans and the inspector had been on the phone. Just as Mika was about to discuss reparation for all damages caused, the line went dead, they had lost the connection.

'Sasha, are you still there?' Mika said.

'Yes,' he said, though his tone made it sound like he wished he wasn't.

'What a fucking mess, perhaps we should send someone over to help sort this mess out?'

'Yes, I agree.'

Before they could discuss the matter further Hans had managed to reconnect with a landline; his cell, he explained, had run down.

The conversation concentrated on the practicalities of the aftermath of Yvetta's outburst: repairing the damage, and smoothing over issues with both Hans and Inspector Gramman.

The staff would have to be found, Sasha and Mika wanted to help out where possible they did not want to leave anything their sister may have done unturned or started unfinished.

They were left with the most troubling question, where could Yvetta be? The rest of the damage could thankfully be repaired with money (and, lord knows, Hans thought, the Rubicovs had no shortage of that) and a bit of damage-control where Hans and the inspector were concerned. The staff and their children would be financially compensated, neither wanted to leave behind a bad impression of their family or the Russian people; there was enough of that around the world already.

Kolya was the only person Mika trusted to do a perfect damage control exercise on the family's behalf. Mika did not want Kolya to wait for flights, and so he chartered his own jet for Kolya to fly to Namibia. He wanted Inspector Gramman to have no doubts about the Rubicov family paying their debts to whomever their sister had harmed, owed money to, or needed looking after. It would be taken care of generously; no quibbling would be needed about the financial costs.

Chapter 17

Kolya had instructions to discuss matters with Hans. The gallery would have to be sold or closed down, all decisions would have to be made while he was out there. The family did not want any loose ends; everything had to be sorted before Kolya flew out of Namibia.

Next they needed to speak with Janus, another trusted friend and associate they had worked with successfully. The Rubicov family owed Janus's company an enormous debt, as did Sasha personally. Luckily for the Rubicovs, Janus was a pragmatic man not an emotional one, unlike most Russians, who found it hard to separate business from their private affairs. Payback was in their blood, if anyone crossed them personally or in business.

Fritzi was someone who had crossed them personally, and she had now got what she deserved; yet here they were, once again, left with the Yvetta problem. They needed to find Yvetta before she found them, especially if she believed they were responsible for weaving the web Fritzi got herself caught up in, which, knowing paranoid, angry Yvetta, was entirely possible. As for the Fritzi problem, it had ended in her deportation to a very secure Russian jail. In the process they had notched up quite a few favours from various law enforcement agencies around the globe, which would make finding Yvetta a walk in the park for Janus's people.

The word had gone out to all agencies to keep Yvetta under lock and key; until the family had made arrangements for a secure clinical institute to take her on, once more, they were left with no other options. Yvetta had played her last card, or so they hoped. But for all the most sophisticated surveillance systems in the world, for all of the international agencies and their all-seeing eyes, they had no idea where Yvetta was.

Unknown to the family, Yvetta had flown to a therapeutic horse farm in the Montana mountains. She had heard about it from a friend in Namibia; more than anything she wanted to be away from everyone and everything, she needed quiet (something she had become accustomed to in Namibia), somewhere to hide from her family (whom, she knew from experience, would soon attempt to make contact with her and ferry her away yet again to another nuthouse somewhere) and from life. That is why she left Namibia before anyone could set the wheels in motion to track her movements down. It was time for Yvetta alone to take control, for long last and for good. After all, who knew better than she what she wanted?

Maybe Montana would be what she needed, communing with nature, alone in the wilds, nowhere near most human beings (such an overrated species, Yvetta thought, human beings). She had loved the wild life in Africa; it had an amazing, calming effect on her emotional state after arriving in Namibia with Fritzi, after the institutions her family had locked her away in. The last one had been outside of Moscow, an awful place where the psychiatrists were too clever for their own good, trying to delve into her mindset at every God-given opportunity, such idiots, did they really think she would let them mess around with her head? She alone knew that she was smarter than all of the psychiatrists, and fooling them was an easy (if rather tiresome) game. She would entertain them with what they wanted to hear, cry when it was called for, and show anger when she knew they expected it. More than that they never got.

Now what she needed was to get well again to face the world without Fritzi, the only person she had ever trusted and loved. Had she been wrong to trust Fritzi? It was a good question. Fritzi had abandoned her, too, how could she be such a stupid bitch, didn't they have everything they could possibly need in Africa? Fritzi was too smart for her own good, and then, when it came down to it, a creature of instinct and habit, Fritzi wasn't that smart at all.

In the end, Yvetta was certain, it was Fritzi who trapped Fritzi. Fritzi always needed more; like herself (or one of her many selves), she could not leave her old life behind. Just thinking about Fritzi made Yvetta feel angry – and sad. She had been such a huge part of her life, the defining part, for so long, and now she was gone, just like that. Yvetta would never forgive Fritzi for ruining their perfect paradise, continuing to work for those dangerous business associates. What happened to Fritzi was a betrayal to Fritzi (who, Yvetta felt certain, was done in by one of her business associates), and a betrayal also to Yvetta.

Somehow it proved Fritzi did not find loving her enough. She was a traitor; it meant she had never loved her enough. Getting herself caught up in illegal adventures outside of their relationship (it was worse than having an affair, if you thought about it; and who knew what Fritzi got up to – and with whom – when she was away from Namibia for long stretches of time). No, Yvetta decided, she would never forgive her, never!

Once she had contacted the Montana Horse Ranch, Yvetta knew what she had to do. Staying at the horse ranch would enable her to vanish until she was ready to make the Rubicov family pay for their years of neglect, disrespect, and abuse. And she knew who would help her with her plot. Her cousin Pasha would be loyal; he hated the Rubicovs as much as she did; after all, they had blamed him for her father's heart attack, they had cut him out of the family, too, robbed him of a large part of his inheritance. Yvetta could see it now: they would plan their revenge together.

Yvetta was sure her family were to blame for Fritzi's arrest, enabling those who wanted to trap her in a web of deceit. She had time now to consider the situation from multiple angles, to give it a great deal of thought. Never had she witnessed Fritzi as disturbed by anything as much as she had been in the last six months. She knew better than to ask Fritzi to betray her contacts, but she heard enough through Fritzi's closed office door (Yvetta pressed against the other side, often for long minutes at a time) to know she was rattled by something.

The staff had caught her listening outside Fritzi's door and she had sworn them to silence, threatened them with consequences if they betrayed her confidences. They seemed surprised that Yvetta would spy on her partner. Clearly these people were not from Russia, where, historically, everyone spied on everyone else. Still, Namibia had originally been a German colony, so you would think its inhabitants would know a little something about authority.

Yvetta knew they looked to Fritzi for guidance in all things, but felt her threats were sufficient to keep them stum. She had heard them discuss her anger spells with Fritzi in the past, and she had heard how Fritzi had calmed their fears by making light of it with her German expressions, more than once but she never imagined they would run out on her, the bastards, after what she had done for them and their kids, who also abandoned her in the end. Faithless and abhorrent, she decided, like all the others. Best to give them no more thought.

Yvetta had been at the ranch for just four weeks, weeks which passed pleasantly and with a gentle rhythm that suited her well. She felt safe. Obviously no one had managed to track her down yet, which proved the ranch was a sound decision on her part. This validated her understanding. Independently wealthy she did not need her families money, she had her trust fund but over the years she had with Fritzi's help and business acumen opened numbered accounts in tax haven's to avoid her family's help at all costs.

She had booked for six weeks so far. It had proved to be a fantastic experience. Much to her surprise, she loved life on the ranch. Much like in Namibia, no one tried to delve into her affairs, no one cared who she was or why she was here. They left her to herself, and, for the most part, they kept to themselves as well. Yet she found working with the horse's pure joy. She wished people would be as trustworthy, as innocent, as respectful as these humble, beautiful creatures. And was disgusted and mortified that she had in her moment of anger hurt those innocent birds, something she would have to live with her demons were out of control. Why was it a shock when people were cruel to animals, was it their demon's controlling their lives. Yvetta reflected, look how cruel people were to one another! She felt a deep bond with at least one of the horses, and looked forward each morning to greeting him, riding him, caring for him. Here, perhaps, at last, she had found a home.

Surprisingly, the ranch had helped her shed some useless beliefs she was unwittingly holding onto, and which she would never have willingly discarded before.

The others on the ranch thought she was from the U.K., which suited her. If anyone came asking, they would not know she was from Russia; using an abbreviation of her surname when signing in would throw anyone off the lead; deciding to use Rubin rather than Rubicov made it easier to pronounce, and less difficult to explain, if questioned.

So far all of her experiences at the ranch were positive. At first, she did not join in campfire group discussions, which occurred almost every night. Then, she got caught up in one, late one evening on return from a long hike into the mountains with the horses. They had stopped at dusk to water and rest the horses, when the group leader suggested they camp for the night under the stars. Apprehensive about sleeping out in the open, she found many of the others shared her anxieties. But the inclusiveness of the group relaxed her doubts. They were all so open and honest, and spoke with such frankness. She wasn't that different to anyone else, everyone there had some kind of grudge against life, or lack of self-belief; many kept their issues under wraps, like her, many seemed to want to hide. As a result, no one would think her strange.

Yet she remained vigilant, careful not to make the crucial mistake of being careless, of becoming lazy and letting down your guard. She would not allow herself to fall into a malaise; the longer people stayed, the more relaxed they became about 'sharing their shit,' as some liked to call it. This was absolutely not the reason for her being there, she had to keep that uppermost in her mind. This was not another clinic, or facility for endless discussion and group-geared talk that accomplished exactly nothing.

She was hiding from her family they would try to track her down once they learnt she had vanished. She was convinced they were behind her lover's arrest. Who else could have helped the authorities to hone in on Fritzi, but Mika, Sasha, or her mother.

Eating around the campfire that particular night became highly charged with camaraderie; everyone partook in passing a hookah, mellowed after a meal of rice and beans rounded off with some sweet coffee.

Grant, a particularly gangly, rugged, handsome 50-year-old, brought out his mouth organ and began to play Bob Dylan and Willie Nelson songs, everyone hummed or sang along. The camp leader, Manoosh, as he wanted to be called, had been in the States only fifteen years. He had an incredible backstory, and many rumours circulated about him, which he dispelled effectively. He did this by retelling his story to the group round the campfire, which, Yvetta realised, helped encourage others, in turn, to 'share their shit.'

Manoosh had left Afghanistan during the first Taliban excesses, when he and his family trekked across the rugged mountains into Pakistan. Luckily for his family, they lived in a small village close to the border. This was a dangerous place to be, but knowing the terrain well, they managed to escape. His family resettled in Lahore, but he wanted to escape the injustices shown to Christian minorities, and so left for the United States, with the help of a relative who sponsored him; he had never looked back.

Manoosh enjoyed the outback, it gave him back what he missed growing up in the mountains. He took the job at the horse ranch five years ago, working the ranch every summer, until he was appointed camp leader three years ago. There was nothing he loved more, it enabled him to practice his natural ability to help others share their stories, a tribal ritual he had grown up with amongst his people. Manoosh was a man of few words, yet he managed to instil a charismatic trust and openness amongst the visitors who entrusted their time on the ranch with him.

On that particular evening Yvetta experienced a revelation. Had she shared her Eureka moment, Manoosh and the others may have been alarmed; they may even have managed to dissuade her from following the plan she was forming to get back what she considered rightfully hers.

All she had to do was relax on the ranch for her remaining time there, heal her broken heart, and formulate her revenge on her heartless family.

She wasn't falling for any of the pathetic namby-pamby weakness of the others, prepared to forgive and let live and all of that stuff – sharing their shit was just that, it was shit. Her Russian blood and heritage ran far too deep. People had to be made to pay for stealing her livelihood and her life, cutting away at her charisma and her personality in the process, making her a shadow of herself. Too many had disappointed and abandoned her over the years; there was no one left to trust but herself – and the horses, perhaps.

Janus met with Mika both men were in New York on business and so set up a lunch meeting at the Rubicov restaurant. Almost six weeks had passed with no conclusive lead to help them track down his wayward sister.

They had followed her flight path to London, from where the lead had run dry. The travel authorities had no one of her surname on their computers flying out of London. After she reached LHR the lead ran dead.

Mika knew that Yvetta would avoid Valentina, or anyone who had family connections. She may take any number of routes out of the U.K. Some had even suggested she may have hired a car, it was easy to cross the channel undetected.

The family home in Moscow had not yet been sold, they still owned the apartments run by Rubicov investments, but her cousins were all over the world, building their businesses and carrying on with their lives, so they knew Yvetta would give any of these a wide birth.

The only home they were in the process of offloading was the Dacha, and there had been no sign of Yvetta going there for shelter. Perhaps it was stupid to think she would go to Moscow, but they had to follow all leads.

Sasha knew his sister was inventive; there was no one more equipped to outsmart them than she was.

A list was made of all the people they thought she might try to contact to help her, but no one on that list had heard from Yvetta, either. It seemed she had dropped off the radar altogether, an extremely dangerous situation for them, especially for Anna and Safi, her stated nemeses.

The best they could hope for at this stage was for Yvetta to get careless; eventually something would turn up, Janus assured Mika. After all, she needed to pay for stuff, she would call someone sometime, she would get tired or scared, she would long for the good life again, she would let her guard down. Until then everyone would have to be on their toes. Sasha had organised for a security guard to be on duty at the gallery. He had organised a front-desk person at their building, ex-police, to be briefed to question anyone who asked for them by name.

Mika had persuaded Anna to agree to more security around her villa in the South of France.

It saddened him that the person they were protecting their family from was a daughter and a sister. How had they reached such a sad state of affairs?

Mika had his own security; Kolya had returned from Namibia, having taken care of all outstanding debts. He now briefed Mika on the trip. The staff had been compensated handsomely, the gallery had been gifted back to Hans: it was, after all, his life's work. He would no longer have money issues; they had left him with a comfortable payoff to live out his old age without financial difficulties. It was the least they could do for his services.

All repairs, replacement furniture, and decorations were to be billed to the Rubicovs for the damages to the rented property. The owners were more than compensated, and had not yet returned. Instructing their estate agents to oversee the works and appoint builders of their choice, Kolya had done an exemplary job on damage control.

With Inspector Gramman's help they had managed to keep most of the lurid details out of the local papers, and off the Namibian radio stations. The evening before his departure, Hans had invited Kolya to his favourite bar and restaurant. Here, Kolya had run across a number of acquaintances made by Fritzi and Yvetta. Amongst them was a young surfer, called Zyron who had apparently taught Yvetta to surf, amongst other sports. He questioned and discussed Yvetta's sudden departure with Hans, trying to gauge when Yvetta would be returning (apparently, Yvetta had not completed a surfing course she had paid for). Hans looked briefly at Kolya, who pretended he did not know who they were referring to. He overheard the surfer mention a horse ranch in Montana. The surfer wondered whether she had taken his advice and gone for an extended period; the ranch had an 'awesome reputation,' after all, and one or two of his clients had experienced a bush like Namibian rebirth of mind and state changing experience.

At the time, Kolya had not given it much thought, but now he wondered whether the information about the horse ranch might be relevant, another lead they could investigate. The perfect place for her to lie low. Lie low while riding high. Yvetta had never been anyone's fool; she would want to remain out of reach, especially from her family, not wanting to be returned to another psychiatric clinic for the rest of her life.

Mika listened with interest to Kolya's train of thought, and decided it was worth a try. But first they had to establish which horse ranch the surfer had recommended.

The ranch could be one of many in Montana; the surfer had not been specific about an exact ranch, but had recommended Montana as a place high on the list for those in search of spiritual guidance and healing. It was an avenue worth exploring.

Janus was informed and they set about investigating the ranches in that area of Montana that were known for healing work. Mika was not surprised to learn that no one of their surname had checked into any of the ranches.

By now they were familiar with Yvetta's case history. They decided the best course of action was to have a number of people visit every ranch that met the surfer's description; if she was at one of them, it would not take long to find her; they would have her photo.

Outside communication was not allowed on many of the ranches; anyone who needed to make an urgent call had to take the ranch bus into town, or, if all else failed, the main hub would allow calls to be made from their landline.

Knowing this, they were supplied with hidden cameras. A photo would rule out any mistakes. Mika did not want any publicity.

Once a photo-fit had been identified, the next step would be to follow Yvetta from the ranch. The family wanted her movements tracked. The agency had managed to book their agents into a number of well-known ranches in the area of Montana. If they had missed Yvetta altogether, it would be difficult to find whether she had been, or where she might have gone.

Their computers would have to be compromised to obtain a list of all their clients within the last six to eight weeks. Janus was certain they would be able to identify any alias Yvetta might have used; in his experience people always left a familiar clue to their original name.

After returning from the campfire with Manoosh the previous day, Yvetta did not leave as many of the people from their hike had stayed the usual ten days; she wasn't aware anyone had remained as long as she had. Perhaps this in itself made her suspicious, marked her out. Perhaps it was time to leave. Still, she liked it here, had found a familiar rhythm. She liked, most of all, the fresh air and endless expanse of sky. Her last week was coming up. She didn't yet know where she would go from here. She would be greeting the second group of people since her arrival at the ranch. One or two left or joined midweek, but not many. There wasn't much she had not done on the ranch, apart from cattle Ranching on horseback, something that did not appeal to her much. Boredom was setting in and she decided to give it a try; most would be as nervous as she was, if she lagged behind with the newest recruits.

They set out at dawn, the pack horses carrying food supplies, all bleary-eyed following the trails through the ravine, to where the cattle were grazing; probably a half a day's riding before they located any cattle. The ravine was pretty narrow, only allowing one horse in front of the other until they dismounted near a shallow, fast-running stream to rest the horses and break for coffee.

She was the only female on the cattle trail. She guessed the other woman shared her feelings about this particular activity and had stayed away as she had done up until now. Sitting on one of the small boulders, cupping the first coffee of the morning while watching the sunrise slowly over the mountains was pretty spectacular, she had to admit. She inhaled the crisp air. Just as she had begun to take this place for granted, it surprised her anew.

'Pretty damn mind-blowing, right?'

It took Yvetta a moment to register that someone had spoken; she had been in a world of her own.

'Uh huh,' she said, not sure she even wanted a conversation right now, annoyed she had been taken out of her reverie.

'Oh, sorry, shouldn't have broken the spell. Takes a while to get into the swing of things.'

Shit, she wanted to enjoy trekking out into the wilderness without distractions. She had to plan her next move. It was the perfect headspace she needed, and what she didn't want was someone yapping in her ear. Perhaps she could ignore them. Give them the silent treatment and they would get the message and move on to someone else.

'This your first week, too?'

No point being offhand, it might attract too much attention, she guessed. Once they were back in the saddle, she would have time enough to concentrate on her strategy.

'Actually, no, my last week, though, so I thought I'd try the tougher stuff, see if I can hack it like the rest of you guys.'

'Do I detect a slight accent?'

'What do you mean?'

'Well, besides the British accent, I thought I heard something else in there.'

'Really?' Was this just a normal chat? Perhaps, but it seemed to be straying into uncomfortable territory. No one else had asked her these questions before, or asked her much of anything. She didn't know whether to enjoy the attention, or to be especially on-guard. She didn't smile, but she didn't turn away, either. She didn't want to bring more attention to herself, not now.

'Eastern European, perhaps?'

Yvetta suddenly felt a shiver run down her spine; no one had detected her Russian accent before, everyone she spoke with thought she was British.

'That's really amusing, no. Perhaps it's because I went to school in Aberdeen, Scotland.'

'Now it's my turn to be amused.'

'Why? Yvetta suddenly took interest who was this person, he looked pretty ordinary in his windbreaker and jeans, a bland face no particular characteristic stood out his accent American.

'Well, you do not have a trace of Scots in your accent.'

Shit, this guy was pissing her off now.

'Ah, that's because it was a private boarding school. They cultivated an English accent where I went, you see.'

'Ah, so you're saying the Scottish accent you had was weaned out of you by the school?'

'Exactly, that's why you probably hear a trace of another accent.'

'Hmm, usually. I am pretty spot-on with accents,' he smiled thinly. 'I must be getting rusty'

'Perhaps, yes.'

They stood around for another 10 minutes, before mounting the horses for the final half of the trek; in that time, neither said another word, yet she had the feeling he was observing her. She didn't care if this oaf did not believe her, fuck him, she would be gone by the end of the week, and he would be staying on, no need for her to worry. Maybe he'd even meet people who would engage him in endless conversations. Maybe he was looking for a woman.

She gave him a winning smile.

'Cheerio, hope you have a fun ride, old chap.'

Perhaps she was overdoing the stiff upper lip, dismissive Hooray Henry stuff, but the guy was bugging her. With luck it would make him uneasy around her; she bloody well hoped so.

The next half of the journey dragged out, though she did not catch sight of the guy who had recognised her Russian accent. In fact, she totally forgot about the whole episode once they were in sight of the cattle. That was when suddenly everyone and everything became madly chaotic as they tried to chase the cattle into another field, where the ranchers with great skill and ease managed to gather them into a pen, the odd stray cow expertly lassoed and brought in line.

Yvetta found the experience exhilarating. She gave lassoing a go, almost catching one of the stray cattle. She was pleased none of the men had done any better; in fact, she thought her efforts were far superior.

On the way home she rode ahead of the line for a while, keeping up with their rancher, then purposely falling back to allow the others to pass her, taking note of each one as they rode alongside. Still, she did not catch sight of the guy. Some of the riders had kerchiefs over their mouths to stop the dust from kicking up into their faces. Even so she would have noticed his lime-coloured windbreaker and LA cap, there was no one of that description amongst the group.

She rode for a while deep in thought: where could that shithead have disappeared to? Surely someone would have noticed if he had hot-tailed it back to the ranch. Maybe she was being unnecessarily paranoid, and especially guarded, it getting so close to her leaving. Did it really matter who this guy was? She would be gone soon. She wasn't going to let this shithead ruin everything for her.

She decided to cut her week here short. After all, she had done everything there was to do, and she craved some luxury and deserved a treat. Yes, a spa was her next port-of-call on her journey to find her dearest brother, Sasha. He would be the first to pay for abandoning her to a fate worse than death in those bloody awful clinics, not to mention giving her beloved galleries away to that bitch from England. Sasha and Safi, the two of them had ruined her life. He had tried, at every opportunity, to sideline and destroy her. Well, now it was her turn. She had absolutely nothing left and nothing to lose now that Fritzi had left her as well; there was no one to trust or rely on but herself.

With this decided, she felt at peace again. The horse cantered along behind the other horses, all she had to do was hold onto the reigns. The ranch-house loomed up ahead, she had been so deep in thought the ride back had flown by.

Yvetta suddenly spotted the lime-coloured windbreaker. He had been somewhere amongst the pack after all, she just hadn't noticed him until this moment; still, she had to remain vigilant. She had come too close to slip up now. He had noticed Russian in her accent; she just felt something wasn't quite right, it was too much of a coincidence, too long of a conversation, not an idle chat; she knew it would only be a matter of time before her family tracked her down, they had an arsenal of independent help at their disposal and all the money in the world. She only had her wits, and she would outwit them in the end. The gallery was hers, she had started it and under her guidance it had become an international success. She was determined to get back what rightfully belonged to her, come hell or high water, to say nothing of her good name.

So as not to arise suspicion, it was best to join them for dinner before retiring to her room. It did not matter if she left her identity documents behind; she had the use of a number of passports, and thanks to Fritzi they all appeared authentic. Having settled her bill in cash (also thanks to Fritzi, who had left enough cash for her to live on for a considerable time). At least Fritzi had honestly cared about her, this was incontrovertible and more than she could say for her own family. If she needed more, she would draw from her numbered accounts spread around the world – again, she had Fritzi to thank for this; but she did not want to dwell on Fritzi, it was upsetting her all over again. She had to concentrate only on her true objective; nothing mattered now. She would do it for herself, and for Fritzi. She would finally get her revenge.

The agent sent the information out to the agency; when it was confirmed he would be informed as to what his next move would entail. The woman he had encountered was one of many, other agents had probably found similar matches; it was a matter of waiting before knowing if his instincts had put him on the right track. He had seldom been let down by his instincts, sniffing out those who did not want to be found.

He had selected her as the only one worth pursuing, after carefully discarding the others on his first day. It was easy to gauge which activity she had chosen; then he had signed himself up for the same activity. After speaking with her he was convinced they had found their quarry; her appearance was somewhat different to the photo-fit, but he knew from experience this was never conclusive. After all, people adjusted their appearances, they grew their hair long, or cut it off entirely. They dyed their hair, or wore lenses on their pupils, or did anything to hide their real identity. The difference between blending in or being discovered could be the difference between life and death.

Bill was not a patient man. In all the years he had been doing detective work for government agencies he had found the machinery much too cumbersome. Now he was an independent contractor working for foreign agencies, making it easier to follow his quarry without first getting the go-ahead. It was less frustrating, more efficient. This one was easy; he only needed to find and pass on information, get the thumbs-up, and the rest wasn't his problem.

He decided to remain in one of the reclining chairs facing the outhouses; from the wooden patio of the main house, he would be able to see any movement late into the night. It would look as if he was resting, perhaps even meditating. Many others sat here all the time. If he had to depart at short notice, he was always ready, keeping his light backpack at hand wherever he was.

He did not want to attract attention, neither did he want to leave his vantage point. Taking his LA cap off, he positioned it over his lap, covering the banned cell phone, and read the message. Smiling, he settled back in his chair. Snoozing wasn't an option. He was sure of one thing, the target wasn't going to hang about; the agency had confirmed the photo, his job now was to alert them she had flown the coop. This would clearly be her next move.

He did not have to wait long, she had obviously decided to check out early. Noticing the rucksack over one shoulder and a handbag slung over the other, Yvetta furtively searched whether anyone was still up to notice her departure. It was not unusual for people here to leave shortly after dawn. The agent would not have been visible from his vantage point; relaxing, he watched as she made her way down the path to the exit gate at the end of the property. Then he flagged the agency as arranged. And, just like that, his job was done.

Yvetta had put a call through to Uber to pick her up at the entrance gate to the ranch; once she received their text, she made her way to the end of the property to pick up her ride.

The agency had placed sleepers in many of the car companies over the years, especially since Uber came into being. The only way Yvetta could possibly leave from the ranch was by car. They immediately placed a call through to the company headquarters, asking for an update on any calls made for a pick-up from ranches in the area; when this particular call came through, they had contacted the agent to send an alert when Yvetta made her move to leave.

Mika wanted her found, and the whole process had taken much longer than planned. Now they had a sighting, what seemed like a positive identification, they were not going to take the chance of losing her again. The Uber agent would let them know where they had dropped her off.

Yvetta climbed into the Uber, pleased to have shirked anyone who might have been sent to follow her; they would never expect her to leave before her last week was up, or without some duplicated, unimportant personal papers she had left behind in their safe. She would call the ranch once she was settled to ask them to destroy her documents, then discard this cell, for another pay as you go.

The Uber dropped her at the bus station. The best way for her to keep a low profile, travelling across the country in a Greyhound bus would give her the opportunity to chill out, lie low, and get her mind in gear for the next stage of her plan.

Yvetta had gone onto the web to track down her cousin Pasha. She did not want anyone in the family to know if she made contact with him, who was almost as hated amongst the Rubicovs as she was. This was precisely why they could be perfect partners. Pasha had built up an online company doing profitable business selling cultural Russian icons. Yvetta was proud of him for having stuck two fingers up at the family, not accepting financial help, going it alone, and by all accounts making it work. He had thrived without the family; she could do so, too. They had tried to break him, but they hadn't succeeded, not even close. If she enquired about an icon, he would answer her query with a bit more than the usual feedback.

It had only been a few hours since her enquiry to Pasha. Sitting on the bus she opened her pocket iPad; sure enough, there the email was. Excitedly, she opened it and started to read. At first she thought he had missed the message she had added at the end of the enquiry, but no, here was his reply:

> Dear Ms Rubanofsky,
> You certainly know your Icons. Such detail could only be picked up by an expert in this field, I await your order with great enthusiasm.
> Best regards 'always' Pasha.

Yvetta smiled, thrilled that Pasha knew it was from her. Thank God, she would send one more email to make sure before setting up a permanent dialogue.

> Dear Pasha,
> Thank you for the immediate reply to my query
> Shipment details to New York or anywhere else in the States would
> be helpful,
> Best Ms Y Rubanofsky

She pressed 'send' and sat back in her seat, mesmerised by the purplish-blue mountains coming into view as dawn faded. The sun would be up by the time they crossed over the state line into North Dakota on her way east to New York City: lots of time to gather her thoughts, before she visited her gallery in Manhattan. After that, things would happen very quickly, and soon she would be on top of the world again.

Yvetta drifted in and out of sleep. She found her wakeful moments akin to living in a twilight zone. At intervals the bus would stop to fill up with gas, and the passengers (those unlucky enough to be awake) would take the opportunity to stretch their legs or buy fresh supplies to munch on as they worked their way east.

There had been no reply from Pasha. Finding this out of character, she pressed 'Resend.' The ping on her iPad brought an immediate smile to her face.

> Dear Ms Y,
> New York would be best option for shipment
> Shipment problems may arise in Florida?
> Best of luck,
> Pasha

Thank you, Pasha. Obviously, Sasha and the bitch Safi were now living in New York. Pasha was warning her not to run into Mika. Well, she had no intention of alerting Mika before she had a chance to create trouble for her little brother Sasha and Miss (now Mrs) Perfect. When she carried out her plan, they wouldn't know what hit them, that was for sure, the element of surprise was paramount. Once she had removed them permanently from her life, she would work on Mika and then reclaim her galleries. Her mother would have no option but to sign them over to her if she wanted to see her darling sons alive again.

Yvetta had a plan formulating though not yet perfected she was confident her contact would co-operate. Fritzi had taught her a thing or two about revenge over the years, they had more successes than losses. With her watertight contact in New York, she had little doubt her plan would succeed. He had been open to bribes in the past, that much she had found out through Fritzi having a reputation to protect. He was the obvious patsy for her plans.

As the bus rolled on towards its destination, she closed her eyes, imagining scenarios unfolding in bright Technicolor in her mind's eye. They always ended with her brothers begging for mercy as she stood triumphantly over them, waving a signed document.

Ramsey boarded the bus East to New York. As the bus dropped off passengers, picking up a few new people, it was easy to keep a low-profile amongst the others journeying East on the mind-numbing, endless highway to its final destination. They always tried to take a seat next to her, but she made it patently clear the seat had been bought and paid for to remain empty of passengers: the only occupants her rucksack, iPad, and the odd snack.

Once or twice, on the occasions Yvetta had vacated her seat to use the onboard toilets, the agent would lean across, while everyone slept, to check for anything useful. On each occasion they found Yvetta had taken the iPad along with her. The rucksack, though, had been left behind, but to their frustration, every document in the folder was written in Russian, a language none of the agents that boarded the bus to replace the agent disembarking, was familiar with. They could have tried to have the documents translated or taken a photo copy but head office were sending a Russian, so they waited.

On the last leg of the journey, a Russian agent boarded the bus: the woman casually took the seat beside him, the agency having sent a photo she obviously knew him right off.

He had kept the document from Yvetta's rucksack in his own carry-on. Having weighed the options, he ultimately decided to take the documents and replace them with empty pages, putting the folder in her rucksack, with the hope that the replacement would not be discovered until they had a chance to replace the originals, once the agent had the opportunity to go through them. Ramsey had noticed Yvetta busy on her iPad, then taking up the empty hours writing in a journal, which unfortunately she kept on her person at all times.

The woman made her way to the back of the bus with the documents, brushing past Yvetta on her way back to her seat. Bumping into each other, Yvetta dropped her journal; the agent apologised as she bent to pick up the journal, purposely kicking it under one of the seats, she gasped in frustration, swearing in Polish.

'Not worry, I will get book, stupid clumsy, sorry.'

Yvetta stood helplessly as the agent crept under the seat to retrieve her journal. At first she did not react to her accent; then she panicked as she realised the woman was Eastern European.

There was absolutely nothing she could do until the stupid woman handed back her journal after crawling on her hands and knees to retrieve it from under the seats where it had lodged itself.

Svetlana was a quick reader, but she had to use all of her resources to take a cursory glance at some of the written pages before handing them back to Yvetta without her becoming suspicious.

As she extricated herself from under the seats, she straightened up, handing the journal back to Yvetta with a flustered, apologetic smile, brushing off her dusty knees in order to deflect more conversation or attention to the incident. Yvetta grabbed the journal, returning to her seat highly agitated. Mumbling, she grabbed her rucksack and replaced the journal safely inside.

The incident had provided some amusement for others on the bus, and Ramsey watched Yvetta closely for any signs of suspicion, but saw nothing but anger at Svetlana's clumsiness. He remained in his seat for a few minutes, then made his way to the back of the bus to wait for Svetlana to emerge with, he hoped, some names or numbers for them to pass on for investigation.

Svetlana handed him a list of names, one number, and email contacts. She returned to the seat, grabbed her bag, and took the seat behind, which was vacant (she did not want to antagonise Yvetta, or have her feel uncomfortable by her close proximity across the aisle).

The bus trundled on into blackness, its final stretch of the journey before the passengers were dropped at dawn just outside Manhattan to find their own way into the dense built-up modern metropolis.

There were a few photos stuck inside the journal, which Svetlana decided to take. She was considering how to return them in an artful manner, while with sleight-of-hand they replaced the files before she had time to become suspicious.

On returning from the toilets with her washbag, Svetlana leaned over Yvetta, handing her the photos with one hand, while obscuring the vacant seat with her jacket hanging over the rucksack in the adjacent seat, 'I found these on the floor they must have fallen out of your journal.'

Yvetta stared at Svetlana, took the photos from her, staring down at Fritzi's face, then looked up at Svetlana again, who was still leaning over Yvetta, waiting for her to confirm they were her photos. When Svetlana was sure Ramsey had replaced the files, she straightened up and returned to her seat.

Once they arrived at the bus station, everyone dispersed in various directions. But Yvetta remained seated, sorting out her belongings, before making her way into the city. She had not set eyes on either the woman or the man who had sat on the opposite aisle. but the whole saga on the bus had unnerved her more than she realised. Trusting only her instincts, she would remain where she was until sure no one from the bus had remained, lest they follow her.

The Upper East Side was where some in her family had stayed for Sasha's engagement to that British brat. She wished she could return to the Rubicov apartments, where her own luxurious apartment sat vacant – not yet, to go back now would be to tempt fate, but she would in time reclaim what was rightfully hers.

Once her week at the spa was over, she would be ready to make contact with those who had zero choice in carrying out her instructions; she would then be ready to make her move.

The smartly dressed elderly man on the curb entered the dark-windowed Uber as it slid to the sidewalk next to him. The yellow cab ahead had pulled away as the Uber slowly made its way into the traffic, where it was instructed to remain a few cars behind the cab until it reached its destination.

The W Hotel was obviously the cab's destination, and he remained seated in the car until the woman in the yellow cab had disappeared inside.

Near the reception picked up the *New York Times* from a complementary pile on the front desk, and found a seat, watching the woman as she checked in.

Four days had gone by without any sign of the woman he was sent to follow. Never before had he lost sight of his quarry; either she had checked out without his knowing, or something was wrong.

He decided to wait one more day, lounging about the foyer unobtrusively. Luckily most Manhattan hotel lounges were used by passing traffic on a regular basis for meetings or general use even to use laptops for hours on end, so he wasn't worried about hanging around. If she was there, he would know. He watched people come and go; no one resembled the female he had followed into the hotel. He was about to admit failure when he noticed a petite, beautifully coiffed blonde walking out of the revolving doors into the midday Manhattan heat. At first it did not register, but then he noticed the same lime-coloured folder protruding from the LV shopper slung over her shoulder.

She had certainly undergone a transformation since he had last seen her, but there was no mistake: same height, same slender figure, and same walk; it was Yvetta with blonde hair.

As he walked a short distance behind, he wondered whether he had missed seeing her due to the obvious change of hair colour. Had she been wearing wigs? Perhaps, but one thing was for sure: he wouldn't be thrown off the track again; hopefully valuable information had not been lost in those four days.

Janus had met and briefed him during his time at the hotel; he had not been pleased Yvetta had given him the slip, but now they were back in business.

Thankfully she had not yet turned up anywhere near the family. In fact, the Rubicovs had been in disagreement about how to apprehend her. Janus had suggested they take her into custody; he could arrange for her to be off the streets, all he needed was confirmation from them.

Anna had wanted to meet with Yvetta; she had been following Yvetta's life since leaving the clinic in Moscow for Namibia, through updates from the agency, which had been instructed to keep Anna informed. Not satisfied with the professional data on her daughter, Anna had made contact with Hans without anyone's knowledge. Hans and her had chatted once a week on FaceTime. Often the conversation veered off subject; both enjoyed chatting about life in general. Anna loved hearing about Hans involvement with her daughter, he seemed to know a different person from the one the family had grown used to
dealing with.

In their last conversation, Hans believed Yvetta may have found peace living in Namibia. Anna was once again shocked to the core to learn of her daughter's out-of-control, violent behaviour; after all this time, she never knew how news of Yvetta would affect her.

At times she would feel total despair, not being able to reach her; at other times she would be resolute, believing her only option was to keep a quiet distance. Yet one thing was constant, she missed her daughter. In some ways, Yvetta was still, and would always be, her little girl. She believed Yvetta loved her family. All evidence proved the contrary yet she would never give up on her daughter, she was such a beautiful happy little girl.

When she was told Yvetta had disappeared from Africa, she wondered whether she would try to find her, come home, maybe find comfort with her. Still, Anna had to admit that her hopes at reconciliation with Yvetta were a pipe dream, she had learnt to have low expectations.

Now Yvetta had turned up in New York, and the immediate family wanted to take her back to one of those awful institutions; this time she may be admitted indefinitely, especially after the destruction she had left behind in Namibia. Anna was convinced Yvetta was in New York to reclaim her gallery. Moscow was out of the question, but the Manhattan gallery would enable her to regain control of her life, and Anna felt that was a good idea?

'Why not give back the galleries to Yvetta now?' Anna said to her sons during one of their FaceTime calls. 'Perhaps it's just what she needs to regain some semblance of normality and peace in her otherwise fractured life.'

Her sons listened, but knew, of course, that this wasn't a possibility.

'Mom,' began Mika.

'I don't think it will work,' Sasha said. 'Anyway, Safi has signed papers at the reading of the will, to look after the galleries until we, as a family, decide what to do, and when to give them back to Yvetta.'

'Sasha,' Anna said slowly, 'I know and I understand. We owe Safi a huge debt. She is now my daughter, too, by marriage to you. But those galleries are Yvetta's by right.'

Mika sighed. 'Mom, let's not do this again. We settled all of this with the lawyers. It will take time and, of course, and agreement from Safi.'

'Safi is having a baby. She will be a mother soon, her priorities will change, and she has Sasha. What does Yvetta have?'

There was a long silence on the line. Anna watched her sons; modern technology made it so easy to feel closer than one was. She wanted to reach through the screen and put her arms round them, hold them close, and encourage them to soften towards their sister. This battle they were raging with her daughter since she had attacked her with Fritzi in their family home in Moscow all of those years ago… it was time if not to forgive, then to move forward. She was old and wanted the family rift healed before she died.

Maurice did not agree with her wishes; neither did Janus, who had seen at first-hand Yvetta's dangerous behaviour.

Anna found Janus an odd man. He seemed to have no anger in him at being jilted (most unusual in an alpha male, which was very much what he gave every indication of being); in fact, he was completely against allowing Yvetta anywhere near Safi, over whom he was still most protective. Anna wondered if he was still in love with Safi, but then why had he conceded her to Sasha so easily, and why did he appear to have so little anger? Perhaps he just cared for her deeply; goodness knows, Anna reflected, the young British girl seemed to make an impression on everyone she met. Still, Janus had made it most clear that he did not trust Yvetta in the same city as Safi; no one, he insisted, could take such a gamble, especially since Safi was almost due to have her baby.

In the past month and a half, Safi resembled a house. She was huge. It was summer and the heat out was oppressive. She chose to remain at home as much as possible, and conducted most of her business on the computer. When she was needed at work, she no longer walked the 12 blocks to the gallery, but called an Uber, sliding with ease from one cool space to the next, hardly feeling the hot air as she stepped from the entrance of her building into the waiting car and into her icy gallery.

A stalemate on the Yvetta situation was not an option; Janus had made it clear he needed to have a clear directive from the family before he was able to stop Yvetta in her tracks. After all, he said, one could hardly catch someone if one did not know what to do with them next.

'Mom, look at this photo we have of Yvetta,' Mika told his mother excitedly on a FaceTime call one afternoon. 'This is what she looks like at the moment; as you can see her appearance has changed drastically. She has a folder containing the numbers and email addresses of some of the most dangerous, ruthless Russian gangsters living in New York. This points to some danger, don't you agree?'

Anna asked to see the photo again. Staring at it on her cell phone while chatting on the iPad, she could not help commenting on her daughter's new feminine appearance.

'Blonde actually suits her. She looks so well, don't you think?'

'Oh, Mom!'

'Okay, I agree she is up to something,' Anna conceded unhappily. 'Could we not stop her if we interjected by offering her what we know she won't refuse – the gallery? If she were to sign an agreement never to harm or work against the family, knowing that if she broke the terms of the agreement, she would not only lose the galleries, but her freedom and no support from the family.'

'Okay, Mom, we will come back to you. First, we have to go over the legal possibility of such a deal.'

Chapter 18

Yvetta felt light-footed as she made her way towards the gallery. She had not been to her gallery in New York before, and the thought of actually entering the space made her temples throb with excitement. She felt elated being in Manhattan, a city bursting at the seams with possibility, at the best of times, but this was something else entirely. Her heart was racing; soon this space would be hers forever.

She felt confident that no one would recognise her with blonde tresses, dark sunglasses, and a pretty floral summer dress (something she would never wear; one thing she never wore was floral or girlie, flimsy Barbie fashion). But now she was embracing the anti-her to outsmart her family, to reinvent herself anew, to take control of her own life once and for all. Her family would never in a million years know it was her striding confidently into the gallery. The spa had successfully (albeit expensively, but nothing came cheap in this part of New York) helped her to make the transformation. She had had her hair bleached blonde with extensions added; it hung past her shoulders in bouncy layers.

When she looked at her appearance in the mirror her hand had flown up to her mouth. The person staring back at her was a million miles from the persona she liked to project. Gone was her short brunette hair, her eyebrows had been thickened and made darker, as had her eyelashes. She had a permanent lip-liner filled in with what the makeup artist called 'aubergine.' Green eyes were staring out at her, made up in a smoky, dark-grey shadow. Standing back, she whistled at her own reflection; she looked hot.

The stylist had brought a number of dresses for her to try, helping with a complete wardrobe change. She now resembled a rich pampered Manhattan babe, wearing strappy high heel sandals instead of her usual Converse or thick-soled lace-up boating shoes, she had got use to wearing with everything in Namibia.

Together with the stylist she had chosen a dozen outfits: trousers, shorts, skirts, tops, and shoes, all brought over by a stylist from various stores in the area. She disregarded all of the usual designers she used to patronise in her youth: Chanel, Prada, or Celine. She had loved everything they designed, but those high-fashion days were over for good. So was the old Yvetta. Now she was someone new, sleek, smart, and impossible to outmanoeuvre.

Now she wore her hair pulled back in a high pony tail. Depending on what she chose to wear, the stylists had given her some amazing insights into the kind of woman she had chosen to mimic. Very little makeup most days, only a healthy glow, amazing eyes, and moist lips; a ridiculously 'natural' appearance that took for ever to achieve and lots of money. The painted lips and smoky eyes were for evenings; days were pared down. As she made her way to the gallery, she felt wonderful for the first time in weeks. She happily met the admiring glances from men and woman as they passed by. Fritzi would have had a field day teasing her, but Yvetta did not want to go there, not now, not again; her life was about to change for ever.

She stopped to view the gallery from the opposite pavement, her resolve ebbing slightly; she hadn't eaten since breakfast. She sat down at a pavement café. She needed to collect her thoughts before she made her presence felt in her gallery, she wanted to appear calm; right now, she was too nervy and excited.

The waiter flirted confidently at every opportunity; she was enjoying the attention, it was, she found, quite fun when she knew who was in control she didn't have the slightest interest in men, not even this oversexed, handsome hunk of a waiter – but she would leave him a big tip for calming her nerves. Men, she thought, such silly animals. Not that some women were any better, she reflected, thinking again about Safi.

Leaving the restaurant she crossed over the road, pushed the heavy glass doors to the gallery open, and stood surveying the space before diverting her eyes to the work hanging on the walls. She couldn't help it – she loved art more than anything, she always would. The gallery receptionist did not bother to look up; many didn't until the punter showed interest in a particular work.

She noticed one other man in the gallery. slowly making his way around the exhibit; for some reason she was pleased not to be alone. Sleek and surprisingly spacious for Manhattan, it was a beautiful space, she had to admit. She wasn't even envious to admit it, after all, all of this would be hers soon.

She loved the space, it was impressive compared to her gallery in Moscow; it had a far more contemporary feel. All of a sudden Yvetta realised how much she missed this world. Being in Namibia, even in Namibia's tiny art world, hadn't quite cut it. She missed the shows, she missed the travel, she even missed the artists. But most of all she missed being around art that mattered.

Most artists were a pain in the neck, to be sure. Gallerists established a love-hate relationship with their artists. Once signed to a gallery, each became demanding on his or her own terms. The artist wanted to be feted. The gallery mostly wanted to sell out a show with many commissions to follow, which rarely happened, but when it did both artist and gallery would gain hugely.

The artist could have their work picked up by museums; for the artist this would be reaching the pinnacle of their career; for the gallery it would be finding a diamond amongst semi-precious stones and may guarantee their reputation and their income for years to come. Neither could survive in the wider world without the other; the star artist would dictate their terms to the gallery, but the semi-precious artists would be at the gallery's mercy, always fighting for a show, for their work to be better represented. It was a tough existence, to be sure, but one she had relished. She was a fighter, but she also loved art, and this business was a combination of both.

As she moved from one exhibit to another her mind raced with memories of her life before she left Moscow: the shows she had attended around the world; the artists she loved and represented; how had she managed to lose so much in such a short time. Never had she hated anyone more at that moment than she hated Safi; she had stolen her life right from under her, and her family had assisted in the theft, she hated them even more, much more, for supporting that bitch now married to her brother.

She noticed the other man in the gallery on an earphone, shaking his head vigorously, obviously buying for a client. She used to have to do the same many years ago when she attended shows in Europe.

The agent in the gallery was listening to his next move from Janus directly; he was to make sure Safi was not in the gallery at same time as Yvetta. Safi was out of contact, not at home. Everyone was frantic, especially Janus and Sasha.

At that moment gallery doors swung open and a heavily pregnant woman entered.

'I believe the subject has just walked into the gallery,' the agent said into his headset. He watched the exchange between the two women; it appeared normal, neither reacted to the other, apart from a casual greeting. The pregnant woman had a word with the girl at the front desk, and moved to the back of the gallery.

There was a gasp and a sharp intake of breath from Janus who controlled the operation on the other end of the line, but as the agent related the scene the agent could hear his controller getting back on track.

He was ordered to remain in the gallery for the duration of Yvetta's visit, not to apprehend but to follow her from the gallery, to take clandestine photographs, and to report back.

Janus was frustrated beyond belief; the family were at a stalemate how to proceed with Yvetta, and he could not make a move without hearing their decision. Janus would not stand by while this unstable woman hurt the only person in the world he loved. Janus had given in graciously when Safi left him for Sasha, believing he would not be able to make her happy, and that this was in fact the right thing to do. After all, Safi was a normal young woman and deserved to have children.

Safi thought the reason Janus did not have children was because of his dedication to his art and to his agency, his two loves, but sadly this was not true. As it happened, he had only one real love, and this was Safi.

Having measles as a teenager had ruined Janus's chances of having a family; he would never experience being a father. When he was a young man, it had not bothered him unduly. But after meeting Safi he had endured a battery of tests, which unfortunately turned out to be negative. He had never stopped loving her, never would, and, wasn't going to allow his own emotions to destroy something he wanted to be a part of. He never wanted there not to be a Safi in his life, for whatever reason. She was the only woman he had ever met that was genuinely warm hearted and loyal to those she loved, even under extreme pressure she never complained and as far as he was concerned, she was the Lotus flower that made even the muddiest water flow clearly, she was his angel the person he most admired and loved.

They had become firm friends in work and socially. At the same time, he could not find fault with Sasha; he believed him a good man. Sasha would be a great father, but he, Janus, would be a great godfather: Safi had asked him, he could not refuse her, it would be his only chance to experience the love of a child through someone he loved, close enough to be his own child.

Dax and Dan were visibly upset at not having been first choice, but Safi had promised they would be joint godfathers to her next two babies; she was determined to have three children, which, she had told Janus, had made them happy enough to stop sulking.

'Though you might as well know,' she had informed Janus, 'you have a tough act to follow replacing the two D's.'

Janus had not declined when invited to be godfather; he surprised even himself by being so elated at the opportunity, it was more than he could have hoped for.

Janus felt they were playing with fire allowing Yvetta to get so close to Safi. It was beyond belief that they had allowed her to leave the loft for the gallery at this, or any, time in her pregnancy, He was beside himself with dread. After all, Yvetta was capable of anything; she had tried once before to take Safi out. He was behaving like the expectant father, he had to remain calm, it was his job to handle these situations. Never before had he felt so utterly helpless; it would be impossible to forgive not only himself but Sasha as well, for not warning Safi about Yvetta being in Manhattan.

Sasha had not known Safi had decided to leave for the gallery; he had been on a conference call with Mika and his mother, when he heard the elevator.

When he found she forgot her cell he panicked; she had become quite forgetful since falling pregnant. Still, he doubted she would be out for long in the suffocating heat.

Sasha had never heard Janus distressed. Normally, the man was unbelievably calm, to the point of being wooden. Now he had him on the line, almost screaming.

'Why the fuck have you allowed Safi to go to the gallery when you know Yvetta is in New York! She has just walked into the gallery. Your sister is in the gallery!'

Sasha went cold, his heart raced; grabbing her cell, he dialled the gallery number.

'Lucky for you,' Janus continued, 'my agent was there. There was no sign of recognition on Yvetta's part, but it won't take Yvetta long to work out who she is.'

Safi picked up the call from Sasha that her assistant buzzed through,

'Yvetta is in the gallery,' Sasha said, speaking quickly and softly, 'don't whatever you do go out into the gallery. The agent is there should she try anything. Why the hell didn't you tell me you were going to the gallery today?'

'Oh my God, that was Yvetta. Last moment decision, sorry.'

'You left your bloody cell behind, too.'

'Oh God, I am so forgetful at the moment. So sorry, Sasha, this is awful. What are we going to do about Yvetta? I would never have recognised her is she the pretty blonde I noticed walking around, never. She looks completely different.'

Yvetta continued to look at the work she was studying as the pregnant woman greeted her. It took her a moment or two before it registered it could be Safi. She tried to remember Safi's face, but couldn't quite – it had been a long time, after all – and the woman passed her by too quickly. Had it been her, Yvetta thought, she would surely have known. Safi was tall, slim, had long black hair; this woman had a sharp bob, her face was bloated, she looked fat; it couldn't be her, and if it was she was beyond recognition, ugh!

How could her brother love a woman so huge and ugly, pregnant or not; Yvetta knew Sasha would never tolerate any woman he was with looking like a fat frump.

The man was still in the gallery on his speaker phone with the cord hanging off his ear, his clients obviously were difficult to satisfy. She noticed him studying her, looking in her direction, something she did not like to encourage. Turning promptly to leave, she stopped at the front desk, asking for a printout of the prices and a synopsis of the artist, then casually asked when the 'gallerist' (a very American term) would be in.

She noticed the receptionist looking up at the man as she handed Yvetta the paperwork. Yvetta turned in his direction, too, wondering what the man was up to, when the girl leaned over to answer her question.

'Oh, she is away right now, but if there is anything you need to know, please don't hesitate to let us know.' Her voice was bright but her words had a slightly rehearsed quality to them. Yvetta looked at the man again; he had his back turned, but had moved closer, almost diagonally across from where they were standing, peering intently at a huge canvas.

'I am sure you will be offloading a number of works,' Yvetta said. 'He has been here a long time talking on that wire of his, good luck!'

The receptionist smiled thinly as Yvetta turned to leave.

Once she was out of sight the receptionist ran to the back of the gallery to tell Safi the coast was clear, and the man in the gallery walked briskly out of the gallery after Yvetta.

'Thank you,' Safi said with relief, 'I have been a bag of nerves the whole time those two were in here. I have no idea what I would have done if it were not for Janus's agent. He picked up her trail. I would never in a million years have recognised her. How did you know to tell her I wasn't in town? That was clever of you'

'Well, the agent was nodding his head violently from side to side when she asked the question about the gallerist, so I got the picture. He was watching her the whole time she was in the gallery, every move. I am so surprised she did not notice. And then Sasha called to warn me, so I knew something was up. Who is she?'

'Oh, it's a very long story. I will tell you, but not now. If she comes in again, though, it will mean trouble, I am sure. Best to tell her the gallery is closing, apologise profusely, but lock the door. Make any excuse, but don't allow her in, okay?'

'Right,' the receptionist said. 'Gosh, you will have to fill me in soon. I don't think I can take the suspense. Why have you come in today, anyway. You must be so close now to the birth date?'

'Well, stupid, really. I got tired of hanging around at home. I have wanted to be here for a while. I will explain, I promise, but not now. I am waiting for Janus, he won't allow me to leave the gallery unescorted. Let me know when he arrives.'

Yvetta hailed a cab, leaving the agent frantically trying to get one, too. Ramsey watched as her cab stopped at the first set of lights; as they turned green he managed to hail a limo. 'I want you to try and catch up to that cab with the ad on top if you can,' Ramsey said. 'I will pay double if we don't lose it.'

'Right, you're on.' The limo slid into the traffic; speaking to another limo ahead, the driver was making sure he didn't lose the cab. As the lights changed he drove up the outside lane bypassing cars and narrowly missing loading vehicles on the sides; the black limo ahead was now in front of the yellow cab, slowing it down, They were abreast of Yvetta's cab now, and the agent leant back for the first time.

'Good job,' Ramsey said. 'Your friend did us a huge favour.'

'No problem, man. I can see why you want to catch that cab, she sure is a pretty lady.'

'Right, let's not lose her again. I want to see where she gets off, you understand. Drop me just ahead. close to that corner.' He threw $50 at the limo driver.

'Thanks man,' the driver said, 'you want me to wait?'

Shaking his head, he called out to Janus the name of the building she had gone into, to find out whether it had any significance.

He did not need to wait long for the answer; it was someone called DuPont, who had offices in the building. They wanted Ramsey to check whether Yvetta had, indeed, gone up to DuPont's offices, or had headed somewhere else.

He let the limo go; there was no point in it waiting, he had no idea how long this would take. Yvetta disappeared through the doors into the building; he waited a few moments before following her in, stood to the side of the long reception desk, watching as she entered the elevator. He noted which floors it stopped at, and was relieved to see it had gone right to the top without any other pickups.

He walked over to the desk, from where a battery of stunning girls smiled up at him. He chose the least attractive; it usually worked.

'Can you tell me, does Mr DuPont have offices here?'

The girl hesitated for a moment

'Why yes. Do you have an appointment?'

'I forget which are his offices.'

He knew he was taking a chance; smiling, he waited

'Well, I'm not supposed to say, okay, just don't repeat anything. Top floor.'

Bingo!

He smiled his most winning smile of gratitude, then turned to leave.

Yvetta casually sauntered into DuPont's offices. Reaching the outer office and reception, she was greeted by a sharp-looking American girl. 'Can I have your name, please?' the girl inquired.

'Tell Mr DuPont that Yvetta Rubicov is here to see him, yes?'

'Is he expecting you today?'

'Go and deliver my message, please, then come back and ask me that question.'

Tossing her silky black ponytail like a thoroughbred stallion, the girl marched off in her too-high heels and tight-fitting skirt. Yvetta watched her hips sway from side to side and shapely legs as she disappeared from view. Not since Fritzi had she looked at another female, but this one merited a 9 out of 10. She was fierce, in her way, and Yvetta enjoyed that. She might even flirt with her when she returned.

The girl returned, now all smiles. She stood in front of Yvetta as she tried to attract her attention, while Yvetta purposely kept turning the pages of the magazine, pretending not to notice.

'Ms Rubicov, can I show you the way, please.'

'You may. Do you speak Russian?'

'No, I am an American.'

'Ah, but so beautifully Russian-looking.'

As the girl opened the door to allow Yvetta past, Yvetta's hand brushed her pubic area. She could feel the girl jump. Smiling apologetically, she winked and walked into the vast open-plan room with a flourish, hand hesitantly outstretched and a fake smile to cover his nerves DuPont came to greet her from behind his desk.

'Yvetta, how lovely to see you. To what do I owe this unexpected pleasure?'

'So many questions, everyone has questions, but what I want is some answers. Perhaps you will be able to help in that regard?'

'I will try my best. A drink, perhaps? May I say you are looking ravishingly beautiful. Have you changed the colour of your hair? I remember it darker.'

'Questions again., the answer is yes, and I will have a small vodka, please'

'Another question, then you have the floor: are you still gay or have your tastes changed since we last met?'

Yvetta threw back her head and gave a throaty laugh,

'I see you have not changed, still trying to seduce, even at your advanced years to seduce.'

'I am French, no, you wouldn't expect anything less.'

'Well, you never know. If you give me what I want, I may consider giving you what you want. How's that for an exchange?'

'I'm all ears,' he said, passing her the drink with a wicked gin.

Seated on his soft white leather designer sofa, with DuPont directly opposite, his knees almost touching, Yvetta straightened, allowing her back to arch slightly, crossed her shapely legs, leaned forward, showing bronzed cleavage as she put the empty tumbler down on the side table.

'Well,' Yvetta began, 'as you know, the galleries have always been mine. My father left them to me in his will, but there was a caveat. I did not agree to it, I had no choice then, but I do now.'

Despite his pretention of flirtatiousness and amiability, DuPont felt deeply uneasy. She was trouble. He knew from past episodes that she could not be antagonised. Worst of all, she was unpredictable. He would have to play this with kid gloves.

He smiled, encouraging for her to continue.

'I would prefer this exchange to go smoothly,' she said softly, 'without threats or violence, you understand. This is where you come in!'

He nodded, preferring to give her his full attention. Best not to comment.

'I want you to convey a message to them directly in person.'

'What would that be, Yvetta?'

She leaned in more closely, stretched out a hand, touching his knee. A feeling of dread enveloped him as he remembered how Fritzi had threatened him and his career not so very long ago.

'This is what I want you to tell my family,' her voice was no longer soft.

'I want my galleries back now, not when it suits them to give them back, but right now. If they do not comply, they will leave me no other choice but to attack in a way that may change their lives for ever. If I cannot get what I want, neither will they!'

'What do you mean by that, Yvetta? I would love to assist you in getting your galleries, but I cannot threaten your family. Surely you would be more successful negotiating less aggressively. I could help you do this.'

A dark, threatening look crossed her face. She was so often frightening that it was difficult to remember how truly pretty she was. He moved back in his seat, waiting for her to explode. Instead, she jumped out of her seat and crossed over to the sofa, sitting up close to him. She took one of his hands in hers: at first it seemed a passive gesture, gentle even, then he felt pressure on his palm; a sharp pain shot up his arm. Pulling his hand away, he was horrified to see blood seeping from a cut across his palm. Staring at his hand in disbelief, he got up and grabbed a wad of tissues from his desk to quell the bleeding.

Yvetta was sitting on the seat, quite composed, smiling sweetly.

'Ah, you are shocked. This is a small sample of what I am capable of, if you do not pass on my message. I am also capable of ruining your illustrious career. Fritzi mentioned you in some of her smuggling deals. Wouldn't your clients love to know what you sell has no authentic provenance. They are just fakes to cover thefts ordered by many gallerists, you included.'

'I have never done business with Fritzi,' DuPont said slowly, his hand still aching, every trace of charm having left his voice long ago, 'nor have I bought antiquities without proper provenance. You cannot prove this; more to the point, I think you are a danger not only to me, but to anyone who does not agree with you. I have pressed an alarm; the security will be here to remove you any moment. I advise you to leave before they get here, if you do not want to be arrested.'

'You pressed an alarm?' she said.

'Yes, with the hand that you cut.'

Yvetta fumbled in her handbag, brought out a small revolver, and pointed it at DuPont.

'If you do not want to be shot, tell them it was an error, now!'

There was a loud knocking on the office door. DuPont made his way over to the door.

'Oh, sorry, guys, but my hand brushed against the alarm by mistake. As you can see all's well.' Yvetta sat smiling as two huge men poked their heads round the door to look inside, making sure no one was hiding inside.

After they departed, closing the door behind them, Yvetta walked over to DuPont and slapped him in the face, her ring with the blade slashing his cheek.

DuPont's hand flew up to his cheek, blood seeping out. God, this woman was mad; he was desperate to get away from her.

'Okay, Yvetta, you have made your point. I will do as you want.'

'NOW.'

He fumbled for his cell, dialled Sasha's number.

'Hi, it's DuPont. I want you to listen carefully. I have a message.'

But Sasha had something to tell him first. DuPont listened as Sasha told him Yvetta was in town and had been followed; they knew she was with him. Trying not to let on what he had been told, DuPont continued with the message.

'Yvetta wants her galleries back now. If you do not comply, she will harm the family in a way that will change your lives, as you have done to hers.'

He saw Yvetta smile approval.

'Okay! Tell her okay, are you alright?'

He turned towards Yvetta, but she was nowhere to be seen. Thinking she may have gone into his private bathroom, he cautiously checked, but she had vanished.

Shaking with fright he slowly sat down at his desk, hand on his face, tissues soaked with blood in his palm.

She is truly mad; they had not exaggerated, after all. Safi had told him of Yvetta's attack on her. At the time he had thought it odd; now he knew first-hand just how dangerous she was.

Yvetta found the assistant who had shown her into the office. Smiling suggestively, she requested the assistant show her another way out of the building; she said she wanted to avoid her brother, who was waiting at the reception.

Not thinking anything of it, Gina walked Yvetta to a single elevator that would take her directly down to the underground car park.

As the doors opened, she pulled the assistant in with her. Startled, Gina felt Yvetta rip her blouse open. Jamming Gina against the back of the elevator, Yvetta lifted her skirt and dropped to her haunches. Pulling the girl's panties off, she spread her legs, massaging her until she could hear Gina moan, throbbing. Yvetta stuck her tongue deep into her, sucking her until Gina dropped onto the floor, gasping. Yvetta straddled her, kissing her mouth; when Gina responded, she forced her head down, allowing Gina to kiss her until she convulsed with orgasmic pleasure.

She had jammed the elevator as it reached the car park; now she straightened her clothes, ordering Gina to check if the coast was clear for them to exit.

Trying to compose herself Gina peered around. Tidying her hair, she stepped out. No one was about. She beckoned to Yvetta, who grabbed her again, pushing her against a pillar, and kissed her on the mouth.

'You were delicious. Pity we can't do this again. Bye honey, don't say a word when asked about me or the back elevator.'

Once outside Yvetta hailed a cab, re-entered the hotel, asked for her bill, and checked out. In her suite she packed her few belongings, and left through the restaurant on the ground floor, hailed another cab, and booked into a new hotel Uptown. If anyone tried to follow her, she would hopefully have given him or her the slip.

The agent had waited for Yvetta in the lobby. When she did not appear, he asked them to call up to DuPont; he wanted to make sure the man was okay.

DuPont was in shock. Normally unflappable, charming and cool and in control, he was now on the point of paralysis, a shivering shell of himself. The agent found him lying on the sofa, a damp hand-towel draped over his face, blood seeping from the wad of tissues in his hand. His arm hung over the edge of the sofa, almost touching the floor. He ran over to DuPont, picked up his arm to feel his pulse

'No, no, I am okay, just in shock,' a small, almost unrecognisable, voice said.

'What happened here, did Yvetta do this to you?'

DuPont slowly raised himself to a sitting position. Facing the agent, he explained the events as they had occurred.

'She is a very dangerous young woman,' DuPont said, still in disbelief. 'I believe they were correct to have her committed. She may resort to anything if she does not have her way.'

'How on earth did she get away?'

'While I was on a call to her brother Sasha, repeating her threats, she must have slipped out and found the service elevator to the car park. That's why you missed her, she exited on a side street.'

Realising Yvetta had given him the slip, he had called for reinforcement to be sent to the W Hotel, but they must have arrived too late. Once the call to Sasha was made by DuPont, Janus had been given carte blanche. Learning of the attack on DuPont, they decided Anna's reluctance to commit Yvetta was a mistake. Yvetta was clearly not coping well (or at all) in society, their mother would be as saddened as they were, but Yvetta's recent behaviour had given them no option. She had proven she had not changed her old ways at all.

They had lost the lead and Janus was livid, total incompetence on his part.

'I want you both out of Manhattan now,' he informed Safi and Sasha on the phone.

'Janus, I am having a baby, in case you haven't noticed, and you are going to be her godfather; where would I go at this late stage?'

'I had noticed,' Janus replied, 'which makes this even more urgent. Los Angeles. Mika will send his plane to fly you. I have contacts in Layout have absolutely nothing to fear, you will be very well cared for, Safi. You will be safe.'

'I can't take this happening, and now of all times. I don't want to leave my home. I don't want to run away to LA. I want to bring my baby home to her nursery here in Manhattan, our home, her home! I have nothing in LA and nowhere to go once I've had my baby. My parents will be arriving in a month to be with us, they will be staying here with Sasha and me; what are they to do now?'

'They will have to change their plans, Safi. You too. This is a matter of urgency.'

'No,' she said firmly. 'Yvetta has upended my life too many times before. I refuse to allow this to change our lives. You will just have to find her. I will remain a prisoner in my own home until you do.'

'Can't we go to Mika in Florida instead,' Sasha said. 'The house is large enough to accommodate us all.'

'No, Sasha, that is a bad idea,' Janus said. 'Yvetta knows Mika is in Florida, she has been to the house, it's not safe. Need I remind you what happened in that house last time the family was gathered together.'

Janus did not need to further remind Sasha of this incident, an incident that Sasha had missed out on due to his absence, but which Janus had been there to witness. He felt bad for reminding Safi of it, but, in this case, it had to be done. They should be under no illusion as to how dangerous Yvetta was.

They sat in silence, obviously a stalemate.

'OK,' Janus said finally, 'but Safi, if you remain here, I am putting a 24-hour watch on this place, in the apartment and at the front entrance.'

DuPont had called to assure Safi he was okay, albeit still shocked at her sudden violent behaviour towards him.

'She has to be found, Safi. You and Sasha are not safe while that crazy person is out there. I suggest you close the gallery until she is tracked down.'

Gina was appalled when she learnt what the women who seduced her had done to her boss. Embarrassed about her sexual tryst, she only told him that Yvetta had escaped via the service elevator to the car park.

Yvetta knew she had burnt her few remaining bridges. Attacking DuPont was not her intention. Still, the man irritated her beyond belief; he was so full of himself. And he hadn't changed at all, in the years she had known him. If anything, he had got worse. She noticed those photographs on full display in his office, photographs of her gallery in Moscow, a searing jealously seethed through her being. In the photograph DuPont stood with a group of celebrities, with Safi at the helm at her Moscow gallery, attending an opening for Dax, the American artist.

Smiling for the press, standing together, Safi and DuPont. In others photos she saw her family with the artist and again DuPont. It was her gallery, Yvetta reminded herself. Blackness descended over her, she wanted to strike out; the pain she felt was overpowering.

She had intended soliciting DuPont's help and advice persuading her brothers to hand back the galleries. After all that, she was now alone. She knew she was destined to be alone. Why did she even bother? At least she would have her gallery back soon. That was enough.

Fritzi had been taken from her. Handing back her galleries would at least allow her a future, something she would be able to build on; perhaps she would even open another gallery in London? She wasn't averse to leaving the New York gallery for Safi to run, but she wanted the legal documents to have her name as owner, they were hers by right, left to her by her father.

She felt cheated, having signed that caveat under immense pressure from her mother and the lawyers, at Mika's home in Florida. She had burnt her bridges then, too, by attacking Safi, but what did they expect, giving that imposter power of attorney over Yvetta's inheritance, until they thought she was mentally able to take over. Who the hell did they think they were to judge her mental state? She would show them once and for all not to mess with a Rubicov.

She sat on the bed in the new hotel suite. All the contacts she thought she had were Fritzi's. She had made a grave error contacting Fritzi's lot they were dangerous to be sure. Fritzi had been arrested as far as her contacts were concerned, they had cut Fritzi off, she no longer had leverage. She thought she may have opened Pandora's box by contacting Fritzi's people, putting herself at risk from being taken out, if they thought she knew anything about their operations.

Yvetta was told to destroy all numbers in her possession. If she called again, she would find the numbers were no longer in operation, and if she disobeyed she would suffer the consequences. She sat on her bed for a few moments, shaking with fright. She had not expected to be threatened. They were dangerous. Fritzi had told her often enough, now she realised they were serious about getting rid of her, maybe they would do so anyhow, she had stolen Fritzi's contacts.

She had been mad to open Fritzi's personal files, she would have to prioritise tackle one thing at a time to keep a clear head!

Exhaustion took hold, it had been a long, stressful day, she did not have the will or energy to find another hotel. Walking to the window she dropped Fritzi's cell, seeing it shatter as it hit the roof below. It was no longer in her possession, they would not be able to track her.

Yvetta jumped as the phone in her suite rang. Should she answer it? Still not sure, partly out of instinct, she picked up the receiver.

'Reception here, we wanted to know if you were happy with your room, Ms Ruben?'

'Actually no, I would like to move to the executive floor, would that be possible?'

'Would you want to be doing so right now?'

'Yes.'

'Hold one moment, please, while I check.'

'Yes, we have another suite on the executive floor. The rate is $1000 a night.'

'Not a problem.'

'I will send a porter up to help with the move'

'No, that won't be necessary, thank you. I will come down.'

She tore the page with names and numbers from Fritzi's file out of her diary, put the page into the trash can, lit a match, watching the paper burn to a cinder, then shut the door behind her. Now she was on the move, perhaps she should walk out of this hotel and into another, there were so many in the area. As the elevator descended to the lobby she had made her decision; leaving was the only option open to her now.

A profile of Yvetta had been passed to all private security agencies Janus and Mika could think of in Manhattan. The police had been ruled out; the family did not want Yvetta behind bars, they wanted her to be in a proper, secure mental institution. If Yvetta went through the courts, her lawyers might persuade her she had a case, putting the family's private affairs on trial at great cost.

Mika had consulted with their lawyers, all agreed it would be preferable for their sister to be dealt with privately; if the courts were involved it could take years before any decisions were made. They would have to have her mental state revaluated by various doctors; this could prove to be controversial given the family dynamics.

Safi was getting closer to her due date. Irritable with being housebound, she spent her time reading and watching videos, trying to keep off her swollen ankles.

The heat out on the pavements were suffocating; in the evenings Sasha and Safi would be escorted to and from restaurants by security. These outings gave relief from cabin fever, and an opportunity to socialise with friends. No one mentioned the security following their every move; even in the restaurant they would have a security guard sitting at a table watching, it was relentless, 24/7. Ten days had gone by with no word of Yvetta, she was proving very hard to track down, with no reported sighting.

The hotels in the areas closest to the gallery and their home was scoured and questioned about guest lists: some would not divulge their guest's identities, others were more forthcoming. The family's best chance was to grease the palms of the doormen and the limo drivers who worked for the hotels; with luck something would fall into their laps.

Janus was desperate to track her down, fearing that the Rubicov's would doubt his ability. He was doubting his own resourcefulness and feeling he was letting Safi down. Disappointing the family and himself, he felt unusually drained.

He had instructed Ying to find an excuse for him not to attend his latest show in Berlin. It was the first show he had agreed to attend; with luck the organisers would put it down to his eccentricity, an image he preferred to foster. It was, after all, preferable to the truth about his other profession.

Chapter 19

She checked out, left through a back entrance, hailed a cab and walked into the Waldorf. The Waldorf was old but it was huge; it gave the anonymity she was after. If the Waldorf didn't work, she would move to Times Square, her best option. No one would find her there. Endless tourists would be her best cover, and no one would be searching for a redhead. She would invest in some wigs, wear shades, and a cap that should confuse anyone searching for a petite blonde with shoulder-length hair.

At the Marque on Times Square she moved to a suite on the 'Executive Floor.' This gave her access to food and drink without having to go through the hotel. It was private, one needed a card to use the lounge on the executive floor.

Ten days had passed and no one had tracked her down. Yvetta felt lonely, her well-thought-out plan had failed, and her confidence took a dive. Visits to the gallery were unsuccessful; each time she passed the gallery she lost her nerve. She could not go near DuPont again: he would have her arrested, but she longed to see Gina, his assistant. She craved company. She felt restless and still simmering with an anger that would not escape her.

Gina left the office at 6.30. The weather hot, she decided to walk to a nearby street café, one of her favourites. Taking a seat outdoors she ordered espresso and a salad. She noticed an attractive, petite woman in skinny white jeans, a pale pink silk top with an expensive shopper, take a table alongside. Swiftly, elegantly, the woman leaned over, commenting on her salad, wanting to know what she had ordered.

When the exact same order arrived at the woman's table, Gina glanced over fleetingly; the woman had moved one table closer, right next to her.

They ate in silence for a few moments, when Gina noticed the woman's lustrous short red hair shining as the last rays of sunlight caught her. The woman smiled at her in a familiar way. Where did she know her from? Gina wondered. The neighbourhood? The office? It was bothering her. Slightly uncomfortable but aroused, Gina called for the bill. That was when the woman leaned in.

'Let me get that,' she said in a strange, low, whispery voice that was nonetheless familiar, too, 'no need for you to pay. I would be happy to buy you dinner every night, if you promise to let me make love to you again.'

Gina hesitated, still not recognising this woman. She had had many lovers, but none quite as brazen or beautiful. Who was this person? It was delicious to be teased in this manner, but cruel and frustrating, too.

'Ah, you don't recognise me. That's good, Gina, it means my transformation is successful?'

'Oh my God, Yvetta?' Gina said, realising it was her with a start. It all came back to her, thrillingly, in a rush of illicit images – the elevator, the woman's touch and kiss, and so much more, their bodies coming together at breakneck speed. It had all been so sudden and so sexy and so strange. And it had almost cost her her job. Her pulse quickened and she felt elated but also a touch of fear.

'The very same, I miss you.'

She moved to the seat next to Gina, putting her hand onto Gina's leg slowly, moving her fingers up under her skirt. As the skirt covered her hand she touched Gina lightly, brushing her hand softly against the mound of hair. It was hot and pulsating. Gina's eyes wide, she was biting her bottom lip, as her hand shot down to stop Yvetta.

Gina gasped. 'Stop, please stop.'

'Why? You like it, right, we had great sex, Gina.'

'I know, but you attacked my boss.'

'I know, he will survive. He deserved it, helping my brother's wife take away my gallery. Come back to my place and I will tell you the whole story, then you will understand.'

Yvetta paid the waiter, leaving a huge tip; he smiled, winking at them, having seen what was happening.

'God, I'll never be able to come here again,' Gina said, regretting her decision already. She knew she shouldn't go, but she couldn't help herself. 'Let's go.'

Yvetta smiled and slipped her arm through Gina's as they hailed a cab.

In the hotel Gina, hot with desire, gave into Yvetta's lovemaking. She was wild, aggressive, yet gentle at the same time knowing every place to touch, every crevice to lick. Exhausted and happy, Yvetta ran them a bath and ordered room service.

'Spend the night, Gina. I need a friend, and we are so good together, we can have such incredible fun. I am rich, I will keep you in any manner you desire. I promise you won't be disappointed.'

'First you have to tell me what's going on.'

'I will, I promise, tomorrow,' Yvetta said soothingly, caressing the other woman's hair.' We can spend the whole day together, it's Saturday.'

They woke to a grey, muggy day, the rain pelting against the windows. A perfect day to stay in bed, make love and watch movies, something Yvetta longed to share with someone. She had not realised how lonely she had been since she had left Namibia. Here in New York City, you got to see so many people, yet not know any of them. The busiest city in the world, Yvetta thought, was also one of the loneliest. It was lonely because it was busy, not in spite of that fact. The opposite of Namibia, already so removed for Yvetta.

They were sitting at table for two in the executive lounge, looking out at the scene far below, where the tourists sheltered under dripping awnings and the streets resembled streams as the rain poured down, another world.

Yvetta felt safe, happy, and cosy in her cocoon, away from the mayhem down in the streets below, she no longer felt afraid, she was convinced she would be able to persuade Gina to stay, she would make it worth her while.

Yvetta told her story to Gina, a very different tale to the one known to others. She described her life in Russia, her home in Moscow, her schooling in England. Her visits home, where she was raped by one of her cousin's time and time again. She could never tell her father, whom she adored. One had to understand, she informed Gina, in Russia they viewed things very differently. Her cousin would be seen to be the injured party, she the temptress who had seduced him, they were both teenagers. She was only thirteen and Pasha was sixteen. He was always wild like her they had what one could call a love hate relationship, he wanted her and she needed him, it was and wasn't consensual, when no meant yes, and she wasn't wilful enough to stop him needing the attention, and the closeness, and physical connection they continued when and wherever Pasha wanted sex, but Yvetta's struggle against his passion was useless, she hated being weak feeling it was wrong but it continued, until Pasha lost interest and moved on leaving her ashamed and a confused adolescent just beginning her teenage years.

Her mother was never home and never seemed to care about her anyway (she was more interested in running the Rubicov empire. Both her parents were oligarchs, their empire ranked in importance above her and her brothers, although Mika was much older and his own man. Then she met a German woman who she fell in love with; she went on to describe Fritzi who had given her back her sexuality and her confidence. Fritzi was everything Yvetta wasn't self- assured and, charismatic a temptress and lover who made her feel she was the centre of her world. She worked for the gallery and they built up a formidable international business together.

Fritzi had always had business dealings of her own on the side, which she had not paid much attention to, but it turned out Fritzi was also working for illegal art smugglers.

Her parents never approved of her affair with Fritzi; they found her choice of lifestyle abhorrent and embarrassing.

She explained her fights with her mother, who she hated, and how she and Fritzi had bungled an art heist at her family home. It all came pouring out not meaning to tell Gina every detail but the tap had been opened and now there was no stopping her, Gina was hearing every detail, how her father had trapped them turning their lives upside down into a hell hole for them both.

Fritzi sprung her from every institution, in the States, in Switzerland and from Moscow. Her lover had been sent to jail in America and Russia, always escaping to save her. Meanwhile, her brother who she used to love dearly, had taken up with this English rose called Safi. Took her back to Moscow, where she took over and stole her gallery in her absence.

Gina sat spellbound while Yvetta, who obviously needed to tell someone her side, continued to regale Gina with the details of her many incredible escapes with Fritzi over the years from the clinics her family had incarcerated her in, the last being in Moscow, an amazing story in itself.

She touched on her brother Sasha's capture by Russian smugglers, adding she did not believe Fritzi could have had a hand in this as she had been in an American jail at that time (due to the involvement of Gina's boss, DuPont).

She spoke of their wonderful year in Africa together; then, somehow, at some point, Fritzi had become embroiled once more with the smuggling ring. captured in a sting, a combined effort by insurance and art fraud police, and Yvetta confided that she would not be surprised if her own family were involved in her partner's capture.

Yvetta wiped tears from her eyes as she relived her life, in all this time she had never told the full story to anyone, never trusting the shrinks.

'I am here to reclaim what is rightfully mine,' Yvetta said finally, after her story was over, 'the galleries were left to me by my father, Alexi, when he died. But because they had me committed, they gave Safi power of attorney over my inheritance – until those bastards think I am fit to inherit.'

Gina was visibly moved she went over to Yvetta, holding her close. Yvetta had been staring at a fixed point from an arm chair at the window, while Gina had remained in the armchair opposite.

'I am so sorry, Yvetta, I wish I could help?'

Gina's tenderness and understanding penetrated a chink in the wall Yvetta had built over the years. The dam broke and she howled uncontrollably; this time she did not resort to anger or a tantrum that resulted in displays of violence. She lay on the unmade bed, her head buried deep in the pillows, sobbing for what seemed to be hours.

Gina sat by helplessly, stroking her hair until Yvetta's sobs subsided.

A soft voice with no anger or arrogance became audible from the pillows she had her head buried in. 'Gina, can you help me? Please don't tell DuPont about me. I should never have attacked him. I went to ask for his help to reclaim my galleries. Then I saw those photos on his wall taken at my gallery in Moscow. I just lost it.'

They sat for a while, Gina holding Yvetta's hand in hers; she needed to absorb the whole sorry saga. It was so much – perhaps too much – for her to get her head around. How could one person go through all of this, and come out on the other end alive, no less? She felt for Yvetta, she liked her, the sex was great, the question was: did she see a future with this person, did she want to get involved? This wasn't her style, she enjoyed her freedom, enjoyed being single even, and the single-girl life in Manhattan. Yvetta knew nothing about her, she hadn't asked not even one question about her life, zero.

It meant two things: either she wasn't interested, or she was a total narcissist with a really bad temper (according to DuPont's diagnosis). Neither of which Gina found attractive in a person; she had had a few long-term relationships, and all had ended badly. How was she going to play this?

Yvetta was a devastatingly good lover and Gina was indisputably attracted to her; did she want to walk away? The sex, oh, the sex! She would be stupid to walk away, but she would have to navigate this relationship very carefully. Right now, she wanted nothing more than sex, wonderful, sensuous, slow sex.

Gina climbed in next to Yvetta, pulled her close and held her for a while. Then she went beneath the covers until she felt Yvetta's back arching, shudders passing through her body as she let go of all the sadness and disappointment.

Yvetta grabbed her hair, pulled her up until she was sitting on her face. She held onto the headboard as Yvetta found her spot and sent her into a frenzy of orgasms. God, this was much too good to ruin. There and then she decided she would stay whatever happened; Yvetta would become hers, she would teach her how to love again, how to navigate life without anger. There was no one better than her for the job; after all, she had dug herself out of many black holes.

Gina called in sick on the Monday; she had spent Sunday shopping with Yvetta; the girl had an insatiable appetite for shopping and good taste, not caring about cost. They returned to the hotel laden with parcels from designer shops Gina had never ventured into, where she was treated like a celebrity. She could get used to this lifestyle, she thought.

To her delight, over an early dinner on the executive floor, Yvetta wanted to know all about her life. They found a secluded corner and she opened up to Yvetta.

Her life was dull in comparison to Yvetta's but she had a few stories of her own, had gotten herself pregnant at an early age, kicked out by her family she had the baby adopted through a Catholic organisation, something she regretted but hoped one day to track her down. She was from a small hick town in California, with small-minded values. The nuns had given her money to start a new life after the baby was adopted, payment from the family who adopted her baby. Found her way East, went to college where she realised, she liked women. Fell in love with an older professional woman who taught her about life, but they split when her partner went back to her former lover.

She'd been working with DuPont for three years, staying away from long-term relationships concentrating on learning about the art world which she loved, and was thrilled Yvetta was in the same business.

Yvetta listened with wonder she could not believe her luck for once in her life she had made the right choice. Gina was who she needed someone she could help, someone she could look after and, someone who loved her world.

On Tuesday Gina strode into work wearing her designer gear, a Bottega Veneta tote bag and Manalo's on her feet; she felt and looked amazing! Her sharp new bob completed the makeover, now sporting blonde highlights streaked through her otherwise dull brown hair.

'Wow, you look wonderful, Gina,' DuPont said. 'Perhaps a new love interest, why not, you are a very attractive woman.'

She smiled warmly at DuPont: he was so very French, no American man would ever say such a thing and get away with it. Still, he managed to be charming without being a letch. Yvetta and Gina had discussed what to do about Gina working for DuPont; both agreed it could work into their plan nicely.

They decided Gina would continue her job while Yvetta looked for an apartment. Gina would give up her small studio in the Lower East Side and move in with Yvetta. They both wanted to live in Chelsea, a thriving gay community with great bars, cafés, and cutting-edge galleries, a domain Yvetta felt comfortable in.

She transferred money from an off-shore account into a foreign private bank in New York. The bulk of her money and investment portfolio was still with her Russian contacts in London, who had always looked after her financial affairs.

They were discreet above all. She could do business with them, they understood each other; whenever she had problems accessing her funds, they had found a way to assist her. She trusted them explicitly: they knew how to evade rules without breaking the law, which suited her lifestyle. If anyone put a trace on her funds they would send up a flare; no one would mess with the Russians, especially not with a Rubicov, they were valuable customers to any financial institution.

Yvetta employed a realtor who knew the Chelsea area; she told him what she needed and spent the following week searching for apartments.

She chose a relatively new block with every amenity, something she knew Gina would love: it had its own gym, pool, and doorman. After viewing it with Gina, she secured the lease with an option to buy, after which she employed an interior designer, recommended by the agent.

Nothing needed fixing. The place was unfurnished: an entrance hall with guest bathroom, open-plan kitchen and living area. There were two double bedrooms with walk-in closets, and a smaller room perfect for a study or TV room.

Her apartment at the Rubicov building was stunning, it had incredible art on the walls; she wished she could ransack it for this apartment, such a shame and a waste not being able to stay there, but this place in Chelsea had its benefits. The Rubicov apartment was larger, but one day she would move back or do with it as she wished; after all, it belonged to her.

The designer met Yvetta at the apartment. They discussed the brief and Yvetta sent her to the Rubicov building to get an idea of the décor she liked, telling her to ask at reception whether it was possible to view one of their apartments for a client, preferably number 62a, the Rubicov apartment.

'If he asks questions, please tell him Sasha sent you,' Yvetta informed the designer.

The designer returned totally blown away by the art, the furnishings, and the attention to detail and finishes.

'The doorman told me Daniel Westfield was the designer,' the designer told Yvetta excitedly. 'I know his work. Actually, we have worked together on quite a few projects.'

At first Yvetta was taken aback, then decided not to acknowledge she knew both Dan and Dax; no one need know that they were well-known to her.

She left the designer to get on with the brief, returning to her hotel suite to wait for Gina to finish her day at work.

Yvetta had almost forgotten her reasons for coming to the States, her deep anger at her family felt less urgent since meeting Gina, she was enjoying life again, even relishing it. Something surprising had happened in the last few days, she did not understand it fully, but she felt liberated from beliefs she hadn't realised had been consuming her every thought.

Fritzi had been part of her life for so many years, and her anger at the family had been bound up in her love for Fritzi. Yet now with Gina, she felt somehow, finally, released from the past. Her ideas had moved on, her father had passed away, her mother had remarried, Sasha was no longer living in Moscow. It seemed everyone and everything had changed, apart from her, that is. She, was living in the past, and holding onto endless grudges while everyone moved on with their life. It came as a shocking revelation to Yvetta: she had been holding onto issues that no longer mattered to anyone else but her. Perhaps it wasn't other people holding her down, perhaps – just perhaps – she was holding herself down.

Gina walked into the hotel suite in her designer clothes; her day had been more than wonderful, everyone had noticed the change in her. She no longer felt like a loser who would never make it, she had met a wonderful person who had lifted her from a life of servitude and drudgery. With dedication and a little luck, she might have joined the world of a lucky few, who had more than a little choice in how they lived their lives.

Yvetta greeted her with affection and they spent time going over their respective days, both excited to share humdrum details that may otherwise seem boring, with someone else.

'Did DuPont ask you any leading questions about your new wardrobe?'

'Well, he guessed I must have met a new love interest, was quite encouraging really.'

'Did he say anything about me?'

'Well, yes, actually he did, but I do not want to upset you.'

'Oh, Gina, it's a strange thing, really, but I no longer feel the hate I harboured for my family in the same destructive way, not since I met you.'

'You have no idea how happy I am to hear that, because what DuPont said was pretty similar to what you have just voiced.'

'Really?'

'DuPont told me he thought you were your own worst enemy by turning against your family, I did not want to pry or make my interest obvious, though he did give me an opportunity to continue the discussion.'

Yvetta gave her an encouraging smile to continue.

'I agreed with him, wanting to show interest so he would give me an opportunity to ask questions. We may yet be able to solicit his help if that's what you want?'

For the first time she had an ally and a friend she could rely on to help her find a way out of this quagmire she was stuck in: how to approach her family, how to win their trust to get back what was rightfully hers without a fight. She would surely lose, or, worse, end up locked away for ever in some mad house again.

She understood she had put them through hell at times, especially her mother and father. It was too late to make amends with her father, but she could somehow try to with the rest of her immediate family. She needed help – and neutral territory, where she did not feel threatened, where she could make amends with dignity. To do that, she needed an intermediary she could trust. DuPont was still the only person she could turn to. She realised now that she had been so stupid to let her anger and jealousy take over. Why did it always get the better of her, that urge to strike out when vulnerable, when she felt loss or at a loss, when her identity was challenged.

Fritzi had always encouraged her to separate from her family, not to allow them to dominate her life, to fight them at every opportunity. Now that Fritzi was out of her life, Yvetta started to see things more clearly. Gina had had a much tougher life, she was from a poor narrow-minded family, kicked out for being pregnant at a young age having to give up her baby yet, had chosen a different path? How much of Yvetta's past reaction to her family had been a result of Yvetta's own actions, as opposed to Fritzi's machinations? How deeply involved was Fritzi in all of this, and for her own ends? Perhaps blaming everything that happened on her family was to please Fritzi. She had always seen her family through Fritzi's eyes and not her own, believing Fritzi knew better. To Yvetta, it had always been her family plotting against her – but perhaps it was more of a case of Fritzi plotting against her family.

True, Fritzi had saved her from her cousin's ownership of her, his belief that she belonged to him even if he wasn't demanding sex, he demanded controlling her when he felt like it. Pasha had backed off once Fritzi had come onto the scene, but she had never healed from that experience, had never told anyone. She had allowed the pain and sense of violation to grow like a cancer, secretly blaming everyone for allowing it to happen, especially her mother. Yet she had made up with her cousin Pasha they were now frenemies with a shared hatred for family.

As Gina's words sunk in, Yvetta was shaken out of her reverie.

'You know, Yvetta, I was wondering why you turned against your family. They sound so very supportive and loving. Please don't get angry with me, but as you know my family kicked me out when I most needed them, so it's hard to understand why you hate them so very much.'

'Yes, you are right,' Yvetta conceded slowly, 'I was young when my resentment started, and it just continued to build unchecked. Then I met Fritzi. She saw it from her point of view, and supported all my efforts, thwarting any kind of working relationship with my family.'

'I understand, really I do,' Gina said, 'you are angry at your family for locking you away in those awful places. I believe they were trying desperately to help you, don't you think?'

Gina thought she had overstepped some boundaries as Yvetta fell into a deep silence. Afraid of causing any more damage, she sat quietly by waiting. Eventually, Yvetta shuddered and looked up at Gina

'You know being able to speak this freely and safely without recriminations has brought home to me the awful terrible things I have done. I am not sure they will forgive me. Maybe one day I will be able to tell you about them without the fear of losing you?'

'Yvetta, I need you as much as you need me. Believe me when I tell you I have absolutely no family. I am here in New York on my own, trying to make a life to support myself. I will be thirty-two soon. Where has it gotten me so far, not very far?

I have gone from one awful relationship to another, but with you I feel we are sort of equally needy, we are good for one another in a positive way. So let's work towards a good outcome for both of us with this problem, so our relationship can grow without fear of losing each other. The thing is, if you can make amends with your family and they with you, and you win their trust back, who knows, you might have a wonderful future to look forward to.'

'What happens if they arrest me and put me in some awful institution again, what then? How can I take that chance?'

'Have you done something so awful to warrant that? Sorry, but I need to ask?'

'Yes, you do need to ask, and yes, perhaps I have. I hate to my mother, I hate Safi and I hurt them all, including Dupont.'

The full scope of everyone she had hurt came into focus for her now, and was too much for her to bear. But she couldn't afford to ignore it, not any longer. It was time now to acknowledge, to confront (herself, for once), to address and redress, to make amends.

'I seem to go over the edge whenever I am challenged. I don't know why I have such strong feelings. When challenged it makes me feel as if I am drowning. My only defence is striking back. When I feel I have been hit, I want to hit back three times as hard, to do real damage, to knock out, to kill even. Maybe it is myself I want to hurt. Maybe it is self-destructiveness turned inside out. But others bear the brunt, and that's unfair, I know that now. I've known that for a long time, I feel. But coming to terms was difficult … it's still difficult. I feel so insignificant to everyone else.'

Gina took everything said on board, she remained silent for a while. She wasn't sure how to answer, did not want to put a foot wrong, not sure what response she may elicit from Yvetta, still a stranger to her in so many ways, though a person she had already begun to love. But so far, in spite of everything DuPont had told her, things were heading in the right direction, Yvetta was seeing the light. The therapy or the horse ranch had obviously awakened some awareness of her past behaviours.

Gina herself had experienced hatred towards her folks for rejecting her attempts at reconciling. Had tried to find her child without success, tried to form relationships with older women, hated men, yet she had failed at all of them. Although she was considerably younger than Yvetta, this also seemed her last chance, she felt something for Yvetta, something really strong and sweet, it wasn't all one-sided, they needed each other. Perhaps if she could help Yvetta through this, they'd embark on something really good together.

'Yvetta, I don't know the answers to those questions, but the way your family have stuck by you in the past, I bet they would be more than happy to have you back in the fold, as the Yvetta they need to hold close and love, as the daughter, sister and family member they have always hoped for. I don't have those same choices you know, my father was a drunk and my mother resented having me, it ruined her chances of becoming a singer. I grew up in an endless circle of resentment, something I knew I had to escape from to survive'.

'Perhaps you are right,' Yvetta said, facing each other in the same armchairs. 'I hate therapists. Do you think I should see one try and get rid of my anger and to understand why this has happened to me. I worry it will do the opposite and trigger my anger. But maybe this time will be different,' she said hopefully. 'I had the opportunity at those places they stuck me in, but fought against help, did not believe I was to blame, was made angrier by my incarceration, my alienation, my lack of control. Everyone seemed to be controlling my life – everyone but me, that is. Things will be different now. They have to be. But now I think I am ready to talk to someone. I want to start over – to start better.' Saying these words was, in itself, a small relief. She smiled, and Gina was smiling, too.

'Well, there are enough therapists in this town, you shouldn't have a problem.'

They both laughed

'I'm starving,' Yvetta said. 'Do you want to order in, or should we go and get some air?'

'Out, let's go out.'

Sitting in the corner out of sight was DuPont. Gina was with her new paramour, there was no mistaking the relationship between them. He had not known Gina's sexual orientation, although was certainly not surprised she was gay (so many people were in the art world). DuPont found something familiar about Gina's partner: the way she moved, the way she smiled. Small, lithe, inarguably pretty. He had met her before, but where? A gallery opening, no doubt. On closer inspection, he could have sworn it was Yvetta. Shocked, he brushed away the possibility. Unless, of course, she had changed her appearance to avoid recognition.

He thought of asking the waiter to convey an invitation for them to join him at his table; if it was Yvetta, she may make a run for it. No, he would surprise them, see what happens, he felt betrayed by Gina, after all if it was Yvetta, he felt her loyalty was questionable.

Gina's head shot up as her boss materialised at their table, her face drained of colour, and she noticed Yvetta pretended to study the large Thai and Ramen menu, hiding her face.

'Ah, 'ello, what a happy coincidence, please join me at my table, I insist.' DuPont picked up their drinks and walked towards his table, not giving them much choice. Gina was in a terrible situation; she grabbed Yvetta's hand as she got up to leave.

'No,' she whispered, 'don't run, maybe this is your chance to persuade DuPont. He has not recognised you. It gives you the advantage to catch him off-guard, apologise, explain, beg for his help.'

Yvetta stood momentarily, not knowing which way to turn; thoughts raced through her mind, flight the strongest. Gina was right, she needed to show she could be rational – this was the new Yvetta, after all. Her mind hurt, this was so hard, so many of her instincts and emotions still belonged to the old Yvetta, but she wanted to change, she was tired of fighting and running. She needed to try Gina's way. Shaking with fear, she followed behind Gina to DuPont's table.

On the way over to DuPont's table Yvetta was formulating her defence, how was she going to approach him, get him on-side. As they took their seats at the corner table, Yvetta immediately leaned over and took DuPont's hand. He tried to jerk his hand back. Oh my God, she thought, he knows it's me, she held onto his hand.

'DuPont, please accept my apology,' she said, the words tumbling out very rapidly. 'It was a terrible way to behave, an awful thing I did. What I really wanted was your help. After seeing you in the photos with my family in my gallery in Moscow, I stupidly lost it. Not that that is an excuse for my actions, but…'

'Really, my dear,' he said in a manner that made Yvetta feel he had recognised her some time ago, his voice soft and grave but not without his customary gentle cadences, 'what about all the other attacks on your family, and on Safi, for that matter. You nearly killed her for God's sake?'

She tried to push her demons aside, face her accuser without defending her actions. She felt the blood rising, the anger building. She summoned every ounce of strength to remain calm; her first instinct was to attack her attacker, but she did not want the same outcome, she had to be clever to get what she needed. Don't attack, a small voice inside her was screaming.

Gina and DuPont watched Yvetta visibly struggle with her demons, as expressions of anger then acceptance flashed in her eyes.

'Yes, I know, DuPont, I am trying to face my demons. Gina has helped me face them. I have some way to go, I am trying to understand, and I will seek help. I do not want to end up in another institution. I want my life back. I want my galleries back, but mostly I want to make peace with my family. Will you help me, please, I have no one else?'

'Do you know they are looking for you after your attack on me?' DuPont said, moving his chair around to face her closely. His eyes glinted and he too seemed excited, or unnerved. 'They have 24-hour protection for Safi, who is about to give birth any day now. Their lives have become intolerable, being cooped up like prisoners in their own home, because of your threats and attacks on your family in the past, and on them now.'

Gina, rigid with fear, sat bolt upright, listening to the accusations DuPont was throwing at Yvetta. She had already learnt of some, and now she was learning about others that were even more shocking.

Yvetta and DuPont stared at one another in silence; both wondered whether he had gone too far. Would she strike out again? This seemed to be the only way she knew how to defend her actions of the past.

Gina was praying Yvetta would be able to see the bigger picture for once, to put a cap on her feelings of inadequacy, vulnerability, and hurt, wanting to protect that little girl inside. She seemed to feel she had been trampled on by her family and others, justifying her anger at them.

She gingerly took Yvetta's hand to give comfort, encouraging her. But Yvetta's hand remained limp, no reaction was forthcoming.

DuPont had waved away the waiter, who took the hint and stayed back, watching them from a distance and from time to time checking whether he could approach with their order.

Her small frame began to shake, her head dropped onto her chest, large tears welled up in her eyes, then dropped down her cheeks into her lap. They sat by helplessly watching Yvetta cry silently. DuPont offered his napkin, but he kept up a harsh front.

'I hope those tears are for your family, who have suffered for years from your and Fritzi's attacks. Even I have suffered an attack from both of you myself. Why should I want to help you, you tell me that, Yvetta, why?'

A thin voice fought its way through the tears. 'For the Rubicovs, help us reunite, do it for them not for me.'

'Ah, noble Yvetta, very noble of you, make peace only to win your inheritance back, is that it?'

Gina couldn't stand it any longer. God, he was being cruel. 'DuPont, please!'

'No, Gina,' Yvetta said, 'it's okay, I deserve this hatred, I do. It's all true, apart from not wanting to make peace. I want to make peace with my mother mostly. And, yes, I do want my inheritance. It's mine, why shouldn't I want what's mine?'

DuPont had to give it to Yvetta: if this was an act, it was a pretty formidable one. She was taking his accusations on the chin, rather than taking everything unbearably personally and lashing out violently. Something had obviously changed.

'Okay!' DuPont said finally. 'You have convinced me. I will do my best.'

The waiter, sensing an opening in their heated discussions, hurried over with the bowls of Ramen soup and departed quickly.

It was almost midnight, too late to call anyone, apart from Janus, who had told DuPont to call any hour if he had any leads – but he wasn't going to do that. Things had changed and DuPont had decided to help them both. After all, DuPont was a romantic at heart, and he thought Gina deserved a break. Yvetta did, too. Something good could come out of this for everyone involved.

He had had many liaisons, but the one he regretted the most was with Safi. He owed the Rubicov family something, and this was his opportunity to make up for seducing her so wickedly. The family had introduced him to influential new clients, elevating his own business into the stratosphere. He owed them, it was payback time.

Yvetta met with DuPont the following afternoon. He had Gina alter his schedule so as to finish his meetings earlier in the day. This left the late-afternoon to discuss strategy with Yvetta. Yvetta asked for Gina to be there for their meeting, saying she felt it would make both her and DuPont feel more at ease, and hurry the negotiations along.

At the meeting it was suggested Yvetta meet with the lawyers before making contact with her family, and that she should write a letter to her family, with an unreserved apology for her behaviours in the past. She should ask for their forgiveness, personalising the letter with a special paragraph to each member of the family she had upset or harmed in some way.

'How do you see this playing out for you Yvetta?' DuPont said, giving Yvetta a hard stare, trying to determine just how much (if at all) Yvetta had changed.

'I am more than happy to meet with the lawyers to write this letter to my family,' Yvetta said, trying to signify by her resolute tone that she had, indeed, changed, She, understood that DuPont was suspicious, but was eager to appease him – and everyone else as well. She gave him her flirtatious smile, then rearranged her mouth somewhat, realising that technique would no longer work, not even with DuPont. With a serious face she said slowly, 'I understand the ramifications involved. Mostly I am hoping they will be willing to give me another chance after reading the signed letters from the lawyers to each member of my family.'

'In those letters I believe you need to be humble,' DuPont began, 'admit to your past behaviours, apologising unreservedly with the understanding that some you apologise to may not be that willing to accept your apology.'

'Are you referring to Saffron and Sasha?'

'Yes,' he said, almost curtly. 'Are you prepared for rejection?'

Gina shook her head to encourage Yvetta to accept whatever her family decided.

'May I say something here please, Yvetta?' Gina said. Yvetta signalled for her to continue.

'I believe right now you need them to stop their search for you.' Gina was talking to Yvetta but for some reasons she was looking at her boss, looking for encouragement. 'Put their minds at rest that you will not be planning any more attacks on your family for whatever reason. Those days are behind you for ever, aren't they?'

Gina needed confirmation, too, she did not want to embark on a relationship with someone who had violent tendencies. God knows, she had been involved with enough screwed-up people over the years. She wasn't looking for any more drama, just stability and happiness with someone who loved her every bit as strongly as she loved them. She hoped Yvetta, without Fritzi in her life, had put all that behind her. And yet experience also told her that old habits die hard, and that people were fixed to their traits – even, perhaps especially, their worst traits.

Shocked, Yvetta remained silent. Never had anyone put her behaviour to her in quite that way. Certainly not someone she felt deeply for – and she did feel deeply for Gina, she realised suddenly. What the two of them had, from the start, was the real deal rather than some passing fling. She had always thought her behaviour to be justified by others, her reactions caused by their actions, as though she was a little more than a helpless bystander sometimes, someone who had life happen to them rather than wholly take control. For the first time, Yvetta was realising no one else quite saw things the way she did. The revelation itself came as a complete shock. Why had she never been able to see this before? And why this clarity only now, in New York, after so much turmoil in her life? Was she being rewarded – or punished – by this moment? She wasn't sure, but Gina, and this sudden, overwhelming self-awareness certainly felt like a reward.

Shaking her head in agreement, Yvetta said, 'I am beginning to understand this now. The attacks on my family were unjustified, I was wrong, and I behaved like a bad person, what I can't understand is, why it seems so clear to me now? It never has before.'

Both DuPont and Gina were speechless at her admission. This was the first time DuPont, who had known Yvetta for years, had seen her anywhere close to being self-aware. There was even humility in her shaken voice. Gina made an attempt at answering the question, not sure whether it was rhetorical, aware she had not known Yvetta that long, despite their intense intimacy of the last few days. She needed to give Yvetta encouragement, some positive feedback to continue on the path she found herself.

'Perhaps the sessions you had at all those institutions may have helped,' Gina suggested in a soft voice. 'Living in Africa may have been healing, too, in some way.'

But Yvetta did not seem to be listening. 'I did some terrible things before I left Namibia,' Yvetta continued. 'Our staff would not even remain in the house to look after me without Fritzi, you know?' Now, she sounded almost embarrassed. Contrition filled her voice and was clear in her face, her eyes, too. Gina reached out and touched her hand, but it was limp, unresponsive. Yvetta was lost in thought.

'Yvetta,' DuPont continued, you can discuss all these issues with your therapist. Right now, we need to assure your family of their safety, especially Saffron's safety. You know she is expecting her first baby. And the safety of Anna, your mother, who you have treated so shabbily over the years.'

These names – Saffron, Anna – and Yvetta's anger towards, and actions against, them filled her head now. Were any of her actions justified? Had she been wrong all along? Had Safi really attempted to remove her from her job, from her life in the art world, or is that merely how it had appeared to Yvetta? Had Yvetta lost her position because of Safi, or because of her own misdeeds? And if it was the latter, had she been wrong to blame Safi all this time?

'This is what you told me you wanted more than anything, isn't that right?' DuPont concluded.

Yvetta sat quietly, staring into the distance, not sure where the two of them were going with all of this. Feeling ill-equipped to deal with her professionally, they waited anxiously to see whether she would revert back to her out-of-control raging tantrums.

They needn't have worried: Yvetta had only one objective, and that was to have her family stop shutting her away in clinic after clinic. She wanted her freedom, to live as she wished and to be given her inheritance. The galleries were hers, not Saffron's, but hers. That was undeniable, as far as she was concerned. But that did not mean that Saffron deserved her hatred. After all, the family's decision about the gallery aside, what had Safi ever done to her? She had disliked Safi on sight because she appeared so sweet. It had to be a ruse, right? But maybe she really was that sweet. Maybe she was sweet enough to forgive Yvetta, for instance. Maybe there was still time to turn everything around, to make amends, to start anew.

'I need to get this settled before the end of this week. I am being pursued by my brother Mika and his men. They are following me. They think I don't know, but I know. I want my life back. This has to stop!'

'Right,' DuPont said forcefully, 'let me call the lawyers and set up an appointment. We will go from there.'

'How does that suit you, Yvetta?' Gina said, her voice softer than her boss, but her gaze no less firm.

'Today, can I see them today?' Yvetta asked.

'I will suggest it,' DuPont said.

DuPont suggested Gina take Yvetta for a coffee break. He needed time to organise the meeting and to make some calls before he accompanied her to the law offices – that was if he could persuade them to see Yvetta at such short notice.

He had called Safi on a daily basis since she had become housebound. He knew she would find it odd he had not yet called today. Their conversations never lasted long, but he knew she enjoyed receiving the calls; it broke up her day and helped her feel connected.

Sasha answered the call, slightly breathless. 'We are on our way to the hospital. Safi is in labour. We will call you later, hopefully with some happy news.'

Feeling elated but also anxious, DuPont next called the law firm in NY who worked for the Rubicov family and asked to speak to John Borland.

Borland answered and they exchanged pleasantries, DuPont remembering that time was money, and that Borland charged a lot. DuPont got straight to the point. John Borland was one of those at Mika's home when the terrible attack by Yvetta on Safi had occurred. For this very reason, DuPont was not at all sure how John would view his suggestion.

DuPont heard an intake of breath on the other end and a few moments of silence ensued, 'Right, obviously I wouldn't normally deal with this,' Borland said finally, 'but under the circumstances, be at our offices by five pm today. I will see to this myself.'

DuPont agreed to the time, then decided to ask whether Yvetta would have the same client privileges as the rest of the family: meaning privacy and discretion, before her presence at the meeting was disclosed.

He further explained that Saffron Rubicov had just gone into labour, and he did not want to alarm the family.

Until Yvetta's letters were received and further legalities dealt with, DuPont requested they only then divulge where she was living in Manhattan. John Borland thought it was more than Yvetta deserved, having seen her actions close up, much closer than he would ever have liked. He would not easily forget that afternoon when Yvetta had attacked Safi at Mika's Florida home. Keeping up to date with the family's concern, he was privy to the hunt for Ms Yvetta Rubicov, and was going to make bloody sure, when she signed the document, that she knew what it meant when it said that it was legally binding in every sense of the word. Should Yvetta lift as much as a finger against anyone in her family, they would be able to throw away the key before she could blink; furthermore, her precious galleries would then be lost to her for ever.

Yvetta had a tough four hours with John Borland and his team. She had not been scrutinised so often, and by so many people, since her stint in the clinic in Switzerland. It was as if the Spanish Inquisition had donned suits and flown down to Manhattan. They grilled her intentions. Dictated most of the terms in the letters she wrote to the members of her family, which she signed with little hope of reconciliation, apart from perhaps being left alone, free to live her life and hopefully, in time, be allowed her inheritance in full, as her father intended.

DuPont and Gina were not privy to the meeting with the lawyers. DuPont left for another appointment, while Gina spent her time hanging about for hours, waiting anxiously for Yvetta, she was dying for a smoke, pleased she had none else she would have re started a habit she had kicked with great difficulty a year ago. She had never set foot in such plush offices, DuPont's offices looked shabby in comparison. Ambling about, trying not to think of cigarettes, defeating the urge to gnaw on well-manicured nails, she found a lounge with a TV screen, even a kitchen where she helped herself to some beverages to tide her over. After all, a diet soda was still preferable to a smoke.

Almost two hours later, relieved to have Gina waiting for her, she felt depleted of all energy. Being confronted by herself for so long, all she wanted now was a warm bed and a soft embrace. They hailed a cab directly to the Marquee on Times Square. In their suite they found umpteen messages from the agent and the designer who needed Yvetta's signature before she could complete any orders to be delivered for the apartment. The agent needed her final signature on the lease, together with assurances and signed copies from people prepared to vouch for her character.

Too tired to even talk, let alone type a message, she ignored all calls on her cell phone, and asked Gina to order food from room service while she ran a bath.

The waiter rolled in the food trolley, laid the table in their suite, and left with a hefty service tip. Ravenous, they both ate in silence. Gina, not wanting to pry and tired herself, tried to make light conversation, which soon petered off into another extended silence. Yvetta was a different person now, more like a ragdoll than a human being. Finally, Yvetta pushed her chair away from the table in the small open-plan lounge, walked through the double doors into their bedroom, and climbed onto the bed, knees pulled up to her chest, the bath robe enveloping her small body. She lay with her head on the piled-up pillows, dwarfed by the huge king-size bed.

Gina, not sure what was still needed, watched as this vulnerable, petite, beautiful woman go through emotions she couldn't possibly understand. She realised that she was in the very early stages of recognising and accommodating Yvetta's moods and emotions. She realised, too, that there was much work, and nothing would be accomplished quickly. Still, she was willing to do the work, to take these risks. She felt sure – she *knew* – that Yvetta was worthwhile. Showered and ready for bed, she walked in to find Yvetta curled in a foetal position in the middle of the bed, Gina stood momentarily, then climbed onto the bed, helping Yvetta under the covers, holding her tightly until they both fell asleep.

Safi lay in the hospital bed, tired but glowing with pride, holding their son to her breast. Sasha had slept over; the experience had been life-altering, he never imagined he would feel so elated, watching his son being delivered, watching his wife as she bravely pushed until a slimy pink little head appeared. It had been a long night, but the most rewarding of his life.

The delivery suite already covered in flowers, the new parents were expecting an onslaught of visitors: Anna, Bernard, together with her parents would be visiting today. The door opened with a nurse carrying yet another huge basket of flowers with a teddy and blue balloons attached.

Sasha opened the card, stopping mid-sentence as he read it out to Safi.

'Who is it from, you look shocked?' she said.

'I am. It's hard to believe this, but it's a message wishing us all the happiness in the world, with our new little bundle of joy and signed, wait for this: "Hugs and Kisses, Yvetta. Letter of apology to follow from our lawyers."'

Safi stared at Sasha, not able to take in the message. 'Read that to me again.'

He did, and Safi said, 'My God, I am not sure how I am supposed to feel about that gift or card. You better check it over in case she has put some device in the teddy bear or balloons.'

'I wonder what she was doing at our lawyers,' Sasha said. 'What apology, exactly? I am going to call Mika and Janus, perhaps they know something we don't?'

The visit from their respective parents should have been about their grandchild; instead, the only topic of conversation was the hand-delivered letters the aggrieved members of their family had all received from Yvetta that morning.

Anna was overcome with emotion. She had a beautiful new grandchild, and, it seemed, a daughter who wanted her back in her life.

Everyone was cautious: they had been through so many different sagas with Yvetta over the years, periods of stability followed by long, seemingly never-ending periods of mayhem. All were anxious about welcoming her with open arms, but Anna wanted them to move forward, without recriminations.

She sat beside Safi, holding her beautiful new grandson, tears of joy running down her face.

'I will understand, Safi, if you do not want Yvetta in your life,' Anna said slowly. 'She does not deserve to be, but you must understand, she is my only daughter.'

'I do, Anna, I do,' Safi replied, looking at her own son. 'Especially now, it means so much more.'

Yvetta's letter to Safi was short and to-the-point. The lawyers wanted her to make it clear to Safi that she understood the ramifications of her actions.

She did not ask for forgiveness. Only an apology for the unnecessary suffering she had caused Safi.

With the physical attack on Safi, at her brother Mika's home, Yvetta stressed that she now understood Safi was not her enemy, but rather the guardian of her galleries. She wished her well and only happiness for the future. She wanted only to make amends, especially with immediate family.

Yvetta and the lawyer had co-signed the letter.

In addition, there was a legal document signed by Yvetta. To say that if she was ever to veer from her pledge of peace and goodwill she stood to lose her freedom and her inheritance. In this event, the NYC gallery would be controlled by Safi only, who had sole power of attorney to sign all documents, and who would hand over ownership to Yvetta when she saw fit.

Safi was livid; she knew she had agreed to the arrangement at the reading of Alexi's will. She did not envisage signing over the galleries to Yvetta, just yet, or, in fact, ever.

On the other hand, she felt elated to be safe again, elated with her life and her baby, elated to have Sasha back, elated to have a loving family and, friends in her life. But for how long could she feel safe? To what extent could she trust anything Yvetta said, even if she said it in a legal document, overlaid with (often incomprehensible) legalese?

She wasn't elated to have Yvetta in her life, she was mad, angry and hurt. This was a woman who had tried to kill her, and done a damn good job of it, by all accounts. And now she was asking for forgiveness and everyone was jumping to comply, to forgive her everything, to start afresh. Was this not another ploy by Yvetta? After all, she had long ago proven that she was shrewder and more resilient than anyone else. What next did she have in mind?

Her emotions were all over the place. She knew it had to be the hormones coursing through her body, but she wanted to cry from relief and exhaustion.

Being kept prisoner and cooped up for the last month, the uncertainty Yvetta brought to their lives made her feel only hatred towards the woman; more than that she saw the NY gallery as hers, not Yvetta's! She had put blood, sweat, and tears into it – and now what? Nothing. She must just walk away, just like that, because of some lawyer's letter?

She had worked her fingers to the bone with Alexi's blessing and help – Alexi, who her son was named after, and who had loved Safi like a daughter; why should Yvetta get her Manhattan gallery?

Yvetta already had the Moscow gallery which Ilona was managing efficiently without Yvetta, she did not want to make a fuss in front of Anna or her parents. She bloody well would when she was less emotional; she wasn't going to take this lying down, or on the chin. She was a fighter, like Yvetta, only she didn't fight dirty.

Being a Rubicov did not give Yvetta the right to come swanning back into their lives when it suited her, demanding to have the NYC gallery when she had nothing to do with building it up from scratch into what it was today, a major player in the art world and one of the city's hottest art spots.

She was now a Rubicov herself, with an heir to continue their vast business empire. She would use her stature from a position of strength not weakness. The galleries were a tiny part of their empire, but to Yvetta it was everything – and to Safi as well. She would bloody well fight tooth-and-nail to keep her Manhattan gallery.

As far as Safi was concerned, this was not going to happen the way Yvetta played it out in her mind. It was going to be a fight. Unless they could come up with an agreement or solution that suited them both.

She was happy for Anna and the larger Rubicov family; she didn't begrudge Yvetta happiness or getting her life back together. Though somehow, she wasn't buying this "new Yvetta: routine; Safi felt sure that it was just a matter of time before she reverted to the crazy person she was. Since she arrived in Moscow with Sasha, all those years ago, young and green about life in general, she had learnt to avoid Yvetta altogether.

It was a cliché to speak of avoiding someone like the plague, but that was exactly what Yvetta had been on Safi's life, a plague. And now, as far as Safi was concerned, Yvetta was trying to infect her all over again, albeit from a different angle. Killing with kindness. But Safi wasn't so naïve. Yvetta had shown her true colours right off by creating mayhem with her tantrums and lack of emotional control.

The nurse had warmed her not to become overly excited or to become unnecessarily upset: lactating milk had a strange way of drying up when a mother became unduly strung out. She tried to push the whole business out of her mind. She wanted to concentrate on her baby, Alexander Rupert Bingham Rubicov, the future of the galleries, and Yvetta would have to wait. Yvetta wasn't the whole show anymore, and the sooner she knew that the better.

They named their beautiful little boy Alexi, after his grandfather and uncle Rupert, Dan's dad, who they all missed. Bingham was a name Safi wanted out of the blue; she loved the name, it reminded her of Brighton, and sounded so terribly British.

The two D's had been round, cooing over the baby. They couldn't wait for the cousins to have a playdate, a whole new world Safi was happy to get used to.

Sasha would be round in an hour to take his new family home. The nursery had taken all of Safi's energy in the last few weeks; it was a haven of baby heaven. Dax had excelled in reverting his artistic talents, painting a mural of oversized baby toy animals, plants, and stars on a wall. White baby furniture had been installed, with soft lighting, a comfortable feeding rocker, and, a daybed to accommodate both herself and Sasha when little Alexi woke at ungodly hours. Endless gift baskets and gifts from the baby gift-list had started to arrive, all the fun stuff she would have to sort when home, including thank-you cards to write. She never managed to have a baby shower, it was not safe.

Dax had insisted on sorting out all the packaging that Sasha found overwhelming to cope with. Safi tried to concentrate her mind on the good stuff, but the bad stuff kept on creeping in. The more Safi tried to shift the gallery from her thoughts, the more it seemed to pop up when she least expected: when feeding Alexi, for instance, and he would feel her tenseness and lose his grip on her nipple. At that moment, she found her whole world of contentment crumbling into a snotty mess of tears.

Sasha walked in to find the nursing sister leaning over Safi, trying to calm the unhappy mother and baby down. He waited patiently until Alexi managed to feed contentedly, with his mother exhausted with emotion.

The nursing sister left the new parents together, closed the door behind her. Once alone, Sasha sat quietly by until Alexi was back in his cradle sleeping peacefully.

Safi tried unsuccessfully to make light of her emotional state, but his mother had already warned him: Safi had been heading towards a relapse, not being able to come to terms with Yvetta's claim on the gallery.

Not used to seeing Safi so unhappy, especially now, when he imagined mothers would be glowing with happiness, he decided the sooner they met with the lawyers to knock out an agreement Safi could live with the better.

Safi settled into a pattern with the help of a baby nurse, who she found invaluable, calming her down when the legal ramifications got too much for her to handle. She thankfully did not have to meet with Yvetta. A face-to-face meeting with her nemesis would have dried up her milk in an instant, anyway that was Safi's mantra when Sasha went to meet with his sister together with his mother and Mika.

She wasn't in the habit of trying to understand her inner ramblings of why things happened the way they did, yet over the years she had tried to sort out what felt right for her. This included why she needed to follow a certain path, especially when warned by some to walk in another direction – and many had warned her of just this, and still were advising her to grasp happiness with both hands, to walk away from the galleries, to hand them over to Yvetta. After all, Safi had done the job she was hired for by Alexi Senior all those years ago.

She did not blame her mother or father when they pointed out that she had more than most and did not need the galleries in her life, especially now with a new baby. After all, her mother said, she could choose to do anything with her life, she certainly had the resources and resourcefulness. She had made a great success of the galleries (and not just in Manhattan, but in a country as utterly foreign and alienating as Russia), had more than proved her capability, her creativity, her assuredness. Perhaps she could begin a new project now – anything else, but something less freighted with family politics. Did she need that stress, now? Being a wife and now a mother might seem fulfilling enough, a whole new set of challenges for which no young women was truly prepared.

Her parents informed her that Alexi would be a full-time job for a while, at least until he was a little older. Not a fashionable suggestion in today's world, they knew, but, with regards to Yvetta, who had given even Safi's parents so much second-hand trauma, begged Safi to let sleeping dogs lie. Why take on such a stressful legal situation when she could let it go, enjoy life, spend more time with her group of friends and making the most of Manhattan, concentrate on the stable lifestyle she so craved in the lonely years when Sasha disappeared.

It made sense, of course it did, but it did not stop the frustration she felt having everyone tell her how to live, how to feel, what to do? She was being childish, perhaps, but wasn't that the whole reason for trying to make it on her own, to grow herself up and become her own woman, not to have anyone, especially her folks, advise her on how to live or conduct her life?

Yvetta had thrown her right back to that place she'd tried so hard to escape from, the child inside fighting to be free; yet she didn't know what she was trying to be free from? She also didn't know why she felt the way she did, and what was it she was running away from or, towards. At times the path she wanted appeared so clearly; then it suddenly vanished and, she was left floundering all over again, not knowing why she wanted certain things, why it rose up and made her feel she had to fight tooth-and-nail to achieve this or that in the past, before it felt as if the itch had been scratched, only to return again.

She was expecting DuPont to arrive; he had been out of town when the baby was born, having left Yvetta in the hands of the lawyers, he was no longer needed. Yvetta was single minded about achieving her goal and, Safi was surely safe from her madness, he decided to take himself out of the scrum.

'Beautiful baby,' DuPont said, 'he looks like his mother.'

Alexi was whipped away by the nurse to have his sleep, having already been fed and burped. Safi, on the other hand, was tetchy and in need of some alone time.

'You are looking radiant, motherhood suits you.'

Safi remained quiet, looked at him closely. Was DuPont being DuPont, or had he picked up on her mood of discontent?

'Well, spit it out,' she said. 'I can see you have picked up on my inner rumblings.'

'Not at all, Safi it's your natural state of being once you have achieved everything you have set out to do.'

'What do you mean exactly?'

'Well, let's see, where should we begin? No, it's much too long a story, my dear Safi, you are like an artist stuck in the midst of creating a masterpiece: it's going so well, then all of a sudden, he freezes, loses the state he felt free to create in, and is once more in the zone of frustration, battling through until he breaks into the space where he feels free again, where everything flows.'

She waited for a long time, before answering, sipping the ice tea they were both drinking.

'What the hell are you on about?'

'You are frustrated, no?'

'Why should I be frustrated? I have no need to be.' A long pause. 'Yes, you are right, I am more than frustrated, I feel ignored.'

'Ah, now we are starting to step out of the frozen zone, continue before you slip back in, it happens.'

'Yvetta, the galleries, it's driving me insane not being the master of my own destiny, yet again. I am at the mercy of losing what I have worked so hard to build up and, with your help, succeeded at. I admit that, but all the same I have enabled artists to become successful, Dax and Janus, to name a few. The gallery is widely respected, why should I throw that success into the wind because the galleries are run by a family decree, kept in the family and ultimately will go back to Yvetta, who is a Rubicov. But so am I.'

'Yes you are.'

'Right, well, I do not feel like a Rubicov. I should but I don't not really, I feel as if I am still the outsider, looking in.'

'Why?'

Safi remembered why she loved DuPont. He understood her, or at least made her feel understood. He was easy to talk to, empathic, but also, when he needed to be, firm, even severe. Most importantly, she had no doubt that he had her best interests at heart. And he had lived a life, there were few things he wasn't experienced in.

Totally frustrated but comfortable in DuPont's company, Safi voiced for the first time why she felt so low, unhappy and frustrated with everyone around her, including herself. No one understood her the way DuPont did. She wasn't sure why, perhaps he was removed enough not to be emotionally stunted by the predicament she was in.

'Well, perhaps it was wrong to confide my feelings to my folks, as well-meaning as they are, their advice threw me straight back into my childhood anxieties. They always make me feel ungrateful for what I already have. They don't mean to, but they do. I guess one always reverts to a childlike state when dealing with one's parents. Sasha and his family, understandably, are so overcome with joy to have Yvetta back in the fold and more or less functioning. They have completely dismissed my feelings about the whole issue of handing over the galleries. More than that, Sasha thinks I am being selfish and paranoid. So, you understand why I hate Yvetta more than ever, even when she isn't a threat to me physically she is still a threat. Whenever she turns up things go haywire, everyone becomes her slave, she holds us all captive to her will, one way or another.'

'Safi, I know you are upset,' DuPont said gently, 'and perhaps this is not the right time to examine the situation pragmatically. Why not let it run its course, see what the lawyers come up with. Give them some credit, after all they know all the legalities of the will and present situation.'

'Yes, of course, you are absolutely right, I know you are, but it hasn't stopped me from wanting to scream, fight to be noticed, and recognised. I feel invisible, no one gets how I feel, perhaps not even you.'

'The galleries are yours, no?'

'Yes, sorry but fuck, YES!'

DuPont sat back, then stood, paced a bit, walked to the windows, watched the panoramic cityscape beautifully spread out, a stunning view from so high, moving in complete silence to its own rhythm.

'No, it was never yours, not legally,' he said in a low voice.

Safi looked deflated, tears welled up, dropping down into her lap. 'God, I am a fool.'

'Why? You are not a fool at all. To me you are a complex, wonderfully beautiful woman, sweet, naughty, but above all a good person, a loyal person, ready to jump in where no one else would, take chances, leap in with both feet, and, when it gets rough, you dig your heels in and see it through. Does that sound like someone who is foolish?'

'Yes, for deluding myself that the galleries would one day be mine.'

'Ah well, don't be too hard on yourself, Safi, dear, because you worked hard. No one can point a finger at you. In all but name they are yours. You signed on the dotted line, remember, agreeing to the contract?'

'Stupid me.'

'Again, try to be patient, let's see what comes out of these meetings, then we can discuss this issue again. Until then, why don't you concentrate on that beautiful baby I can hear crying for attention.'

Yvetta had met with her family, and with the lawyers. Gina had held her hand all the way through, keeping the lid on her partner's emotions, soothing over Yvetta's paranoid feelings of losing control over her life, her family loomed large making her feel diminished, non-existent, her needs were never a priority in the scheme of things when it came to the Rubicov business empire, it was always the whole rather than the individual that counted.

She had, together with Gina's encouragement, visited a therapist, who, surprisingly, she liked. She was American, which made a change from the Russian and Swiss and German therapists. She was an attractive older woman, non-threatening and easy to talk to, in a cosy relaxed atmosphere. She knew nothing of Yvetta's background, her family's connections or their enormous wealth.

Mrs Leibovitz listened, it did not matter what she chose to talk about, present or past concerns, together they would endeavour to analyse her concerns and emotions, allowing Yvetta to form her own answers to muddled emotive thinking. Almost in spite of herself, in certain situations, she found her sessions liberating and enjoyable enabling her to feel confident in her future. She was starting to view certain moments in her life differently.

Gina helped by being in her life, listening to whatever she chose to share, never disapproving in her responses. Yvetta felt as if she was climbing out of the dark into the light, her life was taking a turn she never envisaged.

The relationship with Anna had never been easy, but her mom had grown older, become less critical, softer somehow. Yvetta finally felt she might be able to forge a closer bond, given the chance. She needed her mother in her life, she discovered to her surprise during one of her sessions with the therapist.

Negotiations with the lawyers for the return of the galleries wasn't going all Yvetta's way. Something that Yvetta, in her years of anger, had failed to take into account: Safi was now a Rubicov, no longer an outsider; a big deal in the scheme of things, at least where her family were concerned. Certainly, to Yvetta's family circle, Safi had always been special, mystifyingly so. But Safi's opinions now mattered even more than before, and, her wishes were complicating a clear-cut hand over to Yvetta, a clause her father had insisted on before he died.

Safi refused to meet with Yvetta in order to thrash out a deal that suited them both at the lawyers; this meant that everything was taking twice as long.

Yvetta understood she had to keep calm above all else she could not show any sign of anger or emotional weakness; she had to prove that the old Yvetta was a thing of the past. If she slipped up now, she would almost certainly lose everything. She knew this was her last chance, and was therefore animated with an unusual sense of electricity and anxiety. Gina helped her see this fact more clearly than anyone. Indeed, Gina was bringing her to a new stage of self-awareness, and of feeling self-contained, too. Besides, it was not just her family that Yvetta had to contend with, but the law, too: if she lapsed into her accustomed state of hitting out at those who upset her, she would never be able to break the caveat in the will. The very caveat that Safi held over her. She needed her signature to release all hold over the galleries, without that she wouldn't be able to move forward with the profession she loved.

Anna had suggested she move back into her apartment in the Rubicov building, which had been kept under lock and key for years. Yvetta hesitated at the suggestion. After all, she had forged ahead with the new apartment in Chelsea, they were comfortably settled. The new place did not have the art or the rich warmth her other apartment had, but it was theirs, something they shared and had furnished together, and it was starting to feel like home.

Gina and Yvetta moved into the new apartment the moment it was habitable, they shopped for the things they liked, chose rugs, pillows, throws, and fun objects in the markets and stores. The experience of setting up home together brought them untold pleasure., Gina insisted on contributing to the costs. This was a welcome change from Fritzi, who showed little conscience when it came to spending Yvetta's trust fund, calling it 'The Rubicov Leichtes Geld or Taschengeld,' which translated as 'easy money' or 'pocket money' to the Rubicovs.

Gina had never not paid her way or worked for what she wanted. In fact, paying her way gave her a sense of worth. Never having had it easy, she did not think it wise to take the easy life for granted now.

Together they visited Yvetta's old apartment in the Rubicov Towers. They ate in the restaurant, chatting to the staff who welcomed her back. Yvetta told Gina to choose anything she liked from the apartment for their new place. But in the end they left emptyhanded, locking the door behind them as if starting afresh, something they both felt was needed.

For Yvetta having freedom to go places together without hiding once more became an aphrodisiac. Her medication was helping, she was coping pretty well with difficult situations, and with people crowding in on her (something that was inevitable in New York City); feelings of losing control were easier to deal with. Life in general started to feel right. Once they reached a compromise with Safi, she was sure things would work out with the galleries, too.

An insanely good idea had been suggested by DuPont, which Yvetta put forward in a matter-of-fact way, showing an agreeable side without rancour. The will stated clearly the galleries had to revert to a Rubicov, and at the time the will was drawn up, that person was Yvetta. What the family would be able to do to contest that was an unknown at the moment. The problem was that Safi was now a Rubicov, too.

Yvetta hoped the will Alexi drew up while he was alive could not be contested when ownership came into play. After all, she was the daughter not the daughter-in-law. Gina had introduced DuPont's suggestion one evening while placating Yvetta, helping her understand it mattered now more than ever how she behaved. Yvetta had to put forward her best self, to gain what she wanted; the caveat could only be overturned if a consensus was reached about her mental state.

Namibia had been a pipe dream, her life with Fritzi had always been insecure for a myriad of reasons, nothing was ever stable when it involved Fritzi's work. Yvetta now realised she would always have had to fit in with Fritzi's varied and many commitments, the syndicate took priority over everything else in their lives.

Yvetta tentatively started to discuss her past with Mrs Leibovitz. Fritzi still loomed large in her thoughts. After all, she had depended on Fritzi for so much of her adult life, especially when she was forcibly stuck in the clinics against her will. Fritzi was always the one to set her free. Fritzi was a larger-than-life character with a force of nature so powerful and charismatic it wasn't easy to expunge her from one's life. But Yvetta had to admit that she was slowly beginning to understand what part Fritzi had played in her past, not always beneficial or healthy.

Mrs Leibovitz, she could tell, found her anecdotes of the crazy things Fritzi got away with fascinating. Fritzi was more than just fascinating, she was a chameleon who changed for every role she took on with the intensity and gravitas of an Oscar performance, pulling the wool over the eyes of her ardent critics, turning them into victims long before they became aware they had been thoroughly duped.

With no small amount of sadness, Yvetta now wondered how her lover of old would cope with the unforgiving jail system in Russia. It was known to be particularly harsh for those who had managed to cheat the system, and Fritzi had managed spectacularly in the past, escaping right under the authorities' noses from a secure jail. She was someone who never took no for an answer, believing utterly in her own ability. If there was anything Fritzi guarded more than her life it was her finances.

There wasn't any way to find out how her old lover was. She did not know the type of people who could find out; they had always lurked in the shadows during her relationship with Fritzi, and Yvetta wanted it to remain so. Still, Yvetta's loyalty to Fritzi was on the wane. Gina had come at the right time to fill that void. With Gina she shared life; with Fritzi she merely followed, never questioning the other woman's lead. As a result, Yvetta was experiencing an equal partnership for the very first time. Together the two women made and discussed all decisions. Yvetta's finances did not particularly loom large in their lives, and Gina had no desire to exploit her family. Gina had simple tastes, preferring the ethnic restaurants, art galleries, and museums. They attended the odd, off-Broadway play, and loved art house movies. They were able to share their wardrobe, too: Gina, to Yvetta's delight, enjoyed girlie clothes as much as she did. Fritzi had her own androgynous, inimitable, hip sexuality. No one could carry off Fritzi's style she stood out as only she could in her high art editorial choices, never failing to turn heads. She was one of a kind in everything she did, for better and – too often – worse. But maybe it was time to have a more normal girlfriend, to give stability a shot.

The thought of Fritzi rotting in some jail was hard to imagine; secretly she hoped Fritzi's reputation would beat the odds of an extended stay. She still had some feelings for Fritzi, that much was for sure. But Fritzi had played such an overlarge role in her life, this was only natural – and even these feelings seemed to be slowly subsiding. Yvetta was, on her own terms and in her own time, moving on.

Between visits with the legal team Yvetta indulged Anna with her presence only in the company of Maurice, Gina, or Sasha. Anna never pushed for a meeting, always leaving it to Sasha or Gina, who were both encouraging Yvetta to make peace with her mother.

No one understood Yvetta's reluctance to forgive her mother, everyone was a better parent with the benefit of hindsight, and Anna was no exception to the rule.

Anna was keen to visit Yvetta's therapist, finding it hard to understand why Maurice had advised against it, it was Yvetta's personal space, until Yvetta suggested they see her therapist together.

Anna was happy to acknowledge her shortcomings as a parent. Yes, being a full-time businesswoman gave her little time for Yvetta or Sasha. Mika was the only sibling to grow up in Moscow being older and the first, his parents were more present in his life. She could never understand why Sasha was so well adjusted yet Yvetta not. Both had the same opportunities, both went to the best schools and universities, yet Yvetta chose to spurn her advantages by sabotaging her own family at every given opportunity, especially after she took up with Fritzi. Of course she knew that all children, even children who shared the same parents and background, were inherently different. But nothing had ever prepared her for Yvetta's antics and moods. Anna hoped her daughter would eventually work through her issues before she was too old, that they could reunite finally and for good. She was yearning to put her arms around her daughter, to tell her she loved her, but Yvetta had only started to acknowledge her in very small ways (calling her mom was, to Anna, a huge step in that direction). But Anna had suddenly become pressingly aware of time – that she did not have too much left.

Yvetta had skirted round issues about her mother when seeing Mrs Leibovitz. She knew the family expected her to make things better with Anna, yet the place where she kept those emotions frightened her. She was reluctant to delve too deeply, she wasn't yet ready to face her past, her actions and reactions, her guilt, her anger, her fear.

The family had opened their homes to Yvetta and Gina. Welcoming Yvetta back into the fold meant a great deal, yet Yvetta (as advised by Mrs Leibovitz) needed to keep her distance when the feeling of losing control overwhelmed her. Yvetta felt that they just expected too much of her, and she wasn't able to give that much. She did not trust her own emotions. She realised that she was still struggling with feelings of inadequacy when it came to her family, what did they expect from her anyway? How did they perceive of her, really? And how did she perceive of them?

Gina was baffled by Yvetta's reluctance to embrace her family, who she found on the occasions they visited or met warm and accepting of the two women's relationship. To her mind one could not ask for more, yet Yvetta tried to avoid their welcoming attitude, declining most invitations and continuing to badmouth family members to Gina. But, Gina thought, Yvetta's family was a breeze compared to Gina's. A pity she could not make Yvetta see this. But she also understood that most people had deep and specific gripes about their family, gripes that were not always easy to heal.

Unknown to Yvetta, Gina had met Anna for tea. Gina found Anna kinder and softer in nature than she imagined. Anna extended friendship and warmth to Gina, never criticising her daughter, careful only to convey acceptance and love for Yvetta.

Gina had run into Anna on the street, both recognised one another. Talking was unavoidable and when Anna extended an invitation for a cup of coffee, Gina felt she could not refuse. It was an impromptu meeting but an important one that neither wanted to waste.

Sasha and Anna tried to soften Safi's immovable stance on signing the caveat in the will drawn up by the lawyers after Alexi's death. She stood her ground, wanting every legal angle covered. Nor was she prepared to budge where the NY gallery was concerned. After all, she had worked her butt off building up the reputation of that gallery when she did not know what life had in stall for her with Sasha's disappearance. At the time she was not legally a Rubicov, but she was now, and felt it should count for something, if not everything.

Besides Yvetta had tried to kill her – with luck on her side, she might have succeeded. Safi had Janus to thank for saving her from death at the hands of Yvetta. Safi had little time or sympathy for Yvetta on all levels, her faux-wholesome, entitled attitude, not to mention her selfish, spoilt indulgent grab for what she had not worked for.

To their credit, the lawyers made it easier by not insisting on Safi's presence at any of the meetings when Yvetta was present.

They covered each meeting she missed in minute detail from a legal perspective; so far, the caveat Safi had agreed had not been contested by Yvetta.

Yvetta was, they explained, being more than agreeable to find a solution they could both accept, until Safi was ready to sign.

Compromises included opening a new gallery in Brooklyn, that would be Yvetta's, DuPont suggested.

DuPont's contribution to the impasse, gave Safi time to come to terms with the suggestion, which could be worked out to suit both parties. And so the negotiations moved forward at a snail's pace.

Little Alexi took up most of her day. Safi found motherhood wonderfully satisfying. Since Alex's birth she had rekindled her closeness to the two D's, and to Lauren and Bianca. Her childhood friends had visited over the years, and, they had kept in touch, albeit irregularly; they still kept up with milestones and children, just enough not to lose touch entirely.

Her brother Jake, who had moved to Melbourne, had visited with his partner fleetingly, but mostly Safi kept up with his life though her folks. It was a strange phenomenon but since Alexi's birth those close to her became so much more important. Suddenly she wanted to know more about her friends and family, why this was she had no idea. All she knew was that she needed to forge closer relationships. Having closer relationships made her feel more connected. More than anything, she wanted to share her joy and the birth of Alexi with others.

Yvetta's claim on the gallery she had worked so hard to establish put a dampener on her happiness. Sasha knew his sister needed to feel worthwhile above all else, perhaps more than anyone else in the family. For Yvetta, achieving success in the art world to Yvetta meant she could hold her head up with the rest of the family, being successful in her own right.

In Moscow the gallery struggled to make ends meet; Yvetta supported Russian artists around the globe. Alexi had always indulged her, believing her intentions noble. Then Fritzi came into the equation and a switch flipped, Yvetta had changed from a manageable hothead to a crazy unmanageable dangerous person. From there, her life slowly disintegrated spectacularly, affecting all of the Rubicovs and others in their circle.

Safi was aware not only of Yvetta's history, but also of her place in the Rubicov family hierarchy. Yvetta was a blood relation, whereas she had only married into the family. Safi's position in the family did not stand up in the scheme of things – or did it? Mika had never married, neither had Yvetta; Safi was setting a new precedent which they were obviously grappling with.

Sasha got back in the scrum of running the Rubicov conglomerates, flying with Mika to Europe, Russia, and the Middle East, negotiating new deals and consolidating their huge assets around the world. Their properties in London, Paris, and the United States were growing at a steady rate. She had no idea what they owned around the globe, but knew it to be considerable, and the brothers kept a tight rein on their ever-growing empire.

Mika enjoyed flash assets, he had planes and boats and homes in all the major capitals around the globe; a battery of staff were employed to keep them ready for any member of the family to use at any given time.

Mostly Russians were employed by the company; some had followed the family when their jobs had been terminated in Russia. The family diversified and restructured their assets, but the underlying strength was Alexi's core family. The Rubicovs ran a tight ship; work ethic was valued above all, for young and old.

They played hard and they worked even harder. Holidays were few and far between. So far Sasha had not yet made use of any of the chateaus or villas in Italy or France. Sasha liked to live comfortably but simply, without Mika's taste for grandeur, which suited them both. Neither Sasha nor Safi wanted their offspring palmed off to staff to care for. Still, she had noticed since Alexander's birth that their staff had grown. Sasha was converting the floors below and Dan was busy designing the considerable square footage of a skyscraper of apartments overlooking Central Park for Sasha.

It was obviously an amazing contract for Dan, who was on the site often, popping in to visit Alexander and updating Safi on the amazing progress of their soon-to-be stunning home, with a full-size Olympic pool, gym, and its own small cinema, none of which Safi cared for, but knew it was for Sasha and his family. Property in Manhattan, as in London, needed to be designed to the highest standards.

Safi felt her life racing to a place she never envisaged; she was struggling to keep up with the changes.

Anna loved her villa in the South of France, but since Sasha's return and her grandson's birth had moved into the Rubicov Tower to be near Alexander and to build on her relationship with Yvetta. She now spent only winters in France, sharing her time between New York and Florida when in the States.

The Rubicov family had regrouped since their departure from Moscow and St Petersburg. Many of the family were in the States and Mika's Floridian Mansion became a meeting place for the Rubicovs on a regular basis. It was a vast and close extended family. Safi thought she had met most of the cousins in Russia, but realised more and more were coming to the fore and Alexander had taken pride of place in their affections. Safi was finding her days away from the gallery taken up with playdates, catered teas in their various homes. One thing was for sure, her children would never run out of offspring to play with.

Education was discussed, only the best was considered, and they intended to have all the offspring educated at the same illustrious institutions. It was of primary importance they forge good alliances and mix with the best brains in the country.

They would donate generously to smooth the path for those who came after to follow in their parents' footsteps. Safi wondered whether this would ever be the case going up to Oxford or Cambridge; somehow, she doubted it. Intelligence was valued above all, the trick was to know your mind and being able to use it (more than anything, perhaps, this was the skill that would suit you well in life), besides having good grades, of course. She might have gone to Oxford, but that was long past now – a whole other life, almost unthinkable – from what she had learnt the interview process alone was harrowing, if you were lucky enough to get one.

If Safi had not been preoccupied with Alexander, with the legalities piling up daily with running the gallery, and the complications arising with Yvetta, she might have found the family she had married into a little suffocating and oppressive.

Her life with Janus, who she often met to get away from the Rubicovs, would have been by far simpler to deal with, she had to admit. He was the same handsome hunk she had fallen for in Sasha's absence, and by all accounts, happy with his role as Alexander's godfather. He often mentioned their time together as the happiest in his life, but now had little time for relationships. His art had once more taken over as his raison d'être and Ying was his constant companion. She organised his life the way he liked it. Janus often hung out with Safi in the gallery during his shows. They had managed to overcome the awkward stage, even joked about their brotherly-sisterly friendship. Janus had always been self-deprecating, reminding Safi they both had had a lucky escape. She knew life with Janus would never have panned out, he never wanted a family and she did. And how glad she was that she had had a child. She could not imagine her life without little Alexi now.

Her two closest and most trusted friends in NYC, she realised, had both been her lovers. Not sure what to make of this, she preferred to ignore their complex, insouciant, untroubled friendships without trying to overanalyse it.

Separately both men had been advised that a quick settlement with Sasha's sister, whatever the outcome, would be preferable to the time-consuming impasse they found themselves in. Safi had stipulated no to a face-to-face meeting with Yvetta, not wanting to agree to any deal, and not signing the caveat, which would turn over all Rubicov art galleries to Yvetta.

The suggestion of a subsidiary to the Manhattan gallery in Brooklyn had been put forward. The complications were endless, but Safi had agreed to consider it on a conditional basis. Safi stipulated that Yvetta would have no influence over the Manhattan gallery; the two galleries had to be independent, with the exception of the names, of course: Rubicov Manhattan Gallery and Rubicov Brooklyn Gallery.

Yvetta had agreed to Safi's stipulations, but a major stumbling block remained: signing the caveat eventually handing over all control of ownership to Yvetta. She was no longer estranged from the family, which had been the original intention of the caveat in the will. It had been set up with Safi's signature as the only principal who could overturn the caveat.

After the attempt on her life by Yvetta, Safi's signature remained the only one which could overturn the agreement. Anna had the power to co-sign while she was alive, but only Safi had the power of attorney to hand over the galleries once Anna was no longer alive.

It was hugely complicated: if Yvetta proved her worth running the Brooklyn gallery, Safi thought she might consider signing the caveat handing over ownership to Yvetta.

Safi intended to keep it that way. She held the cards. Yvetta had much to prove before she signed the caveat which would hand the galleries over to her, an eventuality Safi dreaded, and still felt conflicted.

Sasha and Mika stayed away from the legalities, having agreed the issue was for Safi and Yvetta to sort out with their lawyers. The brothers decided they would agree to anything as long as both parties were in agreement. They had had enough of the drama, the rancour, all the years of antipathy. Neither wanted to drive a deeper wedge between the sister-in-laws. They had to respect their father's wishes, and they did not have a right to insist that Safi forgive Yvetta's attempt on her life.

Yvetta had a great deal to overcome. The family had accepted her back into the fold, but they were not prepared to indulge her every whim, and their patience had worn thin. Safi deserved their respect, and to make her own decisions where the galleries were concerned. The Manhattan gallery's success was only due to her hard work and dedication under difficult circumstances. Safi, who had come in as an amateur to the art world, had learnt on the fly – and fast. And the results had been astounding. The brothers would have gifted the gallery to Safi, but no one could or would go against Alexi's will.

In fact, the galleries were not a major asset in the Rubicov Empire, and were of little importance in the scheme of things. Still, to Safi and Yvetta, they were a huge deal. Safi needed recognition from the family for her achievements, while Yvetta needed the challenge and the stability of being responsible for running a successful business on her own once more. To achieve this, she knew, she was going to have to remain stable for a long period of time.

Setting up the Brooklyn gallery would go a long way in helping her regain the trust from the Rubicovs and help her gain self-respect. The test was her fortitude and maturity in dealing with the lawyers when the ownership of the galleries was not automatically signed over, even when it had been bequeathed in her father's will. She would have to show respectful restraint while the negotiations progressed, something she had never been able to do.

Sasha passed his wishes onto the legal team. Not wanting to become, involved he made sure they negotiated the finer points with both Safi and Yvetta on separate visits before any financial agreement was entered into by Yvetta for the second Rubicov Gallery. The running of the Brooklyn gallery would be separate from the Manhattan gallery and controlled by the family's lawyers at all times.

The negotiations took a full year before Yvetta got the go-ahead to look for property to open the new Rubicov gallery in Brooklyn.

In all this time, Yvetta remained dutifully faithful to Gina, and Mrs Leibovitz became a constant in her life with thrice-weekly visits.

There had been a few incidents Gina found impossible to deal with; she had left Yvetta on more than one occasion, one of which resulted in Gina being invited to visit Mrs Leibovitz with Yvetta. It took months until they were able to work together to stop Yvetta's unreasonable jealousy, a jealousy no one else (and, it often seemed, not even Yvetta herself) understood or shared.

Unknown to DuPont, Gina had stayed over at the office over weekends to escape Yvetta's anger. At times Yvetta's paranoid fantasies due to insecurity would result in her aggressively blaming Gina for her unhappiness.

She always turned up waiting for Gina at her work, with her tail between her legs, begging her to return. In the end Gina gave Yvetta an ultimatum: they see her therapist as a couple, or Gina would move out and they separate.

Yvetta hated sharing her safe space, but she did not dare take the risk of losing Gina. She knew Gina was her anchor; without her she would be adrift, losing everything she had worked so hard to regain once more.

Her relationships had improved with Anna and Bernard. Both kept a polite distance, allowing Yvetta to call the shots when or where she chose to see them.

Sasha and Mika were less forgiving. Yvetta was seldom included in family gatherings, and never when Safi was present. Yvetta had little or no interest in Alexander, which suited Safi but irritated Sasha. He insisted she behave like a proper family member, respecting the milestones of her immediate family, including Alexander's birthdays. Whenever her brothers read her the riot act, Yvetta would rant to Gina, who had learnt to listen without comment. It took time and lots of patience, but mostly Gina enjoyed her relationship with Yvetta. Still, she had doubts whether it would have longevity, it was always Yvetta's way and to keep the peace she had mostly given in. It was tiresome folding over and over, losing your voice, giving someone else the upper hand just because you didn't have the energy to be part of another fight you were sure to lose.

Yvetta, she found, was an ironic contradiction, sometimes arrogant yet insecure, authoritarian yet anxious and often indecisive, ruthlessly tough but also needy: the one did not necessarily outweigh the other, both garnered equal amounts of her attention and nerve. The question was, was Gina strong enough to handle Yvetta. Not sure where her life was heading, she often confided in DuPont. He was a wonderful listener, never critical yet always empathic and intuitive, understanding her dilemma.

Gina had to admit that life had improved. She no longer felt alone. She cared for Yvetta more than she liked to admit, yet she did not care to have her personality or life completely submerged in Yvetta's world. Continuing to work with DuPont helped keep her grounded – or as grounded as one could be in Manhattan.

Gina had rejected Yvetta's offer to run the Brooklyn Rubicov gallery with her. She expected that her reasons would never be accepted, yet she hoped it would not be the wedge to drive them apart.

Yvetta's petty jealousies were becoming legendary and tiresome; she no longer wanted to play the supporting role to her ridiculous rages.

Without Yvetta's knowledge, Gina had started to see her own therapist. Walking on eggshells constantly took its toll. She needed to have guidance, someone to lean on for support, and DuPont was, she knew bored, with the whole sorry saga.

Gina also knew that the only reason he indulged Gina was to keep up with Yvetta's erratic mindset. DuPont was always considering Safi's wellbeing, to the point where Gina had begun to wonder whether DuPont had a thing for the beautiful Safi. He was always cooing over everything she did, especially the baby, who he seemed not to get enough of. Whenever Gina walked into his office, he seemed to be chatting to Safi and Alexander on FaceTime. It was DuPont who had advised Gina to seek out the guidance of a therapist, perhaps because he was tired of taking on that role.

Still, Gina had to admit that the sessions with the therapist were helping a great deal. She no longer initiated discussions with Yvetta (however gently) she knew would turn into a heated argument, and she no longer criticised Yvetta or found fault with her (something that always ended in a flameout). Instead, she complimented Yvetta first, then suggested they attempt another way to deal with whatever wasn't working in the first place, leaving the decision to Yvetta, who invariably came up with the same opinion as if it were her idea, which suited Gina perfectly. It was sometimes thankless and often exhausting, but Gina was learning how to negotiate her way around Yvetta's stubbornness to have her own way. But at what cost? Gina sometimes wondered. From time to time, it felt that, by giving all to Yvetta at these moments, her own identity was being diminished.

Both women were both working things out with the guidance of their therapists. Yvetta, it appeared, was now dealing with certain issues in a less confrontational way, too.

Yvetta's days were now taken up visiting end-of-year degree shows and artists' studios whose names were recommended to her, she was slowly building up a list of artists to represent whose work she found interesting and cutting-edge.

The Rubicov Gallery in Moscow was her fall-back; it was still run by Ilona, who she trusted and remembered well. Yvetta did not want to return to Russia, and Ilona helped her source Russian artists abroad who she might want to represent. She made contact with all of the London galleries she had worked with in the past, letting them know she was opening her own gallery in the States.

Her days were filled with overseeing the new building and space the gallery was moving into. It had taken a long time to reach this stage. Yvetta felt a lightness of spirit; she walked with a spring in her step. She loved the art world, she loved her work, it gave her untold pleasure to be back in the profession, and most of all she felt free and alive. She hoped she would remain unscathed by Fritzi's reputation, this was a new beginning, living in New York and together with Gina; Yvetta felt her life couldn't get any better.

Establishing the Brooklyn Rubicov filled every waking hour. Safi could hold onto the Manhattan gallery, Yvetta thought. She had what she wanted: freedom to be her own person once more. The therapist helped her manage her doubts, kept her grounded, helping her to navigate her way out of personal challenges, instead of attacking, overreacting, always being on the defensive and suspicious of others' intentions. She hated taking the medication, but it was a necessary evil; without it her family and the lawyers were unlikely to accept her anew. All in all, life was on its way up, that was indisputable. This was something new for her: she had always been so attuned to the downs, now each day mattered.

Gina's loyalty to DuPont was an irritant, but she let the issue lie; perhaps it was best if she and Gina did not work together. Instead, Yvetta employed a qualified post-graduate curator from Goldsmiths who had just completed a year working for Christie's, and who had also worked at one of the major hip galleries in London. She offered him a salary he could not refuse. James was what she needed: tall and attractive in a typically clean-cut American way, and not gay. She did not have to worry about bumping into him on weekends, he hung out where he could pick up girls rather than boys. Yvetta also valued his dual passport status: having studied both in the States and abroad (mostly in London), he would understand what she was after.

The art scene had moved on. It was no longer static, it had become multi-sensory and interactive. People wanted more than just to stand in front of a work. They wanted it to reach out with sound and movement, alerting one's sensory perceptions and emotions. The art world still remained mostly in galleries or museums, places many still felt uncomfortable with. And some of the buildings were forbidding, too, overpowering to walk in off the street, housing only the big hitters, *oligarchs*, as they called them in Russia.

Yvetta wanted to encourage a welcome, casual-social environment, the standard of work high and cutting-edge, but also a place that was socially inviting, a place to hang out in. Together with James, Yvetta scoured the States for new work; they flew to Korea and China, Mexico and Argentina, and even Brasilia, where she discovered artists working not only in exciting new materials but also breaking barriers with sound, especially the environmental artists. They brought their work close with sound and smells invoking lush jungle canopies and spaces turned into deserts of arid land flattened by over-forestation.

Some believed that the environment was highly contentious, yet this art reflected only what the artist perceived by relating the beauty of the landscape reminding us of the delicate balance affecting not only wildlife but indigenous people. The end result left the viewer with a sense of hope, which Yvetta related strongly to: there had to be hope for humanity. Hope, buoyancy, a sense of possibility after great difficulty, a new life. This was Yvetta's story, too.

The gallery opened with a major show from Brazil featuring the work of three artists covering the same subject in a myriad of different ways. One artist only worked with sound, the second with photographs. The third artist used thick, textured paint on vast canvasses textured and over laid with animal bones, burnt earth, and cloth peeling off the canvasses with debris from war-torn areas of the world, yet there was always a plant or flower showing through, hope never died.

It was a powerful show to open with and Yvetta dedicated every second of her waking hours joyously re-establishing her name in the art world.

All else was forgotten as she drew on every possible contact she had left who remembered her from past associations. James was worth every dollar: he hired the right people for the gallery, organised the staff to send out invites to those who mattered for her first opening, and oversaw the shipping and storage of the works until the gallery was ready for the show.

When the doors opened to the public, it was for a private, catered viewing by invitation only. The artists worked with James and Yvetta until they were satisfied their work had been hung and presented to their specification.

The gallery was a vast warehouse converted into four major spaces: the front entrance was a casual seating area for coffee and wholefood snacks. This area encompassed large, playful, interactive sculptures which led to the three remaining spaces, each large enough to house major works.

It took Yvetta months to complete the space; simply finding, engaging, and in many instances sweet-talking and cajoling the artists took months of travelling abroad, shared dinners, kind words, many, many bottles of expensive wine, and ingratiating emails filtered through agents and art directors. The final six months was spent organising the first exhibition, then signing up other artists to follow over a five-year period, including artists from Yvetta's native Russia with the help of Ilona (who, Yvetta was happy to find, had lost none of her rigour, speed, or efficacy).

When Yvetta finally opened her gallery, Safi was nearing the end of her pregnancy with their second child. She had kept up with the gallery news through Sasha and, of course DuPont. In fact, Yvetta had called DuPont in to pass judgement before the gallery opened.

He arrived at the doors with Gina, only to be greeted by the handsome James to escort them round before the art had been hung. DuPont viewed the massive space with overhanging, moving lights and shifting walls.

Yvetta's family had been supportive, though remaining quietly in the background, watching as the gallery developed and Yvetta's exhaustive plans were put in place, her dream every day becoming more real. Unknown to Yvetta, the family were on top of every move she made, watching her like a hawk. They had employed someone similar to Kolya to report back on all of Yvetta's dealings and business relationships. No one wanted a repeat performance, if Yvetta went off the rails they wanted to be close enough to step in to pick up the pieces and to clean up the mess.

Mika was delighted to learn his sister conducted herself with typical Rubicov shrewdness, each negotiation worked out to the last cent. The occasional unpredictability and eccentricity seemed to have been replaced with a hard-nosed pragmatism and unflagging vision that would have made Alexi proud.

The lawyers and the accountants were equally impressed by her professionalism. She conducted her business with tremendous energy, leaving very little to chance, and, for the first time in her career, paying close attention to business ethics and professional conduct. She covered all of her tracks with up-to-date paperwork, leaving no room for error or confusion.

Anna followed her daughter's progress with more than a smattering of pride, admitting proudly to Mika and Sasha that their sister had what it took to run a smart operation. It felt good to feel proud of Yvetta again and after all this time. It was enormously satisfying, this pride mixed with gratitude and relief. Yvetta was a chip-off-the-old-block, a Rubicov not unlike her mother when she was at the helm of one of the toughest conglomerates in male-dominated Russia.

Still, the family wondered whether it would last. Would Yvetta put her wasted years behind her now and, move forward with her life, no longer sabotaging herself at the least provocation by judging everyone in a limited, one-dimensional way? Gina made a huge difference to her wellbeing, too, this seemed beyond doubt. With Fritzi out of her life, Yvetta had managed to scrape herself off the floor to join the human race, or so it now appeared.

Gina found Yvetta fired up, almost manic at times, but she understood the urgency of her almost childlike exhilaration with her new life. She reminded Gina often enough how free and energised she felt to have her life back. And Gina, for her part, gave Yvetta a reason to enjoy her new-found happiness.

Their visits to the therapists continued. For the first time, Yvetta understood the importance her medication made to her life; it kept her on an even keel. She now negotiated with Gina when things upset her; they had boundaries which Yvetta adhered to, much like an alcoholic understands that one drink could send them over the edge.

Gina accompanied them Yvetta and James on one of their art journeys to Brazil, which happened to be during the Carnival. This turned out to be one of the most incredible experiences of Gina's life. James was tremendous fun and together they kept Yvetta on the straight and narrow. She still had flights of fancy, which were often due to overexcitement when the pressure reached boiling point. Thankfully, James had the charm and guts to handle her when she became overpowering with ideas that did not fly, he would bring her back to earth without loss of face.

The gallery opening was arranged for a Thursday, a popular late-night gallery day when many of the galleries held cocktail evenings to encourage the public to cross their thresholds for some bubbly and cheese snacks.

It took three years after the original proposal by the lawyers for Safi to agree to the contract. Yvetta was prepared to agree to almost anything to make it impossible for Safi to find fault, which would no doubt delay the opening of the Brooklyn Rubicov Gallery, costing them precious time and momentum as the new kid on the block.

Besides, Yvetta had her family in her corner; what could Safi do, apart from refuse to sign over the Manhattan gallery? Still, Yvetta had enough to contend with and there sometimes seemed no end to the stress. Not knowing one way or the other how the contract negotiations would turn out was worst of all. At least she had the support system of Gina and now James.

Gina and the lawyers guided Yvetta to build the reputation of the new gallery and bide her time. She was in no hurry for Safi to sign the caveat; even if it took years, it would eventually be her gallery, much as the gallery in Moscow was hers. She would then have three galleries, and, if all went as she wished, she would open a fourth in London. Yvetta was only 36, many years lay ahead to reach her goal, her life had taken such a dramatic turn – or series of turns, really. It was inconceivable for her to believe that she had vengeance in her heart.

Now she understood, had glimpses of her former self, a self she did not want to return to. She had positive energy and she had benefitted from giving instead of taking for the first time in her life. Attack had always been the way she saw everything when she was with Fritzi, who was now in a prison somewhere deep in Russia, while she, Yvetta, was free forging ahead with her life. Fritzi would never believe it, and Yvetta hoped she never had the opportunity to do so. At the thought of this, a foreboding shiver ran down Yvetta's spine. She found Gina in bed, lay down beside her, and nestled her head under Gina's arm. Yvetta could not remember ever feeling more content; for the first time ever, life was unbelievably good.

She was able to allay her fears by opening up to her therapist and to Gina. They gave her a new perspective, instead of polarising all her energies into seemingly endless problems.

Step by step, her therapist helped her to question her fears, allowing her to see a way through, instead of repeating the never-ending circle of behaviours and negative traits, which, in turn, always ended badly. Treating people badly and seeing herself as a victim was an addiction, she had to break free of.

Yet still Fritzi loomed large in the shadows. She had had an enormous influence over Yvetta's life, no doubt about it. Yvetta felt a mass of mixed emotions when it came to her old lover, some were guilt-ridden, others were filled with admiration – but mostly she felt fear. Not understanding her feelings, Yvetta worked her way through her spider web of emotions, examining her love for Fritzi's strength, her admiration, and her total capitulation to her every whim, like a fly in a web she allowed her old lover to consume her without a thought for her own safety.

As one passed through each exhibit, becoming one with the sounds and smells of the endangered species deep in the Brazilian jungle, a powerful piece and visually stunning, more and more so as one ventured deeper into the jungle, emerging finally into the light.

Each artist left James in no doubt about the way their work was hung or put together to maximise the impact. The end result was powerful and visually exciting, and the urgency of the subject of climate change made the work more impactful still.

The Brazilian artists were relatively unknown outside of their own country. Yvetta wanted the artists to receive maximum exposure to art critics and the public, to help bring new talent into the world. The opening evening was well-attended, but as the week progressed word had spread about the exhibition, and the gallery was receiving fantastic editorials in many local papers and magazines. People were pouring in through the doors to see the new gallery. The Brazilian exhibition had been an excellent choice and a great success.

Yvetta was concentrating on her next show: bringing in cutting-edge artists from Russia. With the help of Ilona, they were able to move forward at a faster pace than her first exhibition. The exhibition had to be in the bag well before the Brazilian show came down, and so Yvetta found her days and weeks were completely occupied with work and sharing her life with Gina.

The lawyers were suitably impressed with the gallery's success, and so were Yvetta's family (many of whom had forgotten how innovative and well-executed her exhibitions had always been). Of all her kudos by far the most surprising was a congratulatory card from the Rubicov gallery in Manhattan, which she valued above many of the others she had received. But she was too busy to dwell too long on the significance of this – the coming exhibition took up all of her time. The card was something she would have to analyse later with Mrs Leibovitz.

Chapter 20

Safi was in her third trimester, delighted to be having a girl whose name she had no trouble choosing, and thrilled that her little Amelia Arianna Rubicov would be born in cooler weather. True to her word, she asked Dan and Dax whether they would be joint godfathers to her little angel.

Amelia was born towards the end of September, a healthy 7lb 5oz baby. Her baby brother Alexander thought she was the funniest little thing he had ever seen; they encouraged him to play gently with his sister, who he wanted to kiss constantly, and she seemed to warm to his attention.

The naming party had been organised and invitations had already gone out to family and Safi's close friends, everyone had such busy lives.

She loved being a mother, and Sasha was a hands-on father, always happy to take Alexander to whatever play group he was invited to when Safi was busy in the gallery with a new show.

Life had changed for both Safi and Sasha: they preferred to be home for bath time, happy to get up in the middle of the night when Alexander did not settle. The nanny and Safi saw to Amelia's needs.

When Alexander started nursery school, both Safi and Sasha walked there in the mornings to drop him off, leaving pickup time for the nanny.

Life had become baby-orientated. Safi and Sasha's every conversation always came back to Alexander or Amelia; they were completely and utterly besotted with their small brood.

Safi understood the family were ecstatic about Yvetta's turnaround from a lunatic to what could only be described as less of a lunatic than usual, far be it from Safi to pooh-pooh Sasha and Anna's praise for Yvetta's accomplishments with the new gallery, but Safi was not going to join in on the praise, and refused to set foot over that gallery's threshold (just saying the name 'Brooklyn Rubicov' was bad enough), they would have to attend the opening evening without her. Yvetta, she was sure, would not be disappointed. No excuse had to be made for Safi's absence; she had just given birth to Amelia, after all.

According to DuPont, the opening evening went without incident, and he added that Yvetta was lucky to have James, an incredible find. Safi had read the critics' reviews: most were favourable. Only one art magazine had an axe to grind, questioning why the gallery chose to open with a Brazilian art exhibition, rather than homegrown American art, or, the critic argued snidely, perhaps Russian art would have been more appropriate.

Safi did not agree: true art was borderless, and besides, did the Whitney Museum not promote American art? Luckily, the critic in question did not have the clout of a Clement Greenberg in the early 1940s. The master art critic of modernism at that time would have put a quintessentially American perspective on all modernist or avant-garde works. Yet the Brazilian artists exhibited by Yvetta's gallery proved art had no borders, and that environmental problems were global. The environmental threat had always existed in some form (though now it was a larger issue than ever), and how an artist chose to interpret the work was their choice alone.

Safi wondered whether she and Yvetta might not have become firm friends had circumstances been different. A sadness settled into her as she read the reviews and, listened to DuPont's chatter about everything from the new gallery to his assistant, Gina, who had moved in with her 'sister-in-law.' Safi's head shot up at the word, she had never thought of Yvetta as her sister-in-law, but that is exactly what she was, and she was also Alexander and Amelia's aunt. Sasha tried to remind Safi of this from time to time, but she blanked out any conversations to do with his sister; indeed, just thinking about Yvetta sometimes darkened her mood, the Florida incident always returning to haunt her, touching her throat.

Saturdays she had her babies all to herself; the nanny had a few hours off, and Sasha played tennis with his old university pals. This left Safi free to do whatever she chose. The November weather was unseasonably mild and she decided to take both Alexander and Amelia for a stroll. For once Alexander had no parties to attend and Amelia was asleep. Alexander was his usual chatty self as Safi pushed the double buggy through the colourful orange and yellow fall foliage covering the sidewalks.

She bent to pick up a handful of leaves, letting them slip between her fingers like confetti as she crushed them in her palm, Alexander found the whole performance hilarious and wanted her to do it again and again.

'Hello, little man, did you find that funny?' a strange voice said. On inspection, it was not strange at all.

Emerging seemingly out of nowhere and chortling sweetly as she leant into the pram to take a closer look at Amelia.

Safi was not sure what to do, this was the first encounter she had had with Yvetta, and here she was alone with her children, no one to turn to for assurance or advice. She had to deal with the situation whether she liked it or not.

Before she could say a word, Yvetta stood a safe distance away from Safi, with an understanding, almost cautious, look on her suddenly soft face.

'They are very beautiful children,' Yvetta said quietly. 'I hope you do not mind. I'm sorry to have disturbed you. It was lovely to see them at last. I will be on my way.' Momentarily speechless, the encounter happening so fast, Safi surprised herself by saying,

'Actually, Yvetta, I am about to stop for a coffee at that café,' she pointed across the street, at a French-style lighted signboard, 'if you wish you could join us for a few moments. I am sure Alexander would love to chat to his aunt.' Shocked at what she had just suggested, as though it had been voiced by someone else entirely and now, she was little more than a passive bystander who now had to deal with the consequences, she waited for Yvetta's reply. Attempting to conceal her anxiety, still second-guessing her own suggestion, Safi busied herself tucking Amelia in. Clearly Yvetta was shocked by the suggestion, too, for it took her a long moment before she responded.

'Oh my God, yes, I would love to join you,' Yvetta said, now surprising Safi with the sheer level of her enthusiasm. Perhaps she had changed after all, even her appearance had undergone a major transformation, gone was her aggressively cutting-edge clothing, replaced by a tailored chic winter white coat and designer shawl, Yvetta's hair was blonde now long and luxurious, she was definitely a head-turner.

Safi could tell Yvetta was overcome with shock at receiving an invitation to join her sister-in-law for coffee, nervously chatting away to Alexander. To Amelia she mostly spoke nonsense words, with some Russian and even German terms of endearment thrown in for good measure. The small child shared none of her mother's reservations about the other woman; she smiled broadly and gurgled.

They found a table to accommodate the buggy. Alexander climbed out of his pushchair and straight onto Yvetta's lap. Not sure how Yvetta would respond, Safi was about to pull him off when she realised that Yvetta was overcome with joy. She kept kissing his cheeks and pulled faces, hugging him tightly to her bosom. Overjoyed, too, and feeling Yvetta's warmth, Alexander tightened his grip on Yvetta. Safi sat in stunned silence, watching the scene in front of her. It was hard to conjure up the vicious woman who had tried to throttle her, no matter how often Safi tried to remind herself. That memory, that Yvetta, became more and more distant. Was that a different Yvetta? Or was Safi just naïve? Was this yet another ploy? No, this loving Yvetta seemed entirely genuine. A warmth like this could not be faked. Eventually Alexander's snack arrived and Safi offered to take him from Yvetta.

'He will dirty your outfit,' Safi said, almost as a prelude to an apology she knew she would soon have to offer.

'Oh, this old thing, it's fine. I am enjoying holding him. I never thought I would enjoy holding any baby, but he has melted my heart.' She looked at Safi, and though she still radiated a strange sense of happiness, there was pain in those eyes, too. 'He is truly adorable, and so good. He reminds me of Sasha quite a lot.'

Safi resigned herself to the situation. As long as Alexander was happy, she thought. After all, she had invited this woman to join them for tea. What had possessed her to do that she still could not fathom. Perhaps she was still a young, overly trusting girl at heart; perhaps she had not grown up so much after all. Or perhaps, deep down, she wanted to think the best of people, and perhaps this new Yvetta wanted to do that as well.

The situation became awkward, neither woman knowing how to move forward.

'Thank you, Safi, for asking me to join you,' Yvetta said gently. 'This,' and she gestured to the children, her hands then taking in the larger café, 'means a great deal to me, and has made me incredibly happy. Maybe one day you will allow me to tell you how sad I am for what happened back then. I don't expect you to forgive me, but perhaps you could try – if not for me, but to heal the family rift.'

'Well,' Safi said slowly, careful to choose the right words, 'I may consider that. In fact, I have considered it, or else I would not have invited you to join us. What happened was awful for me, horrendous really, Yvetta, but perhaps you know that?'

'Mummy cross?' Alexander said.

'Oh no, no, darling not cross, just chatting,' Safi said, her tone reminding her of her mother's all of a sudden.

'Mummy kiss, mummy not cross.'

They both stared at Alexander nonplussed about what to do next.

Yvetta bent over to hand Alexander back to Safi. As Yvetta reached her, she gave Safi a light peck on the cheek.

'See, aunty Yvetta gave mummy a kiss on the cheek.'

He clapped his pudgy little hands in glee, laughing delightedly at the game he had started.

Safi smiled thinly.

'Yes, darling, she has.'

'Mummy, kiss Auntie Etta.'

'Oh, that's okay, darling, another time. Aunty Etta has to go now,' Safi said.

Yvetta bent forward again, rustled his hair, giving him a smackeroo of a kiss on his cheek, which sent him into fits of laughter.

'Safi,' Yvetta said, standing up, 'I hope one day we can share our interest in art.' She surprised Safi one last time, this time with a parting smile. 'It is fantastic, quite amazing, we both love the same profession.'

This was true, and something Safi too often forgot, amid the rancour, violence, and provocations of recent years. Those provocations, Safi reminded herself, were Yvetta's, never hers. Still, it all suddenly seemed rather far away. The past – she felt tired just thinking about it. If Yvetta was a different person, wasn't Safi, now the mother of two children, a different person, too? Perhaps it was time for everyone to start again. Autumn, a time when old things became brittle and died. Old feuds, old slights, the heaviness of the past.

After Yvetta departed, Safi sat motionless for quite some time, until Amelia started to make stirring noises. She paid the bill quickly after insisting, since she extended the invitation and made her way back to their home before Amelia started howling, hoping the movement of the pushchair would help her nod off again.

Sasha came to greet them as the elevator opened, Alexander now out of his chair and Amelia shrieking her head off. He swept Alexander off his feet and into his arms, kissing him on the cheek. Alexander wriggled to be put down, still giggling and chatting away; at first Sasha did not catch what he was saying.

'What did you say, darling, tell daddy again.'

'Auntie Etta kiss.'

'Whose Auntie Etta?' Looking at Safi. Sasha said playfully, trying in vain to conceal his confusion, 'She must be a good kisser'

Nodding, Alexander ran off to his playroom. The nanny would be back to bath Amelia after Safi finished her feed.

Sasha held Amelia for a while before the nanny came in to fetch her for a bath. Both enjoyed bathing her, but Sasha had not spoken to Safi all day and wanted to catch up with her.

'Am I imagining it, or are you a bit out of sorts? Did she cry a lot while you were out?'

'No, she was perfect, but I have something to tell you. I can't quite come to terms with what happened yet. I'm still processing really.'

'Aunty Etta, by the way, is Yvetta.'

'What are you telling me? You spoke to her?'

'More than spoke! We ran into her on our walk, and she was so lovely with the kids that I am not sure what came over me, I invited her to join us for tea.'

Sasha sat dumbfounded, momentarily lost for words.

'What happened?'

She gave him a word-for-word replay of Yvetta's obvious joy at Alexander climbing on her lap, putting his pudgy arms around her neck, giving her a sloppy kiss on the cheek, and all about their kissing game and how they had parted.

'Well, what the hell came over you?' Sasha said. 'Must be the baby hormones.'

'Actually, perhaps you have hit the nail on the head,' Safi said softly, 'because I still have not worked out why I asked her to join us.'

'Where does this leave us with the Yvetta situation?' Sasha asked. 'My mother will be ecstatic, you realise that.'

'Not so fast,' Safi cautioned. 'Leave things for the moment, until I have had a chance to catch up with myself.'

Monday the gallery was closed to the public. Still, Safi couldn't help but be on her phone. Listening to her messages, Safi immediately recognised Yvetta's voice; she pressed replay to catch the message again.

'Hi, Safi, I hope you don't mind this call? I just had to ask you, please, it would mean so much, if you would come and see the gallery, anytime that suits you; although, of course, I would love to accompany you round the exhibition. I am so proud of Rubicov Brooklyn, showing it to you would mean a great deal. I look forward to hearing from you, Yvetta.'

This was it, Safi supposed: the time had come to move forward. Yvetta had changed, she clearly regretted what had happened between them.

Safi's hand went to her throat involuntarily. Was she ready to bury the hatchet? What would the consequences be if the two women started this new chapter in their relationship, acknowledging each other's existence? It could end up with Rubicov Brooklyn having a closer liaison with Rubicov Manhattan? Her mind took flight about the two galleries cooperating on a business level. The more she thought about it, the more it made perfect sense for both galleries to cooperate, even support one another.

Not accepting the invitation would be mean-spirited and small-minded, Safi decided, and it would send the wrong message. Following her instinct and rejecting this opportunity would be awful for everyone involved; Sasha, for one, would encourage her to move forward; he more than anyone else had the closest bond with Yvetta. She could tell he was elated at the sudden change in circumstances.

She decided that she should strike while the iron was hot; if she waited any longer, she would change her mind about the whole thing.

Yvetta picked up on the first ring.

'Oh, you called. That means you have decided to come and see the gallery, am I right?'

'Well, yes, Yvetta, I would actually love to see the Rubicov Brooklyn. We are both closed today. If you are free, perhaps you could show me around this afternoon. I could ask the nanny to stay on after picking up Alexander from nursery, and Amelia has a feed, so that would work for me.'

'Absolutely,' Yvetta said excitedly, 'any time you arrive will be fine with me. I will be here waiting. Please ring the bell on arriving, although the camera will pick you up outside the door.'

Safi arrived at the double-height glass doors just after three. Looking up she knew her arrival had been noted as the huge doors started sliding back.

She entered a cavernous space filled with massive, fully grown trees in vast concrete pots. Marble tables and chairs were scattered around under the green foliage, a sky light above lit the space with natural light. Yvetta came from behind a long white bar with tubular light sculptures hanging the length of the bar, creating a playful mobile. Yvetta had two espressos on the bar and was sitting on one of the tall chrome concave bar stools.

While drinking her coffee, she allowed her eyes to take in the whole ambience of the entrance to the gallery. It had a communal feel, very welcoming. She loved what had been achieved.

The massive, coloured climbing sculpture and a wall of coloured interactive blocks made it a friendly, yet sophisticated, family environment. There was an enormous white wall full of installations with furry textures inviting people to make their own art by moving the fur about with a large comb hanging off the sides. Huge silver and gold balls dwarfed the viewer, encouraging one's eye to travel skyward, where massive white bird mobiles hung catching the sun through the skylight, throwing shadows across the floor and walls of the birds as they moved in the breeze. Yvetta looked expectantly at Safi as she turned around. Not a word had passed between them, and Yvetta knew better than to break the spell while Safi took it all in.

'I am speechless,' Safi finally said. 'I had no idea.'

'Well?'

'It's incredible, quite a feat.' Readjusting to the reality of the moment, Safi tried to find the right words to express herself. 'The space is everything a gallery should be. Welcoming to the public, it has sophistication, but is not at all foreboding, which most gallery spaces can be.'

'Yes, thank you,' Yvetta said, smiling, her pale, fragile face relaxed at last, 'we are both gallerists, and both in charge of Rubicov galleries. The Manhattan gallery fits the status of New York, sleek and serious. The Brooklyn gallery is more casual and inviting, a perfect foil. Don't you think they complement one another perfectly?'

Safi nodded in agreement; Yvetta had a point, and a good one.

'Can I confide in you?' Yvetta said, surprising Safi once again. 'I would like to share my vision with you for the future. I have never dared to share this with anyone.' This was new to Safi: Yvetta, formerly a self-appointed enemy, now asking to be her confidante, her co-conspirator, her colleague and even her friend. 'If I am successful, I would love to open an auction house in London, where we sell important work from around the globe. What do you think?'

Safi was impressed. Yvetta was thinking ahead, she was planning, and she knew what she wanted. If Yvetta was able to keep her mind focused, Safi had no doubt that she would succeed in achieving her dreams. And Yvetta's dreams were not so different from Safi's. Perhaps they shared the same goals, and, working together, could benefit both of their careers.

'Yvetta,' Safi said slowly, sympathetically, 'I believe you'll succeed if you stay focused on your dream. It will materialise with patience and hard work.'

Yvetta reached over the bar to put her hand over Safi's. Safi noticed that Yvetta's eyes were brimming with tears.

'I have no right to ask for your forgiveness. I now see a therapist three times a week, and I am on medication – new medication, medication which might actually be working. For the first time in my life I feel whole, I feel healthy, happy in my relationship and on top of things, you know, in control of my own destiny. Maybe we could never be friends,' her voice softened, 'but we could help each other out, join the galleries through literature, clients, and I am sure you have great ideas as well.'

She held up her hand as if not finished.

'I know I am running when I should be crawling. I do not want or need you to sign the caveat, not until it suits you to do so. I am actually more than happy with the way things are – truly I am.'

'Yes,' Safi said, trying not to show her surprise at this new and totally different Yvetta, not to mention how impressed she truly was by the space, 'I have thought about the galleries being linked. It really is best for all three galleries, and Ilona could do the same in Moscow. It would be incredibly beneficial. I agree. Now, could you show me the exhibition and the rest of the gallery. I need to get back to the children by 4.30.' Looking at her watch, she noticed they had been chatting for nearly an hour.

Using her mini iPad, Yvetta made a quick call for James to join them. She wanted Safi to meet him, and also for him to walk her round the exhibition.

James was charming and a delight, everything Safi had heard, and more. The show needed more time than she had, but she thought it was perfect for the gallery and hoped they would continue in the same vein. Promising to return to see the show again before it came down, and stressing that she needed to give it the time it deserved, Safi said her goodbyes. They walked her to the doors and she could tell Yvetta was unsure how to end their meeting. James did the usual European thing by kissing her on both cheeks. When she held out her hand to Yvetta, she leaned in, covered both of Safi's hands with her own, and, looking directly into her eyes, and pecked her lightly on the cheek.

'That's for Alexander,' Yvetta said brightly.

Safi could not help laughing, it was a sweet thought and she found she did not mind. After all, this was a completely different Yvetta:, how or why, Safi did not know, but whatever it was, she was happy to accept this new person into her life. More than that, the gallery would benefit from the cooperation. So far, things seemed to be working out. Sasha would be pleased, but Safi was not going to let her guard drop just yet. The truth was, they had a long, long way to go before she could ever trust Yvetta again, that was for sure.

Working together for the business was different, however. Rubicov Manhattan was Safi's responsibility, and she would continue as if the gallery was a Saffron Rubicov gallery, not an Yvetta Rubicov gallery. In time she hoped it would result in the ownership being split, but that had to be Yvetta's idea. The way things were proceeding, Safi hoped that time would not be too far away; now she could discuss her ideas with Sasha without him behaving as if blood were thicker than water. When they had a difference of opinion about anything to do with any member of his family, it always appeared as if he sided with his family.

Safi tried to keep Alexander and Amelia busy while she waited for Lee, one of her old school friends from Brighton, to meet them for lunch. They had not seen each other in years but had kept up with each other's offspring and lifestyles. Safi always tried to keep her news light. Lee, on the other hand, let it all hang out; she had never been as reserved as her other English friends, probably the reason Safi and her got on so well. Safi kept everything close to her chest while Lee jabbered away about almost everything, without a single shred of shyness or self-consciousness. Lee's openness about life, good or bad, never felt ashamed, as long as one picked oneself up, dusted oneself off, and got on with it.

She had separated from her husband Charlie soon after her son Jason was born, and had remarried a year later. No foul play on either side, Lee and Charlie just didn't much like one another anymore, had fallen out of love. Charlie had been pretty good about the whole thing and settled generously without a fight. The lawyers were the only ones to lose out in their divorce. All round he was a pretty good sort, really, according to Lee, whose real name was Lisbeth. Safi could not wait to get the second instalment in Lee's life with her new husband.

Alexander, now four, was a pretty handsome chap; it was school break and he wasn't that keen to accompany his mother for lunch, but when she mentioned Serendipity, he immediately cheered up. After all, who would turn down a trip to chocolate heaven? Even adults were addicted to the place. The sugar rush wouldn't help later, but it was worth it to have Lee meet her kids. The nanny was picking them up in an hour so they would have plenty of time to catch up.

Serendipity was on the tourist map, one reason Safi hardly ever took the kids, but Lee insisted, being a chocoholic and an out-of-towner too, who was sick of hearing about the place and wanted to try it out for herself.

Safi was a few minutes early and pointed out all the tooth rotting candy displayed everywhere to the kids, not to mention the ice cream Sunday's being delivered to the wrought iron tables close by. Chatting away to her children, she noticed a tall, elegantly dressed man. She thought he was a man, at least. He looked quite effeminate wearing a herringbone, tightly tailored trouser suit, two-tone tan, and cream-coloured canvas and leather Brogues. The shirt was interesting, too: small, purple paisley-patterned print, high collar with different printed cuffs and cufflinks. Very debonair, very stylish, even for this always-stylish part of Manhattan. The briefcase was soft kid, understated: Smithson's, or something similar.

Safi found him fascinating; he was obviously a visitor. Straining to hear the accent and tone of the voice to make sure of the gender, he or she was paying the bill, she hoped Lee would not decide to arrive as he walked past. Or maybe if she got up to greet Lee, she would be able to get a closer look. He looked familiar, perhaps a celebrity or star. As he rose Safi noticed a slight unsteadiness and a cane she had not previously noticed. He was incredibly skinny, almost skeletal, the suit was obviously doing a great job of covering it up. His hair was white-blonde and brush cut close to his head. It was hard to tell his age. She noticed he wore a huge diamond in one ear.

As he swept past, she stared transfixed; she noticed others following his receding back as he left the restaurant.

Alexander was restless so Safi decided to order. Lee was obviously going to be late, she wanted the kids to finish their treats before the nanny arrived to pick them up.

Lee walked in just as the kids were off with the nanny. The kids had a few moments to say hello, thrilled with their London T-shirts gifts, they disappeared up the stairs with the nanny for their different activities.

'Did you see that rock-star-looking guy?' Lee asked almost as soon as she arrived. 'Is he someone famous? Was he in here? He took my cab as I arrived. He's skinny as a rake but incredibly sexy. I'm sure he's someone famous. I stood on the sidewalk watching him ride off, but I just couldn't place him … anyway hi, so wonderful to see you. God, you look amazing. I want to hear everything.' Lee talked like this, all in a bubbling rush. 'First I have to tell you about husband number two,' she said, sitting down at last. 'He is everything Charlie wasn't, loves life and loves me, which is even better.'

Laughing, Safi said, 'Lee, you never change. It's such a pity we are so far apart. I'd just love it if you lived closer, and yes that guy or woman maybe, was in here, and I couldn't take my eyes off him, either. He seemed familiar to me, too. Anyway, let's hear about you and hubby number two.'

On the way home Safi had an uncomfortable thought, but pushed it out of her mind as being completely ridiculous. Still, it nagged continuously, like an old itch that just wouldn't go away. There was nothing much she could do about it, unless she saw the 'rock star' again. She never caught his accent (the kids were just too noisy), but there was something Fritzi about him. A stupid thought. Ridiculous. Fritzi was in another country, in jail. She knew by the time she jumped out of the cab the thought would be replaced by a million other things, like what to make the kids for dinner. Something they loved to do was dine together; after Amelia went off to bed, Safi and Sasha tried to have a sit-down meal each evening when home with Alexander, who would regale them with stories of his day, and loved having their attention to himself.

Sasha would read him a bedtime story and then switch off his light, which left the rest of the evening for them to relax together, something they were able to do, in fact more now that the kids were getting older.

Amelia had always been a good sleeper; she loved her bed, all she needed was her favourite bear, that was it. According to Fiona, Safi had been the same way as a child. She liked nothing more than to be left alone to snuggle down for the night.

Alexander was a different story. He liked to play until he was ready to sleep, and Safi had learnt to let him do his thing; usually it was colouring in or playing with his latest action hero. Whatever it was, he did it on his own, happy to be left in peace. They often found him asleep on his bed, too tired to get under the covers. Sasha would tuck him in before coming to bed. They had their routine, life was full if a little repetitive at times, but they were happy with the tranquillity, both having experienced enough upheaval in the past.

The builders had left and Dan was thrilled with the result; he had surpassed his usual brilliance, the place was amazing. He had managed to turn four storeys into a home. They would never have to move, not while they remained in Manhattan. It suited their needs perfectly.

The kids had their own play area, they had plenty of space to do their own thing, Safi and Sasha each had an office. The family area was a huge open space encompassing the kitchen, dining, and family room. The formal areas for entertaining were hardly ever used. The floor below them had all the bedrooms and bathrooms, and the floor below that housed the swimming pool and gym, which everyone loved using. Sasha swam at dawn each day, and the kids had swimming lessons in the pool on weekends. Safi tried to use the gym every day before leaving for work. The basement was used for storage, bikes, kids' stuff, and sport paraphernalia, plus a laundry room, all cleverly hidden behind sliding doors,

The elevator was used by all, apart from the cleaning lady and the nanny, who were fitness fanatics; much to Safi and Sasha's chagrin, they didn't break a sweat when reaching the top floor via the stairs.

The Rubicovs had settled comfortably in the States, Russia was the past. The family remained close. Safi had to get used to lavish family celebrations, it was always someone's birthday, anniversary, or a new baby to celebrate. The younger set were getting married, the Rubicovs were marrying (mostly Americans), the family were, according to Sasha, becoming international.

Yvetta now attended all family occasions with Gina; they were tolerated by the older Rubicovs and welcomed by the younger set. Safi and Yvetta remained cordial when meeting at family gatherings; everyone seemed to make a collective sigh of relief to have the ugly rift in the family healed.

Yvetta was for the first time enjoying being welcomed into the bosom of her family with her partner, belonging was a new experience, one she found she loved.

The Brooklyn Gallery was a great success, the subsequent shows had caused further interest, and there was a steady stream of people through the gallery: an objective she had achieved beyond her wildest dreams. She was back on her feet again – and then some. She was flying. The prints from all three galleries were now on sale, and were themselves flying out of the door to the younger set, who could not afford to buy the original works. The cooperation between the three galleries was beneficial to all three people who managed them. Things were harmonious, seemingly for the first time.

Yvetta was given more leeway now that the gallery started paying for itself; the investment made by the Rubicov family was starting to pay off handsomely. All were happy, or so it seemed to Safi, who still harboured doubts since she had seen that man in Serendipity, it had continued to bug her, whenever out on the street or in stores, and certainly when she was at restaurants, she kept her eyes peeled in case she spotted him again. She needed to put her nagging suspicions to rest.

March had swung by and they were attending another Rubicov family gathering to celebrate Anna's 70th. This time the family decamped to Mika's new mansion on Jupiter Island, where Mika had bought a new property larger and more lavish than the first.

This one had its own helicopter pad, its own private beach, not to mention the 8ft natural coral tropical fish tanks on either wall, as one walked through to the vast foyer. A curved marble stair-case with a double-height ceiling, and stained-glass dome. It was all breathtakingly spectacular.

Mika had not held back, allowing his natural exuberance and epicurean tastes for design art and glamour to shine through. It was all a little too tasteful, Safi decided, but she had to admit that Dan and Dax had excelled their brief, the vast Floridian villa ('chateau,' as Safi liked to refer to the orange distressed walls of the vast pillared structure). The interior was filled with a great mixture of old and new, with Russian artefacts perfectly placed in the mix.

The art works alone were worth a fortune; many pieces were from the Rubicov Brooklyn gallery, and she could not miss Janus's works (indeed, she was thrilled to see them given pride of place). Personal touches helped to make the rooms inviting; nothing appeared too precious, the place had a lived-in feel, quite a feat to accomplish with such a vast home.

The tennis court and swimming pools were surrounded by magnificent gardens. The chateau had 15 bedrooms, two cottages on the estate, and enough place for the family. The pool cabanas could sleep more. The estate had its own boat dock for Mika's super yacht, upon which they were to celebrate part of Anna's birthday, sailing up the coastal waters to a restaurant reserved for the occasion.

The family were suitably coiffed and dressed, the weather was cool for Florida, with a wonderful breeze coming off the ocean. Safi wore a long, light, silk, cerise Carolina Herrera dress with split sleeves to the cuff, showing her toned arms as the breeze caught and billowed the skirt, exposing her tanned legs.

To Safi's surprise, Yvetta wore a high-fashion, printed catsuit pantaloon with ankle cuff in a wild print with a low back, her tiny waist was cinched with a metallic gold belt and the jewellery was chunky turquoise stone, ethnic Gucci. She looked stunning, taller than usual in high strappy gold sandals. She noted Gina chose to wear a nude lace top tucked into a knee-length, flirty swing lace skirt, probably Leger. Standing on the deck of the boat leaning against the banisters she was able to admire the stunning couture gowns the Rubicov women were wearing; they were long limbed, refined, and beautiful.

Safi's folks were chatting away to Anna and Bernard; Fiona and Leonard had aged but were holding up well, her dad was in semi-retirement. Both were tanned, having just returned from Melbourne, where they stayed part of the year to be close to her brother Jake and his girlfriend, Bonny.

Safi felt proud of her achievements and she was sure her parents no longer felt disappointed in her choices. She had given them two beautiful grandchildren, but more than that she was capable of supporting not only herself but, if they ever needed it, she would never hesitate to look after them, too.

Yvetta disengaged herself from Gina. As she walked over to Safi, Safi noticed her hair had grown to below her shoulders and was combed off her face, bouncing in soft curls as she walked towards her. She looked like a movie star, the high cheek bones and chiselled, heart-shaped jaw line and green eyes were mesmerising. It was hard to believe she was the same crazy girl who had almost killed her several years ago.

Yvetta had shown without reservation she was capable of turning her life around. Not only her life, but also her character had changed out of all recognition. She was now less thin-skinned, and had even developed a sense of humour and become quite self-deprecating. Bernard, Anna's partner who had sent Yvetta to the clinic in Moscow, was completely astounded at the change. Yvetta appeared to hold no grudge against him; they never mentioned the episode, everyone preferred to forget it ever happened, and this obviously suited Yvetta.

As she strode towards Safi, she once again wondered about that young man she couldn't sweep from her mind; it kept popping up like a bad penny, catching her off-guard. So far, she had not mentioned it to anyone; now she wondered whether she could share her feelings about this person with Yvetta, or whether doing so would prove to be a huge mistake.

Yvetta pecked her lightly on the cheek. As the waiter passed, they both took fresh glasses of champagne to toast Anna. Mika was about to make an announcement. Sasha joined them against the railings. Surveying the scene in front of them, he turned to face Yvetta. As he stood in the centre, he grabbed both women round the waist as the photographer pointed his camera at them. This was an historic shot, something he never imagined happening, and he wanted it recorded.

The evening was joyous. Sasha's mother, in her element, looked incredible for 70. She had had some work done, as all Russian women of means did, did but it wasn't at all noticeable (he only knew because she had confided in Safi, still her preferred confidante when it came to matters that did not involve the immediate family).

The restaurant overlooked the bay. Their private party was set up outdoors, with fires burning in an outdoor cauldron. Candles lined the route to their long table with stunning flowers running the length of the table, separated with tea lights flickering in the breeze. The setting was perfect for the evening and the occasion. Anna did not want anything lavish, only family were invited with their partners and the children were included, young and old. It was, she said, the happiest night of her life to have her nearest and dearest there. It was a new Russian restaurant they owned, so the menu included all of Anna's favourites. Of course, the usual caviar over ice was the first course, with lots of vodka shots between each course. The laughter caused by speeches made by Sasha and Mika was infectious. Soon everyone was howling with laughter. It was a far cry from the sadness Anna had endured before they had left Moscow, and, worse still, after Sasha had been abducted.

Anna was a different woman; her family were all around her and together again. She had everything she ever wished for. Safi noticed how relaxed Anna was reclining in her seat happy to soak up the fun around her. Safi was tearfully thrilled for Anna. She knew now – had always known really, but now fully understood – that Yvetta added a great deal to that happiness.

Yet she also had an awful feeling of foreboding. It had been her experience that so much happiness never seemed to last; there was always disaster lurking around the corner – or was she being morbid? She furtively looked over at Yvetta, who seemed to be enjoying the evening as much as anyone else – laughing and chatting away to her aunts, cousins, and half-sister Marina – and engaging Anna in conversation, which Safi knew was a huge leap for both mother and daughter.

She wasn't the only one to notice. Others appeared to be very mindful not to interrupt their exchanges, allowing the conversation between them to flow.

Something had changed – everyone could tell. Yvetta had, without a doubt, turned a corner, and Gina, her new partner of almost five years, was a huge part of Yvetta's transformation. Gina was a girl with both feet firmly on the ground, and she gave Yvetta the stability she so needed. Still, Safi needed to share her anxiety, and the only person she wanted to share her premonition with was Yvetta. Why this was Safi had not fathomed, but she knew she wanted to protect her sister-in-law. God knows why, Safi thought, maybe for Anna's sake? She felt that, if the person she had seen over two months ago had indeed been Fritzi, Yvetta would be the one most in danger.

Of course, the truth was that they were all in danger, there was no other reason for Fritzi to enter the States and thus endanger herself anew. But Fritzi would put her life in danger to endanger others. She would stop at nothing to get revenge – she was devious, even violent, and she was good at it. She was a criminal, had been through their prison system. If she came into the USA she would have done so under false pretences. Safi wouldn't put it past Fritzi to enter illegally through Mexico; as everyone knew, Fritzi was capable of almost anything, a master at disguise and subterfuge. Someone who had no conscience and no shame.

She had felt a powerful familiarity with that person at Serendipity, a kind of déjà vu, not immediately but the moment the person left and for a long time afterwards, an eerie sensation, attracting the attention of the whole restaurant in the way he walked, with those long strides, head held high and hips thrust forward, a kind of 'see if I care' attitude rang a bell for Safi – a bell that hadn't stopped ringing since. And the way that person looked at Safi's table, not directly at her but a definite acknowledgement. A sideways glance. Her stomach flipped and, she wondered then but put the thought aside until she was in the cab on the way home. The whole episode replayed in her mind and she became certain, who else in the world had that kind of chutzpah and style, having others believe who she wanted them to see?

Yvetta, she was sure would be her target, Fritzi would see her as a deserter jilting her for a new lover, forgetting about her rotting in that Russian jail, she just had to warn her.

The morning after Anna's party everyone would be returning to their various homes around the United States; Safi was flying home with Sasha and the kids. Perhaps she would wait until they were back in Manhattan, she would make an appointment to see Yvetta at the Brooklyn Gallery; it would not be construed as odd since the two galleries now collaborated frequently.

She had her secretary make the appointment for the first Monday after they returned, always a quiet day at work. The only problem she had was that she had never seen this Serendipity person again, and, how would they have known she was going to be in that restaurant on that particular day at that particular time? All the same she was going to share her premonition, and they would take it from there.

Safi walked into the Gallery in Brooklyn unsure of her mission. Yvetta met her with warmth and obvious delight. Even though they never met on a one-to-one basis after her initial visit to the Brooklyn gallery, their gallery staff cooperated so Safi herself never felt the need to have any contact apart from the odd meetings at family homes, where they usually kept their distance.

They sat at the bar, each with a coffee, facing one another. Yvetta tried light chatter. She immediately sensed something was bothering Safi and allowed her to open the conversation.

Safi felt there was only one way to broach the subject, and that was to repeat the scene in the restaurant a few months back and allow Yvetta to draw her own conclusions. Halfway through the story, Yvetta's hand shot up to her mouth.

'Oh my God, it's Fritzi. It had to be, no one else could create such an impression, and you felt it – you *still* feel it. Why else would you be here? Have you told Sasha and Janus? You must tell them! *We* must! She will harm all of us, I am sure of that.'

'No, I haven't told anyone. I have come to you because you know her the best, and I wanted to make sure you felt the same way I did. My only reservation is how would she know where I would be that day, and why hasn't she shown herself again?'

Yvetta snorted, and her warm and pleasant expression had been replaced by a frightened one that more closely resembled the Yvetta of old. She was sitting upright and her left hand shook slightly. With alarm Safi noted the manic motions of the coffee cup. 'None of that is a problem for Fritzi, she is a master strategist, and if she wants to know something, she has her ways of finding it out.'

'So why do you think we haven't seen her again?'

'She plans her attacks meticulously, to the last detail. We will all have been under surveillance. I am convinced it's her, but what I am not sure of is why I have not seen her in one of her guises. Of all the people who would recognize her in any disguise, it should be me.'

They sat silently. For quite some time neither spoke.

'Perhaps she has been observing us from a safe distance,' Safi said after a long moment of thought. 'That's why you haven't seen her, she wouldn't take the chance of you recognising her. Then the game would be up. It would all be over for her. She only has one shot at this, if you think about it. She thought I wouldn't recognise her, but I had quite a lot to do with her when I needed information about Sasha's disappearance. I visited her in jail quite a few times, she used seductive, sexual innuendo and charismatic smarts to throw me off-balance, but I was pretty tough. She never unnerved me then, but she was behind bars, it's quite different now.'

The Windhoek episode came to mind, but she wasn't going to let Yvetta know they had been spying on her; it would be a huge mistake, that part of her life was over, yet Fritzi always seemed to turn up when least expected.

Safi had been so absorbed in her own thoughts, she had not noticed Yvetta, who was whiter than a sheet.

'Are you alright? You are very pale.'

'I'm not sure,' she said, and her voice now was low and grave. An echo of the old Yvetta, full of anxiety, resignation, regret. 'I suddenly feel quite ill, my stomach is in a knot. Luckily, I am seeing my therapist this evening. This whole thing is doing my head in. I am not sure how I am going to cope with all of this, to be honest.'

She glanced at Safi. 'I can be honest with you, Safi, now – I know that. I never understood why my mother confided in you so easily and so much. I always envied that aspect of your relationship, I'm embarrassed to admit. But now I understand it. You are a good person, a good listener. Compassionate. And smart, too. You don't judge – unless you absolutely have to, of course.' Her words were soft, but still, she did not smile. 'I really don't know how to cope with this new development. Maybe I should go away for a while?'

Yvetta was beginning to panic. Her face was still pale, her hands continued to shake though the coffee (a bad idea, in retrospect) was long finished. Her whole body seemed to shake now, her anxiety level high. Safi reflected that perhaps it was a mistake to have taken her into her confidence; she may not be strong enough to withstand her old lover's overpowering personality. The last thing anyone needed was for Yvetta to revert to her former self. Still, Safi reassured herself, it was the right thing to do to warn Yvetta? Or was it? She was beginning to doubt herself.

'Let's not jump the gun, Yvetta,' Safi said, trying to keep the quiver out of her own voice, 'we need to keep our heads and work together, don't you think?'

She shook her head in agreement, yet her eyes told a different story. Her body language had become introverted, it was as though she was regressing, reverting to her old self right in front of Safi. It was the opposite of an evolution, it was a deterioration, an erasure of a better self. Safi noticed she was visibly shaking. She had never touched Yvetta but how could she leave her this way. She had to do something.

'Yvetta,' Safi said, trying to keep her voice strong, trying to put a good spin on a bad situation, and, above all else, trying not to reveal her own fear to Yvetta, to play her anxiety down, 'why don't you come home with me, and we will tell Sasha what we both surmise. We can then plan how to protect ourselves, how to move forward in the event this is true. Janus might be able to check, through his contacts in Russia, whether she is still in that prison. If we have that confirmation we will know, what do you think? What we need now is solid information, not anxiety and supposition.'

She shook her head dejectedly, moving to collect her things. James was in his office, he would deal with everything. She dialled up to let him know she was leaving for the day on an urgent matter.

Sasha sat in shock listening to Safi retell the story. He was aghast to see his sister and Safi collaborating, not sure he understood why Safi had chosen to break her suspicions of Fritzi to Yvetta, seeing his sister in his home invited by his wife was in itself unreal. And coping with the news that Fritzi might have come back to haunt them was unbelievable; she had been sent to jail for far longer than six years, which in itself was chicken feed. The Russian system did not work that way; if she had managed to escape, they would know soon enough.

The wheels were put in motion to find whether they were imagining the person to be Fritzi but he knew better than to doubt Safi's powers of recognition, or Yvetta's certainty; if anyone knew Fritzi, she did.

'Well, hopefully we will know within a few hours, if not tomorrow,' Sasha assured the two women, 'until then there isn't much any of us can do. Turning to his sister, he tried to keep his tone calm, even as he suddenly suspected the worst about Fritzi. How are you coping, Yvetta? I imagine Fritzi will know by now you have a new partner. I think you better warn Gina and DuPont. None of us will be immune from an attack of some kind, its best we are all on our guard. When we have sufficient evidence that she is no longer in jail we will get Janus involved and listen to what he suggests.'

Yvetta left for her appointment. On her way she called Gina, who was working late that evening. Yvetta had moved her appointment to an earlier spot with her therapist, and would go onto DuPont's offices after.

Sasha had insisted on sending her with a driver and security guard who would remain until she was dropped off at home.

They decided it was best for Yvetta to inform Gina and DuPont of their suspicions. Sasha had suggested Yvetta should no longer travel by public transport. It was arranged for her to have security while everything was up in the air. But Sasha needn't have worried; Yvetta was not arguing. Obviously she no longer wanted anything to do with Fritzi. At long last, Sasha thought. This was the proof the family had been looking for that she really had turned a page; there could be no doubt now that she was a new, improved, reformed Yvetta. She accepted being ferried to and from work. It was a welcome change to have her accept his brotherly concern for her safety. Life had changed for all of the Rubicovs. No one needed the additional anxiety. They had all been through quite enough, especially himself and Yvetta, caused by Fritzi. She would have to be stopped before she was able to wreak havoc once again.

The Russian police were taking their time to get back to Sasha: why, he had no idea. Surely they would know if Fritzi was no longer in their system. Russia had changed, but the prison system remained pretty antiquated. Not wanting to wait any longer, Sasha pulled his weight, calling the head of the elite police in Moscow. After Sasha had finally been released from captivity, he had developed a camaraderie with Inspector Ivanov. The Rubicovs had given Ivanov more than a little kudos with his superiors, the Russians' information about the rebels had given them the element of surprise, resulting in a successful sting.

Ivanov was alarmed at his suspicions about Fritzi's escape: how could such a thing occur; something had gone very wrong if she had managed to escape from jail and, leave Russia without causing alarm in the prison system. The whole thing smelled of corruption.

Ivanov did not know whether he would be able to extract the information as fast as Sasha needed it. He would have to investigate, it could take some time to get the truth; such corruption would probably be well-hidden within the system. He imagined no one would want to take responsibility for the escape of such a high-level prisoner; he suggested they operate their own security at the highest level.

On learning of Fritzi's escape, Janus arrived promptly in Manhattan. He had little interest in confirmation from the Russians, knowing he was unlikely to get an honest answer out of them and having decided if Safi thought it was Fritzi and Yvetta had little doubt than it was, in fact, Fritzi.

They needed to operate as if a positive sighting had been made, something he reiterated to Safi and Sasha.

Mika was the only person who doubted it was Fritzi and doubted she was capable of launching an attack on their family on her own, unless she did not care if she was caught. He doubted she would get away with whatever she might be planning, the whole scenario was unrealistic.

He suggested they decamp to Florida while Janus and Kolya, the only one who would be able to recognise her on sight, returned to work in Manhattan. The suggestion to decamp to Florida went down like a lead balloon. No one wanted to change their lifestyles; they were going to put a brave face on it and hope Kolya, Janus and his agency would be successful.

DuPont understood Yvetta's concern for Gina's safety. His solution was to send Gina to Paris for a while. The trip made practical sense as well: he needed some work done, and she could be useful remaining on to finish the job after he returned to New York. She could live with his family while there.

Neither women wanted to part (they had grown incredibly close, and the mere thought of losing each other was traumatic), but Yvetta knew it was the best solution.

Safi now had a shadow wherever she went, which she hated but had sadly become familiar with. She understood the need. When she went out, she couldn't help staring at every eccentric tall person she happened to spot; any tall guy or woman was instantly under suspicion. The gallery staff were handed photos of Fritzi with instructions to alert security even if in doubt, and on no account to attempt to approach or apprehend any of the public themselves.

An answer from Moscow was inconclusive. No one, it appeared, could pin down exactly where Fritzi had been sent. She had apparently been in a number of different prisons; to Ivanov's frustration they had lost track of her after the third move. He imagined it was a ruse to put them off any incriminating evidence of her disappearance. All the prisons were put on alert to find Fritzi in their jails. Ivanov did not have high hopes of ever finding out. The system would close ranks, she would vanish without a trace, perhaps even turn up 'dead.' He would not believe a word, and advised the family to remain on guard at all times.

Gina enjoyed travelling with DuPont; he was a fantastic raconteur and a minefield of information. She had been to London and Madrid, but never to Paris. This would be her first time and she was buzzing with excitement. DuPont's family were charming; their Paris flat in the 6th Adornment, right in the heart of Paris, was breathtakingly chic. Her FaceTime calls to Yvetta were overflowing with praise, even the Metro was so much nicer than in New York. She loved the Left Bank. They just had to spend time in Paris, she excitedly informed Yvetta, and her enthusiasm was infectious, it was the most romantic city ever. Gina imagined wandering the narrow, gorgeous, winding Parisian streets with Yvetta, streets full of history, surprises, and their own particular flavours. Well, the streets were certainly narrow compared to Manhattan, where every major street could be legitimately called Broadway.

'Oh, sorry, Yvetta, I know I am being self-absorbed,' Gina said in a hurried, apologetic, but still clearly excited manner, 'What's been happening? Any sightings yet?'

'None. The Russian system stinks, and they are all covering for one another; no one can find her.' Yvetta realised she was talking too fast, realised, too, how much she missed Gina. She wondered and worried that Gina was not missing her as much as she should; Paris could be very alluring, she knew that all too well; even more alluring than Manhattan in some ways. 'I can believe that. Really, Russia hasn't changed that much, still singing to the same old Communist tune. They pretend to the rest of the world that the country has changed completely, but that's all it is, pretend, make believe. You know that old expression, from Shakespeare, I think – the lady doth protest too much.' Yvetta suddenly thought about Fritzi again, about Fritzi's many schemes and dreams – and lies. Whole sentences without a shred of truth to them. Fritzi protesting. Yvetta believing everything – and nothing. Yvetta being cajoled, and deceived. Yvetta being lied to, and then lying to others. A vicious circle. A cruel world. And yet Gina lightened all of that, made the world seem a happier place, changed everything and for the better. 'I am missing you madly, but I am happy that you are safe. And in beautiful Paris no less, so you might as well have a good time. We will go to Paris together, I promise, maybe next summer, that's if my old lover doesn't catch up with me, who knows what's she's capable of.'

'Please don't say that Yvetta,' Gina said softly, uneased all of a sudden, even here in the City of Lights. 'It frightens the hell out of me, we need to grow old together, I love you.'

There was a pause in which Gina could tell Yvetta was struggling: she had never actually told Gina that she loved her, something she found hard to do.

'Me too, I miss you like hell,' finally came the stifled response.

That was all she was going to get, Gina knew. Still, it was pretty close, she wasn't going to make a fuss. Yvetta had enough on her plate, but Gina would raise the question back home, once this bloody cloak-and-dagger thing was over and done with.

Fritzi's supposed return had a serious knock-on effect. The whole Rubicov family had upped their security arrangements; the galleries had extra security, each building they inhabited had security placed in the foyers, and planted with the reception staff. No leaf was left unturned and a great deal of money was spent. The Rubicov building had its own security in place, including in the restaurant; they placed waiters with security training among its staff. The memory of the Moscow restaurant skirmish, which Fritzi planned, came to mind, amongst other attacks on their family, both in Moscow and London; they needed to be on alert to avoid any other attempts.

No one knew where or when Fritzi would strike. If it was indeed Fritzi, all they knew was that she would eventually do something. Safi decided she was going continue her daily life, as did Sasha and Yvetta. DuPont was nervous; he had suffered from Fritzi's devious interference with his business on previous occasions. Most of all, he did not want to be dragged into the Rubicov fight with Fritzi yet again.

Her ingenious, twisted mind would no doubt catch them all on the hop, he just hoped the Rubicovs would not be harmed in any way. For the first time in their long relationship, life for Sasha and Safi had become normal.

Yvetta had made a miraculous recovery. DuPont felt Gina should remain in Paris. He was able to use her skills there, and it made little difference to him if she was not in New York. His wife enjoyed Gina's company, commenting on how friendly and grateful the American girl was. Their daughter was now married and settled, all the senior DuPonts hoped for was a grandchild. Things were chugging along nicely, no one needed any unnecessary upheaval. The sooner Fritzi was put out of action, the happier everyone involved would be. The endless threat to all of them was becoming tiresome, he would even say old hat, an English expression he enjoyed using, but, like it or not, they had all become victims, suspended in nowhereland waiting for her next move.

DuPont figured out that Fritzi had allowed Safi to see her, knowing it may take a while before the penny dropped. Even if she thought better of it, the seed would have been planted. She had started the ball rolling by letting them know she was in town and watching. Fritzi had the upper hand, they in turn were at her mercy and he knew it may take months before she made her move, an unnerving prospect for the Rubicovs – and, indeed, for him. He suspected she may know many people in New York, people who no doubt thought she was sexy and charming and had no idea what she was capable of, and no desire to report any aspect of her life to the authorities. She could no doubt afford to float around Manhattan for a good long time. Or, rather, a bad long time. He would do everything in his power to help, he had grown to love and admire Safi over the years, valued her friendship more than anyone he knew, and did not want to see her life turned upside down again. To endure more than she already had would be inhuman, even impossible.

In many ways, the Safi he knew today was still the young, charming, headstrong Safi he had met all of those years ago – only better. Safi had kept her head and feet firmly on the ground, an admirable characteristic in his book. Many in her situation would have thrown in the towel and become a lady of leisure, but that wasn't Safi's style, or the Rubicov work ethic. And besides, she had gone from being a newbie in the art world to one of Manhattan's most respected and buzzed-about gallerists.

Sasha, Safi and Yvetta met Janus for an early morning breakfast at their home. Janus wanted to outline his plan to set a trap for Fritzi, one she may not be able to ignore, judging by her vanity and ego, driven no doubt by self-belief to outsmart everyone.

They wanted Yvetta to hang around in the gay bars; all the girls she took up with at the bars would be highly trained to combat any attack on her. Janus was convinced she would find it almost impossible not to show herself, perhaps even to try pick Yvetta up herself, in a disguise she may believe foolproof from recognition. She was, after all, a superb actress and chameleon, even her adversaries could attest to that.

At first Yvetta balked at the suggestion, not sure whether she was strong enough. Fritzi had always been in control in their relationship, and Yvetta had always felt powerless with Fritzi allowing her to make all decisions. Power was Fritzi's addiction and aphrodisiac, what she craved most in the world.

So far, she had not ventured far from the gallery or her apartment, keeping her time filled with work. Talking to Gina about a planned visit to Paris as soon as this sting (which she secretly believed Fritzi would never fall for) was over.

'How will I recognise these agents when I arrive at the bar?' she asked Janus.

'Not a problem. I will supply a photo of each woman, what they will be wearing. You will have it on your cell phone, which you will be able to double-check once inside the bar.'

'How long will I have to do this for?'

'If we're in luck, not long. She probably hangs out at the bars close to your area. We have scoured them but have not picked up any sign. If she gets word, you are hanging out in the bars, we are sure she will show up.'

'So, you do not think she is working alone?'

'She has more than likely made contact with her acquaintances from prison, and perhaps others. The people she worked for won't touch her with a bargepole any longer. The sting in Switzerland and Lichtenstein would have sent them running for cover.'

'Fritzi has enough money,' Yvetta offered, 'she doesn't need to work for anyone, she loved the cloak-and-dagger stuff they were involved with. The money wasn't her main objective. Only when that huge sum suddenly turned up in her Swiss account, she had to find out who could have wired it to her private account without her knowledge. That was a mistake, she thought it was the syndicate setting her up for a fall.'

Janus did not want to divulge their involvement in this plot. Instead, he shook his head as if hearing this for the first time, 'Should we begin tonight,' he said quickly. 'I have three agents ready to roll. Don't worry, it won't be obvious. They will invite you to join them at their table for a drink, then all you have to do is flirt with them, then wait to see if anyone approaches you, or if you notice anyone interested in your table.'

'What do I do if someone does approach the table or I notice anything?'

'Absolutely nothing. At that point, the agents will take over.'

'You will move on to two other bars with the agents, staying for an hour or so in each.'

Before she had time to express any second thoughts, she found herself agreeing to the plan.

Yvetta dressed in her slinkiest jeans and over-the-knee boots with a sheer blouse and her Burberry fur-trimmed denim jacket.

Her anxiety was high but she held her nerve, else she would turn and run. She had no desire to come face-to-face with her old lover. The first bar was at the end of her block, and mostly gays hung out here. At a table facing the entrance she noticed three women waving at her to join them. Pretending she was meeting friends (Yvetta could act, too; Fritzi had not trained her all of those years for nothing), she made her way through the crowd and over to their table. She recognised them immediately from the cell phone pictures. Joan hugged her, and the other women leaned over to greet her with friendly, touchy-feely hugs and kisses. Yvetta thought these women looked pretty ordinary, attractive but not what she expected, hardly tough enough to take on her tiny frame, but Fritzi was six feet tall.

The hour went without incident, and by 10pm they made their way to the next bar. The woman all stood to leave together. As they made their way to the main exit, Yvetta noticed a person seated at the far end of the bar near the sliding glass doors, opening to a small garden patio. The women followed Yvetta's gaze, not making their interest obvious. One of the agents engaged the barman, while another made as if to use the bathroom; the third remained with Yvetta, just inside the entrance lobby close to the bar.

As she passed the woman at the far end of the bar, she took a photo with a hidden camera. No one noticed the woman leaving, but she was not at the bar by the time the agent returned to join them.

The second bar went without incident. Yvetta, by now used to the setup, sipped at the wine, taking in the scene. Hanging out at bars wasn't something she had ever got into, but it wasn't boring, either, at least not yet. Once her eyes focused in the dim light she noticed the same tall girl hanging out with some tattooed woman in a biker jacket. She pointed it out to one of the agents.

'Well spotted,' the agent replied brightly. 'You go, Annie, check them out.'

'Should I engage them in conversation?' Annie asked.

'Play it by ear. Drop something, then engage them casually, see how it goes.'

Annie sauntered over, making her way past the bar close to where the group of tattooed females were chatting. As she closed in, she dropped her purse, and leaned down to retrieve it. But the tall one they had seen at the first bar beat her to it, handing the purse to her.

They could see the exchange, but Annie did not hang around.

'What the fuck is she up to? That was a perfect opportunity to chat to those bitches.'

Annie slowly made her way back to their table, threading through the crowd towards them; as she approached, she shook her head,

'Not our target, they are all German, I think – foreign anyhow.'

Yvetta gasped. 'What are you talking about? Fritzi is German. You haven't been very well briefed, have you?'

The three agents stared at Yvetta. 'Damn.'

'This is a waste of my time. I am going home.'

'Hold on a moment. We know she is German, but Annie here was the replacement by another agent at short notice, our mistake for not giving her all the info.'

Yvetta, not impressed, remained adamant she wanted to go home.

'Hold on,' the agent said quickly, 'now I will check them out on my way to the bathroom and engage them on some level. Now that Annie's purse was handed to her by the tall one, I have a reason to say thanks, right?'

Yvetta was doubtful, and not only of the strategy, but of the whole operation, after such a profound and unprofessional mistake. Unless the agents weren't telling her something – but what? She knew, too, that Fritzi would gobble these stupid agents up and spit them out. They weren't smart enough to do battle with someone like Fritzi, that was for sure. They were pygmies compared to her abilities in the field of stakeouts and outsmarting the authorities.

They watched as Brandy made her way towards the bathroom, taking a detour past the group of tattooed females downing Heineken from bottles.

Brandy touched the tall woman's sleeve as she spun round to face her. Brandy could be seen talking to her, then she was offered a bottle of beer. Accepting, and now holding the beer in her right hand, she remained there chatting, obviously enjoying their company as her head fell back laughing at whatever they were saying.

Another agent decided to check out the scene. Yvetta watched the tall woman in the group, looking out for any signs of body recognition. Fritzi had certain ticks: she would often touch her mouth with her forefinger, a suggestive stance when engaging someone in conversation; or she would lean in close, taking up (or, perhaps, taking over; with her lust for dominance) their personal space. But Yvetta noticed none of these, or any of the others she had become familiar with over the years.

Annie joined the group, as if to retrieve her friend. That was when Yvetta noticed the tall woman turn around, hand on lips, acknowledging their table, at the very moment that Annie pointed out they were about to move on to the next pub.

A cold shiver ran down Yvetta's spine, dismissing the stance as a mere coincidence, her heart rate slowly returning to normal, concealing her rapid breathing and her look of fright behind her vodka drink. The woman in question did not resemble Fritzi, yet no two people could have that habit, it had to be her. Yvetta's head was a whirlwind. The woman's look in their direction had been fleeting, disinterested (or was that calculated disinterest? the illusion of indifference). Yvetta felt unsure and deeply nervous. She would wait to hear what the agents had to report. There had been no sign of recognition at seeing Yvetta, the woman behaved like a stranger would have. So maybe that is exactly what she was, a stranger.

As soon as the agents returned to their table, Yvetta became agitated, demanding to know every word of the conversation.

'Well, what happened?' Yvetta said hurriedly, her fingers still trembling around her glass. 'I want to hear absolutely everything that tall woman said, every word. And not just what she said, but how she said it, and how she looked at you.' She realised that she sounded obsessive, but could not help herself. More than anything, perhaps, she was reverting to the bullying old Yvetta. 'Every little detail, don't leave anything out. You may have noticed in her body language.'

The three agents exchanged a glance.

'Yes, they are German,' Joan said slowly, 'but speak English perfectly. None are gay, all have husbands, but happen to be staying in the area. The tall one showed me photos of her family living in Stuttgart. Not our target,' she concluded with an almost aggressive air of finality.

But Yvetta was not convinced.

'You do have a photo of her, right?' Yvetta said, trying to control the anxiety in her voice, her face. 'You got one when we saw her at the first bar.'

'I have dispatched it on to the agency,' Joan said, and she seemed all of a sudden to be the most senior agent of the bunch, 'they have not come back to us yet.'

The third bar was small in comparison, and it was easy to spot everyone in it. The bar was long and narrow. Yvetta had no intention of remaining any longer. It was late now, after 11 and she wanted to go home. This new, domesticated, genteel Yvetta liked an early night and a lot of rest.

A man walked in, tall, elegant, not someone one would see in a bar, certainly not a bar like this one. He leaned with his back towards the bar, surveying the scene. Yvetta noticed his elegant hands as he accepted the tall champagne flute from the barman. He remained with his back to the bar, crossing his legs at the ankle, something Fritzi would do, as he sipped. His eyes settled on their table, but the women gathered around it did not appear to interest him all that much. Noticing he was being observed, a flicker of a smile crossed his face. Turning, he put the flute down on the bar, had a word with the barman, then in a slow, leisurely, unhurried fashion he strode out of the bar. But, when he was in their eyeline for the final time, a finger came up to his lips fleetingly and he was gone.

'Oh my God, Jesus Christ,' Yvetta said, unable to contain herself now, 'that is the same person we saw in all three bars. That was Fritzi, you have absolutely no chance of catching her, she is far too clever for any of you. Shit, shit shit. I am dead, we are all going to die. Fritzi has just let me know she is here.'

The agents looked shaken at Yvetta's outburst, disbelieving, even. After all, they had been briefed on Yvetta, too: she wasn't exactly the most stable person. Were the Russian and the German working once again in cahoots, perhaps? Or was this all an elaborate ruse to get Yvetta some much-needed attention? Was it all a game?

'How can you be sure it's the same person?' Annie asked.

'*How?*' Yvetta spat out. 'How you are asking me how?'

'Yes,' Annie asked slowly but not exactly kindly, 'I am asking you *how*, and please I know you are upset and all, but can you calm the fuck down.' It wasn't a question.

'Don't you dare speak to me like that, you stupid idiot,' old Yvetta suddenly said out of nowhere. 'I did not expect this of Janus to employ such brainless assholes.'

The agents stared at Yvetta. Brandy and Annie rose from the table.

'Okay, you're on your own, Maggie, we are not taking any more of this rich bitch's tantrums.'

Yvetta was visibly shaking. Maggie was the only one employed by Janus, the two who had walked were doing Maggie a favour: a huge mistake, she now realised, to bring them along. They were pretty green behind the ears, rookies from the local police force doing her a favour.

Maggie put her hand over Yvetta's.

'Sorry about that. Friends from the local precinct doing me a favour on their night off. Huge mistake on my part. Maybe they didn't want to be here after all. I apologise for the way they spoke to you. If that woman is the same person, we are sure dealing with the best in the field. An expert at subterfuge, one hell of a ballsy operator for sure. Now how do you want to play this?'

Yvetta nodded, then she called Sasha on her cell.

The agent received a text at the same time from Janus' agency.

'A positive ID had been made, it was the same person.'

She was shocked, the three women were visibly different in every way

Only someone who knew her intimately would be able to tell; it seemed likely she wanted Yvetta to recognise her, she had given her a signal of some sort. And Yvetta had passed the test.

'Kolya will pick us up, Janus wants to speak with you,' Maggie said.

They sat in silence until Kolya walked in, Yvetta speaking in Russian told him she wanted him to remain with her until Fritzi was caught; he was the only one who knew her well enough to understand the danger she faced.

Kolya knew better than to argue with Yvetta; he had been with the Rubicovs a long time, had seen some things he'd rather not remember, and others he wouldn't repeat to his best friend. They were a complicated family, but he would die for them if he had to. They were the closest thing he had to a family, and they were very, very good to him. He lived like a king compared to his old life. He loved America, the land of the free. Russia had a long way to go, even the ordinary people here lived like rich people: they complained, but they had it all. The truth was that no one was ever satisfied, but Kolya was more satisfied with his life than he'd ever been, living in sunny Florida, a truly beautiful place.

Yvetta, on the other hand, was exhausted; all she wanted to do was cry, her old life flashing before her once again. The life she thought she had overcome – its shame, its many fears – seemed to have returned to stalk her, to gloat and remind her daily of her past self, her past sins. She felt punished, and – worse – terrified. She knew what she had to lose: happiness, contentedness, stability, even love. She had her life back, and it was better, and yes, she loved Gina, truly, and she wasn't about to let Fritzi take all that away from her; she would do anything to keep them all safe.

They were waiting for them: Mika, Sasha, and Janus. Safi had retired for the night. They were in Sasha's office, a comfortable room filled with books and Russian artwork, his private place and unlike the rest of his home; his Russian roots were proudly on show everywhere. His desk displayed a huge framed photograph of Alexi, sitting behind his own desk, smiling with a huge Cuban cigar. Yvetta wished she could reach out and touch him; a deep sadness clutched her heart. Her father had died and she hadn't even been at his funeral. How much strife had she given him? And how much guilt did she now have to bear? Had she ruined his life? No, her father was eternally (and sometimes cheerfully) at war – with the establishment, with his rivals, with his own family even. But she had certainly made his hard life even harder. And for that she felt great pain.

The other photos were of their childhood in Russia: the long, bright summers shared space with surprisingly bright photographs of dark, wintry days. But even here the family always seemed happy, young, attractive, sitting together, their child smiles mirroring their father's larger, broader, more all-encompassing, adult smile.

Sasha kept his Russian photos on one side of the desk, and his present life with Safi on the other. Two sides, two separate lives perhaps. The only sign of the family union was his engagement party; so much had happened since that day. Had Safi known what the future held, she might have run for her life, Yvetta thought, but she doubted that somehow; Safi was a loyal, kind person, she saw that now – regrettably late, true, but she was just glad that they had finally reunited and that Yvetta was part of the family again at last.

Between and behind the fear and the guilt there was enormous gratitude and warmth. Yvetta felt deeply ashamed of her treatment of her English sister-in-law, who she had grown very fond of. Who would ever have believed that possible? Grateful once more that her life had changed out of all proportion, she hugged herself and relived her father's smile. He was smiling at her, she decided, from up above. He was proud of her. And for her part, she was proud of herself. Pulling away from the photos on the desk, she settled down to concentrate on the debriefing.

Janus fired question after question at Bonny, covering the minute details. He remained disapprovingly silent when she mentioned the rookie policewoman on the mission. His thin face became thinner still, and his eyes were unusually cold. He was obviously displeased.

He turned to Yvetta and said in a taut voice, 'When did you realise it could be Fritzi?'

'Well,' Yvetta said, feeling immediately uncomfortable under this withering stare, 'in the first bar she was noticeable because of her height and slenderness, but there were no other similarities. She had long dark hair there. I did notice her all the same. In the second bar she had on a biker's jacket, her hair was up in a ponytail. She wasn't trying to hide, but she was the same woman we saw in the first bar, on purpose, I guess, not to throw us off the scent.' Yvetta finally lowered her gaze, wiped her brow. Only then did she speak again. 'She wanted us to believe that she was bar-hopping, had met friends, was perhaps a tourist. In other words, she had another identity, or persona, worked out, and she wanted nothing to disturb that. In the third bar she was a man, elegantly dressed, casual, no socks, yet very bisexual in a feminine way. She was always brilliant at crossdressing to suit her persona, she had a short grey brush-cut, and a huge diamond stud in one ear.'

They did not interrupt Yvetta, she was in a world of her own, recalling every detail.

'I noticed she was the same person in the second bar, and when I heard she was German from that rookie policewoman I became suspicious, so I watched her body language. There was nothing at first, but then she put her finger to her lips, the way she does when she is flirting, being sensual, drawing you into her world. Still, I wasn't one hundred percent certain. And then she leaned in close to the policewoman. Well, that triggered something in me. Fritzi always liked to dominate one's personal space, to be the centre of attention the centre of anyone's world. It was becoming too much of a coincidence. In the third bar we noticed this elegant man sauntering past us in a nonchalant way, as if he owned the place but simultaneously did not belong. He leaned with his back against the bar, champagne flute in hand, surveying the scene, looking completely out of place. As he sauntered outside, he looked straight at me, as if he knew me, as if we had a secret to share, and his finger went to his lips. It was Fritzi alright. She was sending me a message loud and clearly, that it was her. She wanted me to know it was her!'

Janus nodded and said, 'Safi noticed that he had a huge diamond stud in one ear when she first saw him at Serendipity. She was sending a message, she wants us to know.' His eyes were still glinting but his voice seemed more relaxed now. Still, Yvetta noticed, he did not smile once. 'Yvetta is right, otherwise why wear the same disguise, use the same body language discreetly, and indicate she has seen you, make herself known to you?'

'She is playing a cat-and-mouse game,' Mika said firmly, 'but what are her intentions? She has been in a jail for the last several years. We have no idea where she has been since out of jail, or indeed how long she has been out – until she turned up here, that is. My guess is that she has been doing her homework. She was always fastidious, right?' He was looking at Yvetta now. 'She knows exactly what her game plan is, and she is letting us know – letting us in on her plan, not completely, but just enough to warn us, to unnerve us – giving us fair warning, but why?'

'Or about what?' Sasha said, agreeing with Mika

'I agree, unless we are able to apprehend her before she strikes, there is very little we can do,' Yvetta said, her words betraying how tired she suddenly felt. Tired of Fritzi, of these games, of the implicit danger – of everything. She felt the game was up, Fritzi would make her move now, she had shown she has the upper hand. Perhaps no one really knew Fritzi, but certainly Yvetta knew her better than anyone else.

'Janus, I know Fritzi intimately, she is no one's fool. I guess you realise there isn't a chance in hell that she will show herself again. I believe her next move will be to strike. We won't even know she is around. It's the worst situation any of us could be in, we are sitting ducks.'

Janus didn't like the odds, either: Manhattan was small, yet she could be anywhere and they would not know who she was at any given time. All the family had to go on was someone tall, and there were thousands of tall people around. She changed from male to female, from fat to thin, wore eyeglasses, false teeth, facial hair, and wigs. She changed with such ease and aplomb – and with such enjoyment.

If it was a game, she was clearly the winner and she knew it, and she seemed to want to play over and over. In one evening, she had changed three times, and each transformation had fooled them all, until she chose to show her disguise to the person who knew her best. Then the veneer cracked – or did it? Had she slipped up, or was this part of the plan, too.

'The third bar,' Janus said, 'was it crowded when you noticed the man at the bar?'

'Yes, there was only standing room left, and Fritzi found a spot where she could observe us. How long she had been there is anyone's guess. We only noticed her because she was the only person with her back to the bar. We only realised it was the man we noticed walking past when he faced away from the bar. In other words, she wanted us to notice her!'

'When you realised it was Fritzi, what did the policewoman Maggie do?'

'Well, she rushed after, but by the time Maggie squeezed past everyone, this mysterious person had disappeared, vanished into thin air.'

'Yes, Maggie told me she ran to the corner, hoping to catch sight. She surveyed the whole area for 10 minutes but concluded she had missed her.'

'Lucky for me, she did not double back,' Yvetta said. 'I would not have put it past her. If she had realised Maggie was no longer with me, she might have. I would have had little option but to go with her' The thought made Yvetta shiver.

Janus could tell Yvetta was exhausted. He made his voice softer.

'She probably calculated there wouldn't be enough time to double back. Besides,' he said with a semblance of warmth, giving Fritzi the benefit of the doubt, 'I am sure you would have kicked up a mighty stink.' He paused to survey a room full of exhausted faces. It was not just Yvetta, everyone seemed tired.

'Right,' Janus said, 'we will reconvene here tomorrow, once I have spoken with the agency. I presume you are staying over here, Yvetta, it might be the safer option.'

She shook her head in agreement and made her way to the guest room, feeling dispirited. They were up against a master operator, and, until she made her move, there was almost nothing they could do. She knew almost everything about them at this point. And what did they now know about her? Almost nothing.

Two weeks after the bar sighting, strange things started occurring. A bag of putrid entrails was left at the entrance to the Manhattan Gallery one chilly Thursday morning. Yvetta found another at the Brooklyn Gallery. Another parcel had been dropped off at the reception of the gallery, too. Another parcel had been left at Sasha's home, and at Yvetta's home they found a package waiting, addressed to Yvetta.

Janus's men collected all five packages: the last three had not been opened, but they all contained the same disgusting entrails. No message was ever attached, but it was clearly a dire warning to the Rubicovs of what was to come. She was planning some violence of some kind, and it wasn't going to be pretty when it happened. She wanted them all dead, or badly injured. A messy revenge on people she loathed more than she valued her own freedom, and escape from a Russian hellhole.

Janus' agency had been in contact with their people on the ground in Moscow and further afield in Russia, hoping to find out how Fritzi had managed to escape a secure prison in one of the most inhospitable areas of Russia.

This was Janus's third assignment for the Rubicov family: each had involved threats of violence, either from outside or within the family; he wondered whether Safi could deal with much more. Safi was stronger than most people, certainly, but she wasn't superhuman, and he knew she was more sensitive and fragile than many people knew. He truly felt for her and the whole family; there seemed always to be someone who wanted to harm them.

He would gladly lay his life down for Safi, take a bullet if he had to; there wasn't another woman he respected and loved more. It had almost destroyed him to let her go back to Sasha but he had to be honest with himself, he wasn't able to give her what she needed. Seeing her on weekends suited him, it was something only his physician knew about, that he had a non-existent sperm count, and a very low sex drive. He had long ago decided (and comforted himself with the information) that, once she found out the news, Safi would never have stayed with him. And he never wanted to find out, either.

Sasha had saved him from facing the inevitable truth, and from breaking her heart when he had to confront her with it, or regurgitating his excuse for not wanting to have kids. Safi had been the only woman he had ever considered marrying: it was a weak moment, a mad decision, in his otherwise ordered life. Sadly, it would never have worked, he had to let her go, the only solution that wouldn't ruin their friendship, something he never wanted to be without her. She remained a constant in his life and Alexander was his godchild, and he loved them both. Everyone saw him as a strong man, but he wasn't strong, or not entirely.

People had layers of intrigue, secrets, one reason why he had gone into the espionage game all of those years ago. Rarely was someone what they first appeared. He could live with his physical shortcomings, but not without love in his life, and Safi had given him that. And he would never, ever forget it, or stop loving her.

If the truth be known, it was the reason he had always shied away from woman who were attracted by his looks, an irony that he had them falling at his feet yet didn't have the power or ability to take advantage of their advances.

Safi had been different from all of those other women. She needed his help, which he was able to give. She had turned around his career, and for the first time in his life he had trusted a woman and trusted his ability to perform like a man, but it never lasted. She had never suspected it had been a struggle, or that if not for Viagra he would never have been able to perform like a proper, virile man, although he sure looked the part.

It was his secret to take to the grave. It had not bothered him, his life had been more than full. The agency gave him the adrenalin and excitement he needed, and his art gave him the spiritual fulfilment. Alexander came into his life when he most needed to have someone to love – a beautiful, entirely unconditional, and very special love – and, he had Safi to thank for that. He owed her more than she would ever be aware of.

This was the first time he felt vulnerable, perhaps he was too close to the problem. He was not supposed to care about his cases. And yet he did care, he cared enormously, it was more than another job.

Chapter 41

Mika wanted to transport his whole family to Florida. As far as he was concerned, they could spend the rest of their lives living in Villa Fort Knox. As Mika aged, he felt the need to envelope his family in a safety net, having them remain under his protection forever. Sadly, though, he knew this wasn't realistic. The Rubicov family had to continue with their lives, to work and play and socialise as usual, to be fully functioning people. Fritzi would have to be caught before she managed to do any more damage. He had not yet fathomed how they could beat her at her own game, but he would sure as hell try, she remained a formidable opponent for sure.

Cameras were installed on all of the Rubicov properties, but even if they caught Fritzi on camera, there was no lead to follow as yet. She had not opened a bank account or used credit cards, a tough thing to accomplish in the States. According to Yvetta, she had a safety deposit box in New York City, probably at Grand Central station in some locker, with enough money to live on for years, she had this safety net in every major city in the world.

Every hotel in Manhattan had been alerted to watch out for a tall, German-speaking woman or man. Many leads had turned up nothing; all of the computers had failed to make a positive iris identification.

The Rubicovs would have to wait for her to make the next move. Until then, the family had personal security wherever they went, and this would last, Mika had told them all, until Fritzi was stopped. This made her arrest even more urgent. Like it or not, the security would remain in place. Janus wasn't convinced the security was a safety net; the whole scenario gave him sleepless nights, he spent every spare hour going over Fritzi's methods, praying for a break. All Fritzi had to do was show the smallest crack in her armour, a weakness in her strategy. Fritzi was smart, sure, but perhaps not as smart as she thought she was. Her plot could not be fool-proof. They had to find that chink in her arsenal of tricks, that one loose thread that would unravel the entire garment. And they had to be ready when she became overconfident in her ability, sloppy in her arrogance to outwit them all.

There was no question she was playing with them, rubbing their noses in it, enjoying her vignettes of ingenious disguise, playing different characters but always leaving a calling card, a wink here, a tic there. She knew Yvetta would be familiar with these tics, these gestures, motions, personas, and set pieces. She would vanish into the crowd when it suited her to watch over them, always be one step ahead of them, alert and ever-calculating, learning their habits, getting to know them intimately without them being aware of her, above them, around them, like a leopard on a hill surveying what it would soon kill. It was frightening, they were her prey and she would strike when it suited her, the question was how would she choose to strike – and when. And who would she choose to strike: just one of the family, or more? And would she strike to injure or to kill? There were so many questions, so much uncertainty, so many variables, so much to process, and so much of it felt incomprehensible. And all the time the fear hung over everything.

He needed more information to work with – and there was no time. Or too much damn time, depending on how you looked at it. Their only hope was that she would fail in her mission to hurt the Rubicov family, who had escaped many hits on their family from different groups, including the Russian government covert but enormously damaging attacks on their companies. Fritzi had outwitted almost every one of them, they were not dealing with an amateur, but an expert at what she did.

With the help of international insurance companies, the agency's expertise had succeeded in trapping her. But now they were on their own, with nothing to work with. Manhattan was a small island, the agency was they hoped more familiar with its ways than Fritzi, the police and the authorities were perhaps their next step, she was in the US illegally, it would not hurt to have them on the lookout as well.

Dax and Dan were beside themselves with worry. They wanted Safi and Sasha to move to Rupert's home upstate. If Fritzi turned up it would be far easier for the police and Janus to trap her before she was able to catch them off-guard.

Janus had offered for them to move to his home upstate, but Safi and Sasha kindly rejected the offer. Safi had Art Americana opening in a week, anew exhibition and Yvetta's Brooklyn Gallery were liaising with the Moscow gallery for an upcoming exhibition showing only new Russian art. Neither wanted to be away from their work, or saw why they should upend their sanity and routines for Fritzi's schemes – wasn't that giving her what she wanted? Both wanted to live their lives normally; they had had too much turmoil for too long, and they were tired of it. Staff in both galleries were aware of the situation, the family had no choice but to brief them about the gallery being targeted, after the entrails had been left on the doorsteps, at which point Fritzi's threat became no longer just a distant nuisance but a criminal act being investigated by the authorities.

The police had been notified by Janus and were co-operating. Fritzi would notice the security had been stepped up, she no longer had it all her own way. The ante had been upped. Anna had returned to her villa in Le Cannes. Fritzi would not leave the States until she had made her point. And then, there was no guarantee she would be able to leave without being caught; she would be on all immigration and police databases. Even if she were to appear different, they had all her biometrics There was no way she would be able to enter or leave the States in any official way.

Sasha thought Fritzi might try to kidnap Yvetta. the relationship between the two women was very one-sided. Fritzi treated his sister as her property. Even though Sasha knew she cared for his sister, it had never been a healthy relationship; Fritzi manipulated Yvetta's illness to suit her own ends. Before Yvetta and Fritzi planned the attack on his family home and their mother, Fritzi completely monopolized and controlled the operation. Yvetta had become distant, more erratic in her behaviours. Fritzi never gave up on Yvetta, she had gone to extraordinary lengths, successfully kidnapping her from two institutions, one in the US and the other in Moscow.

When luring Fritzi into their sting, the insurance agencies had never recovered all the pilfered art, but they had managed to infiltrate the ring. He believed Fritzi would not want her former criminal contacts to know she was free; they would consider her a danger to their operations. She had more than likely used hired hands to do her dirty work. So far she had not shown her usual ingenious mastery, or creative flair; perhaps she had become rusty while in prison, or she wanted to strike without any chance of being caught, mix things up, upend expectations.

A month had come and gone without any other sign or sightings or sign of Fritzi stalking them. She had left no more unsavoury, frightening threats. Instead, the silence had become ominous, the uncertainty its own kind of punishment. Sasha did not feel comfortable with Safi or Yvetta relaxing their lifestyles. He was sure Fritzi was using the lull in activities to unnerve them, or to catch them off-guard, relaxing their diligence, making them easy prey. Nothing with Fritzi was ever an accident or unprepared. She was taunting them by doing nothing. He remembered that her planning was meticulous, she took her time doing everything that mattered, and never hurried anything unless she had to. She relished the build-up, then catching everyone off-guard before they had a clue something had gone down or changed without their knowledge.

He had an insight into her mindset: she was after Yvetta, he was surer of this every moment he thought about it. He thought about his own experience with Fritzi in Moscow; how she had masterminded Yvetta's escape from the clinic to the deserts of Namibia before anyone had realised, she was posing as a fake doctor from Montreal.

He recalled sitting right next to her in that office, almost being taken in by her act himself.

She had crossed over into Russia, even though she knew if she were caught, they would throw away the key or have her killed, but she had risked everything to free Sasha from the rebels before he was disposed of; she needed him in her plan to free his sister, and it had worked.

Not being able to contact his sister on her cell, Sasha called James at the Brooklyn gallery to ask if Yvetta was around. She might be working with one of the artists; he knew Safi never wanted to be disturbed when she was working in the gallery, setting up a show. Yvetta was probably the same.

'Hold on,' James said in his brisk, prompt, ever-professional voice, 'I will go and take a look and get back to you.'

After a minute James was back on the line, a little more breathless this time, his voice just a tad less smooth.

'She isn't in the gallery. Apparently, she has left for an appointment with Safi at the Manhattan gallery.'

'Did the security accompany her?' Sasha said, taking in this information.

James leaned over the open gallery to look 'I don't think so.' There was a note of concern in his voice now. 'I'm not sure how she managed to get out alone, but Yvetta's security detail is still sitting in his usual place.'

Sasha could not believe that Yvetta would be foolish enough to venture out on her own. He worried they were falling right into Fritzi's lap – or web. Fritzi no doubt hoped her long hiatus had made them careless. For his part, Sasha hoped she had given up in the face of all the private and police security, but he doubted any of that would bother Fritzi.

Sasha did not want to waste time trying to get anyone on the phone, discussing his premonition. He left with his own private security for the Manhattan gallery, wanting to make sure both Yvetta and Safi were safe. He entered the gallery, not even stopping to notice the new artwork that hung above the front desk, below the "Rubicov Gallery" written in elegant lettering.

The only person he noticed as he strode through to the back was an elderly man with a lot of facial hair, pamphlet in hand and deep in thought while examining one of the sculptures. As Sasha stepped behind the wall to enter the office, he peeked around the corner to take another look at the man, but he had now moved out of sight.

He found both women in the office studying the new Russian art on a computer screen that was almost as large as a television. Relieved, he threw himself down in the armchair opposite them.

'What's with you?' Yvetta asked in an exasperated tone.

'I think I know why Fritzi is here,' Sasha said, 'and that is only for you, Yvetta. Her other tactics are merely to throw us off her real objective. Think about it: she has gone to incredible lengths to help you escape from two very secure institutions. Why would she not want you back in her life? After all, you have said yourself she doesn't like losing, and she must feel as if she has lost you. She will want her revenge. It must infuriate her that you moved on while she was stuck in some hellhole in Russia. As far as she is concerned, you are her property, you belong only to her.'

Yvetta nodded. 'I know,' she said, 'that has already occurred to me, but she has disappeared. Perhaps she has given up now that the police are involved.'

'Stupid thought,' Sasha said, and his firm tone had a brotherly note of resolve. 'And to leave your gallery to come here without your security – not a good move. There is one thing I know for sure: she is waiting. Don't leave yourself so exposed again, ever, unless you want to be caught by that monster so please take more care in future.'

Yvetta did feel stupid – it was never a good feeling to be admonished by your brother, or anyone, really. Like Fritzi, she detested criticism or the idea that she was anything less than ideal. Still, she had come to accept her imperfections, and that was the beginning of her recovery, of becoming whole. True, she should have known better than leave the gallery alone, but she was sick of having a shadow wherever she went. Besides, she was about to fly off to Paris to be with Gina once the new exhibition went up. Fritzi, she knew, would not be able to follow her to Europe, and they would be safe there.

Turning to Safi, he said, 'More reason to be suspicious of everything and everyone. Do you know who that old man scuffling round in the gallery is, Safi?'

They all walked back into the gallery. There were four security men standing about. Safi assured them they were quite safe. The old man now had an elegant attractive grey-haired older black woman with him. The two of them were deep in conversation, unaware of their presence at the back of the gallery. They were a tall couple, which made Sasha uncomfortable all over again, suspicious and overprotective of his wife and sister. He examined the couple from head to toe. Right now everyone was a suspect.

An alarm sounded close by. The security guards in the gallery went to check outside. There had obviously been some incident nearby. This was not in itself unusual. Manhattan was never without a cacophony of fire engines roaring past, police sirens, ambulances blaring and honking their way down the streets. It was an everyday occurrence Sasha had never quite got used to, despite his many years in the city. The noise had always put him on edge and today wasn't any different.

The elderly couple had moved to the windows to observe the drama outside. Protected from within, they all moved to the windows to watch as the firemen tore into the building attached to the gallery. Sasha just hoped the smoke wouldn't affect the work. As they were watching, a policeman entered the gallery and ordered them out onto the street, for safety. Everyone within close range had been evacuated and were standing around on the pavement.

They allowed the couple in the gallery to exit first. Locking up behind them, they joined the rest of the throng outside. As New Yorkers do everyone was complaining, but took the proceedings in their stride; they had seen it all before.

Their security had surrounded them as they stood about on the opposite pavement. Sasha noted the elderly couple had vanished. Still, his mind kept returning to them for some reason. Something about them felt odd, but what? He couldn't say. He searched amongst the crowd, trying to spot them. But they had moved on, no doubt preferring to be away from the mayhem.

Their bodyguards were not happy with the situation, there were too many variables, too much movement, too much chaos, too many people, too much could go wrong at any moment. Crowd control was never an easy situation, especially not in an amplified moment like this. The guards hadn't been on the pavement five minutes when a scuffle broke out as one of the bodyguards, elbowed someone out of his way. The man, a burly, bearded fellow in his mid-fifties or thereabout, took a swing at the bodyguard and before anyone knew what was happening a fight was in progress. There were gasps from the crowd, radio static from the assorted police equipment, more noise. With Safi in tow, Sasha tried to duck the flying blows now reigning freely about them. As they fled from the crowd, Safi noticed Yvetta struggling. Being tiny she was finding it hard to push through the crowd. Safi thought she noticed a hand grab Yvetta from the back and yank her back into the crowd.

'Sasha,' Safi screamed amid the noise, 'someone just grabbed Yvetta and yanked her back into the crowd. It might have been the bodyguard.'

'Go into the coffee bar and wait for me,' Sasha shouted back. 'I need to make sure Yvetta is okay.'

Some semblance of order had ensued, he could tell the bodyguards were searching frantically for the three of them, towering above everyone around them.

'Have you seen Yvetta?' Sasha called out to the bodyguard 'Someone yanked her back into the crowd.'

He threw himself back onto the pavement; the crowd watching had doubled in size. It was a terrible situation to be in, and a perfect moment for Fritzi to grab Yvetta. He was frantic, scanning the crowd, struggling to see clearly in front of him. When he reached the other security guard, he gave instructions to question anyone who looked suspicious.

He stood in the road, feeling helpless, desperate, lost. The traffic had been halted; there were flames shooting out of the windows on the opposite side of the street. Several firemen were allowed close to the building. The rest of the fire crew were controlling the crowd, cordoning off areas too close to falling glass as the heat buckled the window frames.

The crowd were enthralled and ten-deep. If Yvetta had been dragged into the crowd on the pavement, there was no way she could step free without being seen. She must have been dragged into the road. Two blocks had been closed off; there was nowhere to go save for a coffee shop further down the road. But anyone leaving the pavement would have to fight their way through to the end of the block and cross the road. Everything was cordoned off for the fire engines, and now other emergency services were using every available space in the area to assist those who had suffered smoke inhalation or had been hit by flying debris.

Noticing a small blonde at a strange angle, Sasha leapt into the crowd, elbowing his way through a mass of flesh, pushing people as he made his way towards the spot where he had glimpsed his sister. He was convinced it was Yvetta. As he caught sight of her Burberry mac, he leaned into the crowd, grasping, struggling. Grabbing hold of the raincoat to stop whoever he thought it was pulling his sister by the hand. That's when he lost his balance as a hard object hit his head.

The forty-eight hours after Sasha had been shot were the toughest Safi had ever endured. Sasha lay in a hospital bed in NYU Langone Health on life support. The object that hit his head had entered his skull at close range. The surgeons were amazed the bullet had not shattered his skull, but as luck would have it (if one could call it luck), the tiny bullet had entered the back of his skull at a strange angle and gone straight, through hitting a person close by in the leg.

The bullet had injured part of his spinal cord; part of his skull had been damaged, but it was intact, thank God. The doctors didn't know when Sasha would come out of the coma or if he would ever be able to walk.

The family were flying in from all over the world, including Safi's parents to give support and be by Sasha's bedside at the neurological unit.

Yvetta was stricken with grief. Sasha had almost lost his life to save hers.

The old couple in the gallery had obviously been Fritzi and an accomplice. The black woman had been Fritzi; the old man had not been that old, and the facial hair was false. When Sasha had noticed Yvetta struggling, she was being held in a vice-like grip from behind by the old man, while Fritzi tried to work their way through the crowd. Thankfully, they were thwarted at every escape route by police who were pushing the crowd back. The bodyguards had noticed Yvetta at the exact moment Sasha had, and they had launched into the crowd to grab her almost simultaneously. When Sasha was shot, the bullet had hit the bodyguard in the shin as it flew through the back of Sasha's head. Due to the fire, the emergency services were close by and Sasha was rushed to hospital with the bodyguard in an ambulance.

Safi sat in the coffee shop unaware of the catastrophic events taking place outside. The bodyguards, with the police in tow, found her sitting in a café. A police officer knelt next to Safi, quietly breaking the news about Sasha.

The next few hours became a nightmare. She barely remembered the events that followed while she sat waiting for her husband to be brought out of surgery, trying to come to terms with what had happened. Everything was an awful blur.

The Rubicov family took care of Alexander and Amelia (or Amy as everyone now called her). Safi sat alone and lost, not knowing what to expect. Everything had changed in an instant; one moment he was there and, the next he was in surgery, fighting for his life. She kept seeing him beside her in the crowd, and then, suddenly, noise, commotion, confusion, and he was gone. And even when that crowd had long broken up, the sense of confusion remained for her. And a sense of terror, too.

Yvetta had been taken to an emergency station. Her shoulder had been dislocated while she tried to free her arm from the old man's vice-like grip when she saw Sasha fall to the pavement and the bodyguard lurching towards them. The old man pushed Yvetta into the crowd, hoping to stop their advance, but the crowd close by had heard Yvetta scream as Sasha hit the ground. In the ensuing chaos, Yvetta and Fritzi locked eyes. In that instant she saw her old lover with new eyes. The fear she experienced left her speechless. Her mind raced to catch up, but it was too late: Fritzi had melted away with her accomplice. All Yvetta cared about was Sasha at her feet, bleeding and unconscious.

At the hospital Yvetta found Safi sitting in an empty hospital room, waiting for Sasha to return from surgery. Later they both acknowledged that this was the moment they bonded; the tragedy drew them together as the past faded into the distance. They sat side by side, holding hands late into the night, until Mika arrived. Anna was in mid-flight, trying to reach her son, not knowing whether he would live or die.

Safi remained at his bedside for a week, sleeping on a recliner, watching him breathe, kept awake half the time by the noise of the machines and her own beating heart. Yvetta and Mika kept vigil while she bathed or stretched her legs. Anna had to be sedated; the shock of losing Sasha once more proved to be too much for her. The tough Anna the children knew from previous years was now gone; in its place was only a mother who worshipped her children and grandchildren.

The day Safi's parents arrived from Australia, having been told to wait as the Rubicov family were flying in and Safi wanted her parents to herself, she did not think she would be able to hold it together if she saw them, so soon after the shooting. Sasha had been in a coma for almost a month, but it was the day she would remember forever. It was late in the afternoon when they walked into Sasha's hospital room. Safi's tears had dried up, but when her mother and father held her close, she dissolved into uncontrollable, heart-wrenching sobs. A strange guttural sound stopped everyone in their tracks. As they turned, they found Sasha staring at them, trying to speak – but the words wouldn't come.

That was the beginning of Sasha's long journey to recovery, with his family remaining at his side every step of the way. For the next two weeks he slept most of the day. Each time he woke the family thought he appeared to be more alert, though he still could not speak, or move. It was an agonizing period, not knowing whether he would recover his speech or his motor skills.

Mika had every expert around the world on the phone. Some flew in to see Sasha, but none were able to give any conclusive diagnosis. It was a waiting game. The injuries may heal over time or not, the experts all said, one at a time and in more or less the same words, there was nothing to do but wait.

After six weeks of hospitalisation the doctor allowed Sasha home with twenty-four-hour nursing care. The kids were sensitive and careful around their father, but above all loving. They had missed him dearly. Questions were asked and answers were given; they knew as much as they could at their ages, and perhaps intuited much more. Most importantly, they gave him the love and attention he deserved, even in his new, diminished state. They accepted Sasha as he was. Alexander now fourteen would sit by his father for hours on end reading to him, talking with him about his days at school, sports, even the girls he liked but was too shy to approach or talk with.

Amy would climb onto his bed and lie next to him, give him hugs and kisses whenever she ran in to say hello. She would bring her dolls in to show him their latest outfits or her latest craze. The children never seemed to tire, and Sasha would lap it all up with his eyes. They learnt to read his expressions better than anyone – better than Safi, even.

Alexander was a handsome boy, he resembled Sasha, Amy had a bit of both parents in her: Safi's eyes but her father's exuberant personality.

A neurological team would arrive daily to work with Sasha. A slight improvement in his motor skills had been noted after several weeks, which was encouraging.

The gain in his motor skills was marginal, his language skills remained unchanged, but Sasha was relentless with his exercise routine. Safi remained home with Sasha to organise the daily onslaught of medics and visitors; it became an uphill battle to keep him mentally stimulated and occupied.

Mika would arrive every month for a week to be with his brother. He would go over business with Sasha as if Sasha, a silent partner now in almost every sense, was able to contribute, and slowly Mika started to notice that he was, indeed, contributing in small ways, not only listening, but he was able to agree or disagree with certain complex issues, by writing his thoughts down.

Six months flew by. Safi returned to the gallery, only for a few hours a day. She worked from home and allowed DuPont or Yvetta to deal with transactions she herself could not do in person when needed, he had remained as an art appraiser and advisor to the Rubicovs.

With the assistance of the police, Janus had managed to track down the person Fritzi had paid to accompany her to the gallery wearing an old man's disguise. Tony, in his forties and, an out-of-work actor whom Fritzi had hired, knew almost nothing about Fritzi, only that she paid handsomely for something that at the time seemed like a piece of cake; he had not expected her to shoot anyone.

He thought Fritzi a mesmerising fascinating creature, herself theatrical, only needed to rescue her sister from her drug-addicted lover. Fritzi had informed him that the sister needed to be put in rehab before it was too late; if she struggled to get free, he was to hold onto her, which he did, until the shot was fired, felling her supposed lover right in front of him. He had freaked out and made a run for it. The whole episode left him in a terrible way, he said. It had not taken the police long to track him down. In the places he hung out, everyone knew the story.

Fritzi still remained off the radar. She had failed in her attempt to abduct Yvetta. There was a warrant out for her arrest for attempted murder. The police had her profile from the FBI. She would be caught eventually, she was on every database throughout the world; even with her skills she would find it difficult to remain in hiding for ever.

Janus's contacts in Russia had only recently managed to track down some information on Fritzi's disappearance from their prison system. She had worked with an unknown group in Russia who they believed had links to many criminal organizations around the world. How this group managed to help her escape the secure prison remained a mystery: money, lots of it, was the only answer. The prison authorities were tight-lipped and in denial; as far as they were concerned Fritzi would be found: only her papers had vanished, not their prisoner.

Whatever happened, the search in Manhattan continued. The authorities still hoped she would surface on their radar. A net had been thrown far and wide, Fritzi would have to be invisible to get past the intelligence.

Yvetta now had Kolya with her almost 24 hours a day. He knew Fritzi better than most and was sure to recognise her in any disguise she chose to show up in. Kolya had studied her body language for many years after her attack on the Rubicov family home, but had never had the opportunity to put his skills into practice; now that he had been trusted with Yvetta's protection, he became supersensitive to whoever came within a foot of her.

Paris came and went in a blur for Yvetta. She ached to be with Gina, and understood the need to leave Manhattan after Fritzi's insane behaviour. The two women embraced tearfully, made love often, and walked the streets of Paris for hours on end, going over every detail of what had happened the day Sasha was shot. Many suspected that Fritzi had caused the fire in the adjacent building as a decoy to kidnap Yvetta.

Still, the city's report on the fire had not been conclusive in its findings. The evidence pointed to old wiring, yet Yvetta and the rest of the family were convinced Fritzi had had something to do with the fire. Why else would she be in the gallery at that exact moment? She was waiting for her opportunity to grab Yvetta, that was for sure. Yvetta believed that the shooting was a random unplanned occurrence. It was very unlike Fritzi to behave in such an erratic manner, or to endanger herself to such a degree with such a public act of violence. She was obviously desperate. Perhaps Fritzi was not as in control as she liked everyone to think she was.

Yvetta had seen the frantic fury in Fritzi's eyes. The mere thought of failure or walking away emptyhanded caused Fritzi's uncharacteristic behaviour. Fritzi did not like losing and as a result Sasha became her victim. Someone in the Rubicov family had to pay.

On Yvetta's return from Paris, the sadness she felt when seeing Sasha motionless in the hospital bed had been overwhelming. Anna, Mika, and Safi sat her down to listen to her synopsis of the events of that day, how she could have saved Sasha had she not dislocated her shoulder. She replayed certain moments over and over in her mind. She second-guessed and reassessed everything, doubted herself, and was full of guilt once again. But her family allowed her to understand that it was not her fault, that she could not be held responsible for Fritzi's actions. She understood all of this, and yet the guilt and self-doubt still lingered, impossible to erase.

'I was right there when it happened,' Yvetta said, her voice weighed down by pain, 'and still I was paralysed with fear when I saw that revolver in Fritzi's hand. I was convinced she was going to kill me. Then, in a flash, Sasha fell to the pavement, everything went blank, I couldn't remember the sequence of events for the longest time, it was all muddled up in my head. I slept all the way to Paris, but when I started to recall the events, I saw them so clearly, almost in slow-motion: Fritzi with that tiny revolver in her hand, pointing it. I should have realised she was pointing it at Sasha and not at me. Why didn't I see that?'

It took a lot of convincing to help Yvetta understand there was not enough time for anyone to do anything. It was that split second that enabled Fritzi to escape. She shot Sasha to save herself from being caught, another subterfuge to cause maximum mayhem. She would never have harmed Yvetta, Sasha just happened to be closer at the time, and she shot him.

Yvetta spent every day at Sasha's bedside with the rest of the family. Once he returned home, she remained a constant visitor, bringing gifts of Russian delicacies he liked, or audio books in Russian, anything to help him recover. She even joined Anna on her trips to the Russian Orthodox Church to pray and light candles for a miraculous recovery.

Throughout Sasha's torturous uphill climb, during a very dark period in their lives, Safi held onto every scrap of hope and positive thinking.

'Who knows whether prayer helps, but it certainly concentrates the mind,' Safi said. Sunlight streaming through the window interrupted her reverie. She looked up, caught Polly's gaze. 'Someone once told me that prayer and cosmic energy are connected. The universe is listening. One grabs onto anything when in a dire situation. After months of therapy and prayer Sasha did begin to improve. It was slow but it was happening. His speech was slurred at first, but he was able to form words, and the words turned into short sentences. The short sentences became long sentences, and in no time, he was talking again. The doctors were encouraged, X-rays were made of his brain and spinal cord. There was no doubt in anyone's mind things were improving, he was slowly healing. For the first time everyone was hopeful Sasha would return to full health, eventually.

His motor skills had been improving. He could eat on his own: messily at first, but improving slowly. His body refused to respond and they had to keep his water mattress, turning him constantly in case of bedsores. The nurses cleaned him and bathed him, and the work to improve his condition continued relentlessly for a year before Sasha turned the corner and was able to stand with the aid of the nurses.

Once he believed in his own recovery, there was no stopping, Sasha. They would exercise in the pool twice a day. Special hoists were installed and the water was kept at a certain temperature. Sasha remained stoic throughout, his frustration at his slow progress only witnessed by the medical staff, who used their professional expertise not only on his body but on his mind and spirit. Above all else, they wanted to keep him from sliding into a depression. They were the angels sent through those, who kept the prayer vigil going, that's what I like to believe, anyhow.'

The pool therapy started to pay dividends, and Sasha was back on his feet, with a cane at first, then managing on his own. His physical ability rapidly improved by leaps and bounds. Only his anxiety remained. He avoided large groups of people outdoors, and strangers made him uncomfortable. He avoided going out on his own for months. In time this passed, too. Sasha had beaten the odds, he was going to be fine, life was returning to normal.

Safi turned to face Polly. She had to continue, they were almost at the end, yet she found it almost impossible to utter the words swirling around in her brain. The next stage of her life became incomprehensible after Sasha's mammoth uphill fight to regain his former physical strength only to be extinguished just as he started to plan ahead, holidays to Australia were booked and paid for, a move to California was under discussion, owning a vineyard appealed to them both, everything had become a possibility, yet it all fell away, leaving Safi in the depths of despair.

Alexander found Sasha floating face-down in the pool. Nothing could be done. He had had a brain seizure while doing his laps early one morning. After the security dragged him from the water the paramedics pronounced him dead on arrival.

The entire family were suspended in disbelief. It was hard to grasp that such a terrible thing could happen after his brave fight to survive, beating the odds stacked against him. Sasha had just begun to enjoy life, in all its forms, with the kids, with his family, and with his friends, but most of all with Safi. They loved each other more than ever, having gone through so much together, and apart. They were planning exciting changes, to relax more, spend time with the children surrounded by nature rather than a concrete jungle.

The funeral came and went. Life carries on, the living continue doing what they do, but for Safi life stood still. She spent hours, then days, then months on automatic pilot; until one morning she could no longer get up or wash or comb her hair. It all stopped that day. She found her body just couldn't, wouldn't, continue.

It took time and care in hospital, then recuperation somewhere outside of Manhattan, where she sat staring at nothing for hours. People visited, family spent hours sitting by her side, the children were cared for by family. Janus became a surrogate father to both Alexander and Amy, the children spent time at his ranch, riding horses, rapidly adjusting to life as children do. Both Alexander and Amy visited with Mika in the winter months at his Florida villa, cosseted by the rest of the Rubicov family. Yvetta now ran both the Manhattan Gallery and the Brooklyn Gallery, what she had most wanted had come to pass, but she wanted Safi back things had moved on and she valued her friendship with her sister in law more than she could ever imagine.

One morning Safi woke to a world of colour. A year after her breakdown, she noticed the leaves on the trees were burning gold and green in the sunlight, food tasted delicious once more, she had returned to the land of the living.

The flight to Sydney with Alexander and Amy and their grandparents, Leonard and Fiona, was their very first holiday together without Sasha. It was tough in many ways, but they got through it. Everyone loved being Down Under. They saw the Outback, travelled to the Gold Coast, and enjoyed Australia's many attractions. Not long after returning home to Manhattan, Safi planned another trip for the following school break, this time they remained in the States, flying to California, where they drove in an open-topped car, enjoyed the wine route, and stayed at small inns and hotels along the way, visiting vineyards that Janus recommended. Janus flew out to join them for part of the trip.

They visited his famous agency, built into the hills with its underground tunnels and glass walkways, staring in wonder at banks of computers, screens, and state-of-the-art technology. Janus had found a special place in the hearts of Alexander and Amy. It was obvious that they adored him. Like Mika, Janus took his responsibility of the kids to heart. When it came to sports or events at school that Sasha would have attended, Alexander never felt isolated or forgotten. Mika and Janus made sure they were around when he needed them; but mostly it was Janus who filled Sasha's shoes.

He never put any pressure on Safi, but as time marched on they became inseparable. Janus became known as Safi's partner, and neither felt the need to contradict that view.

Slowly, surely, one thing led to another. It happened over many years, but Janus's love for Safi had never dulled. He wanted to be there for her when she needed him. It was a natural process – for Janus, at least. But not for Safi, who took five years to realise Janus was the person she wanted to share the rest of her life with.

They had an intimate wedding with all their nearest and dearest present. Gina and Yvetta had tied the knot. Safi marvelled at the same-sex couples at their wedding, the two D's with their two children, Yvetta and Gina, and Lauren and Bianca and family. Safi's brother Jake and his fiancé Maggie flew over for the occasion, and the whole Rubicov family were present to give their blessing.

DuPont arrived with his wife and daughter, who flew out from Paris especially for the occasion. It was a casual, fun, happy event, out in the open; spring was in the air and the kids were ecstatic to see the young foals running with their mothers in the fields.

Safi's father got the chance to walk her down the aisle, while her mother, together with Anna, Mika, Yvetta and her suddenly very grown-up children filled out the retinue, and made the wedding a warm, fun-loving occasion.

Sasha's memory never overshadowed the happy occasion. Indeed, Safi would never allow his memory to die and she encouraged the children and everyone who knew him to speak of him as often as they chose to remember him. There was sadness and tears during the speeches, but that past, too, and then they partied late into the night.

There was never any question where the family home would be. The Manhattan apartment became their weekly residence, while the ranch provided a welcome refuge from the urban jungle.

Janus had a second studio built below the ground floor, and spent many hours working while Safi continued to head up the gallery, but the evenings were theirs to spend together.

Life was so unpredictable and insane, she had odd moments wondering if she was hallucinating, if she had dreamed up her experience ever since she had arrived in New York. Things had turned out bizarrely, who would have believed she would end up marrying both Sasha and Janus?

A year before they married, Janus had to broach his concerns about their sexual lives, but to his relief it was a non-event.

'I've been down the wild sex road,' Safi said. 'What matters is that the children love you, I love you, and whenever we get the urge to make love, whatever you have to do, we'll be doing it together. I thank God every day that we have you. Anyway, to be honest, if you had not confided your medical history, I would never have guessed.'

Polly and Safi sat in silence for a while. Both needed time to reflect, and absorb the details of Safi's life story.

'Well, this may only be the first instalment,' Polly said finally, closing her notebook with aplomb. She smiled warmly and Safi was reminded of when she first met her, all those years ago, when shortly after she arrived in New York. 'The next chapter of your life will have to be written by my replacement, sadly, but given your resilience to bounce back, it will never be dull.'

Fritzi remained out there somewhere. Every lead had run cold. It was rumoured by some that she had put down roots in Central America, if not further afield.

Yvonne Spektor was born in South Africa but moved to the UK in the 1970s. The Royal Academy of Arts named her Woman Artist of the Year in 2002. She lives in London with her husband Ken and cockapoo Shandy.

Printed in Great Britain
by Amazon

Inglés Básico
PARA HISPANOHABLANTES

Autora: Sila (Silvia Mascaró)
Diseño y maquetación: Eva Reina
Colaboradora y asesora pedagógica: Amelia Sánchez Brito
Fotografía de portada: Óscar García Ortega

Agradecimientos:
Este proyecto no se hubiera podido llevar a cabo sin el apoyo de dos grandes profesionales como son Eva Reina y Amelia Sánchez. Ambas han contribuido con su trabajo, talento y entusiasmo para conseguir que este libro que tienes entre tus manos sea una pequeña joya. *I admire you both!*

También debo agradecer a mi príncipe de ojos azules su apoyo incondicional y sus largas horas de soledad esperando a que este libro saliera publicado de una santa vez.
Du bist der Beste!

Y cómo no, quien se lleva mi más profundo agradecimiento, sois vosotros: los seguidores de aprendeinglessila.com Los que cada día me proporcionáis fuerza y motivación para seguir enseñando inglés de una manera diferente 😊

Cheers!

Copyright © Sila Inglés, 2016
Reservados todos los derechos.

No se permite la reproducción total o parcial de esta obra, ni su transmisión en cualquier forma o por cualquier medio (electrónico, mecánico, fotocopia, grabación u otros) sin autorización previa y por escrito de los titulares del copyright.

La infracción de dichos derechos puede constituir un delito contra la propiedad intelectual.

Para más información, contacte con el departamento de márketing de aprendeinglessila.com:
marketing@aprendeinglessila.com.

Hello!

Soy Sila Inglés y aquí os presento una guía de inglés básico para empezar a meterle caña al inglés.

Desde que creé mi blog aprendeinglessila.com, han sido millones de personas las que se han paseado por sus categorías buscando respuestas a sus dudas sobre temas de inglés, tanto de gramática, como de vocabulario, slang o pronunciación.

Esas personas, aparte de encontrar respuestas a sus preguntas, han encontrado a una compañera que les ha explicado varios temas de inglés de una manera diferente, como si fuera una amiga, más que una profe.

Un tono fresco, ameno y directo, que pretende acercar el inglés a los hispanohablantes en un "de tú a tú", sin tapujos, sin rodeos aburridos.

Yo misma, en mis años de colegio e instituto, odiaba la asignatura del inglés más que ninguna otra... bueno casi tanto como las mates 😒 pero con los años, este idioma me empezó a fascinar.

Lo que en realidad odiaba y me aburría a más no poder, era como estaban planteadas las clases, no el idioma en sí.

Mi propósito es conseguir que el inglés no sea un tostón, que le encuentres ese puntillo tan *cool* que tiene y que te contagies de mi pasión por el idioma.

Con esta guía de inglés básico, espero que te inicies con el inglés o que le des un repasillo a todo eso que aprendiste en tus años de colegio, pero que esta vez, lo disfrutes tanto como yo lo estoy disfrutando ahora. 🙂

Enjoy!

Índice

Introducción 9

NIVEL: NO ME ENTERO DE NÁ

1. **Artículos y pronombres** 13
   - Artículos 14
     - Determinado *'the'* 14
     - Indeterminado *'a/an'* 15

   - Pronombres 16
     - ¿Qué son los pronombres? 16
     - Pronombres Personales y estructuras 17
     - Pronombres Interrogativos 19

2. **Sustantivos** 23
   - Género de las palabras en inglés 24
   - El plural en inglés 27

3. **Preposiciones** 29
   - Introducción 30
   - Lugar 31

4. **Adjetivos** 35
   - Introducción 36
   - Adjetivos Comparativos de Igualdad 37
   - Adjetivos Demostrativos 38
   - Adjetivos Demostrativos vs Pronombres Demostrativos 40

5. **Adverbios** 43
   - ¿Qué son y cómo se usan? 44

6. **Verbos** 47
   - Las conjugaciones en inglés 48
   - Tipos de verbos:
     - Regulares 50
     - Irregulares 53
   - El verbo *'to be'* 58
   - *There is/There are* 61

7. Tiempos Verbales 63
  • Presente Simple 64
  • Pasado Simple 69

8. Pronunciación 73
  • ¿Por qué nos resulta tan difícil pronunciar bien en inglés? 74
  • Alfabeto 79
  • Símbolos fonéticos 80

NIVEL: VOY PILLANDO ALGO

1. Pronombres 85
  • Pronombres Acusativos 87
  • Pronombres Reflexivos 88

2. Sustantivos 91
  • Contables e incontables: Introducción 93

3. Preposiciones 97
  • Tiempo 99
  • Preposiciones en medios de transporte 102

4. Adjetivos 105
  • Adjetivos Comparativos 107
  • Adjetivos Superlativos 109

5. Adverbios 113
  • Formas Irregulares y excepciones 115
  • Formas Comparativas y Superlativas 117

6. Verbos 119
  • El verbo *'to have'* 121
  • *Have got* 123
  • Los verbos *'do'* y *'make'* 124

7. Tiempos Verbales 127
  • Presente Continuo 129
  • Presente Simple vs. Presente Continuo 130
  • El Futuro en inglés: *'will'* y *'going to'* 131

8. Pronunciación 135
  • No hablan como leen 137

NIVEL: ¡VAMOS A TOPE!

1. **Pronombres** 143
   - Pronombres Posesivos y Genitivo Sajón 145

2. **Sustantivos** 151
   - Contables e Incontables: excepciones y problemas 153

3. **Preposiciones** 157
   - Lista de 40 preposiciones básicas 159

4. **Adjetivos** 161
   - 100 Adjetivos básicos en inglés 163

5. **Adverbios** 169
   - Adverbios de Frecuencia 171
   - Adverbios de Grado 174

6. **Verbos** 177
   - Condicional Cero y Uno 179
   - Introducción a los verbos modales: *'can'* y *'could'* 181
   - *Phrasal Verbs:* introducción 183

7. **Pronunciación** 187
   - Letras mudas en inglés 188

8. **Vocabulario** 195
   - Inglés de supervivencia 197
   - Días de la semana: un paso más allá 200
   - *False Friends* 204
   - *Idioms* básicos del inglés 206

Un último consejo 211

Introducción

Muchas veces me preguntan: "¿cómo puedo aprender inglés desde cero?"

La verdad es que "desde cero" hay muy poca gente que empiece a aprender inglés.

Es decir, aunque no lo hayan estudiado en la escuela, como por ejemplo los de la época en que aprendían francés, pocas veces se empieza desde cero con el inglés.

Porque el mundo está "anglofonado" (creo que me acabo de inventar esta palabra).

En nuestro léxico español tenemos una infinidad de palabras que acaban en *"-ing"* que es una desinencia inglesa: *camping, marketing, parking, etc...*

También, sin darnos cuenta, utilizamos una cantidad inmensa de anglicismos en nuestro día a día: *chat, hobby, show, shorts, barman, top, etc.*

Por eso, el que dice que empieza desde cero con el inglés no es consciente de que lo habla cada día, al menos un poquito...

Sin embargo, para aquel que quiere empezar con los temas básicos de gramática, vocabulario, pronunciación, estructuras y demás, necesitará una guía para poder adentrarse en el maravilloso mundo del inglés con un itinerario bien trazado, sin salirse demasiado del camino (o que siempre regrese a él).

Y esto es lo que pretendo hacer con esta guía: daros las pautas básicas para arrancaros con el inglés...

Let's start!
(¡Empecemos!)

Inglés Básico
PARA HISPANOHABLANTES

Nivel:
No me entero de ná

Artículos y Pronombres

Artículos y pronombres

✱ Artículos Determinados e Indeterminados.

Vamos a empezar con los artículos del inglés.

Tenemos dos tipos: el artículo determinado '*the*' y el artículo indeterminado '*a/an*'.

El determinado equivaldría a nuestros **"el, la, los, las"**.

La casa ⟶ *The house*

El indeterminado son nuestros **"un, una, unos, unas"**

Una casa ⟶ *A house*

Las reglas que siguen estos artículos son muy similares a las del español (por ejemplo, siempre van delante del sustantivo), por lo que no tendréis problemas en entenderlo.

"THE": Artículo determinado

Cuando hablamos de algo conocido o mencionado anteriormente utilizamos el artículo determinado **'the'**.

Se utiliza tanto para el singular como para el plural:

THE students are listening ⟶ Los alumnos están escuchando
I need A book. Is THE book available? ⟶ Necesito un libro. ¿Está el libro disponible?

En este último ejemplo, la primera vez que se menciona al libro, se utiliza el artículo indeterminado **'a'**; una vez mencionado, 'libro' va acompañado del artículo **'the'**.

¿Te das cuenta de lo simple que lo pone el inglés?
Solo usa una palabrita para todo, mientras nosotros usamos tropecientas mil dependiendiendo de si el sustantivo que sigue al artículo es masculino o femenino, plural o singular. ¡En inglés no!

14 | Inglés básico para hispanohablantes | Articulos y pronombres

The house, pues *the house. The houses*, pues **'the'** también. *The boy* y *the girl, the boys, the girls* , nada de 'él', 'la', 'los' y 'las'... *'the'* y punto.

En inglés no se complican tanto como nosotros (en algunas cosas 🙂)... o sea que vamos a aprovecharnos de esas partes fáciles y dominarlas en un plis.

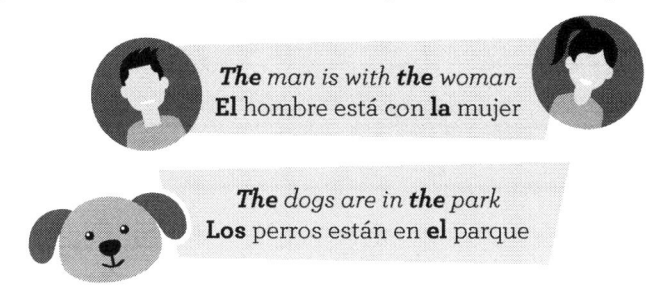

The man is with **the** woman
El hombre está con **la** mujer

The dogs are in **the** park
Los perros están en **el** parque

"A/AN": **Artículo indeterminado**

El artículo indeterminado *'a/an'* se utiliza, como en español, cuando hablamos de algo NO conocido ni mencionado anteriormente.

Siempre se refiere al singular.

La forma correcta *'a'* o *'an'* dependerá del primer sonido del sustantivo (o adjetivo si éste estuviera presente) que le sigue.

1) Si el primer sonido es un sonido consonántico, el artículo correcto es *'a'*:

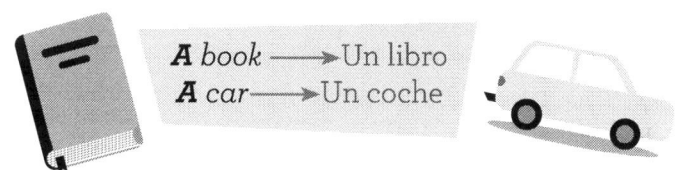

A book ⟶ Un libro
A car ⟶ Un coche

2) Si el primer sonido es vocálico, el artículo correcto es *'an'*:

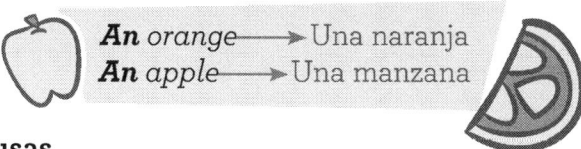

An orange ⟶ Una naranja
An apple ⟶ Una manzana

Palabras confusas

Algunas palabras pueden llevar a confusión, ya que pueden comenzar con una consonante que se pronuncia como vocal o una vocal que se pronuncia como consonante. Os doy algunos ejemplos, pero es un tema más avanzado, entonces, no te preocupes demasiado por ahora.

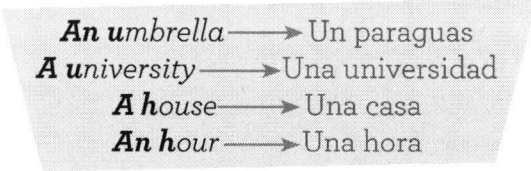

An umbrella ⟶ Un paraguas
A university ⟶ Una universidad
A house ⟶ Una casa
An hour ⟶ Una hora

Pronombres

¿Qué son los pronombres?
Los pronombres sustituyen a los nombres.

> Por ejemplo, en vez de decir **"María es alta"** (*Maria is tall*), puedes decir **"Ella es alta"** (*She is tall*).
>
> **"Ella"** (*she*) es el pronombre personal.

Generalmente los pronombres son palabras cortas.

Si no tuviéramos pronombres, tendríamos que repetir sustantivos mencionados anteriormente en la frase, lo que nos haría repetitivos y muy pesados.

Aparte de los pronombres personales que son los más conocidos **I, you, she,** etc... hay muchos más tipos de pronombres: pronombres, acusativos (u objeto), posesivos, reflexivos, relativos, etc...

Algunos ejemplos:

Pronombre Sujeto	Pronombre Objeto	Pronombre Posesivo	Pronombre Reflexivo
I	Me	Mine	Myself
You	You	Yours	Yourself
He	Him	His	Himself
She	Her	Hers	Herself
It	It	(Its)	Itself
We	Us	Ours	Ourselves
You	You	Yours	Yourselves
They	Them	Theirs	Themselves
One	One	---	Oneself

Inglés básico para hispanohablantes | Articulos y pronombres

✲ Pronombres Personales y estructuras

La lengua inglesa es una lengua con estructuras muy sencillas y fijas:

She is tall (Ella) es alta
Sujeto / Verbo / Complemento (objeto)

He lives in Valencia (Él) vive en Valencia
Sujeto / Verbo / Complemento (objeto)

En este sentido el inglés es muy diferente al español.

En español se puede cambiar el orden de los componentes de una frase; en inglés este orden siempre es el mismo.

Hay algunos trucos para recordar estas estructuras; el orden de las frases afirmativas se puede recordar con las siguientes iniciales:

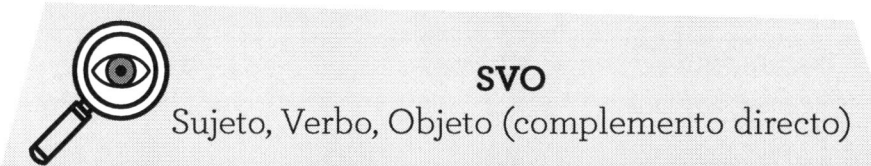

SVO
Sujeto, Verbo, Objeto (complemento directo)

El **Sujeto,** aquél que realiza la acción, no se puede omitir como se hace en español y siempre aparecerá delante del **Verbo.** El **Objeto,** aquel que recibe la acción, a veces no está presente, pero si aparece, siempre irá detrás del verbo.

She eats (Ella) come
Sujeto / Verbo

They know my brother (Ellos) conocen a mi hermano
Sujeto / Verbo / Objeto (Complemento)

Los pronombres personales nos ayudan a ver claro esta estructura básica del inglés.

I know that woman ⟶ (Yo) conozco a esa mujer
I like her ⟶ Me gusta (ella)
He hates you ⟶ (Él) te odia (a ti)

NOTA:
El *'Subject Pronoun'* (pronombre personal que funciona como sujeto) realiza la acción y siempre precede al verbo.

El *'Object Pronoun'* (pronombre personal que funciona como complemento) recibe la acción y siempre irá detrás de él.

Con estos pronombres personales **Se Ve O**tra vez lo fijas y simples que son las estructuras en inglés:
SVO: Subject + Verb + Object

Articulos y pronombres | **Inglés básico para hispanohablantes**

✱ **Entonces, ¿cómo se forman las frases?**

Esta es la estructura:

Subject Pronoun + Verb + Object Pronoun

S   V   O

S	V	O
I (Yo)	*know* (conozco)	*me* (a mí)
You (Tú)	*know* (conoces)	*you* (a ti)
He (Él)	*knows* (conoce)	*him* (a él)
She (Ella)	*knows* (conoce)	*her* (a ella)
It (Eso)	*knows* (conoce)	*It* (eso)
We (Nosotros)	*know* (conocemos)	*us* (a nosotros)
You (Vosotros)	*know* (conocéis)	*you* (a vosotros)
They (Ellos o Ellas)	*know* (conocen)	*them* (a ellos o ellas)

Como puedes ver, los pronombres personales en inglés se utilizan para sustituir la parte de la frase que ya es conocida, ya sea sujeto u objeto.

Recuerda que, a diferencia del español, el sujeto en inglés no se puede omitir, así que los *'Subject Pronouns'* se usan muy frecuentemente.

Otra diferencia con el español es que el *'Object Pronoun'* siempre va detrás del verbo:

They have it

mientras que en español suele ir delante:

Ellos/as lo tienen

El *'Object Pronoun'* también es el pronombre personal que sigue a preposiciones:

You talk to them ⟶ Vosotros habláis con ellos

Pero eso ya lo veremos más adelante ☺

Inglés básico para hispanohablantes | Artículos y pronombres

✱ Pronombres Interrogativos

Para iniciarnos con los Pronombres Interrogativos, vamos a ver una serie de preguntas y respuestas básicas que te ayudarán a entablar una conversación:

>**How** are you? ¿**Cómo** estás?
>**Where** are you from? ¿De **dónde** eres?
>**Where** do you live? ¿**Dónde** vives?
>**What**'s your job? **What** do you do for a living? ¿A **qué** te dedicas? (¿**Cuál** es tu trabajo?)

Las posibles respuestas serían, respectivamente:

>*I'm fine, thanks, and you?* Estoy bien, gracias, ¿y tú?
>*I'm from Menorca/I am Menorcan* Soy de Menorca/Soy menorquín/a
>*I live in New York* Vivo en Nueva York
>*I'm a teacher* Soy profesora

Siempre que sea políticamente correcto, les puedes preguntar por su edad:

>**How** old are you? ¿Cuántos años tienes?
>*I'm thirty years old* Tengo treinta años

NOTA:
Literalmente la frase **How old are you?** se traduce al español por:
¿**cómo** de viejo eres?, por eso la respuesta literal en inglés es:

Soy 21 años viejo ⟶ *I am 21 years old*

Por eso cuando contestamos a esta pregunta en inglés, al principio los hispanohablantes nos liamos y decimos:

~~*I have 21 years*~~
Tengo 21 años

¡Pero está maaaal!

En inglés NO "**tienes**" x años, "**eres**" x años viejo.

*You **are** 38 years old*

Articulos y pronombres | Inglés básico para hispanohablantes

✱ Sigamos...

Si la conversación va por otros derroteros y quieres profundizar aún más, puedes preguntar:

> **Why** are you in Madrid? ¿Por qué estás en Madrid?
> **Who** are you with? ¿Con quién estás?
> **When** are you leaving? ¿Cuándo te marchas?

Las respuestas pueden ser muy variadas, pero a la primera se contestará empezando por la palabra **because** (porque)-pronunciada /bɪ'kɒz/ (BICÓS):

> **Because my brother lives here**
> Porque mi hermano vive aquí

Al aprender estas preguntas, no sólo serás capaz de llevar una conversación básica, sino que también habrás aprendido algunos de los pronombres interrogativos de la lengua inglesa.

Con ellos, podrás realizar cualquier tipo de pregunta.

CÓMO SE UTILIZAN

Estos pronombres siempre van al principio de la pregunta, incluso cuando haya una preposición, que, a diferencia del español, no se podrá poner delante del pronombre, sino que irá al final de la pregunta:

> **Who** are you talking to? ¿Con quién estás hablando?

Vamos a profundizar entonces en el tema de los Pronombres Interrogativos y veamos para qué se utilizan cada uno de ellos:

What (Qué)
Se utiliza para preguntas generales, sobre todo relacionadas con la acción:
> **What are you doing?** ¿Qué estás haciendo?
> **What are you eating?** ¿Qué estás comiendo?

O para preguntar por cosas:
> **What is this?** ¿Qué es esto?

Where (Dónde)
Con este pronombre preguntaremos por lugares:
> **Where is the toilet/restroom** (AmE)? ¿Dónde está el lavabo?

Inglés básico para hispanohablantes | Artículos y pronombres

How (Cómo)
Con él podemos preguntar de qué manera se hace o es algo:
How do you open this door? ¿Cómo se abre esta puerta?

Why (Por qué)
Este es el pronombre que utilizaremos para preguntar la razón de algo:
Why are you asking? ¿Por qué lo preguntas?

Who (Quién)
Utilízalo para preguntar por personas:
Who is that girl? - ¿Quién es esa chica?

When (Cuándo)
Este pronombre se utiliza para preguntar por el momento en que algo ocurre:
When does it start? - ¿Cuándo empieza?

Ejemplo de diálogo:

Carlos: *Good morning*
Ana: *Good morning*
Carlos: *My name is Carlos, **what**'s your name?*
Ana: *My name is Ana, **how** are you?*
Carlos: *I am fine, thanks, and you?*
Ana: *I am tired*
Carlos: *May I ask you **how** old are you?*
Ana: *I am thirty five years old, **what** about you?*
Carlos: *I am forty years old.*
Ana: ***Where** are you from?*
Carlos: *I am from Italy, and you?*
Ana: *I am Mexican, but I live in Germany, **where** do you live?*
Carlos: *I live in Washington. **Why** do you live in Germany?*
Ana: *Because I work there as a nurse, **what**'s your job?*
Carlos: *I am a dentist*

¿Entiendes la conversación? ¿Crees que podrías traducirla?
Aquí puedes ver un glosario de las palabras utilizadas en el diálogo:

Glosario

Good morning: buenos días
Fine: bien
Thanks: gracias
Tired: Cansado/a
May I ask you...?: podría preguntarle...?
Thirty five: treinta y cinco (35)
What about you?: ¿y tú/usted?
Forty: cuarenta (40)

Italy: Italia
Mexican: mexicano/a
Germany: Alemania
Work: trabajar
There: allí
Nurse: enfermero/a
Job: empleo
Dentist: dentista

Sustantivos

2 Sustantivos

✱ Género de las palabras en inglés

Si tuviésemos que clasificar los sustantivos según su género, podríamos hacerlo de la siguiente manera:

1. **Palabras de género masculino**
   Son palabras que designan una entidad masculina, por ejemplo: *boy, man, lion, actor...*

2. **Palabras de género femenino**
   Son palabras que hacen referencia al sector femenino: *cow, woman, girl, waitress, queen...*

3. **Palabras de género común**
   Son palabras que se pueden referir tanto al género masculino como al femenino: *student, child, teacher, friend, person...*

4. **Palabras de género neutro**
   Normalmente en inglés, los sustantivos que hacen referencia a objetos no llevan ninguna marca para determinar su género.

   No podríamos diferenciarlos ni con la ayuda del determinante, ni con la del adjetivo ya que son invariables.

   House: *The house is green.*
   Pen: *The pens are blue.*
   Sea: *The sea is calm.*
   Street: *The streets are dirty.*

¡Ojo a las excepciones!

- **Sustantivos colectivos:** Aunque se refiera a un grupo de personas, siempre serán de género neutro: *army, police, family...*

- **Sustantivos únicos por su grandeza o poder:** Se considera que tienen género masculino: *the Sun, time, death, winter...*

- **Sustantivos que destacan por su belleza y singularidad**: Se considera que tiene género femenino: *the moon, the earth, solidarity, spring...*

En cuanto a la formación de algunos sustantivos, podemos decir que:

1. Hay palabras que cambian totalmente según el género:

Man (hombre) ⟶ *Woman* (mujer)
Girl (chica) ⟶ *Boy* (chico)
Cow (vaca) ⟶ *Bull* (toro)

2. A veces nos vemos obligados a añadir algún elemento para especificar el género: *male o female* (macho o hembra) o *boy o girl* (chico o chica):

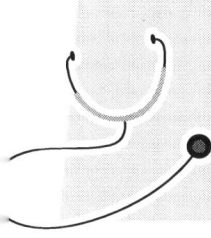

Boy-scout ⟶ *Girl-scout*
Boyfriend (novio) ⟶ *Girlfriend* (novia)
Male doctor (doctor) ⟶ *Female doctor* (doctora)
Male singer (cantante) ⟶ *Female Singer* (cantante)

3. También el sufijo **"-ess"** se utiliza en algunas palabras para formar el femenino usando como base la palabra del masculino:

Waiter (camarero) ⟶ *Waitress* (camarera)
Actor (actor) ⟶ *Actress* (actriz)
Prince (príncipe) ⟶ *Princess* (princesa)

4. Al revés también, aunque mucho menos frecuente, se utiliza como base la palabra del femenino para formar el masculino:

Widow (viuda) ⟶ *Widower* (viudo)

** Aquí os dejo una muestra de algunos sustantivos masculinos y su correspondiente versión femenina:

Dog ⟶ *Bitch* (perro/a)
Horse ⟶ *Mare* (caballo/yegua)
Wizard ⟶ *Witch* (brujo/a)
Gentelman ⟶ *Lady* (caballero/dama)
Monk ⟶ *Nun* (monje/a)

Sustantivos | Inglés básico para hispanohablantes

5. Y realmente, donde es más evidente esta diferencia entre palabras para el masculino y para el femenino es en los parentescos. Y, ojo, reconozco que si ya de por sí son un poco lío en nuestra propia lengua, en inglés también lo son... y de muestra...

Desde los más cercanos:

Madre ⟶ Padre
Mother ⟶ ***Father***

Hijo ⟶ Hija
Son ⟶ ***Daughter***

Abuelo ⟶ Abuela
Grandfather ⟶ ***Grandmother***

Tío ⟶ Tía
Uncle ⟶ ***Aunt***

Sobrino ⟶ Sobrina
Nephew ⟶ ***Niece***

Hasta los más lejanos:

Suegra ⟶ Suegro
Mother-in-law ⟶ ***Father-in-law***

Nuera ⟶ Yerno
Daughter-in-law ⟶ ***Son-in-law***

Inglés básico para hispanohablantes | Sustantivos

✲ El plural en inglés

¿Qué significa que una palabra está en plural?
Pues que indica más de un elemento. En singular, sólo indica uno:
Casa - casas (singular - plural)

Veamos rápidamente cómo se forma el plural:
La manera fácil: **se le añade una '-s', como en español.** ☺

House ⟶ *Houses* (Casa/s)
Book ⟶ *Books* (Silla/s)

Ahora veremos maneras un poco más fastidiosas

1. Si la palabra acaba en **'-sh', '-ch', '-s', '-x', '-z'**, se le añade **'-es'**
   Glass ⟶ *Glasses* (Vaso/s)
   Tax ⟶ *Taxes* (Impuesto/s)

2. Si la palabra acaba en **'-o'** también se le suele añadir **'-es'**
   Hero ⟶ *Heroes* (Héroe/s)

   Aunque hay muchas excepciones a esta regla:
   Piano ⟶ *Pianos* (Piano/s)
   Photo ⟶ *Photos* (Foto/s)

3. Cuando la palabra acaba en **'y'** tras consonante, se sustituye la **'y'** por una **'i'** y se le añade **'-es'**.
   Party ⟶ *Parties* (Fiesta/s)
   Body ⟶ *Bodies* (Cuerpo/s)

4. Algunas palabras que terminan en **'-f'** o **'-fe'** forman el plural sustituyendo la **'f'** por una **'v'** y añadiendo **'-es'**.
   Life ⟶ *Lives* (Vida/s)
   Thief ⟶ *Thieves* (CuchilloLadrón/es)

   Pero otras no:
   Dwarf ⟶ *Dwarfs* (Enano/s)
   Roof ⟶ *Roofs* (Techo/s)

5. Y también tenemos plurales irregulares.
   Veamos algunos de ellos:
   Child ⟶ *Children* (Niño/s)
   Man ⟶ *Men* (Hombre/s)
   Woman ⟶ *Women* (Mujer/es)
   Foot ⟶ *Feet* (Pie/s)
   Deer ⟶ *Deer* (Ciervo/s)
   Fish ⟶ *Fish* (Pez/ces)
   Sheep ⟶ *Sheep* (Oveja/s)

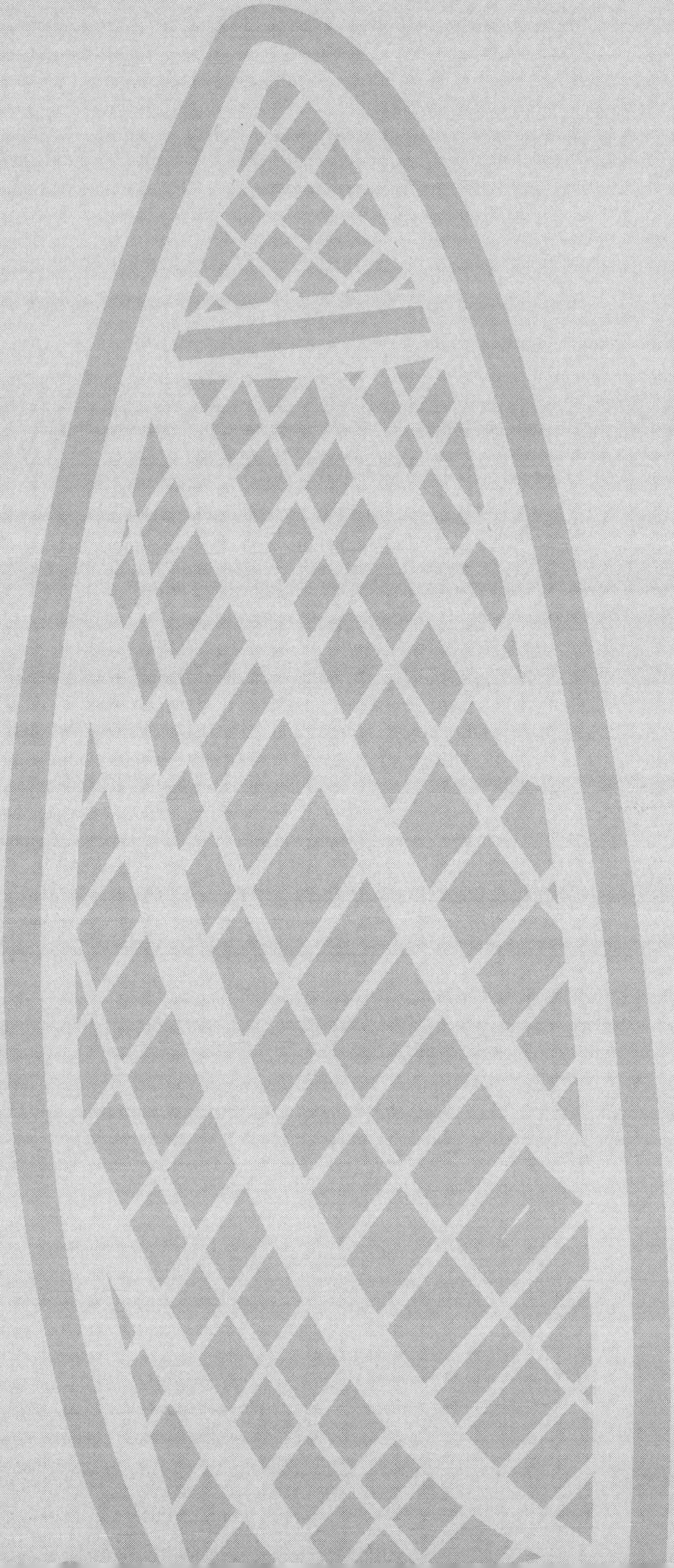

Preposiciones

3 Preposiciones

✱ Introducción

El uso de las prepos suele ser bastante confuso para los hispanohablantes.

Aunque, en general, su posición en una frase es igual que en español, tienen un par de reglas muy diferentes a las nuestras que siempre hacen que se nos crucen los ojos y nos quedemos locos.

La posición normal de las preposiciones es, como es español, delante de un nombre, o más de uno, con sus complementos incluidos:

At home
En casa

In the garden
En el jardín

Since last week
Desde la semana pasada

Between that red car and your bike
Entre ese coche rojo y tu bici

Hasta aquí todo bien, ¿verdad?

Pues vamos a empezar a ver algunos tipos de preposiciones y contrastarlas con el uso que hacemos de ellas en español...

Are you ready? ☺

✷ Preposiciones de lugar

Muchas veces necesitamos decir dónde está algo, o alguien, en relación a otra cosa.

La preposición 'en' de la frase, por ejemplo, "estoy **en** mi casa", se traduce al inglés de diferentes maneras.

Vamos a verlo:

En

- **'En'** sería *'in'* cuando las cosas están dentro, ya sea de un sitio cerrado (p.ej. edificios) o delimitado de alguna manera (p.ej. un parque, sobre todo si está vallado):

    *The book is **in** the bag*
    El libro está **en** la bolsa

- **'En'** será *'on'* cuando algo está encima de otra cosa, por lo que también podemos traducir *'on'* como 'encima de':

    *Your money is **on** the table*
    Tu dinero está **en/encima** de la mesa

- *'On'* también se traduce como nuestra preposición **'a'** en expresiones como a la derecha/izquierda:

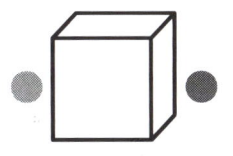

    *You'll find it **on** the right*
    Lo encontrarás **a** la derecha

- **'En'** se dice *'at'* cuando no sabemos si es dentro, fuera, al lado..., pero es por ahí.

    Hay ciertos lugares que siempre van con esta prepo:

    *I left my computer **at** home*
    Me dejé el ordenador **en** casa

Ahora veamos un par de preposiciones más para aprender la base de este tema, pero sin agobiar al personal 🙂

...o sea que tampoco me pasaré, Ok?

Preposiciones | Inglés básico para hispanohablantes   31

Debajo (de) / abajo

En inglés no se suelen ver dos preposiciones juntas, así que nuestra combinación "debajo + de" se traduce por una sola prepo: **'under'**.

*Mary's sitting **under** that tree*
Mary está (sentada) **debajo de** (bajo) ese árbol

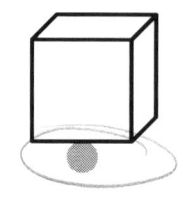

Detrás (de) / atrás

Como pasa con la prepo anterior, **'behind'** es la traducción de "detrás de", sin tener que añadir nada que represente a 'de':

*Your son is hiding **behind** the curtains*
Tu hijo está escondido **detrás** de las cortinas

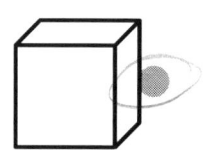

Al lado de / junto a

Pues ahora viene la excepción que todos esperábais... esta vez si que se nos juntan dos preposiciones y si que hay una representación de 'de', ya que al lado de 'o' junto 'a' se traduce por **'next to'**:

*Fetch the box which is **next to** the bed*
Coge la caja que está **al lado de/junto a** la cama

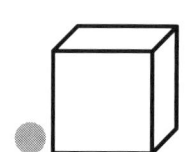

Entre

Esta prepo, como pasa también con **en**, tiene varias traducciones al inglés. A los angloparlantes a veces les gusta ser muy específicos, así que dependerá de la posición de lo que estamos situando:

'Entre' sería **'between'** cuando queremos situar algo entre otras dos cosas:

*The cinema is **between** the bank and the shop*
El cine está **entre** el banco y la tienda

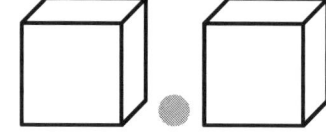

'Entre' será **'among'** cuando el objeto a situar se encuentra entre un número de elementos.

*The bear is hiding **among** the trees*
El oso se esconde **entre** los árboles

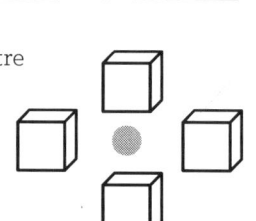

Seguiremos viendo más preposiciones de lugar y sus usos cuando toque subir al nivel intermedio, por ahora, tenemos **'enough'** (suficiente) ☺

Inglés básico para hispanohablantes | Preposiciones

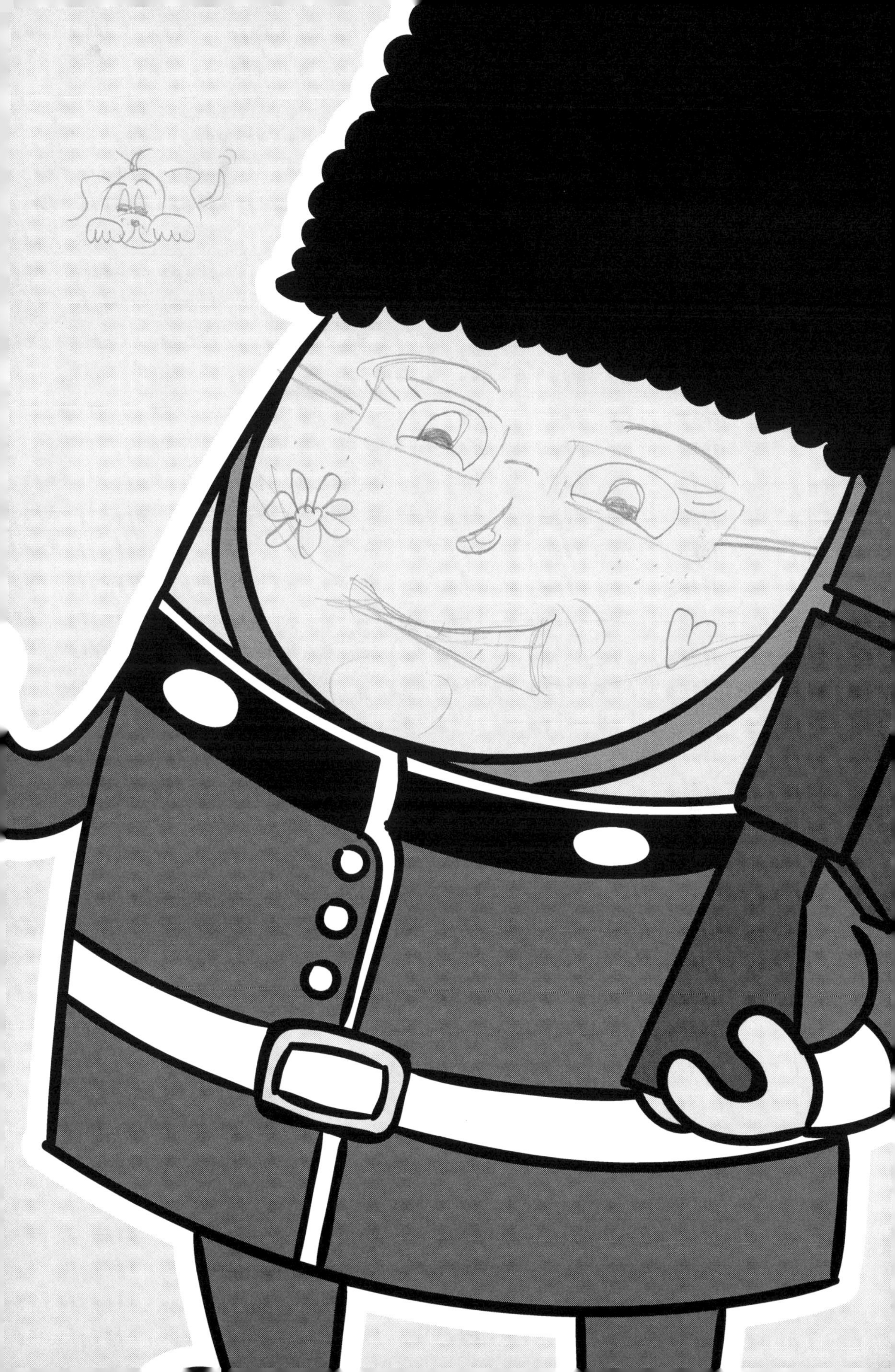

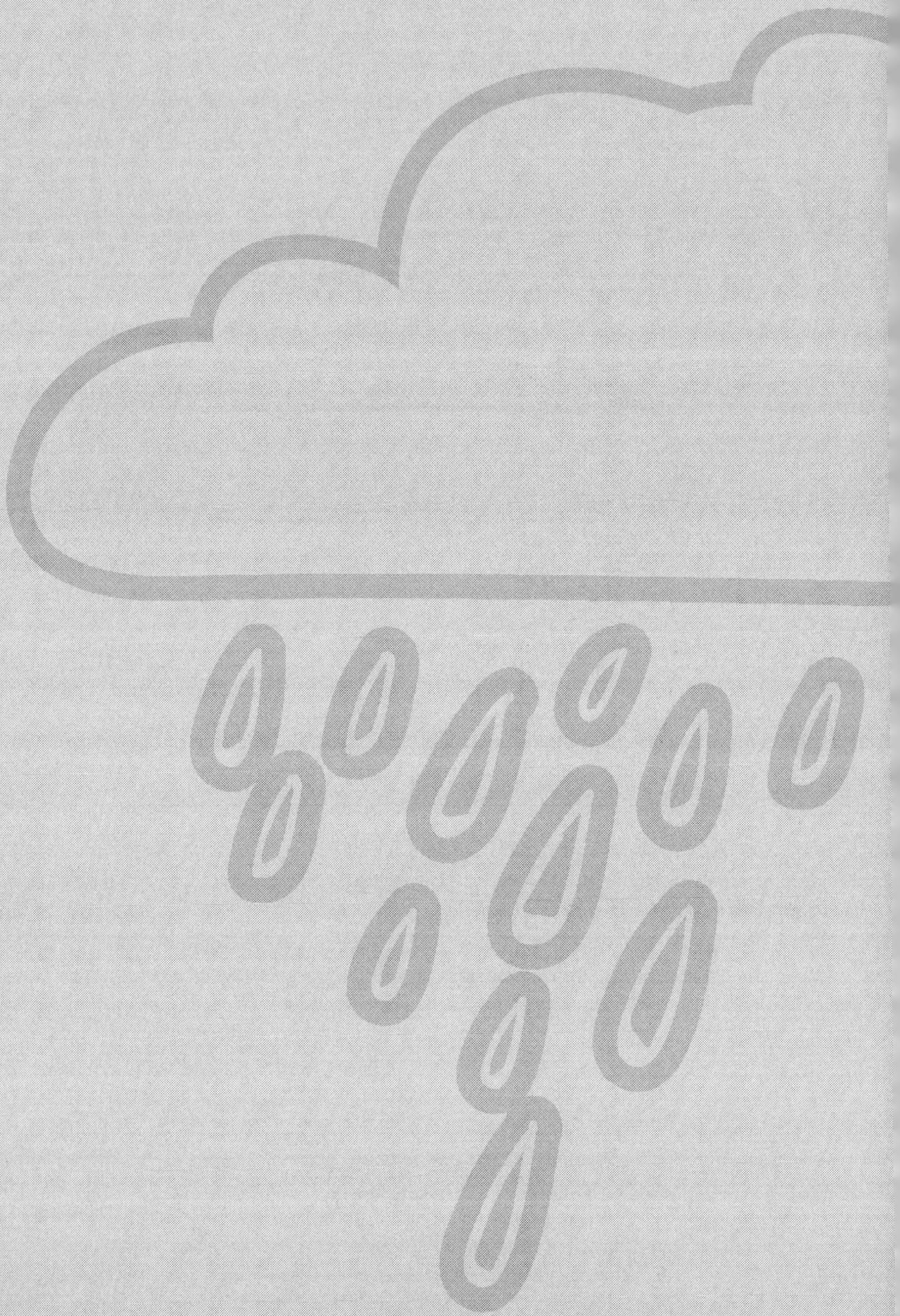

Adjetivos

4 Adjetivos

✱ ¿Qué son los adjetivos?

Los adjetivos son esas palabras que acompañan a los sustantivos y que designan alguna cualidad de ese nombre.

Por ejemplo, "una flor roja" *"a red flower"*.
"Roja" (**red**) es el adjetivo.

¿Cuáles son las diferencias entre los adjetivos en inglés y en español?
En español sabemos que el adjetivo suele ir justo detrás del sustantivo, pero en inglés nos cambian el orden: el adjetivo se colocará siempre antes del nombre que describen.

A tall woman Una mujer alta
The black cat El gato negro

En español debe existir una relación entre el objeto/sujeto y el adjetivo.

Por ejemplo:
"Flores roja" es incorrecto porque el adjetivo debería ser plural **"rojas"**.

Otro ejemplo:
"Él es alta" es incorrecto porque el adjetivo debería ser masculino **"alto"**.

En inglés el tema de los adjetivos es bastante sencillo porque no tenemos que usar ni masculino, ni femenino, ni plural; sólo usamos el adjetivo en singular, aunque el nombre al que acompaña sea masculino, femenino, o plural.

Red flower ⟶ *Red flowers*
Juan is tall ⟶ *María is tall*

VS

Flor roja ⟶ Flor**ES** roj**AS**
Juan es alt**O** ⟶ María es alt**A**

Inglés básico para hispanohablantes | Adjetivos

✱ Adjetivos Comparativos de Igualdad

La forma comparativa de igualdad la utilizaremos cuando queramos comparar dos o más cosas, para decir que son iguales.

Mira el ejemplo:
*Marta is **as** thin **as** Carmen* ⟶ Marta es/está **tan** delgada **como** Carmen

Se forma así:
As + *Adjetivo* + as...
(Tan + *Adjetivo* + como...)

Si la frase es en forma negativa:
Not as + *Adjetivo* + as...
(No tan + *Adjetivo* + como...)

*Marta is **not as** thin **as** Carmen* ⟶ Marta no es/está **tan** delgada **como** Carmen

✱ Adjetivos de Inferioridad

Cuando comparamos dos nombres y una de ellos tiene un grado inferior al otro utilizaremos ***"less"*** "menos".

*Marta is **less** pretty **than** Antonia* ⟶ Marta es **menos** bonita **que** Antonia

Se forma así:
Less + *Adjetivo* + than...
(Menos + *Adjetivo* + que...)

✱ Adjetivos Demostrativos

Los Adjetivos Demostrativos son:

**This / That
These / Those**

Estos adjetivos nos ayudarán a posicionar diferentes objetos, cosas, o personas en la distancia.

Con los adjetivos demostrativos sólo tendrás que aprenderte cuatro formas, ya que no se distingue entre femenino y masculino como en español, ni si la distancia, cuando es lejos, es más o menos lejana (eso vs aquel).

Veamos unos ejemplos:

This *bed is very comfortable* ⟶ **Esta** cama es muy cómoda
*Please, sit on **that** chair* ⟶ Por favor, siéntate en **esa** silla
*I like **these** shoes* ⟶ Me gustan **estos** zapatos
Those *houses are very expensive* ⟶ **Esas** casas son muy caras

En el siguiente cuadro veremos los diferentes significados de los demostrativos:

	NEAR (cerca)	FAR (lejos)	NOUN (sustantivo)
SINGULAR	**This** (esta)	**That** (esa, aquella)	**bed** (cama)
PLURAL	**These** (estas)	**Those** (esas, aquellas)	**bed<u>s</u>** (camas)

Cómo se usan

1. Es muy fácil entender y recordar este tipo de términos en inglés, ya que no haremos distinciones entre masculino y femenino:

   This *bed is uncomfortable* - **Esta** cama es incómoda
   This *book is useful* - **Este** libro es útil

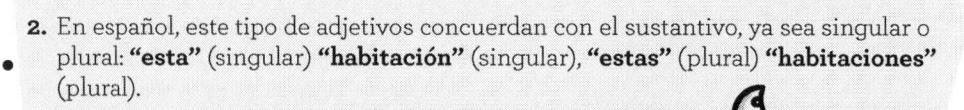

2. En español, este tipo de adjetivos concuerdan con el sustantivo, ya sea singular o plural: **"esta"** (singular) **"habitación"** (singular), **"estas"** (plural) **"habitaciones"** (plural).

   En inglés, también concordarán en número:

   That *bottle is big* - **Esa** botella es grande
   Those *bottles are big* - **Esas** botellas son grandes

Inglés básico para hispanohablantes | Adjetivos

3. Importante: Como hemos visto, existen plurales que son irregulares. Estos tendrán que concordar en número con el adjetivo demostrativo.

These men *are tall* - **Estos** hombres son altos
Those women *are beautiful* - **Aquellas** mujeres son preciosas

5. El sonido de la **'th'** inicial de estos pronombres se pronuncia casi como una **'d'** española.

Digo casi, porque es un sonido más suave (/ð/ es interdental), es decir, la punta de la lengua se coloca entre los dientes, casi como cuando pronuncias la 'd' entre vocales en español.

Lo que pasa es que en inglés se expulsa más aire y esto crea fricción.
Es es sonido 'd' de "i**d**ioma", no el sonido 'd' de "**d**ónde"

En inglés no pronuncias igual:
"day" /deɪ/ (dental) que *"this"* /ðɪs/ (interdental)

Por tanto:

This	/ðɪs/
That	/ðæt/
These	/ðiːz/
Those	/ðəʊz/

Luego ya veremos los símbolos fonéticos ☺

✱ Pronombres Demostrativos vs Adjetivos Demostrativos

Los pronombres demostrativos son los mismos que los adjetivos demostrativos **this, that, these,** y **those,** lo que varía es su uso.

Pero es muy fácil de entender porque nosotros hacemos la misma distinción en español.

Lo que tenemos que tener en cuenta es que los pronombres sustituyen al nombre, mientras que el adjetivo lo acompaña.

Por tanto, si los pronombres demostrativos son **this, that, these,** y **those,** esta vez, como pronombres, los usaremos para sustituir al nombre.

Este pronombre en inglés nos indicará si a lo que sustituye es singular o plural, y si la cosa está cerca o lejos.

Veamos la diferencia entre pronombres y adjetivos más claramente en esta tabla:

ADJETIVO	PRONOMBRE
This house is very big Esta casa es muy grande	*This is very big* Esta es muy grande
*You can see **that castle** from here* Puedes ver **ese castillo** desde aquí	*You can see that from here* Puedes ver eso desde aquí
These glasses *are expensive* **Estas gafas** son caras	*These are expensive* Estas son caras
*Bring me **those shoes*** Traéme **esos zapatos**	*Bring me those* Traéme esos

Inglés básico para hispanohablantes | Adjetivos

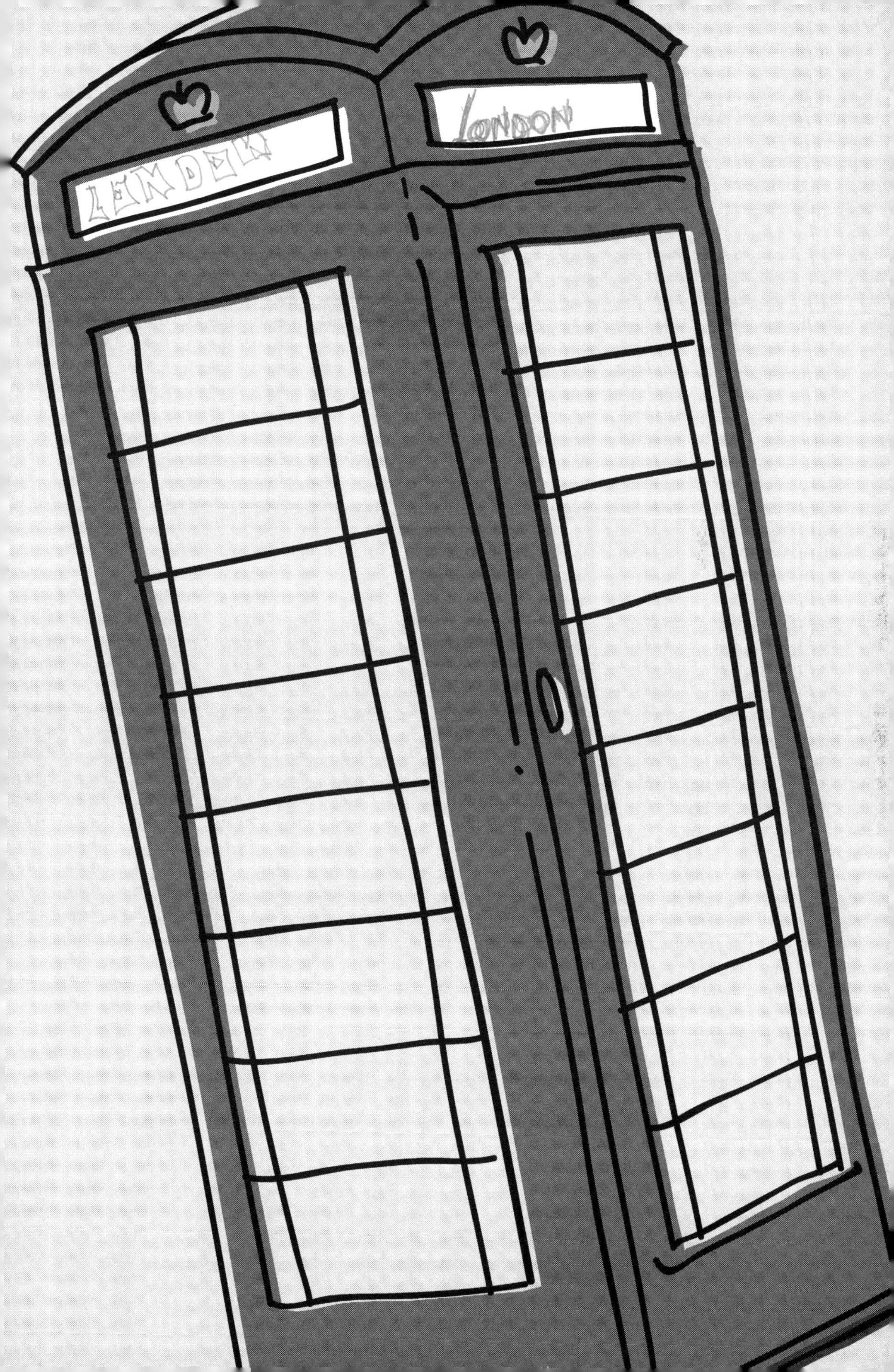
LONDON
London

Adverbios

5 Adverbios

¿Qué son los adverbios?

Los adverbios nos indican de qué manera alguien hace algo o de qué manera algo pasa. En español estas formas suelen acabar en **"-mente"**, por ejemplo "amablemente" *(kindly)*.

Los adverbios pueden modificar verbos, adjetivos y otros adverbios:

1. Modifica al verbo (detrás del verbo).

*Ana woke up **early*** ⟶ Ana se despertó **temprano**

2. Modifica al adjetivo (antes del adjetivo).

*Raquel is **extremely** thin* ⟶ Raquel está **extremadamente** delgada

3. Modifica a otro adverbio (antes del adverbio principal).

*Lucía drives **extremely** slowly* ⟶ Lucía conduce **extremadamente** despacio

¿Cómo se forman los adverbios?

1. Para formar un adverbio, generalmente se añade **'-ly'** a un adjetivo:

Inglés: **adjetivo + '-ly'**.
Español: **adjetivo + "-mente"**

Soft ⟶ *Softly* / Suave ⟶ Suavemente

Suavemeeeeente, bésame, que quiero sentir tus labios besándome otra vez...

Inglés básico para hispanohablantes | Adverbios

Pero cuando el adjetivo...

ACABA EN:	SE FORMA CON:	EJEMPLO:
-y	-ily	Happy - Happily (Feliz - Felizmente)
-ic	-ally	Magic - Magically (Mágico - Mágicamente)
-le	Cambia a -ly	Simple - Simply (Simple - Simplemente)
-ll	-y	Full - Fully (Entero - Enteramente)

** Pero cuidado, hay excepciones. Por ejemplo:
Shy - Shyly (Tímido - Tímidamente)
True - Truly (Verdad - Verdaderamente)

Adverbios | Inglés básico para hispanohablantes

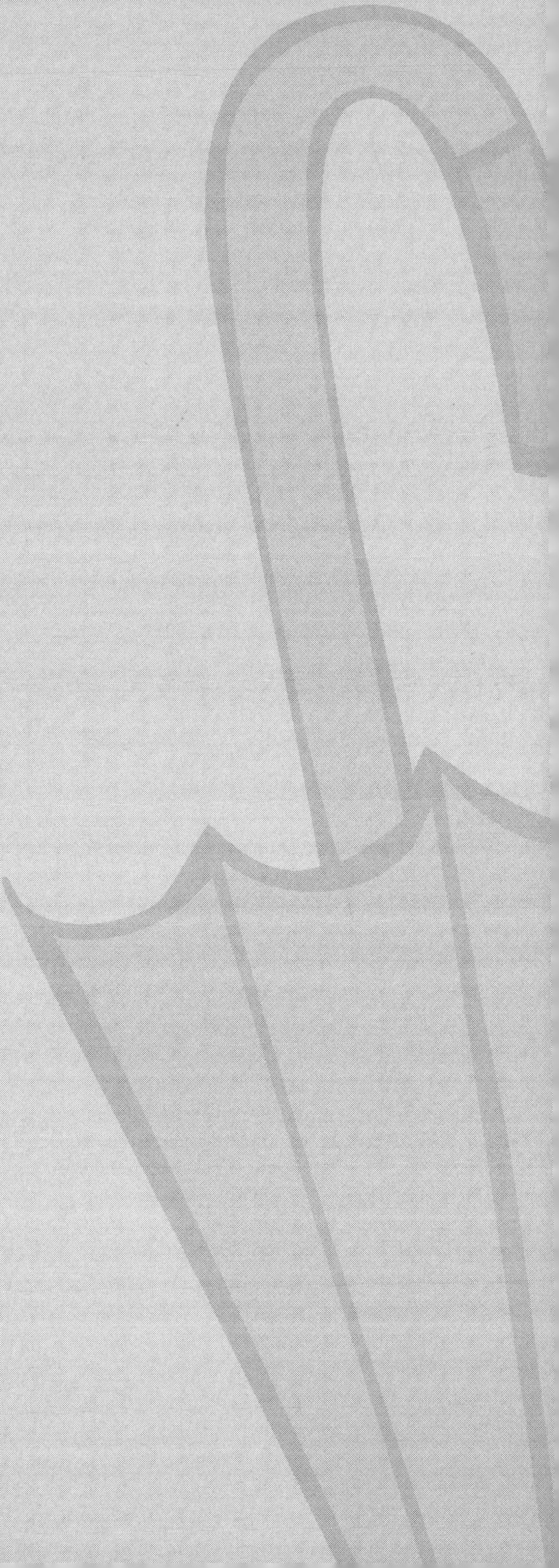

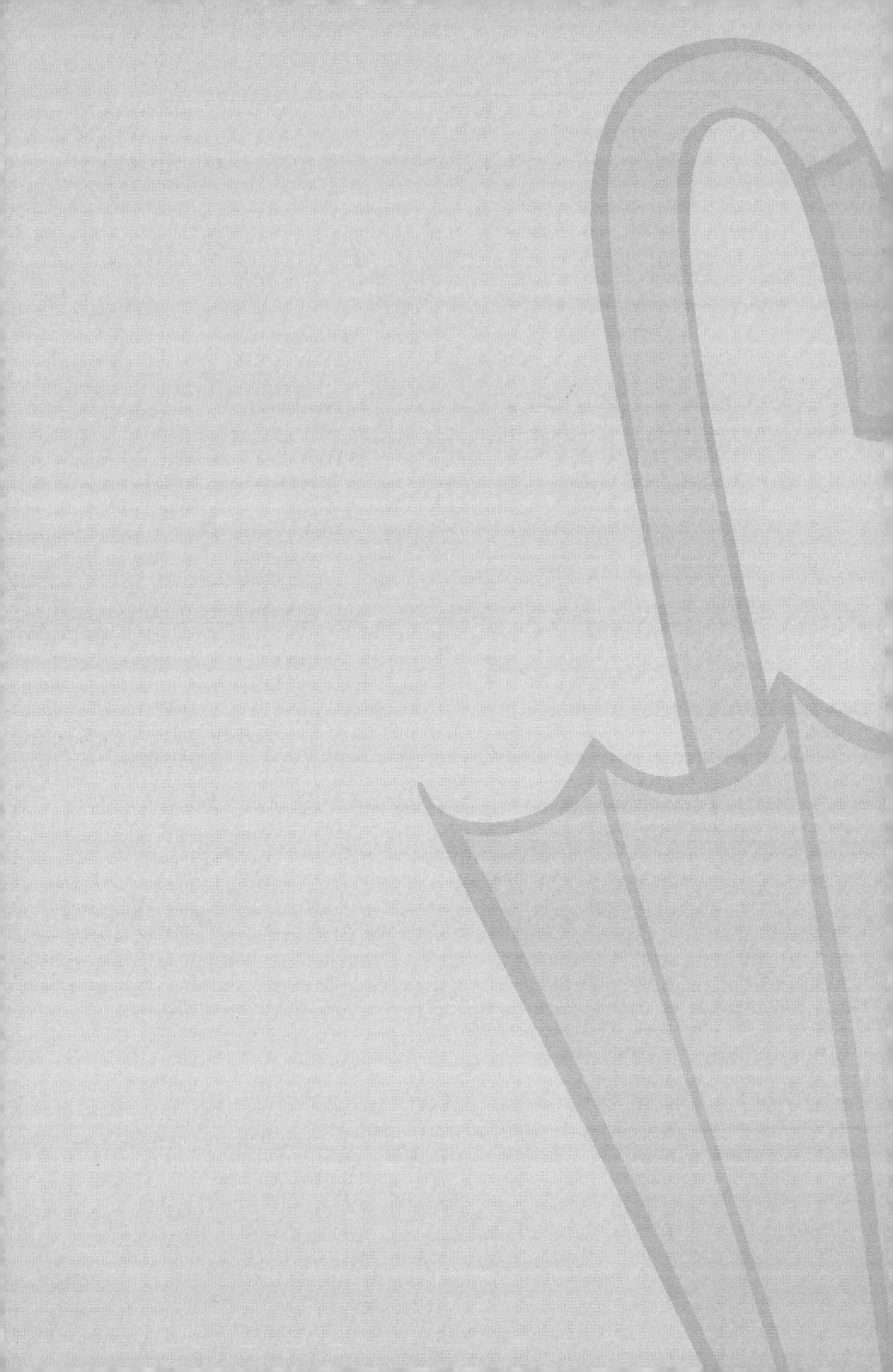

Verbos

6. Verbos

El tema de los verbos ya lo tengo ampliamente desarrollado en mi libro LOS VERBOS EN INGLÉS, pero no está de más tocar los puntos básicos de las formas verbales para que vayáis abriendo boca.

✳ Las conjugaciones en inglés

Cuando uno está estudiando gramática inglesa y le toca el tema de las conjugaciones en inglés, solo piensa "vaya tostón toca ahora"...

Tenemos "miedos" y prejuicios con este tema, pero siendo hispanohablantes, no me extraña... (ahora me explico, *don't worry*).

¿Por qué tenemos tanto miedo a las conjugaciones?

El tema de las conjugaciones nos parece complicado porque en español es una auténtica tortura, pero os aseguro que los tiempos verbales y las conjugaciones en inglés es uno de los temas más fáciles de entender y aprender del inglés.

Yo diría que es el idioma que lo pone más fácil de todos.

Siendo hispanohablante, este tema está chupado porque nuestro idioma sí que tiene telita...y si hemos sido capaces de entender y organizar en nuestra mente las conjugaciones en español, las del inglés nos las comemos con patatas ☺

¿En qué me baso para realizar esta afirmación tan rotunda?

Una de las grandes diferencias entre la estructura del inglés y nuestra lengua, es "la cantidad de información que contiene cada palabra en español".

Una palabra en español engloba mucha más información gramatical y semántica que una palabra inglesa.

Por ejemplo, si yo digo **'bebo'** en una palabra estoy dando esta información:

Verbo: beber
Tiempo: presente
Persona: Primera del singular (yo)

48 Inglés básico para hispanohablantes | Verbos

En cambio, si en inglés digo **'drink'**, solo sabemos que se trata del verbo 'beber' pero poco más.

Verbo: *drink*
Tiempo: no sabemos.
Persona: no sabe/no contesta

Si a **'drink'** no le acompaña nada más, no tenemos demasiada información, ¿verdad?

Para que **'drink'** signifique **'bebo'**, hay que agregarle un pronombre y decir **'I drink'**.

Otro ejemplo:
Verbo: **'ir'** - **'go'**

El verbo 'ir' en inglés se traduce como **'go'**. Hasta ahí guay.

Ahora vamos a conjugar ese verbo en inglés:
Go, goes, went, gone, going...

Eso es TODO, no hay más... sólo 5 formas... Y es de los verbos "complicados" porque es un verbo irregular. 🙂

¿Es más difícil el inglés o el español?

Go, goes, went, gone, going

Ir, yendo, ido, voy, vas, va, vamos, vais, van, iba, ibas, íbamos, ibais, iban, fui, fuiste, fue, fuimos, fuisteis, vaya, vayas, vayamos, vayáis, vayan, fuera, fueras, fuéramos, fuerais, fueran, fuese, fueses, fuésemos, fueseis, fuese, fuere, fueres, fuéremos, fuereis, fueren, id, etc...

Wait, WHAT?

Sígueme en:
aprendeinglessila.com

Realmente, este es el tema más fácil de aprenderse en inglés, porque en este idioma casi no usan conjugaciones, al menos comparado con el español.

Entonces, si el español es tu lengua materna y te sabes la mitad de las conjugaciones que existen en español, verás que el tema de los verbos en inglés, aunque tenga alguna peculiaridad, está bastante chupado.

✱ Tipos de verbos: Regulares e Irregulares

✱ Verbos Regulares

En inglés existen dos tipos de verbos: **los regulares y los irregulares.**

Los regulares son los "facilitos" porque tienen la peculiaridad de que tanto su forma pasada como de participio, terminan en **'-ed'**.

Por ejemplo, el verbo 'jugar': ***play - played - played***

Lo único que puede complicar este tipo de verbos, aparte de tener que memorizarlos, es la pronunciación, ya que, depende del sonido final del verbo antes de **'-ed'** se pronunciará de una manera o de otra.

El problema real es que muchos hispanohablantes nos fijamos en la letra que precede **'-ed'**, no en el sonido, ya que seguimos el mismo patrón que seguiríamos en español que una letra generalmente equivale a un sonido determinado.

En inglés no porque hay letras mudas, o que se pronuncian de diferente manera, por ejemplo el verbo **'dance'** (bailar).

'Dance' acaba ortográficamente con la vocal "e" pero resulta que esa "e" es muda en inglés, no se pronuncia.

Por tanto, **'dance'** acaba con el sonido de una **'s'** ⟶ /dɑːns/

Una vez visto esto, veamos rápidamente las reglas de pronunciación de estos verbos, pero no te agobies demasiado.

Aprender a pronunciar estos verbos correctamente se consigue con la práctica, pero al menos ya lo tienes aquí para recordar la regla 😊

Estas son las 3 posibles pronunciaciones:

Se pronuncia:	'ed' ⟶ /t/	'ed' ⟶ /d/	'ed' ⟶ /id/
En palabras que acaban con el sonido:	Sonidos sordos: p, k, ch, sh, s, f, h y θ	Sonidos sonoros: Vocales y consonantes b, g, z, v, m, n, l, r, w, j, ð	't' o 'd'
Ejemplo	*Dance* /dɑːns/ *Danced* /dɑːnst/	*Opened* /ˈəʊpən/ *Opened* /ˈəʊpənd/	*Paint* /peɪnt/ *Painted* /ˈpeɪntɪd/

Inglés básico para hispanohablantes | Verbos

Por tanto, una vez visto el punto de la pronunciación, os dejo una lista de algunos verbos regulares comunes, indicando qué tipo de pronunciación tienen:

ESPAÑOL	INGLÉS INFINITIVO	PASADO Y PARTICIPIO	PRONUNCIACIÓN TERMINACIÓN
Actuar	Act	Acted	id
Sumar, Añadir	Add	Added	id
Preguntar, Pedir	Ask	Asked	t
Responder	Answer	Answered	d
Llegar	Arrive	Arrived	d
Cepillar	Brush	Brushed	t
Pertenecer	Belong	Belonged	d
Suplicar, Mendigar	Beg	Begged	d
Creer	Believe	Believed	d
Cerrar	Close	Closed	t
Cocinar	Cook	Cooked	t
Llamar	Call	Called	d
Cambiar	Change	Changed	d
Cargar, Cobrar	Charge	Charged	d
Limpiar	Clean	Cleaned	d
Llorar	Cry	Cried	d
Bailar	Dance	Danced	t
Vestir	Dress	Dressed	t
Morir	Die	Died	d
Secar	Dry	Dried	d
Disfrutar	Enjoy	Enjoyed	d
Explicar	Explain	Explained	d
Seguir	Follow	Followed	d
Terminar	Finish	Finished	t
Ayudar	Help	Helped	t
Esperar, Desear	Hope	Hoped	t
Suceder	Happen	Happened	d
Imaginar	Imagine	Imagined	d

Verbos | **Inglés básico para hispanohablantes**

ESPAÑOL	INGLÉS INFINITIVO	PASADO Y PARTICIPIO	PRONUNCIACIÓN TERMINACIÓN
Besar	Kiss	Kissed	t
Matar	Kill	Killed	d
Reir	Laugh	Laughged	t
Gustar	Like	Liked	t
Mirar	Look	Looked	t
Extrañar	Miss	Missed	t
Casar (Se)	Marry	Married	d
Abrir	Open	Opened	d
Jugar, Tocar	Play	Played	d
Preferir	Prefer	Prefered	d
Prometer	Promise	Promised	t
Repetir	Repeat	Repeated	id
Llover	Rain	Rained	d
Recordar	Remember	Remembered	d
Sonreir	Smile	Smiled	d
Estudiar	Study	Studied	d
Fumar	Smoke	Smoked	t
Detener, Parar	Stop	Stopped	t
Conversar	Talk	Talked	t
Agradecer	Thank	Thanked	t
Tocar, Palpar	Touch	Touched	t
Usar	Use	Used	t
Visitar	Visit	Visited	id
Esperar	Wait	Waited	id
Querer, Requerir	Want	Wanted	id
Caminar	Walk	Walked	t
Lavar	Wash	Washed	t
Observar, Mirar	Watch	Watched	t
Desear, Anhelar	Wish	Wished	t
Trabajar	Work	Worked	t

Inglés básico para hispanohablantes | Verbos

✱ Verbos Irregulares

Los verbos irregulares se nos complican un poco más en cuanto a forma, porque el infinitivo, el pasado y el participio suelen ser diferentes el uno del otro, y con ello, la pronunciación.

Y el incordio es no se rigen por ninguna regla para formar el pasado o el participio, por lo que deben memorizarse.

Es mejor siempre memorizarlos en contexto, pero existen otras técnicas mnemotécnicas para acordarse de ellos, por ejemplo, agruparlos dependiendo de cómo se forman o de cómo se pronuncian.

En este capítulo, en vez de pasaros una lista de verbos irregulares ordenados alfabéticamente y ya está, os agruparé algunos de los verbos más comunes para que sea mucho más fácil acordarse de ellos.

Pero antes de nada, tengo que mostraros unos verbos irregulares súper comunes en inglés.

Estos sí que toca memorizarlos *"a pelo"*. ☺

ESPAÑOL	INGLÉS	Pron.	PASADO	Pron.	PARTICIPIO	Pron.
Conseguir	Get	ˈget	Got	ˈgɒt	Got / Gotten (AmE)	ˈgɒt / ˈgɒtn̩
Haber o Tener	Have	hæv	Had	hæd	Had	hæd
Hacer	Do (Does)	duː (dʌz)	Did	dɪd	Done	dʌn
Hacer	Make	ˈmeɪk	Made	ˈmeɪd	Made	ˈmeɪd
Ir	Go (Goes)	gəʊ (gəʊz)	Went	ˈwent	Gone	gɒn
Ser / Estar	Be / am, are, is	Biː / æm / ɑː / ɪz	Was / Were	wəz / wɜː	Been	biːn

Verbos | Inglés básico para hispanohablantes 53

Forman el **infinitivo,** el **pasado** y el **participio** de igual manera:

ESPAÑOL	INGLÉS	Pron.	PASADO	Pron.	PARTICIPIO	Pron.
Golpear	Hit	hɪt	Hit	hɪt	Hit	hɪt
Cortar	Cut	kʌt	Cut	kʌt	Cut	kʌt
Cerrar	Shut	ʃʌt	Shut	ʃʌt	Shut	ʃʌt
Poner	Put	ˈpʊt	Put	ˈpʊt	Put	ˈpʊt
Costar	Cost	kɒst	Cost	kɒst	Cost	kɒst
Herir	Hurt	hɜːt	Hurt	hɜːt	Hurt	hɜːt

El grupo *'come'*:

ESPAÑOL	INGLÉS	Pron.	PASADO	Pron.	PARTICIP.	Pron.
Convertirse	Become	bɪˈkʌm	Became	bɪˈkeɪm	Become	bɪˈkʌm
Vencer, superar	Overcome	əʊvəˈkʌm	overcame	əʊvəˈkeɪm	Overcome	əʊvəˈkʌm
Venir	Come	kʌm	Came	keɪm	Come	kʌm

Estos verbos se asemejan entre ellos porque **comparten la pronunciación del Pasado y del Participio.**

ESPAÑOL	INGLÉS	Pron.	PASADO	Pron.	PARTICIPIO	Pron.
Beber	Drink	drɪŋk	Drank	dræŋk	Drunk	drʌŋk
Cantar	Sing	sɪŋ	Sang	sæŋ	Sung	sʌŋ
Correr	Run	rʌn	Ran	ræn	Run	rʌn
Empezar	Begin	bɪˈgɪn	Began	bɪˈgæn	Begun	bɪˈgʌn
Encogerse	Shrink	ʃrɪŋk	Shrank	ʃræŋk	Shrunk	ʃrʌŋk
Hundirse	Sink	sɪŋk	Sank	sæŋk	Sunk	sʌŋk
Llamar por tlf	Ring	rɪŋ	Rang	ræŋ	Rung	rʌŋ
Nadar	Swim	swɪm	Swam	swæm	Swum	swʌm

Inglés básico para hispanohablantes | Verbos

El **Infinitivo** se pronuncia con una *'i'* larga. El **pasado** y el **participio** con una *'e'*.

ESPAÑOL	INGLÉS	Pron.	PASADO	Pron.	PARTICIPIO	Pron.
Alimentar	*Feed*	fiːd	*Fed*	fed	*Fed*	fed
Criar	*Breed*	briːd	*Bred*	bred	*Bred*	bred
Dejar	*Leave*	liːv	*Left*	left	*Left*	left
Dormir	*Sleep*	sliːp	*Slept*	slept	*Slept*	slept
Encontrarse con	*Meet*	miːt	*Met*	met	*Met*	met
Guiar	*Lead*	liːd	*Led*	led	*Led*	led
Leer	*Read*	riːd	*Read*	red	*Read*	red
Mantener	*Keep*	kiːp	*Kept*	kept	*Kept*	kept
Sangrar	*Bleed*	bliːd	*Bled*	bled	*Bled*	bled
Sentir	*Feel*	fiːl	*Felt*	felt	*Felt*	felt
Significar	*Mean*	miːn	*Meant*	ment	*Meant*	ment
Soñar	*Dream*	driːm	*Dreamt* *Dreamed (AmE)*	dremt driːmd	*Dreamt* *Dreamed (AmE)*	dremt driːmd

Verbos que el Participio acaba en *'-n'* con una *'o'* en el pasado

ESPAÑOL	INGLÉS	Pron.	PASADO	Pron.	PARTICIP.	Pron.
Conducir	*Drive*	draɪv	*Drove*	drəʊv	*Driven*	ˈdrɪvn̩
congelar	*Freeze*	friːz	*Froze*	frəʊz	*Frozen*	ˈfrəʊzən
despertarse	*Wake*	weɪk	*Woke*	wəʊk	*Woken*	ˈwəʊkən
elegir	*Choose*	tʃuːz	*Chose*	tʃəʊz	*Chosen*	ˈtʃəʊzən
escoger	*Choose*	tʃuːz	*Chose*	tʃəʊz	*Chosen*	ˈtʃəʊzən
escribir	*Write*	ˈraɪt	*wrote*	rəʊt	*Written*	ˈrɪtn̩
hablar	*Speak*	spiːk	*Spoke*	spəʊk	*Spoken*	ˈspəʊkən
jurar, blasfemar	*Swear*	sweə	*Swore*	swɔː	*Sworn*	swɔːn
Llevar puesto	*Wear*	weə	*Wore*	wɔː	*Worn*	wɔːn
Montar	*Ride*	raɪd	*Rode*	rəʊd	*Ridden*	ˈrɪdn̩
olvidar	*Forget*	fəˈget	*Forgot*	fəˈgɒt	*Forgotten*	fəˈgɒtn̩
Robar	*Steal*	stiːl	*Stole*	stəʊl	*Stolen*	ˈstəʊlən
romper	*Break*	breɪk	*Broke*	brəʊk	*Broken*	ˈbrəʊkən

Otros verbos comunes que el **participio** acaba en **'n'**.

ESPAÑOL	INGLÉS	Pron.	PASADO	Pron.	PARTICIPIO	Pron.
Caer	Fall	fɔːl	Fell	fel	Fallen	ˈfɔːlən
Comer	Eat	iːt	Ate	et	Eaten	ˈiːtn̩
Dar	Give	gɪv	Gave	geɪv	Given	gɪvn̩
Esconder	Hide	haɪd	Hid	hɪd	Hidden	ˈhɪdn̩
Perdonar	Forgive	fəˈgɪv	Forgave	fəˈgeɪv	Forgiven	fəˈgɪvn̩
Prohibir	Forbid	fəˈbɪd	Forbade	fəˈbæd	Forbidden	fəˈbɪdn̩
Ver	See	ˈsiː	Saw	ˈsɔː	Seen	ˈsiːn

Pasado '-ew', Participio '-own'.

ESPAÑOL	INGLÉS	Pron.	PASADO	Pron.	PARTICIPIO	Pron.
Crecer	Grow	grəʊ	Grew	gruː	Grown	grəʊn
Saber/Conocer	Know	nəʊ	Knew	njuː	Known	nəʊn
Soplar	Blow	bləʊ	Blew	bluː	Blown	bləʊn
Tirar	Throw	ˈθrəʊ	Threw	θruː	Thrown	ˈθrəʊn
Volar	Fly	flaɪ	Flew	fluː	Flown	fləʊn

Pasado y participio acaban en '-ught'.

ESPAÑOL	INGLÉS	Pron.	PASADO	Pron.	PARTICIPIO	Pron.
Buscar	Seek	grəʊ	Sought	gruː	Sought	grəʊn
Comprar	Buy	flaɪ	Bought	fluː	Bought	fləʊn
Enseñar	Teach	tiːtʃ	Taught	tɔːt	Taught	tɔːt
Luchar	Fight	bləʊ	Fought	bluː	Fought	bləʊn
Pensar	Think	nəʊ	Thought	njuː	Thought	nəʊn
Traer	Bring	ˈθrəʊ	Brought	θruː	Brought	ˈθrəʊn

Inglés básico para hispanohablantes | Verbos

Cambia de *'-ell'* a *'-old'*.

ESPAÑOL	INGLÉS	Pron.	PASADO	Pron.	PARTICIPIO	Pron.
Decir	*Tell*	tel	*Told*	təʊld	*Told*	təʊld
Vender	*Sell*	sel	*Sold*	səʊld	*Sold*	səʊld

El **infinitivo** acaba en *'d'*, pero el **pasado** y el **participio** acaban en *'t'*.

ESPAÑOL	INGLÉS	Pron.	PASADO	Pron.	PARTICIPIO	Pron.
Doblar	*Bend*	bend	*Bent*	bent	*Bent*	bent
Enviar	*Send*	send	*Sent*	sent	*Sent*	sent
Prestar	*Lend*	lend	*Lent*	lent	*Lent*	lent
Gastar	*Spend*	spend	*Spent*	spent	*Spent*	spent
Construir	*Build*	bɪld	*Built*	bɪlt	*Built*	bɪlt
Dormir	*Sleep*	sliːp	*Slept*	slept	*Slept*	slept
Mantener	*Keep*	kiːp	*Kept*	kept	*Kept*	kept

✱ El verbo 'to be'

El verbo **'to be'** nos ahorra a los hispanohablantes aprendernos varios verbos diferentes en inglés, porque se traduce al español como los verbos ser, estar, tener, etc...

I am pretty ⟶ Soy guapa

John is twenty years old ⟶ John tiene veinte años

Sam and Mary are Spanish ⟶ Sam y Mary son españoles

Observa esta tabla:

Sujeto + Verbo **'to be'** + Complemento

I (Yo)	**am** (soy/estoy)	
You (Tú)	**are** (eres/estás)	
He (Él) **She** (Ella) **It** (Eso)	**is** (es/está)	**Tired** (Cansado)
We (Nosotros)	**are** (somos/estamos)	
You (Vosotros)	**are** (sois/estáis)	
They (Ellos o Ellas)	**are** (son/están)	

Tal como en español, el verbo **'to be'** se utiliza para describir estados relativamente permanentes:

She is Spanish ⟶ Ella es española

o estados transitorios:

We are happy ⟶ Estamos felices

✲ Contracciones, Negación e Interrogación

En inglés, a diferencia del español, es muy habitual contraer dos palabras mediante un apóstrofe (').

Cómo se contrae el verbo *'to be'*:

NORMAL	CONTRACCIÓN
I am	I'm
You are	You're
He is / She is	He's / She's
It is	It's
We are	We're
You are	You're
They are	They're

young (joven)

NEGACIÓN

Para negar el verbo *'to be'* se le debe añadir la partícula *'not'*.

Cuando queremos contraer la negación se le añade *'-n't'* unido al verbo (excepto en la primera persona del singular: *'am'*).

NEGACIÓN	CONTRACCIÓN
I am not	I'm not
You are not	You aren't
He is not / She is not	He isn't / She isn't
It is not	It isn't
We are not	We aren't
You are not	You aren't
They are not	They aren't

sad (triste)

INTERROGACIÓN

En inglés no existe el símbolo de interrogación de principio de frase como en español (¿)

En inglés sólo se utiliza el símbolo del final (?) por lo que, para saber que una frase va a ser una pregunta desde el principio, debemos fijarnos en el orden de las palabras.

En las oraciones interrogativas cambiaremos el orden de las palabras y colocaremos el verbo al principio seguido del sujeto:

You are short ⟶ Eres bajo (lo afirmo)
Are you short? ⟶ ¿Eres bajo? (lo pregunto)

* Fijándote en el orden de las palabras en inglés puedes saber fácilmente, desde el principio, si se va a formular una pregunta o una afirmación.

✱ 'There is' y 'There are'

Pues vamos vamos a enlazar el tema del verbo **'to be'** con el tema también muy importante de **'there is'** y **'there are'** (hay).

Cuando queremos decir que hay o no hay algo o alguien, utilizaremos **'there is'** (para el singular) y **'there are'** (para el plural).

1. En español decimos **"hay"** tanto para el **singular** como para el **plural**:

   There is *a cow (**There's** a cow)* ⟶ Hay una vaca
   There are *some cows* ⟶ Hay algunas vacas

2. La negación se forma **añadiendo "NOT"** tras **"is/are"**:

   There is not *a horse (**There isn't** a horse)* ⟶ No hay un caballo
   There are not *any trees (**There aren't** any trees)* ⟶ No hay árboles

3. Para construir la forma interrogativa de esta expresión simplemente debemos **invertir el orden**:

   There is *a wall.* Hay una pared.
   Is there *a wall?* ¿Hay una pared?

Verbos | Inglés básico para hispanohablantes

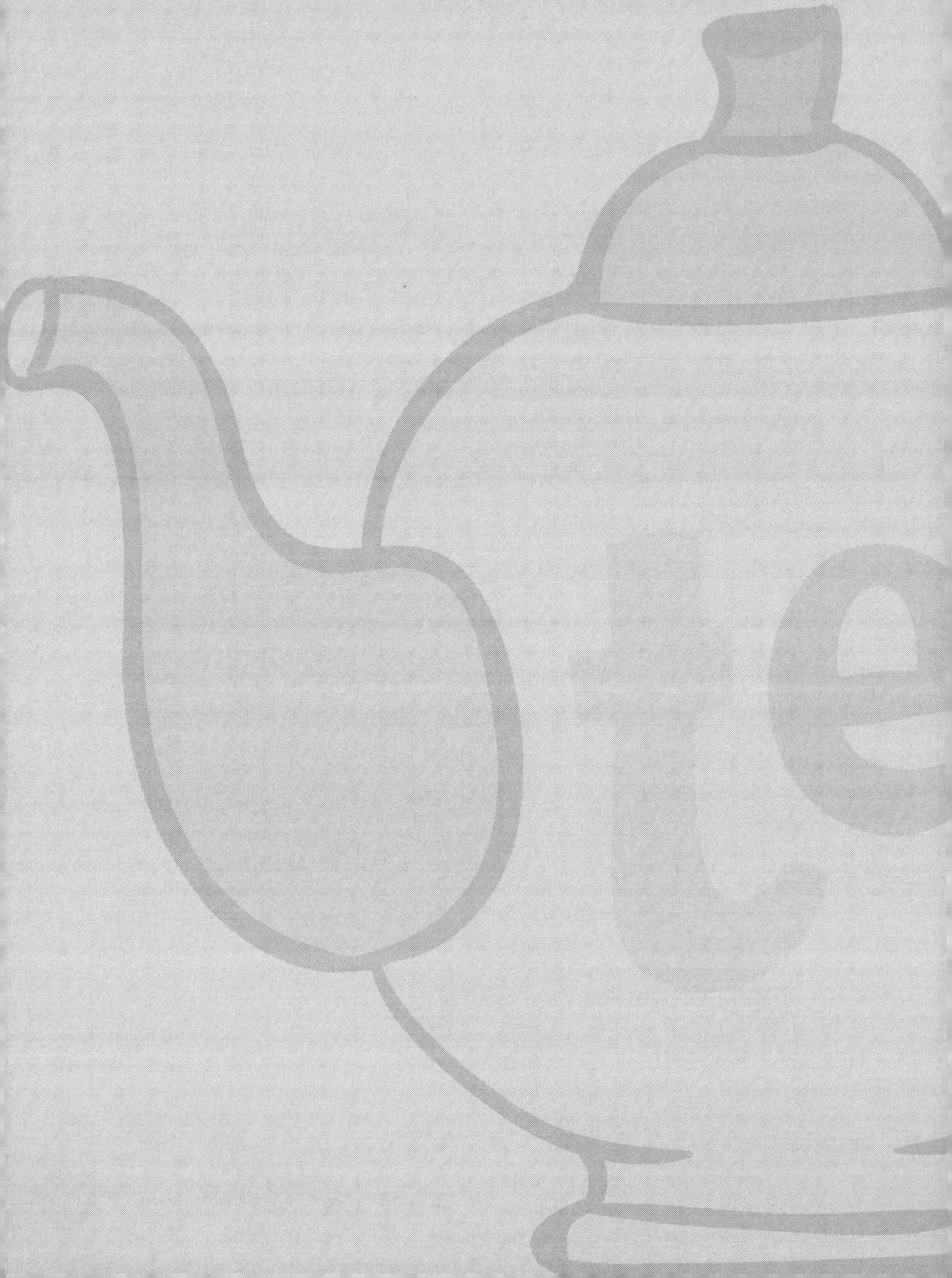

Tiempos Verbales

7 Tiempos Verbales

✱ El Presente Simple: Introducción

Si comparamos la formación del Presente Simple en inglés y en español podemos atrevernos a afirmar que resulta mucho más sencilla la versión inglesa.

Ahora veremos por qué:

I eat at 2 o'clock ⟶ (Yo) como a las 2 en punto

Esta forma verbal se emplea para referirnos a:

1) Verdades Universales:
   Water boils at 100 degrees - El agua hierve a 100 grados

2) Hábitos o costumbres
   We drink water every day - Nosotros bebemos agua cada día

3) Gustos o estados
   Children like summer - A los niños les gusta el verano.

Si nos fijamos en los ejemplos vemos que los verbos permanecen invariables en casi todos los casos. Veamos la estructura:

Sujeto + Verbo + (Complemento)

I send emails (Envío emails)
You send emails (Envías emails)
He/She sendS emails (Envía emails)
We send emails (Enviamos emails)
You send emails (Enviáis emails)
They send emails (Envían emails)

Y bien, ¿veis como en español es bastante más complicado?

Cada persona lleva una terminación diferente.

En inglés esto se simplifica al máximo así que no os podéis quejar.

64 Inglés básico para hispanohablantes | Tiempos verbales

La única forma verbal que se diferencia de las demás es la tercera persona del singular, **'He/She/It'** en la que se le añade una **"-s"** al final del verbo.

He works - (Él) trabaja.

Aunque admito que no todo es tan fácil.
Existen algunas excepciones a la hora de formar la tercera persona del singular.

Excepciones:
1) Cuando el verbo acaba en **-sh, -ch, -s, -x, -z, -o** se le añade **"-es."**

   TO WASH - **He washes** the dishes. Él lava/friega los platos
   TO CATCH - **The dog catches** the ball. El perro atrapa la pelota
   TO WAX - **She waxes** her legs. Ella se depila las piernas

Usamos esa **"-e"** + **"s"** como forma de facilitar la pronunciación.

Intentad pronunciar la tercera persona de cualquiera de los verbos anteriores sin esa **"-e"** de apoyo: *washs, *catchs, *waxs...

No solo sería muy complicado sino que pareceríamos serpientes siseando.
Así que si no queréis pareceros a esos agradables bichitos...

¡recordad añadir '-es'!

2) Cuando la palabra acaba en **"y"** tras consonante, se sustituye la **"y"** por una **"i"** y se le añade **"-es"**.

   TO STUDY - **He studies.** Él estudia

   Pero NO en:
   TO PLAY - **She plays.** Ella juega
   TO BUY - **She buys.** Ella compra

... porque la **"y"** no va seguida de consonante, sino de vocal.
El Presente Simple: Negación e Interrogación

Antes de acabar, debéis saber que hay dos verbos que cambian en algunas personas:

1. El verbo *'to have'* (tener) es irregular en la tercera persona del singular *'He/she has'*

I have
You have
He/she/it has
We have
You have
They have

2. El verbo *'to be'* (ser/estar) también es irregular:

I am
You are
He/she/it is
We are
You are
They are

✱ El Presente Simple: Negación e Interrogación

Hemos visto cómo se forma el Presente Simple, en su forma más simple (valga la redundancia).

Ahora vamos a ver cómo se forma la negación e interrogación en Presente Simple.

Para negar o preguntar hay que añadirle un verbo auxiliar a la frase.

> Utilizaremos el auxiliar **'do'**
> ***You don't speak French*** - (Tú) no hablas francés
> ***Does she speak French?*** - ¿Habla (ella) francés?

1. Para formar la **negación**
   Si quieres negar algo en Presente Simple deberás añadir verbo auxiliar **'do'** más **'not'** después del sujeto y antes del verbo.

   Do es simplemente eso, un auxiliar, algo que nos ayuda a formular preguntas y negaciones pero NO se traduce.

   You do not know Peter (You don't know Peter) - Tú no conoces a Peter
   * El verbo deberá ir en infinitivo.

   Así se forma:

   Sujeto + *don't/doesn't* + Verbo (Infinitivo) + (Complemento)

   I don't eat meat - (Yo) No como carne
   You don't eat meat
   He/She DOESN'T eat meat
   We don't eat meat
   You don't eat meat
   They don't eat meat

* Os habéis fijado que otra vez lo único que ha cambiado es la tercera persona del plural **'He/She'** (se usa **does + not = doesn't**) igual que con **'it'** (eso):

It doesn't rain much in summer - No llueve mucho en verano.

2. Para formar la **interrogación**

La primera diferencia que se percibe a simple vista es que, en inglés, sólo hay un signo de interrogación al final de la oración pero, si además nos fijamos en el orden de las palabras, vemos que el sujeto ya no encabeza la frase sino el auxiliar:

> **Does** para la tercera persona y **Do** para el resto.

Do they live in that building? ¿Viven (ellos) en ese edificio?
Does he like pop music? ¿Le gusta la música pop?

Sin embargo, si hubiera algún pronombre interrogativos **(Wh-words)** este tendría que anteponerse al propio auxiliar. Fijaos en cómo quedaría la estructura:

> **(Wh-word) + Auxiliar (do/does) + Sujeto + Verbo (Infinitivo) + (Complemento)?**

Where do I live? - ¿Dónde vivo?
Where do you live? - ¿Dónde vives?

¡atención!

Where DOES he live? - ¿Dónde vive?
El verbo en 3º pers. no lleva **"-s"** porque ya está en el auxiliar.

Where DOES she live? - ¿Dónde vive?
Where do we live? - ¿Dónde vivimos?
Where do you live? - ¿Dónde vivís?
Where do they live? - ¿Dónde viven?

SHORT ANSWERS

Los anglosajones tienen fama de ser extremadamente educados así que si no quieres desentonar, recuerda que cuando contestes a una pregunta, es de mala educación decir un simple **'yes'** o **'no'** a secas.

Para responder preguntas que empiezan por el verbo auxiliar **'to do'**, tenemos que utilizar **'short answers'** (respuestas cortas).

Estas respuestas cortas se forman diciendo 'sí' o 'no' seguido del sujeto y la forma correcta del auxiliar **'to do'**:

- *Do you* like reading? - ¿Te gusta leer?
- *Yes, I do.* - Sí.
- *No, I don't.* - No.

Inglés básico para hispanohablantes | Tiempos verbales

✱ El Pasado Simple *(Past Simple)*

Para hablar de acciones que se completaron en algún punto del pasado utilizamos el Pasado Simple.

Hay dos maneras de expresar el pasado, con verbos regulares o irregulares.

Cómo se forma
En el pasado simple no se hará distinción con la tercera persona del singular *('he', 'she' and 'it')* como hacemos con el Presente Simple.

A todas las formas personales les corresponderá la misma forma del pasado:

I BOUGHT a T-shirt. Compré una camiseta.
She BOUGHT a T-shirt. (Ella) compró una camiseta.
They BOUGHT a T-shirt. (Ellos) compraron una camiseta.

Negación e Interrogación del pasado simple

Esta parte os va a resultar muy fácil, ya que las reglas para formar negación e interrogación en pasado son muy similares a las que explico en el capítulo del *Present Simple.*

AFIRMACIÓN:
I saw your brother - Vi a tu hermano.

NEGACIÓN:
She didn't miss the train - (Ella) No perdió el tren.

INTERROGACIÓN:
Did you watch that film? - ¿Viste esa peli?

Cómo se forma
Para formar tanto la negación como la interrogación del pasado simple también utilizamos el verbo auxiliar *'do'* y el verbo deberá ir en infinitivo, como ocurría con el Presente Simple.

Esta vez, tendremos que utilizar la forma en pasado del auxiliar *('did')*, la cual, al estar en pasado, no distinguirá entre las diferentes formas personales.

Y esto es una gran ventaja porque le podremos decir **bye-bye** a la **–s.**

Vamos a ver cómo funciona:

Negación

Sujeto + *did not (didn't)* + Verbo (Infinitivo) + (Complemento)

SUJETO	NEGACIÓN	CONTRACCIÓN	COMPLEMENTO
I	did not	didn't sleep (no dormí)	
You	did not	didn't sleep (no dormiste)	
He/She/It	did not	didn't sleep (no durmió)	last night (anoche)
We	did not	didn't sleep (no dormimos)	
You	did not	didn't sleep (no dormisteis)	
They	did not	didn't sleep (no durmieron)	

Interrogación

(Wh-word) + Auxiliar (did) + Sujeto + Verbo (Infinitivo) + (Complemento)?
Where   did   you   go   yesterday?
¿Dónde fuiste ayer?

Truco

Hay un truco para acordarse del orden de las palabras en la preguntas tanto en presente como en pasado simple. Solo hay que acordarse de la palabra QASI (casi).

Q	A	S	I	
Question Word	Auxiliary verb	Subject	Infinitive	
Where	**do**	**you**	**study?**	¿Dónde estudias?
Why	**did**	**she**	**shout?**	¿Por qué chilló?

Para responder preguntas que no lleven pronombre interrogativo, es decir, aquellas que empiezan por el verbo auxiliar **'did'**, tenemos que utilizar respuestas cortas.

Did she call you? - ¿Te llamó?
Yes, she did - Sí.
No, she didn't - No.

Inglés básico para hispanohablantes | Tiempos verbales

Otro truco mnemotécnico
Como nos encanta haceros las cosas más fáciles, aquí os dejo otro truquillo para recordar el orden de las palabras en este tipo de preguntas.

Esta vez hay que acordarse de la palabra ASI.

A	S	I	
Auxiliary verb	*Subject*	*Infinitive*	
Did	**they**	**leave?**	¿Se marcharon?
Do	**we**	**stay?**	¿Nos quedamos?

Pronunciación

8 Pronunciación

✳ ¿Por qué nos resulta tan difícil pronunciar bien en inglés?

Millones de personas en el mundo están estudiando inglés y quieren aprender a pronunciarlo de una manera, como mínimo, *"correcta"* (es decir, hacerse entender).

Otros pondrán toda carne en el asador para aprender a pronunciar inglés como un nativo (tanto sea americano, británico, australiano, o la versión que sea...) y, por eso, incluso existen *"coaches"* y cursos específicos que te ayudan a desprenderte de tu acento nativo *(Accent Reduction)*.

El tema de *Accent Reduction* simplemente significa que reduces tu acento nativo (en nuestro caso el español) y empleas un nuevo sistema de sonidos (fonología).

Para conseguir el acento deseado uno debe:

- Cambiar la manera en que usa los órganos de articulación (los labios, los dientes, la lengua, etc..) para formar vocales y consonantes desconocidas hasta ahora.

- Modificar la entonación y los patrones de acentuación.

- Cambiar el ritmo del habla.

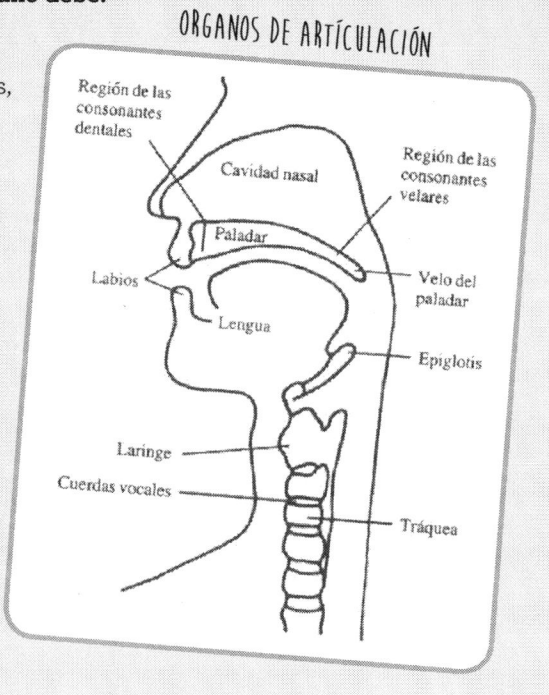

ÓRGANOS DE ARTICULACIÓN

Región de las consonantes dentales
Cavidad nasal
Región de las consonantes velares
Paladar
Labios
Velo del paladar
Lengua
Epiglotis
Laringe
Cuerdas vocales
Tráquea

Mucha gente quiere aprender a pronunciar "más a la inglesa" porque les
da vergüenza tener un acento demasiado "español".

En mi vida como profe me he encontrado con alumnos de todas las edades y
estamentos sociales (incluso algún profe de inglés) que controlaban el tema
del *reading* y de *gramática,* pero que a la hora de expresarse (o de entender a alguien
hablando inglés) se perdían en jardines muy floridos... ☺

Cuántas veces me he encontrado con gente que me dice: "Nooo, si yo leer inglés puedo,
es hablar o entender a un inglés lo que me cuesta..."

El problema de fondo no lo arreglaremos en los cinco minutos que tardes en leer este
capítulo. Es un tema que viene de largo, del énfasis que siempre se ha puesto (al menos
en España) en aprender la gramática, olvidándose de la importancia del *listening* y
del *speaking*.

Por eso, si no aprendemos a pronunciar bien en inglés, más nos costará entender esa
misma pronunciación en alguien que nos hable en inglés con un acento cerrado de, por
ejemplo, Glasgow.

Tampoco digo que aprendiendo a pronunciar bien, entiendas a un grupo de escoceses
en un bar a las 3 de la mañana, no...
Yo tenía un novio de Londres al que le costaba entender el acento escocés en ese tipo
de situaciones (es como un catalán intentando entender a un grupo de menorquines
hablando rápido en las fiestas de Sant Bartomeu). Ese no es el tema...

La cuestión es que aprender a pronunciar bien en inglés te ayudará a distinguir esos
mismos sonidos en los demás.

Serás capaz de reconocerlos más fácilmente que si te limitas a "yo leo bien en inglés
pero ni lo hablo ni lo entiendo".

Y no es fácil.

Fácil podría ser, pero requiere un esfuerzo de tu parte. Aquí no se regala nada.

Obviamente, el inglés escrito y el hablado son muy diferentes.
Son como dos temas (asignaturas) casi independientes.
Un estudiante, a diferencia de con el español, tendrá que aprender, por un lado
a leer (con su *spelling*) y, por el otro, a pronunciar/escuchar con sus sonidos específicos.

Es importante tener en cuenta que el *writing/reading* no va tan ligado al *speaking/
listening* cómo nos creíamos...

¡esto no es Spanish, señores!

En inglés, la vista (leer/escribir) y el oído (hablar/escuchar) forman parte de dos
dimensiones separadas.

Historia real:

Conocí a una señora en Londres, llamda Adelina, que limpiaba la escuela donde yo trabajaba de secretaria. Esta señora había estado currando en el mismo puesto de trabajo durante más de 30 años.

Adelina era una señora gallega y analfabeta que se había ido a Londres hacía muchísimo tiempo con su marido para buscarse la vida en una época donde la gente huía de una España en corrupta y en crisis.

Llegó allí con sus cuatro pesetillas ahorradas y empezó a trabajar de limpiadora en una escuela. Treinta años después de que Adelina llegara a Londres, yo la conocí. Seguía sin saber leer ni escribir, pero se comunicaba en inglés con un acento casi perfecto.

Había aprendido inglés de oídas, no se confundía (como yo) con palabras que se escribían y pronunciaban de diferente manera en inglés, ¡porque no sabía leer!

En ese tiempo yo (todavía sin haber estudiado la carrera de Filología Inglesa y sin conocer todas las teorías académicas que apoyaban mis "descubrimientos") me dí cuenta de que, de alguna forma, esa era la manera perfecta de aprender un nuevo idioma, desde cero, de una manera pura, sin contaminaciones lingüísticas, como empieza un bebé a aprender su primera lengua, "analfabéticamente" (esta palabra creo que me la acabo de inventar).

Era más importante aprender imitando inglés que no leerlo (porque el lío y la confusión se apoderaban del "aprendiz").

- Si se escribe **'hiccough',** ¿por qué tengo que pronunciar "híccap" ?

Y de ahí muchas frustraciones y mucha gente que tira la toalla y se queda con el tema de que "el inglés es muy difícil de pronunciar" o "Yo sé leer pero no hablar".

Adelina me enseñó la asignatura más importante de mi carrera de una manera práctica.

Ella decía *"Richard"* a la inglesa, yo a la española.

Yo no la entendía.

Ella lo decía bien, yo no (ya que estaba contaminada por los "Richards" y las "Jeniffers" españolas).

Inglés básico para hispanohablantes | Pronunciación

✳ El oído

El lenguaje empieza por el oído.

Cuando un bebé empieza a hablar lo hace a través del oído; escuchando los sonidos que hace su madre e imitándola.

Si un bebé nace sordo no puede oír estos sonidos y por tanto no puede imitar y por tanto no podrá hablar.

Pero los bebés que nacen sin este tipo de limitaciones, pueden oír e imitar; son imitadores geniales y, este don de la imitación, que nos proporciona el don del habla, dura muchísimos años.

Es de sobra conocido que un niño de siete años puede aprender cualquier lengua perfectamente, pero cuando pasan los años, la habilidad de la imitación disminuye.

Bien lo sabemos los que pasamos de una cierta edad y nos damos cuenta de lo que nos cuesta pronunciar inglés de una manera "inglesa".

Hay gente que tiene más facilidad para imitar y dominar el tema de la pronunciación que otros.

Les resulta menos complicado, pero, ¡CUIDADO!, nunca resulta fácil, solo menos difícil...

¿Por qué este don de la imitación que todos tenemos de niños va desapareciendo con los años?

¿Por qué un adulto no puede pillar un sonido determinado a la primera y repetirlo sin problema como hace un niño?

La respuesta es que nuestra lengua materna no nos lo permite (más bien, nos crea obstáculos).

Para cuando somos "adultos", los hábitos y patrones de nuestra propia lengua son tan fuertes que son difíciles de romper.

Es como si en nuestra mente tuviéramos un número reducido y determinado de combinaciones de sonidos y no pudiéramos huir de ese círculo vicio-lingüístico.

Tanto es así que los sonidos que escuchamos (sean en la lengua que sean) los organizamos en nuestro cerebro dentro de ese patrón de nuestra lengua materna, y todo lo que decimos, sale de ese mismo círculo (por tanto, sonando igual).

Un **ejemplo práctico** antes de acabar con este rollazo de hoy 😊

> El **sonido /ɜː/** (de ***word, bird, turn***) **no existe en español,** entonces cuando lo oímos, lo **convertimos en una 'o', en una 'i' o en una 'a'...** porque esos sonidos sí existen en nuestro círculo vicio-lingüístico.
>
> En otras palabras, oímos ese sonido pero no lo reconocemos porque no lo tenemos guardado en nuestro disco duro y lo archivamos en una carpeta de algo que se le parezca.
>
> Guardado ahí, cuando debemos utilizarlo, lo convertiremos al sonido que consideremos más adecuado y parecido a algo dentro de nuestra red de "sonidos guardados".
>
> La solución para pronunciar bien en inglés es crear un nuevo disco duro en el que almacenaremos todos los archivos con nuevos sonidos y así poder romper el círculo vicioso de sonidos "solo en español".

¡EYY!! NO ES FÁCIL, PERO TAMPOCO ES IMPOSIBLE, ¿EH?

Se trata de romper viejos hábitos para crear unos nuevos y tener una mente abierta para dejar que nuevos sonidos formen parte de nuestro cerebro.

Para ello tenemos que escuchar en inglés, practicar nuestro *listening* como si fuéramos bebés. Despojarnos de antiguos patrones y escuchar al mundo con nuevos oídos.

Necesitaremos trabajar duro (nadie dijo que romper viejas costumbres fuera fácil), pero somos seres humanos y por tanto *"adaptables"*.

Podemos adaptarnos a nuevos *inputs,* adaptar nuestra percepción, escuchar con una nueva perspectiva e interiorizar sonidos que hasta ahora ni siquiera oíamos.

Vamos a empezar a escuchar (no solo a oír) los sonidos del inglés.
Vamos a crear un nuevo disco duro en nuestro cerebro al que llamaremos **English Sounds** y dentro de éste guardaremos archivos de vocales, diptongos y consonantes inglesas.

PERO POCO A POCO, PASO A PASO, NO HAY PRISA.

No se debe intentar romper hábitos de toda una vida en un día. Tenemos tiempo.

Adelina todavía debe estar en Londres, jubilada, viviendo de rentas y sonriendo como siempre con su Ramiro. Quiero que todos nos convirtamos en Adelina y ¡pronunciemos *"Richard"* como se tiene que pronunciar!

Inglés básico para hispanohablantes | Pronunciación

✱ Alfabeto

Es importantísimo que te aprendas de **memoria el abecedario inglés,** poniendo especial énfasis en letras con las que los hispanohablantes nos confundimos.

Nos liamos un montón con:

1) Las vocales **"A", "E" y "I"**
2) La **"B"** y la **"V"**
3) La **"W"**
4) La **"C"** y la **"S"**
5) La **"K"** y la **"Q"**
6) La **"R"**
7) La **"Y"**

ALFABETO INGLÉS CON PRONUNCIACIÓN

A [eɪ]	B [biː]	C [siː]	D [diː]	E [iː]	F [ef]
G [dʒiː]	H [eɪtʃ]	I [aɪ]	J [dʒeɪ]	K [keɪ]	L [el]
M [em]	N [en]	O [əʊ]	P [piː]	Q [kjuː]	R [ɑː]
S [es]	T [tiː]	U [juː]	V [viː]	W [dʌbljuː]	X [eks]
Y [waɪ]	Z [zed]/[ziː]				

http://aprendeinglessila.com/

✶ Símbolos fonéticos

Como has visto en el cuadro del alfabeto del capítulo anterior, todas las letritas van acompañadas de unos símbolos que pudieran parecer jeroglíficos egipcios...
Sila, **¿por qué debajo de la 'o' me pones esto [əʊ]?**

Pues son los famosos símbolos fonéticos que utilizo un montón en mis clases, en mi blog, en mis lecciones, en todoooo.

¿Por qué?

Es súper importante que conozcáis los símbolos fonéticos para que aprender inglés sea mucho más directo, rápido y sencillo.

Conociendo un poco los símbolos (... no hace falta que os saquéis un máster en alófonos), seréis capaces de pronunciar las palabras en inglés en un segundito.

Es necesario que os familiaricéis con la tabla fonética del inglés, por tres razones (como mínimo):

1) Para que vayáis practicando los diferentes sonidos y así vais creando ese disco duro de *English Sounds*.

2) Porque conociendo los símbolos fonéticos seréis capaces de pronunciar cualquier palabra en inglés con una simple ojeada al diccionario.

La mayoría de diccionarios contienen la transcripción fonética de las palabras.

3) Porque si no conoces los símbolos fonéticos no te enterarás de que el símbolo /θ/ se refiere a nuestra **«z»** española, que el símbolo /z/ es una **«s»** sonora y que el símbolo /ʃ/ se pronuncia **«sh»**.

Hay sonidos bastante complicados para los hispanohablantes, por ejemplo los diferentes tipos de **"íes"**.

Para aprender los símbolos fonéticos, existen millones de recursos en Internet en sitios como la BBC o Cambridge English.

Suelen poner un cuadro como el que ves abajo, pero en plan interactivo.

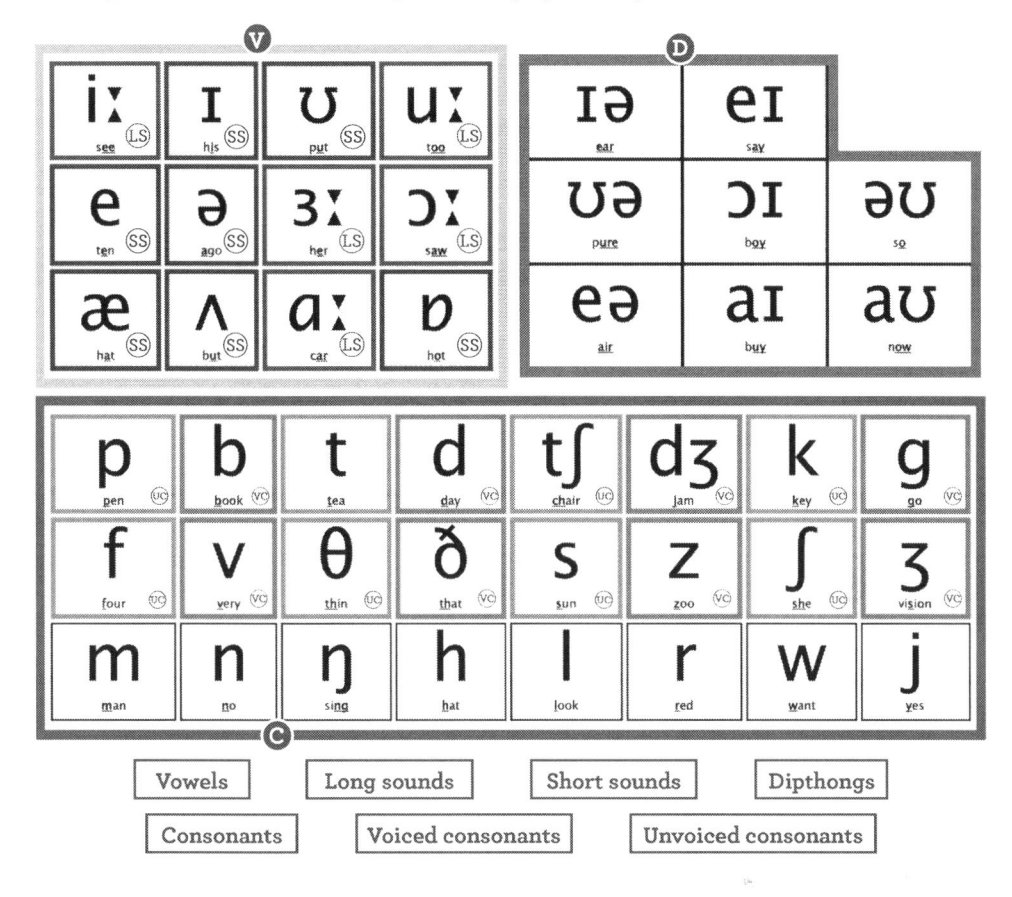

iː see (LS)	ɪ his (SS)	ʊ put (SS)	uː too (LS)		ɪə ear	eɪ say	
e ten (SS)	ə ago (SS)	ɜː her (LS)	ɔː saw (LS)		ʊə pure	ɔɪ boy	əʊ so
æ hat (SS)	ʌ but (SS)	ɑː car (LS)	ɒ hot (SS)		eə air	aɪ buy	aʊ now

p pen (UC)	b book (VC)	t tea	d day (VC)	tʃ chair (UC)	dʒ jam (VC)	k key (UC)	g go (VC)
f four (UC)	v very (VC)	θ thin (UC)	ð that (VC)	s sun (UC)	z zoo (VC)	ʃ she (UC)	ʒ vision (VC)
m man	n no	ŋ sing	h hat	l look	r red	w want	j yes

- Vowels
- Long sounds
- Short sounds
- Dipthongs
- Consonants
- Voiced consonants
- Unvoiced consonants

Lo que yo hacía para aprender las diferencias entre sonidos era pinchar en los símbolos, repetir, escuchar y así una y otra vez y vuelta a empezar hasta que al final aprendí a discernir las diferencias (a veces súper sutiles) que existen entre los diferentes sonidos del inglés.

Ahora cierra el libro y busca esta tabla fonética y empieza a escuchar y repetir los sonidos del inglés.

Mañana seguimos, ¿ok? ☺

ˈsiː ju ˈleɪtə

Pronunciación | Inglés básico para hispanohablantes

Inglés Básico
PARA HISPANOHABLANTES

Nivel:
Voy pillando algo...

Pronombres

1 Pronombres

En la sección anterior hemos visto:

- ¿Qué son los pronombres?
- Pronombres Personales y estructuras
- Pronombres Interrogativos

✱ Pronombres Acusativos

Los Pronombres Objeto o Acusativos los hemos visto anteriormente, pero les vamos a dar un repasillo, también son conocidos como Pronombres Personales Complemento.

En vez de explicaros otra vez cómo se usan estos pronombres, lo repasaréis mucho mejor viendo su uso en contexto:

En esta tabla se pueden ver estos pronombres con su traducción en español y un ejemplo de cómo se usan:

Me	me, mi	*Can you pass **me** the salt?* ¿**Me** puedes pasar la sal?
You	te, ti	*I want to go without **you*** (Yo) quiero ir sin ti
Him	le, lo, él	*I know James, I live with **him*** Conozco a James, vivo con él
Her	le, la, ella	*Who is your sister? - I don't know **her*** ¿Quién es tu hermana? –No **la** conozco
It	le, lo, él, ella, ello	*I have a new book. I have **it** here* Tengo un libro nuevo. **Lo** tengo aquí
Us	nos, nosotros, nosotras	*Sarah wants to see **us*** Sarah quiere ver**nos**
You	les, los, os, vosotros, vosotras, ustedes	*If you all want to go, I'll take **you** there* Si todos queréis ir, **os** llevaré allí
Them	les, los, las, ellos/as	*Where are my keys? I can't find **them*** ¿Dónde están mis llaves? No puedo encontrar**las**

Pronombres | Inglés básico para hispanohablantes

✱ Pronombres Reflexivos

Los Pronombres Reflexivos son aquellos que se refieren a uno mismo o a otro/s.

Myself	Me o Yo mismo
Yourself	Te, Se o Tú mismo
Himself	Se o Él mismo
Herself	Se o Ella misma
Itself	Se o A sí mismo
Ourselves	Nos o Nosotros/as mismos
Yourselves	Os o Vosotros/as mismas
Themselves	Se o Ellos/as mismos

Los Pronombres Reflexivos se utilizan para:

1. Referirse al sujeto ya mencionado. Es decir, cuando el sujeto y el objeto son el mismo.

I cut myself ⟶ Me corté (yo mismo).
He shot himself ⟶ Se disparó (a él mismo = se suicidó).

2. Enfatizar el sujeto (nadie lo ayudó a hacer tal o cual cosa)

The child got dressed (by) himself ⟶ El niño se vistió él mismo (sin ayuda de nadie).
My sister cooked this meal (by) herself ⟶ Mi hermana cocinó esta comida ella misma (sin ayuda de nadie).

3. Cuando el sujeto y el objeto son el mismo se pueden utilizar como el objeto de una preposición.

I bought a book for myself ⟶ Me compré un libro (para mí mismo)
That mad woman is talking to herself ⟶ Esa mujer loca está hablando consigo misma.

4. Intensificar el sujeto, como diciendo: "**Él en persona/Personalmente**"

The President himself wrote the letter ⟶ El Presidente (personalmente) escribió la carta.
The Queen herself knocked at the door ⟶ La reina en persona llamó a la puerta.

Cómo se forman:

SINGULAR	My Your Him Her It	+self
PLURAL	Our Your Them	+selves

Ahora vamos a ver una expresión muy común en inglés que utiliza un pronombre reflexivo:

By oneself: Sólo (sin compañía)

Entonces:

I am by myself	Estoy solo
You are by yourself	Estás solo
He is by himself	(Él) está solo
She is by herself	(Ella) está sola
We are by ourselves	(Nosotros) estamos solos
You are by yourselves	(Vosotros) estáis solos
They are by themselves	(Ellos) están solos

Sustantivos

2 Sustantivos

En la sección anterior hemos visto:

- Género de las palabras
- El plural en inglés

✱ Sustantivos Contables e Incontables

El tema de los sustantivos contables e incontables, nos resulta un tema un poquillo difícil de entender.

En español también tenemos sustantivos contables e incontables.

Además, muchos coinciden en ambas lenguas.

Ojo que he dicho muchos, no todos. Es ahí donde tenemos que tener cuidado. Hay ciertos sustantivos que en español son contables y en inglés no.

Incluso hay algunos que pueden ser contables e incontables a la vez.

Pero vayamos por partes. Empecemos con lo fácil.

Contables

- Tiene una forma de singular y otra de plural. Cuando no conocemos la palabra, generalmente la **-s** final ya nos da la pista de que puede ser plural y, por lo tanto, contable.

- Ante una forma en singular siempre utilizamos el artículo indeterminado **'a/an'** o el determinado **'the'** y, ante la forma en plural, podemos especificar el número o no.

    A dog / three dogs ⟶ un perro / tres perros

- Recuerda que el artículo determinado **'the'** va delante de sustantivos contables tanto en singular como en plural.

    The apple / the apples ⟶ la manzana/las manzanas

- No es posible usar un sustantivo contable en singular por sí solo, como ocurre en español.

    Necesito cebolla ⟶ ***I need an onion***

- Sin embargo, cuando se usan en plural sí pueden utilizarse solos.

    I need onions

- En caso de que sea plural pero NO se especifique el número, podrá ir precedido de **'some'** o **'any'**.

    I bought some pears - Compré (algunas) peras

- **'Some'** (alguno/a) se utiliza cuando el sustantivo es plural:

    Some biscuits - Algunas galletas

- **'Any'** (ninguno/a, alguno/a) se usa cuando el sustantivo es plural y la oración negativa o pregunta:

    There aren't any sweets - No hay ningún caramelo (no hay caramelos)
    Are there any sweets left? - ¿Queda (algún) caramelo?

- **'Many'** (muchos/as) se usa cuando el sustantivo es plural y la oración negativa o pregunta.

    There aren't many chairs in the classroom - No hay muchas sillas en la clase
    Are there many chairs? - ¿Hay muchas sillas?

Incontables

- Los sustantivos incontables siempre son singulares, incluso cuando parecen lo contrario.

> ***Chinese people eat rice every day*** - Los chinos comen arroz todos los días
> ***I need money*** - Necesito dinero

- Los sustantivos incontables funcionan gramaticalmente como los contables en singular en la concordancia con el verbo, ambos concuerdan con un verbo en tercera persona del singular.

- Aunque concuerden con un verbo en singular, nunca podrán llevar un artículo indeterminado.

> ***~~A music~~*** - Una música

- Tampoco pueden llevar delante un número, ya que nos referimos a algo que no se puede contar.

> ***~~Two waters~~*** - Dos aguas

- Pueden ir precedidos del artículo determinado 'the' o de 'some', cuando hablamos de un caso real, o no llevar nada delante

> ***There is salt in the sea*** - Hay sal en el mar
> ***There is some salt in the kitchen*** - Hay algo de sal en la cocina

- **Sustantivos incontables**
  Los agruparé por categorías para que os sea más fácil de recordar: Aunque ya nos ayuda bastante el hecho que hay sustantivos que son incontables tanto en inglés como en español.

  - **Líquidos:** *milk* (leche), *water* (agua), *juice* (zumo), *coffee* (café), *tea* (té)
  - **Granos:** *salt* (sal), *sugar* (azúcar), *rice* (arroz), *sand* (arena).
  - **Sentimientos:** *love* (amor), *hate* (odio), *hunger* (hambre)
  - **Sustantivos abstractos:** *beauty* (belleza), *intelligence* (inteligencia)...
  - *Bread and butter* (pan y mantequilla)
  - *Meat* (carne), *cheese* (queso) y *pasta*
  - *Money* (dinero)

- Cuando queramos referirnos a "mucho/a" no usaremos ***many***, sino **'*much*'**.

> ***I don't eat much bread*** - No como mucho pan

Por ahora ya hemos visto suficiente de este tema, más adelante nos volvemos a meter...

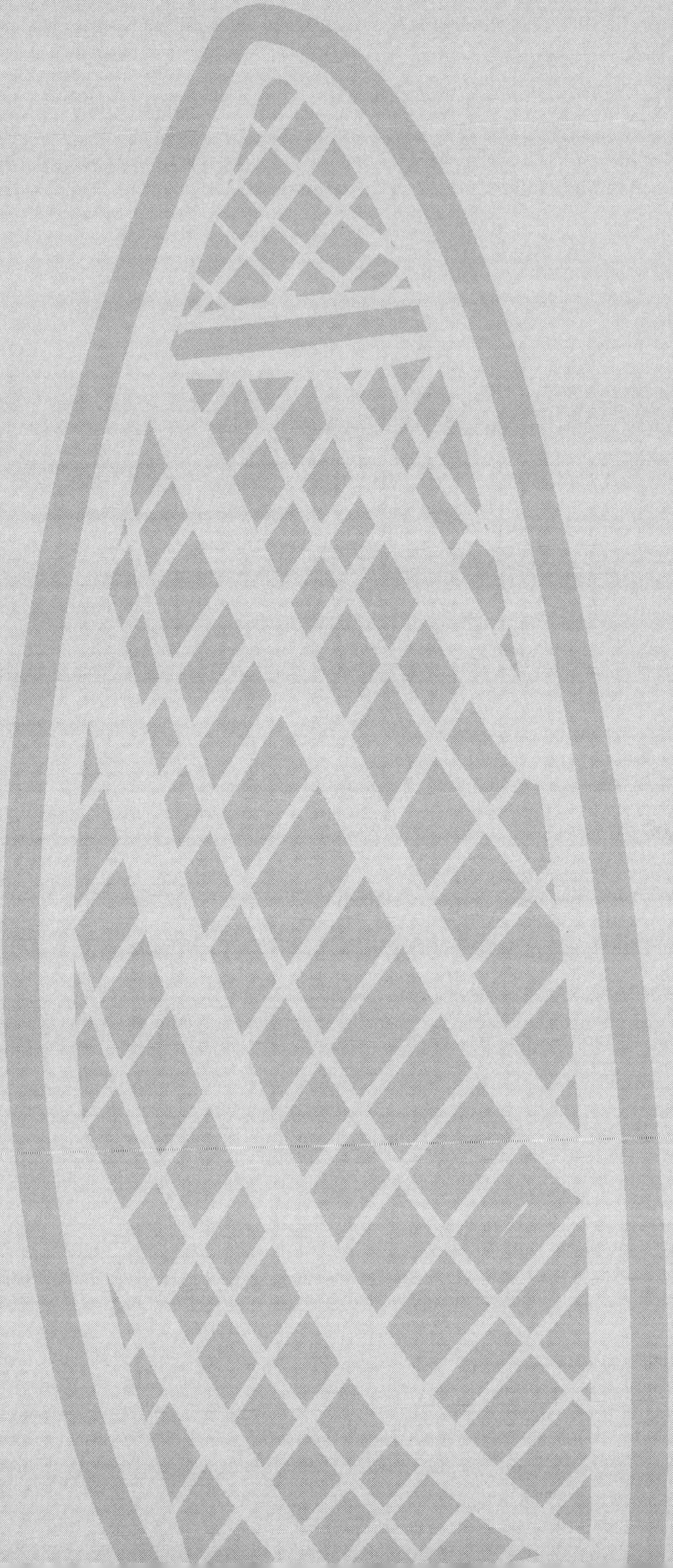

Preposiciones

3 Preposiciones

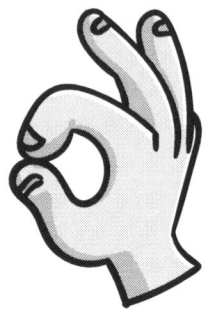

En la sección anterior hemos visto:

- Introducción
- Preposiciones de Lugar

✷ Preposiciones de Tiempo

Ahora vamos a entrar en el tema de las preposiciones de tiempo.
Como hemos visto anteriormente, las preposiciones *at*, *in* y *on* se pueden traducir al español por 'en'.

En cuestiones de tiempo, estas mismas preposiciones también nos tocan la moral ☺

At

Días festivos	*At Christmas*	En Navidad
Fin de semana	*At the weeekend* (En inglés americano se dice 'on the weekend')	El fin de semana
Horarios de comidas	*At dinner-time*	A la hora de la cena
Horas	*At 7 o'clock*	A las dos en punto

On

DÍAS	*On Friday*	El viernes
UN DÍA PARTICULAR	*On October 18th* *On New Year's Day*	El 18 de octubre El Día de Año Nuevo
DÍA + PARTE DEL DIA	*On Tuesday afternoon*	El martes por la tarde

In

AÑOS	*In 1789*	En 1789
ESTACIONES	*In (the) summer*	En verano
MESES	*In July*	En julio
SIGLOS	*In the 19th century*	En el siglo XIX

Preposiciones | **Inglés básico para hispanohablantes**

Ten en cuenta una cosa muy importante.

La preposición *'in'* se utiliza con algunas partes del día:

In the morning - Por la mañana (5h a 11:59h)
In the afternoon - Por la tarde (13h a 18h + o -)
In the evening - Por la tarde (18h a 20:30h + o -)

...pero con otras partes del día se utiliza 'at':

At noon/*at* middday - Al mediodía (12h a 13h)
At night - Por la noche (20:30h >23:59h)
At midnight - A medianoche (12h)
At dawn - Al amanecer

Y ahora veamos otras preposiciones de tiempo básicas

Antes/antes de
Se traduce al inglés como *'before'* y se coloca tras verbos y sustantivos

Your father arrived before one o'clock.
Tu padre llegó **antes que** de la una

Después / después de / tras
En inglés se dice *'after'* y también se coloca tras verbos y sustantivos.

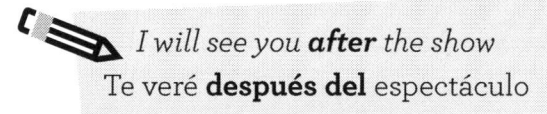

*I will see you **after** the show*
Te veré **después del** espectáculo

Durante *(during)*
En inglés lo traducimos como *'during'* y puede ir seguido de verbos y sustantivos.

*Jane watches TV **during** lunch*
Jane mira la tele **durante** la comida (mientras come)

Durante *(for)*
También se puede traducir por *'for'* aunque no tiene el mismo matiz que *'during'*. Éste se utiliza para expresar un período de tiempo ya sean días, horas, meses o años.

*I lived in London **for** five years.*
Viví en Londres **durante** cinco años

Te dejo un resumen, para que veas la diferencia entre estas dos últimas preposiciones:

Diferencia entre: DURING - FOR

DURING

durante

during
+
sustantivo

Para exponer CUÁNDO algo pasa

> Jane usually watches TV during lunch.
> Jane generalmente mira la tele durante el almuerzo
>
> Nobody spoke during the presentation.
> Nadie habló durante la presentación

FOR

durante

for
+
duración de tiempo

Para exponer DURANTE CUÁNTO TIEMPO algo pasa

> She usually watches TV for 3 hours a day.
> Ella generalmente mira la tele durante 3 horas al día
>
> We waited for 15 minutes outside your house
> Esperamos durante 15 minutos fuera de tu casa

✱ Preposiciones y medios de transporte

Ahora nos vamos a adentrar en un tema que es de inglés básico pero que tiene telita... como todo lo que tiene que ver con las preposiciones en inglés, jeje...

Generalmente con los medios de transporte usamos el verbo *'to get'* (a veces *'to go'*) acompañado de las siguientes preposiciones:

Dependiendo del tipo de medio de transporte que utilicemos, en inglés, se utilizará una preposición u otra.

Generalmente si nos referimos a un medio de transporte, y no al vehículo en sí, se usará *'by'*.

> *To go by car, train, plane, bus, ship, bicycle*
> Ir en coche, tren, avión, autobús, barco, bicicleta
> Sin embargo se dirá *on foot* (a pie)

Si nos referimos a un vehículo concreto usaremos:

In
Con: *'car'* y *'taxi'*.
En coche, en taxi.

On
Con: *'bus'*, *'train'*, *'ship'*, *'horse'*, *'bicycle'*, *'motorbike'*, *'plane'*
En autobús, tren , barco caballo, bicicleta, moto, avión

Para subir o bajar de un medio de transporte
Dependerá, al igual que antes, del tipo de vehículo.

Subir
Get in (to) + car, taxi
Subir a un coche, taxi

Get on + bus, train, bicycle, horse...
Subir a un autobus, tren, bicicleta, caballo...
Con los barcos se utilizará *go on board* (embarcar)

Bajar
Get out of + car, taxi
Bajar de un coche, taxi

Get off + bus, train, bicycle, horse...
Bajar de un autobus, tren, bicicleta, caballo...

Quick tip...

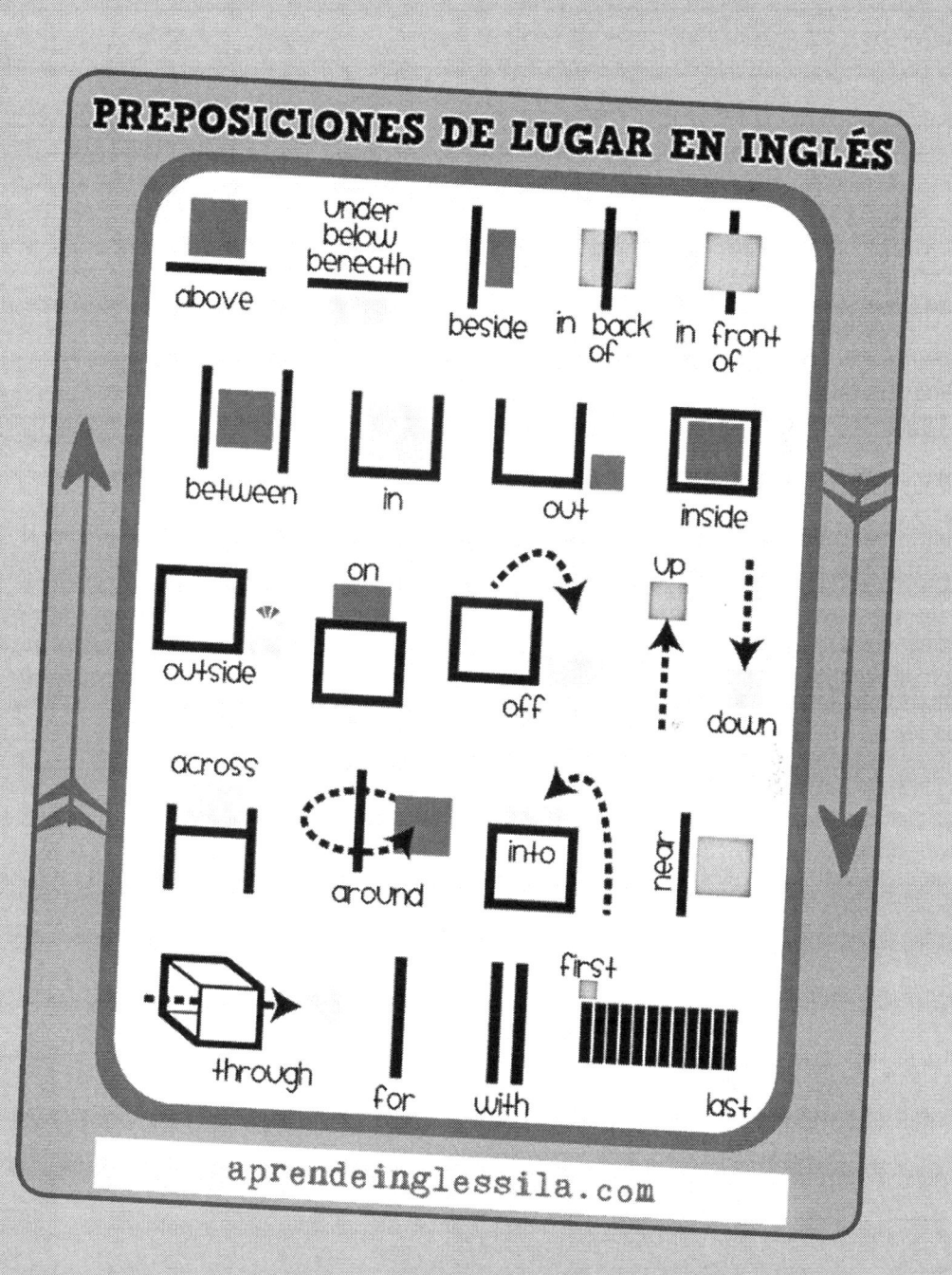

PREPOSICIONES DE LUGAR EN INGLÉS

- above
- under / below / beneath
- beside
- in back of
- in front of
- between
- in
- out
- inside
- outside
- on
- off
- up
- down
- across
- around
- into
- near
- through
- for
- with
- first
- last

aprendeinglessila.com

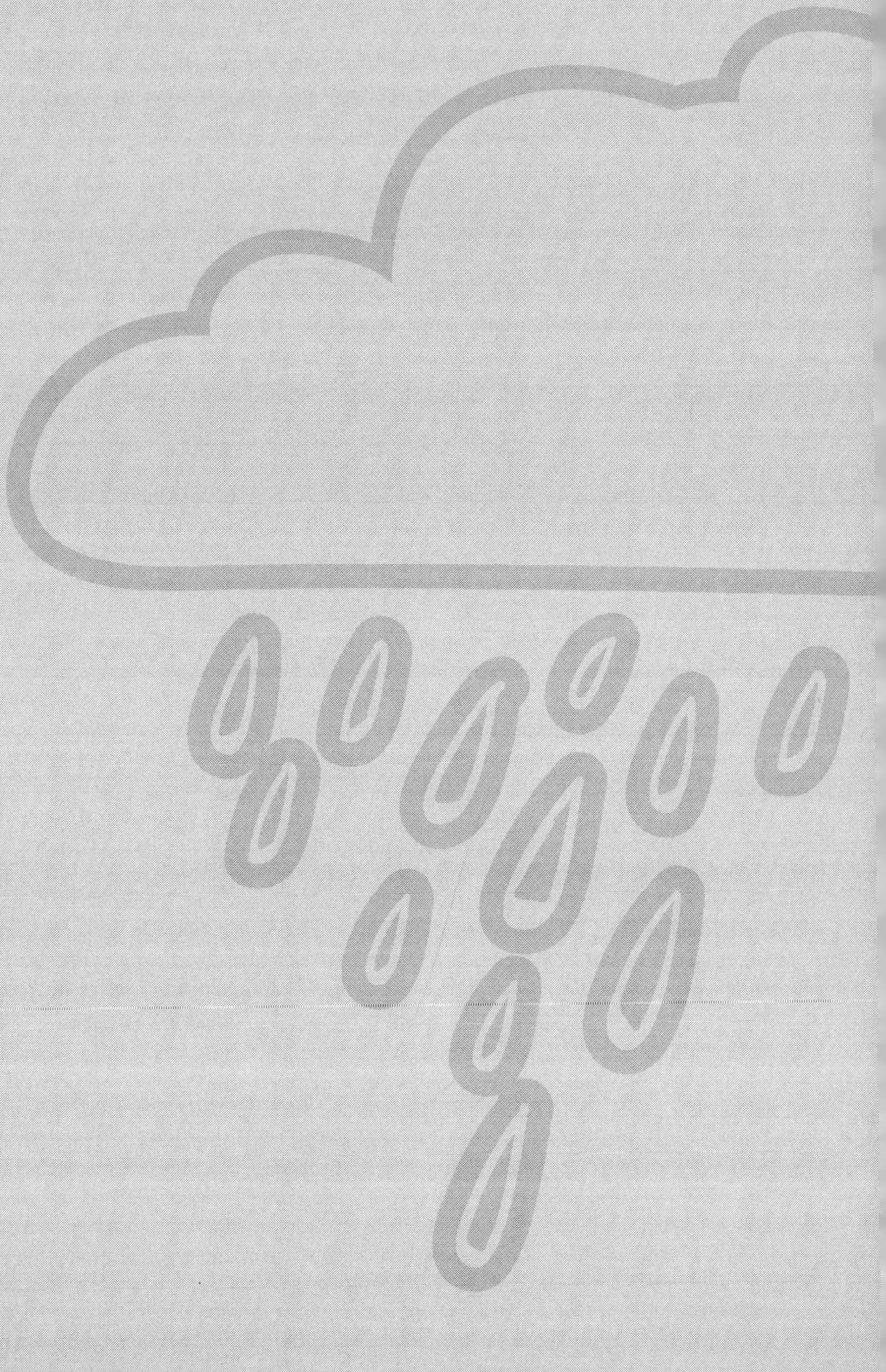

Adjetivos

4 Adjetivos

En la sección anterior hemos visto:

- Introducción.
- Adjetivos Comparativos de Igualdad.
- Adjetivos Demostrativos.
- Adjetivos Demostrativos vs Pronombres Demostrativos.

✱ Adjetivos Comparativos

Como ya hemos aprendido, los adjetivos los podemos utilizar para comparar cosas, personas, conceptos, etc.

Ahora vamos a ver cómo funcionan los Adjetivos Comparativos y los Adjetivos Superlativos.

Nos vamos a centrar en aprender a decir que una cosa es "más" que otra.

Para eso debemos utilizar la forma comparativa del adjetivo.

Cats are faster than dogs - Los gatos son más rápidos que los perros

¿Cómo se forman?
Lo vemos clarito en un cuadro:

NÚMERO DE SÍLABAS	COMPARATIVO	EJEMPLO
UNA SÍLABA	+ *"-er"* *Fast* Rápido/a	*Cats are faster than dogs.* Los gatos son más rápidos que los perros
UNA SÍLABA ACABADA EN CONSONANTE (que vaya precedida de vocal)	Doblar la última consonante + *"-er"* *Big* Grande	*Ciutadella is bigger than Ferreries.* Ciutadella es más grande que Ferreries
UNA o DOS SÍLABAS Y LA ÚLTIMA LETRA ES "-Y"	Quita la *"-y"* + *"-ier"* *Easy* Fácil	*English is easier than Mathematics.* El inglés es más fácil que las matemáticas
DOS O MÁS SÍLABAS	*More ... than* *Expensive* Caro/a	*Cars are more expensive than bikes* Los coches son más caros que las bicis
IRREGULARES	*Worse / Better* Peor/Mejor	*My teacher is better than yours* Mi profesor es mejor que el tuyo

** Pero, como siempre, hay excepciones. Por ejemplo, existen varios adjetivos de dos sílabas que aceptan ambas formas.

Ej:

Simple: *simpler / more simple*
Clever: *cleverer / more clever*

Además, adjetivos tales como **unhappy** (3-sílabas) se formaría así: **unhappier.**

El inglés tiene más excepciones que reglas. ☺

* A diferencia del español, en el que podemos dividir las palabras por sílabas, en inglés las palabras se separan por golpes de sonidos.

Por ejemplo, la palabra *phone* no la dividimos así: *pho-ne*, porque esta palabra está compuesta por un sólo golpe de sonido **/fon/**.

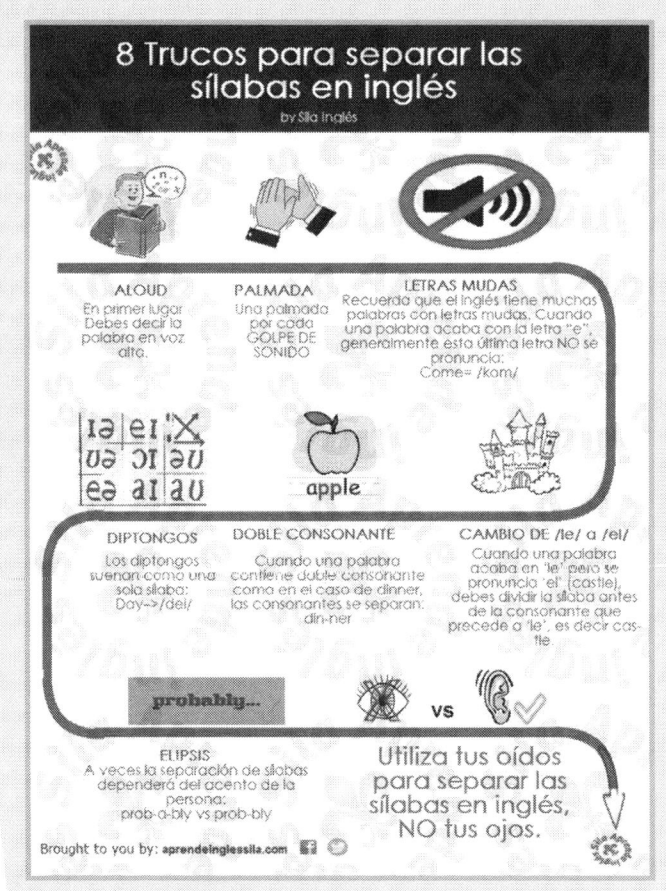

8 Trucos para separar las sílabas en inglés
by Sila Inglés

ALOUD
En primer lugar. Debes decir la palabra en voz alta.

PALMADA
Una palmada por cada GOLPE DE SONIDO

LETRAS MUDAS
Recuerda que el inglés tiene muchas palabras con letras mudas. Cuando una palabra acaba con la letra "e", generalmente esta última letra NO se pronuncia:
Come= /kom/

DIPTONGOS
Los diptongos suenan como una sola sílaba:
Day→/dei/

DOBLE CONSONANTE
Cuando una palabra contiene doble consonante como en el caso de dinner, las consonantes se separan: din-ner

CAMBIO DE /le/ a /eI/
Cuando una palabra acaba en 'le' pero se pronuncia 'eI' (castle), debes dividir la sílaba antes de la consonante que precede a 'le', es decir cas-tle

ELIPSIS
A veces la separación de sílabas dependerá del acento de la persona:
prob-a-bly vs prob-bly

Utiliza tus oídos para separar las sílabas en inglés, NO tus ojos.

Brought to you by: aprendeinglessila.com

Adjetivos Superlativos

Los Adjetivos Superlativos nos servirán para decir que algo es "lo más...".

> **The cheetah is the fastest animal**
> El guepardo es el animal más rápido

* Delante del adjetivo siempre se pone *'the'* (el, la, lo).

¿Cómo se forman?

NÚMERO DE SÍLABAS	SUPERLATIVO	EJEMPLO
UNA SÍLABA	+ *"-est"* **Tall** Alto/a	***Ana is the tallest in her class*** Ana es la más alta de su clase
UNA SÍLABA ACABADA EN CONSONANTE	Doblar la última consonante + *"-est"* **Sad** Triste	***This is the saddest poem*** Este es el poema más triste
UNA o DOS SÍLABAS Y LA ÚLTIMA LETRA ES "-Y"	Quita la *"-y"* + *"-iest"* **Pretty** Guapa	***My cousin is the prettiest girl in the world*** Mi prima es la chica más guapa del mundo
DOS O MÁS SÍLABAS	*The most* **Handsome** Guapo	***Tobías is the most handsome man in the world*** Tobías es el hombre más guapo del mundo
IRREGULARES	***Worst / Best*** El/la Peor/ El/la Mejor	***My teacher is the best*** Mi profesor es el mejor

Como hemos visto en las últimas filas de los cuadros, existen adjetivos irregulares que crean la forma comparativa y superlativa sin seguir un patrón determinado.

Estos verbos se deberían aprender de memoria, pero no os preocupéis, no son muchos y son fáciles de aprender.

Vamos a ver los más comunes:

Forma Simple	Form Comparativa	Forma Superlativa
Bad Malo	*Worse* Peor	*The worst* El peor
Good Bueno	*Better* Mejor	*The best* El mejor
Little Poco	*Less* Menos	*The least* El menos
Many Muchos	*More* Más	*The most* La mayoría
Much Mucho	*More* Más	*The most* La mayor parte
Far Lejos	*Further o Farther* Más lejos	*The farthest o the furthest* El más lejano

Inglés básico para hispanohablantes | Adjetivos

Quick tip...

Expresiones útiles en inglés para...

Pedir la opinión:

What are your thoughts on all of this?
What do you think about (that)?
Could you tell me your opinion about...?
Wouldn't you say?
How do you feel about (that)?
What's your view on...?
Do you agree?

Mostrar desacuerdo:

I don't agree
I don't think so
No way
(I'm afraid) I disagree
I really can't agree with you there
I totally disagree
I see your point but...
I beg to differ
I'd say the exact opposite
Not necessarily
That's not always true
That's not always the case
No, I'm not so sure about that
That's out of the question!

Mostrar acuerdo:

I (totally) agree
You have a point there
That sounds good
I couldn't agree with you more
That's a great idea
I agree with you 100 percent
You're absolutely right
That's fine
That's OK with me
No doubt about it
Tell me about it! (informal)

aprendeinglessila.com

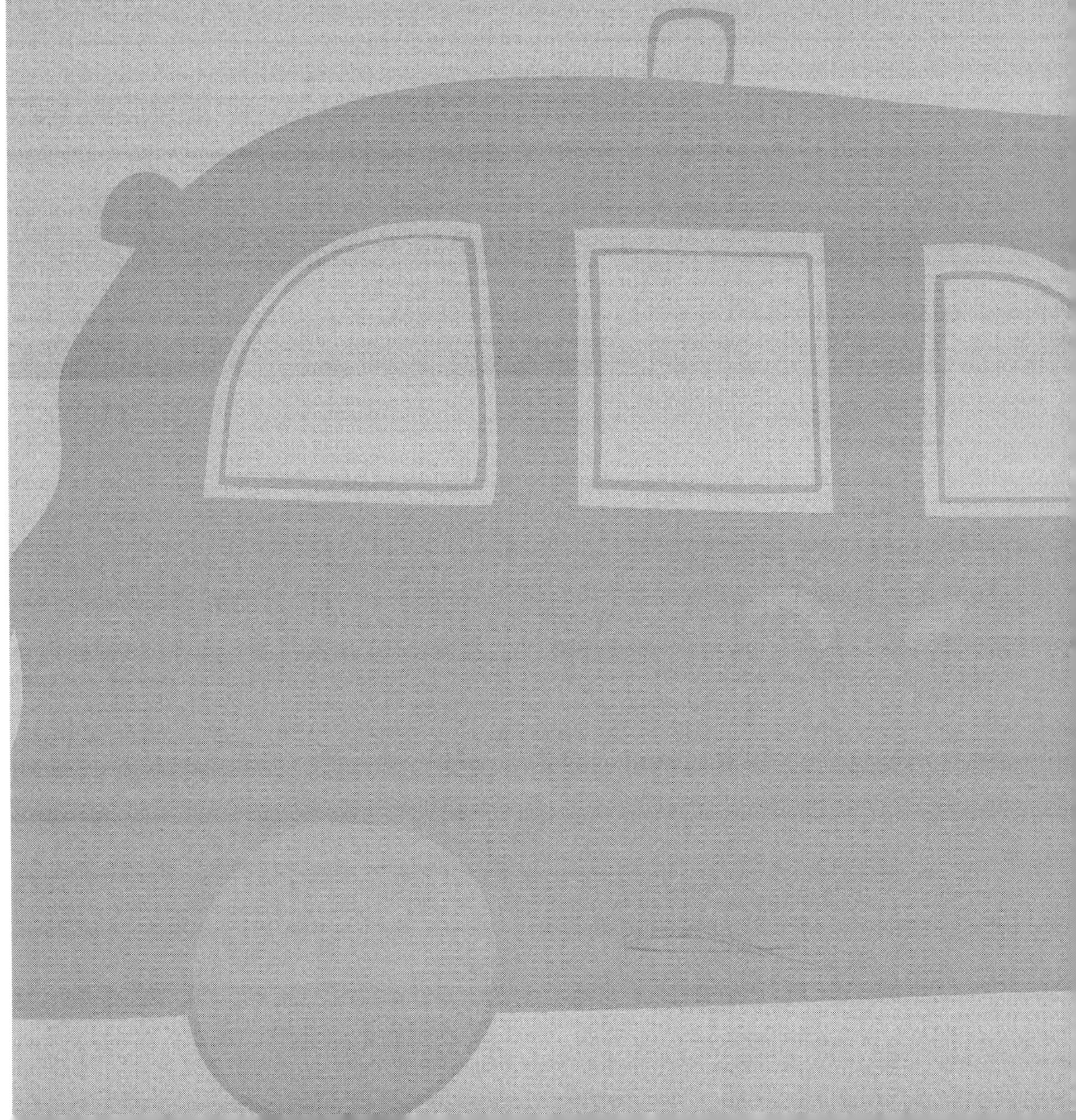

Adverbios

5 Adverbios

En la sección anterior hemos visto:

- ¿Qué son los adverbios y cómo se usan?

✱ Las Formas Irregulares y excepciones de los adverbios

¡Excepciones!....¡Cómo no!

Sería raro que todo fuera tan fácil y no aparecieran esas 'irregularidades' taaaan típicas del idioma inglés...

Veamos este tema con un *Truth or False*:

¿VERDADERO O FALSO?

1. **Todas las palabras que terminan en '-ly' son adverbios.**
   FALSO
   Hemos visto que los adverbios generalmente terminan en "-ly", pero no todas las palabras terminadas en "-ly" son adverbios.

   Por ejemplo las palabras **'friendly'** (simpático) y **'ugly'** (feo) ¡NO LOS CONFUNDAS! son adjetivos aunque terminen igual que un adverbio.

2. **Los adverbios y adjetivos son fáciles de diferenciar.**
   FALSO
   Algunos adverbios tienen la misma forma que el adjetivo, por ejemplo:

   Fast (Rápido / Rápidamente)
   Straight (Directo / Directamente)
   Far (Lejos / Lejano)

   * Algunos adjetivos cambian la forma completamente cuando se convierten en adverbios: **Good- Well** (Bueno-Bien)

3. **Los adverbios formados a partir de un adjetivo siempre conservan el significado original.**
   FALSO
   Hay adverbios formados a partir de un adjetivo que cambian el significado cuando se convierten en adverbios. Vamos a ver algunos ejemplos:

   Late (Tarde) - **Lately** (Últimamente)
   He was late (Llegó tarde)
   Vs
   Lately, he's late (Últimamente llega tarde)

   Near (Cerca) - **Nearly** (Casi)

   John lives near the park (John vive cerca del parque)
   Vs
   We spent nearly $100 in books (Gastamos casi $100 en libros)

4. Todos los adverbios se forman a partir de un adjetivo.
FALSO
Como hemos visto con los adverbios de frecuencia, hay adverbios que **no** se forman a partir de un adjetivo.

Vamos a ver algunos ejemplos más:

Adverbios de tiempo:
1. *Today*: Hoy
2. *Tomorrow*: Mañana
3. *Yesterday*: Ayer
4. *Now*: Ahora
5. *Soon*: Pronto
6. *While*: Mientras
7. *Still*: Todavía

Adverbios de lugar:
1. *Here*: Aquí
2. *There*: Allí

Todas eran *'False'*

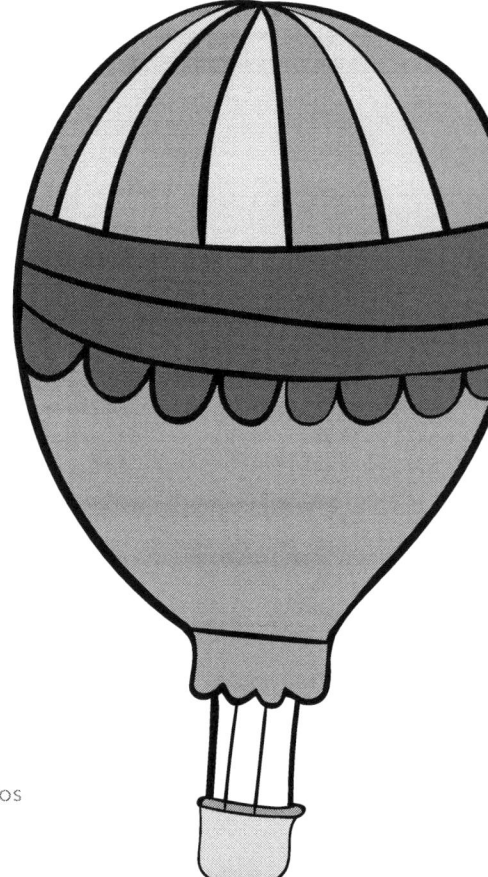

✻ Las formas Comparativas y Superlativas de los adverbios

1. Para construir la forma comparativa y superlativa de los adverbios seguiremos exactamente el mismo patrón que utilizamos para crear sendas formas en los adjetivos.

   Es decir, añadiremos *"-er"* y *"-est"* a los adverbios monosilábicos y *'more'* y *'most'* al resto.

   1 Sílaba:

ADVERBIO	COMPARATIVO	SUPERLATIVO
Fast	Faster	The fastest

   2 o más sílabas:

ADVERBIO	COMPARATIVO	SUPERLATIVO
Efficiently	More efficiently	Most efficiently

2. Como en los adjetivos, también tenemos adverbios con formas irregulares:

ADVERBIO	COMPARATIVO	SUPERLATIVO	OTRAS FORMAS
Well (Bien)	**Better** (Mejor)	**Best** - el, lo, la, los, las mejor (es)	
Badly (Mal)	**Worse** (Peor)	**Worst** - el, lo, la, los, las peor (es)	
Much (Mucho)	**More** (Más)	**Most** - el, lo, la, los, las más...	*Mostly* (La mayoría de las veces)
Little (Poco)	**Less** (Menos)	**Least** - el, lo, la, los, las menos	

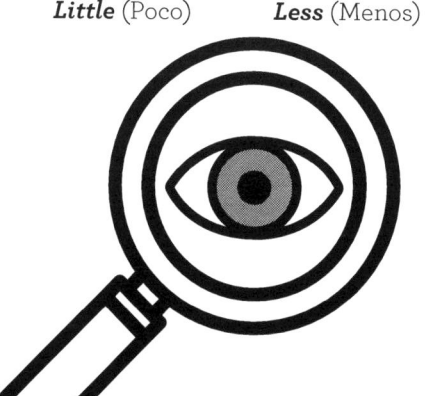

Adverbios | Inglés básico para hispanohablantes

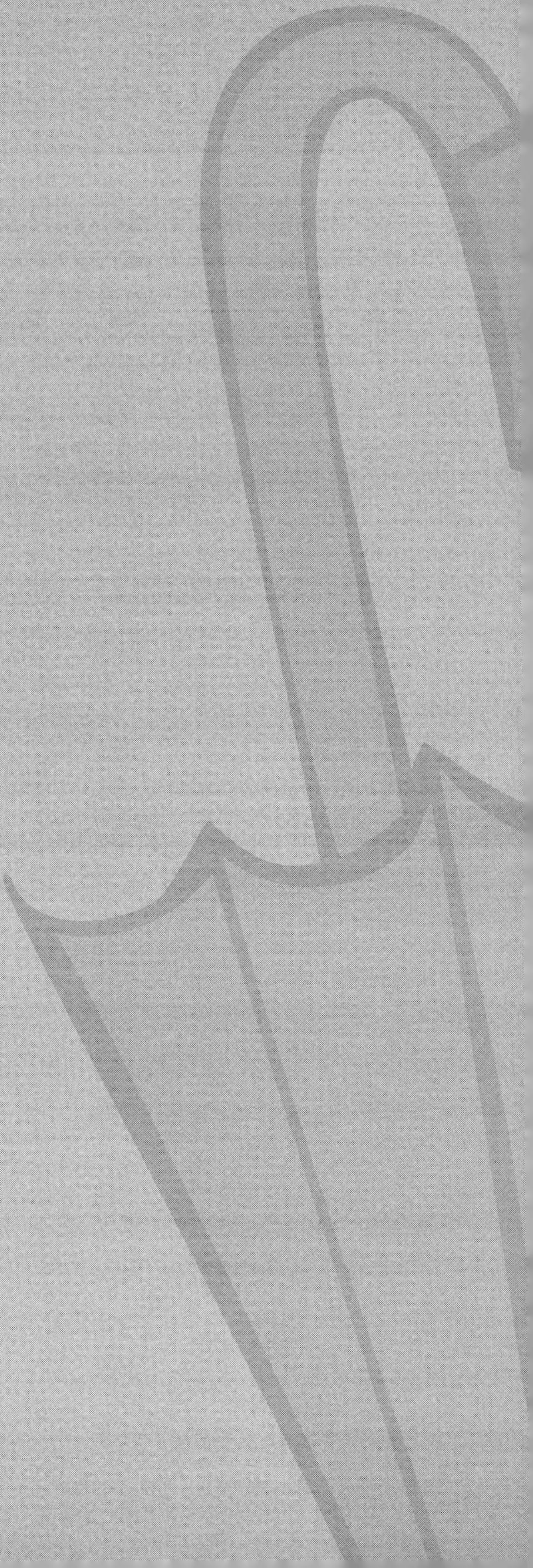

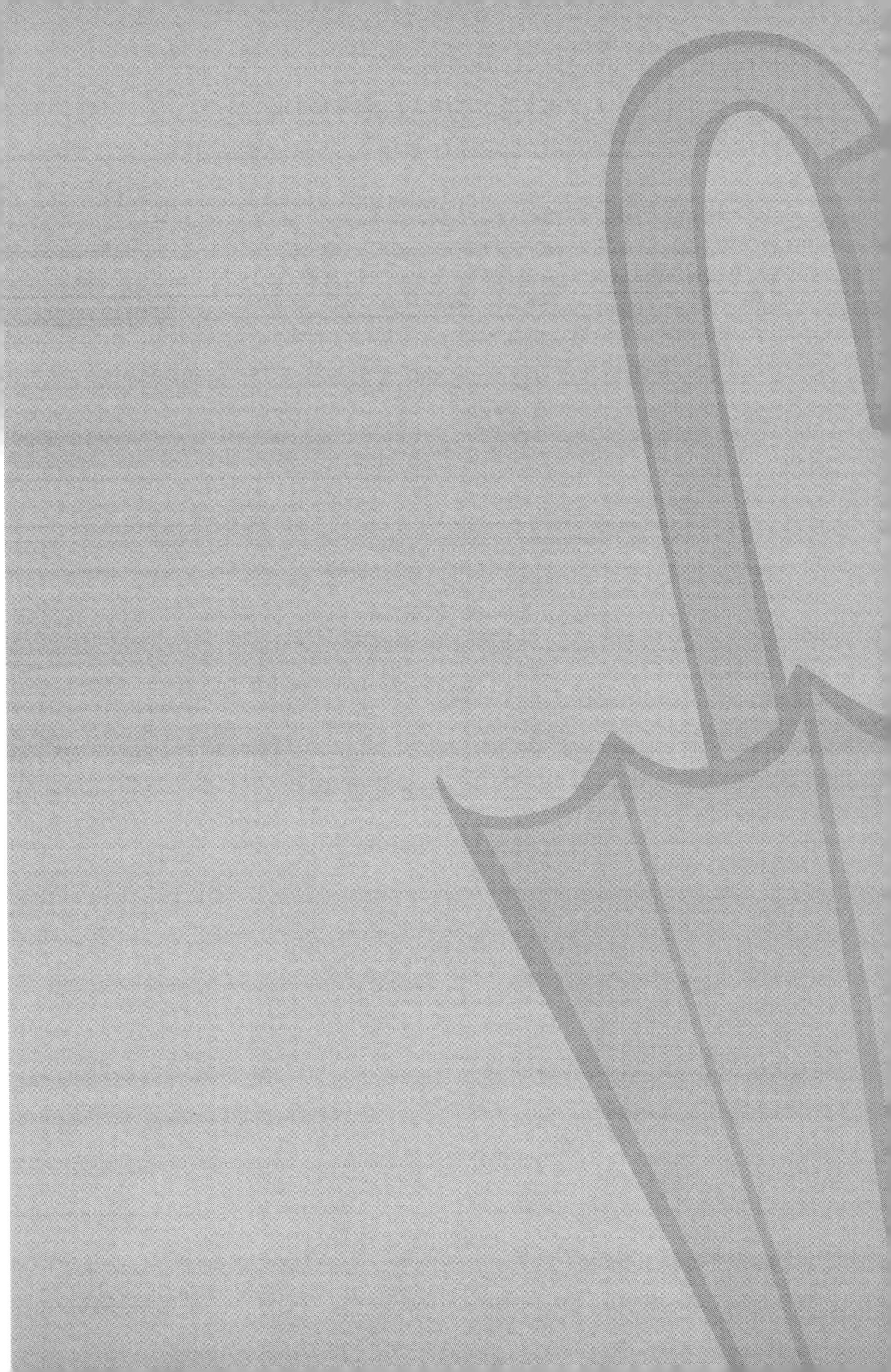

Verbos

6 Verbos

En la sección anterior hemos visto:

- Las conjugaciones en inglés
- Tipos de verbos:
  - Regulares
  - Irregulares
- El verbo *'to be'*
- *There is / There are*

✶ El verbo *'to have'*

El verbo *'to have'* en inglés es equivalente a los verbos "haber" y "tener" en español. Su conjugación en el presente del indicativo (*Simple Present*) es la siguiente:

Yo he/tengo	*I have*
Tu has/tienes	*You have*
El/ella ha/tiene	*He/she/it has*
Nosotros hemos/tenemos	*We have*
Vosotros habéis/tenéis	*You have*
Ellos/ellas han/tienen	*They have*

Como contracciones de estas formas se utilizan:

I / you / we / they have	*I / you / we / they've*
He / she / it has	*He / she / it's*

Su conjugación en Pasado Simple (*Simple Past*) tiene una única forma:

Yo había / tenía (hube / tuve)	*I had*
Tu habías / tenías (hubiste / tuviste)	*You had*
El / ella había / tenía (hubo / tuvo)	*He/she/it had*
Nosotros habíamos / teníamos (hubimos / tuvimos)	*We had*
Vosotros habíais / teníais (hubisteis / tuvisteis)	*You had*
Ellos / ellas habían / tenían (hubieron / tuvieron)	*They had*

El verbo 'have' más 'to' se usa, como en español, para decir 'tener que':

I have to write a letter
Tengo que escribir una carta

I have to buy a house
Tengo que comprar una casa

Como verbo auxiliar, 'to have' se utiliza para construir las formas compuestas, pero ese es otro tema para el próximo libro ☺

I have read your book
(Yo) he leído tu libro

'Have' nos sirve de base para construir muchísimas acciones más con otros significados distintos a "poseer":

Have breakfast / lunch / dinner
(desayunar / almorzar / cenar)

Have a drink / a coffee / a sandwich / a cigarette
(tomar una copa / un café / comer un sandwich / fumar un cigarrillo)

Have a bath
(darse un baño)

Have a baby
(dar a luz)

Have a good time
(pasar un buen rato)

Have fun
(divertirse)

Inglés básico para hispanohablantes | Verbos

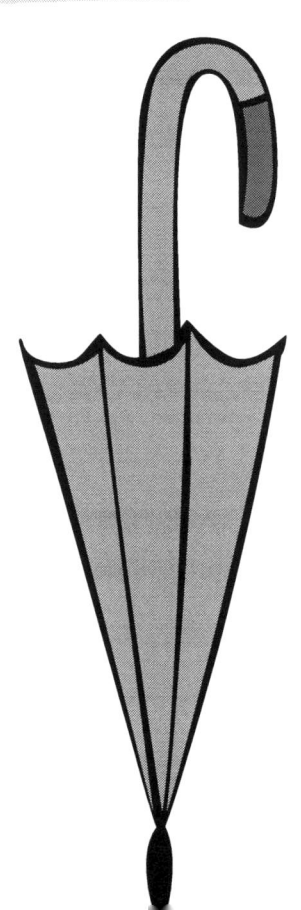

✱ Have got

Para indicar posesión usamos el verbo compuesto 'have got' (BrE) o 'have' (AmE), aunque los dos pueden utilizarse indistintamente, por ejemplo:

> **I have got a big house / I have a big house**
> Tengo una casa grande

'Have got' es frecuente en el inglés británico y 'have' es habitual en el inglés norteamericano.

Pero, ¡mucho cuidado!

Cuando digo que se puede escoger una u otra, no quiero decir que las dos tengan la misma estructura. Ojo a las diferencias:

Have got	Have
(+) She has got a red dress.	(+) She has a red dress.
(-) We haven't got a car. She hasn't got a car.	(-) We don't have a car / She doesn't have a car.
(?) Has he got a dog? Have you got a dog?	(?) Do you have a red t-shirt? Does it have a red t-shirt?

'Have got' es menos formal que 'have':

> **Do you have some coins? / Have you got some coins?**
> ¿Tienes algunas monedas?

HAVE GOT

Do y make

Make /meɪk/: hacer
Do /duː/: hacer

DO & MAKE

Diferencia principal:

- **Do:** este verbo significa "hacer" en el sentido de "realizar una actividad en general, ejecutar, llevar a cabo" como por ejemplo:

  Do homework: hacer deberes
  What did you do yesterday?: ¿Qué hiciste ayer?

- **Make:** este verbo significa "hacer" en el sentido de "fabricar algo o crear algo que no existía" como por ejemplo:

  Sam makes tables: Sam hace (fabrica) mesas.
  I will make a cake: Haré un pastel

Collocations

Una *collocation* es la combinación de dos o más palabras que a menudo se usan juntas, están 'colocadas' juntas.

Con los verbos *do* y *make*, existen un montón de estas *collocations* que debemos aprendernos de memoria para no cometer errores gramaticales del tipo *"to make a favour"* en vez de *"to do a favour"* (hacer un favor).

Para facilitaros la tarea de memorizar las más comunes, os las muestro justo aquí:

Con el verbo *TO DO*

INGLÉS	PRONUNCIACIÓN	ESPAÑOL
To do a favour	tə də ə ˈfeɪvə	Hacer un favor
To do a job	ə dʒɒb	Hacer un trabajo
To do an exercise	ən ˈeksəsaɪz	Hacer un ejercicio
To do an experiment	ən ɪkˈsperɪmənt	Hacer un experimento
To do homework	ˈhəʊmwɜːk	Hacer los deberes
To do some exercise	səm ˈeksəsaɪz	Hacer ejercicio (físico)
To do something	ˈsʌmθɪŋ	Hacer algo
To do the shopping	ðə ˈʃɒpɪŋ	Hacer la compra
To do the washing-up o to do the dishes	ðə ˌwɒʃɪŋ ˈʌp - ðə ˈdɪʃɪz	Lavar los platos

124 Inglés básico para hispanohablantes | Verbos

Con el verbo *TO MAKE*

INGLÉS	PRONUNCIACIÓN	ESPAÑOL
To make a cake	ə keɪk	Hacer un pastel
To make a complaint	ə kəmˈpleɪnt	Hacer una queja
To make a decision	ə dɪˈsɪʒn̩	Tomar una decisión
To make a mistake	ə mɪˈsteɪk	Cometer un error
To make a wish	ə wɪʃ	Pedir un deseo
To make money	ˈmʌni	Hacer dinero
To make plans	plænz	Hacer planes
To make tea	tiː	Preparar té
To make the bed	ðə bed	Hacer la cama

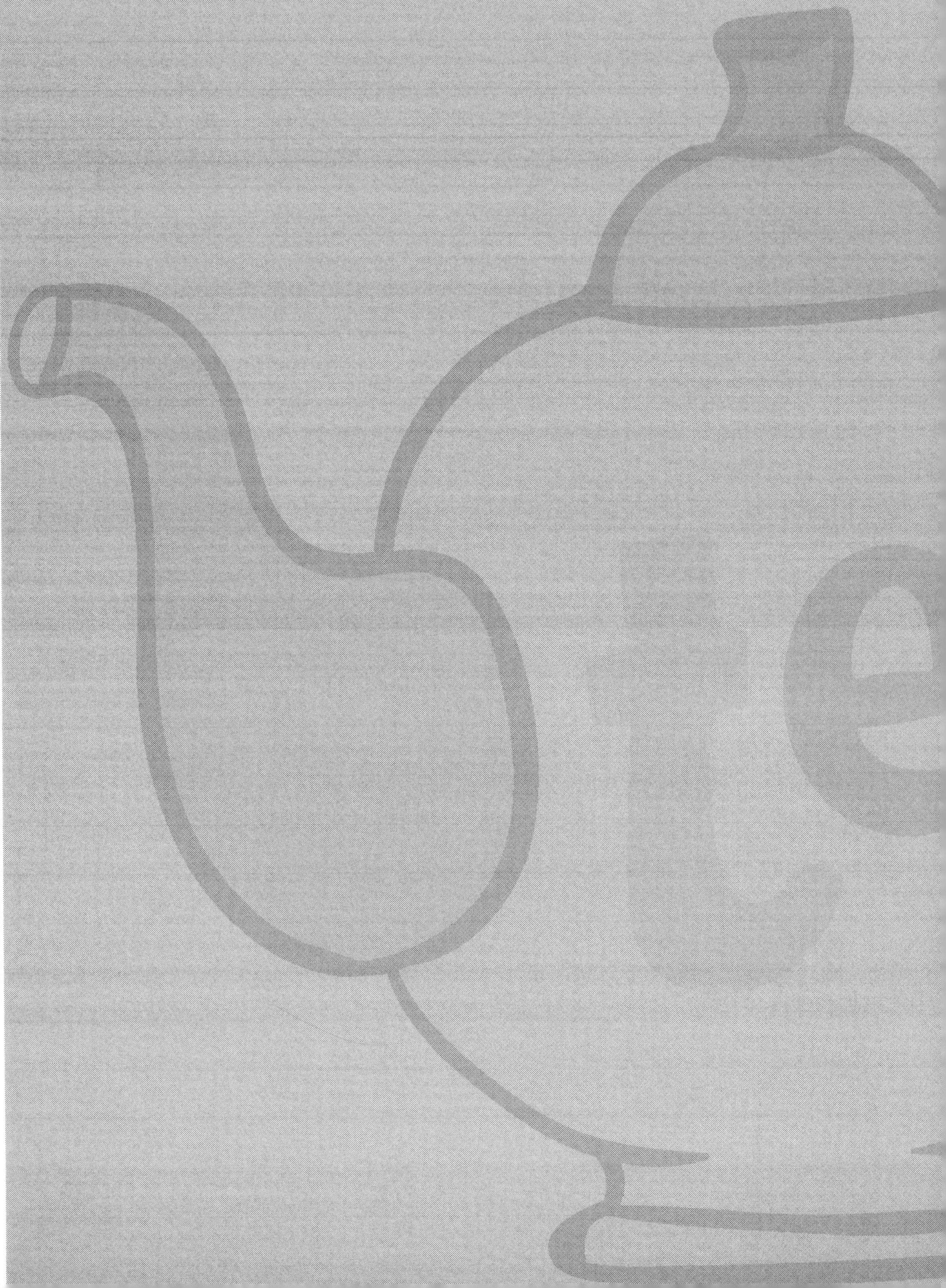

Tiempos Verbales

7 Tiempos Verbales

En la sección anterior hemos visto:

- Presente Simple
- Pasado Simple

✶ El Presente Continuo *(Present Continuous)*

Una vez ya hemos visto las formas del Presente Simple, ahora vamos a aprender la forma verbal del Presente Continuo (o Progresivo).

El *Present Continuous* generalmente se refiere a acciones que están en progreso, o sea, que están ocurriendo en el momento justo en el que estamos hablando.

Pero mira todos los usos del Presente Continuo:

1) Situaciones temporales:
   Manuel is studying English - Manuel está estudiando inglés

2) Pueden estar pasando en ese mismo instante:
   I am talking to Javier - Estoy hablando con Javier

3) Acciones que se repiten:
   They are always helping each other - Siempre se están ayudando el uno al otro

Cómo se forma

$$\text{Sujeto} + \textit{To Be} + (\text{Verbo}) \text{ '-ing'}$$

We + are + reading
1. Primero el sujeto: *we* (Nosotros)
2. Segundo: la forma presente del verbo *'to be'*: *are* (estamos)
3. Tercero: El verbo en gerundio (Verbo + '-ing'): *reading* (leyendo)

* También podemos usar la forma contraída del verbo *'to be'*:
   He's drinking a glass of wine - (Él) está bebiendo una copa de vino
   They're playing - Están jugando

Negación e Interrogación

1. Para crear la forma negativa del presente continuo sólo se debe insertar la partícula *'not'* entre el verbo *'to be'* y el verbo en gerundio:

   He is not jumping - No está saltando

2. Para crear la forma interrogativa, tal como en el verbo *'to be'*, se invertirá el orden de la frase y se pondrá primero el verbo *'to be'* y luego el sujeto:

   You are reading - Estás leyendo
   Are you reading? - ¿Estás leyendo?

✷ Presente Simple vs Presente Continuo

Ya sabemos cómo se utilizan el Presente Simple y el Presente Continuo. Ahora vamos a compararlos para no confundirlos.

Diferencias:

1. Estos dos tipos de presente sirven para diferenciar entre una acción que se realiza con frecuencia (Presente Simple) y una que se realiza temporalmente (Presente Continuo).

   *Ben usually **drinks** water* (P. Simple), *but today **he's drinking** beer* (P. Continuo)
   Ben generalmente **bebe** agua pero hoy **está bebiendo** cerveza

2. Otra diferencia es que utilizamos el Presente Simple para cosas que se hacen con frecuencia (o no se hacen: *'never'*) y el Presente Continuo para lo que se está haciendo ahora.

   *Ben is **having dinner** at home, he **never goes** to restaurants*
   Ben **está cenando** en casa, *(él)* nunca **va** a restaurantes

Vamos a ver un poquito más claro cómo funcionan:

Presente Simple	Presente continuo
Jack always takes his dog for a walk	*Jack is taking his dog for a walk*
Jack siempre saca a su perro a pasear	Jack está sacando a su perro a pasear (ahora mismo)

Presente Simple	Presente Continuo
Peter never listens to you	*Peter is not listening to you*
Peter nunca te escucha	Peter no te está escuchando (ahora mismo)

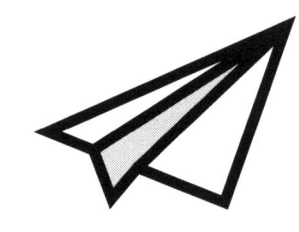

✱ El Futuro en inglés: 'will' y 'going to'

Ahora vamos a ver cómo se forma el futuro en inglés con 'will' y con 'going to'.

Primero un cuadrito:

will + infinitivo	be (am, is, are) going to + infinitivo
(+) **I will eat**	(+) **I'm going to eat**
Comeré	Voy a comer
(-) **He won't eat**	(-) **He isn't going to eat**
No comerá	No va a comer
(?) **Will they eat?**	(?) **Are they going to eat?**
¿Comerán?	¿Van a comer?

* Mucho cuidado porque siempre hablamos de la forma '**going to**' pero debéis saber que es '*BE going to*' y que esa forma verbal tenemos que conjugarla: *am, is o are*, para que concuerde con el sujeto.

El error habitual es olvidarnos del verbo 'to be': **I going to buy those shoes*.

En español no tenemos tantos problemas para distinguir el "yo iré" (*I will go*) frente al "yo voy a ir" (*I'm going to go*).

No vemos que se diferencien tanto, salvo por ese matiz de certeza que da el "ir a hacer algo".

Veremos que cuando estudiamos una forma frente a la otra, todo parece más sencillo de entender:

1. **Acciones planeadas vs no planeadas.**
   Usamos el '*going to*' para hablar de actividades futuras planeadas.

   > ej. ***I'm going to travel to New York next month. I've already bought the tickets.***
   > Voy a viajar a Nueva York el próximo mes. Ya he comprado los billetes.

   Con este ejemplo en concreto, vemos que se trata de una decisión planificada, puesto que ya tengo los billetes comprados.

   A veces (¡¡OJO QUE NO HE DICHO SIEMPRE!!) son frases más largas porque se añade una explicación para que quede claro que ha habido cierta planificación.

Usamos el *'will'* para hablar de actividades repentinas. NO planeadas.
Se usa para ese tipo de actividades que surgen de manera espontánea.

> ej. ***It's cold. I'll close the window.***
> Hace frío. Cerraré la ventana.
>
> ***Someone is at the door. I'll open!***
> Alguien está en la puerta. ¡Abriré!
>
> ***Those bags look very heavy. I'll help you!***
> Esas bolsas parecen muy pesadas. ¡Te ayudaré!

Con estos ejemplos vemos que ninguna de estas tres acciones han sido planificadas. Fijáos en el ejemplo de arriba.

No he decidido de repente irme a Nueva York, puesto que he comprado los billetes con anterioridad.

En este caso ocurre todo lo contrario, se trata de una reacción espontánea, nada planeada.

Surge porque algo la motiva: el frío, el timbre o ver a alguien cargado de bolsas.

También debéis prestar atención al uso de la forma contraída /aɪl/ que hace que la pronunciación sea algo más inmediata que un *"I will"*.

2. **Predicciones vs Evidencias.**
Usamos el *'will'* para hablar de predicciones futuras.

> ej. ***You will be rich some day*** - Algún día serás rico
> ***Next week it will rain*** - La semana que viene lloverá

Si os hablo de predicciones, ¿qué es lo primero que os viene a la cabeza?

Algunos pensarán en videntes y otros en el hombre del tiempo.

Con todos mis respetos a las dos profesiones, una con más aciertos que la otra, la probabilidad de que se den las situaciones de los ejemplos puede ser algo incierta en según qué casos.

Usamos el *'going to'* para hablar de acciones futuras pero basándonos en evidencias.

> ej. ***Look at those black clouds!! It is going to rain soon.***
> ¡Mira esas nubes negras! Pronto va a llover.

Si comparamos el último ejemplo de arriba con este, podemos ver que las probabilidades aumentan porque me baso en una evidencia (los nubarrones).

Inglés básico para hispanohablantes | Tiempos verbales

Con esto no quiero decir que esté 100% segura de que los hechos se vayan a producir pero sí que hay más posibilidades.

Hasta aquí los grandes bloques que diferencian el *'will'* del *'going to'* pero también os enumero otras pistas para saber cuándo debemos decantarnos por *'will'*.

.A.

Dijimos que con predicciones va *"will"*, por lo tanto también irá con verbos predictivos como: *hope* (tener la esperanza), *expect* (esperar), *think* (pensar), *believe* (creer)...

ej. ***I think I will go to your party*** - Creo que iré a tu fiesta

Y con adverbios del tipo: *maybe* (quizás), *perhaps* (quizás), *probably*...

.B.

¿Recordáis el famoso tema de la malograda Whitney Houston? Pues eso, con promesas también :

I will always love youuuuu...

.C.

Así mismo dijimos que con decisiones repentinas, no planeadas va *'will'* pues por eso lo podemos relacionar con peticiones, ofrecimientos o invitaciones:

Will you help me? - ¿Me ayudarás / Me ayudas?
I will be there when you need me - Estaré ahí cuando me necesites
Will you come with me? - ¿Vendrás conmigo?

.D.

En el primer condicional (este lo vemos luego):

If you study, you will pass - Si estudias, aprobarás

Pronunciación

8. Pronunciación

En la sección anterior hemos visto:

- ¿Por qué nos resulta tan difícil pronunciar bien en inglés?
- Alfabeto
- Símbolos fonéticos

✱ No hablan como leen

Aunque los hispanohablantes creamos que aprender español es fácil, en realidad es un idioma sumamente complicado, no sólo por su inmenso vocabulario, sino también por todas las reglas gramaticales que implica.

Como hemos visto en el capítulo **Las conjugaciones en inglés**, es muy difícil para un anglosajón aprenderse todas las conjugaciones de los verbos en español ya que ellos tienen un número muy limitado de formas verbales.

Sin embargo, una de las cosas más fáciles que caracteriza a la lengua española es que "hablamos como escribimos" (discutible en según que acentos), es decir, que leyendo una palabra ya sabemos cómo se pronuncia exactamente.

Esta es una de las grandes diferencias que distingue el inglés del español ya que en inglés la pronunciación de las palabras dista mucho de sonar cómo se escribe.

Pongo el ejemplo de la terminación *-ough* (un caso bastante extremo):

Mira esta lista de palabras:

INGLÉS	PRONUNCIACIÓN		ESPAÑOL
Hiccough	HÍCCAP	/ˈhɪkʌp/	Hipo
Plough	PLÁU	/plaʊ/	Arado
Lough	LOJ o LOK	/lɒk/	Lago
Through	ZRUU	/θruː/	A través de
Tough	TAFF	/tʌf/	Duro
Thorough	ZÁRA	/ˈθʌrə/	Meticuloso / Minucioso
Thought	ZOT	/θɔːt/	Pensar (en pasado)
Though	DÓU	/ðəʊ/	Aunque

Todas ellas acaban igual (o casi) pero se pronuncian de una manera totalmente diferente.

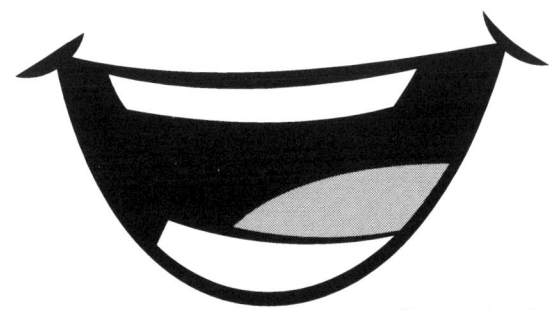

NOTA: La pronunciación es aproximada, pues depende del acento inglés que se utilice.

Con esto solo quiero avanzaros que, con el tema de la pronunciación, a diferencia del tema de las conjugaciones verbales, sudaréis, a veces os parecerá una tortura, a veces pensaréis en tirar la toalla y enviar los sonidos del inglés a freír espárragos pero....

Espérate...
¿Y lo divertido que resultará?
¿Y el reto que supone?

Si fuera fácil, todo el mundo hablaría (y pronunciaría) inglés perfectamente...

Tómatelo como un reto y disfrútalo.

Te digo por experiencia que ¡es un camino realmente fascinante!

Don't ever give up! ☺
Nunca te rindas

Quick tip...

Errores comunes en inglés

- ~~People is...~~
- People are ✓

- ~~I lost the bus~~
- I missed the bus ✓

- ~~I am agree~~
- I agree ✓

- ~~I'm going to the bed~~
- I'm going to bed ✓

- ~~I have 38 years~~
- I am 38 years old ✓

- ~~I make homework~~
- I do homework ✓

- ~~I have others books~~
- I have other books ✓

- ~~You are happy?~~
- Are you happy? ✓

- ~~My mother is teacher~~
- My mother is a teacher ✓

- ~~The dog black~~
- The black dog ✓

- ~~On fridays I study english~~
- On Fridays I study English ✓

Inglés Básico
PARA HISPANOHABLANTES

Nivel:
¡Vamos a tope!

Pronombres

1 Pronombres

En la sección anterior hemos visto:

- Pronombres Acusativos
- Pronombres Reflexivos

✱ Pronombres Posesivos

Antes de mostrarte los pronombres posesivos, quiero enseñarte cuáles son los Adjetivos Posesivos:

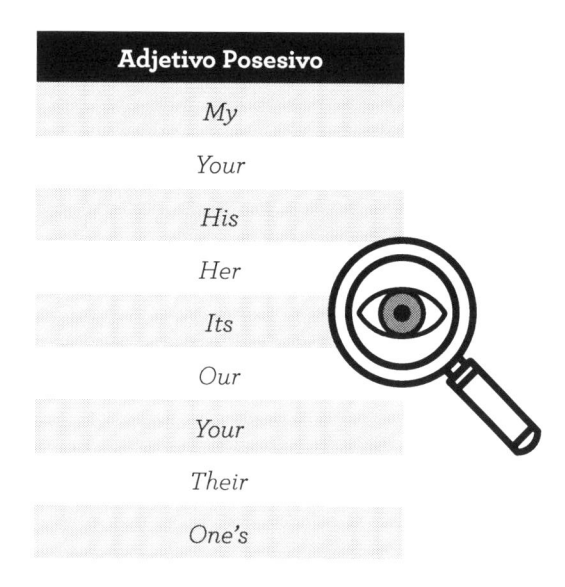

Adjetivo Posesivo
My
Your
His
Her
Its
Our
Your
Their
One's

Los pronombres posesivos sustituyen al nombre y se usan para evitar repetir información que ya está clara o que es obvia. Los adjetivos posesivos acompañan al nombre.

Lo hemos visto con los Pronombres y Adjetivos Demostrativos:

> ***Bring me those shoes*** (Traéme esos zapatos - adjetivo)
> ***Bring me those*** (Traéme esos - pronombre)

Con los adjetivos y pronombres posesivos pasa lo mismo.

Por ejemplo, si en español dijéramos:
Este libro es **mi** libro, no **tu** libro
('mi' y 'tu' acompañan al nombre 'libro')

Queda raro, ¿no?... Pues en inglés también suena fatal.

En español diríamos:
Este libro es **mío**, no **tuyo.**
('mío' y 'tuyo' sustituyen al nombre 'libro')

Y en inglés pasa lo mismo. La siguiente frase suena rarísima:

> ***This book is my book, not your book***
> (*'my'* y *'your'* acompañan al nombre *'book'*)

En cambio, sí decimos:

> ***This book is mine, not yours***
> (*'mine'* y *'yours'* sustiyen al nombre *'book'*)

De esta manera estamos yendo al grano de una manera gramaticalmente correcta, usando *'mine'* y *'yours'* (mío y tuyo).

Veamos gráficamente la difrencie entre los adjetivos posesivos y los pronombres posesivos:

ADJETIVO POSESIVO	Ejemplos	PRONOMBRE POSESIVO	Ejemplos
My (mi)	**My book is here** / Mi libro está aquí	**Mine**	**Mine is here** / El mío está aquí
Your (tu)	**Your house is big** / Tu casa es grande	**Yours** (Tuyo/a)	**Yours is big** / La tuya es grande
His (su-de él)	**It's his dog** / Es su perro	**His** (Suyo/a-de él)	**The dog is his** / El perro es suyo
Her (su-de ella)	**It's her scarf** / Es su bufanda	**Hers** (Suyo/a- de ella)	**The scarf is hers** / La bufanda es suya
Its (su –neutro-)	**The dog ate its bone** / El perro se comió su hueso	**Its** (Suyo- neutro)	**That bone is its, not mine or yours** / El hueso es suyo, no mío o tuyo
Our (nuestro/a)	**This is our bed** / Esta es nuestra cama	**Ours** (Nuestro/a)	**This bed is ours** / Esta cama es nuestra
Your (vuestro/a)	**That is your phone** / Ese es tu teléfono	**Yours** (Vuestro/a)	**That phone is yours** / Ese teléfono es tuyo
Their (su –de ellos)	**It's their car** / Es su coche	**Theirs** (suyo/a -de ellos)	**The car is theirs** / El coche es suyo

Inglés básico para hispanohablantes | Pronombres

✻ Genitivo (propiedad o posesión)

En inglés podemos referirnos a la propiedad o posesión de dos maneras distintas.

Por una parte, podemos hacerlo añadiendo 'of', que vendría a ser nuestro 'de' en español.

Por ejemplo:

> ***The door of the car***
> La puerta del coche

Por otra parte se puede utilizar el **"Genitivo Sajón"**.

En español no tenemos ningún equivalente a esta forma, por lo que nos puede resultar un poco más complicado, pero con un poco de práctica seguro que lo dominamos.

Veámoslo:
El Genitivo Sajón se forma de manera muy sencilla.
Primero se le añadirá **'s** a quién posee y la posesión irás detrás.
La posesión no lleva artículo:

El que posee 's + Posesión

My sister's shirt - La camisa de mi hermana
Peter's car - El coche de Peter

Si el sustantivo está en plural terminado en **"-s"**, se añadirá el apóstrofo (') pero no la **"-s"**:

Books ⟶ *Books'*　　　　*Glasses* ⟶ *Glasses'*

My parents' friends - *Los amigos de mis padres*

> **¡Repetimos!**
> Al nombre del que posee se le añade un apóstrofo y una '-s' ⟶ ('s)
>
> Ese nombre con ('s) (**Juan's**) siempre va delante de lo que es poseído *"Juan's hat"* "El sombrero de Juan".

Vamos a ver unos ejemplos para aclararlo un poco más:

> ***My mum's dog is old*** - El perro de mi madre es viejo
> ***Eva's house is expensive*** - La casa de Eva es cara

El posesivo también se utiliza para indicar relaciones familiares:

> ***That man is Marisa's father*** - Ese hombre es el padre de Marisa

* La traducción la haremos de atrás hacia delante:

Marisa's father ⟶ Padre de Marisa

No se debe confundir el posesivo ('s) con la contracción del verbo *'to be'* en tercera persona.

> ***Where is his mother's book?*** ⟶ Posesivo
> ¿Donde está el libro de su madre?

VS.

> ***She's my grandmother*** ⟶ *'To be'*
> Ella es mi abuela

Quick tip...

EN INGLÉS NO DIGAS...DI...

NO DIGAS: FOOTING
DI: JOGGING o RUNNING

NO DIGAS: ZAPPING
DI: CHANNEL-HOPPING

NO DIGAS: PUENTING
DI: BUNGEE JUMPING

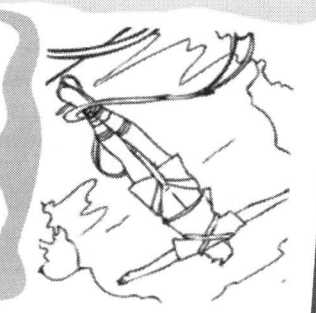

NO DIGAS: CRACK
DI: STAR, ACE, CHAMPION

Messi is a crack
En inglés significa:
Messi es una grieta

Sustantivos

2 Sustantivos

En la sección anterior hemos visto:

- Contables e incontables: Introducción

✱ Sustantivos contables e incontables: Excepciones y problemas

Vamos a ampliar un poquito más el tema de los sustantivos contables e incontables.

Tranquilos, no os asustéis, no pretendo que os lieis, tan solo que conozcáis algunas de las **excepciones y problemas** que presentan ciertos sustantivos:

1) Concordancia

Ciertos sustantivos parecen ser plurales (y por lo tanto aparentemente contables), aunque el verbo se mantiene en singular:

The news is good - Las noticias son buenas
La "-s" final no siempre es indicativo de plural.

2) Convertir a contables.

Aunque afirmemos sin dudar ni un momento que *bread* (pan), *water* (agua) o *coffee* (café) son sustantivos incontables, puede darse el caso de que se puedan convertir en contables.

¡QUE NO CUNDA EL PÁNICO!
¡TODO LO QUE YA SABÍAIS SIGUE SIENDO VÁLIDO!

Ciertos sustantivos admiten que los acompañe una palabra que ayuda a su contabilización:

A loaf of bread - Una rebanada de pan
A slice of pizza - Una porción de pizza
A tin of tuna - Una lata de atún
A bag of food - Una bolsa de comida
A carton of milk - Un cartón de leche
A bar of chocolate - Una tableta de chocolate
A glass of water - Un vaso de agua

En determinados contextos se puede dar la situación de tratar sustantivos incontables como si fueran contables. Digamos que esto se debe a un fenómeno llamado omisión.

Imaginaos en una cafetería:
Can I have two coffees and one tea, please?
En ambos caso se han omitido *"cups of"*.

Puede ser para otorgarle de mayor inmediatez a la oración y además porque tanto el hablante como el oyente, dado el contexto, entienden perfectamente la intención del mensaje.

En español pasa lo mismo...

3) **Ampliemos un poco más nuestra lista de sustantivos incontables.**

Os los agrupo en categorías para que os resulte más fácil de recordar.

Líquidos y sustancias más cremosas: *jam* (mermelada), *cream* (nata), *youghurt* (yogur), *honey* (miel), *sauce* (salsa), *oil* (aceite),...

Gases: *oxygen, smoke* (humo), *air* (aire),...

Sustantivos abstractos: *music, work - homework / housework* (trabajo), *advice* (consejo), *art, information, time* (tiempo), *luck* (suerte), *fun* (diversión),...

Materiales: *wood* (madera), *fabric* (textil), *ice* (hielo), *stone* (piedra), ...

Fenómenos atmosféricos: *rain* (lluvia), *snow* (nieve), *fog* (niebla),...

Colectivos: *furniture* (mobiliario), *luggage* (equipaje), *traffic, rubbish* (basura), *equipment* (material),...

4) **Por último, solo me queda hacer mención al *pluralia tantum*.**
Esta palabreja designa un grupo de sustantivos que, pese a tener una forma aparentemente plural, son singulares.

Por lo tanto, no podríamos usar a/an, sino que tendríamos que valernos de alguna expresión de cantidad para contarlos.

Socks (calcetines)
Shoes (zapatos)
Trousers (pantalones)
Jeans (vaqueros)
Glasses (gafas)
Pyjamas (pijama)
Scissors (tijeras)
Shorts (pantalones cortos)
Leggins
Binoculars (prismáticos)
Headphones (auriculares)

Así que no sería correcto decir: ~~I bought two jeans~~ sino ***I bought two pairs of jeans.***

Quick tip...

No cometas estos ERRORES en INGLÉS...

I'm thinking to go...

I'm thinking about going...

When I arrived to Paris

When I arrived in Paris

I don't mind to work

I don't mind working

Can you take us a photo?

Can you take a photo of us?

He explained us the book

He explained the book to us

We are 3 in my family

There are 3 of us in my family

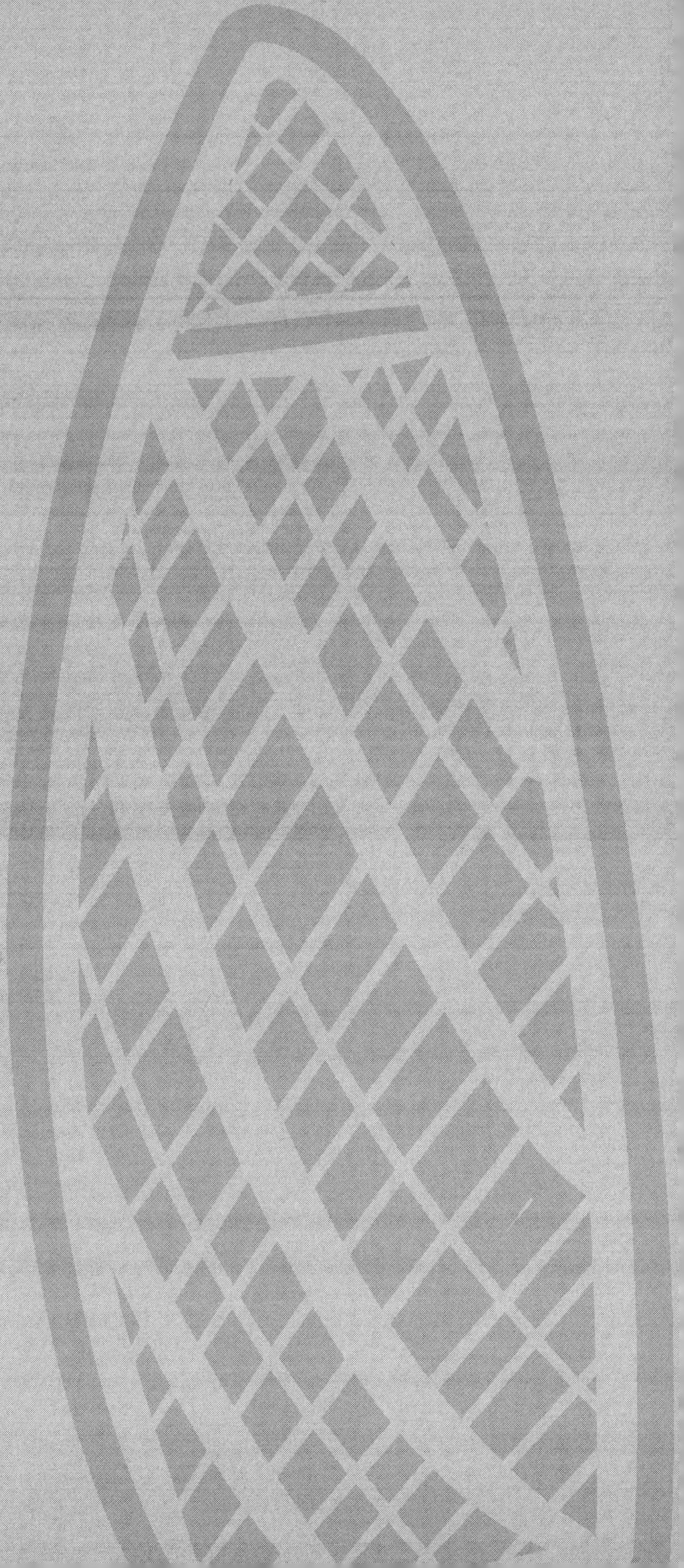

Preposiciones

3 Preposiciones

En la sección anterior hemos visto:

- Tiempo
- Preposiciones en medios de transporte

✶ Lista de preposiciones básicas en inglés

En esta tabla te presento una lista de 30 preposiciones básicas en inglés, para que te vayas familiarizando con las prepos más comunes. ☺

INGLÉS	PRONUNCIACIÓN	ESPAÑOL
Above	əˈbʌv	Encima, encima de, más de, por arriba de, por encima de
Across	əˈkrɒs	A través de, al otro lado de, a lo ancho de
After	ˈɑːftə	Después de, detrás de, según, tras
Around	əˈraʊnd	Alrededor de, en torno de
At	æt	En, a
Before	bɪˈfɔː	Ante, antes de, delante de
Behind	bɪˈhaɪnd	Detrás, detrás de
Below	bɪˈləʊ	Debajo de
Between	bɪˈtwiːn	Entre (entre dos o más)
But	bʌt	Sino, sin, excepto, salvo, menos
By	baɪ	Al lado de, por, junto a
During	ˈdjʊərɪŋ	Durante, en el transcurso de
For	fɔː	Para; por; a causa de; durante
From	frɒm	De, desde, a partir de
In	ɪn	En, dentro, dentro de; hacia adentro
Inside	ɪnˈsaɪd	Dentro, en, dentro de, en el interior
Into	ˈɪntə	Dentro de, hacia dentro, hacia el interior de
Near	nɪə	Cerca de
Of	ɒv	De; en; por
On	ɒn	Sobre, encima de; de; al; en
Out	ˈaʊt	Fuera de; afuera de
Over	ˈəʊvə	Encima; encima de; a más de; demasiado
Since	sɪns	Desde
Through	θruː	A través de; dentro de; por
To	tuː	A; en; hacia; hasta; para
Under	ˈʌndə	Bajo; debajo de; en; por; mediante; so
Until	ʌnˈtɪl	Hasta
Up	ʌp	(Movimiento) por; en lo alto de; hacia arriba; arriba de
With	wɪð	Con; por medio de; mediante; de; entre
Without	wɪðˈaʊt	Sin; fuera, fuera de; desprovisto de

Preposiciones | Inglés básico para hispanohablantes

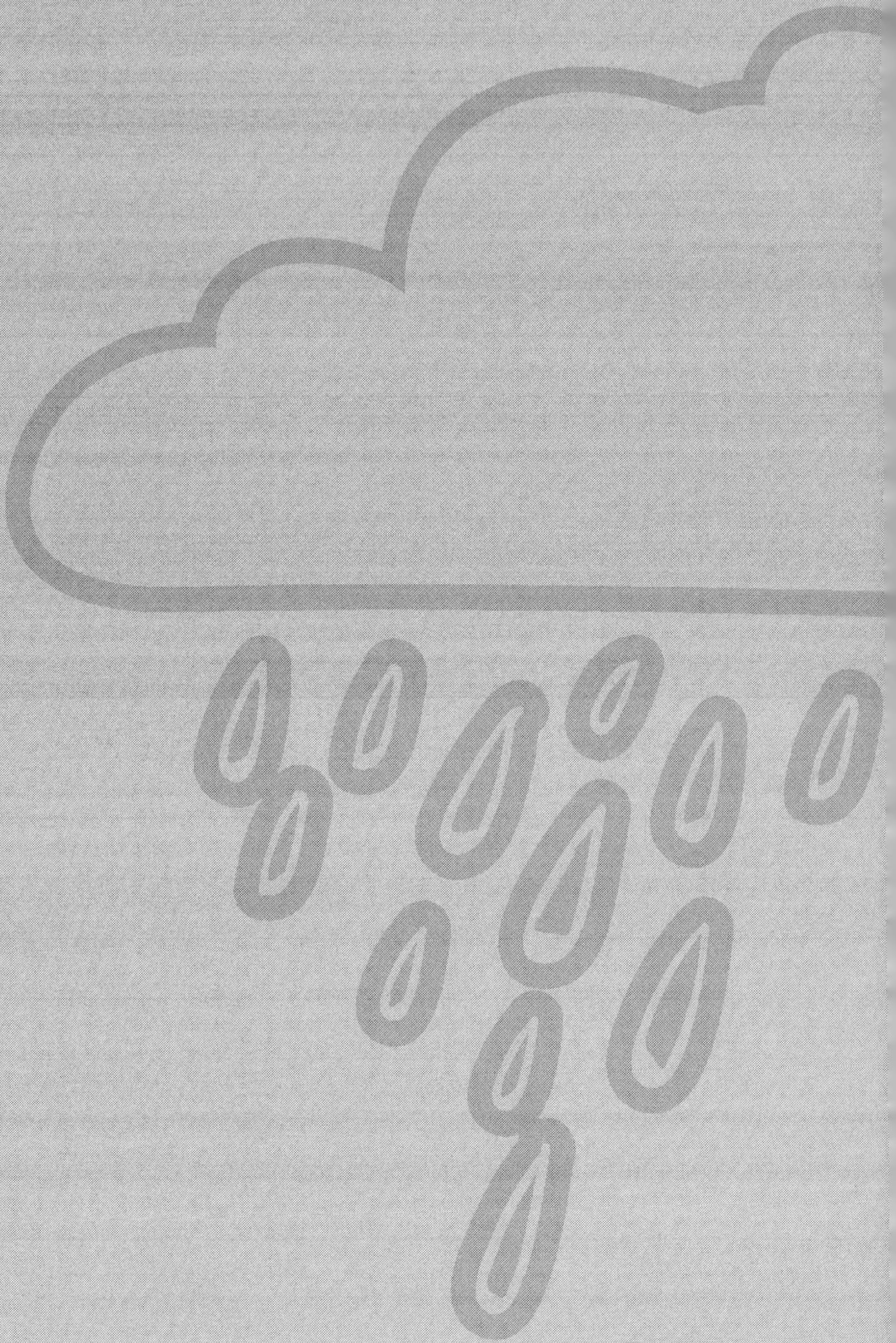

Adjetivos

# 4 Adjetivos

En la sección anterior hemos visto:

- Introducción.
- Adjetivos Comparativos.
- Adjetivos Superlativos

✱ 100 adjetivos en inglés

Aquí presento una lista de 100 adjetivos en inglés que todo estudiante de inglés debería conocer para tener unas bases de vocabulario en la lengua inglesa.

Faltan muchísmos adjetivos, pero estos son de los más comunes y acordes al nivel que estamos viendo y además... más vale aprenderse unos cuantos al dedillo y luego ir avanzando poco a poco que no intentar abarcar demasiado (*don't bite more than you can chew*).

Es importante fijarse bien en su pronunciación.
No sirve de nada saber el significado y ortografía de estos adjetivos si no los pronuncias correctamente.

ESPAÑOL	INGLÉS	PRONUNCIACIÓN
Abierto	*Open*	ˈəʊpən
Ácido	*Acid*	ˈæsɪd
Afilado	*Sharp*	ʃɑːp
Agrio	*Bitter*	ˈbɪtə
Alto	*High*	haɪ
Alto	*Tall*	tɔːl
Amable	*Kind*	kaɪnd
Ancho	*Wide*	waɪd
Áspero	*Rough*	rʌf
Bajo	*Low*	ləʊ
Bajo	*Short*	ʃɔːt
Barato	*Cheap*	tʃiːp
Brillante	*Bright*	braɪt
Bueno	*Good*	gʊd
Cálido / Caluroso	*Warm*	wɔːm
Caliente	*Hot*	hɒt
Cansado	*Tired*	ˈtaɪəd
Ceñido / Apretado	*Tight*	taɪt
Cerrado	*Shut*	ʃʌt
Claro	*Clear*	klɪə
Contrario	*Opposite*	ˈɒpəzɪt
Corto	*Short*	ʃɔːt
Cruel	*Cruel*	krʊəl

Adjetivos | **Inglés básico para hispanohablantes**

ESPAÑOL	INGLÉS	PRONUNCIACIÓN
Débil	Feeble	ˈfiːbl̩
Delgado	Thin	θɪn
Delicado	Delicate	ˈdelɪkət
Delicado / Fino	Smooth	smuːð
Derecha / Correcto	Right	raɪt
Despierto	Awake	əˈweɪk
Diferente	Different	ˈdɪfrənt
Dulce	Sweet	swiːt
Duro	Hard	hɑːd
Empinado	Steep	stiːp
Enfadado	Angry	ˈæŋgri
Enfermo	Ill	ɪl
Enorme	Huge	hjuːdʒ
Erróneo	Wrong	rɒŋ
Especial	Special	ˈspeʃl̩
Estrecho	Narrow	ˈnærəʊ
Estupendo	Great	ˈgreɪt
Extraño	Strange	streɪndʒ
Falso	False	ˈfɔːls
Feliz	Happy	ˈhæpi
Físico	Physical	ˈfɪzɪkl̩
Frío	Cold	kəʊld
Fuerte	Strong	strɒŋ
Gordo	Fat	fæt
Grueso / Espeso	Thick	θɪk
Hueco	Hollow	ˈhɒləʊ
Húmedo	Wet	wet
Importante	Important	ɪmˈpɔːtnt
Izquierda	Left	left
Joven	Young	jʌŋ
Largo	Long	ˈlɒŋ
Largo	Long	ˈlɒŋ

Inglés básico para hispanohablantes | Adjetivos

ESPAÑOL	INGLÉS	PRONUNCIACIÓN
Lento	*Slow*	sləʊ
Libre	*Free*	friː
Ligero	*Light*	laɪt
Limpio	*Clean*	kliːn
Lleno	*Full*	fʊl
Malo	*Bad*	bæd
Natural	*Natural*	ˈnætʃrəl
Necesario	*Necessary*	ˈnesəsəri
Normal	*Normal*	ˈnɔːml̩
Nuevo	*New*	njuː
Oscuro	*Dark*	dɑːk
Paralelo	*Parallel*	ˈpærəlel
Pegajoso	*Sticky*	ˈstɪki
Pequeño	*Small*	smɔːl
Pesado (de peso)	*Heavy*	ˈhevi
Picante	*Spicy*	ˈspaɪsi
Plano / Llano	*Flat*	flæt
Pobre	*Poor*	pʊə
Posible	*Possible*	ˈpɒsəbl̩
Precioso	*Beautiful*	ˈbjuːtəfl̩
Preparado	*Ready*	ˈredi
Privado	*Private*	ˈpraɪvɪt
Profundo	*Deep*	diːp
Rápido	*Quick*	kwɪk
Recto / Directo	*Straight*	streɪt
Repentino	*Sudden*	ˈsʌdn̩
Ruidoso	*Loud*	laʊd
Sabio	*Wise*	waɪz
Saludable	*Healthy*	ˈhelθi
Seco	*Dry*	draɪ
Seguro	*Safe*	seɪf
Serio	*Serious*	ˈsɪərɪəs

ESPAÑOL	INGLÉS	PRONUNCIACIÓN
Simple	*Simple*	ˈsɪmpl̩
Sólido	*Solid*	ˈsɒlɪd
Suave	*Soft*	sɒft
Sucio	*Dirty*	ˈdɜːti
Tarde	*Late*	leɪt
Temprano	*Early*	ˈɜːli
Tieso	*Stiff*	stɪf
Tonto / Insensato	*Foolish*	ˈfuːlɪʃ
Tranquilo	*Quiet*	ˈkwaɪət
Triste	*Sad*	sæd
Verdadero	*True*	truː
Viejo	*Old*	əʊld
Violento	*Violent*	ˈvaɪələnt

Quick tip...

Frases para ROMPER EL HIELO
break the ice

Las típicas-tópicas:

What's your name?
¿Cómo te llamas?

Where are you from?
¿De dónde eres?

Where do you live?
¿Dónde vives?

What do you do for a living? What's your job?
¿De qué trabajas?

Al terreno personal...

What's your favourite food?
¿Cuál es tu comida favorita?

Do you have a pet?
¿Tienes mascota?

What's your favourite sport?
¿Cuál es tu deporte favorito?

Do you have any brothers or sisters?
¿Tienes hermanos?

What's your favourite film?
¿Cuál es tu peli favorita?

Hablando del mundo...

How many countries have you visited?
¿Cuántos países has visitado?

If you could live anywhere, where would you live?
Si pudieras vivir en cualquier lugar ¿Dónde vivirías?

Which country would you like to visit?
¿Qué país te gustaría visitar?

Do you like the town where you live?
¿Te gusta la ciudad donde vives?

Al terreno (casi) íntimo...

Do you have any tattoos?
¿Tienes algún tatuaje?

Do you have boyfriend/girlfriend?
¿Tienes novio/a?

Are you religious?
¿Eres religioso?

What are you scared of?
¿Qué te asusta?

Are you religious?
¿Eres religioso?

Have you ever been drunk?
¿Alguna vez te has emborrachado?

Do you smoke?
¿Fumas?

Hemos ligado...

Has anybody ever told you that you have the best smile?
¿Alguien te ha dicho alguna vez que tienes la mejor sonrisa?

How are you still single?
¿Cómo que todavía estás solter@?

When can I see you again?
¿Cuándo puedo verte otra vez?

Adverbios

5 Adverbios

En la sección anterior hemos visto:

- Formas Irregulares y excepciones.
- Formas Comparativas y Superlativas.

✳ Adverbios de Frecuencia

Los Adverbios de Frecuencia se utilizan para definir la periodicidad con que se realiza una actividad determinada. Se usan habitualmente con el Presente Simple.

El Presente Simple se utiliza para hábitos y costumbres, por tanto, los adverbios de frecuencia nos indicarán cuán a menudo realizamos estas acciones.

Vamos a ver algunos ejemplos.

> *I **always** go to sleep early* - Siempre voy a dormir temprano.
> *You **never** listen to her* - Nunca la escuchas.

En principio parece bastante simple aprenderse los Adverbios de Frecuencia y colocarlos en la frase, pero... los hispanohablantes tenemos un pequeño problema con el tema de la posición de los adverbios dentro de la frase.

VEAMOS LA RAZÓN

¿Dónde se colocan los Adverbios de Frecuencia?

Vamos a verlo en la frase:

> *Carlos is **often** late*

En español podemos decir:
- A menudo Carlos llega tarde
- Carlos llega tarde a menudo
- Carlos a menudo llega tarde.

Es decir, en español podemos organizar la estructura sintáctica de la frase (el orden de las palabras) de una manera más flexible que en inglés.

En el caso de los adverbios, su posición dependerá del verbo al que acompañe.

Con el verbo *TO BE*

1) El adverbio va siempre detrás del verbo si la frase es afirmativa o negativa.

> *I **am always** happy* - Siempre estoy feliz.
> *He **isn't usually** bored* - Normalmente no está aburrido / No suele estar aburrido.

2) Si es una pregunta, el adverbio ira detrás del sujeto

> *Are **you sometimes** sad?* - ¿A veces estás triste?

Con verbos en Presente Simple
En este caso, dependerá del tipo de oración.
Sí, ya sé que es un lío, pero si te re-lees este capítulo un par de veces seguro que te queda más claro. ☺

Veamos:

1) Si la oración es afirmativa o interrogativa, el adverbio irá entre el sujeto y el verbo principal:

> *I **hardly ever** drink beer* - Casi nunca bebo cerveza
> *Does **she often snore** at night?* - ¿A menudo ronca de noche?

2) Ten en cuenta que en las negaciones, el adverbio va entre el verbo auxiliar y el verbo principal:

> *I **don't often go** to visit my grandmother* - No voy a visitar a mi abuela a menudo

Preguntar por la frecuencia
Si quieres preguntarle a alguien con qué frecuencia hace una cosa o la otra, utilizas el pronombre interrogativo 'how' seguido del adverbio 'often':

> ***How often** do you go to Menorca?* - ¿Con qué frecuencia vas a Menorca?
> *I go to Menorca twice a month.* - Voy a Menorca dos veces al mes.

Aquí tenéis una lista con los adverbios de frecuencia más frecuentes (valga la redundancia).

Always: siempre
Usually: habitualmente
Often: a menudo
Frequently: frecuentemente
Sometimes: a veces
Seldom: casi nunca
Never: nunca
Everyday: cada día/Todos los días
Every Thursday: cada jueves
Every morning: todas los mañanas

Every summer: todos los veranos
Every year: todos los años
Every once in a while: muy de vez en cuando
Once a day: una vez al día
Twice a week: dos veces a la semana
Three times a month: tres veces al mes
Four times a year: cuatro veces al año

** Ten en cuenta que 'una vez' es '*once*' (pronunciación: UANS) y no ~~one time~~.

De la misma manera, 'dos veces al día' se dice '*twice a day*' (TUAIS) y no '*two times*'.

Existe una manera de decir 'tres veces al día' en inglés '*thrice*' (TRAIS) pero su uso es muy poco común. Aquí sí puedes decir '*three times a day*'.

Y recuerda el refrán: *Better late than never!*

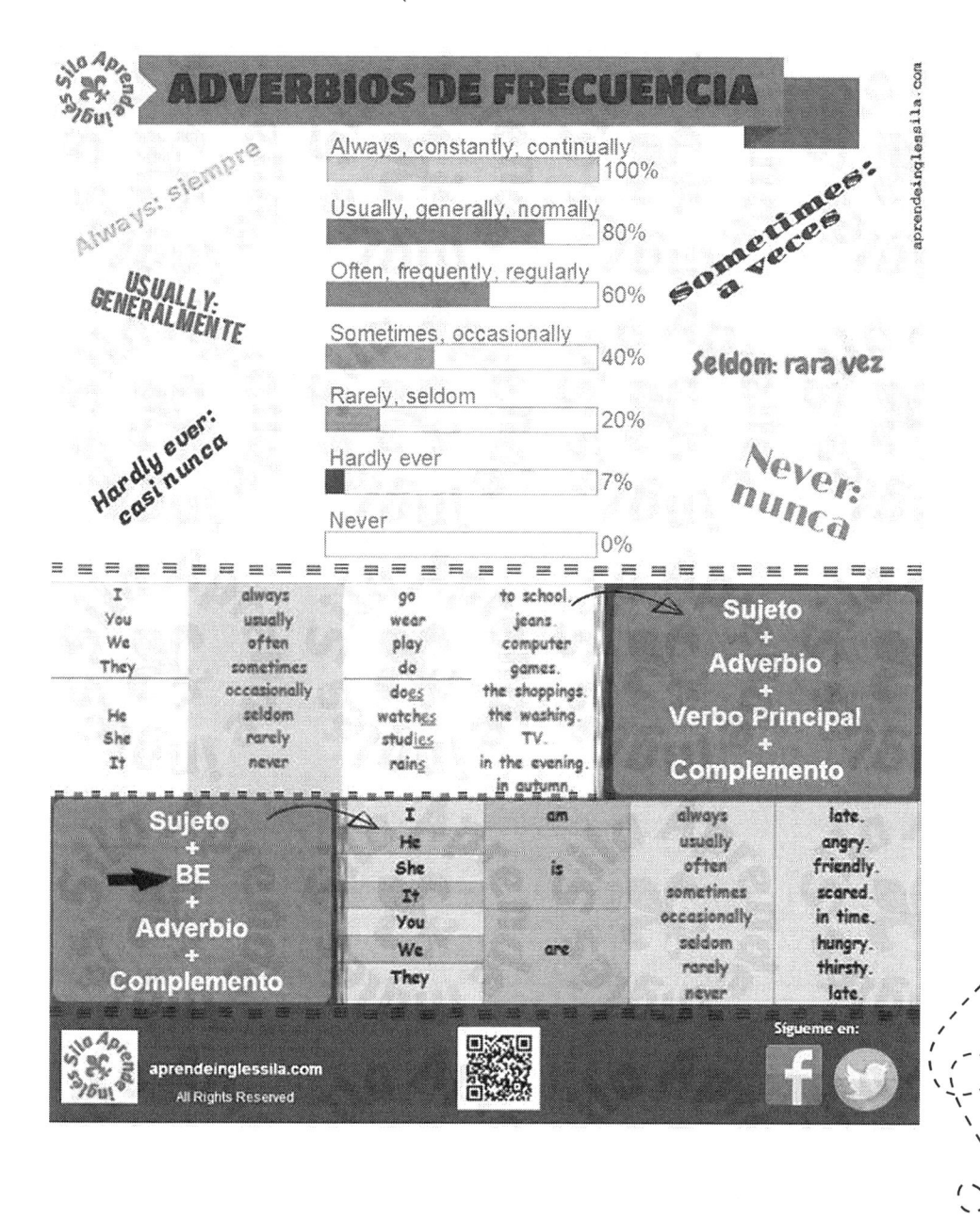

ADVERBIOS DE FRECUENCIA

Always: siempre

- Always, constantly, continually — 100%
- Usually, generally, normally — 80%
- Often, frequently, regularly — 60%
- Sometimes, occasionally — 40%
- Rarely, seldom — 20%
- Hardly ever — 7%
- Never — 0%

Sometimes: a veces

Usually y: generalmente

Seldom: rara vez

Hardly ever: casi nunca

Never: nunca

I / You / We / They	always / usually / often / sometimes / occasionally / seldom / rarely / never	go / wear / play / do	to school. / jeans. / computer games. / the shoppings.
He / She / It	seldom / rarely / never (does / watches / studies / rains)		the washing. / TV. / in the evening. / in autumn.

Sujeto + Adverbio + Verbo Principal + Complemento

I	am	always	late.
He / She / It	is	usually	angry.
		often	friendly.
		sometimes	scared.
You / We / They	are	occasionally	in time.
		seldom	hungry.
		rarely	thirsty.
		never	late.

Sujeto + BE + Adverbio + Complemento

aprendeinglessila.com
All Rights Reserved

Sígueme en:

✱ Adverbios de Grado

Ya hemos visto qué son los adverbios y hemos analizado los Adverbios de Frecuencia en inglés.

Ahora nos vamos a centrar en los Adverbios de Grado.

Veremos cómo se usan y sus diferentes tipos.

¿Para qué se usan?
Se trata de un tipo de adverbio usado para determinar el grado de intensidad del adjetivo, adverbio o verbo al que acompaña.

Para entenderlos mejor vamos a dividirlos en tres grupos:

1. Adverbios de Intensidad o intensificadores
   • **Very** (muy) : *I am very happy.* (Estoy muy contento)

   • **Really** (muy): *He talked really fast.* (Él hablaba muy rápido)

   • **Quite** (bastante): *We all felt quite tired.* (Estábamos bastante cansados)

   • **Pretty** (bastante): *She was pretty rude with him.* (Fue bastante grosero con ella)

   • **So** (tan/muy): *Her house was so far away.* (Su casa estaba tan/muy lejos)

   • **Rather** (bastante): *He was rather annoyed after what she said.* (Estaba bastante molesto al oír lo que ella dijo)

   • **Even** (incluso): *The experience was even better than we thought.* (La experiencia resultó ser incluso mejor de lo que creíamos)

   • **Too** (demasiado): *It was too difficult to explain.* (Era demasiado difícil de explicar)

   • **Enough** (suficiente): *You aren't old enough to drive.* (No eres lo suficiente mayor para conducir)

2. Adverbios terminados en -ly
   • **Fairly** (bastante): *The exam was fairly difficult.* (El examen fue bastante difícil)

   • **Completely** (completamente): *The room was completely full of people.* (La habitación estaba completamente llena de gente)

   • **Extremely** (extremadamente): *Last summer was extremely hot.* (El verano pasado fue extremadamente caluroso)

   • **Hardly** (casi no/apenas): *I hardly ate anything.* (Apenas comí)

Inglés básico para hispanohablantes | Adverbios

- **Nearly** (casi): *I nearly forgot to close the door.* (Casi me olvido de cerrar la puerta)

- **Mostly** (casi/prácticamente): *My homework is mostly finish.* (Mis deberes están prácticamente terminados).

Much, more, less y little

- **Much more** (mucho más): *The book is much more interesting.* (El libro es mucho más interesante)

- **Much less** (mucho menos): *That is much less common nowadays.* (Eso es mucho menos común hoy en día)

- **Little less** (un poco menos): *She should be a little less shy.* (Ella debería ser un poco menos tímida)

- **Far more / less** (mucho más / menos): *Diving is far more dangerous than playing golf.* (Bucear es mucho más peligroso que jugar al golf)

Al comparar estas dos oraciones:

> *We were happy to hear that*
> *We were really happy to hear that*

Es cierto que podemos llegar a pensar que, como el sentido general no varía al añadir el adverbio de grado, no resulta de mucho interés aprender a usarlos.

Sin embargo, resulta evidente que la segunda oración de nuestro ejemplo ha ganado en intensidad.

De ahí la utilidad a la hora de incorporarlos a nuestros *writings* ya que les aportará esa vidilla necesaria para hacerlos más atractivo al lector/examinador, lo que, académicamente hablando, se traducirá en una mejor valoración de vuestro trabajo... así que ya sabes: *Be **very** creative!*

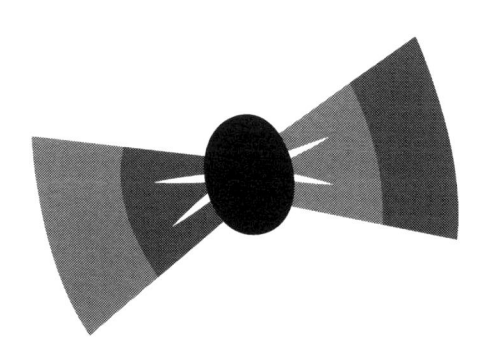

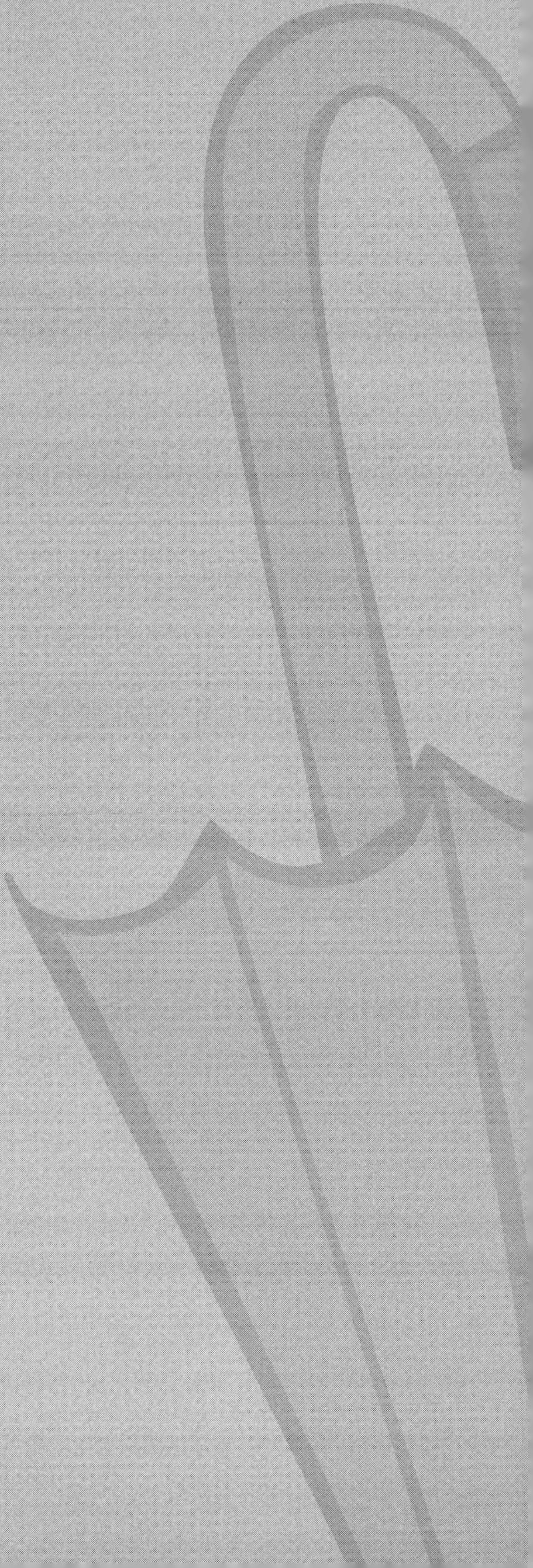

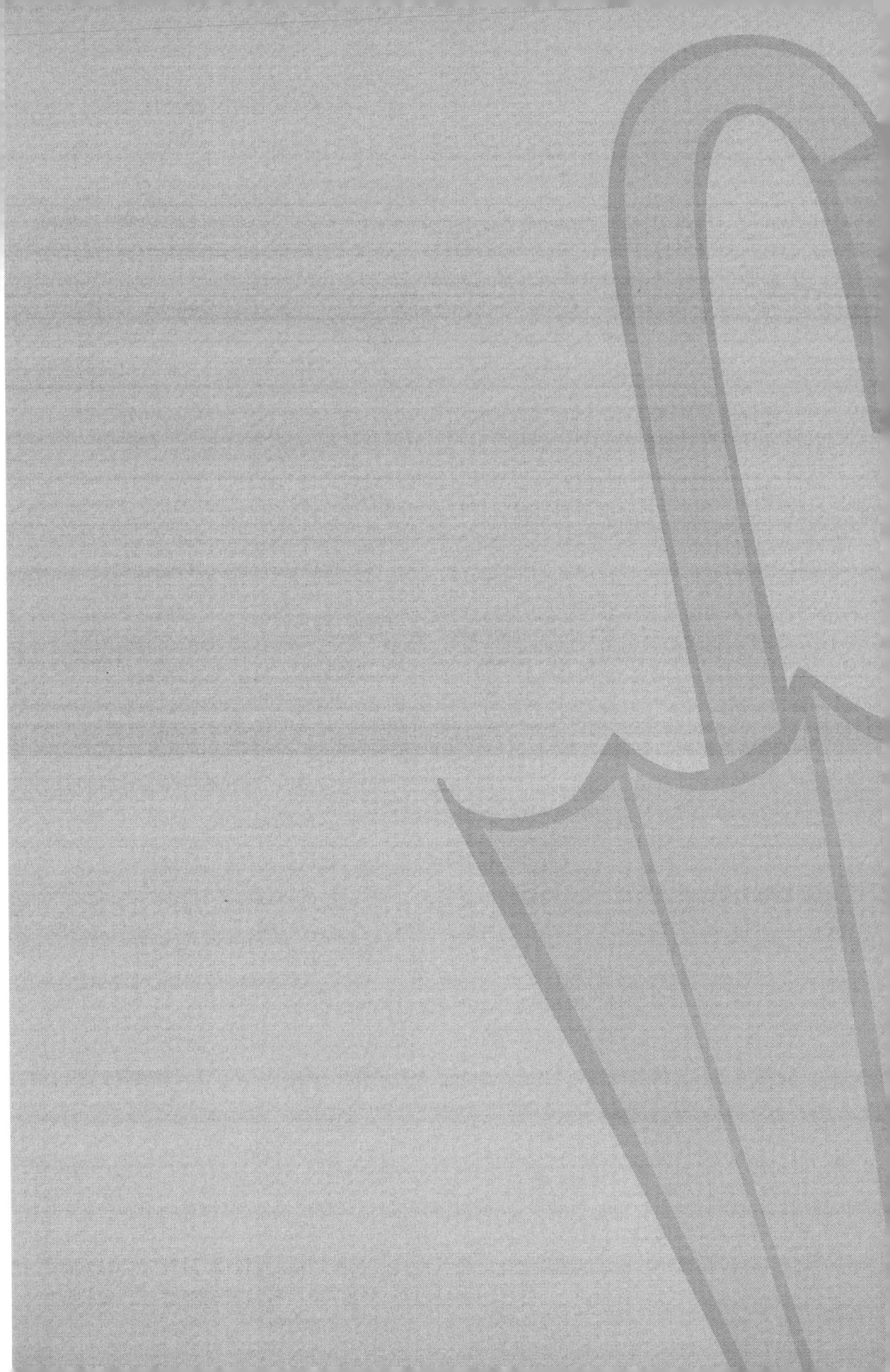

Verbos
Tiempos Verbales

6 Verbos / Tiempos Verbales

En la sección anterior hemos visto:

VERBOS
- El verbo *to have*
- *Have got*
- Los verbos *do* y *make*

TIEMPOS VERBALES
- Presente Continuo
- Presente Simple vs Presente Continuo
- El Futuro

✱ Las formas Condicionales

Los condicionales se emplean para teorizar sobre de lo que podría pasar, lo que puede haber pasado y lo que desearíamos que pasase.

En inglés, la mayoría de las frases que usan el condicional contienen el término *'if'* (si): *If I go home...* (si voy a casa...)

Existen cuatro formas condicionales, pero en este nivel nos vamos a centrar en el condicional 0 y en el 1.

¡PUES VAMOS ALLÁ!

✱ Zero Conditional

Es el que se refiere a las verdades universales, es decir, lo que ocurre siempre que se dé esa condición.

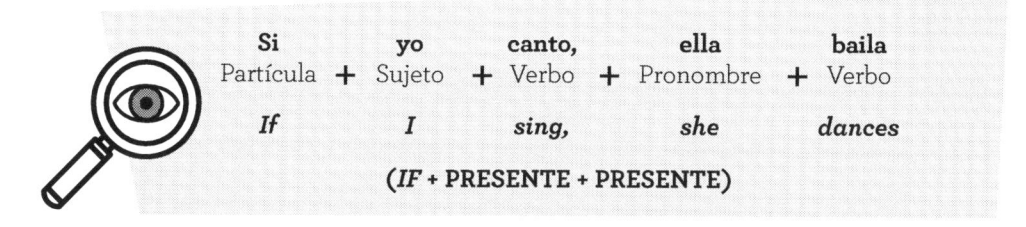

Si	yo	canto,	ella	baila
Partícula +	Sujeto +	Verbo +	Pronombre +	Verbo
If	I	sing,	she	dances

(*IF* + PRESENTE + PRESENTE)

Cada vez que canto, ella baila... siempre ocurre.

Vemos que la estructura coincide con el español.

El verbo en las dos oraciones está en Presente Simple.

Este uso es parecido (y a veces se puede sustituir) por una frase subordinada que empiece por *'when'* (cuando):

When I chop onions, I cry
Cuando corto cebollas, lloro

o

If I chop onions, I cry
Si corto cebollas, lloro

✶ First Conditional

A este condicional también se le llama Condicional Real porque el que usamos para hablar de hechos reales o probables que se pueden dar en el futuro.

La estructura es similar a la anterior pero le añadiremos algo nuevo: el *will* como marca de futuro.

Si	+	yo	+	canto,	+	ella	+	bailará
If		**I**		**sing,**		**she**		**will dance**

(IF + PRESENTE + WILL + INFINITIVO)

Es probable que si canto, ella baile. Es una acción que se producirá en el futuro (aún he empezado a a cantar).

NOTA: En el Condicional 1 generalmente usamos la preposición *unless* (a menos que).

Es decir, "a menos que se de prisa..." (*unless he hurries up*) también se puede decir: '*if he doesn't hurry up...*" (si no se da prisa...).

You'll be sick unless you stop eating
Te pondrás enfermo a menos que pares de comer

Veamos otros ejemplos de Condicional 1:

If you don't hurry, you will miss the bus
Si no te das prisa, perderás el autobús

If it rains today, you will get wet
Si hoy llueve, te mojarás

If John is late again I will get angry
Si John llega tarde otra vez, me enfadaré

If the boss is busy now, I will come back tomorrow
Si el jefe está ocupado ahora, volveré mañana

✱ Introducción a los verbos modales: *can* y *could*

Los verbos modales son unos verbos especiales en inglés.

Vamos a centrarnos en *'can'* y *'could'* para introducir el tema

Una vez entendamos como funcionan, para que sirven y como se usan nos será muchísimo más fácil de entender todos los demás.

Cómo se forman
Como ya hemos dicho, los verbos modales son verbos especiales que funcionan de manera diferente a los demás verbos en inglés. Son mucho más simples porque no se conjugan.

LOS VERBOS MODALES:

1. Se colocan antes de otro verbo en forma infinitiva (sin *'to'*)

   I can swim ⟶ Puedo nadar
   We can sing ⟶ Podemos cantar

2. Nunca se les añade "-s" en la tercera forma del singular:

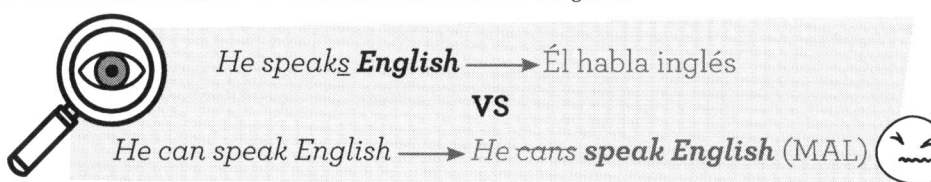

   *He speaks **English*** ⟶ Él habla inglés
   VS
   He can speak English ⟶ *He cans speak English* (MAL)

3. Para crear la forma negativa de los verbos modales se le añade *'not'* después del verbo modal y antes del verbo léxico (el que proporciona el sentido a la frase). También los modales tienen una forma contraída.

   I cannot go - I can't go ⟶ No puedo ir
   I could not go - I couldn't go ⟶ No pude ir

'CAN'
'Can' (en presente) se utiliza para expresar permiso, habilidad o posibilidad

1) Permiso
   Can I go to the beach? No, you can't. - ¿Puedo ir a la playa? No, no puedes

2) Habilidad
   Margot can play the piano - Margot sabe (es capaz de) tocar el piano

3) Posibilidad
   It can get very cold in this house - Puede (llegar a) hacer mucho frío en esta casa

'COULD'
El verbo modal *'could'* se traduciría de diferentes maneras:

1. 'Poder' en español: Pretérito Perfecto e Imperfecto del Indicativo

> ***They could sing like angels*** - Podían cantar como ángeles
> ***I couldn't see you through the window*** - No pude/podía verte a través de la ventana

2. 'Poder' en español: Condicional

> ***Could you pass me the salt, please?*** - ¿Podrías pasarme la sal por favor?
> ***We could go to New York on the weekend*** - El fin de semana podríamos ir a Nueva York
> ***It could rain tonight*** - Esta noche podría llover

3. Como en español, utilizamos *'could'* tanto para formular preguntas más formales y educadas,

> ***Could you pass me...?*** VS ***Can you pass me...?***
> ¿Podrías pasarme...? **VS** ¿Puedes pasarme...?

...como para indicar una posibilidad:

> ***I could write a letter to the president*** - Podría escribirle una carta al presidente

* Como has visto en los ejemplos, para crear la forma interrogativa, solamente se invierte el orden del verbo y del sujeto. Nada nuevo ahí, ¿verdad?

> ***I can go with you*** - Puedo ir contigo
> ***Can I go with you?*** - ¿Puedo ir contigo?

✱ *Phrasal Verbs:* **introducción**

Los *Phrasal Verbs* son verbos a los cuales se le añade una (o dos) partículas (preposición o adverbio).

El problema es que, al unir ese verbo con una partícula determinada, el significado del verbo suele cambiar completamente y no se puede interpretar su nuevo significado ni por lógica ni por intuición.

Por ejemplo: **run out**

Si fueras a traducirlo literalmente, sabes que *run* significa 'correr' y *'out'* implica 'fuera'... ¿lo traducirías como "correr afuera"?

Errooooor

'Run out' significa "quedarse sin, agotarse algo"

We have run out of milk
Se nos ha acabado la leche

En español no tenemos *Phrasal Verbs*, y por eso nos cuesta tantísimo a los hipanohablantes usarlos correctamente, porque con este tipo de construcciones verbales no nos queda otra que aprendérnoslas de memoria.

Aquí propongo algunos ejemplos de *Phrasal Verbs* comunes, pero hay muchísimos más...

NOTA: solo pongo un signifiado de cada *Phrasal*, pero para torturarnos un poco más, tened en cuenta que algunos *Phrasal Verbs* tienen más de un significado y de dos, y de tres...

Call off
Cancelar
The meeting was called off
La reunión se canceló

Come back
Regresar
Samuel is leaving on Tuesday and coming back next week
Samuel se va el martes y vuelve la semana que viene

Get on
Llevarse bien
Maria y Ricardo don't get on. They're always arguing
María and Ricardo no se llevan bien. Están siempre discutiendo

Go on
Continuar
The show must go on
El show debe continuar

Move in
Mudarse
I've got a new flat. I'm moving in on Monday
Tengo un piso nuevo, me mudo el lunes

Put up with
Tolerar, aguantar
I won't put with your behaviour
No toleraré tu comportamiento

Take off
Despegar
The planes is about to take off
El avión está a punto de despegar

Tell off
Regañar
Her mother told her off
Su madre la regañó

Quick tip...

MISS vs LOSE: PERDER

MISS

- the bus / el autobús
- the train / el tren
- the chance / la oportunidad
- the meeting / faltar a la reunión
- the post / llegar tarde para recoger el correo
- the point / no comprender algo
- the forest for the trees / no ver mas allá de las narices

LOSE

- one's appetite / el apetito
- one's keys / las llaves
- interest / el interés
- weight / peso
- the game / el juego
- one's head / la cabeza
- track of time / la noción del tiempo

aprendeinglessila.com

Pronunciación

7 Pronunciación

Letras mudas

En inglés existen muchas palabras con letras mudas, es decir, que están escritas pero que no se pronuncian.

Por ejemplo, island /ˈaɪlənd/, walk /wɔːk /

¡Qué complicados son estos ingleses!, ¿no?

Si ponen la letra que la pronuncien y, si no la pronuncian, que la borren **GRRR...**

Pero, tranqui, todo tiene un motivo.
Primero veamos algunos ejemplos y luego ya explicaré las razones.

Antes de empezar es importante que entiendas y te familiarices con los símbolos fonéticos en inglés. Sí, esos que hemos visto hace unas cuantas páginas 😊

Y ahora, *let's start!*

Aquí va una lista de las combinaciones más comunes con letras que **no** se pronuncian:

B muda
La B no se pronuncia cuando está precedida por una M al final de la palabra, incluso si se le agregan sufijos:

- *climb* /klaɪm/ - *climbing* /ˈklaɪmɪŋ/ *climber* /ˈklaɪmə/: escalar, escalando, escalador
- *crumb* /krʌm/: miga
- *dumb* /dʌm/: tonto, mudo
- *comb* /kəʊm/: peine

C muda
La C no se pronuncia en la terminación 'scle':

- *muscle* /ˈmʌzl/: músculo

D muda
La D no se pronuncia cuando está precedida o seguida de N en una misma sílaba:

- *handkerchief* /ˈhæŋkətʃɪːf/: pañuelo
- *Wednesday* /ˈwenzdeɪ/: miércoles
- *sandwich* /ˈsænwɪdʒ/
- *grandmother* /ˈgrænmʌðə/: abuela

188 Inglés básico para hispanohablantes | Pronunciación

E muda
La E no se pronuncia cuando está al final de una palabra y precedida por una consonante:

- *drive* /draɪv/: conducir
- *gave* /geɪv/: dio (verbo irregular: 'dar' en pasado)
- *write* /ˈraɪt/: escribir
- *site* /saɪt/: lugar

G muda
La G no se pronuncia cuando va seguida de una N:

- *foreign* /ˈforən/: extranjero
- *sign* /saɪn/: señal
- *feign* /feɪn/: fingir

GH muda
En muchas palabras la GH no se pronuncia cuando va seguida de T:

- *thought* /θot/: pensar en pasado (verbo irregular)
- *through* /θru:/: a través de (preposición)
- *daughter* /ˈdɔ:tə/: hija
- *light* /laɪt/: luz, ligero,...
- *might* /maɪt/: ser posible (verbo modal)
- *right* /raɪt/: derecho/a, correcto
- *fight* /faɪt/: luchar

H muda
La H generalmente no se pronuncia cuando va precedida por la W:

- *what* /wot/: qué (pronombre interrogativo)
- *when* /wen/: cuándo
- *where* /weə/: dónde
- *whether* /ˈweðə/: si, tanto si
- *why* /waɪ/: por qué

La H no se pronuncia al comienzo de estas palabras y sus derivados:

- *hour* /ˈaʊə/: hora
- *honest* /ˈa:nəst/: sincero
- *honour* /a:nər/: honor
- *heir* /eə/: heredero

K muda

Pronunciación | Inglés básico para hispanohablantes

La K no se pronuncia cuando va seguida de N y al principio de una palabra:

- *knife* /naɪf/: cuchillo
- *knee* /nɪː/: rodilla
- *know* /nəʊ/: saber
- *knock* /nɒk/: golpear
- *knowledge* /ˈnɒlɪdʒ/: conocimiento

L muda
La L generalmente no se pronuncia cuando va seguida de M, F, K, D

- *calm* /kaːm/: calma
- *half* /hæf/: mitad, medio
- *walk* /wɔːk/: caminar
- *talk* /ˈtɔːk/: hablar
- *would* /wʊd/: verbo modal
- *should* /ʃʊd/: debería

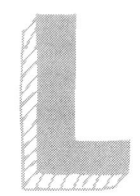

Así que, nada de pedir un Johnny /WOLKER/ en el bar!!!!!!!

N muda
La N no se pronuncia cuando va precedida por una M al final de una palabra:

- *autumn* /ˈɔːtəm/: otoño
- *hymn* /hɪm/: himno

P muda
La P no se pronuncia en palabras como:

- *raspberry* /ˈrɑːzbəri/: frambuesa
- *cupboard* /ˈkʌbəd/: despensa
- *sapphire* /ˈsæfaɪə/: zafiro
- *receipt* /rɪˈsiːt/: recibo

Ni en palabras con los prefijos "psych" y "pneu":

- *psychiatrist* /saɪˈkaɪətrəst/: psiquiatra
- *pneumonia* /nʊˈmɒnɪə/: pneumonía
- *psychotherapy* /saɪkəʊˈθerəpi/: psicoterapia
- *psychotic* /saɪˈkɒtɪk/: psicótico

S muda
La S no se pronuncia en:

- *island* /ˈaɪlænd/: isla
- *isle* /aɪl/ (Observen que aquí no se pronuncia la 'e' tampoco)

T muda
La T no se pronuncia en palabras como estas:

- *castle* /kæzl/: castillo
- *Christmas* /ˈkrɪsməz/: Navidad
- *fasten* /ˈfɑːsn̩/: abrocharse
- *listen* /ˈlɪsn̩/: escuchar
- *often* /ˈɒfn̩/: a menudo (en algunos acentos la «t» sí se pronuncia)
- *whistle* /ˈwɪsl̩/: silbar
- *thistle* /ˈθɪsl̩/: cardo
- *bustle* /ˈbʌsl̩/: ajetreo
- *rustle* /ˈrʌsl̩/: crujido
- *hasten* /ˈheɪsn̩/: apresurar
- *glisten* /ˈglɪsn̩/: relucir
- *wrestle* /ˈresl̩/: luchar

U muda
La U no se pronuncia en las combinaciones 'gue' y 'gui':

- *guess* /gez/: adivinar, suponer
- *guidance* /gɪˈtɑː/: guía
- *guitar* /gɪˈtɑː/: guitarra
- *guest* /gest/: invitado

W muda
La W no se pronuncia al principio de una palabra cuando va seguida de R:

- *wrap* /ræp/: envolver
- *write* /raɪt/: escribir
- *wrong* /rɒŋ/: equivocado

Y en los siguientes pronombres:

- *who* /huː/: quién
- *whose* /huːz/: de quién
- *whom* /huːm/: a quién

Pronunciación | **Inglés básico para hispanohablantes**

¿Por qué no pronunciamos estas letras en inglés?
Estas omisiones tienen un motivo y una causa, no están ahí sólo para volvernos locos...

Los sonidos se han omitido para:

- **Distinguir palabras muy similares**: *whole* de *hole*, *plum* de *plumb*, *hour* de *our*, etc.

- **Para diferenciar las vocales con sonidos cortos de las vocales con sonidos largos**: rid/ride (cuando la palabra termina con una 'e' muda, la vocal anterior suena como en el alfabeto y es larga /rid/-/raid/)

- **Para diferenciar las consonantes suaves de las duras**: *guest/gest* (/gest/ - /dʒest/)

- **Para conectar diferentes formas de la misma raíz**: *resign/resignation*

Las causas de estas omisiones son:

- **Cambios a lo largo de la historia**: con el tiempo el sonido desapareció pero se mantuvo la letra *(light, hope, knot)*.

- **Similitudes**: para hacer la palabra más parecida al latín o francés se agregaron letras pero no se pronuncian *(debt, victual, island)*.

- **Combinaciones complicadas**: por combinaciones demasiado difíciles de pronunciar *(handkerchief, sándwich)*

- **Préstamos**: se han tomado prestadas muchas palabras de idiomas extranjeros *(champagne, kaki, myrrh)* y se mantuvo la escritura original pero se le dio una pronunciación inglesa.

Quick tip...

Pronunciación de los VERBOS REGULARES en pasado

La pronunciación de las palabras acabadas en "-ED" depende del sonido final.

Hay 3 maneras de pronunciar –ED:

aprendeinglessila.com

SONIDO FINAL | EJEMPLOS

'ed' se pronuncia /t/
Tras sonidos *sordos:

p, k, ch, sh, s, f, h, θ

(este último sonido suena como una 'z')

*Sonido sordo: NO vibran las cuerdas vocales

Stopped (stopt)	/stɒpt/
Checked (chekt)	/tʃekt/
Washed (wosht)	/wɒʃt/

'ed' se pronuncia /d/
Tras sonidos sonoros:

vocales +
b, g, z, v, m, n, l, r, w, j, ð

(este último sonido suena como una 'd')

Listened (lisend)	/ˈlɪsnd/
Called (coold)	/kɔːld/
Grabbed (grabd)	/græbd/

'ed' se pronuncia /id/
Con verbos que terminen en:

't' o **'d'**

Started (startid)	/ˈstɑːtɪd/
Decided (disaidid)	/dɪˈsaɪdɪd/

aprendeinglessila.com

Vocabulario variado

Introducción

En este apartado no os voy a poner listas interminables de vocabulario básico del inglés.

No me quiero meter en historias de colores en inglés, ropa, partes de una casa, etc... Para eso existen millones de libros de vocabulario, *flash cards*, apps y miles de páginas webs con toda la información y dibujitos interactivos y demás.

No, en esta sección, simplemente introduciré algunas partes de vocabulario que os ayudarán a ampliarlo y, espero, a ponerlo en práctica.

Por eso incluyo:

Inglés básico de supervivencia
Una lista de palabras y expresiones básicas pero súper útiles para el día a día.

Días de la semana
No es una lista de los días de la semana. Voy un poquito más allá y os explico el origen y la pronunciación (que es complicadilla) de estos términos.

False Friends
Una pequeña introducción a los False Friends para que no metáis demasiad la pata al hablar inglés :)

Idioms **básicos del inglés**
Frases idiomáticas variadas para que le vayáis pillando el truquillo a las expresiones hechas.

INGLÉS BÁSICO DE SUPERVIVENCIA

ESPAÑOL	INGLÉS
¿Cómo funciona?	How does it work?
¿Cómo se deletrea?	How do you spell it?
¿Cómo se pronuncia?	How do you pronounce it?
¿Cuánto cuesta?	How much does it cost? How much is it?
¿Cuánto tiempo se tarda?	How long does it take?
¿Cuántos hay?	How many are there?
¿De dónde eres?	Where are you from?
¿Dónde está el baño?	Where is the toilet / restroom (USA)?
¿Dónde está/n...?	Where is / are...?
¿Habla español?	Do you speak Spanish?
¿Me puede despertar a las siete?	Can you wake me up at seven o'clock?
¿Podría repetirlo, por favor?	Could you say that again, please?
¿Por qué?	Why?
¿Qué hora es?	What's the time? What time is it?
¿Qué significa...?	What does... mean?
¿Quién?	Who?
¿Tienes...?	¿Do you have...?
Adiós	Goodbye
Aeropuerto	Airport
Agencia de viajes	A travel agent's
Antes	Before
Aquí mismo	Right here
Buenas noches	Good night
Buenas tardes	Good afternoon / evening
Buenos días	Good morning

Vocabulario variado | **Inglés básico para hispanohablantes**

ESPAÑOL	INGLÉS
Cama de matrimonio	A double bed
Carné de conducir	Driving licence
Carné de identidad	Identity card
Con permiso	Excuse me
De nada	You're welcome / Not at all
Derecha	Right
Después	After
Estoy perdido	I am lost
Gracias	Thank you
Habitación doble	A double room
Habitación individual	A single room
Hasta luego	See you later
Hasta mañana	See you tomorrow
He perdido mi…	I have lost my…
Izquierda	Left
La cuenta, por favor	The bill, please
La embajada española	The Spanish Embassy
La estación de autobuses/trenes	The bus / train station
Lo siento	I'm sorry
Más despacio por favor	Slower please
Me gustaría…	I would like…
Me han robado mi…	I have had my… stolen
Me llamo…	My name is…
Muchas gracias	Thank you very much
No entiendo	I don't understand

Inglés básico para hispanohablantes | Vocabulario variado

ESPAÑOL	INGLÉS
No hablo inglés (muy bien)	*I don't speak English (very well)*
No importa	*It doesn't matter.*
No lo sé	*I don't know*
Oficina de correos	*A post office*
Pasaporte	*Passport*
Por favor	*Please*
Que pase un buen día	*Have a nice day!*
Quiero cambiar euros	*I want to change some euros*
Quiero...	*I want / I would like*
Reembolsar	*To refund*
Seguro de viaje	*Travel Insurance*
Sí	*Yes*
Tal vez	*Maybe*
Tengo 30 años	*I'm thirty years old*
Vale	*OK*

Vocabulario variado | **Inglés básico para hispanohablantes**

DÍAS DE LA SEMANA

Vamos a ver un tema que parece facilito, pero que tiene algunas complicaciones: **los días de la semana en inglés**.

Algunos de mis alumnos continúan confundiendo el martes (*Tuesday*) con el jueves (*Thursday*).

Otro problemilla es el dichoso Miércoles (*Wednesday*) que para pronunciarlo bien en inglés uno se tiene que comer media palabra.

Antes de empezar veamos algunas cositas que debemos tener en cuenta:

1. Todos los días de la semana en inglés acaban con la terminación -*day*, que quiere decir "día". En español la terminación es "-es", como en lun-es (excepto los días del finde). «-Es» es una abreviación de la palabra latina *dies*, que quiere decir "días").

2. En inglés, a diferencia del español, los días de la semana y los meses se escriben en mayúscula.

3. ***'Days of the week'*** y *'weekdays'* no es lo mismo.
   'Days of the week' son los días de la semana, es decir los 7 días de lunes a domingo. *'Weekdays'*, en cambio, son los "días entre semana" (5 días de lunes a viernes).
   Al fin de semana (sábado y domingo) se le llama *'weekend'*.

4. Los días de la semana tradicionalmente empezaban en domingo (esto no hace falta tenerlo en cuenta, pero es curioso).

Los orígenes de los nombres en inglés son los siguientes:

Sunday /ˈsʌndeɪ/
Day of the Sun (Día del Sol). Proviene de la diosa Sunna. Entre los siglos III y VI, las lenguas romance cambiaron el nombre de este día para llamarlo "El día del Señor" (*dominicus dies* en latín)

Por ejemplo:
Domingo: español y portugués
Domenica: italiano
Dimanche: francés
Diumenge: catalán

En alemán mantiene su nombre germánico ***Sontag.***

Inglés básico para hispanohablantes | Vocabulario variado

Monday /ˈmʌndeɪ/

Day of the Moon (Día de la Luna). Proviene de la diosa Máni de la mitología germánica (en alemán es *Montag*). Aparte del portugués, en las lenguas romance también se refiere a la luna.

Por ejemplo:
Lunes: español
Lunedi: italiano
Lundi: francés
Dilluns: catalán
Luns: gallego

Tuesday /ˈtjuːzdeɪ/

Day of Tiw. Día de la guerra Tiw/Tyr. Proviene de la mitología nórdica y equivaldría al dios romano de la guerra Marte. La mayoría de las lenguas romance mantienen la conexión con este último dios:

Martes: español
Martedi: italiano
Mardi: francés
Dimarts: catalán

Wednesday /ˈwenzdeɪ/

Day of Woden. Proviene del dios Odin de la mitología nórdica y está conectado al dios romano Mercurio. Este dios le dio el nombre a la capital de Escocia, Edimburgo (*Edinburgh* /ˈedɪnbrə/).

La mayoría de las lenguas romance mantienen la conexión con el dios Mercurio.

Let's have a look!

Miércoles: español
Mercoledi: italiano
Mercredi: francés
Dimecres: catalán

Thursday /ˈθɜːzdeɪ/
Day of Thor. Thor, dios en la mitología nórdica es el equivalente a Jupiter, del cual nosotros pillamos nuestro "jueves". Compáralo con el escandinavo *Torsdag* y con el alemán *Donnerstag*. La mayoría de lenguas romance tomaron el nombre de la mitología romana:

Giovedi: italiano
Jeudi: francés
Dijous: catalán
Xoves: gallego

Friday /ˈfraɪdeɪ/
Day of Frig. Esta divinidad era la diosa nórdica del amor, la belleza y el sexo. Equivale a la diosa romana Venus. El planeta Venus dio nombre a este día a varias lenguas romance:

Viernes: español
Venerdi: italiano
Vendredi: francés
Divendres: catalán
Venres: gallego

Saturday /ˈsætədeɪ/
Day of Saturn (Saturno). Es el único día en inglés que ha mantenido su conexión con la mitología clásica romana. Compáralo con algunas lenguas romance que hacen referencia al Sabbat (*Sabbath*) judío:

Sábado: español, portugués y gallego
Sabato: italiano
Samedi: francés
Dissabte: catalán

Inglés básico para hispanohablantes | Vocabulario variado

Aquí un resúmen / esquema:

Dies Solis	**Sun day**		**Sunday**
Dies Lunae	**Moon day**		**Monday**
Dies Martis	**Mars's day**	*Tiw's day*	**Tuesday**
Dies Mercurii	**Mercury's day**	*Woden's day*	**Wednesday**
Dies Jovis	**Juputer's day**	*Thor's day*	**Thursday**
Dies Veneris	**Venus's day**	*Frigg's day*	**Friday**
Dies Saturni	**Saturn's day**		**Saturday**

Abreviaturas de los días de la semana

Aquí te dejo una tabla de cómo abreviar los días de la semana.

Día	
Monday	*Mon*
Tuesday	*Tue*
Wednesday	*Wed*
Thursday	*Thu*
Friday	*Fri*
Saturday	*Sat*
Sunday	*Sun*

FALSE FRIENDS

Los "*False Friends*" (Falsos Amigos) son palabras del inglés (o de cualquier otro idioma, pero ahora estamos aprendiendo inglés) que se parecen, en la escritura o en la pronunciación, a palabras del español, pero que tiene un significado diferente.

¿Os podéis imaginar lo que implica?

Confusiones a raudales y metidas de pata extremas 😊

Hay muchísmos *False Friends*, pero aquí os voy a mostrar algunos de los más comunes para evitar que metáis la pata desde el principio jeje

Actually no significa 'actualmente', sino ➤ **'en realidad'**

Assist no significa 'asistir', sino ➤ **'ayudar'**

Avocado no significa 'abogado', sino ➤ **'aguacate'**

Bland no significa 'blando', sino ➤ **'soso'**

Carpet no significa 'carpeta', sino ➤ **'moqueta'**

Compliment no significa 'complemento, sino ➤ **'piropo'**

Constipation no significa 'constipado', sino ➤ **'estreñimiento'**

Diversion no significa 'diversión', sino ➤ **'desviación'**

Embarrassed no significa 'embarazada', sino ➤ **'avergonzado'**

Exit no significa 'éxito', sino ➤ **'salida'**

Fabric no significa 'fábrica', sino ➤ **'material'**

Large no significa 'largo', sino ➤ **'grande'**

Lecture no significa 'lectura', sino ➤ **'conferencia'**

Library no significa 'librería', sino ➤ **'biblioteca'**

Once no significa 'once', sino ➤ **'una vez'**

Parents no significa 'parientes', sino ➤ **'padres'**

Preservative no significa 'preservativo', sino ➤ **'conservante'**

Resume no significa 'resumir', sino ➤ **'reanudar'**

Sensible no significa 'sensible', sino ➤ **'sensato'**

Realise no significa 'realizar', sino ➤ **'darse cuenta'**

Record no significa 'recordar', sino ➤ **'grabar'**

Inglés básico para hispanohablantes | Vocabulario variado

Quick tip...

Saludos informales en inglés

ESPAÑOL	INGLÉS
¡Hola Sara!	Hey/Hi Sara!
¿Cómo está(s)?	How are you?
¿Qué tal la vida?	How's life?
¿Todo bien?	You alright?
¿Cómo te va todo?	How is everything?
¿Qué tal?	What's up?
¿Cómo va hoy?	How are you doing today?
¿Qué hay?	What's cracking?
Me alegro de verte	Good/nice to see you
Ha pasado tiempo…	It's been a while…
Ha pasado mucho tiempo	It has been a long time
¡Cuánto tiempo!	Long time no see!
Hace siglos que no nos vemos	It's been ages (since I've seen you)
¿Cómo te ha ido?	How've you been?
¿Dónde te has metido?	Where have you been hiding?
¿Por qué nunca te veo?	How come I never see you?
¿Qué hay de nuevo?	What's new?

aprendeinglessila.com

IDIOMS BÁSICOS DEL INGLÉS

Las frases idiomáticas, refranes o *"idioms"* en inglés, son unas frases hechas con un significado propio que puede ser bastante diferente de lo que algunas de las palabras que hay en ellas pueden dar a entender por separado.

Hay una gran cantidad de *idioms* en el inglés y se clasifican según refieran a ciertas realidades de nuestra vida, como pueden ser partes del cuerpo, con los colores o con los números, entre otras muchas más.

Aquí encontraréis algunos idioms muy comunes con su traducción al español y algunos ejemplos de cómo usarlas dentro de una conversación.

Idioms relacionados con partes del cuerpo

To cost someone an arm and a leg: Costar a alguien una gran cantidad de dinero importante.

> ***The house cost me an arm and a leg.***
> La casa me costó un ojo de la cara/un riñón.

Be hand in glove with someone: Tener una muy buena relación con alguien.

> ***She is hand in glove with her mother.***
> Ella y su madre son uña y carne.

To give/lend someone a hand: Ayudar a alguien.

> ***Jane gave him a hand to end the homework.***
> Jane le echó una mano para acabar los deberes.

To catch someone's eye: Atraer la atención de alguien o hacerse notar en un sitio.

> ***If I could catch Lina's eye, I'd like to ask her to go out***
> Si pudiera atraer la atención de Lina, me gustaría pedirle para salir.

To have eyes in the back of one's head: Estar muy atento, darse cuenta de todo lo que sucede alrededor de uno.

> ***My mother always knows what I do;***
> ***she must have eyes in the back of her head!***
> Mi madre siempre sabe lo qué hago;
> es como si tuviera ojos detrás de la cabeza.

Inglés básico para hispanohablantes | Vocabulario variado

Idioms relacionados con los colores

To have blue blood: Ser de la aristocracia (sangre azul)

Victoria has blue blood.
Victoria tiene sangre azul.

To look/feel blue: Sentirse triste o deprimido.

Susana looked so blue that we prepared a surprise party for her.
Susana staba tan deprimida que le preparamos una sorpresa.

Once in a blue moon: Muy raramente.

The teacher is in a good mood once in a blue moon.
El profesor está muy raramente de buen humor.

To be in the red: No tener dinero.

This month I will have problems; I am in the red.
Este mes tendré problemas; estoy en números rojos.

As white as a sheet: Quedarse pálido como consecuencia de un shock o del miedo.

When we told her what happened, she went as white as a sheet.
Cuando le contamos lo que había ocurrido, ella palideció.

Idioms relacionadas con los números

To be in two minds about sth: Estar indeciso en algo

I am in two minds about my studies; I do not know what to do.
Estoy indeciso con los estudios; no sé qué hacer.

To be two-faced: No ser sincero; tener dos caras; ser fals@ e hipócrita

Be careful with Eva; she is two-faced.
Ten cuidado con Eva; tiene dos caras.

Vocabulario variado | Inglés básico para hispanohablantes

At sixes and sevens: Estar desordenado.

> ***All her documents were at sixes and sevens.***
> Todos sus papales estaban completamente desordenados.

A nine day's wonder: Algo que es una maravilla y que nos gusta mucho pero que es de muy corta duración.

> ***Being with him was a nine day's wonder.***
> Estar con él fue una pequeña maravilla.

Existe una laaaarga lista de *'idioms'* que los angloparlantes usan a diario. Para ellos no es nada raro usar estas expresiones, de la misma manera que en español también usamos miles de ellas sin apenas darnos cuenta.

Por eso, para una persona que esté aprendiendo inglés, escuchar estas frases en una conversación o leerlas en un libro, puede hacer que esta pierda todo el hilo de la conversación o de la lectura.

Por tanto, uno de los mejores ejercicios que se pueden hacer para aprender los *'idioms'* es, en primer lugar, organizarlos en tu cabezal mismo tiempo que los escuchas y utilizas en contexto.

"Ufff qué complicado", pensarás... no te voy a mentir, no es fácil memorizar un montón de expresiones, ¡pero esa tampoco es la idea!

Tienes que ir introduciéndolos en tu léxico poco a poco, sin forzarlos...

Quick tip...

IDIOMS en inglés relacionados con la memoria

Come/spring to mind
Ocurrir, venir a la mente

I'd like to get him a special birthday present, but nothing **springs to mind**

Me gustaría comprarle un regalo especial para su cumpleaños, pero no se me ocurre nada

Your mind goes blank
Quedarse en blanco

When I read the exam questions, **my mind went blank**

Cuando leí las preguntas del examen, me quedé en blanco

Ring a bell
Sonar

The name **rang a bell** but I couldn't remember where I had heard it before.

Me sonaba el nombre pero no recordaba donde lo había oído antes

A train of thought
El hilo de la conversación

Oh no! I've lost my **train of thought**

¡Oh, no! He perdido el hilo de la conversación

Rack your brains
Estrujarse los sesos

I've been **racking my brains** all day but I can't remember her name

He estado estrujándome los sesos todo el día, pero no me acuerdo de su nombre

On the tip of your tongue
En la punta de la lengua

Her name is on the **tip of my tongue**

Tengo su nombre en la punta de la lengua

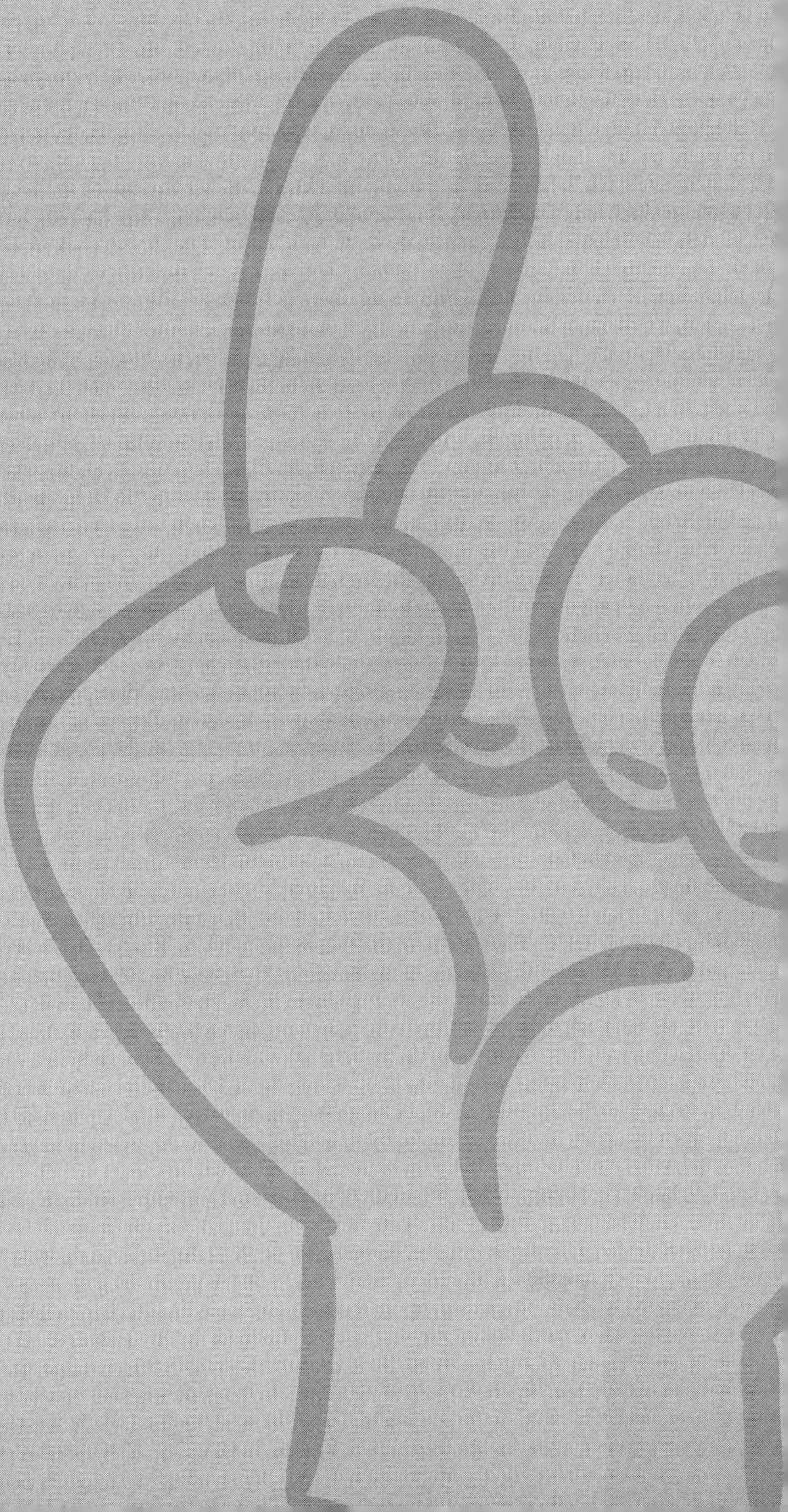

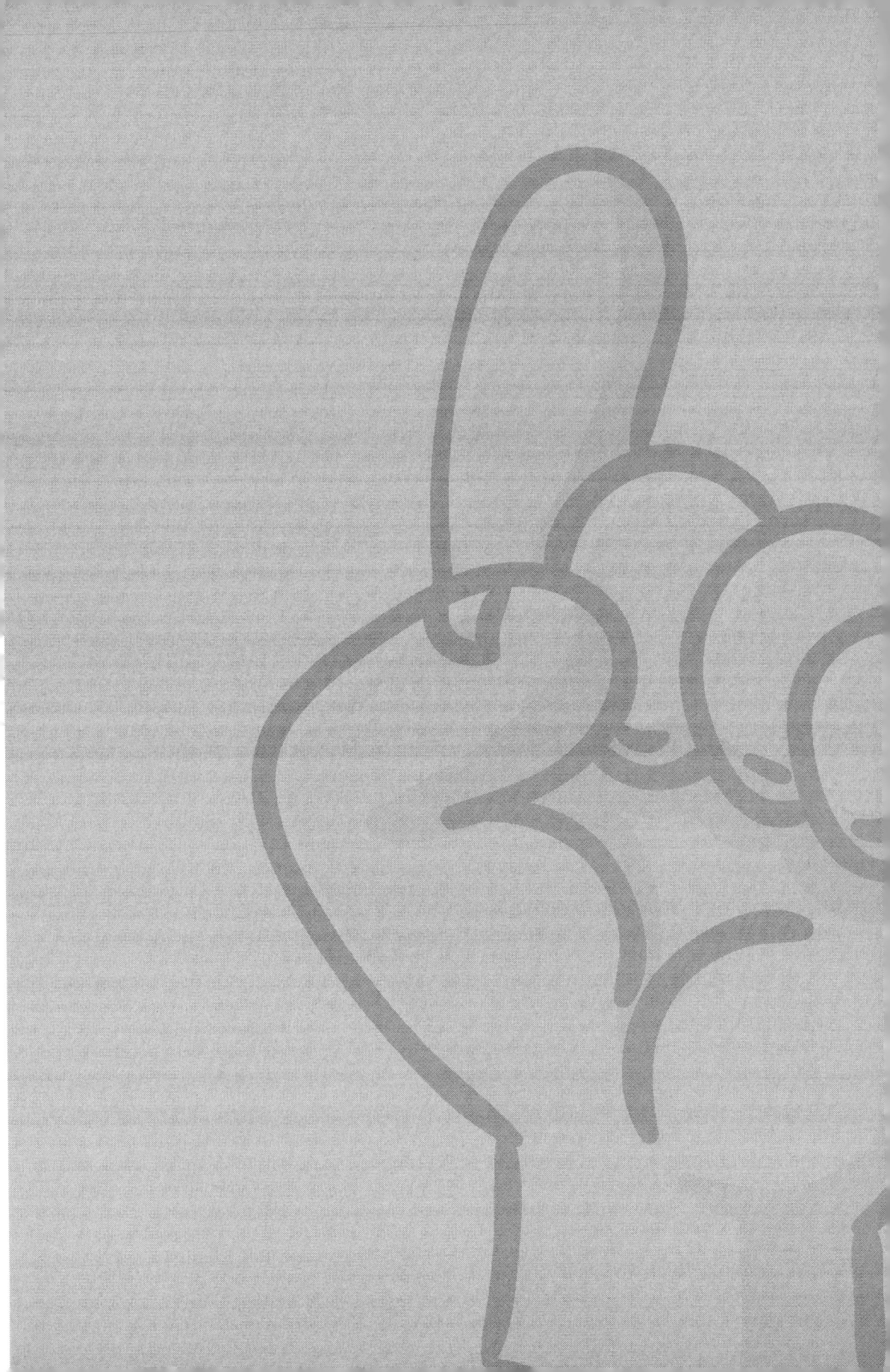

Un último consejo...

¡¡IMPORTA

Si has llegado hasta aquí, te habrás dado cuenta de que aprender inglés no se consigue de un día para otro, que requiere práctica, motivación y ser muy cabezota.

Por eso, vamos a ver unos trucos para ir practicando lo que hemos aprendido hasta ahora y para aprender mucho más.

Y no se trata de ponerle codos y machacar con la gramática, se trata de pasarlo bien y disfrutar del aprendizaje.

Para practicar todo lo aprendido hasta ahora:

Escucha música en inglés
¿Te gusta escuchar música?

Primero escucha la canción y luego busca la letra y ve siguiendo la letra al ritmo de la música.

Escuchando y cantando canciones mejorarás tanto la pronunciación como el vocabulario y encima te lo pasarás bien.

Escucha y repite, escucha y repite, escucha y repite.

Mira películas en versión original
Si te gusta el cine, esta es tu oportunidad para mejorar tu inglés. Intenta ir a cines donde se proyecten películas en versión original. Si el presupuesto no te lo permite, busca en tu televisión la opción de ver las películas en versión original.

Te recomiendo que empieces con películas subtituladas, pero a medida que vayas acostumbrando el oído, quita los subtítulos. Intenta ver pelis tanto americanas como británicas, australianas o canadienses para ir acostumbrándote a los diferentes acentos.

Intercambio de idiomas
Hay muchos angloparlantes que viajan a nuestros respectivos países para aprender y practicar su español. En Internet encontrarás miles de anuncios de gente que quiere intercambiar idiomas, además puedes encontrar un montón de páginas que precisamente ofrecen intercambio de idiomas (Language Exchange).

Lee tu libro favorito... pero ahora en inglés
Una de las cosas que les pido a mis alumnos es que lean en inglés aunque les resulte difícil y aburrido. Yo les presto libros adaptados a su nivel, pero, si mis alumnos no se "enganchan" a estos libros, rápidamente se aburren y dejan de leer.

Hace un tiempo una alumna me explicó que se estaba aburriendo con la versión de nivel intermedio de *Frankenstein* de *Mary Shelley*.

Entonces le pregunté cuál era su autor favorito y me dijo: *Ken Follet*.

Su libro favorito era Los Pilares de la Tierra y, de hecho, le gustaba tanto el libro que se lo había leído dos veces.

¡Ahí encontré mi oportunidad!

Le presté el libro en inglés. Lo ojeó y espetó con frustración: "¡Ufff, que difícil!... el vocabulario es demasiado complicado".

Yo asentí y le expliqué que el vocabulario de ese libro no estaba adaptado a su nivel, pero que ella, al conocer y disfrutar de ese libro, iría entendiendo el argumento de la historia. ¡Especialmente porque se lo sabía casi de memoria!

Marchó de clase con el ceño fruncido y un libro enorme bajo el brazo...

Al siguiente día de clase regresó emocionada.
Le encantaba el libro y lo entendía casi todo. Las palabras que le impedían entender oraciones, las buscaba en el diccionario, pero las demás palabras extrañas las interpretaba por el contexto.
¡Se pasaba el día leyendo!

Moraleja: Redescubre tus libros favoritos en inglés. No dejes de leer porque un libro sea aburrido. **Aplica el idioma a tus gustos y personalidad, y no al contrario**. No permitas que aprender un idioma se vuelva aburrido.

EVÍTALO. ¡TÚ ERES LA ÚNICA PERSONA QUE SABES LO QUE TE ENTUSIASMA!

Ve a ver obras de teatro y musicales en inglés
Aprovecha cuando alguna compañía extranjera venga de gira a tu ciudad o, cuando vayas tú a un país anglosajón, no te pierdas una buena obra de teatro.
Si no te llega el presupuesto, infórmate por Internet de obras de teatro representadas por *amateurs* (muchos actores aficionados son mejores actores que algún actor profesional...).

Juegos
Si te gustan los juegos o videojuegos, esta es una oportunidad magnífica para practicar tu inglés. Empieza por cambiar el idioma de las instrucciones...Si buscas por Internet encontrarás miles de juegos gratuitos que te ayudarán aprender y practicar inglés. No dejes de navegar por la red hasta encontrar el tipo de juego que más se adapte a tu personalidad y nivel. Aprender jugando es una de las mejores maneras de practicar, ¡te lo aseguro!

Revistas y periódicos
Si te gusta el cotilleo o siempre estás al tanto de las últimas noticias, ¿por qué no pruebas a leer revistas y periódicos en inglés? Con ellos aprenderás un montón de vocabulario y siempre estarás al día de nuevas palabras y expresiones.

No te preocupes si no lo entiendes todo, verás como poco a poco irás pillándole el truco y identificarás elementos que has aprendido en esta o aquella frase.

Si tienes alguna revista favorita en español, búscala en inglés. Muchas veces se hacen vesiones en diferentes idiomas.

Escucha emisoras de radio en inglés
Cuando estés en el coche, en casa, en la bañera, no pierdas la oportunidad de sintonizarte la radio en ingles. Por Internet encontrarás miles de emisoras que valen la pena.

- *BBC Radio Station*
- *3TFM (Glasgow)*
- *Capital London*
- *LBC News*
- *Fox News*

Vete a tomar una copa
¿En tu ciudad hay pubs ingleses o irlandeses?
 Si no los hay, seguro que conoces algún bar que sea frecuentado por 'guiris'. Vete para allá, pídete una *'pint'* **/paint/** y atrévete a entablar conversación con algún asiduo/a.

Además de practicar tu inglés, seguro que haces amigos.

Sé especialmente amable
Ofrece ayuda a los turistas que veas perdidos. Si ves a un señor con sandalias, calcetines y una cámara de fotos, tiene todas las probabilidades de ser anglosajón... No te cortes, pregúntale *'Do you need any help?'*

Luego tendrás que intentar hacerte entender... a parte de la mímica, también puedes practicar frases como:

Follow the signs for: sigue las señales hacia.
Continue straight on past some traffic lights: continue recto tras pasar varios semáforos.
Turn left: gire a la izquierda.
Turn right: gire a la derecha.
Take the second exit at the roundabout: tome la segunda salida de la glorieta.

***Recuerda, el gran TRUCO para aprender inglés es practicar, practicar y practicar.

Otros libros de Sila Inglés

Printed in Great Britain
by Amazon